THE VENOM FACTOR

A MARVEL OMNIBUS

NOVELS OF THE MARVEL UNIVERSE BY TITAN BOOKS

Ant-Man: Natural Enemy by Jason Starr
Avengers: Everybody Wants to Rule the World by Dan Abnett
Avengers: Infinity by James A. Moore
Black Panther: Tales of Wakanda by Jesse J. Holland
Black Panther: Who is the Black Panther? by Jesse J. Holland
Captain America: Dark Design by Stefan Petrucha
Captain Marvel: Liberation Run by Tess Sharpe
Civil War by Stuart Moore
Deadpool: Paws by Stefan Petrucha
Morbius: The Living Vampire – Blood Ties by Brendan Deneen
Spider-Man: Forever Young by Stefan Petrucha
Spider-Man: Kraven's Last Hunt by Neil Kleid
Spider-Man: The Darkest Hours Omnibus by Jim Butcher, Keith R.A. Decandido, and
Christopher L. Bennett
Spider-Man: The Venom Factor Omnibus by Diane Duane
Thanos: Death Sentence by Stuart Moore
Venom: Lethal Protector by James R. Tuck
Wolverine: Weapon X Omnibus by Mark Cerasini, David Alan Mack and Hugh, Mathews
X-Men: Days of Future Past by Alex Irvine
X-Men: The Dark Phoenix Saga by Stuart Moore
X-Men: The Mutant Empire Omnibus by Christopher Golden
X-Men & The Avengers: The Gamma Quest Omnibus by Greg Cox

ALSO FROM TITAN AND TITAN BOOKS

Marvel Contest of Champions: The Art of the Battlerealm by Paul Davies
Marvel's Spider-Man: The Art of the Game by Paul Davies
Obsessed with Marvel by Peter Sanderson and Marc Sumerak
Spider-Man: Hostile Takeover by David Liss
Spider-Man: Miles Morales – Wings of Fury by Brittney Morris
Marvel's Guardians of the Galaxy: No Guts, No Glory by M.K. England
Spider-Man: Into the Spider-Verse – The Art of the Movie by Ramin Zahed
The Art of Iron Man (10th Anniversary Edition) by John Rhett Thomas
The Marvel Vault by Matthew K. Manning, Peter Sanderson, and Roy Thomas
Ant-Man and the Wasp: The Official Movie Special
Avengers: Endgame – The Official Movie Special
Avengers: Infinity War – The Official Movie Special
Black Panther: The Official Movie Companion
Black Panther: The Official Movie Special
Captain Marvel: The Official Movie Special
Marvel Studios: The First Ten Years
Spider-Man: Far From Home – The Official Movie Special
Spider-Man: Into the Spider-Verse – The Official Movie Special
Thor: Ragnarok – The Official Movie Special

MARVEL

SPIDER-MAN

THE VENOM FACTOR

A MARVEL OMNIBUS

by Diane Duane

TITAN BOOKS

Spider-Man: The Venom Factor Omnibus
Print edition ISBN: 9781789094596
E-book edition ISBN: 9781789094602

Published by Titan Books
A division of Titan Publishing Group Ltd
144 Southwark Street, London SE1 0UP

First edition: March 2020
10 9 8 7 6 5 4 3 2

© 2020 MARVEL

Special thanks to Lou Aronica, Lucia Raatma, Eric Fein,
Danny Fingeroth, Julia Molino, Ginjer Buchanan, Eileen Veith, Ken Grobe,
Stacey Gittelman, Mike Thomas, Steve Behling, Steve Roman, Carol D. Page
and the gang at Marvel Creative Services.
Original trilogy edited by John Betancourt & Keith R.A. DeCandido.

FOR MARVEL PUBLISHING
Jeff Youngquist, VP Production Special Projects
Caitlin O'Connell, Assistant Editor, Special Projects
Sven Larsen, Director, Licensed Publishing
David Gabriel, SVP Sales & Marketing, Publishing
C.B. Cebulski, Editor in Chief

Spider-Man created by Stan Lee and Steve Ditko.

A CIP catalogue record for this title is available from the British Library.

Printed and bound by CPI Group (UK) Ltd, Croydon, CR0 4YY

THE VENOM FACTOR

Book One

THE VENOM FACTOR

Diane Duane

PROLOGUE

IT was very cold three hundred feet down, very dark; but not very quiet. Outside the skin of the sub, the noise of near-shore seas rumbled and clattered and moaned against the hull—a muted chainsaw rattle of engine noise from ships passing overhead, the clunk and burp of bells or horns from nearby and distant buoys, even the occasional soft singing moan of a whale going about its lawful occasions. The man in the center seat of the submarine's bridge looked thoughtfully at his charts. He sighed at the thought of his upcoming leave and of the relative peace and quiet of being surrounded by air instead of water.

The spot where he sat was not really the center seat, of course. Not yet: his boat was still three years off its refit. Eventually all U.S. subs' bridges would come to resemble the original one of a famous television starship, the circular design having eventually been appreciated by the powers-that-be as the best and most efficient presently available. But right now, the bridge of SSN-45, the USS *Minneapolis,* was still a tangle of panels and conduits arranged around the obstructive central column of the periscope. The captain's chair was no plush overseeing throne, but a folding chair stuck under the lighted chart table: not very aesthetic, not very comfortable. It was not meant to be. Captains spent most of their time on their feet.

Right now, though, Captain Anthony LoBuono was sitting and didn't care who saw him. He could not wait to get this boat into dock and out again. Eight days from now, after final unloading at Greenland, he would get his butt off her, and the back cargo section emptied out once and for all. *Never again,* he thought. *Never again.*

Realistically, though, he might be commanded to carry such a cargo again, and he would take his orders and do as he was told. In fact (and the thought made him twitch) it occurred to Captain LoBuono that, since he had managed this mission well enough, he might easily be given the same task again at some later date.

He swore gently under his breath. He would not soon relish another week and a half like the last one. His crew were on edge, which was no surprise, for *he* was on edge: and such things communicated themselves, no matter how hard you tried to keep them under wraps. *You should be grateful,* he thought to himself. *It's one of the things that makes your crew as good at their jobs as they are. They hear you thinking, anticipate you, jump faster when they have to.*

All the same, he would have preferred to pass on this last week's case of nerves.

His Ex appeared at his shoulder. LoBuono looked up. Bass Lorritson— no one called him Basil, no one who didn't want a drink later spilled on them "accidentally"—favored his captain with a calm look that fooled LoBuono not at all. "Coming shallow as scheduled at the north end of Hudson Canyon, sir," he said. "Do orders mandate a specific course, or are they letting you play this one by ear?"

LoBuono smiled grimly. "We're inside the limit," he said, "and safely under the birds by now. No mandate, except to avoid the Hudson Canyon/Barnegat lanes—too much routine traffic there. Plot us in toward the Coast Guard beacon at Democrat Point, and then take your preferred route to the Navy Yards."

Bass raised his eyebrows, thought a moment. "Jones Inlet," he said, "East Rockaway Inlet, Rockaway Point, Ambrose Light, Norton Point, Verrazano Narrows Bridge, and up."

LoBuono nodded. "Don't stop to pay the toll this time. How's the tide at Ambrose?"

"About three knots, the CG says."

The captain nodded. "Coast-creeping. I guess it suits the situation. Call Harbor Control and give them our ETA. Then call New York Yards Control and tell them I want that stuff waiting at the dock and loaded no more than fifteen minutes after open hatches."

"Yes, sir."

"I'm not fooling around, Bass. I don't want to linger."

"I'll tell them so, Captain."

"Go."

Bass went. Captain LoBuono got up and stepped over to the periscope. "Depth," he said.

"Two hundred, Captain," said Macilwain on the number-two radar. "Periscope depth in half a minute."

LoBuono waited, staring at the shiny scarred deck-plates. It seemed about a hundred years, now, since he had reported aboard the *Minneapolis* at Holy Loch after returning from his last leave and had been handed the sealed envelope. That aspect of his life he was used to: usually a whole looseleaf binder full of mission info stamped "SECRET," which in the present scheme of things normally meant "not very." But this envelope had not been the usual color, but an eye-rattling air-rescue orange, and it had had the new barcoded utter-security seals in it. Two sets of seals: one for the envelope itself, and one for a package which had been waiting on a lowloader by the dock. The package had been about eight feet square, a metal case with a very large cordon of armed and jumpy MPs around it—an escort which, in a lighter mood, would have suggested to Captain LoBuono that possibly the President himself was inside. As it was, he went down belowdecks, swiped the barcode through the reader in his quarters, opened the envelope, swiped the barcode on the inside envelope, opened that, sat down, and read.

And swore. But then, as now, there was nothing he could do about it, any of it—not the envelope, the box, or either of their contents. The box was loaded on, and he had told his crew not to ask questions about it because he had no answers for them. Then *Minneapolis* had headed out.

The door of the secure-cargo compartment way in the back, where the uneasy MPs had deposited the box, was now sealed with the second set of barcode seals, and a sign which one of the MPs had slapped on the door at eye-height: "DANGER—RADIATION," with the familiar three triangles, red on yellow. At the bottom of this sign, over the past few days, some wit had scrawled in ballpoint, "SO WHAT ELSE IS NEW?" Whoever had done it had a point: *Minneapolis* was an attack sub and carried nuclear-tipped torpedoes—what her crew did not know about radioactives would fit in a very short book indeed.

"FULL ALERT," his orders had said, "HOLY LOCH TO GREENLAND: TRIPLE WATCHES: RADIO SILENCE UNTIL

COASTAL WATERS NY." And so it had been done. LoBuono had known what effect this would have on his crew. They were an intelligent and stable bunch—no news there: neither the stupid nor the unstable were allowed on nuclear-armed submarines. But it made them uneasy to be carrying out secret orders. It made them feel as if their superiors didn't trust them, and they didn't know which superiors to be annoyed with— the brass higher up or their captain.

For his own part, Captain LoBuono knew how they felt. His annoyance was more focused. Without knowing what he carried, it was hard for him to take all possible and prudent precautions, thus jeopardizing the mission itself.

"Periscope depth, sir," said the number-two radar man.

"Thank you, Mr. Macilwain," LoBuono said. "Up periscope."

It slid up before him, and he draped himself over its handles and peered into the hood. Someone had left the starlight augmenter on, so that everything in view glared green. He *hmphed* to himself, toggled it off, and looked again.

Dead ahead of them he could see Ambrose Lightship, some six miles away, rocking slightly in the offshore swells despite its anchoring. He looked north toward Norton Point, got a brief glimpse of Coney Island, walked around the 'scope housing a little, gazing to northeastward, and saw the brick tower in the middle of Jones Island, with its pointed bronze-green top. He smiled slightly. It was a long time since he had pestered his folks on summer weekends to take him down to Zachs Bay near that tower, where he could sail his toy boats in the quiet water near the Playhouse—

"… don't know," he heard someone whisper off to one side, partly behind him.

"You think he does?" the whisper came back from down the Bridge.

Silence: probably the sound of a head being shaken. "I think that's what's steaming him these last couple days—"

This was the other thing Captain LoBuono hated about sealed-orders runs: the rumor mill that started running when the engines did and didn't stop until some time during the crew's next leave, if then.

"I heard different." Another voice, whispering too.

"What?"

"Some kind of *thing* they're studying. Something they found."

"Thing? What kind of *thing*?"

Captain LoBuono swung gently around so that his back was broadside-on to the conversation. He looked idly south toward empty water, then swung slowly around to gaze westward, spotting the familiar landmarks: the Coast Guard observation towers on Sandy Hook, and the Sandy Hook Light, oldest in continuous use in the country; the low rise of the Highlands of Navesink, marking the southern boundary of New York Harbor.

"I don't know. Something—not from *here*."

A little further around LoBuono swung, toward the conversation. It stopped.

"Verrazano Narrows," his Ex said.

"So I see," said Captain LoBuono, looking through the periscope at the graceful upstrokes of steel and curves of cable. "Got five bucks, Bass?"

There were smiles around the bridge. Three trips ago, they had come this way, and Bass had been easing *Minneapolis* out of harbor in storm weather while LoBuono attended to paperwork business in his quarters. A nasty unsuspected riptide had pushed *Minneapolis* into one of the stanchions of the Narrows Bridge. She had taken no damage worse than a good scrape on the hull, but Bass had been mortified, and the crew had teased him good-naturedly and offered to pay the toll for him if he wanted to get onto the Bridge that much.

"Fresh out of small bills, Captain," Bass said.

"Good man. Sound surface. Steady as she goes, then twenty degrees starboard."

"Sounding surface." The usual clangor began. "Twenty degrees aye. Yard Control says our packages are loaded and waiting for us, Captain."

"Very well, Mr. Lorritson. Surface. Anything from Harbor?"

"Routine traffic west of Gowanus Bay," Macilwain said. "We pass eastward, starboard of the separation zone. Course to Buttermilk Channel and north to the Yards is clear."

"Proceed," Captain LoBuono said.

They sailed on up out of the Lower Bay and into New York Harbor proper, taking their time. LoBuono turned a bit again to admire the view of the skyscrapers towering up over lower Manhattan, or to seem to. He heard no more talk behind him, though, except the normal coming-to-berth chatter. "Tide's at two," said Loritz, the second navigator, one of the crewmen who had been whispering before.

"Mind the Spider," Bass said. LoBuono's mouth quirked. The treacherous crosscurrents of that name, which ran to the starboard of Governor's Island, were what had caused Bass his old trouble with the bridge. But this time of day, with high water still two hours off, they were at their least dangerous.

Without more incident they sailed on up through the East River and under the Brooklyn Bridge. Traffic on the bridge slowed down as motorists, seeing the *Minneapolis*'s sail, braked to stare and point. Captain LoBuono smiled slightly with pride, but the pride did nothing to ease his tension. *The sooner we're loaded and out of here,* he thought, *the better I'm going to like it.*

A few minutes later they passed under the Williamsburg Bridge, where the same slowing occurred, and then turned slightly out of the main East River "deepwater" channel.

"Wallabout Bay," the second navigator said.

The Navy Yards at last. "Down scope. Pop the top," Captain LoBuono said. "Mooring crew to the aft hatch. Down to one knot, Bass."

"One knot aye. Mooring crew reports ready."

"What's our berth?"

"Sixteen."

"Take us in."

They crept slowly through the outer Shipyard harbor mole. Not much business came this way anymore, what with defense cutbacks and other curtailments on spending: the Brooklyn Navy Yards, once the talk of the world, full of half-laid keels and the rattle of rivets and air-hammers, were now mostly home for mothballed ships and massive lifting cranes whose hooks swung empty in the wind off the Harbor. Still, the Navy used the Yards for occasional nontechnical repairs and provisioning work.

"Twenty-five degrees right rudder," Bass said. "Half a knot."

"Five hundred yards, sir."

"Very good. Rudder back."

A crewman was working the wheel that popped the forward hatch. Captain LoBuono waited for him to get out of the way, then went up the ladder to get a look at the day and the mooring.

There was a brisk wind blowing: it had already mostly dried the sail and the superstructure. LoBuono leaned on the sail's "balcony rail" and gazed down at the dock to the starboard of slip sixteen as *Minneapolis* sidled gently into it. The dock was stacked with plastic-wrapped crates and packages on dollies, ready to be hauled up onto the superstructure and passed down the hatches. Very slowly, very gently, the boat nudged sideways into the dock.

Bump.

And then, abrupt and terrifying, came the screaming hoot of collision alarms. The whole ship shook, abruptly, and shook again. "What the—" LoBuono started to mutter, and didn't bother finishing, as he dove down the ladder again.

By the time he reached the bridge, Lorritson was already running out of the back of it, toward the source of the alarms. "Hull breach!" someone yelled at the Captain as he raced past them.

"Bass!" LoBuono yelled at the back of his Ex, running in front of him.

"Not me, Captain!" Bass yelled back. They kept running.

Ahead of them they could hear the most dreaded sound of boat men, the thundering rush of uncontrolled water. They could also hear a slightly more reassuring sound, that of watertight compartments with automatic doors, dogging themselves closed. First Bass, then Captain LoBuono came to the final door, the one down at the far end of the weapons room, and found it closed as well. Behind it, they knew, lay the door with the "DANGER—RADIATION" sign. They looked at each other as they stood there.

LoBuono grabbed a mike that hung nearby and thumbed its "on" button. "Bridge! Everybody accounted for?"

"All accounted for, sir," said the Crew Chief's voice. "No one's back there."

"Get someone out in the water and have them see what the damage is!"

"I've got a man out there now, Captain," the Crew Chief said. "One moment—" There was an unintelligible squawking of secondhand radio conversation. Then the Crew Chief said, "We've got a breach about a foot and a half by two and a half, from the looks of it. Deck crew are getting a temp-patch on it. We can pump out the aft compartment in a few minutes."

"Go," LoBuono said.

He looked at his Ex. Lorritson opened his mouth, and the Captain said, "Sorry, Bass. The currents in the Narrows are one thing, but I know you'd never make a goof like that in dock." He made a slightly sour smile. "Put it down to nerves."

Lorritson nodded. "It's been—difficult," he said.

"All around—"

"Patch is in place," the Crew Chief said. "Pump's started."

They heard the throb from the in-hull pump motors starting. For a few minutes more they hummed unobtrusively. Then LoBuono heard the coughing noise that meant they were running out of anything to pump.

"Right," he said, and turned to Lorritson. "Got your dosimeter?"

Bass patted his pocket, where the little radiation-sensitive patch hung.

"If it turns any interesting colors, get your butt out of here," the Captain said. He turned the wheel to undo the door.

Clunk! went the latch. LoBuono pulled; the door swung slightly open. He peered around its edge.

His dosimeter, one of the new ones with a sound chip in it which essentially made it a small geiger counter, ticked gently to itself—a slow watch-tick, serious enough but hardly fatal. "Let's keep it short," the Captain said, stepping through and looking around cautiously.

There was nothing to be seen but wet floor, wet walls, wet ceiling, and the silvery-gray metal crate in the middle of it all, as wet as everything else. Slowly LoBuono walked around it. The front was fine. The sides were fine.

The rear of it, though, had an oblong hole about a foot and a half wide and two and a half feet long punched through it. The bent rags and tags of metal around the hole in the crate were all curved outward. LoBuono's dosimeter began to tick more enthusiastically, as did Lorritson's when he came up beside the captain and peered through the hole in the crate. There was nothing inside.

They looked at the hole in the hull, now sealed with pink plastic fast-patch. It very closely matched the one in the crate, both in size and in the direction of impact—from inside, punching toward the outside. Whatever had been in the crate, it had waited until the most opportune moment and then had left under its own power...

Lorritson looked at the hole in the hull, reached out to touch it, thought better, and let the hand drop. "I guess we'd better call the lost and found."

Captain LoBuono shook his head. "The lost part we seem to have handled," he said sourly. "We'll be in enough trouble for that very shortly, I would imagine. As for the found part—are you sure you would *want* to?"

Lorritson shook his head like a man unsure of the right answer. "Come on," LoBuono said, "let's get on the horn to the brass. We might as well start the trouble ourselves as wait for it to come to us."

But as they walked to the Bridge, LoBuono found himself wondering again, against his own orders, just what *might* have been in that box… and he shuddered.

ONE

HE had been in many strange and terrible places, in his time. He had been off Earth, on other planets, to other galaxies, even. He had faced threats terrible enough to make all Earth shudder, and had come away from them alive. All in all, he didn't have a bad record so far.

But right now, Peter Parker stood outside the doors of the 48th Street midtown branch of the First Manhattan Bank and cursed at the way his palms were sweating.

Behind him, the city made its accustomed roar. People on the sidewalk rushed past, going about their business, no one noticing the young man standing there paralyzed by his own unease—he refused to call it "fear." *I'm a super hero,* he thought. *Why am I standing here twitching?*

No answers came. Peter scuffed one sneaker on the sidewalk, staring at the chrome and plate glass of the bank. He had never been entirely comfortable with the term "super hero," at least not as applied to himself. Some of the other people he consorted with in his line of business— mutants or other humans unusually gifted with extraordinary powers— seemed to him really to merit description with the word "hero": many of them exhibited a level of courage or nobility which inspired him and sometimes shamed him. In his own case, "super" couldn't be argued with. But the way he often felt while out on his rounds—frustrated, enraged, sometimes terrified—struck him as less than heroic. *This kind of thing… this is different. Harder, in a way. This is just life.*

The people on the sidewalk just kept streaming past him. It was lunchtime, and they had more important things to pay attention to than a reluctant super hero, had they even recognized one in his street clothes. Peter let out a long sigh, squared his shoulders, and walked into the bank.

He made his way through the soulless cheerfulness of the front of the bank, filled with gaudy posters shouting about mortgages and favorable interest rates, and went to the customer service counter. For all the attention anyone paid him for the first five minutes, he might as well have stayed outside. The young woman who finally came over to him did so with the air of someone engaged in much more crucial matters than serving a customer. "Yes?" she said, and popped her bubble gum.

"Mr. Woolmington, please?" Peter said.

"He's out to lunch."

This chimed well with some of Peter's private opinions about the man, but he was hardly going to say as much in public. "Can you tell me when he'll be back?"

"Dunno," said the young woman behind the counter. "This afternoon sometime." She turned away.

"Can you take a message for him, please?"

Popping her gum in a manner which suggested she had been a machine gun in an earlier life, the young woman said, "Yeah?"

"Please tell him—" Peter had a powerful urge to say, *Please tell him that Spider-Man was here to see whether his debt-consolidation loan's been approved yet, or whether he has to get one of the Avengers to cosign for it.* He restrained himself. "Please tell him Peter Parker stopped in to see if there was any news on his loan approval."

"Uh huh," said the young woman, and she turned away again.

Peter watched her go, then walked back out to the street again, feeling—actually, a little grateful. He was so sure the answer was going to be "no" when it came, that not finding the guy there to give him the bad news was a blessing, in a way.

He walked on down 48th Street toward Fifth Avenue, hands in his pockets, staring at the sidewalk—as much from self-defense as anything else. No matter how much you fined people for not cleaning up after their dogs, it never seemed to help much.

Banks.... Peter thought. This had been just one more of many situations in his life lately which had made him wonder whether being able to invoke the inherent cachet of superherodom openly would be any use. Or, would it just make matters worse? There were some heroes who functioned without secret identities, and when you saw them socially—if you did—they seemed to be managing okay. All the same, Peter suspected their answering machines were always full when they got home from heroing, or even from doing the shopping, and the thought of how much junk mail they must get made him twitch. Even without anyone knowing his own secret identity, Peter got enough to make his trips to the recycling bins a trial for anyone, super hero or not. And when you added MJ's endless catalogs to the pile....

He smiled slightly as he crossed Madison and headed on along toward Fifth. Mary Jane Watson-Parker was quite a celebrity in her own right—or had been, until she had left the soap opera *Secret Hospital*. Even before that, she had been well enough known for her modeling work. As a result, every mail-order house in the country, it seemed, sent her notifications of its new product lines... and she went through every one lovingly, pointing and oohing at the goodies.

But, of late, not buying from them. Things had gotten—well, not desperate, but tight. It was easy to forget how lavish money from TV work was until you lost it. Until then, MJ had spent some months persuading Peter to lighten up a little, to go ahead and spend a little money, buy himself that jacket, eat out more often. Peter had resisted at first. Finally, because it made her happy, he had given in—gotten used to enjoying himself, gotten used to having more funds to work with, gotten out of the habit of dreading the time the credit card bills came in.

And then, just as he had gotten used to it, it had all changed.

Now the mailbox was once again a source of uneasiness. The rent on the apartment, easy enough to handle on the combined incomes of a minor TV star and a freelance photographer, had now become a serious problem. Breaking the lease before it expired so that they could move somewhere smaller and cheaper was proving near impossible. So was keeping up the rent on just a freelancer's salary. They had some savings: not a huge sum, but it would last a while. MJ was out there getting every interview and audition she could scrape up. She was getting depressed, too, at not having been hired for something else right away. But Peter, just as nervous about it all as she was, had been purposely staying cheerful, trying to keep her spirits up and prevent her from getting discouraged. At the same time, he desperately wished there was someone to keep *him* from getting discouraged.

Being a super hero is all very well, he thought. *I just wish it paid better. I wish it paid,* period!

He stopped at the corner, waiting for the light, while around him people hurried across anyway, daring the oncoming traffic. Whether heroing paid or not, he had to do it. Just as he had to take pictures, because he loved to, whether he got paid for them or not. Just as he had to study science, whether there seemed to be a job in it for him later or not. The old habit, the old love, went back too far, was too much a part of him now to let go.

He just had to make everything work together, somehow.

The light changed. Peter crossed, heading up Fifth to West 49th, then over to the shop where he usually got his photographic supplies. He had a couple of hours' work in the darkroom before him. Usually he tried to wind that up before MJ got home from her day out and complained about the smell of the developing solution (as well she might). It wasn't always easy. Darkroom business had become a lot more complicated, and more expensive, since the *Daily Bugle*'s front page had gone color. Now a photographer who aspired to lead-story work had to be able to manage quality color processing at home—a one-hour place wouldn't cut it. And color chemicals were four times the cost of black-and-white.

Nothing he could do about it, though. Peter swung into the store, waited a few moments: Joel, the owner, was busy trying to sell a guy in a leather jacket a large and complicated camera case. After a few minutes the guy shook his head and went off.

"Hey, Petey," Joel said, "you need a camera case?"

Peter snorted. "That thing? With the plastic hardware on it? It wouldn't last a week."

They both laughed. It was an old game: Joel would push something useless at Peter; Peter would push it back. Then they would gossip a while. Peter had learned not to cut the gossip short—Joel sometimes knew about potential news stories in the area, and once or twice Peter had been able to bring in hot pictures to the *Bugle* as a result, before anyone knew anything about the news story in question.

"Hey," Joel said, bending down to rummage under the counter for a moment. "Got that gadget you were asking me for."

"Which one?"

"Wait a sec." Joel vanished below the counter, and things began to appear on it: rolls of film, brushes, lens caps, lens hoods, and lots more small pieces of equipment. After a moment he came up with a little black box with a clear plastic lens on the front.

"Strobe slave," Joel said.

"Got one already," Peter said. It was a useful accessory for a photographer, a second flash cabled to his camera and "slaved" to the first, so that they went off together. That way you could add light to a dark scene, or fill in unwanted shadows from the side.

"Not like this, you haven't," Joel said. He picked up the little box and turned it to show Peter a tiny secondary lens on the side. "Wireless. It goes off when your flash does by sensing sudden changes in the ambient light."

Peter picked it up and looked at it thoughtfully. He had been thinking about some improvements to his present rig. "Any way you could hook a motion sensor to this, you think?"

Joel nodded, pointing to a jack socket on the back of the slave flash. "One of my other customers did something like that. Nature photographer. He picked up one of those passive infrared things, you know the kind— the doohickey that turns on your outside lights when someone gets close to the door. Saved him having to watch the birdie so much." Joel chuckled. "The bird moves, the camera takes its picture before it flies the coop."

Peter smiled. "I can use this. How much?"

"Forty."

He sighed, did some hurried addition in his head and pulled out his credit card. "Okay. And give me another package of three-by-five stock and a bottle of three-fifty, would you?"

"No problem." Joel went back to the shelves, came back with the gallon bottle of developer solution and the photo paper. For a moment he worked at the cash register. "Your lady find work yet?" he said.

Peter shook his head. "Still hunting."

"Hmm. You know, I have a guy comes in from the network place around the corner, the studios for the daytime stuff. Yesterday he told me they're hiring actors all of a sudden. Some kind of high-class soap, he said." Joel chuckled. "*Is* there such a thing?"

"You've got me. But I'll tell MJ to check it out."

The cash register dinged. "Sixty-two thirteen," Joel said.

Peter winced and handed his credit card over. "Did the price of the three-fifty go up again?"

"Yup. Another four bucks. Sorry, Petey."

"Not much we can do, I guess," Peter said, as Joel swiped the card through the reader.

"Don't I know it. The distributor says he can't do anything since the manufacturer's raised *his* prices…" Joel sighed. The reader beeped twice: Joel looked down at it, then raised his eyebrows. "Uh oh. They declined it."

Peter swallowed. "Didn't get the payment yet, I guess."

"Wouldn't be surprised. Did I tell you I sent my sister-in-law in Brooklyn a birthday card two weeks early, and it didn't get to her until two weeks *afterwards*? I ask you. You'd think we were in Europe or something. Come to think of it, I get letters from my cousin there *faster* than I do from Cecile."

Peter dug out his wallet and produced the necessary cash, noting sadly that this process left him with the munificent sum of one dollar and sixty cents. "Yeah," he said. "Here you go."

"Right." Joel handed him his change. "Hey, Petey—" Peter turned, already halfway to the door. Joel waggled his eyebrows at him. "Don't let it get you down. It can only get better."

Almost against his will, Peter smiled. "Yeah. See you, Joel."

"See you."

All the same, as he walked on down the street, it was hard for Peter to see any way that things would get better any time soon. *There's only one thing*, he thought, *that's going to make it seem worthwhile.*

Tonight….

The apartment was empty when he got there. It was big and roomy, with a nice enough view of the skyline, and a slightly less impressive view of the next-building-over's roof, about ten stories below their own and in this weather well covered with people in bathing suits trying to get a tan through the smog. The apartment's big windows let in plenty of light on white walls and a polished oak floor. There, as in some of MJ's show-business friends' apartments, it might have stopped, finding not much else to shine on. But unlike them, MJ had no patience with the presently fashionable minimalist school of decorating which considered one couch and one throw rug "enough furniture" and left the place looking barren as a Japanese raked-sand garden. Mary Jane Watson had been something of a packrat—though in the best possible taste—and Mary Jane Watson-Parker remained so. Her tastes ran more toward Laura Ashley than Danish Modern: big comfy sofas and chairs to curl up in, cushions scattered around, lots of bookshelves with lots of things on them—vases, bric-a-brac old and new (mostly old), and lots of books. It made for a comfortable and welcoming environment, though it was a pain to keep properly dusted.

Dusting, though, was not on Peter's mind at the moment. The new strobe slave was. Peter made his way back to the darkroom, unloaded the developing chemicals and the paper, and went back out to the front of the apartment to see what the answering machine had for him. Two invitations to subscribe to the *New York Times* (which they already did), one offer to clean their carpets (there weren't any), two anonymous please-call-this-number messages (probably bill collectors: sighing, Peter took the numbers and wished the machine had thrown one of its occasional fits and lost the messages). No offers of work, no parties, no sudden legacies, no good news.

Oh well. Tonight....

Peter got up and went back to the table where he had dropped the new strobe slave. It was often difficult to take decent pictures when you weren't behind the camera, but in front of it as Spider-Man. It was tough to pay much attention to *f*-stops and exposure times when you were duking it out with some bad guy. It was the devil to keep the camera pointed at the action when you were swinging by your webline from one rooftop or another. Also, criminals, both the elite super villain types and your ordinary garden-variety crooks, were generally not very amenable to staying in the camera frame while you were having it out with them. Peter had been trying to find a solution to both of those problems for some while.

Now, though, I might have one. On the table, left over from where he had been fixing MJ's sunglasses the other night, was a set of ultra-tiny screwdrivers which he also used for jobs like maintenance on his web-shooters and getting the faceplate off the microwave when its LEDs failed. Now he picked up the third-largest of the group, undid the screws on the bottom and sides of the strobe, and carefully pried the backplate off, taking a long look at the insides. It was a fairly straightforward array, though some of the soldering on the chip at its heart was slapdash. A transistor, some assorted diodes, all labeled for a change; an LED to tell you when the gadget was armed; the light sensor; and a bypass circuit to take it out of commission when you had some other triggering mechanism jacked into the input.

Fair enough. Peter had one other piece of hardware which would communicate with this readily enough, with some programming. Miniaturization had worked enough wonders of late, but there was one that not a lot of people but researchers in the sciences knew about. To take up less room on the lab benches, some bright guy in the Far East had taken a whole PC computer motherboard and worked out how to fit it on a board the size of two cigarette packs laid end to end. That, with enough RAM chips, was enough machine-smarts to run a fairly sensitive motion-control apparatus—and that was what Peter had been working on for a while now. The Engineering Department at Empire State University had assumed that one of the doctoral candidates was doing a little good-natured slumming when he came down to pick their brains about the fine points of motion control programming. Privately they thought that the guys up in Nuclear Physics were getting twitchy about handling the radioactives themselves, and were trying to teach the computers how to do it for them. They could hardly have suspected the real purpose of Peter's visits. Pretty soon, though, he would have something of considerable use to a photographer who was also a crimefighter. Bit by bit, he was building a camera which, with the right motion sensor attached, would turn by itself to follow the action taking place around it, and which could be remotely triggered, and which (if the aforesaid crimefighter got too busy) would follow his movements and fire at preset default intervals. Once this creature was built, his bosses at the *Bugle* would have fewer complaints about the poor composition of Peter's shots compared to other photographers'.

And his credit card company would be *much* happier with him.

For half an hour or so he fiddled with the slave strobe. The actual movement-controlling hardware, the guts of an old portable telescope's cannibalized and much-altered clock drive, had been ready for a while. All Peter had needed was a suitable actuator. This new slave would do fine until something more sophisticated came along. The afternoon shadows moved across the apartment, and finally the windows lost the sun. Peter barely noticed, finishing his adjustments to the slave itself and then going to fetch the system's moving parts and the camera itself. It was his best one, a Minax 5600si, with an extremely advanced automatic exposure- and shutter-control system—which it would need, when its owner was hanging by synthesized spiderweb from the top of some building, swinging after a crook, tens or even hundreds of yards away. The camera screwed into a little platform with a ball-and-socket joint able to yaw, roll, and pitch. That, in turn, screwed into the top of a small collapsible tripod which had the motion-control motors and the teeny PC motherboard, each bolted to one of the tripod's legs in a small shockproof case. The whole business, when collapsed, would fit comfortably into a backpack or one of the several elastic pouches that Peter had built into his costume over time.

Finally, there it all stood, ungainly looking but theoretically functional. He took the camera off its stand, popped off its back, rooted around in a nearby desk drawer for some of the time-expired film he used for tests, loaded the camera, and seated it on the stand again.

The instant the camera was turned on, it whirled on the stand. The camera's inboard flash went off as it took his picture, and another one, and another, and another....

"Oh jeez," he muttered, "cut it out." He stepped away, trying to come around the setup sideways to turn off the slave. Unfailingly the camera followed, taking pictures as fast as it could wind itself, about one per second. The flash was beginning to dazzle Peter. He jumped over the table and took a few steps further around it. The camera tried to follow, fouled itself on its own motion-control cables, and got stuck, still taking picture after picture, its motor making a pitiful and persistent little *hnh, hnh, hnh* noise as it tried to follow him right around the table. Peter reached out and caught the tripod just as it was about to fall over.

It *hnh, hnhed* in his hands for a few more seconds before he managed to pull the motion control system's jack. *Well, it works,* Peter thought, turning back toward the table. *Even if it is a little light on the trigger. I'll take it out tonight and see how it does.*

A key turned in the apartment door, which then obligingly opened. The camera in Peter's hands flashed. MJ stood in the doorway, caught open-mouthed with a couple of heavy bags of groceries, and looked at Peter curiously.

"It's not my birthday," she said. "And I don't remember calling the media. What's the occasion?"

"Your glorious homecoming," Peter said, putting the camera down. "C'mere. I want a hug."

MJ offloaded the bags onto a table near the door, and Peter collected the hug, and a couple of serious kisses, while behind them the camera flashed and flashed and flashed. After a few seconds, MJ detached herself by a few inches, took his face between her hands, and said, "Gonna run the batteries down that way."

"What, mine?"

She laughed. "Not yours, lover. Eveready, that's you. Just keeps going, and going, and..." Peter poked her genially in the kidneys, and MJ squealed slightly and squirmed in his arms. "What, what, why are you complaining? It's a *compliment*. Lemme go, the frozen stuff's going to defrost. It's like an oven in here. Didn't you turn the air-conditioning on?"

"I didn't notice," Peter said, letting her go. He picked up one of the bags while MJ got the other, and they headed into the kitchen.

"It may be just as well," MJ said as she started unpacking one of the bags: salad things, a couple of bottles of wine, ice cream, sherbert. "I turned the air conditioner on this morning and it didn't go. Made a sort of gurgly noise for a while, but no cold air. I shut it off—thought it might recover if I left it alone."

Peter sighed. "That's what it did the last time it broke. The compressor, wasn't it?"

"Yeah. The guy said it might not last much longer...."

She reached down into the bag for a couple of cheeses, then picked the bag up and started to fold it. Peter opened his mouth to say something about how they really couldn't afford to have the air conditioner break just now, there were too many other bills... and then he stopped. MJ looked so tired and woeful. Perspiration and the heat of the day had caked the makeup on her, her hair was all over the place, and she had a run in her stocking. He knew she hated looking like that, and she was so worn down and miserable that she didn't even care.

He went to her and hugged her. Somewhat surprised, MJ hugged back, and then she put her head down on his shoulder and just moaned softly, a little sound that hurt him as badly as any super villain tapdancing on his spleen.

"Nothing today, huh?" he said.

"Nothing," MJ replied, and was silent for a little while. "I can't stand this much longer. I *hate* this. I'm a good actress. At least, they all used to say so. Were they just saying that because they wanted to stay on my good side? And if they weren't just saying it, *why can't I find another job?*"

Peter didn't have any answers for her. He just held her.

"I've been all over this town," MJ muttered. "I'm either too tall, or too short, or too fat, or too thin, or my hair's the wrong color, or my voice is wrong somehow. I wouldn't mind if I thought the producers *knew* what they wanted. But they *don't* know. They don't know anything except that I'm *not* what they want. Whatever that is." She breathed out, hard. "And my feet hurt, and my clothes stick to me, and I want to kick every one of their sagging, misshapen butts."

"Oh, come on," Peter said, holding her away a little now, since her voice told him it was all right to. "Their butts can't *all* have been misshapen."

"Oh yes they can," MJ said, straightening up again and reaching for the second paper bag, while Peter still held her. "You should have seen this one guy. He had this—"

"Who's all this food for?" Peter said suddenly, looking at the counter, which was becoming increasingly covered with stuff. Chicken breasts, more wine—dessert wine this time—fresh spinach, cream, fresh strawberries. "Is someone coming over for dinner, and I forgot about it? Ohmigosh, you said we were inviting Aunt May—"

"It's for *us*," MJ said. "Why do we only have to have nice dinners when people are coming over? Besides, May is *next* week. You have a brain like a sieve." She folded up the other bag, picked up its partner, and shoved them into the bag drawer.

"No question about that whatsoever," Peter said, abruptly glad of an excuse not to have to tell her immediately about the bank, or the credit card, or the answering machine. "Sieves R Us. What's for dinner, sexy?"

"I'm not telling you till you set the table. And tell your little droid friend out there that he doesn't get a high chair. He can sit in the living room and I'll give him a can of WD-40 or something." She hmphed, an amused sound, as she pulled a drawer open and started taking out pots and pans. "Flashers. I have enough problems with them in the street without finding them at home."

Peter chuckled, picked up the camera tripod and its associated apparatus and carried it into the living room, where he left the camera with its face turned to the wall. Then, humming, he went to get the tablecloth.

Tonight, he thought. *Tonight we'll see.*

Much later, well after dinner, the lights in the front of the Parker apartment went out.

The lights in the back were still on. MJ was in bed, propped up in a nest of pillows, reading. If someone heard about this tendency and asked her about it, Peter knew, MJ would tell them one version of the truth: that she was just one of those people who found it constitutionally impossible to get to sleep without first reading something, *anything.* The other truth, which she only told to Peter, and no more often than necessary, was that she needed to do something to take her mind off his "night job," as opposed to his day job. His night job's hours were far more irregular, the company he kept was generally far less desirable, and sometimes he didn't come back from it until late or, rather, early. Peter knew MJ restrained herself from saying, much more often, how much she feared that one night he would go out to the night job, and *never* come back from it. He had learned to judge her level of nervousness by how big a book she took to bed with her. Tonight it was *The Story of the Stone,* a normal-sized paperback. So Peter went out in a good enough humor, as relaxed as he could be these days, when he was no longer quite a free agent.

It was perhaps more strictly accurate to say that Peter Parker opened the window, and turned off the lights. Then, a few minutes later, someone else came to the window and stood for a moment, the webbed red and solid blue of the costume invisible in the darkness to any putative watcher. It was always a slightly magical moment for him, this hesitation on the border between his two worlds: the mundane standing on the threshold of the extraordinary, safe for the moment... but not for long.

Tonight he hesitated a shorter time than usual. The camera and its rig were collapsed down as small as they would go, slipped into the back-pouch where they would stay out of his way. If anyone caught sight of him on his rounds tonight, they would probably find themselves wondering if they were seeing some new costumed figure who had decided to emulate the Hunchback of Notre Dame. He chuckled under his breath at the thought. *Would one more costumed figure attract any attention in this city anymore?* he wondered. Lately the place had been coming down with them. Meanwhile, there would be the usual stir if one of the natives spotted him, one of the more familiar, if not universally loved, of the super heroes in town.

Under the tight-fitting mask, he smiled. Then Spider-Man slipped out the window, clung briefly to the wall, and closed the window behind him, all but a crack.

Carefully, as usual, he wall-crawled around the corner of the building—theirs was a corner apartment—and around to the back wall, where MJ's bedroom window was. The window was open, in the hope of any cool breeze. He put his head just above windowsill level, knocked softly on the sash. Inside, on the bed against the far wall, the reading light shone. MJ looked up, saw him, smiled slightly, made a small finger-waggle wave at him: then went back to her book. She was already nearly halfway through it. *I still wish she could teach me to read that fast,* he thought, and swarmed up the back corner of the building, making for the roof.

He peered cautiously over the edge of the roof balcony. There was no one up there this time of night: it was too hot and humid, and their neighbors with air conditioners seemed to have stayed inside to take advantage of it.

Can't blame them, he thought. It was a heck of a night to be out in a close-fitting costume. All the same, he had work to do.

About a third of a block away stood a tall office building. Spider-Man shot a line of web to a spot just south of the roofline near the building's corner. *And we're off,* he thought, and swung.

He had five different standard exit routes from the apartment, which he staggered both for security—no use taking the chance someone might see him exiting repeatedly and figure something out—and for interest's sake. Security was more important, though: he didn't want to take the chance that someone would find out where he was living by the simple expedient of following him home.

By now the business of swinging through the city had become second nature, a matter of ease. Tarzan could not have done it more easily, but then, Tarzan had his vines hanging ready for him. Spider-Man made his swinging equipment to order as he went. He shot out another long line, swung wide across Lexington and around the corner of the Chrysler Building, shot another line way up to one of the big aluminum eagle's heads, and swarmed up the line to stand atop the head and have a look around.

This was a favorite perch: good for its view of midtown, and it had other attractions. This was the particular eagle-head on which Margaret Bourke-White had knelt while doing her famous plate photos of the New York skyline in the late forties. Spidey stood there a moment, enjoying the breeze—it was better, this high up—and scanned his city.

It moved, as always it moved: restless, alive, its breath that old soft roar of which he never tired, the pulse visible rather than audible. Red tail-light blood moving below him in golden-lined sodium-lit arteries, white light contesting the pathways with the red; the faint sound of honking, the occasional shout, but very faint and far-off-seeming, as heard from up here; the roar of late jets winding up, getting ready to leap skyward from LaGuardia; lights in a million windows, people working late, home from work, resting, eating meals with friends, getting ready to turn in. Those people, the ones who lived here, worked here, loved the place, couldn't leave—those were the ones he did this for.

Or had *come* to do it for. It hadn't started that way, but his mission had grown to include them, as he had grown.

Spider-Man breathed out. While Spidey had never established a formal communication with the various lowlifes, informants, and stoolies that populated the city, he still heard things. Over the last couple of days, he'd heard some rumblings about "weird stuff" going on on the west side. Nothing more specific than that, just "weird."

Spidey slung a long line of web at the Grand Hyatt, caught it at one corner and swung on past and around, halfway over Grand Central, then shot another line at the old Pan Am building, swung around that, and headed westward first, using the taller buildings in the upper Forties to get him over to Seventh Avenue, where he started working his way downtown. That was something he had learned fairly early on: when traveling by web, a straight line was often not the best way to go. It wasn't even always possible. Buildings tall enough to be useful are not necessarily strung for a webslinger's convenience in a straight line between him and his destination. Over time Spidey had learned where the tall buildings clustered and where they petered out. He learned to exploit those clusters for efficiency, discovering that an experienced slinger of webs could gain as much speed slingshotting around corners as he lost from not being able to go straight as the crow flew.

Shortly he was down in the mid-Twenties, and he slowed down to take in the landscape. This time of night, things were more than just quiet, they were desolate. There were few restaurants in this area, not even many bars, and almost no one lived here, except the occasional tiny colony of homeless squatting in some unused or derelict structure. Not even much traffic passed by. Here the street lighting was iffy at best, the lamp bulbs missing or sometimes blown out by people who liked the dark to work in. The presence of that kind of person was one of the reasons he patrolled here on a more or less regular basis. Left to themselves, the children of the night might get the idea that they owned this neighborhood, and it was good for them to know that someone else had other ideas.

He paused on the roof of one building, looked up and down its cross-street, and listened carefully.

Nothing. He shot out another line of web, swung across another street, and waited. It was not only sound for which he listened.

Nothing.

So it went for some good while. Not that he minded. Every now and then, he lucked into a quiet night, one which left him more time to appreciate the city and required less of his time worrying about it. The problem was that the worry came a lot more easily than it used to. The city was not as nice as he remembered it being when he was a child—and he chuckled softly to himself, remembering what a dirty, crime-ridden place it had seemed to him when his aunt and uncle first brought him from Queens into Manhattan. By comparison, that New York of years ago—and not that many years, really—was a halcyon memory, a pleasant and happy place, where it seemed the sun had always been shining.

Not anymore.

He paused on another rooftop on West 10th, looking around. Nothing but the muted city roar. Locally, no traffic—but he could hear the grind and whine of a diesel truck, one with a serious transmission problem to judge by the sound of it, heading north on 10th Avenue. *We've got a dull one*, he thought. *No "weird stuff" in sight. Normally I'd be grateful.*

Then it hit him.

Several times over the course of their relationship, he had tried to explain to MJ how it felt, the bizarre experience he had long ago started to call his "spider-sense." It was, first of all, very simple: there was nothing of thought or analysis about it. It wasn't a feeling of fear, but rather of straightforward alarm, untinged by any other emotion, good or bad. It was the internal equivalent of hearing a siren coming up behind you when you knew you hadn't done anything wrong. It had seemed to him that, if as simple a creature as a spider experienced alarm, it would feel like this.

It also made him feel as if he was tingling all over. He was tingling now.

He stood very still, then slowly turned. The sense could be vaguely directional, if he didn't push it. Nothing specific northward, nothing to the east. Westward—

He shot out some web and swung that way, over several decrepit-looking rooftops. Unlike the buildings closer to midtown, these were in rather poor repair. There were gaping holes in some of the roofs, places where the tar and shingles and gravel had fallen in—or been cut through. *Looks like there's precious little to steal in most of these, though.*

The spider-sense twinged hard, as abrupt and impossible to ignore as the nerve in a cracked tooth, as he came to one particular building. He had almost passed it, an ancient broad-roofed single-story building with big skylights which looked mostly structurally intact, though most of the glass in them was broken. Well, all right…

He shot out another length of web, cut loose the last one from which he had been swinging, and let it lengthen as he dropped toward the old warehouse's roof. After a second or so he impacted, but so lightly he doubted anyone inside would have heard him.

Softly he stepped over to the skylight with the most broken glass, dropped beside it to show the minimum possible silhouette, and peered inside.

A very old place indeed. Down on the main shop floor, if that was what it was, lay toppled or discarded timbers, piles of trash, and puddles of water from other spots in the roof that leaked. His gaze took in old oil-drums lying on their sides, some of them split and leaking, and old newspapers plastered to the floor and faded by the passage of time.

Spider-Man shuddered. It was in a place very like this one that he had found the man who killed his uncle.

At other times, it all seemed a long time ago. His life had become so busy since. But here, it all seemed very close. The memory was reduced, now, to quick flashes. That afternoon in the science department at college, the experiment with what was mildly referred to as "radioactive rays." He could almost laugh at that, now. It had taken him years of study, nearly to the master's level, to really understand what had been going on in that experiment—and he now knew that the professor conducting it hadn't fully understood what was happening, either. There was more going on than the generation of plain old gamma rays: the radiation source had been contaminated by unusual elements and impurities, producing utterly unexpected results.

A spider had dropped gently downwards between the generating pods and become irradiated. Its DNA so quickly uncoiled and recoiled into a bizarre new configuration that it was actually able to survive for a few moments and bite Peter before the changes in its body chemistry killed it. The memory was frozen in Peter's mind like a slide from a slideshow: the tiny glowing thing falling onto his hand, the sudden rush of pain and heat as their respective body proteins met in what started as an allergic reaction, but turned into something much more involved and potentially deadly. Only the tininess of the spider and the minuscule amount of venom from its bite had saved his life. As it was, the radiation-altered proteins in its body fluids complexed with his own, the change a catalytic one, sweeping through Peter's body faster than mere circulation could have propelled it. Ten seconds later, he almost literally had not been the same person.

Another slide-image: the building he jumped halfway up, frightened by a car horn behind him, his hands adhering to the brick as if glued to it, but effortlessly. A standpipe that he accidentally crushed with what seemed a perfectly normal grip. Soon he had realized what had happened to him and, after the initial shock wore off, decided to market it.

He made a costume, not wanting his quiet home life with his Aunt May and Uncle Ben to be affected, and started making public appearances. The media ate it up. Sudden fame, to a guy who had always been regarded by his peers as a useless bookworm, was heady stuff. So it was, one night after a television appearance, that a man brushed past him and dove into an elevator. The cop in pursuit had shouted at Peter (still in costume at that point) to catch the running man. Peter had let the guy go, not particularly caring about him. He had other business to think about, appearances to plan, money to be made. What was one thief, more or less, to him?

Until a burglar, surprised in the act, shot and killed his Uncle Ben.

Weeping, raging, Peter had struggled into his costume, going to join the pursuit. There was an old warehouse not too far away where the burglar had gone to ground. By ways the police couldn't manage, he had gone in, cornered the burglar, disarmed him, battered him into submission—and then had found himself looking, horrified, into the face of the man he hadn't bothered to stop.

That face hung before him again, now. Other memories might mercifully fade. Not *this* one. Since that awful night Spider-Man had learned the lesson that with great power comes great responsibility. The weight on his conscience of his uncle's lost life had perhaps lightened a little over the intervening years, but he doubted he would ever be completely free of it—and maybe he didn't want to be.

Now he looked down into the warehouse, alert, and saw nothing but what was actually there. *As good a chance to test this as any,* he thought, and silently unshipped the camera apparatus, set it up near the edge of the skylight, checked its view and made sure that the pan-and-tilt head worked freely and without fouling itself. He wasn't using a flash tonight; instead he had loaded the camera with a roll of the new superfast ASA 6000 film, which would let the camera work by available light and keep it from betraying its presence to unfriendly eyes.

Right, he thought. *Now let's see what the story is in here.*

Softly he walked around to another of the skylights and peered inside. There was more glass in this one, and the view through it was somewhat obscured: he rubbed at one pane with a gloved hand and looked through. *Nothing.*

Spider-Man went along to the third skylight. This one, as the first, was missing most of its glass. Now, though, he heard something: voices muttering, the clunk of something heavy being moved, metal scraping laboriously over metal. He peered down. There was a shape on the floor. He squinted.

A security guard in uniform lay askew, crumpled and motionless. *Unconscious? Dead?*

He went through the biggest pane of glass with a crash, uncaring, taking only time enough to leave a strand of web behind him to ride down as it lengthened and break his fall to the floor. Landing, he took in the surroundings in tableau, as if frozen—four men, thuggish-looking, caught in the act of loading big oil-drumlike metal canisters onto a truck backed into the warehouse's loading ramp. Wide eyes, mouths hanging open, certainly unprepared for his arrival.

Not that *unprepared,* Spider-Man thought, as one of them pulled a gun. But the man was moving at merely human speed, and his opponent had a spider's swiftness of reaction. Spider-Man flung out one arm, shot a thick, sticky line of web at the gunman. It stuck to the gun, and Spidey yanked it out of the man's hand and threw it across the warehouse into the piles of trash in the shadows. The man yelped—apparently his finger had gotten stuck in the trigger guard, and now he stood shaking the hand and cursing.

"Serves you right," Spidey said as the others came for him, one of them pulling his own weapon. "But come on, now, didn't you see what just happened?" He threw himself sideways as the second man fired, then came up out of the roll, shot another line of web and took the second gun away, flinging it after the first one.

"Anybody else?" The first of the four came at Spidey in an attempt to get up-close and personal. "Oh well, if you insist," he said, resigned but amused. Spidey sidestepped the man's headlong rush, shot a line of webbing around his ankles, and got out of the way to let him sprawl face-first to best effect. The second one, now deprived of his gun, swung a board at Spider-Man and missed in his excitement. Spidey cocked one fist back, beginning to enjoy himself, and did *not* miss. That sound of a perfect punch landing, so bizarrely like the sound of a good clean home run coming off a bat, echoed through the warehouse. The man went down like a sack of potatoes and didn't move again.

"Glass jaw. Guess the gun is understandable," Spidey said, as the third of the four came at him. This one didn't just dive headlong, but stopped a few feet away, turned, and threw at Spider-Man what under normal circumstances would have been a fairly respectable rear thrust-kick. Unfortunately, these circumstances were *not* normal, as Spidey had been having two-bit crooks throwing such kicks at him since the craze for kung-fu movies had started some years before. While the kick looked good, the man throwing it had obviously never heard about the defenses against it, and Spidey simply stepped back a pace, then grabbed the foot hanging so invitingly in the air in front of him, and pulled hard. The man fell right down off his inadequately balanced stance on the other foot, and straight onto his tailbone with a crunch and a shriek of pain.

"I'd get that X-rayed if I were you," Spidey said, throwing a couple of loops of restraining web around the man before he could struggle to his feet. "Now then—"

His spider-sense buzzed sharply, then, harder than it had on initially seeing the warehouse. Spidey threw himself instantly as hard and as far to the right as he could. It was just as well, for just to his left there was a deafening *BANG!* and an explosion of light, and dirt and trash from the warehouse floor were flung in all directions through a thick roil of smoke.

The light and the noise were horribly familiar: Spider-Man had run into them entirely too often before. *Pumpkin bomb,* he thought. He came up into a crouch, aching slightly from the concussion but otherwise unhurt, and stared through the smoke at its inevitable source. Tearing through the smoke, standing on the jetglider which was one of his trademarks and his favorite way of getting around, was the orange-and-blue-garbed figure of the Hobgoblin.

Spidey jumped again as another bomb hit near him and went off, then leapt one more time to get out of range. "Hobby," he shouted, "why can't you stick to playing with cherry bombs, like other kids your age? This kind of antisocial behavior's likely to go on your permanent record."

A nasty snicker went by Spidey overhead: he rolled and leapt again, to be very nearly missed by an energy blast from one of Hobgoblin's gauntlets. "Spider-Man," Hobgoblin said in that cheerful, snide voice of his, the crimson eyes glinting evilly from under the shadow of the orange cowl, "you really shouldn't involve yourself with matters that don't concern you. Or with anything else but your funeral arrangements."

A couple more energy blasts stitched the concrete in front of Spider-Man as Hobgoblin soared by low overhead. Spidey bounced away from the blasts, hurriedly throwing a glance toward the four thugs. They were already showing signs of recovery, and the webbed ones were struggling to get loose. *Not good.* Spider-Man looked at the truck. *This may not go exactly as planned. I need a moment to plant a spider-tracer on that*—Another pumpkin bomb hurled near him and, warned again by his spider-sense, he jumped one more time, but almost not far enough. He felt the concussion all over the back of his body as it detonated. "Hobby," he shouted, "I expected better of you. How many of these things have you thrown at me, all this while, and not gotten a result?"

"One keeps trying," Hobgoblin said from above, over the whine of the jetglider. "But since you insist—"

Immediately it began to more or less rain small knife-edged electronic "bats" which buzzed dangerously near. It was too dark to see their edges glint, but Spidey had had occasion before to examine them closely, and they were wicked little devices—light graphite and monacrylic "wings" with individual miniaturized guidance systems and razor-sharp front and back edges. *Me and my big mouth,* Spidey thought, resisting the urge to swat at them as they buzzed around him—they could take off a finger, or even a hand, in no time flat. He ducked and rolled out of the way as fast as he could, slipping behind a couple of standing canisters in an attempt to confuse the razor-bats.

"Is this better?" Hobgoblin said sweetly.

Spider-Man didn't answer, intent as he was on dodging the bats. He spared a glance upward. *Came in through the skylight. I wonder,* Spidey thought, *did the camera get him? Well, we'll see. Meanwhile, I want him out of here—he's got too much of the advantage of mobility, and inside here I'm a sitting duck for these things. Also, I've got a better chance of snagging him out in the open.*

Spider-Man shot a line of webbing at the edge of the skylight where the camera was positioned and climbed at top speed. "Coward! Come back!" he heard Hobgoblin screech.

Outside, he looked up and around. Several buildings in this block and the next were ten stories high or better. He shot a webline at the nearest of them and went up it in a hurry. Behind him, to his great satisfaction, he heard the camera click, reposition itself, click again. *Good baby. You just keep that up.*

Hobgoblin, standing on the jetglider, soared up out of the skylight without noticing the camera. *Whatever else happens,* Spidey thought with slightly unnerved satisfaction, *these pictures are going to be dynamite.*

The bright, noisy detonation near him in midair reminded Spider-Man that he had more immediate explosives to worry about. *Now if I can just keep clear of those,* he thought, *long enough to snag that sled.*

For that, though, he needed to get himself anchored to best advantage, ideally in a situation that Hobgoblin would fly into without adequate forethought. Little time to manage such a situation. *All the same,* Spidey thought, *there's a chance. Those two buildings there are pretty close.* He swung around the corner of the building to which his webbing was presently attached, but instead of shooting out more webbing to the next anchorage and continuing around, he pulled himself in close to the side of the building and lay flat against it. Hobby shot on past and kept going, apparently assuming that Spidey had done so as well. *Good. He always tends to overreact a little.*

Now Spider-Man swarmed around the side of the building, back the way he had come, shot several strands of web across to the next building, felt them anchor; moved down and shot a couple of more, anchoring them in turn. In the dark, they were almost invisible. *Now all I need to do is swing across there with Hobby behind me, and one or another of those lines is going to catch him amidships and take him right off that glider.*

He wall-crawled as fast as he could up to the top of the building, peered around, saw nothing. *Good.* He anchored another strand of web, waited—

—and suddenly heard the buzzing all around him. The razor-bats had followed him up out of the warehouse.

Without hesitation he jumped off the building and web-slung for all he was worth, working to shake the things by swinging perilously close to the wall of the next building over. Several of the razor-bats hit the wall, disintegrating in a hail of graphite splinters. But the rest followed, and one of them got in close and nailed him in the leg. He managed to kick it into the building in passing, but his leg had a two-inch-long razor cut in it now, shallow but bleeding enthusiastically. *Next best tactic,* he thought, and shot out another line of webbing, heading upward toward where Hobby was gliding by, watching the fun and laughing hysterically.

"Yeah, this whole thing is just a bundle of laughs, isn't it? Let's see if it stays this funny," Spidey shouted, and made straight for him, energy blasts and pumpkin bombs or not. Even Hobgoblin had cause to be a little twitchy about being caught in a rapidly approaching cloud of his own flying razors. Sure enough, Hobby backed off slightly, tossing spare pumpkin bombs and firing off energy blasts as best he could. Spidey smiled grimly under the mask, noticing that his enemy was swooping toward the space between the two buildings where he had stretched his trap of weblines—

Then, without any warning, Hobgoblin turned, his great cloak flaring out behind him, and threw a pumpkin bomb right at Spidey. Caught up in Hobby's barrage, he was unable to dodge it, and it went off, seemingly right in his face.

He fell. Only an uprush of spiderly self-preservation saved him, the jet of webbing streaking out to catch the edge of the nearest building and break his fall to the roof of the old warehouse. It was not enough to cushion that fall, though. He came down hard and lay there with the world black and spinning around him.

Dead, he thought, *I'm dead. Or about to be.*

He could just hear the whine of the jetglider pausing in midair above and beside him, could just feel the sting of the roof gravel its jets kicked up. He knew Hobgoblin was bending over him.

"It doesn't matter," Hobby said, and laughed, not quite as hysterically. There was purpose in the laughter, nasty purpose, and the sound of genuine enjoyment. "Right now you wish you'd never heard of me, for all your smart talk. And shortly the whole city will wish it had never heard of me." More laughter. "Wait and see."

The laughter trailed away, as did the sound of the jetglider. Spider-Man could just barely hear Hobgoblin scolding his henchmen down in the warehouse, yelling at them to hurry, get themselves cleaned up, get the truck loaded, and get it out of here! He must have passed out briefly: the next sound he heard was the truck being driven away, fading into the greater roar of the city.

It was some while before he could get up. *Click, whirr, click, whirr,* he heard something say. The camera, its lens following his motion, the motion of a very dazed and aching Spider-Man staggering toward it, holding his head and moaning. *Click, whirrrrr,* said the camera. Then it said nothing further. It had run out of film.

He sat down next to it, hard, picked up the camera after a moment, and pushed the little button to rewind the film. *This worked, at least,* he thought. *But whatever else was going on down there, there's no way to tell now. I didn't even have time to put a tracer on that truck. Oh well—I bet we'll find out shortly. Whatever it is, it's big—Hobby wouldn't be involved otherwise.*

Meantime, I'd better get home.

TWO

"AND the WGN news time is one forty-five. It's eighty-four degrees and breezy in New York. Looks like we're in for worse tomorrow—our accu-weather forecast is for hazy, hot, and humid weather, highs tomorrow in the mid-nineties with expected humidity at ninety-two percent."

"I wish to God," said a weary voice off to one side, "that you'd turn that bloody thing off."

Harry sighed and reached out to turn it down, at least. "Can't get to sleep without my news," he said, turning over in the thin, much-flattened sleeping bag.

From his companion, half inside a cardboard box, wrapped in discarded Salvation Army blankets and numerous alternating layers of newspapers and clothes, there came a snort. "I can't sleep with it. Why don't you at least use the earphones, since you've got them? Jeez." There was a slight rustle of the other turning over restlessly in his box.

Harry grumbled acquiescence and started going through his things in the dark, looking for the small bag that contained the earplugs for the transistor radio. The sound echoed through the empty old warehouse: nothing else was to be heard. That didn't stop Harry from wrapping himself in several layers, despite the heat. You never knew what would be crawling around—or who. Best to keep protected, and keep what few possessions you had as close as possible.

He and Mike had been here for about six days now, having wormed their way in through a back-alley service entrance—the door to one of those ground-level elevators which, when they were working, came clanging up through the sidewalk to deliver crates and cartons to the storage area below a building. In the case of this particular freight elevator, it had been many years since it had worked. Some careful prying with the crowbar that Mike carried for self-defense got them in. They squirmed and wriggled their way through and found their way into a subcellar, then up a couple of flights of crumbling steps to the warehouse floor.

It wasn't as old as some of the buildings around here; it looked to have been built in the late forties and fifties, when there was still something of an industrial boom going on in this part of town. To judge from the general look of the place, Harry thought, it had been let go to seed for the past ten years or so. Now it looked like no one had been in to clean or maintain it for at least that long. There were chips and fragments of old paint and downfallen plaster all over the floor, and much of the light-blocking stuff they used on the glass windows had also peeled off. In other places, sun on the other side of the building had burnt the glass to translucent iridescence. There were some big old dusty canisters stacked up against one wall, forgotten, no doubt, by the previous owner, or the present one, whoever they were.

There were no signs of other habitation, which was unusual in this neighborhood. Squatters and dossers were all over this part of town, looking for a place to spend a night, or five, or ten. This building's quiet was a treasure, a secret that Harry and Mike kept very close to themselves and never spoke of when they were out on the street during the day, going through the trash and cadging the cash they needed for food.

"Money you spend on batteries for that thing," Mike muttered, "you could get food for."

Harry sniffed. His friend was single-minded in pursuit of something to eat: whatever else you could say about Mike, he wasn't starving. But his conversation wasn't the best. Harry, for his own part, might be homeless—but he liked to keep up with what was happening around him. He would not be this poor forever—at least, he tried to keep telling himself so.

At the same time, it was hard to predict how he was ever going to climb out of this hole he had fallen into two years ago. Job cuts at Bering Aerospace out on the Island left him an aircraft mechanic out on the street, unable to get a job even at McDonald's, because they said he was too old, and overqualified.

At least he had no family to support, never having married. So, when Harry's savings ran out, and he lost his apartment, there was no one else to feel grief or shame for. He had enough of that for himself. He kept what pride he could. He availed himself of a bath at least once a week at the Salvation Army; he only resorted to the various charities which fed homeless people when he absolutely had no choice. Most of all, he did his best not to despair. He kept himself as well fed as he could, and not on junk food, either. When he had the money, he bought fresh fruit and vegetables to eat. Whereas others might paw through garbage cans strictly for half-finished Big Macs, Harry as often as not would be distracted from his growling stomach by something in print that looked interesting, a foreign newspaper or a magazine. And there were, as Mike complained, nights when Harry went without anything to eat so that he could afford batteries for the transistor. That little radio had been with him a long, long time, a gift from his father many years ago, one of the first truly transistorized radios. It was on its last legs, but Harry refused to throw it away before it gave up the ghost on its own. It was, in a way, his last tie with his old life, and it kept him in touch with the rest of the world as well.

He pushed the earplug jack into the transistor and listened.

"A Hong Kong investment group is close to a deal with Stark Industries to finance a $3 billion housing development on the Hudson River site where real estate developers had once planned to build Television City. The plan for a vast media center on the Riverside between 59th and 72nd Streets foundered nearly a decade ago when attacked by city planners and neighborhood activists as a leviathan that would tax the area's infrastructure and environmental resources. It is believed that Stark's plan to introduce low-income housing for the area will meet with far greater approval—"

"I can still hear that thing," Mike said loudly. "Can't you turn it down?"

Harry was strongly tempted to tell his companion to wrap a pillow around his head and shut up. Since they started dossing here some six nights ago, Mike's constant complaining had been getting on Harry's nerves. There wasn't much he could do about it, though. He was aware that his companion was a bit of a sneak and a bully, and if Harry did anything to push him out of this warehouse, Mike would tell others about it. Shortly thereafter, the place would be full of other people, who would crowd in and steal from each other and get falling-down drunk on cheap booze, or blitzed on drugs, and would generally make the experience even more unpleasant than it already was. So Harry turned the transistor down just as far as he could, and lay there listening.

"*District Attorney Tower has announced that he will be running for another term this year, citing his excellent conviction record and his toughness on paranormal criminals. He is expected to run unopposed—*"

Harry waited to see what Mike would say. For the moment, at least, he lay quiet. At the end of that story, the radio said, "… *and if you have a news story, call 212-555-1212. The best news story of the week wins fifty dollars.*"

Harry yawned. He knew the number by heart, but the odds of him seeing anything newsworthy enough to win such a fabulous amount were less than nil.

"I can't stand it," Mike said. "I can still hear it!"

Harry opened his mouth to say, "You're nuts!" and then shut it again. He knew that he had just recently been discharged from the Payne Whitney Clinic across town. Or more accurately, he had signed himself out, after having been brought in half-crazed from drinking what seemed to have been bad booze—or maybe it had been Sterno. In any case, Mike had taken advantage of seventy-two hours' worth of good food and a cleanup before signing himself out. "Had to get out," Mike had said to him when they met again on the street. "They talk to you all the time—they never stop. I woulda gone nuts for sure. And there were rats in the walls."

Privately, Harry believed otherwise. He was no expert, but he thought that Mike sometimes heard and saw a lot of things that weren't there. The complaining about the radio was probably more of the same.

"I can't turn it down any further," he said.

"Well, you're a bastard, that's all," Mike said mildly, "just a bastard." He crawled out of his box and shed the first two or three layers of his wrappings.

Harry watched warily, wondering whether Mike was going to try to start a fight with him again, as he had a couple of nights ago, when he claimed Harry had been whispering all night. It had been more of an abortive struggle than a fight, but it had wound up with Mike ostentatiously hauling his bedding over to the other side of the warehouse—his mien indicating that this was meant as a penalty for Harry's bad behavior.

"I can't stand the noise," Mike said. "I'm going to sleep over here." And once more he proceeded to drag his box and his various bags full of belongings, one at a time, with a great show of effort and trouble, over by the canisters stacked up against the wall. This left at least fifty feet between Harry and Mike, and Harry was just as glad: it was that much further for the lice to walk.

Mike started the arduous business of rewrapping and reinserting himself into the bedding. Harry, with only a touch of irony, waited until Mike was finished with all this, then shouted, "Can you hear anything now?"

"Nothing but your big mouth," the answer came back after a moment.

Harry raised his eyebrows in resignation and went back to listening to the radio.

"An amino acid has been found for the first time in large galactic clouds, proving that one of the molecules important to the formation of life can exist in deep space, researchers say. Yanti Miao and Yi-Jehng Knan of the University of Illinois at Urbana reported Tuesday—"

"Hey," Mike's voice came from the other side of the warehouse floor, "I hear something!"

Oh, God, Harry thought. *I was almost asleep.* "What?"

"I dunno. I heard something outside the wall—bangin'."

Harry rolled his eyes. This, too, was a story he had heard before. Things banging on the wall, rats, things walking on the roof—"For God's sake, Mike, just wrap a pillow around your head, or something. It'll go away!"

"No it won't," Mike said with almost pleased certainty. "It didn't in the hospital."

Harry sighed. "Look, just lie down and go to sleep!"

"It's still there," Mike said. "Bangin'."

Unutterably weary, Harry took the earplugs out of his ears and listened.

Bang.

Very faint, but definitely there. "You got one this time, Mike," he said softly.

Bang. And definitely harder, so that he felt it through the floor. Bang.

"Now what the hell could that be at this time of night?" he wondered.

The two of them lay there, across the floor from one another, staring into the near-darkness and listening. Only a faint golden light came in through the high windows from outside—the reflected streetlights from the next street over. It gleamed faintly in their eyes as they turned to look at each other.

Then, silence—no more bangings.

"Aah, it's probably someone unloading something," Harry said after a while. "Maybe that Seven-Eleven over in the next block getting a late delivery."

Mike groaned. And groaned again, then, and Harry realized abruptly that it was not Mike at all, but a sound that was coming from the wall itself. A long, slow, straining sound of—metal, perhaps? He stared at the source.

In the darkness, your eyes fool you, so at first he simply didn't believe what he saw. The wall near the canisters was bowing inward toward them, almost stretching as if it were flexible, and being pushed from behind. Then a sudden sagging, the whole shape of the wall changing as it went to powder, and almost liquidly slumped away from itself, bowed further inward—

And then with a dreadful clanging crash, several of the big canisters were tipped away from the wall by what was coming through it, pushing them—the lowest ones fell over sideways and rolled. One of them stacked higher, slightly over to one side, teetered, leaned away from its stack, then crashed to the floor and burst open.

It fell right on the cardboard box where Mike had been sleeping. At the first dreadful noise the wall made, he had scrambled out and was now standing safe from the canister's fall, but not safe from its contents, with which it sprayed him liberally as it burst. A sort of metallic chemical smell filled the air.

Mike shook himself all over and started jumping around and waving his arms, cursing a blue streak. "What the hell, what is this sh—"

The last of the canisters fell down, missing and rolling away, drowning the sound of his cursing. And then something jumped through the hole in the wall.

Harry looked at it, and swallowed—and had to swallow again, because in that second his mouth had gone so dry, there was nothing left to swallow with. In the shadows of the warehouse, the thing that stood there was blacker still. Whatever light there was in there fell on it and vanished, as if into a hole. It was man-shaped, big, and powerful-looking, with huge pale eyes—

Mike, still waving his arms around, jumping and swearing, took a long moment to see it. Harry concentrated on staying very still and very quiet, and not moving in his bag. He might not have a television himself at this point in his career, but he certainly looked at them when he passed the TV stores on the Avenue. And he knew that dreadful shape—it had been in the news often enough lately. A terrible creature, half man, half God knew what. And Mike, infuriated, spotted it, and went at it waving his arms.

For the moment it seemed not to have noticed. It was crouching like some kind of strange animal. From a huge fanged mouth it emitted an awful long tongue, broad and prehensile and slobbering, and it began to lap at the stuff which had burst from the containers. Mike lurched toward it, windmilling his arms inanely as if he were trying to scare off a stray dog.

For a few breaths' worth of time, it ignored him. Harry lay there, completely still, while the sweat broke out all over him, and the blood pounded in his ears. The black creature seemed to grin with that huge mouthful of fangs as it lapped and lapped with the huge snakelike tongue.

But Mike was far gone in annoyance or paranoia, and he went right up to the creature, yelling, and kicked it.

It noticed him *then*.

It noticed his leg first, the tongue wrapping around it and sliding up and down it as if it were thirsty for the stuff which had drenched Mike. Mike hopped and roared with loathing and annoyance, and he batted at the dark shape.

Then he roared on a higher note, much higher, as it pounced on Mike.

It was not long about exercising its teeth on him. Harry lay there transfixed by horror, now, not by fear for himself. Eventually the screaming stopped, as the dark shape ferreted out the last few delicacies it was interested in, and finally dropped the hideous form that had been Mike.

Then it went back to its drinking, decorous and unselfconscious as some beast by a pool out on the veldt. It cleaned up every last drop of the spilled stuff on the floor... not despising or declining the blood.

And then it stood up and looked around thoughtfully, like a man, with those great pale glaring eyes.

Its eyes rested on Harry.

He lay there frozen, on his side, watching, a trickle of drool running unnoticed out of his shocked-open mouth.

The creature turned away, whipped a few more of the nastily dextrous tendrils around several of the canisters, and effortlessly leapt out the hole in the wall with them, silent in the silence.

Gone.

It was a long, long time before Harry could move. When he did, it took him a while to stand up, and he stood still in the one spot, shaking like an old palsied bum, for many minutes.

Then, carefully, avoiding the still-wet spots, and the gobbets and tatters of Mike that lay around on the floor, he made his way out through the hole the creature had left… feeling in his pocket for a quarter to call the radio station, and collect his fifty dollars.

IT took Spider-Man a long time to get up after the fight. First he saw to the camera, unloading the film and tucking it away in his costume, and then he found that he didn't feel very well. He sat down, breathed deeply, and tried hard not to throw up. It was as usual: the reaction hit him later, sometimes worse than other times.

Finally he decided he really had to get himself moving. He started web-swinging his way home, taking his time and not overexerting himself. His whole body felt like one big bruise, and several times he had to stop and blink when his vision wobbled or swam. He found himself wondering whether the pumpkin bomb had possibly left him with a borderline concussion along with everything else. *Hope not,* he thought. *At least I wasn't unconscious at all.* It was a relief. Going to the emergency room as a walk-in patient held certain complications for super heroes with secret identities—especially as regarded sorting out the medical insurance….

The digital clock on the bank near home said 4:02, with two bulbs missing, and 81 degrees. *Lord, the heat….* There was this blessing, at least: the city seemed mercifully quiet as he made his way back.

Very wearily he climbed up the wall toward their apartment, avoiding the windows belonging to the two nurses on four who were working night shift this spring and summer, and the third-floor windows of the garbage guy who was always up and out around four-thirty.

He found the bedroom window open just that crack, pushed it open, and found the lights all out inside as he stepped carefully over the sill and closed the window behind him. He looked at the bed. There was a curled-up shape there, hunched under the covers. He looked at it lovingly and was about to head for the bathroom when the shape said, "Out late tonight...."

"Later than planned," he said, pulling his mask off wearily, "that's for sure."

MJ sat up in bed and turned the light on. She didn't look like she'd slept at all. "Sorry," he said, knowing she hadn't.

She yawned and leaned forward, smiling a small smile. "At least you came back," she said.

The issue of his "night job," and his need to risk himself webslinging for the public good, had been a source of concern. Peter had felt for a long time before they got serious that a costumed crimefighter had no business having a permanent relationship with someone who, by that relationship, would be put permanently at risk. It hadn't stopped him from dating, with various levels of seriousness, both super heroes and mere mortals—something that MJ was always quick to point out when the subject came up. She also pointed out that there were other costumed crimefighters and super heroes who were happily married and carried on more or less normal family lives, even without their alternate identities being known. That much he himself had shared with her. There was no reason they couldn't make it work as well. "All you have to do," she kept saying at such times, "is give up the *angst.*"

Anyway, *now* she said nothing about those other discussions, though the memory of them clearly lurked behind her eyes. "You made the news," MJ said.

"I did?" He blinked as he pulled the costume top over his head. "That was quick. Didn't see any news people turn up before I left—"

"Yup. You made WNN."

"What??" That confused him. "Must have been a pretty slow news night," Peter muttered. "I still don't see how they managed to find out about that—"

MJ laughed at him softly, but there was a worried edge to the sound. She swung out of the bed. "Boy, you must be getting blasé. After what's been going on around this town the past few years, it is *not* going to be considered a slow news night when Venom turns up again—"

"What?!"

The laugh definitely had more of the nervous edge to it. She turned and felt around in the semidarkness for the nightgown left over the bedside chair. "Venom," she said, and then looked at him. Her mouth fell open. "I assumed—" She shut the mouth again. "You *weren't* out fighting Venom?"

"Hobgoblin, actually." But now his head was spinning.

She stared at him again. "It was on the news, like I said. Something about him having been seen at a warehouse downtown. There was a murder—and then he made off with some—radioactive waste, I think they said."

"Who was murdered?"

MJ shook her head. "Some homeless guy."

Peter was perplexed. "Doesn't sound like Venom," he said. "Radioactive waste? What would Venom want *that* for? As for murdering a homeless person—" He shook his head too. "That sounds even *less* like him."

He handed MJ his costume top. "I thought," she said, "when you were out late…." Then she looked down at her hands and wrinkled her nose. "This can wait," MJ said. "I think I'd better wash this thing." She held the top away from her, with a most dubious expression. "And I think you'd better change your deodorant. Phooey!"

"You didn't have the night that I had," Peter said, "for which you should be grateful."

"Every minute of the day," MJ said, with her mouth going wry. "Have you given any thought to making a summerweight one? This can't be comfortable in this weather."

"In all my vast amounts of spare time," Peter said, "yes, the thought has crossed my mind, but picking the right tailor is a problem." MJ winced, then grinned and turned away.

"I'll just wash it," she said. "Did you buy more Woolite yesterday?"

"Oh, cripes, I forgot."

"Oh well. Dishwashing liquid'll have to do. *Don't* forget the Woolite this time."

"Yes, master."

"Have you got everything off of the belt? All your little Spidey-gadgets?"

"Uh huh."

She looked at his abstracted expression and, smiling, handed him back the costume. "You'd better go through it yourself—I can never find all those compartments. The thing's worse than your photojournalist's vest."

Peter took it, obediently enough, and removed from the top a couple of spider-tracers and some spare change. Then he shucked out of the bottom and gave it to her.

"You go get in the tub, tiger," MJ said, turning away again. "You can use a soak to relax."

"And to make me fit for human company?" he shouted down the hall after her.

A slightly strangled laugh came back. "After you're done," she said, "we can look at WNN. It'll be back on again."

Peter sighed, went to the hall closet for a towel, then ambled to the bathroom.

It was just like life to pull something like this on him now. Venom. But he's supposed to be in San Francisco—

Then again, this sudden appearance was not necessarily a surprise. Every time in the past he had thought Eddie Brock, the man who had become Venom, was out of his life, back he would come.

And thinking this, not watching particularly where he was going, Peter tripped on the bathroom threshold and fell flat on the tile floor. Only a quick twist sideways kept him from bashing his forehead on the sink.

"You okay?" came the worried call from down the hall, in the kitchen, where MJ was filling the big sink to wash the costume.

"If 'okay' means lying under the toilet with the brushes and the Lysol, then, yeah…."

He heard MJ's footsteps in the hallway as he started to lever himself up. "You fell down?" she said, sounding confused. "That's not your style, either."

"No," Peter said, getting up and rubbing one of his elbows where he had cracked it against the sink on the way down. "No, it isn't. Ever since—"

And then he stopped. The spider's bite had conferred a spider's proportional strength on him, along with its inhuman agility, and the spider-sense always helped that agility along, warning him of accidents about to happen, non-routine dangers, and even routine ones like trips and falls and people blundering into him. Now it was just gone. Then he remembered that he had also gotten no warning whatsoever when Hobby tossed that last pumpkin bomb at him. He should have received *some* sort of warning. He rubbed his ribs absently, feeling the ache. He said to MJ, "Some time ago when Hobby and I first tangled—Ned, not the current version—he had managed to come up with a chemical agent that killed my spider-sense for a day or so at a time. He used to deliver the agent as a gas out of the pumpkin bombs. However—" He bent over to finger the shallow cut on his leg.

"You're going to need stitches for that," MJ said, concerned.

"No, I won't. It looks worse than it is. But it was deep enough for one of the razor-bats he threw at me to give me a good dose of the anti-spider-sense agent, whatever it is."

MJ looked at him. "How long is it going to last?"

Peter shrugged. "Well, Jason Macendale isn't quite the scientific whiz that Ned Leeds was. If *Ned* were still the Hobgoblin, I'd have reason to expect much worse—an improved brew every year, at least. But I think this'll just last a day or so."

"Well, be careful," MJ said. "Just get yourself into the tub and try not to drown, okay?"

"Yes, Mom," he said with some irony.

He turned on the tub's faucets, put in the drain-plug, and sat and watched the water rise. Hobgoblin was enough of a problem, but the addition of Venom to the equation—if the news story was accurate—made the situation even less palatable.

In a city filled with super heroes with complex life-histories and agendas, and villains with a zoo full of traumas, histories, and agendas almost always more involved than the heroes', and inevitably more twisted, Hobgoblin stood out. Originally "he" had been another villain entirely, one called the Green Goblin, who had taken a particular dislike to Spider-Man early in their careers. He had spent a long time repeatedly hunting Spidey down and making his life a misery. Norman Osborn had been the man's name: a seriously crazy person, but nonetheless a certifiable genius with a tremendous talent in the material and chemical sciences. Like many other super villains, he picked a theme and stuck to it with fanatical and rather unimaginative singlemindedness, establishing himself as a sort of spirit of Halloween gone maliciously nuts—wearing a troll-like costume with a horrific mask and firing exploding miniature "pumpkin bombs" in all directions around him from the jetglider on which he stood. He took whatever he liked from the city he terrorized, and he frightened and tormented its citizens as he pleased.

Spider-Man, naturally, had been forced to take exception to this behavior: and the Green Goblin had taken exception to *him*. Their private little war had gone on for a long time, until finally Osborn died, killed by one of his own devices—but not before he had caused the death of Gwen Stacy, an early love of Peter's.

Peter paused, looking for something aromatic and soothing to put in the bath water. There didn't seem to be anything but a large box of Victoria's Secret scented bath foam. *I can't imagine why she buys this stuff,* he thought. He started going through the bathroom cupboards and finally came up with a bottle of pine bath essence.

Green, he thought. *It would have to be green....* He shrugged and squirted some in, then sat down again, watching the bubbles pile up.

No sooner had the Green Goblin died—and Peter, after a while, had come to some kind of terms with his grief—than history began to repeat itself. Some petty crook stumbled onto one of the Goblin's many secret hideouts, sold the information of its whereabouts to another, better-heeled criminal, who found the Green Goblin's costumes, bombs, energy gauntlets and jet gliders intact and in storage. He had done some minor work on the spare costumes—alterations and changes in color—and had emerged as a more or less off-the-rack super villain, the Hobgoblin.

Hobby had been a reporter named Ned Leeds—ironically, both a colleague of Peter Parker's at the *Daily Bugle* and the husband to another of Peter's early loves, Betty Brant. This man too, in his new identity, began bedeviling Spider-Man in an attempt to keep him busy while Leeds tried to mine the secrets of Norman Osborn's rediscovered diaries—which Spidey feared also might include information on his own secret identity, which Osborn had learned. Leeds also synthesized the odd chemical formula which had given the Green Goblin his terrible speed and strength, but he ignored the warnings in Osborn's journals that the formula might also cause insanity in the person who used it for maximum physical effect.

It did, of course. It made Leeds as crazy as Osborn had ever been, and he too died, killed by a rival criminal. And then the weaponry, the costume, the persona, and the ruthlessly opportunistic and money-hungry personality surfaced again, this time in another man called Jason Macendale. Macendale had eagerly made himself over as Hobgoblin Number Two, or perhaps Two-A. Hobby Two-A thought, in concert with his predecessors, that it would be an excellent idea to get rid of Spider-

Man, one of the most active local crimefighters and the one most likely to cause him trouble on a day-to-day basis.

Peter turned the faucets off, tested the water. It was at that perfect heat where, if you stepped in carefully and lay perfectly still, it would boil the aches out of you, but once in, if you moved, you'd be scalded. He climbed in, sank down to bubble level, and submerged himself nearly to his nose. *Hobgoblin,* he thought and sighed. *Him I could deal with. But Venom, too…*

He closed his eyes and let the hot water do its work on his body, but his mind refused to stay still.

Venom was entirely another class of problem.

The trouble had begun innocently enough, when he was off-planet— Peter chuckled at how matter-of-fact it all sounded, put that way. He had been swept up into a war of super heroes against unearthly forces at the edge of the known universe and conveyed by a being known as the Beyonder to a world out there somewhere. While there, his trusty costume had been torn to shreds and, not being the kind of crimefighter who felt he was at his best working naked, he looked around for another one. A machine on that planet, obligingly enough, provided him with one. It was quite a handsome piece of work, really—that was his thought when he first put it on, and when he wore it during the Secret War, and afterwards, on his return to Earth. It was every super hero's dream of a costume. Dead-black, with a stylized white spider on the chest—graphically, he thought, a more striking design than his present red-and-blue one. Possibly the machine had read the design from some corner of his mind which thought it knew what he really wanted to look like.

The costume was more than just sleek-looking. It responded instantly to its owner's desires. You didn't have to take it off: you could think it off. It would slide itself away from your mouth so you could eat or talk; it would camouflage itself, with no more than a thought, to look like your street clothes; at the end of a hard day, it would slide off and lie in a little puddle at your feet, and you could pick it up and hang it on a chair, where the next morning it would be perfectly fresh and clean and ready to go.

It was *so* accommodating, in fact, that Peter began to find it a little unnerving. He began to have odd dreams about that costume and his old one, engaged in a struggle for possession of him, threatening to tear him apart. Finally he took the costume to Reed Richards, the most scientifically inclined of the Fantastic Four, and asked to have it analyzed.

He was more than slightly surprised to discover that what he had been wearing was not a costume, not a made thing—or *made* it possibly was: but it was not just cloth. It was *alive*. It was an alien creature, a symbiote, made to match his physiology, even his mind. And its intention was to bond with him, irrevocably. They would be one.

Peter shivered in the hot water and then winced slightly as it scalded him. He slowed his breathing down slightly, trying to deal with the heat and the discomfort of the memory.

It had taken a fair amount of work to get the costume off him. He had not been prepared for a relationship of that permanence, intensity, or intimacy—not for anything like it at *all*. It took all Reed Richards' ingenuity to get the symbiote-costume off Peter's body and confine it for further study. Sonics were one of its weak points; against loud noises, and specifically, focused sound, it had no defense. But even when it was finally off him, that did not solve Peter's problem.

The costume desired him, and a great rage was growing in its simple personality. If it ever escaped its durance, it would find him. It would bond with him. It would punish him for his rejection. And in the act, it would probably squeeze the life out of him. The irony, of course, would be that in so doing, in killing the host for which it had been created, it would probably then die itself. But from Peter's point of view, the irony ran out with the prospect of his own death.

The symbiote had eventually escaped, of course—these things have a way of not ending tidily—and it did indeed hunt Peter down. The only way he had been able to get rid of it was to flee into the bell tower of a nearby church, and let the brain-shattering ringing of the bells drive it off him. Most of the symbiote, he had thought, perished. But a drop or two, it seemed, remained. With unearthly persistence it replicated itself—and found another host.

That new host was named Eddie Brock: once a journalist who worked for the *Daily Globe*, the *Bugle's* primary competitor, but who had been fired over a misunderstanding, a misjudgment of a news story he had been reporting. Spider-Man had been involved in a less visible aspect of the same story, which involved a masked killer called the Sin-Eater. Spidey had revealed the genuine identity of the killer to the media, when Brock had thought it was another person entirely, and had written and published his story based on insufficient data.

Once fired, Brock had decided that Spider-Man was the cause of all his troubles and needed to be killed. And one night, in that same church, something dark oozed out of the shadows and found Eddie Brock. He was joined. He welcomed the hating unity that the symbiote offered him—he became one with it, part of it; and it, part of him.

Hatred can be even more potent than love as a joining force. So it proved for Brock. The costume, though not saying as much in words, gave him to understand its hatred for Spider-Man, for whom it had been made, and who, in its view, had heartlessly rejected it. And in Eddie Brock's opinion, anything that hated Spider-Man was only showing the best possible taste.

They were one. Eddie Brock became one of those people who could say "we" and did not need to be royal to make it stick. Since then, he, or they, as Venom, had successfully hunted Spidey down in apartment after apartment in New York—not beneath frightening MJ in their attempts to get at Spider-Man. That dark shadow—black costume, white spider, and the formidably fanged mouth and horrific prehensile tongue that the symbiote liked to grow—that shadow came and went in Peter's life, never bringing less than dread, often terror, sometimes pain and injury nearly to the point of death. They had slugged it out, how many times now? Up and down the city, and each time only skill and wits and sometimes luck had saved Spider-Man's life.

After many encounters, though, something strange had happened. In one final battle on a lonely Caribbean island, Spider-Man (already nearly beaten to a pulp) arranged for Venom to believe he had died in a gas explosion—leaving charred human bones and the remnants of his costume as evidence. He himself swam like mad into the nearby shipping lanes, looking for a ship to take him home, and found one.

And Venom, Eddie, convinced that his old enemy was dead at last, found a sudden odd peace descending on him. For a while he stayed on that island—maybe, Peter wondered, recovering some of his sanity there? At any rate, some time later Eddie turned up in San Francisco. He stayed there only long enough to discover that Spider-Man was still alive, and began hitching his way eastward to come to grips with him one last time.

But on the way, a gang of thugs attacked the kind family which had offered him a ride cross-country. It was here that Eddie began to find a sense of purpose, as Venom stood up and utterly destroyed the thugs attacking this family and the other people in the truckstop. He decided there might be something else for him to do in this life. He would protect the innocent, as (he thought) Spider-Man had betrayed him.

Or, at least, those he thought were innocent. One had to remember that Venom was not remotely sane. Still, he was no longer a figure of pure malice, either. There was an ambivalent quality to his danger now. He would probably always be a threat to Spider-Man, on some level or another. But the poor and helpless had nothing to fear from him—at least as far as Peter understood. That was why this news about some homeless person's murder rang so false.

"How you doing in there?" came the call from down the hallway.

Peter bubbled.

MJ put her head around the corner of the door. "Need anything? Should I scrub your back?"

"Maybe later," Peter said. "Has the news come around yet?"

"No. You just make sure you dry off before you come out, and don't drip all over the floor like last time." She turned away. "Things are wet enough in here as it is."

"From what?"

"Your costume. Keeps trying to climb out of the sink."

"Don't even joke about it," Peter said, and submerged to his nose again.

It was bad news all around. He sighed, bubbling. His spider-sense was gone for at least a day, or so he thought. Even if it had been in working order, his spider-sense didn't react to the symbiote Venom now wore. It had, after all, been designed by that alien machine not to interfere with his own powers.

Bad, he thought. *If I were Hobgoblin, I would be gunning as hard as I could for Spider-Man over the next day. I'm just going to have to be super careful tomorrow. I've got no choice about going out, either.* He looked out at dawn's early light beginning through the bathroom window. *As soon as I get myself out of the tub and dried, I've got to start getting those pictures developed… so I can do something about that credit card bill. Assuming they* want *the pictures.*

He frowned for a moment. The job market had been tightening of late; there were a lot more freelancers competing for the same number of photo slots in any given day's paper. *The competition is fierce now, but it's hard to pay attention to composition,* he thought ruefully, *when someone's lobbing pumpkin bombs at your head.* Peter had a lively respect for the acuity and quality of results that war correspondents got in their photographs. He knew how they felt, and how it felt to be on the firing line… and often he would have given a great deal to be shot at just with bullets, instead of energy blasts or weird gases.

"Yo, tiger! I think it comes on after this bit. C'mon."

Peter got out of the tub, ouching again as the water scalded him, toweled himself passably dry, wrapped the towel around his waist and padded down the hall to the living room. The TV was showing another of those horrifically frequent commercials for something called Flex-O-Thigh, in which people who plainly had no need of physical exercise whatsoever smilingly worked various springy pieces of machinery in an attempt to convince you that the exercise was effortless, and the machinery results beyond your dreams. Toll-free numbers flashed, and a friendly voice urged all and sundry to Call Now!

Then the news came back on again. "Super villain Venom has been implicated in a burglary and murder tonight in New York," said the voice. "Venom, whose last known appearance was in San Francisco, according to California law enforcement officials, allegedly murdered one man in an incident in a warehouse, then stole several containers of what City authorities have confirmed is nuclear waste—"

The camera showed the warehouse: a big jagged hole, but odd in its jaggedness, almost as if the edges had been pulverized—or melted? Peter looked at the picture curiously, but it changed to a view of a sheeted form, surprisingly small, being carried out of the warehouse on an ambulance's gurney and loaded into a paramedic wagon. The announcer said, "An eyewitness was treated for shock at St. Luke's Hospital and later released."

Peter and MJ found themselves looking at a stubbled, shaggy-haired man who was saying, "Yeah, he just came in through the wall—knocked some of the canisters over—and then—" He stammered. "He killed Mike there. He just ripped him up like a paper bag. Little bits came off the Venom guy—you know, like the pictures in the paper from the last time— little bits, they just shredded—" He turned away from the camera, making short chopping motions with one hand. "I'm sorry. I'm sorry, I just wanna go—" He stumbled away.

Peter and MJ looked at each other. "'Shredded'?" she said softly.

"He could if he wanted to," Peter muttered. "But it's just—it's just not like him."

"Maybe he had a bad day," MJ said doubtfully.

"New York City authorities have begun a search for Venom, but reliable sources within the NYPD have told WNN that they doubt the police will have much luck in finding him. Venom's *modus operandi,* they say, has been to lie quiet until some set of circumstances aggravates his old hatred against Spider-Man—at which time Venom makes his presence known abundantly. The people of New York can only hope that Spider-Man maintains a low profile for the immediate future. Lloyd Penney, for WNN News, New York."

"And to think that meanwhile," MJ said, "you've been out aggravating someone else entirely."

"Hush, woman." He chuckled, though it wasn't really all that funny; and briefly he told MJ about the evening's confrontation with Hobgoblin, while WNN went on briefly about the new Madonna movie and details of a press conference the Avengers had recently called. "And there was nothing in there," he said at last, "but some big canisters...." His voice trailed off.

"Like those you just saw on the news?" MJ said, raising her eyebrows.

"Like those.... I can't go to sleep," he said, getting up with a groan. "I've got to get those pictures developed and get them in to the *Bugle,* and I've got to get a look in the morgue—"

"The morgue," MJ said dryly, "is exactly where you're going to wind up if you go out in this condition."

There was no point in arguing with her in this mood, Peter knew. He sat there quietly, thinking about which stock to use for developing the pictures, and drank what MJ gave him. But the decaf coffee was mostly milk, and Peter sat back, just for a few moments....

MJ stood up, smiled, looked at him and shook her head. "It's the hot milk," she said with satisfaction. "That tryptophan does it every time." She went away to get a quilt to cover Peter, turned off the TV, and then slipped into the kitchen to see about her own pot of coffee.

THREE

PETER blinked at the sunshine suddenly filling the living room. He blinked harder. *Oh, God, I overslept.* "MJ, why didn't you get me up?!" he said.

No answer, nor would there be one, he realized. The apartment had that particular empty sound. As Peter sat up on the couch, the quilt fell to the floor along with a note. Moaning a little—the bruises from last night had now had time to stiffen up—Peter bent over to pick it up. "Gone out for *Daily Variety* and *H'wd Reporter,*" it said. "Had hot tip this morning, might mean work. See you later. Love love love love," followed by a little tangle of X's and O's.

Peter dropped the note onto the coffee table, yawned, stretched, moaned again, stretched some more regardless. The smell of coffee was drifting through the apartment. *Just like MJ to have made a pot and left it for me....* He staggered to his feet, wandered into the kitchen, poured himself a cup, added a couple of sugars, stirred and drank. When the caffeine buzz started to hit, he headed down the hall to the bathroom, this time to hunt down the extra-strength aspirin.

Peter took a couple of aspirin and a long drink of cold water, then turned the shower on and climbed in, letting the hot water pummel him into some kind of flexibility again. When he could move without whimpering, he turned the water to cold and let the change in temperature blast him awake. Another fifteen minutes saw him dressed, combed, downing another cup of coffee, and heading for his darkroom.

He turned on the red light and closed the door behind him. He glanced at his workbench, where someone had placed his camera and a plastic-wrapped sandwich on a plate, with a note on top. The note said,

"NOW YOU EAT THIS, DUMMY! XOXOXO," and had a lipstick kiss imprint on the bottom of the page. Smiling, Peter unwrapped the plastic and sniffed. Tuna salad: good enough for breakfast.

He spent a few moments hauling down the jugs of developing chemicals and mixing them, getting them ready in the various pans. Then he pulled the string for the exhaust fan to get rid of the stink, and began to break the camera down, pulling out the rewound film. He stripped it carefully out of the canister, dropped the long coil into the first developer pan, and started the timer.

He chomped down the first half of the sandwich while squinting to see how the negatives were doing. In this light, as usual, it was impossible to tell. For him, this was always the worst part of photography: waiting in hope. A picture that seemed useful at first might have inequities of grain, or color, or contrast, which would turn it into so much mud on the printed page. There was no way to tell until you did the contact prints, and in some cases not even then—sometimes you had to do trial blowups of a print in which you were interested to see whether it would really work— and there was that much paper and chemical gone as a result, money down the drain if the picture was no good. One of the risks of the art....

The timer went off. He reached into the bath with a pair of tongs, swished the film around a little, then hoisted it out and dropped it into the fixer. The first glimpse looked good. A lot of the pictures had strong diagonals, he could see that much even now. Whether the fine detail would be good enough, though, remained to be seen. He started the timer again, and waited.

While watching the timer tick its dial around backwards, Peter started on the second half of the sandwich. *Venom,* he thought. *Now there would have been someone to have pictures of.* The only problem, for him at least, was that when Venom was in the neighborhood, he was usually too busy trying to keep his skin in one piece to worry about photo opportunities of any kind. *If Venom really is in town, though, I'm going to have to deal with him quickly.*

Probably soon, too. When Venom suddenly reappeared, it didn't usually take long for him to hunt Spider-Man down—or worse, to do the same to Peter Parker. That had been one of the worst problems of all. Venom knew his secret identity, knew where to find him, and knew where to find MJ. Venom's big, broad-shouldered silhouette was not one he ever wanted to see on his living-room wall again.

The timer went off. He pulled the film out of the fixer, held it up to the red light, and took his first good look at the negatives. "Awright," he breathed. There were some good jumping shots of him, good shots of the Hobgoblin, and nice ones of the two of them. The motion sensor was doing its work. He wondered if he could slightly improve its effectiveness by adding to the motion-control system some routines from the software which managed his spider-tracers. *Plant one on the super villain,* he thought, *so that the computer keeps him in frame all the time.* He was not so egotistical as to care whether he was in those shots, particularly. The city knew pretty well what Spider-Man looked like; it was the super villains who fascinated them, and in any shot containing both a hero and a villain, it was best to have the villain better centered.

And then he saw something else he had hoped for—one of the first shots in the roll, and as a result one of the last ones he came to—a shot of the robbery actually in progress. "Not bad," he said softly. "This'll get their attention, if nothing else does."

He looked thoughtfully at the big canisters in the photo. One thing the camera was not good at, unfortunately, was zooming. He couldn't really make out much beyond the big "warning—radiation" trefoil on the side. No use trying for an enlargement, really.

Now then—prints. He pulled a pad close and began scribbling notes. *Two, six, seven, eight, nine... fourteen, sixteen... eighteen....* He marked which of them he would print, checked the ones he wanted as eight-by-tens rather than three-by-fives, then shrugged a bit. *A contact sheet, six eight-by-tens, then this one, this one... that one.... Done.*

After that, things moved quickly. Picking the exposures was always the worst part of the work for him. You had to anticipate your editor. Sometimes it was hard to tell what they would prefer: did they want the more carefully composed picture, or the one with more fine detail? The best you could do was pick the best of each, bring a sampling of the others, and a contact sheet. That sheet—which showed a thumbnail of every picture on the roll—had saved his bacon more than once when his editors had chosen a picture that Peter hadn't bothered to make into a print for one reason or another.

He got to work, pulling out his printing stock, setting up the enlarger, cutting the negatives down to more manageable strips of five. The developing took him about another three-quarters of an hour.

The clock was running, now. Two o'clock was the cutoff for the five-o'clock evening edition, and no one would thank a photographer who came in on the stroke of two, just as the big web presses were being prepped. One o'clock would be good, noon better still—but noon was pretty much impossible now. He twitched slightly at the thought of which photographers might have beaten him down to the office with other pictures. Some of the editors at the *Bugle* in particular felt that a picture in the hand was worth any two in the bush, regardless of quality, but there was no telling which editor was going to make the call on your photos, either. If Kate Cushing was in today, Peter knew she liked to have pictures in early, rather than good—though she wanted them good as well.

Shortly the pictures were hanging up on the little "clothesline" of string. Peter snapped the white light on and looked at them, while fanning them dry with his hand. They were a fairly good-looking bunch. It had been a good first test of the camera's motion control. The camera had gotten one particularly good chance shot, a full-face view of Hobby running straight at the camera without his having been aware it was there. Peter looked at the grinning face, slightly strained out of shape by the speed of the turn Hobgoblin had just made, and thought, *That's the one. If she doesn't want that one, I can't imagine what her problem is.* Assuming the editor in question was Kate. She could sometimes be a dreadful stickler for quality—not necessarily a bad thing, when you were in competition with all the other newspapers in town, but annoying to the photographer with credit card bills to pay.

Peter smiled as he took down that head-on shot, and two others: one of Spider-Man leaping directly at Hobby, the webline reaching up and out of frame at a most dramatic angle, another of the warehouse floor, Hobgoblin streaking up and out past the camera's point of view, a very lucky shot both in that Hobby could as easily have come up out of any other of the skylights, and that he might also easily have tipped the camera over as he zipped past. *Gotta find a way to lower the center of gravity on that tripod,* he thought as he took down the last of the prints and flicked its edge with one finger to see if it was still tacky. It wasn't. Peter slipped it and its companions into a compartmented paper portfolio, put that in turn into his leather photo envelope, packed in the negatives as well, and finished the last of the tuna fish sandwich. *Payday today,* he thought, in as hopeful a mood as he could manage, and headed out to the *Bugle.*

HALF an hour later he was standing in the air-conditioning just inside Kate's office door, while one by one she peeled the photos out of the paper portfolio and dropped them on the desk. "Not too bad," she said, dropping the one with the canisters, and "That's OK, a little dark." Then, with an intake of breath and a smile, "What an ugly sonofabitch he is."

Peter heard the faraway sound of cash registers. He knew that smile, slight as it was. "He won't win any beauty contests," he said.

Kate held up the full-face picture of Hobgoblin. "How did you get that one?" she asked, cocking an eye at Peter.

He shrugged. "Long lens," he said.

The look she threw at him was amicably suspicious. "Since when can you afford lenses that give you that kind of detail without grain? Then again, this is that new ASA 8000 film, isn't it?"

"Six," he said. "I got a price break on it."

"You must have," Kate said. "Buy much of that stuff at the regular prices and you just about have to go into escrow. Well—" She held up the Hobgoblin shot. "This one with the canisters—this is the actual robbery itself, isn't it?"

Peter nodded.

Kate looked sidewise at him. "Enthusiasm is a good thing," she said, "but you want to watch you don't get reckless. What you were doing up on that rooftop, that time of night?"

Peter opened his mouth, thought better of it and shut it again. Kate just smiled. "Long lens," she said. "I remember." Then she added: "Came in with this a little late today, didn't you?"

"As soon as I could."

"Yes, well, I sent someone down to the crime scene already," she said. Peter's heart sank. "And he's back, and the pictures are developed, and already in the system for pasteup. Now I'm going to have to get into the system again and pull them out. You could have saved me some trouble by being a little earlier. I hate that damn new software."

Peter smiled. This was a common complaint all over the *Bugle*. They had just gone over to a new computer-based pasteup system, and everyone was moaning about the endless inservices needed to learn how to use it, especially since they were used to the old system, no matter that this one was supposed to be so much more flexible and usable. "Anyway," Kate said, "anybody who's out with this 'long lens' in the middle of the night and gets pictures like this, deserves a little over his rate."

She scribbled for a moment on a pad, looked at the numbers, made a change. "Here," she said, "this should help you get some sleep tonight." She reached for another pad, the sight of which made Peter's heart rise again: it was the voucher pad, and you took the filled-out form on it to the cashier downstairs. Whatever she was writing, Peter could see that it was in three figures.

She tore off the sheet and handed it to him, and Peter could see which three figures. He suppressed the gasp. This figure was half the Visa bill, on the spot. "Thanks, Kate," he said.

She waved a hand at him negligently. "You do the work, you get the pay," she said. "The composition on these is a little better than what you've been showing me lately."

Peter said nothing, but was silently glad that the motion sensor was performing as advertised.

"Initiative, I don't mind. Enthusiasm is fine. Just you be careful," Kate said.

"Yes, ma'am," Peter said, and walked out.

He wandered down the hall clutching the voucher, looking at it once or twice to make sure it wasn't actually a typo or a mistake. But she had written the amount both in numbers and words. As Peter went down the hall, he could hear two familiar voices. Had they been anyone else's, he would have called what he was hearing an argument. As it was, when one of the voices belonged to J. Jonah Jameson, the noise going on was merely a discussion. "What the hell am I paying you for?" J. Jonah was shouting out his open door. This, too, was an indication of the casual level of the discussion; for a real argument, JJJ would have been right out into the hall.

"How could you possibly be so obtuse? Here we have the biggest super villain ever to hit this city, and one of the worst, and you know why he's here."

"I don't, actually," said Robbie Robertson's calm voice. "He seems to have forgotten to fax me his itinerary again."

"Don't get cute with me, Robbie." JJJ emerged into the hall, gesticulating. "All the other papers are going to be all over this like a cheap suit. You know perfectly well that any time Venom turns up, Spider-Man turns up as well, and they begin bashing each other all over this city, trashing buildings, driving the city's garbage-removal budget through the ceiling, and doing all the other kinds of things that make news." He stalked back into the office again, apparently waving disgustedly at the computer. "And we're stuck with two-bit break-ins, and secondhand reporting about flying hooligans zooming around, flinging exploding squash in all directions. We should be coming down a lot harder on this Venom story. It's just not the same as—"

"As the newsworthiness of having the flesh flayed off your bones? No, I suppose not," the answer came back. "But the police are saying that the forensics are looking a little funny. We don't have enough—"

"Funny? Now how can they *not* look funny when the thing that committed the murder is half psychopathic human and half some kind of mind-reading man-eating amoeba with a bad body image? Yet another little present to our fair city from Spider-Man, let me remind you. I tell you, there is not a garbage can in this town that you won't find the damn webslinger at the bottom of it—"

"There is not enough data to lean really hard on the Venom story," Robbie said calmly, "and I would sooner be late than be wrong. Extremely wrong."

"C'mon, Robbie," JJJ grumbled. "Right is doing it first. And I know it's right. I know it's Venom. I can feel it in my bones. This is some kind of plot between Venom and Spider-Man. I've seen it before. One turns up, and the other turns up, and the city gets trashed. And I refuse to miss the chance to cover it in my paper!"

"With all due respect—" Robbie said quietly.

"Yes, yes, with all due respect, you're not going to do what I say, because I'm not editor-in-chief anymore, and you are."

"Something like that," Robbie said, "yes. You can say what you like about it in your publisher's editorials. But while I'm editing, I edit. When I don't think there's enough data to set a story on, I let it build up until there is."

"I don't know what this business is becoming these days," JJJ bellowed, coming out into the hall again, with Robbie ambling along behind him, sucking resignedly on his empty pipe.

Peter was standing nearby, leaning as respectfully as he could on the wall—being careful to put his pay voucher out of sight lest JJJ should get a glimpse of it and start going on about his freelancers being seriously overpaid. He couldn't resist putting in his two cents. "But, Jonah," he said. "Spider-Man—"

JJJ whirled on him. "And what would you know about it?"

"That Spider-Man wasn't anywhere around there," Peter said. "He was off fighting Hobgoblin when Venom showed up."

"Oh? Who says?"

"I saw him," Peter said. "I got pictures of it."

"Did you, now?" Robbie said, his eyebrows going up.

"Hmm," Jonah said. "Think, Parker, use your brains! Don't you know what it means?"

Peter looked at Robbie, who just gave an infinitesimal shake of his head. "No, sir," Peter said.

"It means Spider-Man, Venom, and Hobgoblin are all in it together! Hobgoblin strikes in one spot, then Spider-Man turns up to pretend to fight him, and while they're drawing attention away, Venom is off murdering people on the other side of the city, or committing some other kind of weird crime! Drinking toxic waste, it looks like, for pity's sake. As if that monster isn't enough trouble, without messing with stuff like *that* as well."

"Oh," Peter said, not able to find much to add.

"Oh, go on," Jonah said, glaring at him and gesturing away between himself and Robbie. "I'm tired of looking at you. You just don't have any imagination, that's the problem. And as for *you*," he said, turning to Robbie.

Robbie winked at Peter as Peter slid by. For his own part, Peter was glad enough to escape. When Jonah got on one of these rolls, there was no stopping him. He would blame Spider-Man for the federal budget deficit, global warming, and World War II if he kept going long enough.

I wish I understood it, Peter thought as he made his way down the hall. *It's not as if Spider-Man ever really had it in for JJJ.* Maybe he was just one of those personalities, like the old king in Thurber, who thought that "everything was pointed at him" to begin with. That Spider-Man should be as well would only help him make more sense of the world. But who knew?

In any case, JJJ had long since made up his mind and no longer had any desire to be confused by facts. Peter doubted any fact concerning Spider-Man was big enough to do anything but hit Jonah and bounce at this point.

At any rate, he had other things on his mind right now. First, that voucher. He took himself downstairs to the accounting offices, and took his turn standing in line at the cashier's armor-glass window. Maya smiled from behind the window, and said, "Long time no see!"

It was her constant tease, one she used with all the freelancers. "Yeah," Peter said. He handed her the voucher.

She widened her eyes appreciatively at the sight of it. "That'll buy some cat food," she said.

Peter chuckled. "We don't have cats."

"I know," Maya said. "Which makes you the perfect home for one of the new kittens!"

"Maya," Peter groaned. "Don't tell me you still haven't had her spayed!"

"I just hate interfering with nature," Maya said. Her beautiful Persian had struck up a nonplatonic and extremely fruitful relationship with a handsome black tom from several buildings over, and periodically escaped, the result being litter after litter of gorgeous, long-furred, mixed-color kittens, with which Maya had populated half the *Bugle's* employees' apartments. "No, thanks," Peter said gratefully. "We're a no-pets building."

Maya *tsk*ed, handing him the cash. "Terrible sort of place to live," she said. "You should move out."

Peter just sighed, but thought, *We may have to if Venom finds us again....* He headed off.

"I've got a real cute one!" she shouted after him. "Black longhair!"

Peter just waved at her and kept going. He had a lot more than cats on his mind.

He took the elevator back up to the second floor to the *Bugle's* morgue. These were the archives where earlier editions of the paper were kept. Once upon a time, they had been kept in their original paper format;

later, the archives had gone over to microfilm, but over time, even that had proved too bulky. Now both new paper and old microfilm were being stored on CD-ROM, able to be called up instantly from any terminal at the newspaper. At least, that was the plan. Everybody would be able to do that when the new system was completely installed, but at present the installation was only half done and the staff half trained. And there would always be those who preferred to go down to the morgue as a break from being stuck at their desks. Many claimed that this new system was in fact intended to keep them at their desks, where keystroke-activated "smart" productivity monitoring systems buried in the software would keep track of who was working and who was slacking off. Peter had heard of such things at other companies, but he personally doubted anything like that would be brought online at the *Bugle*. He suspected strongly that JJJ was too cheap to pay for such stuff, preferring to go stalking into people's offices and bug them about their productivity personally.

Peter sauntered into the big airy room. There were only a few people at the scattered workstations. Off to one side, the big mainframe computer sat, making no noise except that of its private air conditioners. The rest of the place, too, was pleasantly cool, the computer's own aggressive air-conditioning keeping the temperature down.

Bob the computer maven wandered over to Peter as he stood looking around. Bob was a big, rugged-looking, handsome Irish guy, another one gone prematurely silver, with a mustache to match, and a big engaging smile. He looked less like a software nerd than anything you could imagine. "You need some help?" he said to Peter.

"Just a spare terminal. I could use a look at today's edition, too," Peter said.

Bob grinned at him. "Why not just pick up a paper?"

"What," Peter said, "and get newsprint all over me?"

Bob snickered. "We could make a software jockey out of you eventually," he said. "Come on over here."

He showed Peter to a spare terminal and handed him a photocopied booklet. "There," he said. "This is the idiot's guide. Control-F1 gives you the main menu. Just page through it and pick the day you want."

The screen in front of Peter was a big handsome one, the size of a full tabloid page. Bob hit the keys for him the first time, and the menu came up on screen: a numbered list of dates, starting with today's and proceeding backwards. "Morning edition okay?" Bob said. "Evening's not out of comp yet."

"Morning is fine."

Bob brought up the page. It appeared in black and white. The front page had a quite well composed but not terribly illuminating photo of the shattered wall in the warehouse, a few canisters still scattered about, all rather dark. *A little hurried*, Peter thought. *If I were him, I would have waited and gone up a couple more f-stops—gotten a little more light.*

He pushed the arrow key to turn the "page," looking for the rest of the story. "Give a shout if you need anything," Bob said, and strolled off to see about something else.

Peter read on through the continuation on page three. The language was straightforward enough. Venom was indeed accused of the murder of a homeless man by his friend squatting in the warehouse, the man whom Peter had seen early that morning on the news. The story gave a little more detail: the address of the warehouse; its owner, Consolidated Chemical Research Corp. in New Jersey; and some detail, rather garbled, about what Venom had looked like to the man. The description mostly focused on the tentacles the man saw. That was accurate as far as it went: the symbiote's tentacles looked like strands and long flowing lines, tendrils that came alive and reached for what they wanted.

But the part of it all which still left Peter most confused was that Venom did this at all. Venom had settled in San Francisco and was supposedly protecting homeless people there. The idea that Venom would kill a homeless person, much less any innocent bystander, was hard for Peter to imagine. One of his few redeeming qualities was his belief that the innocent were to be protected at all costs, that life had given them a hard enough run as it was, and that somewhere they needed a protector.

Something, though…. Peter paged forward to see if there was anything more about the story but filler. Nothing.

He paged back again. *Consolidated Chemical Research*, he thought. *I could have sworn that CCRC had a sign on that warehouse where I was last night.* He pulled out the contact sheet from his portfolio, studied it. Yes, on that photo near the front of the roll, the lens had just caught it. Three letters out of four: CCR…. Right, he thought. And the likeness between the canisters, which MJ had spotted: she had been absolutely right.

And here, that weird detail which the homeless man reported in today's story, that he had seen Venom drink the radioactive toxic waste. Peter sat there and shook his head. *Is this some weird new taste the symbiote's developed?* he wondered.

"How's it going?" Bob said, materializing at his shoulder.

"Not too bad. Is there a way to scan for a specific word or phrase in this thing?"

"Oh, sure. You want to scan for a string? Just take it out of graphic mode. Here." Bob tapped the control key. The screen went mostly blank, except for a C:> prompt up in the corner. Then Bob entered something which didn't echo to the screen—a password, probably. The screen went dark and showed another menu. One option highlighted on it was "string search."

"There," Bob said. "You get, I think, up to sixty-four characters. There are ways to sort for two or three phrases at once, if you want. Just hit this one here and it'll show you the sample screen, with examples of how to enter the stuff so you get what you want."

"Hey, this isn't so bad," Peter said. "Why's everyone complaining about it?"

"Because it's not what they had the last time," Bob said, resigned.

Peter grinned. "That's okay. In five years they'll get used to this, and then Jonah will bring in something newer."

Bob moaned. "Don't tell me," he said. "I know damn well."

Peter turned back to the screen and had a look at the help menu. Carefully, because he knew how relentlessly stupid computers were about typographical errors, he typed, "CONSOLIDATED CHEMICAL RESEARCH."

"One Moment Please," the screen said. "Processing Your Request."

The cursor sat there and blinked at Peter for a little while. Then, up came a list of locations in the text archives where the computer had spotted the name. There weren't that many of them. The company was a newish one, as Peter found from reading the articles, mostly from the financial pages: a small company specializing in radioactive materials of various kinds, tailored isotopes for radioimmunoassay, and the medical equipment and so forth needed to handle them. None of the articles contained anything particularly interesting.

The last two entries on the main menu were: (8) Crossindex to Yellow Pages and (9) Crossindex to White Pages. Peter chose the second. The New York phone directory came up, with a long listing of addresses—corporate headquarters in the city, some other office addresses, and then their warehouses. There were four. One was the warehouse Peter had been in last night. The other one was the warehouse into which Venom had supposedly broken.

He backed up to the main menu again, and this time carefully typed, "VENOM."

"Age Of Story?" the computer prompted.

Peter thought. "THREE WEEKS," he typed.

"Incorrect Entry! Please Try Again," said the computer.

Peter frowned. "21," he typed instead.

"One Moment Please," said the computer. "Your Request Is Being Processed."

Peter waited. At least it didn't play music while processing.

Finally, "ONE REFERENCE," the computer said.

Aha! Peter thought. He hit (1).

The screen filled, and the byline made him catch his breath. "San Francisco—A revolutionary breakthrough in snake-farming techniques means that for the first time, the antidote for rattlesnake venom will not have to be given in multi-vial doses, over the course of days, but in a single injection—"

"Oh, phooey," said Peter. He backed out of that story, went back to its menu and the one before that, and studied the search criteria a little more carefully. But there seemed no way to differentiate between snake venom and the Venom Peter had most in mind. *What this thing needs is a proper name filter,* he thought.

He paused, then typed, "VENOM + SAN FRANCISCO." The computer asked him for days again, and he told it "21."

"ONE REFERENCE," the computer screen said. Peter asked to have that displayed, feeling sure that it was going to be the same snake-venom story.

It was. Peter sat back and looked at the screen. *At least, I think I know what this means. He hasn't been sighted in San Francisco at all. At least—*He backtracked through the computer's menus to the point where one choice offered was Crossindex To Other Newspapers/News Services. Peter chose that, and when the program asked him again for search phrases, once more typed VENOM + SAN FRANCISCO.

"ONE REFERENCE," it said, and once again, it was the snake-venom story.

Not a peep out of him, then, Peter thought. *No one's seen him or heard from him—not the wires, not the papers.*

Which means he really could be in New York....

Or anywhere else, of course. There was no telling, with this dearth of data.

I still don't get it, though. Radioactives....

He sat still and thought for a moment. Radioactives. There was not a lot of radioactive material loose in the city. The stuff in the hospitals—gamma sources for radiotherapy, blood isotope material and so forth—was too developed, too single-purpose, for much criminal use to be made of it. *What a crook would want,* Peter thought, *would be less refined nuclear material, or nuclear material in bulk, or both. And there are only a couple of places in the city, really, where you could get such stuff....*

Peter put that aside for the moment. It was simpler to deal with the facts as he understood them. He knew that two CCRC warehouses had been hit in one night, by different people—or entities, he thought—and possibly for different reasons. Both perpetrators had been interested in those canisters of waste for reasons Peter couldn't yet understand. In the case of the warehouse where the homeless men had been sleeping, who or what the perpetrator had been remained unproven. Peter still couldn't believe that Venom was involved.

As for the Hobgoblin—what would he want with nuclear material? Hobby's motivations were something he had studied in the past. They seemed generally to come down to one thing—money. Either he would steal money directly, or he would steal something which he could ransom or sell to get a lot of money, or he would hire himself out as a mercenary for money. *Nuclear waste, though?* Peter got up from the terminal and hefted his portfolio. It was all very peculiar.

Then an idea, a sort of doomsday scenario, leapt to his mind. *A bomb?* Plans for atomic bombs were not hard to find: high school students had made them. The Freedom of Information Act made it possible to get all the data you needed except for a few crucial bits of information about critical mass and so forth, but those could be worked out by someone with, in one case, no better than high-school physics. The problem, of course, was the size. A bomb of any real destructive power could not be made very small. But small enough. You could hide a fairly damaging nuke in the trunk of a car, a much worse one in the back of a truck. There was certainly no question that, if he felt like it and had the time, Hobgoblin could build such a thing himself.

Even if he didn't want to, there were enough terrorists, cranky underpaid scientists-for-hire, and disaffected high-school physics students whom Hobby could get to do such a job for him. *But why now? It can't be that the idea just occurred to him.* Such do-it-yourself bombs had been in the news for years—either the possibility of them or the actuality. If Hobby were in fact building a bomb, or masterminding one, why right this minute? Why not a long time ago?

Either the talent he needed had just become available—or something else had just become available.

What?

Peter shook his head and waved to Bob, heading out of the morgue. There were still too many pieces missing from this puzzle. What he was sure of, though, was that Venom was not involved in this.

Peter was equally sure, though, that Venom did not like having his name used behind his back. If you mentioned him often enough, he had a way of turning up. And when he did… all hell broke loose.

Just what we don't need right now, Peter thought. Bad enough to have Hobby messing around with some kind of unspecified nuclear material. All we need is old Chomp-'n'-Drool showing up at the same time.

Still, there were at least two very obvious places where nuclear material, in raw and refined forms, was kept and worked with, sometimes even stockpiled. One was Empire State University, where Peter was working on his doctorate. Half the doctoral candidates in the place were working in some aspect of nuclear physics, having sought out the labs there, widely thought to be the best-equipped on the East Coast. The other place—about which he had heard enough complaints over time, from people who didn't care to have nukes so close to New York City—was the Brooklyn Navy Yard. Nuclear subs came there, docked, and were refuelled and defuelled. A visit over there as Spider-Man would not go amiss.

Peter chuckled a little as he walked out of the *Bugle* offices. *The Hunt for Web October, huh?* he thought—

Preoccupied with all this information he'd just processed, he blithely stepped off the curb. The blare of the horn practically in his ear shocked Peter almost out of his skin. He jumped back, almost fell over, reeled to one side and clutched a lamppost to keep himself from ramming into it. "Why don'cha watch where you're going, ya dummy!" shouted the voice of the driver of the truck which had almost turned Peter into paté.

He stood watching the truck roar away. *My spider-sense should have warned me*—But of course, it was gone, still gone, for another eighteen hours at least.

Peter muttered under his breath. *I'm going to have to be a lot more aware of my surroundings until this clears up.* He ostentatiously looked both ways, and crossed the street.

FOUR

MARY Jane Watson-Parker sighed, settled herself in front of the bathroom mirror, and started putting on her makeup. Her thoughts drifted to the apparent reappearance of Venom. Once, long ago, in one of those earlier apartments she and Peter had shared, she encountered Eddie Brock standing over her. Because he knew Spider-Man's real identity, it had been easy for him to track them down. She found herself wondering whether they were going to have to move again, and if so, how the heck they were going to afford it. First-last-and-deposit on anyplace decent was really out of their reach at the moment, unemployed as she was and with Peter's employment on the sporadic side. *But if we have to, we'll manage it. Somehow.* She refused to tolerate the idea that a costumed villain—or, in Venom's case, a villained costume—was going to start invading her and her husband's personal space again. If there was something Peter deserved, it was a quiet place away from the bizarre and dreadful people and creatures with whom his work brought him into conflict.

She got out the mascara, fiddled with the brush to get the usual huge blob off the end of it, and began working on her lashes. MJ had become more philosophical about Peter's work over the last couple of years. There had been a time when she thought perhaps married life would steady him down to the point where he wouldn't need his "night job" anymore, where his family life would be enough to make him renounce those long dangerous nights out. Now she smiled briefly at her own old naïveté. Peter's commitment to what he did was profound, though he covered that commitment with glib, good-natured street talk most of the time as a distraction. Once MJ had come to realize this, life had become both simpler and more difficult. Simpler, because she stopped waiting for something which was never going to come; more difficult, because now she had to struggle for two. They were a team.

The issue of support came up sometimes with some of the women she knew from her television and modeling work. It wasn't that the men weren't trying, holding down menial jobs while struggling to make it. The women, meanwhile, would gather in one of their occasional kaffeeklatsch sessions, in the back of some studio or off to the side of some photo shoot, nodding and grinning a little ruefully at one another as they compared stories.

"It could have been worse," June, one of her cohorts on *Secret Hospital,* told MJ dryly over their last lunch, "you could have married an artist." *She* was married to one, the kind of wildly creative "conceptual artist" whose idea of a meaningful installation was to cover the inside of a plain-walled room with slices of bread stuck to the walls with peanut butter.

At such times, while sympathizing with June, MJ knew that her situation was worse, and there was no way to explain it to the others. So she let them console her on the rising price-per-credit at ESU and the cost of textbooks, and otherwise held her peace on the issues which really concerned her, like patching her husband up after he came home badly messed up following yet another brawl with some intransigent caped kook.

Now, while she knew that one of the worst of them was seemingly in the neighborhood, she had to concentrate on other things, and specifically, work. It was hard enough for Peter to be out and about his personal quest against evil without him having to obsess about the rent as well. That concern, at least, she had been able to keep off his mind while she'd had the job with *Secret Hospital.* But that job was gone now, and it was her responsibility to get employed again as quickly as possible, to leave Peter once again free to concentrate on his work.

MJ checked her face over one last time. Theoretically, she was just going down to the store for the trades, but if she saw something likely in one of them, MJ had to look good enough to walk straight off into an interview or a cold reading with confidence. *Not too bad,* she thought, *for a woman who was up half the night wondering if her husband had fallen off a tall building.*

She went back through the living room, where Peter was still snoring under the quilt, and paused a moment to look at him thoughtfully. *I don't like those circles under his eyes. But then his hours have never been exactly what you'd call regular.*

She picked up her keys and her purse, and headed for the door, locked up, and went down in the elevator.

Their street was still fairly quiet, this time of morning. MJ didn't hurry: there was no need, and the weather was too pleasant. This was the only time today when it was likely to be: the weather report claimed it was going to get up in the high 90s again, and with the humidity they'd been having, the climate would be no joke later.

The thought kept her sighing down to the open door of the store at the corner.

"Morning, Mr. Kee," she said as she passed the owner at the counter.

"Morning, MJ," he said, glancing up from behind the lottery tickets and the chewing gum. "Got your papers in, today."

"Thanks." She paused by the rack, picked up *Variety* and the *Hollywood Reporter,* and turned to the back to have a quick look at the classifieds. There was nothing much in the *Reporter,* and she tucked it under her arm.

"Hey, MJ, you gonna buy that?" Mr. Kee called from the front of the store.

"Oh, no," she said, "I was just planning to stand back here and bend all the pages." She grinned. Mr. Kee was not above teasing her as if she was one of the comics-reading ten-year-olds whom he claimed were the bane of his existence.

That was when her eye fell on the boxed ad almost at the back of *Variety.*

OPEN CALL
Young-looking females, 22–25, for episodic work:
reading & look-over. August 12, 445 W 54th St,
10 AM–2 PM.

MJ blinked and looked up hurriedly into the mirror to see if she looked 22–25. Then she smiled at herself, but the look was wry: these days, it seemed, 22–25 meant "just out of the cradle" to some of the directors she had auditioned for, and despite the fact that she was between the ages in question, the odds were no better than fifty-fifty that she would manage to be cast as such. *Still—nothing ventured, nothing gained—*

She made her way up to the checkout, still staring at the copy of *Variety. Ten o'clock… there's plenty of time to get back up to the apartment, pick up a couple of eight-by-tens and a CV or so… then get down there….*

"Going to walk into a post or something, reading like that," Mr. Kee said, eyeing the two papers. He tapped at the cash register for a moment. "Mmm… three forty-five."

She fished around for the change. "You find anything?" Mr. Kee said.

MJ raised her eyebrows. "I'm not sure. Do I look between twenty-two and twenty-five?"

He shook his head at her, smiling, his eyes wrinking. "Eighty at least."

MJ grinned. "You're no help. If I'm eighty, what are you, chopped liver?"

"Good luck, MJ!" he called after her as she went out. MJ, equipped with copies of her resume and publicity stills and dressed in interview clothes, got on the subway. A half-hour later, she was at the address where the open call was being held.

It looked like any other somewhat-aging office building in that part of the West Side: no air-conditioning, grimy linoleum, broken elevators, windows that appeared to have been last washed around the time the Mets won their first World Series. The only clue to anything interesting was the hand-scrawled sign taped to the elevator which said AUDITIONS— SECOND FLOOR.

MJ found the stairs and climbed them slowly: it was already getting warm, and she didn't want to get all sweaty. She could hear a soft mutter of voices upstairs. *Not too loud, though. Maybe not too many people. That would be good luck for me.*

She pushed open a fire door at the top of the stairs, and the wall of sound, about a hundred voices, hit her. *Well, so much for that*, she thought, as she pushed her way into a hall full of women twenty-two to twenty-five years old, or purporting to be.

A harried production assistant was pushing through the crowd. "Anybody who doesn't have a number yet," she yelled to the assembled actresses, "take a number, will you? Numbers over on the table, ladies."

I am not a number, MJ thought, somewhat ironically, pushing her way over there through the crowd, *I am a free woman*. She grabbed a card, one of only a few remaining on the table. *Free woman number one hundred and six. Oh, joy.* There was no hope of finding anywhere to sit; she resigned herself to leaning carefully against the cleanest piece of wall she could find, and pulled out her much-thumbed copy of *War and Peace.*

An hour and a half later it was about twenty degrees warmer, and all around her the remaining thirty or so women were wilting. MJ was not exactly cool herself, but the combination of images of a Russian winter and the likelihood that absolutely nothing would come of this interview were helping her somewhat.

"One oh four," came the voice from the next room. One oh four, who was certainly no more than eighteen and dressed in the most minuscule possible shorts and a halter, vanished into the room and came immediately out again, looking morose. This had been happening with increasing regularity over the last while, MJ had noticed. The heat, she thought, was beginning to tell on the interviewers as much as on the interviewees. "One oh five," the voice said, and no question that the PA at least sounded weary of the day, if not of life.

One oh five raised her eyebrows at MJ and went in. The door closed. About three minutes later it opened again, and she came out. "One oh six," said the tired PA's voice from inside.

MJ slipped her paperback into her bag and strolled into the room, looking around. The room was bare, except for a table which held the first PA and two other people, a middle-aged woman and a younger man, all of whom looked at her with various degrees of loathing.

Except the middle-aged woman, whose expression changed abruptly. "You were on *Secret Hospital,* weren't you?" she said.

MJ smiled. "Was, yes."

Glances were exchanged at the table. The young female PA held out some sheets of paper. "Would you mind reading from this?"

Cold, MJ thought, not losing her smile in the slightest. *I hate cold reading.* But she took the pages, and started reading after no more than a glance.

It was something to do with social work, some dialogue about homeless people. *Typecasting,* MJ thought, *do I mind? I should think not!* She threw as much feeling into it as she could, recalling the compassion in the voice of one of her friends, Maureen, who had been doing some volunteer work with the homeless and had told MJ some dreadful horror stories about the situations they got into these days. When she finished, the three were looking at her with interest.

"Can you come back Thursday?" the young man said.

"Certainly," MJ said.

"Do you have a CV?"

"Right here," MJ said, and handed it over, along with her still.

And a few minutes later she was out on the street again, staring with mild bemusement at a five-page premise for something called *Street Life,* which was apparently intended to be a dramatic series with a comic edge, and involved a starring role for a female actor who was to play a crusading social worker. There were three more sets of dialogue and half a script to study as well. On Thursday she would read for real.

What happened to the interview? MJ wondered as she walked down the street, trying to recover her composure after the abrupt excitement of the past few minutes. Never mind: she hated interviews. She preferred job tryouts that seemed to actually have something to do with her acting ability, rather than her life experience.

She stopped at the corner, waiting for the light to change, while traffic streamed by in front of her. *This,* she thought, *could* be *something. Now, is that a phone over there? Okay—*

She crossed hurriedly, pulling out her address book. By the time she reached the phone, someone else was using it already, but the guy in question was mercifully brief. A few moments later, she was dialing.

The phone at the other end rang, picked up. The first thing MJ heard was a yawn.

"Mau-*reeeeeeeeeen*" MJ said, very amused, for this sound she had heard often before. Maureen liked to sleep in.

"Oh, MJ," her friend said, "what's your problem? Where are you, anyway? It sounds like a parking lot."

"Nearly. Seventh Avenue, anyway. Look, are you still working at that soup place?"

"The shelter? Yup." Another yawn. "I have a shift this afternoon."

"That's great. Can I come with you?"

Another yawn, mixed with an ironic laugh. "Having a sudden attack of social conscience?"

"I should, I know. But no. Listen, this is what it's about—" She quickly told Maureen about that morning's job-nibble. "It would be real smart if I went into this reading Thursday knowing what I'm talking about as regards homeless people, anyway."

"Stanislavsky would approve, I guess. Listen, no problem. How's your cooking?"

"My *cooking*? Not bad."

"Good. I can always use another hand in the kitchen. Come on by and I'll take you in to the shelter with me, and you can help me out while I'm getting ready. Then you can do your research while we're serving."

"Sounds great. Maureen, you're the best."

"You just keep telling me that. See you in a while."

About two hours later MJ and Maureen were walking in the front door of the Third Chance Shelter on the Lower East Side. MJ had had a mental picture of a dreary, spartan kind of place, but Third Chance totally overturned it. The outer brick wall was bland, true, but inside the front door MJ found herself in a courtyard full of green plants with an open skylight, and beyond that lay several stories' worth of meeting rooms, workrooms, a cafeteria, bedrooms, game rooms, and offices.

"We don't have a lot of beds," Maureen said, leading MJ into the kitchen area of the cafeteria, where people were finishing the cleanup after lunch. "Mostly we're about feeding people, and after that, teaching them new job skills—office work, computing, things like that." She paused a moment by one of the big stainless-steel industrial stoves, tying up her long blonde hair. Maureen was small, with one of those faces that people usually called "severely pretty," and her gorgeous hair went almost down to her knees, causing envy in everyone who saw it.

"That was how you got into this, then?" MJ said. "The job part."

Maureen nodded, pulling out a long apron and handing another to MJ. "They brought me in as a consultant on the computer end. Came to teach, stayed to serve." She chuckled. "Here—"

She pulled a paperback down from the shelf, handed it to MJ. "Potato soup today," Maureen said.

MJ turned the book over. "Alexis Soyer. Why is that name familiar?"

"He was the founding chef of the Reform Club in London. Also the last century's greatest expert on nutrition on the cheap—he got started working in the soup kitchens in Dublin during the Great Famine. '*A Frugal Kitchen*' there is still one of the best sources for recipes designed for maximum nutrition and minimum money."

MJ smiled as she put on her apron. "Better than macaroni and cheese?"

"Much. There's the potatoes. Let's peel."

For at least an hour, they did just that, potato after potato, hundreds of them, until MJ didn't want to see another potato for the rest of her life. Then they started making the broth—chicken broth, as it turned out, using stripped chicken carcasses donated by one of the local places that did "fast-food" roast chicken. Herbs went in, and both sliced and pureed potatoes, and when the soup was done about two hours later, MJ could hardly stay out of it. "Old Alexis," Maureen said, "he knew his stuff. You've got time for just one bowl before the customers start arriving."

MJ was almost drowning in sweat from working over the hot stove in this humidity for two hours. All the same, her stomach growled assertively, and when Maureen handed her the bowl, MJ grabbed a spoon and finished it right to the bottom.

Maureen looked up approvingly. "It's just four-thirty," she said. "First shift will be in shortly. Help me get that pot onto the trolley. We'll take it up front by the serving window."

Together they handled the big twenty-gallon pot onto the low trolley and trundled it forward. As they passed the serving window, MJ saw that there were already a lot of people gathering out on the cafeteria side. She shook her head slightly. "Why do so many of them have their coats on?" she said. "In this weather!"

Maureen looked, shook her head. "Some of them are just old. Others—you can't carry the stuff in your hands all the time, and most of them don't have anywhere they can leave things. Simpler to wear them— even though in heat like this, they get so dehydrated sometimes that they pass out. We go through a lot of bottled water here. Come on—here comes the first shift."

The two of them grabbed ladles and started filling bowls and putting them out on the cafeteria side of the serving window. Other workers were filling water pitchers, or putting out pitchers of homemade Gatorade-type drinks. "Electrolytes," Maureen said. "This weather, you can sweat all your salts out before you even notice, and die of it."

The soup quickly vanished. MJ lost count of how many shabbily dressed people came up to the counter, took a bowl and a spoon, nodded, said a word or two, and went off. She knew that there were a lot of homeless people in the city, but had never had it borne in on her so straightforwardly how *many* of them there were. She started feeling somewhat ashamed of herself for not having noticed. The single lone figures on a streetcorner, in a doorway, you could ignore, turning your head as you went by. But not these.

When she realized there wasn't any more soup, MJ found herself suddenly not having any idea what to do. She looked up into the face of the person standing outside the serving window with an empty bowl, and could only stammer, "Uh, I'm sorry, we're all out—"

The man nodded, walked off. MJ almost felt like crying. "Maureen—" she said.

"I know. Take a break. There's some iced tea out here. Then we'll go out and have a chat with people."

"Do they mind?" MJ said a little shakily, sitting down with the iced tea.

Maureen looked at her with a small quirk of sad smile. "You mean, do they think you're patronizing them? No. Do they know that this hurts, on both sides? Yes. But it's better than doing nothing. Drink the tea."

She drank it. Then they went out into the cafeteria.

It *did* hurt, talking to people who had had busy lives, and proud ones, and who now spent most of each given day working out in which underpass, tunnel, or doorway they would spend that night. But Maureen's example made it easier to listen to them. By and large, though there were angry people in the cafeteria, and sullen ones, most of them were curiously and consciously kind to the first-timer, as if they were more embarrassed for their predicament than for MJ's.

A few of them were people she felt she would have been pleased to meet socially, and the knowledge made her ashamed, considering that had she today met them in the street, MJ knew she would have looked away. *The least I can do is look at them* now, MJ thought, and concentrated on doing that.

Three of the people finishing their soup at one table had waved at Maureen, calling her over: she and MJ sat there, and Maureen made the introductions. "Mike," she said, indicating one big redheaded, broad-faced man, "our newest computer nerd. He's learning C++ during the days. Marilyn—" This was a little old lady of about seventy, from the looks of her, well wrapped in coats and sweaters, thin but apple-cheeked and cheerful. "She's a few months ahead of Mike. Writes the fastest code I ever saw."

"Only problem is," said Marilyn, "to get me employed, we're going to have to pass me off as a twenty-year-old."

"Online," Maureen said, "who'll know the difference until it's too late? And Lloyd." Lloyd was a young handsome black gentleman with a face that reminded MJ of something from Egyptian monumental art, noble and still, except for when the rare smile broke through. "Lloyd is still seeking his *metier*. Typist, possibly. He's got good speed."

The chat came easily enough after that. MJ was instantly recognized and teased about her own job loss: the others seemed to think it made her more accessible, and shortly she found herself talking to them about the difficulty of getting an apartment and keeping it, the fear of losing it, how tough it was to hang on.

They told her how they did it. All of them used shelters when they could: all of them wound up in the occasional favorite doorway or tunnel. Lloyd favored the tunnels under Grand Central. "They keep trying to clean them out," he said, "trying to get rid of us and the cats. Us and the cats, we keep coming back."

"Not so many of us, lately," Marilyn said. "I've been hearing stories—"

Glances were exchanged. "Not the transit police again," Maureen said.

Marilyn shook her head. "Something else. Something big and dark… down in the train tunnels. A couple of people who usually sleep down there haven't been seen, last couple of days."

Lloyd's eyebrows went up. "Not George Woczniak?"

"George," Marilyn said. "Rod Wilkinson, you know Rod, told me he saw some big black guy—not black like you: *black* black—down there on the lower level, not far from the Lexington Avenue upramp where the maintenance tracks are. Saw him the other night, over by where George usually sleeps. Then, the last couple of days—no George. And you know how George is: predictable. This isn't like him."

Mike looked up and said, "Now, you know… that's funny. Jenny McMahon, you know her, the blond lady who stays around 49th and Ninth—she was telling me she'd heard somebody telling some kind of story about something in the sewer tunnels under Second—you know where those access tunnels are—"

"Alligators again," Marilyn said.

Mike shook his head. "Nope. This was going on two legs. Teeth, though. She said whoever told her the story said the thing had teeth like a shark's happy dream. Lots of teeth."

MJ's eyes opened a little at that, but she kept her thoughts to herself for the moment.

Lloyd said, "Some of the regulars told me they didn't want to come up topside now, because of the chance that while they were leaving, they might run across… whatever it was. Makes you wonder whether above-ground might be safer for the time being."

Mike shrugged. "After those two guys got aced in the warehouse last night? Naah. It's just that there's no place safe in this city, not *really* safe. Not an apartment, not the top of Trump Tower, *no* place. The crime rate's a disgrace."

The conversation started to take the same kind of mildly complaining tone to be heard sooner or later from every city dweller anywhere: things are going downhill, the place is a mess, it wasn't like this ten years ago, the city really ought to do something… MJ was having trouble concentrating on it. She was thinking about someone in black, someone with big teeth, someone around whom people vanished. "And the worst of it," Marilyn was saying, "is that all their hair is falling out."

"All of it?" Mike said, unbelieving. "Maybe it's bad water."

"Helen told me Roedean's hair was coming out in handfuls, in patches. And a whole bunch of them over there were coming out in weird splotches on their skin."

"This is over by Penn?" Maureen said curiously.

"Yeah," Marilyn said. "Roedean just moved over there a couple of weeks ago, and it started. Other people took longer, but they're doing it too. Some have moved already—they say they don't care how comfortable the digs over there are."

Maureen shook her head. "Are they all getting their water from a common source?"

"I don't think so—"

"Can't be that, then."

Lloyd shook his head. "Lyme disease, maybe? There was just an outbreak of it up in the Park last year."

Marilyn shook her head. "Takes longer, doesn't it…?"

The conversation wandered on again, and MJ found herself thinking, *Hair falling out. Patches on the skin. Sounds more like radiation.* It was hardly a revolutionary concept for her, or any great leap of imagination. She had married a man who was very interested indeed in the effects of radiation on human beings, for very personal reasons. She had heard more than enough dissertations on the subject. And her thoughts went again to the huge dark shape with the teeth….

Peter, she thought. *Peter needs to know about this, as fast as I can find him. Wherever he is.*

PETER was not available for comment just then. But on the top of a fire-hose drying tower at the southeastern edge of the Brooklyn Navy Yards, Spider-Man crouched and looked out over the place, thinking.

Hard to know where to start. Even the military doesn't routinely paste big signs all over the outside of buildings saying, RADIOACTIVE STUFF, GET IT HERE! But all the same…. He looked over the expanse of the place, considering. *You wouldn't leave it at the outskirts, routinely. You'd put it as far inside the installation as you could—making it as difficult as possible to get in and out without detection.*

Or, alternately, you would keep raw fissile material close to the subs. That's one of the most secure parts of the base. He had seen the anti-dive nets below the surface of the entry to the Yards as he swung in. Those would routinely be moved only when a sub was about to enter or leave. *Keep the fissiles near the missiles.* He grinned under the mask. *And the vessel with the pestle has the brew that is true….*

He shot out a strand of web and began swinging in closer to the heart of the Yards, where the subs would dock. There was only one of them present at the moment, and he intended to take his time approaching it. His reconnaissance was a friendly one, but he wasn't sure the Base security people would immediately recognize it as such.

The Yards were not as easy to swing around in as, say, midtown: there were fewer tall structures, most of the buildings being one- or two-story jobs. Still, you had to work with what presented itself. Dusk was coming on—that much help he had. He busied himself with avoiding lighted windows, staying away from routes passing doorways from which people might suddenly emerge—say, people with guns.

On top of one middle-sized office-type building nearest the docks, he paused, eyeing the local traffic. Not many people were in the narrow streets that went between the buildings. *Dinner time? Staff cuts? No telling.* He pulled out the camera and its tripod from a web pouch slung over his shoulder. This was as good a spot as any—

It was the sudden faint whining noise in the air which brought his head up, not his spider-sense. *That* was still absent. He tracked with the sound, then glanced away and hurriedly turned the camera on too. It tracked as well, following the faint gleam of brightness as something fell down from where the sun still shone between the shadows of the skyscrapers falling across the water. The sun's brightness left the tiny shape, but not before Spider-Man saw it and knew it for the angular arrowhead-shape of Hobgoblin's jetglider.

My hunch was right, he thought. He watched the shape arrow downward, heading right for the sub. *Don't know what good that's going to do him—*

But a closer look at the sub told him. Its biggest hatch, the one used to service the missiles back at the rear end, was open. And anything big enough to install a missile through, was big enough to let the jetglider through as well.

He shot out web and instantly threw himself in Hobgoblin's direction as fast as he could. It was no simpler a business than getting across the base had been, but this time at least he wasn't going to worry about avoiding attention. Hobby was already attracting enough: he could hear shouts below him, and at least once, the sharp crack of a warning shot. *If I can just keep from getting caught in a crossfire. Well, my spider-sense—*

He felt like swearing. *Won't do a thing.*

Never mind!

He swung toward Hobgoblin's plummeting sled. For once luck was with him. Hobby was so intent on the sub that he didn't hear or see Spider-Man coming at him. *I am* not *going to let him just waltz in there,* Spidey thought. *The thing is as full of nukes as a subway car's full of commuters.*

But how to stop him?

Hobby was dropping lower, was certainly no more than a few hundred yards away. *Now here is a truly* dumb *idea,* Spidey thought, *whose time has come.*

He took the best aim he could manage, and shot a line of web straight at the sled. It caught—

He was yanked off the building with dreadful speed in Hobgoblin's wake. At first he had entertained some wild hope that his weight would slow the glider down, maybe even make Hobby fall off, but that was too much to hope for. The thing was fast, overpowered, and adaptable, and it just kept flying. Hobby staggered briefly, turned, noticed what sudden unwelcome cargo he was suddenly dragging behind him like a towed dinghy, and turned hard, so that Spidey was whipped hard to one side at the end of his line of webbing, like a kid at the end of a line of skaters playing snap-the-whip. He hung on desperately, thinking, *This is not a good place to fall off. A hundred fifty feet above land, a hundred fifty feet above water, it's pretty much the same result from this height. Splat*—!

"You just can't keep out of my business, can you?" Hobby yelled at him, curving around so sharply in the air that for a moment Spidey was still going in the original direction while Hobby was going the other way, and they passed one another in the air. For that brief moment, the effect was comical.

It stopped being funny as the snap at the end of the whip caught Spidey again, harder this time. *About 3 g's, if I'm any judge,* he thought, his jaw clenched and his fists locked on the webbing. He thought the jerk as he came around again would break his wrists, but somehow he hung on, even without his spider-sense to warn him of exactly when the most dangerous stresses would come. "Let's just call it civic duty. Hobby," he yelled back. "This is government property—"

The second bullet went *wheet!,* just the way bullets were supposed to go, through the air right past his ear. It had been fired at Hobgoblin, but Hobby had banked hard around again, laughing hysterically. And here came the snap of the whip—

Spidey hung on, eyeing the buildings under him for one tall enough. If he could snag one of them with a webline and mate it with the one attached to the jetglider—*without being pulled in two pieces first like a Thanksgiving wishbone, that is.*

But he didn't have time. The next thing he saw, again without his spider-sense giving him the slightest warning, was a pumpkin bomb flying straight at his head.

Spider-Man let go the web and dropped, spread-eagled—he had learned long ago from watching real spiders, and from experience, that this was the only way to buy yourself a second or two in free fall. Behind and above him, the bomb went off. More rifle fire laced up past him toward Hobgoblin as Spidey looked around desperately for something to web to. One building had a radio mast on it, VHF from the look of it, and fairly sturdy. He shot web at it, felt it anchor, hauled himself in hard, managing to slingshot around it with enough speed and effort to keep himself from crashing into the roof of the building.

He looked up and saw Hobby heading straight down toward the open hatch of the sub. He had just enough time to see some sub crewman look up out of the hatch open-mouthed at the noise, take in the spectacle above, and duck hastily out of sight—but not fast enough to close the sub's hatch. Down the hatch Hobby went, and there followed several seconds of horrible silence.

And a BANG!

Oh God, no, Spidey thought, and swung straight down after him. It was a long shot for the hatch of the sub. He let go of the webbing, casting off as hard as he could to get those last few feet of distance.

He came down hard just at the edge of the hatch as the smoke came boiling up. *Not one of the high-explosive pumpkins,* he thought. *Maybe he's not feeling homicidal today.*

He dropped through the hatch and realized that the lack of spider-sense had betrayed him one more time. The first billow of smoke had been an ignition artifact from the bomb, nothing more. Down in the body of the sub, everything was drowned in a thick fog of gas: people were struggling in all directions, falling over each other. This gas Spidey knew from old experience. At high enough concentrations it paralyzed, even killed—and the bombs usually went off in two stages. He stopped breathing and made his way hurriedly along the way to where the cloud was thickest, squinting through his mask, which gave him some protection. *There—looks like—*He fumbled along the floor, and after a moment his hand came down on the round shape of the pumpkin bomb.

Spider-Man leapt back up the ladder to the hatch in two great bounds, reared back and threw the bomb up and out of the hatch. In midair it detonated again, letting loose its main dose of gas, the one meant to flood the whole place and kill, but the breeze off the bay began to take the big noxious green cloud away immediately.

Not that this solved the problems of the men down in the sub. Spidey dove back down that hatch and started grabbing men any which way, upside down, right side up, a double armful of them. Up the hatch he leapt again, making harder work of it this time, but if a spider could jump around while lifting such proportional weights, so could he. He dropped the men in a heap on the upper hull and dived down the hatch again. A second load, men choking and coughing with tears streaming down their faces, cursing the gas and trying to find out what was happening to them. He leapt back up into the clean air, dumped them by their buddies, took a great lungful of breath and dived back down—and was slammed sideways into the opening of the hatch by Hobgoblin, still laughing, as he rocketed back up into the open with his arms full of something metallic and bulky. He soared away.

Spidey clung to the edge of the hatch and shot a webline at Hobgoblin, furious at one more failure of his spider-sense, desperate not to let Hobby get away. But Hobby veered to one side and was off across the river, heading for Manhattan at high speed, his laughter trailing away as he went. The web fell, useless, not being much good at changing direction in mid-shot.

Spider-Man clambered up out of the hatch and went over to check out the men lying around on the upper deck. They were still coughing and rubbing streaming eyes, but none of them were dead, which was something. "Hey," one of them said, focusing on him when his eyes were working again, "thanks, buddy. Maybe I'll do the same for you some day."

Spider-Man looked around him at the dark elegant bulk of the sub. "You've been doing it for a long while," he said. "I'm just returning the favor."

He heard clanking footsteps on the ladder from the big hatch, and turned. A tall dark man with eyes still wet from the effects of the gas, and wearing a sidearm, had come up out of the hatch and was eyeing him coolly. He said, "Captain wants to see you, Mr.—"

"Your friendly neighborhood Spider-Man will do," Spidey said, trying to sound as cool. "My pleasure. Lead the way."

The sergeant-at-arms went down the ladder: Spidey followed him. Blowers had been activated inside the sub, and the gas was slowly clearing, so that off to his left Spider-Man could see something he would have missed the first time: a large door labeled DANGER—RADIATION, and bearing the radiation-warning trefoil. *Now that's interesting,* he thought. *Hobby never gave that a second glance, if I'm right. Very strange indeed....*

"This way," the sergeant-at-arms said, gesturing Spider-Man rightwards. Spidey went. Around him, in the corridor, men were being helped to their feet by others wearing anti-gas equipment. The corridor ended in what seemed like the bridge of the ship—or, at least, *a* bridge—and standing there was another man wearing an expression entirely too calm for the situation, and triple stripes on the short sleeves of his shirt, which accounted for the expression.

"Spider-Man, I presume," the Captain said. "That'll be all, sergeant-at-arms."

The officer saluted and turned away.

"Permission to come aboard. Captain—"

"LoBuono," the Captain said, and held out his hand. They shook. "Granted. My medic tells me you saved the lives of the men who were stuck aft."

"I think so, Captain."

"Thank you," the Captain said. "We seem not to have sustained any serious damage. But there has been a loss."

"Not of life—"

"No. Your friend there—"

"No friend of mine, sir. Hobgoblin."

"He deserves the name. And worse. He broke into one of the missile silos just forward of the hatch—" A young officer came hurrying up to Captain LoBuono at that point. "A moment," he said. "Report?"

"He got at number three, Captain," said the officer. "Pulled the upper actuator right out."

"Damn him straight to hell," the Captain said, again quite calmly. "Anything else?"

"No, sir. He tried number four as well, but seems to have decided not to bother."

"Doubtless one was enough," Captain LoBuono muttered. "Very well, start decommission procedures on that silo, and notify shoreside and Omaha by the usual procedures. And check number four out. Dismissed."

The officer saluted and went. "Actuator?" Spidey said.

The Captain let out a long breath. "The device that triggers the atomic reaction in a fired missile," he said. "Certainly something which could have other applications."

"For someone like Hobgoblin," Spider-Man said softly, "no question whatever. And over the last day or so, he's been involved with the theft of some nuclear material."

Captain LoBuono looked at him thoughtfully. "Nuclear.... Would you come with me?" he said.

Spider-Man followed him. Further into the body of the sub, air-tight doors had closed and the air was still clean. They went through several of these until they came to the door which led to the Captain's office. The Captain closed the door behind them, gestured Spider-Man to a seat.

He sat down himself, across the desk from him, and paused a moment to run his hands over his face and through his hair. For that second all his dignity didn't so much fall away as relax to reveal beneath it a very tired and upset man. Then he straightened, everything in place again. "I want to thank you again," Captain LoBuono said, "for saving my people."

"Hey," Spidey said, "otherwise I would have kept tripping over them."

The Captain's smile was thin, but amused, that of a man used to seeing people conceal what was going on in their minds or emotions. "We have had some other unusual occurrences here over the past day or so," he said, "and in the light of this, I think perhaps you should know about one of them."

His spider-sense might not have been working, but Spidey could still get that sensation described by some as A Very Bad Feeling, and he was getting it now.

"We had an unusual passenger aboard," the Captain said. "We made pickup—I'm not at liberty to say where—and were to deliver it to a safe location in Greenland. However, our passenger parted company with us very shortly after we docked here."

"'It,'" Spider-Man said.

Captain LoBuono nodded, folded his hands. "You have been to some unusual places," he said, "and you have a reputation for dealing with— unusual people—so I feel safe about imparting this information to you. There are no guarantees that our, uh, passenger, stayed on this side of the river. It may turn up in your bailiwick, as it were."

"What actually *is* your passenger? Or was."

The Captain's face wore a curious expression. "I can't say."

A moment's silence. "Meaning 'shouldn't'?" Spider-Man said.

The Captain nodded. "This much seems plain: it is of extraterrestrial origin."

"It was in that chamber—and broke out—"

"Through the hull of my boat," Captain LoBuono said, for the first time looking annoyed. "Though perhaps I should be grateful."

"Did anyone see it?"

"No. Not from the beginning of the cruise, and not when it left us."

Spider-Man thought about this. "Was it radioactive?"

"Not in itself, no. But its habits require that it stay in a chamber containing radiation."

"And now it's loose," Spider-Man said, "in a city with enough radioactive sources to feed on."

The Captain nodded. "I would say so."

Spider-Man nodded. "Captain," he said, "precisely what am I supposed to do about it?"

Captain LoBuono was silent for a moment. "Watch out for it," he said.

"Just that?"

"Just that. I doubt I have the right to ask much more."

Spider-Man restrained a sigh. "Okay."

"Very well." The Captain stood up. "You can find your way out?"

"Yes, sir."

"Good day to you, then. And, Spider-Man—thank you again."

Spidey nodded, caught between feeling abashed and profoundly confused. He made his way out of the sub to the applause and cheers of the men who saw him go. But it was not until he was away from there again, and had recovered his camera and was web-borne on his way back to Manhattan, that he was able to deal in much detail with the confusion. Plainly the Captain had given him classified information—though not much. A thing that no one had seen, something that could go through the hull of a sub—something fond of radiation, but not radioactive itself—was loose in the city.

He thought suddenly of the warehouse wall he had seen on TV, crumbled or melted, and of the homeless man's story of something lapping at the radioactive waste. *Drinking* it.

Spider-Man headed home in a hurry.

FIVE

IT took Peter several hours to process that evening's film. The photos weren't quite as good as the last batch had been: too much swinging and jumping around, he thought. From the look of things, the camera almost suffered some sort of electronic nervous breakdown as it tried to follow their wild gyrations through the air.

It had, Peter noticed happily, taken an excellent shot of Hobby zooming out of the hatch of the sub with his arms full of equipment, knocking Spider-Man on his butt in the process. Peter felt certain Jonah would feature that shot prominently on the front page, if only to show his old nemesis getting taken down a notch.

He was still fuming over the way he had been unable to stop Hobgoblin from getting into the sub. *The problem,* he thought, hanging up a finished print and eyeing it critically—the composition on some of these was nowhere near as good as it had been on the last batch—*the problem is that I've been depending too much on my spider-sense and not enough on my brains.*

It was useful to have a sixth sense watching his back while he was fully occupied with matters in front, that warned him of dangers and stresses ahead of time. The spider-sense had saved him many times— from unpleasant surprises, from severe or fatal injuries, from the elaborate forms of sudden death his opponents were capable of handing out. But suppose Hobby *had* managed an improvement in the gas that caused this loss of his special sense. The thought of having to do without it permanently gave Peter the creeps. Suppose the loss was irrevocable? Suppose that he was going to have to go through the rest of his career this way…?

He sighed. Right now there was nothing else to do but go about his work as usual, and do it the best he could, and keep himself as far out of harm's way as that work allowed. He had too much going on to be incapacitated due to a sense that wasn't there.

While he worked, he listened eagerly for the sound of the phone going off. It was unusual for MJ to be out so late without checking in.

I wonder if she got *that job,* he thought. Desperately, he hoped the answer was yes. But there was no use getting your hopes up about these things. Too often MJ had stumbled onto what had seemed to both of them a sure thing only to come home afterwards very depressed when it didn't pan out. They had both learned from bitter experience not to raise one another's hopes unnecessarily, for there was never any way to tell when luck was going to strike and too many ways to be mistaken about it.

All the same, I wish she'd get home. I miss *her.*

There was that other thought in the back of Peter's mind as well. *Venom.* Often enough in the past, Venom had put pressure on MJ in order to flush Spider-Man out into the open, where the two of them could tangle. On days like this when she was late and Venom was known to be in the area, he could never quite get rid of the fear that somewhere, in some dark alley or quiet spot where no one would hear her yell for help, that dark shape was looming over her, smiling with all those teeth.

He wouldn't hurt her, Peter thought. *She* is *an innocent. Isn't she?*

That was the question he couldn't answer. As far as Spider-Man was concerned, it was a good question whether Venom considered anyone associated with him to be truly innocent. All the same, Peter's resolve was clear.

If he touches her…

The difficulty with Venom was that the odds were stacked against him. They had fought some desperate battles in the past, and though on some occasions a flash of genius-under-pressure—or just plain luck—had intervened on Spider-Man's behalf, once or twice those capricious dice had fallen favoring Venom, and the result had almost been fatal for Spidey. All the free-flowing hatred of someone who thought that Spider-Man was responsible for the destruction of his career and his life made Eddie Brock and his symbiotic suit a very dangerous adversary.

He hung up the last print and looked at it closely. It showed an enlarged view of Hobgoblin shooting out of the hatch, and Peter looked carefully at the shiny metal box with what looked like some circuit boards and exposed contacts sticking out of the back of it, and a couple of lights and switches on the front. *Probably just yanked it right out of a console. So much equipment has gone modular these days. Easy to remove for repair or replacement, and just as easy to remove for robbery. But if I was suspicious about him building some sort of bomb, this seems to clinch it. First radioactive material, now a trigger. What the devil is Hobby up to this time…?*

He picked up MJ's borrowed hair-dryer and started fanning it over two of the prints to dry them faster. The part of the theft giving Peter the most trouble was the radioactive material itself. Even if you *were* going to build a bomb, you needed the so-called "weapons-grade" fissionable material that thriller-writers were so fond of. You couldn't just make off with a barrel of nuclear waste, hook a fuse and a trigger to it, and hope that the end result would be *boom*. A barrel of gunpowder, yes. But not this stuff.

It would have to be refined. The refining was an expensive, slow, and above all, obvious process, as some countries, never mind crooks, had already learned. Refining uranium ore, or even spent low-grade reactor waste—where part of the process had already taken place—into metallic U-235 needed a linked series of massive heavy-metal separation centrifuges. Such equipment took up a great deal of space and consumed an equivalent quantity of power.

You couldn't build such a facility in a populated area without someone noticing, no matter how much you tried to disguise it. The power drain on the local grid whenever the separation system was running—and it would have to run almost constantly—would tell even the most unimaginative electrical engineer that something out of the ordinary was going on.

Later, Peter thought, *when I have some time, I'm going to look into the thefts at the two warehouses in a little more detail. I want to find out exactly what was in those canisters. More to the point, why is someone storing nuclear waste—nuclear material of any kind—in Manhattan?* Offhand he could think of about six environmental groups that would blow their collective stacks if they found out about it… and were perhaps already doing so. *That's for later,* he thought. *Right now…*

He checked the six best of his prints to make sure they were dry, put them in his portfolio, put the negatives in as well, and headed for the door. As he went, he threw a last look over his shoulder at the stubbornly silent phone. *MJ….* he thought, then shook his head and smiled a bit to himself at his own nervousness. *She's a big girl, she can take care of herself.*

He headed for the *Bugle.*

"YOUR long lens again?" Kate said, looking over his shoulder at the prints as he put them down one after another on her desk. "That one's not too bad." Critically, head on one side, she studied the shot of Hobby coming up out of the sub. "A little underexposed, though."

"They can push it in Comp," Peter said. Kate nodded. Another shadow fell over the desk. Peter turned, and saw J. Jonah Jameson standing there, scowling down at the photos.

"What are these?" he said, picking up the shot of Hobby, the sub, and Spider-Man. "Not again?"

"Why, Jonah," Kate said dryly, "I'd have thought you'd be delighted. We're having a good news day. Look at that; there's your headline. 'Hobgoblin Strikes Again.'"

"Who cares about that creep?" J. Jonah growled. "It's Spider-Man I'm wondering about. What's he doing inside a nuclear sub in the Port of New York? He could have been doing anything in there!"

"Uh, Mr. Jameson," Peter said gently, "it was Hobby who was doing the 'anything.' Seems he grabbed a trigger for a nuclear missile out of there. You can see it in the shot."

"Maybe," JJJ said, frowning. "But I'm still sure Spider-Man wasn't there just for the good of his health."

Peter thought of the noxious green cloud of gas that had enveloped him inside the sub and silently agreed.

"There's got to be some connection," J. Jonah said. "Hobgoblin and Venom and Spider-Man all in the same day. Are you trying to tell me they're not involved with each other somehow?"

Peter agreed with that too, but not in the way that JJJ thought.

"Look, Jonah," Kate said, "that doesn't matter at the moment. We've got the best picture in town for the *Bugle's* front page, and we've got time to run it for the first evening edition. I don't care if those two were getting together for their weekly pinochle game, this picture's going to make *us* look good tonight! You have any problems with it?"

Jonah glowered at Kate. "Well, not *that* way, but—"

"Good," she said with satisfied finality. "That wording sound all right to you?"

"Well, it'll do for the moment, but—"

"Good," she said again, even more satisfied, "then we're set." She bent over the shot of Hobgoblin. "Just let me decide how I want to crop this—"

Just then Harry Payne, one of the junior editors on the City Desk, stuck his head around the edge of Kate's door. "Hey, Kate," he said, "something on the scanner you might find interesting."

"Oh? What is it?"

"There's something going on in the rail yards over by Eleventh Avenue," he said. "I think it's Venom!"

"What?" all three of them said, turning, the photographs forgotten.

"That's what it said on the scanner. 'Unidentified person, big, black, huge teeth, drooling slime.' That sounds like Venom to me…"

Kate shook her head and grinned. "This is my lucky day," she said. "Peter, don't you move until I can find—" She put her head out the door, looked around for a moment, then shouted down the hall. "Ben? *Ben!* Saddle up! You're needed!" She turned back to Peter. "You go with Ben," she said. "Grab a cab. Go!"

"Let me know how it comes out," Jonah muttered, and stalked off down the hall towards his own office.

Kate watched him go, then glanced at Peter. "You know, I wish I could yell 'Stop the presses!' But it's kind of a problem when you haven't started them yet… And what are you still here for? Go *on!*"

Ben Urich was one of the most experienced reporters on the *Bugle*. Peter was uncertain exactly how long he had been in journalism— it might have been thirty years or longer, but there was no telling by looking at him. Ben's age seemed to have frozen at forty-five, a hard-bitten, cool-eyed forty-five that Peter suspected would hold right where it was until Ben was ninety.

By the time Peter got down to the *Bugle's* front doors, it was dark out. Ben was already pacing and looking impatient. He had a cab waiting at the curb. "Come on," he said, "time's a-wasting!"

Peter jumped into the cab. Ben followed. "Go!" he told the driver, who took off and went racing through the traffic.

Ben glanced down at Peter's camera, then pushed his thick-framed glasses back up the bridge of his nose and looked at Peter. "That all loaded up?"

"Yup."

"Nervous?"

Peter looked at him sharply. "If what we think is down at the rail yards is actually there. I'd say we have reason, wouldn't you?"

Ben raised his eyebrows. "*If* it's what we were told."

"You don't think so?" said Peter.

Ben leaned back in the seat and stretched. "Kind of hard to tell at a distance. All we've had so far is hearsay, and extremely odd-sounding hearsay at that."

"Odd-sounding how?"

Ben looked at him, causing his glasses to slip down again. "As I understood it, Venom isn't much the type for killing people who don't need it. These days, anyway."

"That's what I'd heard, too," Peter said. "Still, you don't suppose he could have had a change of heart?"

Ben's mouth quirked, and he pushed his glasses back up. "People change their minds all the time," he said. "Their hearts—not so often."

"If you can call Venom 'people.'"

"Oh, I don't know," Ben said. "There is a human being in there somewhere."

"There's a lot of difference," Peter said, "between being a human being, and being a man."

Ben raised his eyebrows, looking skeptical. "Semantic difference, mostly," he said. "Anyway, we'll soon find out. Assuming—" and Ben looked even more skeptical "—that the man, creature, or whatever does us the courtesy of hanging around until we get there."

Ben leaned forward and gave the cab driver instructions. They pulled into the pickup and delivery entrance for the rail yards. Overhead, the rail yards' huge yellow sodium lights cast a harsh glare on everything, making the buildings look unreal, like a movie set. The red-and-white strobe of several police cars added to the effect, making the whole place seem like a kaleidoscope.

"Now, then," Ben said, and launched himself out of the cab.

"Your friend meeting somebody?" the cabbie said to Peter, as they both stared at Ben's hurrying back.

"I hope not," Peter said sincerely. Sighing inwardly, he paid the fare and got a receipt. He'd have to put in for reimbursement the next time he was at the *Bugle*.

Then he followed Ben into the guard's shack, a long low building full of file cabinets, a couple of ancient formica-and-aluminum tables, and numerous very upset railroad personnel, many of whom were talking to cops. Ben already had his pocket recorder out and was speaking to one of the supervisors who wasn't giving a statement to the police. "It was this tall," the big blond man was saying, indicating a height at least two feet higher than his own head. "And this wide—"

Peter studied the distance in question and wondered if Venom had put on a great deal of weight. Then again, the costume could change shape....

"Where did you see it first?" Ben said.

"Down by the siding," the foreman said, pointing. "At first I thought it was a cat, moving in the shadows down in the mouth of the tunnel. We have a lot of cats down here, they run in and out all the time. But then it came a little closer, and I got a better look at it—and cats don't get that big. It came sliding out of the tunnel, all black—"

"Black," Ben said. "Did you see any designs, any patterns on it?"

"It had these big long arms—"

"Patterns. Did you see any color on it?" Ben said.

"No, I don't think—that is—" The foreman shook his head. "It moved too fast. That was the trouble. It just came storming out of there all of a sudden, you know? And then there was this train coming down the line at it, and it looked at that, and it roared. It didn't like that—"

"It roared?" Ben said. "It didn't say anything?"

"It just kind of yelled—"

Peter, taking pictures of the man for the "our-witness-tells-us" part of the story, had quite vivid memories of that particular roar. It was usually followed by a statement that Venom intended to have some portion of your anatomy for lunch. "So it roared then," Ben said. "*Then* what did it do?"

One of the other rail workers, a small sandy-haired man who had just finished giving his own statement to the NYPD, said, "He jumped. He jumped away from the train that was coming at him—it was heading into the tunnel—and yeah, like Ron says, he roared at it. But then he stood still. He kind of hunkered down and just looked—"

"Yeah," said a third man, small and dark. "He just looked around him."

"Could you see his eyes?" Ben said.

The three men shook their heads. "Just these blank spots," one said. "Pale," another said. "All white. But when he was in the shade, they glowed a little, you know? Kinda fluorescent."

Peter concentrated on taking more pictures of the three storytellers, while thinking that that odd, faint glow was something he had seen or seemed to see before in the costume—possibly a function of its being alive. He wasn't sure. "It was smelling," the foreman said. "Sniffing."

"You heard it?" Ben said.

"No, no," the three men said, shaking their heads, waving their hands. "It was just the way it looked like—with its head, it sniffed, you know—" One of them put his head up and mimicked something smelling the air, looking alertly from side to side, seeking. "Yeah, and pieces sort of came off it, and swayed around—"

"Came off it?" Ben said. "Came completely off?"

"No, just stretched out, you know?"

"You mean it put tentacles out?"

"Like an octopus, or something like—that's right. They sort of waved all around it, like that, as if it was smelling with them. Like a jellyfish, an octopus, yeah. Do octopuses smell with those?"

"I couldn't help you there," Ben said. "Then what?"

"Well, then," said the sandy-haired man, "another train came up out of the tunnel."

"And it smelled at it," said the small dark man, stretching out his arms and wiggling his fingers at Ben in what Peter assumed was an octopus or tentacle imitation. "And it jumped at it—"

"And it knocked the train over," they all three said, more or less simultaneously.

Ben blinked. "The train. It knocked it over?"

"Come on," said the foreman, and he led Ben and Peter out the back door of the building. Behind it was a rust-stained concrete platform, littered with stacks of railroad ties, coils of wire and cable, and some small stacks of track rails further down. From one end of it, to their left, tracks ran down to the railbed. Six tracks ran in parallel here, with two sets of siding on each side.

Between the number one and number two tracks, slewed over on its side, lay the train. Its engine, one of the big Penn Central diesels, had been knocked furthest off the track and now lay diagonally across it, on its right side. The other cars of the train, four of them, had derailed. It looked, Peter thought, as if some giant child had lost patience with his Lionel train set and had given it a good kick between the second and third cars. He started taking pictures as fast as he could, walking down the length of the train, while the railroad workers stopped near the engine with Ben.

"At first we thought it was gonna jump," said the foreman. "But it didn't. It held still, and it crouched down, kinda, and it put out a lot of those arms, tentacles, whatever, and it grabbed the engine—"

"About how fast was the engine going?" Ben said.

The foreman shook his head. "No great shakes. This is restricted-speed track. You can't really open up until you get across the river. About ten miles an hour, maybe."

"Even so…." Ben said. "So a train weighing—how many tons?"

"These diesels are rated for twelve," said the foreman. "It just sort of grabbed the front of the engine—"

"It sort of shied back, shied away a little, when it did that," said the sandy-haired man. "The bell, you know the bell on the diesel goes constantly under fifteen miles an hour—it was going right in front of the guy's face. I don't think it liked that."

Peter's eyebrows went up at that as he continued down the length of the train, snapping images of the huge exposed undercarriages, the wheels in the air. He turned to get another shot of the gesturing men, small beside the huge overturned engine.

"I don't know about that," said the foreman. "I didn't see that. But then it grabbed the engine, and it just hunkered down and"—he shrugged—"wrestled it off the track. Threw it down."

"The engineer's all right?" Ben said.

"Yeah, he climbed out the window when it went over on the other side."

"So it grabbed a twelve-ton train," Ben said slowly, "and pulled it off the track."

"Right," said the small sandy-haired man. "So it stood there a moment, and it smelled around a little more—and then it went straight back to the third car—"

"Ripped the door right off it," said the foreman. "Like cardboard. And then it climbed in, and came out with a little drum of something. An oil drum, I thought at first."

"But not oil," Ben said.

"Nope," said the little sandy-haired man. "It had the 'radioactive' sign on it."

"I pulled the shipping manifest," said the foreman. "Here it is." He reached inside his bright orange work vest, came out with some paperwork.

"Now what's this," Ben said, pointing down the list. "Uranium hexafluoride—"

Peter came back from down the length of the train and looked over Ben's shoulder at the manifest. "It doesn't go in toothpaste, that's for sure," he said. "It's a by-product from the uranium-enrichment process." He looked up at the foreman. "What did it do with the canister then?"

"It tried to bite it, first," said the foreman, sounding understandably puzzled. "With those teeth, I thought we were going to have a spill right here on the tracks. But it looked like it was having trouble. By then, pretty serious noise had started up—the yard sirens and all—and the warning loudspeakers in the tunnel, all that stuff. It looked around, like it didn't like the noise, and it grabbed the canister in some more of those tentacles and ran off."

"Which way?" Ben said.

The foreman pointed down into the tunnels, into the darkness. "Thataway."

"I take it no one followed it," Ben murmured.

The rail workers looked at him, and all shook their heads. "Hey," one of them said, "we've all got families. I know theft from the rail network is a felony, but—no paycheck's worth *that* much."

The small sandy-haired man looked from Ben to Peter, and back to Ben again. "It was him, wasn't it?" he said. "That Venom guy."

Ben looked at his little pocket recorder, switched it off. "Boys," he said, "I'd be lying if I said it didn't sound like it." The three exchanged nervous glances. "But I want to be sure about this. You didn't see any markings on it? Any white in that black?"

The men shook their heads. "Just the eyes," one said.

"And the teeth!" another said, shivering.

They all stood there in silence for a few. "Well, gentlemen," Ben said, "is there anything else you need to tell me?"

They all shook their heads. "Don't want to see him again," one of them said, "and that's a fact."

"I hope you don't," Ben said. He turned to Peter. "Pete, you got enough pictures?"

"More than enough." He handed Ben the film he'd already shot and unloaded: his camera was whining softly to itself as it rewound the second roll. "Will you take this stuff back with you?" he said. "I've got an appointment tonight that I can't blow off."

"No problem," Ben said. "I see you've had a long day, what with one thing and another. Your photos got page one and two today, Kate tells me." He grinned. "Well," he said to the rail workers, "thanks for your help, gentlemen. If I could get your names and phone numbers for questions later on if we need to ask them?"

They spent a few minutes sorting that out. Then Ben and Peter made their way back up through the guard shack and up onto the street again, where they waited to hail a cab.

"This should make interesting reading in the morning," Ben said, tucking his recorder away.

"What's the headline going to be, you think?" Peter said.

"'VENOM,'" Ben said, "with a big question mark after it."

"You're still not convinced," Peter said.

Ben shook his head. "I am not. There were a lot of the right signs there, but not all."

"The costume?" Peter said.

Ben nodded. "Partly that. But also—" He shrugged, looking down the street for any sign of the light at the top of a cab. "Venom has always been a very verbal sort. Not the kind to do something and then just leave without saying anything, let alone bragging a little. Every report I've heard has made him out to be a talker. I just don't know...."

Peter nodded. It was good to hear his own thoughts being substantiated this way. Ben was a sharp thinker. Peter had learned from Daredevil, one of the local costumed crimefighters, that Ben had worked out for himself Daredevil's secret identity from fairly minimal information, when others had had much more and had never made the connection. "Well," Ben said, "J.

Jonah may not like it, but I'm not going to construct a story that's not there. I'll report the news as it was reported to me, and let it do the work itself."

Peter nodded. "When you get back in," he said, "if you want to call Alicia down in Comp, she'll take care of the developing—"

Ben snorted. "I know what *she'll* do—she'll send your film around the corner to the one-hour place! You let me take care of it—I'll see that they're properly developed." He smiled slightly at Peter as a cab pulled up in front of them. "Got a hot date with MJ tonight?"

"That, and other things," Peter said. "Thanks, Ben! I appreciate it."

"Have a good evening, youngster," Ben said. He climbed into the cab and was gone.

Peter watched him go, and then made for the shadows, for somewhere private, where he could change into something more comfortable.

Before too long, he was web-slinging along through the dark city streets, making his way from building to building and thinking hard.

Mostly he was turning over a thought which had occurred to him belatedly, after recovering from the craziness last night. He really did have to find out what that radioactive stuff in the warehouses had been. Taken together, those two thefts raised a nasty question: what was Consolidated Chemical Research Corporation doing keeping radioactive material on Manhattan Island, in such insecure circumstances, in two different places? Environmental groups, when they heard, would go ballistic. So would the Environmental Protection Agency, for that matter. Normally, he thought, so would the city. There should be no storage facilities for such stuff within the city boundaries. The material stolen from the train, on the other hand, had been completely aboveboard, destined for the legal storage in one of the deep disused salt mines down south, where nuclear waste was now kept under controlled conditions and federal supervision.

He was determined to take a closer look at CCRC, from the inside if possible. If a little discreet poking around turned up no evidence of wrongdoing, that was fine. But this whole thing smelled pretty fishy to him.

He crossed the city carefully. His spider-sense showed no sign of coming back yet, which made him twitchy. He tried, as he went, to keep watch in all directions. If there was any time for Hobgoblin to hit him and take him unawares, this was it. *Unless Hobby is off busy somewhere this evening*, he thought, *playing with his newfound toy*.

He shook his head. If Hobby was holed up building a bomb.... *Something else to look into tomorrow at the paper,* he thought. *Check the database again and see if there have been any other recorded thefts or losses of nuclear material elsewhere in the country. Hobgoblin wouldn't necessarily have to be there himself to steal the stuff. He's not above having it stolen for him. And then*—He frowned under his mask. He would have to sit down and work out exactly what critical mass was when you were working with uranium isotopes. It was not a piece of math he could do in his head, unfortunately. The physics of military fissionables was something he paid little attention to, on general principles. Some of his classmates spent happy afternoons working out engineering solutions and materials criteria for battlefield nukes. But Peter was not one who found such work enjoyable. *I'll take care of it when I get home,* he thought.

Right now, though, the warehouse building from which the radioactive material had been stolen loomed ahead of him, and next to it, the office building which housed CCRC's New York City offices. CCRC's headquarters looked a little seedy, but in good enough repair. The police had the street in front of it and the warehouse cordoned off. Yellow "police line" tape rustled slightly in a slight warm breeze coming off the river, and the cops standing out on the street fanned themselves with their hats. This late, there was little traffic. They looked bored.

All their attention was toward the street, so it was no particular problem for Spidey to swing up from behind the building, let go of his last webline, land against the upper part of the outside wall, and cling there. He held still for a moment, waiting to see if anything had been dislodged by his impact, waiting to see if the police had noticed. They hadn't. Faintly he heard a voice come floating up: "So a guy is crossing the street, and he sees this duck—"

He smiled inside the mask. *A bored cop makes a happy Spider-Man,* he thought, and wall-crawled down the building, testing window after window as he went. Only the lower ones had protective grilles over them. The upper ones were all locked, except for one. *Always some careless person,* he thought, *who doesn't think that Spider-Man might visit their building tonight.* He pushed the window open—it was an old-fashioned sash window—and swung in through it.

His feet came down on thick carpeting. He looked around and saw a heavy walnut desk, with matching office furniture all around. *Very nice,* he thought. *That explains the window, too. Some executive who doesn't want his view spoiled by bars—President's office? Vice-president's? Hmm.* President's, or CEO's, probably; it was a corner office. He looked the place over for signs of alarm systems, saw none. *Very lax—especially when you're involved in* this *industry.*

Silently, Spider-Man stepped up to the door of the office, touched it. No contact alarms, either. No wiring on the door betraying a "reed switch" which would be broken when the door opened. He turned the knob: the door opened, and he found himself looking into an outer office, a secretary's office from the looks of it—nearly two-thirds of the size of the office he had just come from, lined with file cabinets all in walnut, more of that thick carpeting on the floor, a big wall unit with a television, sofas, glass tables—a somewhat executive-level waiting room, it seemed, for people seeing the boss. *Now let's see—*

He went over to the file cabinets. These, at least, were locked, but over time he had become fairly expert at lock-picking. Shortly he had the master lock on the first cabinet open, and was rummaging through the drawers, hunting for anything that seemed interesting.

Several drawers down, he came across what, to judge from the thickness of it, must be the incorporation info for the company itself. He pulled the file out and riffled through it thoughtfully. CCRC turned out to be fairly young. The names of its members of the board could have been from anywhere in New York, but he was interested to note that the majority shareholder was not an American citizen: he was Ukrainian.

He worked backwards to the date the company was formed. *The Soviet Union would have just fallen—*

After turning up nothing else of great interest, he put the file back where he had found it. But ideas were stirring in his mind, nonetheless. *One of the things they've been having trouble with in that part of the world,* he thought, *is radioactive material being smuggled out and sold cheap. What was that one report I heard?—how two guys took a near-critical mass of U-235 out of Russia in the trunks of two cars, and wound up abandoning them on the Autobahn in Germany because they misjudged the distance to Berlin, and ran out of gas?* He shook his head. Not everyone dealing in radioactives from behind the former Iron Curtain was that stupid.

He started going slowly and with care through drawer after drawer. There were a lot of file envelopes with English labels, which, when he opened them, he found contained pages and pages of stuff typed in Cyrillic. He *tsk*ed at himself. MJ had been teasing him for some time now about getting so singleminded about the sciences that he was letting the humanities pass him by, the languages especially. Russian was one of the languages she suggested he take—"Because it's one of the hardest," she had said, looking at him as if the sense of that reason should be obvious. Now he wondered whether he should have taken her advice. But Cyrillic or not, digits were the same. Some of the files he looked at, as he went through the drawers, were plainly shipping manifests of some kind: lists of figures, amounts in rubles and equivalent amounts in dollars—that much he could make out plainly. A lot of currency transactions, in fact, and a lot of changeovers from rubles to deutschemarks, and here and there a document turned up in what looked like German.

He was only marginally better at reading German than he was at Russian, but at least here the alphabets were mostly the same. More amounts in deutschemarks appeared, along with references to weights and masses, always in tens or hundreds of kilograms. And here and there, the German word for "nuclear," which he had come to recognize during his doctorate work, having seen it often enough in the titles of dissertations and articles in journals. The names of the transuranic elements were also just about the same in German as in English, and he came across repeated references to U-235, U-238, and the German word for "enriched" U-235—

Each time it was mentioned, somewhere nearby was a column of figures which made it plain that money was changing hands. But nowhere in all those documents did he see anything like a customs stamp or a bill of sale authorized by any government—and governments had to authorize such sales, as far as he knew.

This place, he thought, *is a front, almost certainly, for smuggling the stuff around. The conditions under which they've been keeping it downstairs seem to confirm it. Those canisters had the barest minimum of labeling. They were being kept clandestinely—*

He shut the files, tidied up after himself as best he could, and looked thoughtfully at the computer on the secretary's desk. *Not networked: a standalone. Might have some interesting files in it.* He moved toward the desk.

From downstairs, in the body of the building, he heard a single, hollow booming sound. A door shutting? He froze, listening hard.

The sound repeated itself, just once. *Boom.*

I think I'm just going to look into that. First of all, though, I want a look at that wall next door.

He stepped to the outer office door, silently let himself out, looked up and down the hall. Nobody.

He started looking for a door exiting to a stairwell. At the end of the corridor, he found one, opened it, slipped out, anchored a webline to one of the stair railings, and let himself down, slowly and silently, as far as the well reached: about six stories. When he let go, he found himself looking at a door with a large letter L on it. *Loading?* he thought, holding still, listening. Somewhere in the building, that soft, low *boom* sounded again, much closer—

This level? he thought. *Well, let's have a look.*

Softly he pulled the door open and peered through it. Nothing: a dark first-floor loading area, as he had expected, pillars supporting the ceiling, plain bare concrete floor—and, off to one side, a hole in the wall, with slumped, crumbling-looking edges. Much nearer to him, though, was a big hole in the floor. Its edges had the same look as those of the hole in the wall, and of the picture he'd seen on TV of the warehouse's wall. That hole would be just across the alley from this one, he thought, glancing up.

What the heck are they up *to in here?*

That booming noise came again. *Might be the police,* he thought. *Might be a good time to excuse myself.* But that hole in the floor, the size of it, the look of it, drew him.

He stepped carefully to its edge and looked down. It gave directly into a big brick-lined sewer tunnel which ran beneath this building. A faint smell of sewage floated up out of it. *Radiation,* he thought, *could definitely cause a hole like this—if it was tremendously intense, tremendously confined—causing the material to come apart out of sheer fatigue. A good push would break it after such treatment.*

Boom.

It is *the police, I bet. Well, I'm going to get out of here.* He went hurriedly to the hole in the wall, looked hastily up and down the alley. The yellow police tapes fluttered a bit down at the far end. Being inside them, he had no one impeding him. The coast was clear, so he slipped hurriedly across the alley, through the hole in the far wall, and into the warehouse where the homeless man had died.

The place stank of blood. It was drying, but not fast enough in this humidity, and the place had a dark, desolate feel, very much like the lower level of the next building over. There was nothing to see here.

Boom.

Not in the other building: in *this* one. Possibly a door opening and shutting in the wind? He turned—and saw the dark shape loom out of the shadows, almost directly behind him. There would have been no warning from his spider-sense even if it had been working at the moment. The dark shape, tall, broad-shouldered, fangs like a shark's dream of heaven, splitting in a grin of unholy glee, and the white stylized spider-shape splashed across the chest.

Spider-Man launched himself at Venom and was astounded a second later when Venom merely backhanded him away. The backhand by itself was more than powerful enough to slam Spider-Man into the wall near the big hole, and leave him reeling for a moment.

"We might have thought," said the low, menacing voice, angry but also oddly amused, "that you at least might have learned never to judge by appearances."

Spider-Man leapt again, and this time Venom's dreadful fangs parted in a smile that went so far around the back of his head, the top should have fallen off. Two-handed, he clubbed Spider-Man sideways again, and this time he stepped back. Spidey flew ten feet or so through the air, came down hard on the concrete floor, but rolled and sprang up again. There he crouched, taking a breath to get his composure back.

"I don't care about the smooth talk, Eddie," Spider-Man said, looking for the best place to attack. "Whatever else may be going on, you're a fugitive—"

"Whatever else," Venom said softly. "Then you have some odd suspicions, too."

"Suspicions? About what?"

"That we would never be involved in such as what happened—here." Some of the awful grin faded as Venom looked around him with distaste. "Someone," he said, "did murder here, in our name." He looked sideways at Spider-Man. "And we are not amused."

"Now why should I believe you?" Spidey said.

Venom simply looked at him, folding his arms. "Because you know us?"

Spider-Man breathed in, breathed out. "You've got me there," he said.

"So," said Venom, "you will forgive us for the moment if we choose not to permit your infantile attempts to apprehend us." He chuckled nastily, and the symbiote for its part took the opportunity to wave that horrendous slime-laden tongue at Spider-Man, *wuggawuggawugga,* in straightforward mockery. "Later on we'll have leisure to joint you and nibble the bones. But right now, we have other matters to attend to."

"Is 'we' you or is 'we' us?"

Venom paused a moment, then chuckled again. "A college education just isn't what it used to be, is it? 'We' is us—I think. At least, any information you can share with us will be welcome. Someone here," Venom said, looking darkly around at the spattered walls, "someone here is trying to frame us for the deaths of these innocents—and when I catch them, both for the attempted framing, and for the murders, we shall certainly eat their spleen."

Spider-Man sighed in brief annoyance. "Listen," he said, "hearts, livers, even lungs I could see. But spleens? Have you ever even *seen* a spleen? I bet you don't even know where it *is.*"

"We could find out," Venom said, looking at him speculatively, and that grin went right around his head again. "It would be fun."

"I thought you said you didn't want to do that right now."

"Don't tempt us. Part of us still desires to make peace with you in the most final manner. But that's going to have to wait. We have done some preliminary research on the firm which owns this property and the one next door. Its clandestine associations make us very uneasy."

"The smuggling, you mean," Spidey said.

"You deduced that? Very good."

"Nothing as fancy as deduction," Spider-Man said. "I just went through their files. Their paperwork is lousy with deutschemark and ruble transfers."

"Yes," Venom said. "That would seem to argue a busy trade across the former East German border. Possibly also the hiring of old East German scientific talent for some purpose. There is a lot of that going very cheap now, I hear. Russian as well."

"And Ukrainian," Spider-Man said.

Venom nodded. "The owners." He glowered back at the hole in the wall. "A sordid business, but one with which we would not normally concern ourselves. In our normal haunts, we have other concerns these days."

"You mean that cave under San Francisco?" Spidey said.

Venom eyed him. "It is an underworld," he said, "though not the kind that's usually meant by the term. People who've taken refuge in a part of the city buried and abandoned in the earthquake eighty years ago. We protect them." For a moment there was just a tinge of pride in the voice.

"It's always nice to have a purpose," Spider-Man said, "besides eating people's spleens."

Venom sighed. "You are an insolent puppy," he said. "But you're right about the purpose. There is worthwhile work to be done, down where the innocents have taken refuge from a world too cruel for them. Noble work, building them a better world than the one they've fled."

"I won't argue that," Spider-Man said.

"You'll understand, then," Venom said, gazing around him coldly at the spattered walls, "that all this—" he gestured around with several tendrils "—will sully our image. Whoever is masquerading as us will be unmasked, swiftly, and will pay terribly for the crime."

"Look," Spider-Man said, inching closer, "I understand that this makes a sort of image problem for you. But a lot of other people have had problems with you and that suit. A lot of them haven't survived them. So you'll understand if I have to cut short the chat, and at least try to take you in—"

That was when they heard the voice from outside. "Charley? Charley, is that you down there, or Rod?"

"Nope, Rod's down here," came another voice.

"Then who's in the building?"

Spider-Man and Venom looked at each other, shocked. It was the police this time.

"You'll forgive us," Venom said, "if we don't wait around for whatever it is you're planning to try now. If you cross our path again, Spider-Man— don't cross *us*. We're on business." And he leaped out the hole in the wall and upward into the darkness.

"Rod, you see that?" came the voice from down the alley. The sound of running footsteps followed it almost immediately.

Yeesh, Spider-Man thought, and shot a webline to expedite his departure and chase down Venom.

"There's another one!" the cry went up. "Get him!"

In the alley, Spider-Man looked and saw cops coming at him from both left and right. He shot a line of web up and out, and went up it just as fast as he could, shooting another line across to the CCRC building and then swinging out past it, around a corner and away, just as fast as he could. As he went, he scanned desperately for any sign of Venom, but there was none to see. *Of course,* Spider-Man thought, *he's immune to my spider-sense—even when it is working—and he can make himself look like anyone. I could be staring right at him and not even know it.*

Reluctantly, he started making his way home. The lights were on in the apartment when he got there. He found MJ just dropping her purse on the front table, and bending over the answering machine to get the messages. She looked up with delight at him as he swung in one of the windows which she had just thrown open. "Hey, tiger," she said, "how was your day?"

He pulled off his mask and shook his head, went to her and hugged her. "Not like yours, I bet."

"I bet," she said, stroking his hair. "Listen—get changed and get something to eat inside you. We've got to talk."

He was tired enough at the moment not to argue with her. He changed, and made a sandwich, and ate it—and made another, and ate it. Then they sat down and she told him about her day.

When she was finished, Peter was still blinking from the news that radiation sickness was being reported in the city. While trying to put this together with other facts, he told her about his day, in some detail. MJ's eyes widened considerably when he told her about his conversation with Captain LoBuono, and they widened more yet when he told her about the hole in the sub's wall. Afterwards, his tale of meeting Venom in the warehouse seemed almost anticlimactic.

"Wow," MJ breathed when he had finished. She looked at him, shaking her head. "There's our riddle for today, then. What goes through walls, and likes radioactive stuff, and isn't Venom… and is loose in New York? And comes from another planet."

"It's the first stuff that's our problem," Peter said, leaning back on the couch. "In this town, who cares if you're local? But now we have to figure out what to do next."

SIX

THEY stayed up late that night talking. There was a lot to be gone over; a lot more news than a few minutes' worth of conversation could hope to deal with. And additionally, just because of business, they hadn't had a lot of time to see each other over the past few days. So there was a prolonged period of hugging, snuggling, smooching, and general touchy-feely before they got back on the subject again.

"Slow down with the sandwiches, tiger," MJ muttered, amused, "save some for me." She headed into the kitchen, Peter close behind her. His stomach growled. "You've *been* eating!" she said. "I can't believe you can still be hungry!"

"You haven't had the day I've had," Peter said again and smiled slightly.

"Oh, haven't I? I may not have been swinging all over the city, but boy, do I feel grateful for food right now. And a place to sleep." She cocked an eye at him as she started rummaging in the refrigerator. "Which is something *you* should start thinking about fairly soon. Look at the bags under your eyes!"

"Bags or no bags, I couldn't sleep right now if you hit me with a hammer. I've got too much on my mind."

"That's the problem with you," said MJ. "You wouldn't know what to do if you didn't have something on your mind. Just imagine it for a moment." She shut the refrigerator door and looked at him challengingly. "Imagine a twenty-four-hour period when everything's working. When the rent's paid, and the phone bill's paid, the electricity's paid, and you've got a credit balance in your checking account, and no checks have bounced, and the credit card company is happy—"

Peter opened his mouth.

"Hush," she said, "I'm on a roll." He shut it again. "Where was I…? Oh yes. And there are no super villains tearing the joint up, and no crime—"

"Are you sure this is Earth you're talking about?" said Peter, raising his eyebrows at her. "Gimme that mayonnaise."

"Nothing for you until I'm finished," she said, standing with her back to the refrigerator door, blocking his way. "Think about it. Just—" She put out one hand and pushed him back, then waved a finger under his nose. "Go on, try it. Stand still for a moment and imagine it. One whole day, just one, when everything's all right."

He stood still, and tried, and found it a bit of a strain. "All right," he said. "So?"

"Well, don't just imagine the events. Imagine how you'd *feel*."

Peter looked at her and shook his head. "I have to confess," he said, "that I don't have a clue. I don't believe that it's ever going to happen."

MJ sighed and moved away from the refrigerator. "You'll never get there," she said, "because you can't—or won't—see all of that as something worth imagining. My money says that if it ever actually got that quiet, you'd go nuts. I'd give it about an hour, and then you'd go out into the street and shanghai the first super villain you saw and beg him to start a fight with you."

"I'd do no such thing," Peter said. "I'd sleep. For about a week, and not get up. I presume this wonderful world we're imagining means I don't have to go into work?"

MJ shook her head. "Oh, no. I know you better than that. Work? If you didn't have to do it, if money didn't drive you to it, you'd *dance* into it. You'd be all over this town, taking pictures of everything that moved—and everything that didn't. The film bill alone—"

"A-*ha*!" Peter said triumphantly. "Something to worry about. Now give me the mayonnnaise."

"Here," MJ said in a lordly manner, stepping away from the fridge and getting a loaf of bread. "Take your mayonnaise." She handed him the jar, which hadn't been in the refrigerator after all. "Listen to me, tiger. You're missing my point. I really think sometimes that the way you keep yourself busy, the way there's always something or somebody to run after, always something important to do, is just that. A way to *keep* yourself busy so you don't have to stop and think about things."

"Like what?" Peter laughed. "Is that bologna still in there?"

"Forget the bologna… it looks like a science experiment."

"Let me see."

"I wouldn't, if I were you," said MJ. "Certainly not just before you eat."

"All right then. What is else is there?"

"No more salami. We've finished that. Some sliced chicken?"

"Okay." He rooted around for it, noted the bologna in passing, rolled his eyes, and shut the fridge again. Then he went over to the counter and started constructing his sandwich. MJ got out a cup, filled it with water, and put it in the microwave to boil. She spent a silent moment rummaging in the cupboard and then said, "I'm thinking about the creature on the sub."

Peter nodded, spreading mayo on the bread. "So am I."

"They wouldn't tell you where they found it?"

"Nope. The captain said it wasn't dangerous." Peter laughed. "Well, not in so many words. He implied it, or at least let it be implied. I don't know about you, but I would normally call something that could go straight through the hull of a nuclear submarine close enough to 'dangerous' to make no difference. I think they're worried. And if it was in that warehouse, and if it killed that homeless guy, then it's already meeting my usual definition."

MJ paced in front of the microwave. "He did say that the thing wasn't radioactive."

"So he *said*."

"Then how did it make that hole in the hull? And in the wall of the warehouse, and in the floor there."

Peter had been chasing around those questions as well. "I don't know," he admitted. "Radiation alone can crumble concrete like that after a few years."

"But how can this—whatever it is—do that *without* being radioactive?"

Peter shook his head. "I'm thinking that Captain LoBuono's higher-ups were economical with the truth when they briefed him on what he was carrying. It may not be radioactive all the time, just under certain circumstances—and I can't even begin to guess what those might be." Peter's voice trailed off as he tried to put the jumble of theories into a coherent form. "Maybe it's immune to radiation, the way snakes are supposed to be immune to their own venom."

MJ raised her eyebrows. "Not my favorite word just at the moment," she said. "He *is* here, then?"

"Oh, he's here, all right. Though he didn't seem particularly interested in me."

MJ sniffed. "I suppose we should be grateful for small favors." The microwave went off. MJ got her cup, put it on the counter and started hunting through one of the cupboards for a teabag. "What gets me," she said, dunking the teabag up and down and watching the way the hot water darkened, "is this thing looking like Venom. If it really *is* the same thing that got out of the sub."

Peter made a wry face as he took a bite of his sandwich. The face had nothing to do with the way it tasted. "It gets Venom, too, from the sound of it. But I suppose it's not *entirely* unlikely. From what the others tell me, there's an awful lot of bipedal, more-or-less humanoid life in this arm of the galaxy."

The others was his blanket term for the various super heroes, super-powerful beings, and all the other oddities in and out of costumes that he ran into during the course of his work as Spider-Man. One theory was that one species, many, many millions of years ago, seeded this part of the galaxy with similar genetic material. All the carbon-based planets, anyway. Some others, among them Reed Richards, said that there was no need to postulate a *species ex machina*—that for carbon-based life, the bipedal pattern was merely logical and tended to recur. Whatever the reason, the approximately upright bipedal form with bilateral symmetry was common enough that he had grown used to seeing it in the most unlikely places. And maybe he was growing used to seeing what he *expected* to see.

"My problem is, I need to know what this thing wants. And what to do about it."

"If it's the same thing that came out of the sub," MJ said, "then what it wants seems to be radiation. But why would something that wasn't radioactive itself be attracted to a radioactive source?"

"I'm not sure," Peter said. He took another bite from his sandwich. "I keep thinking of the train worker who said the first thing it tried to do was gnaw the canister open. Then there was the homeless guy from the warehouse, who claimed he saw it licking the stuff up off the floor." He caught an escaping dribble of mayonnaise with his finger and popped it in his mouth, then looked at his finger as if it held the secrets to the universe. "Biting and licking—like I'm doing with this sandwich! Maybe it wants this radioactive material to *eat*." He looked at the chicken sandwich, still dripping mayo from the two big semicircular bites he had taken out of it, and felt his appetite suddenly disappear. He put the remnants down and wiped his fingers on a paper towel, then folded his arms and leaned back in the chair so that its front legs left the floor. "It's an interesting question," he said. "What kind of creature eats radioactive material, but doesn't hold any detectable trace of radiation in its body?" He thought a moment. "*If* it doesn't. Captain LoBuono said that it had to be kept sealed away with radiation because of its habits." He looked sideways at MJ.

MJ sat down and started dunking the teabag in her cup again. "I keep thinking of gremlins. Or tribbles. What if feeding enables it to breed?"

Peter shuddered. "Don't even suggest it. If that thing reproduces, we've got real trouble on our hands. Can you imagine a bunch of those things running around, eating everything radioactive in sight? And the most obvious place for them to start would be the hospitals, looking for X-ray isotopes."

MJ dropped her teabag onto a nearby saucer. "You're so good at imagining the nasty things," she said, "and no good at all at imagining the good ones! There's a definite problem there."

"We'll deal with that later," Peter said. "But its metabolism… Everything has to get energy from somewhere. We tend to think of living things getting energy from food, or from sunlight if they're plants. But what if you had a life form that started out one way and was forced to adapt? To change from what we think of as normal sources of nutrition," he eyed the sandwich again, "and resort to a direct transfer of raw energy."

He stood up, paced around the table, then sat down again. "I'm not even an ordinary biologist, never mind a xenobiologist. This stuff isn't my strong suit, and it's giving me a headache. But radioactivity I know a little about. If there was a life-form that has the physical structure of a living nuclear reactor—" He shuddered.

MJ looked at him sympathetically. "Then maybe you need to ask for advice from somebody who *does* know about that kind of thing. Try Reed Richards. He's always been able to give you some sort of answer before. Why not now?"

"Because right now I don't even know if he's in town. And there's so much other stuff to do. I've got to do some more checking into these CCRC people, and then there's Venom, and there's Hobgoblin—"

"It occurs to me," MJ said, "that if Venom runs into this whatever-it-is that looks like him, there's going to be an almighty ruckus."

Peter nodded grimly. "Yeah. Probably right in the middle of the city, as usual. And in broad daylight. Venom doesn't wait for anything if he thinks the moment's right. Patience isn't something he's good at. And then I have to go after him. I can't just stand by and watch him waltz through and not do something about it." His voice trailed off and he rubbed at his shoulder, still sore from where he had gone crashing into the wall earlier on.

MJ saw the gesture. She walked around behind him and started rubbing his shoulders. "Do you know," she said conversationally, "how many tubes of Ben-Gay we've gone through since we got married?" Peter looked at her, completely confused. "Eighty-six," she said. "Deep Heat, Mentholatum, you name it. Every time I go to the grocery store, I have to buy more. The guy in the Gristede's asks me if I put it in my tea or something."

Peter's only reply was a groan of ecstasy as his wife rubbed the kinks out of his shoulders. He poked at the sandwich, decided not to waste it, and demolished it in about three or four bites.

MJ ceased the shoulder rub and said, "Your spider-sense still isn't back, I take it."

"Nope. It's possible I just got a really heavy dose of whatever Hobby was using last time."

MJ looked at him sadly. "You think that it's gone for good," she said. "At least, that's what's worrying you." He looked at her and she smiled a little, one-sided. "Do you seriously think you can hide that kind of thing from me at this point? I can recognize your 'brave face' at fifty paces. Wait a little longer and just watch your step. That sense is so much a part of your powers that when everything else is still working fine, I can't imagine it's going to be gone for long."

Peter smiled back at her. "It doesn't necessarily follow," he said, "but for the moment, I like your explanation better than any of the ones that I've got. And as for Hobby, he *will* strike again. If he doesn't do it tonight, it'll be tomorrow. And I can't do anything about tonight, because if I don't sleep, I'm going to fall over."

"You got *that* right," MJ said. "You are not leaving this house, no matter *what* happens between now and 8 A.M." Her eyes glinted. "I have plans for you."

"Oh, boy!" Peter said, and meant it, even though he was still somewhat distracted. "Anyway, as for Hobby. I really doubt that he's going to get any more stuff from any more warehouses. Anybody who's running an illegal trade in radioactives in this town will have noticed what's been happening, and they'll have slapped extra security on whatever they've got. So I think we can rule out CCRC or anyone else like them. Which leaves the legal sources." He frowned slightly. "They'll be raising their security levels too, but increased security hasn't stopped Hobby in the past. And I doubt it'll stop him tomorrow. Or the day after. So I'm going to have to do some patrolling myself."

"Do you have a good guess as to where he's going to be?" MJ said.

Peter nodded. "The only big *legal* nuclear research facility in New York right now is at ESU. There's enough material of the kind Hobby will want on campus for him to try making a grab. There's always somebody on the inside who'll talk about where things are for money, or fear… Hobby has a gift for finding people like that. If he doesn't know already where something is, he's going to find out soon."

"And what kind of luck are *you* going to have at finding out where things are?" MJ said.

He yawned, and stretched until his joints went click, then grinned at MJ. "Oh, I'll do all right. Tomorrow I'll stop by the lab, chat with some people, pick up on the gossip, hear what's going on."

"And do a little judicious inveigling of information?" MJ said.

"Oh yeah. I'm sure I can find out what I need to know. Because Hobby will turn up. I'm sure he will."

MJ was sipping her tea again, and looking thoughtful. "What about Venom?" she said.

"One thing at a time, please! I don't think it's a headache at all. I think my *brain* hurts."

"That's it," MJ said, pushing the teacup to one side. "A nice hot tub for you, and your sore head, and your sore muscles. And I'm getting in with you."

"Ooh!" Peter said, grinning at her. "Lucky me!" He got up, wincing at the bone-deep aches he had been trying to ignore, and followed her down the hall.

NEXT morning, after checking the papers and the news to make sure that nothing untoward had happened during the night, Peter betook himself to the groves of academe.

Empire State University was located in Greenwich Village. The main building was an old structure, full of little rooms tucked off into odd nooks and crannies. One tiny broom closet into which Peter had found his way looked down through a small window over at the Science Building. There were endless ways for a Spider-Man, or other unauthorized person, to sneak into or out of ESU's campus, if that person knew where those ways were. And if you were expecting someone who didn't know the ins and outs, you could make their welcome a very interesting one, indeed.

The new annex out back was not nearly so architecturally inspiring as the main building, built as it was during a period when being functional was deemed more important than being stately, but it too had its advantages. Over his years of study, Peter had had plenty of leisure to observe where its ducts went, which grilles led into which part of the air-conditioning system, what roof spaces gave onto rooms through utility traps or openings to attic storage space. A clever and determined person could stay out of sight and out of mind for a long time up in those empty spaces—moving from place to place, keeping an eye on things. That was what Peter had in mind for Spider-Man. But first, he had some things to take care of which Spider-Man couldn't manage with impunity and Peter Parker could.

He headed up the big marble steps, through the front hall and the body of the main building, finally on out the back door to the little square which separated the main building from the annex.

The annex was all very sixties-academic—plate glass, aluminum, and solid blocks of color. Somebody with a strange taste for modern art had erected, in the middle of the square, something which purported to be a stainless steel Tree of Life. The science students claimed that, on moonlit spring nights, coeds danced around it scattering ball bearings. At most other seasons of the year, the thing was festooned with toilet paper. Everyone hated it.

Peter went up the shallower set of steps by the science building, paused by the bulletin board inside the front doors, and looked to see if anything interesting had been posted. This time of year, between the active semesters, there was nothing much to be seen but some outdated flyers about parties, and a university directory of Internet e-mail addresses that had probably been out of date by the end of the week it had been posted. Far down on one page of it, someone had scribbled, FOR A GOOD TIME, CALL PI 3-1417....

Peter went off to the right, where a stairwell led to the classrooms on the second floor, and a door in the wall stood underneath it. This was where the Nuclear Physics department was, for the simple reason that most of the equipment was too heavy to be put any higher.

The door under the stairs was not a swinging door, like most of the others in the building, but required a key to open. Peter pulled his key out of his pocket and let himself in. All the instructors and doctoral and degree students working in Nuke had the keys: they weren't exactly difficult to lay hands on. But that door was a boundary of sorts. Here the construction of the building changed, got abruptly heavier and more solid. Walls were thicker, and in the hall behind the door a wall jutted out into the corridor, covering two-thirds of its width from the left side out. About five feet further on, another wall did the same from the right side. It was good old-fashioned radiation safety. Should some kind of accident occur inside, radiation couldn't just stream through the door and out. The construction and look of it was very fallout-shelterish, and every now and then it brought back Peter's childhood memories of crouching under his desk at school with his hands over his head during atomic war drills. What was the old song? "Duck and Cover?" *A lot of good it would have done us at ground zero*, he thought as he went past the baffle.

He headed on through to the classroom and lab area. The place was utterly quiet. It felt that way even in mid-semester. The machinery here didn't need heavy air-conditioning: most of the machines had few or no moving parts. But the whole place, clean and light and bright as it looked, held a slight edge of threat, of silent power, usable by some, misusable by others, waiting to see which way it would go.

The door at the very end of the downstairs hall was the one Peter was heading for. It, too, was locked. The same key opened it as had opened the outer door.

He put his head in. As he'd hoped, lights were on, shining on the big closed cabinets, the blocky silent machines. "Hello?" he said.

"Yo!" came a familiar woman's voice from the back. "Who's that?"

"Peter Parker."

"Good lord, the wandering boy returns!" the voice half-sang from the back of the room. A cheerful face with blonde hair drawn tightly back in a ponytail peered at him around a room divider.

"Dawn," Peter said. "How're you doing?"

"Not too bad," Dawn said. "Catching up on work—" She put unusual emphasis on the word as she grinned wickedly at him. Peter was hoping that Dawn McCarter—no, Dawn Luks her name was now; he kept forgetting she was married, though it had been more than a year—would still be around working on her dissertation. She was a doctoral candidate in Nuclear Physics, and had one of the quickest, brightest minds he had ever seen, able to move within a second from a learned discussion of supercollider physics to going "ooji-ooji-ooji" at her new daughter. Speaking of whom, he noticed Dawn's baby girl sitting in her carrier on the floor, waving a pink-and-white star-and-heart chew-toy in front of her face, and occasionally giving it a good gumming. "I see you got stuck with the baby this time," he said.

"Ron's deep into work-on-the-computer mode. The kid could drop dead in front of him and he wouldn't notice. Since I'm just polishing off the dissertation work, I figured I'd take her in here for the next week or so. God knows we can't afford a sitter on our stipends. How's MJ? What's she up to, these days?"

"Just fine. She's doing the audition circuit right now."

"What brings you in?" she said. "Didn't think I'd see you until the fall."

"Oh, well, I'm supposed to be meeting with my advisor, but he's running a bit late."

Dawn laughed. "So what else is new?"

Peter wandered around the room. There was a lot of big, bulky, expensive, and difficult-to-move machinery in here. One large installation on the side, a glove-box with three sets of waldoes for working with sensitive material behind leaded glass and concrete. Next to it, a big lead safe for storing radioactive material, with a smaller one beside it; various light sensing equipment here and there; and over in the far corner, about twenty feet away, the thing he was most concerned about, and which Dawn was working with: the casings and materials fabrication unit. After all, you couldn't just carry nuclear material around in a lunchbox, you had to build containers according to the requirements of the sample in question, to handle its specific level of radiation, and to suit the application for which it was to be used. It was a combination isolation box and machine shop, all very compactly made. The whole thing was no more than four feet square, and it had occurred to Peter that, if Hobby were going to steal something at this point, this might very well be it. It would be difficult to move, but far from impossible.

Dawn was busy inside it at the moment, putting the final touches on a small lead-lined carrier box. "For sushi, right?" Peter said, looking over her shoulder through the leaded glass.

"Idiot," Dawn said affectionately. "Here, amuse the rugrat while I'm working on this."

"Hey there, gorgeous," Peter said, hunkering down beside the baby, "how ya doing?" The baby took the chew-toy out of her mouth, looked at it thoughtfully, and offered it to Peter.

"No, thanks," he said, "I'm trying to cut down." He let the baby grab his finger in her fist and shook it around a little. She gurgled.

He turned back towards the blond. "So how goes the dissertation, anyhow? It was something to do with transuranic superconductors, wasn't it?" As he stood up from beside the baby, he palmed one of the spider-tracers from his pocket and stuck it unobtrusively near the bottom of the fabricator unit.

"Yeah," Dawn said, not actually looking at Peter, engrossed as she was. "Most of the papers were saying the lanthanide connection wasn't turning out to be very productive... so I decided to try some of the higher transuranics, and see if sandwiching them together with one of the higher-temp superconductors would produce any results."

"Which one were you playing with?" While he spoke, Peter wandered away from the box and headed over to the safes.

"Americium, mostly."

Peter grinned. "Why don't you just try holding water in a sieve? As I recall, that stuff has a half-life shorter than your kid's attention span."

Dawn grunted. "This *is* a problem. With a ten-hour half-life, you might well invent a revolutionary super-conductor compound, but if you go to lunch at the wrong time you miss it, and the results are dang near impossible to replicate. Oh, well, if that doesn't work"—and Peter saw her grin—"I might try something simpler, like cold fusion."

Peter chuckled. "I can see your point. Well, I hope it works out," Peter said. "You've got to graduate from this place before *she* starts her freshman year, or people will talk. Anything new in here?"

"Not that I've seen," Dawn said absently. "They took out most everything but the project stuff in there."

"So I see," Peter said, his eye falling on a series of little lead canisters all labeled "americium tetrafluoride." There were enough canisters that Dawn wasn't likely to miss one of them, and each was small enough that it would get the attention of anything that liked radiation. Fighting down a twinge of guilt, he palmed one of the canisters, and tucked it in his pocket without Dawn seeing.

Then he leaned over and placed two more tracers on the shelf containing the canisters and on the bottom of the bigger safe. "So, Dawn," he said, "when are you going to come have dinner with us?"

"Oh, Pete, you know how it is," she muttered, still intent on what she was doing in the fabricator. "It's all I can do to drag Ron away from the computers—or his baby daughter." She smiled. "Maybe you ought to make a date with *her*."

"Better not," Peter said, straightening up. "MJ would get after me for chasing younger women. Listen, if I don't see you before then, I'll see you when classes start again, huh?" He waved at the baby. "Bye, gorgeous!"

"Urgle," she commented as he shut the door behind him.

A short while later he was changed into his spider-suit and entered the ducts of the science building. He had leisure to think about a lot of things as he moved stealthily from place to place, checking the ducts to see that they were as he remembered them, peering into this room, out that window. How he really needed to call Aunt May, how he had forgotten to pick up the Woolite again, about many other things. But none of them could quite take his mind away from the little lead canister webbed at his waist. The skin under it itched.

He knew, of course, that there was no possibility of the substance in the canister causing the itch. The canister was solid, the radioactivity inside was fairly low. Nonetheless, he imagined he felt it.

Very slowly, afternoon shaded into evening. Offices started to be locked, lights began turning off, and people went off to dinner. Thinking that a view from outside might be wiser than a view of the inside, Spider-Man took this opportunity to make his way cautiously out of the ducts and back up into the main building, into the little broom closet that looked down on the annex. Its grimy window, when you pushed the sash up, would be more than big enough to let him out. Inside it, he couldn't be seen. He waited there, while the shadows lengthened and leaned toward dusk—

—and something twinged inside him, just faintly, just once: the taste of danger coming.

The chemical has worn off, Spider-Man thought happily. His pulse started to pick up. *My spider-sense is returning!* He didn't even mind that the faint tingle meant trouble was coming.

Outside the window, he heard that faint telltale whine of very small, very sophisticated jet engines.

He couldn't even wait for it to get completely dark, he thought. *Impatient cuss.*

Spidey leaned forward to watch the jetglider settle into the courtyard, with the eerie shape of Hobgoblin standing on top of it. His back was to Spider-Man.

"It's showtime!" Spidey said softly to himself as, very gently and very quietly, he eased the little window open.

Now this is going to be interesting, Spidey thought. While the Nuclear floor of that building had windows, they were very few and small. Most of the light came in via glass brick. Hobby, though, seemed undaunted. He jockeyed the jetglider around to the rear end of the building, where the least important equipment was sited, and very straightforwardly flung a pumpkin bomb at the outside wall.

A tremendous explosion shook the building, and the rear wall fell away in ruins. Alarms started ringing, but Hobby obviously didn't care about those. He zipped in through the opening.

Just as I thought, Spider-Man thought as he leapt from the open window and swung across the courtyard. *Somebody told him where things were. What to worry about damaging, what not to care about.*

Hurriedly, Spider-Man began webbing almost the entire outside of the building, except for the opening Hobby had blown in the back side. The webbing was in the garden-spider tradition, a fairly fine-meshed network anchored to the ground all around. Spidey leapt and bounced from place to place, very glad that he had restocked his web-shooters earlier in the day. When all the rest of that side of the building was covered, he went to the hole and threw a similar webbing across it. He was barely half done when Hobgoblin appeared on his jetglider. He hovered behind the web mesh, staring at Spider-Man with a look of shock on his face.

Spidey was slightly shocked, too, for Hobby had cabled the bigger safe to the bottom of his rocket sled, and to Spidey's astonishment, the jetglider was actually managing to lift the thing off the ground.

"All right, Hobby," Spider-Man said as calmly as he could. "Put it back where you found it."

Hobgoblin's incredulous expression didn't last long. A nasty grin spread over his face. "Surely you jest, Spider-Man," he said, laughing. He pulled out another pumpkin-bomb and lobbed it casually at the nearest wall.

There was another huge explosion. Brick and broken pieces of equipment flew in all directions, and Spider-Man felt a moment's extreme unhappiness over how much it was all going to cost to replace. "Ta-ta, bug," said Hobby as the smoke cleared, and without hesitation, he and his jetglider zoomed straight at the hole he had made.

He should have hesitated. As soon as Hobgoblin came through the hole he'd made, he ran into Spidey's trap full tilt. The webbing caught and held him. Spider-Man moved in fast to finish the job, parting his webbing and leaping through the first hole. From behind, he webbed Hobby up like a neat package. Hobgoblin thrashed and swore, but it did him no good. Within a few seconds, all he could do was glare mutely at Spider-Man, so tightly webbed from toes to mouth that there was nothing he could do. He couldn't reach a bomb to throw, nor deliver any shock from his energy-gauntlets that would do anything but fry himself. The jetglider, tethered now, thumped to the floor with its leaden cargo.

"Now then," Spider-Man said gently. "You and I have things to discuss."

"Perhaps," said a deep voice from behind him. "But we think *our* conversation with this—thing—takes precedence."

Spider-Man turned. There, silhouetted against the webbing and the opening Hobby had made, stood Venom. The symbiote slowly grinned, his terrible snakelike tongue reaching toward Hobgoblin.

"We've got to stop meeting like this," Spider-Man said, annoyed, "or people will talk. This is just a good old-fashioned garden variety theft of nuclear materials. Nothing for you to concern yourself about—"

"We think not," Venom said, stepping slowly toward Hobgoblin, who was so thoroughly wrapped up that he couldn't even speak. Instead, he made nervous, placating-sounding grunting noises.

"The very fact that he is thieving nuclear material," Venom said, "makes plain what he's been up to. The other 'us' that we've been hearing reports of has also been thieving such material, has he not?" Slowly he drew closer to Hobgoblin. "So you kill two birds with one stone. You fulfill whatever nasty mercenary criminal scheme you're working on at the moment, and you also throw the blame on someone else. And they eat it up, don't they? The media." Venom smiled his awful fangy smile, and the symbiote drooled in anticipation. "No one has ever dared try anything quite so audacious with us. Such action on your part would seem to argue that you are weary of your life. That being the case—"

Tendrils from the symbiote streamed off him, grabbed Hobby, webbing, glider, safe and all, picked him up, and shook him as another man might shake someone by the lapels of a jacket. "Before we julienne the flesh off your bones and tie it in bow-knots while you watch—we want to know *why?*"

Hobgoblin made muffled, desperate noises. Venom's dark tentacles begen to edge themselves like razors. They descended on the webbing—sliced it, ripped it, shredded it away.

"Hey, wait a minute," Spider-Man cried. "It took a little doing to get him that way!" He leapt at Venom to pull him off from behind.

Venom's hands were occupied. Some of his tendrils whipped around to deal with Spider-Man—still razor edged, deadly as any knives. Spidey ducked away from them, and managed—but only because Venom was distracted—to throw some of his own webbing around Venom this time.

The struggle that followed was a chaotic sort of thing—Venom tearing at the web, his tentacles wriggling and streaming out from between the strands, trying to reach Spidey, Spidey throwing more web over it all, desperately hoping he wasn't about to run out after all he'd just used on the building. The two of them danced to and fro, spraying webs, cutting webs, tendrils clutching, being tangled, freeing themselves and being tangled again—

—until the whine of the jetglider stopped them both where they stood.

It was a pitiful-looking package which was soaring slowly, but more and more quickly every second, up out of the shattered building. Shreds and rags of web hung off Hobby, the jetglider, and the safe—all ascending as Hobby put on speed.

"Oh, no," Spidey moaned. He dashed out and shot web desperately at the receding form, but the jetglider kinked suddenly sideways, rose over the walls of the college, and was gone.

Glaring terribly, Venom rid himself of the last few rags of Spidey's webbing. "You utter fool. Now he'll get away and finish whatever awful thing he's started! Not to mention going back to impersonating *us*. And there's no telling where he's heading now—"

Spider-Man said nothing. He had seen, as the safe ascended, that his tracer was still on it. When his spider-sense came back fully—which he hoped would be soon—he would be able to track him well enough. He turned to Venom. "You're serious about this. It really *wasn't* you down there."

"You still don't quite believe us," Venom said, his voice a low, angry growl. "O ye of little faith."

"Yes, and the Devil can quote scripture to his purpose," Spider-Man said. *Still,* he thought, *I've been giving him the benefit of the doubt all this while. And now when he comes to me and tells me I was right—I can't believe him?*

"You're telling me that you didn't knock over a train last night?" Spidey said.

Venom's smile was grim, but just a touch more humorous-looking than usual. "Someone who could knock over trains," he said, "would not have had the trouble with your webbing that we just did." He frowned. "We must see about a more effective remedy."

"Let's leave that aside for the moment," Spider-Man said.

"I think we had better. That creature can't continue impersonating us—"

"I'm not so sure it was Hobgoblin," Spider-Man said. "And it would be dreadful to eat his spleen for the wrong reason, wouldn't it?"

"If he's doing what we think he's doing at the moment," Venom said, his tongue flickering in shared rage, "there's reason enough to rip him limb from limb, even leaving personal business out of it. Hobgoblin is almost certainly building a bomb of some kind, wouldn't you agree?"

Spider-Man could only nod at that.

"And the only reason one builds atomic bombs is to threaten other people with their use. And sometimes... to actually use them." Venom glared at Spider-Man again. "We, for one, though we consider this city a Hell for the innocent, and the den of every kind of injustice and crime, would prefer not to see it blown up... it, or any other like it. That Hobgoblin is even willing to threaten to do such a thing, or to help someone else to do it, merits him death. If he would do more—if he would actually detonate a bomb and end millions of innocent lives—then he merits death millions of times over. And we promise to make that death as prolonged and painful as he would make the deaths of many of the people here!"

"Look," Spider-Man said, "I'd agree, but—"

"No buts," said Venom. "We are going after him. This wretched creature has been brought to 'justice' enough times—with what result? *This.* We swear to you, we will find him before you do. By the time we are done with him, he will bewail the fate that kept you from finding him first."

Venom turned and leapt out the blown-out end of the building.

Spider-Man leapt after him.

SEVEN

MJ had seen Peter off that morning in a somewhat mixed state of mind. She had the pleasure of knowing that he was rested, not aching too badly (for a change), he'd had enough to eat, and most important, he'd actually had enough time to digest and consider what had been happening to him for the last couple of days. MJ watched her husband with considerable concern. She was afraid that, if he went out one time too many unrested and without his plans in order, he wouldn't come back.

She knew what he was planning for his day at ESU. She couldn't say she was overwhelmingly happy about it, but he was as well-prepared as he could be; he had a plan. So, there was nothing much more to be said about it. That being the case, she made tea and toast, sat down at the dining-room table with the sun coming in through the window, and paged through the trades she'd bought the other day at Mr. Kee's. There wasn't anything much of interest that she hadn't already seen. News of mergers, buyouts, movie deals—*I'd love to have anything happen to me,* she thought, *that had lots of zeroes after it....*

She made a second batch of toast, buttered it, and sat down when the phone rang. She debated letting the machine take it, then got up and went over to the phone table. "Hello?"

"Ms. Watson-Parker?"

"This is she."

"This is Rinalda Rodriguez, over at Own Goal Productions—"

"Yes," MJ said, and her heart leaped. It was the people who had offered her the audition.

"Listen, I'm sorry to trouble you so early, but we've had a change of plan—"

There it goes, MJ thought. *The whole thing's off.*

"My partner and I have to leave for LA early tomorrow morning—"

I knew it, it was too good to be true.

"—so is there any chance that you could come up to do your audition today?"

"Today?" MJ said, swallowing. "Certainly. I don't see why not. What time?"

"Would after lunch be all right?"

"After lunch—"

There was some babbling in the background. "Oh, no, wait a moment—" The phone was covered, and some words were exchanged. "Actually, three o'clock. How would that be?"

"Three o'clock. Fine. Same place?"

"No, we're moving uptown for this one." The AP gave her an address on the Upper West Side.

"That's fine," MJ said. "I'll be there."

"Sorry again to change plans on you like this."

"Oh, that's all right. It's nice of you to tell me this early," MJ said, meaning it. Some producers she'd known would change plans without warning and then make it sound as if it was your fault somehow when you couldn't meet the new requirements. "I'll see you this afternoon, then. Bye!"

She hung up. *This afternoon. Ohmigosh!*

She had planned to spend a leisurely afternoon, studying the material she'd been given, reading to feel what the material did for her, and working to the mirror, making sure that her expressions were doing what she thought they were doing. Well, it was going to have to be mostly mirror work today, and in a hurry, too. As always, when a crisis like this came up, she was all nerves, all at once. She scooted over to the window, leaned against the windowsill and looked out across the rooftops, twitching slightly. *Peter...* she thought.

But Peter could take care of himself. He had proven that often enough in the past, in one set of clothes or another. Now she was going to have to get out there and do the lioness thing. She would make him proud of her.

She let out a fast, excited breath, then went to get those script pages.

THE time until two o'clock, when MJ needed to leave, flew by. How to read young Dora, the social worker character—that was the main problem. She was young: if the producers were casting actresses 22–25, they meant it. Surely they didn't want Dora too experienced, too knowledgeable. Yet at the same time, someone coming out of school that age could have considerable expertise—and the series bible did emphasize the character's sense of humor. That, MJ thought, was the key. When the character knew for sure what she was talking about, she would be all business and certainty, but when something happened with which she'd had no previous experience, she'd cover with humor while trying to figure out what to do.

As time to leave got closer, it got harder for MJ to concentrate. *I wonder how many other people are auditioning?* she thought. She had trouble dealing with cattle-calls like the one the other day. But surely most of those people had been shaken out. All the same, she didn't like watching a lot of readings before her own—the fear dogged her that she could accidentally adopt someone else's approach when her own would really work better. And at the same time, she was usually forced to see a lot of other readings, because her name began with "W." So she did her best to ignore what was going on around her—but the long wait always made the nervousness worse. *Sometimes I think it would be less stressful to go out and have a fight with a super villain.*

As two o'clock inched closer she read the pages one last time, putting some extra emphasis on the set of lines about hunger, letting the feeling out. There was a lot of it: her close look at the shelter yesterday reminded her how easy it was to forget about the homeless problem completely, and the anger and frustration came up in the reading, she thought, to good effect.

Well, she decided at last, *this is as good as it's going to get. Let's get dressed and head out.*

She had showered and taken care of her hair and makeup earlier. Now she went into the bedroom and hunted through the closet for the right thing. Something attractive, but appropriate for a young social worker. Fawn linen skirt, just barely below the knee; medium heels; white silk shirt. She thought for a moment and pulled out her one and only Hermes scarf, the one with the tigress on it, a present from Peter. She twined it around her neck outside the shirt collar and left it hanging down casually.

There, she thought, looking herself over in the mirror. *A touch of class.*

She went out, grabbed her purse and keys, the script pages and audition pack, and her copy of *War and Peace,* and headed down to catch a cab. Normally, MJ had cab luck. Rain or shine, all she had to do was go out to the curb, stick her arm out, and a cab would materialize from nowhere. Today, naturally, the luck deserted her for all of five minutes, so that she stood there twitching impatiently, thinking. *What if I don't get a cab at all, what if I'm late, what if there's a traffic jam…*

Peter…

She let out a breath, then smiled at herself. At times like this, her free-floating anxiety fastened on anything it could find. Peter was quite probably happily and coolly ensconced at ESU somewhere, biding his time.

A cab finally pulled up. She got in, gave the driver the address, and let him whisk her away. From Peter, her mind jumped again to the homeless people she had met. While she and Peter had been in the tub, they had talked about the radiation sickness—for so it seemed to be—that some of these people were suffering from. *The submarine captain said,* she thought, *that the creature itself wasn't radioactive. And Peter mentioned the hole in the bottom of the warehouse, leading down into the sewers. If that thing's been down in the sewers, and in the train tunnels where some of the homeless people are, doesn't it have to be the cause? But if the captain's right and it's not affecting them, not the cause of their radiation sickness—what is?*

She turned the problem over in her mind, but could find no obvious answer. *Could there be some kind of radioactive waste leaking down into the tunnels and sewers? Could someone be disposing of the stuff illegally?* She knew that toxic waste got dumped in landfills where it didn't belong. Sometimes, tankers full of it just sprayed their contents out on the side of some lonely country road, or into common sewerage, where it just flowed out to sea, untreated. Suppose someone was doing something similar with radioactive waste here in the city?

It would be easy enough to do, and there would be reasons for it. Disposing of nuclear waste safely was expensive: companies that used the legal methods of disposal were charged a lot for it. Why not save the money and just dump the stuff somewhere?

She was too nervous to think clearly about it. There was something nagging at her—the image of people, hungry and homeless to start with, now having to watch the blotches and sores form on their bodies, their hair falling out, feeling themselves getting more ill and weak every day. It didn't bear considering. She hoped somebody—Spider-Man, or the police, or even Venom—would find the creature, if it was the cause of this, and end its threat. *Those poor folks,* she thought and was surprised to find her eyes stinging with tears.

She got a tissue out of her purse and dabbed herself dry again. *Nerves,* she thought. And then, after a few seconds, she shook her head ruefully, catching herself in a lie. Nerves was not what it was about, feeling was what it was about—and there was no need to be ashamed of that.

The cab pulled up in front of a tall old brick building. She paid the cabbie, put herself in order, tossed her hair back, and strode into the building's lobby, smiling and ready.

TWO hours later, she felt a lot less ready, but the smile was still there, mostly.

The reception area was typical: full of comfortable, sleek furniture, big sofas curving around to match the lines of the room, gorgeous modern art on the walls, two separate televisions showing two separate channels, and a busy, expensive-looking receptionist working behind a massive and politically incorrect desk of polished teak that MJ estimated would have cost about a year's rent on their apartment.

The audition room where she and the twenty-three other actresses all gathered to meet the production staff was more of the same: state-of-the-art sound and video equipment all stashed away in absolute tidiness behind a floor-to-ceiling glass wall, not a loose cable or wire in sight. Next, the AP ushered them into a big, bright, clean, carpeted rehearsal space, everything brand-new. There was serious money here and MJ was determined to be part of it, one way or another.

The competition daunted her. She looked good—she knew that—but some of these women looked spectacular, with the kind of effortless beauty that suggested they didn't have to do anything to themselves in the morning but wash their faces and toss their hair back out of their eyes. It was not in MJ's style to be jealous—not after a first flash of emotion which usually simply translated as, "It's not *fair!*" and then melted away into rueful and slightly forlorn admiration. At least ten of her fellow auditioners looked like this. The others were all at least extremely good-looking, and possibly better actresses than she was. And here she was, enduring the Curse of the W's, watching them go in before her, one after another. Why the producers would want to look at her in the face of this competition, she couldn't imagine.

She sighed and determined to raise her mood somewhat. How, though, she wasn't sure. She had already read every magazine sitting out here on the Italian glass-topped tables. *War and Peace* did nothing for her today. The smell of hot coffee in the pot off to one side had been enticing when she came in. Now she was getting sick of it.

She leaned back and looked at the televisions. One of them was showing a large, purple, blunt-faced dinosaur, which was at that moment dancing clumsily and singing a song about how it wanted to be someone's friend. MJ gazed at it and had a sudden bizarre but very satisfying image of herself introducing it to Venom: taking the dinosaur by its pudgy purple hand, turning, and saying very sweetly, "Here, make friends with *this*."

The other television was in the middle of a commercial for a used-car dealership, car after car and license-plate number after license-plate number flashing on the screen, followed by the image of the dealer, a man with one of those faces MJ would *never* buy a used car from. *I don't know how he does it,* MJ thought. *Maybe I'm just suspicious. Must come of having super villains running in and out of Peter's life all the time.*

The screen went mercifully black, then suddenly MJ found herself looking at a card that said, "SPECIAL REPORT." The card was replaced by the image of a newswoman sitting at a desk, an "Action News" logo and the network "bug" in the lower-right-hand corner of the screen. "Reports are coming in of an explosion on the ESU campus in the Village," the reporter said. "Emergency services are responding. Witnesses report substantial damage to the ESU science facility—"

And whatever composure MJ had managed to recover went right out the window.

Peter!

ACROSS town and downtown, Spider-Man was swinging between building and building, scanning the streets frantically for any sign of the dark shape which was his quarry.

That boy really can move, he thought again. One of the most annoying things about having to tangle with Venom was how closely they were matched, in terms of their powers and abilities—and when it came to physical strength, while Spider-Man's strength was proportionally that of a spider his size and mass, the strength the symbiote lent Eddie was another matter entirely. The symbiote's job was to do, literally, whatever its host wanted—and it frequently seemed to bend various physical laws to make it all happen. Having worn the symbiote himself for a little while, he remembered the astonishing feeling of something as light as silk but as strong in its way as a steel exoskeleton—something that flowed around you being as hard or soft, as edged or smooth as it needed to be for the moment's requirements. It looked like whatever you wanted it to look like and *became* whatever you needed. Without thought, without hesitation—just doing it. Wearing that symbiote, you didn't need a weapon. You *were* a weapon.

Going through walls would be no problem for Venom. If he wanted to claim he couldn't knock over a train, well, perhaps that was true—but watching him try would be worth the price of admission, and if bets were being taken, Spider-Man wasn't sure he wouldn't put a five on the symbiote, just to be safe.

In the meantime, there was no telling where Venom had gone. Theoretically, since they were both chasing a flying target, Venom should still be out in the open the way Spider-Man was. But if Hobgoblin had gone to ground, there was nothing to prevent Venom from going right through walls, or the ground, for that matter, to get at him.

Either way, Spider-Man's only chance to find them both was to get some height and cover as much ground as he could as quickly as he could. *So head for the tall timber and start looking,* Spidey thought. There was a good cluster of skyscrapers just west of him, near Columbus Circle. He would go up the old Gulf-Western building, have a look around, and decide his next move before the trail got too cold.

Spider-Man hared off along 57th Street, high up, swinging from building to building, surprising office workers and window cleaners and the occasional peregrine falcon. As he headed westward, he got another twinge, the slightest buzz, from the spider-sense. *Trouble ahead—*

The sense was vaguer, more prolonged, and more directional than usual, possibly a side-effect of its slow return. *This is the right direction, then,* he thought, and didn't bother stopping when he came to the area south of Columbus Circle. He just kept going west. The sense twinged him again, more sharply, as he continued, and Spider-Man kept heading that way, as much for the pleasure of the returned feeling as anything else.

He paused near the corner of one building, and swung out in a partial arc, like a pendulum, to see in which direction the "buzz" was strongest. Straight west—okay.

He continued that way. The buildings weren't as tall here—mostly apartment buildings, pretty nice ones, with rents he didn't even want to think about. At Eleventh Avenue he swung out again, looking all around him—

The spider-sense jolted him, hard. He looked down toward the West Side Highway. At the end of Fifty-Second Street was a horse corral, and near it he saw something black moving, heading for the street. Something two-legged, shining, dark, heading toward a manhole cover.

Not Venom! he thought in triumph—Venom would not have triggered the spider-sense. Instantly he let go of the present line of web and dropped down, cannonballing, his arms wrapped tightly around himself so he would fall faster. A couple of stories above ground, he shot out another webline, caught a streetlight pole, and swung across toward the fleeing figure. He dropped to the ground just in front of it.

It was black. It shone. It looked humanoid, but not quite. The blackness was total, except for the pale, moonlike patches on its head, very much like the eyes on his or Venom's mask. That blackness was not a suit or clothing of any kind. It was the creature's skin, gleaming in the late sun like ebony polished to a high gloss, and it was actually very beautiful. It was bipedal and had arms, but there was something tentative about the hands. The fingers were lithe like tentacles, but sharp-looking like claws.

For only a second it crouched there, looking at him. Then it leapt, to tackle him—

Spider-Man jumped sideways, leaping for the nearby streetlight pole. The creature came down hard where he had been, but not as hard as

Spider-Man had expected. From its body, tentacles erupted, slapping the ground hard and absorbing the shock as expertly as any judo enthusiast would. It bounced to its feet again, casting around it to see where he had gone, lifting its blank-eyed head with the kind of "sniffing" motion that the railroad workers had described.

Its eyes may not be so good, Spider-Man thought. *Could that be one of the reasons it prefers the dark? It doesn't need to see, so much? Or maybe—if it's radiation-sensitive, maybe the presence of the normal background radiation from sunlight and so forth, at ground level, bothers it—*

It leapt at him again, and this time came at him with tentacles and talons both, aiming right for his middle. Spidey jumped straight up this time, pulling his legs up hurriedly as it shot by underneath him. He shot a webline up onto the nearest building and gained himself some altitude, watching his frustrated adversary hit the ground again, roll, and come up to its feet again, "looking" to see where he had gone.

I'm really not sure it's not blind to visible light, Spider-Man thought. *Or else as far as it's concerned, there's so much ambient light, even this late in the day, that whatever it uses for optics are overwhelmed.*

His spider-sense stung him hard, so hard that he simply let go of the webline he was holding and dropped. This was just as well, for right past Spider-Man, whizzing through the air, the creature came plunging past him in a superb and unlikely leap from ground level. Whipping tentacles and claws both lanced out at his waist *en passant.* In midair he twisted aside, cannonballing again to fall faster, then shot out web and caught another light pole. Recovering, he saw the creature slam into the wall of the nearest building, clinging there a moment as if stunned.

Three times was too frequent a hint to miss. *It wants the canister,* Spider-Man thought, leaping away from the light pole again. *It must be really sensitive to the isotopes I'm carrying to be able to pick it out right through lead with all this background radiation.*

The creature dropped down from the building, "seeking" him again. *The thing's a living Geiger counter,* Spider-Man thought. *What on earth are its insides like—or off Earth, rather.* He peered down at it thoughtfully from his light-pole. *And more to the point, now that I've got it, what do I do with it?*

Its head turned blindly toward him, and it started for him across the street. Traffic, which until now had been crawling by at the easy pace New

Yorkers use while rubbernecking, now screeched to a halt as the shining black creature scuttled across the road. Horns blew, and the creature threw its head up and produced a high, piercing soprano roar, a bizarre sound to come from inside a chest so big. It threw itself at the foremost car, a cab, tearing at it with tentacles that suddenly flew from all parts of its body. Pieces of bodywork came off—fenders first, then the roof of the cab, and the hood—and from inside the cab came the indignant yell of the cabbie and the scream of a passenger.

Uh-oh, Spider-Man thought, and leapt down from his streetlamp perch, shooting web two-handedly. The webbing settled over the creature, wrapping it—or trying to. It reared up from the cab, roaring again, and shredded the web all around it, turning and twisting to try to see where the stuff was coming from. Spidey danced around, keeping the webbing coming, and yelled to the people in the cab, "It's a write-off, folks, better get out while you can!"

They did, erupting out opposite sides of the cab, front and back. The elegantly dressed lady in the back, seemingly unhurt, vanished down the nearest side street at high speed, without wasting a second. The cabbie, though, stopped nearby and yelled, "What am I going to tell the insurance company?!"

Spidey shook his head as he kept laying webbing over the creature, which was shredding and shedding it as fast as he spun it. "Don't think they'll buy 'act of God'," he said. "Listen, just get away, this thing's—"

The "thing" abruptly spun into a whipping vortex of activity, throwing off web faster than Spider-Man could lay it down, and at the same time reached out to the cab again with a whole new batch of tentacles, longer and thicker than any it had produced so far. It wrapped these around the cab, and without any apparent effort at all, simply picked the car up and looked around for something to fling it at.

That blank gaze fixed on Spider-Man. The creature heaved—

Spider-Man needed no hints from his spider-sense this time. He simply leapt the biggest leap he could manage off to one side, grabbing the distraught cab driver as he passed, hitting the ground and bouncing again. Behind the two of them, the cab hit the side of the nearest building with a tremendous crash, shattering into enough pieces to stock an auto parts store. The cab's gas tank ruptured in the process, spraying gasoline all over the place, and the gas promptly caught fire.

The honking and beeping and shouting from the backed-up traffic further on down the street got louder. The fire spread over the asphalt of the street, though mercifully not very far, and burned enthusiastically. In the midst of all this the creature stood, some of its tentacles clutching its head, others whipping around it, as if the noise and commotion were all simply too much for it. It "looked" at Spider-Man, and some of the tentacles reached out toward him indecisively.

"Uh-oh," he said, putting the cab driver down. "Mac, you'd better get out of here—I don't know what my buddy there's going to do next. There's a phone down the street. You'd better call 911 before this spreads—"

"No problem," said the cabbie, and got down the street in a hurry, looking glad to get away. Spider-Man turned his attention back to the alien creature. It was staring all around it, and "smelling" as well. Several times, its pale gaze came back to him, but it made no immediate move.

The noise of horns got louder, and the creature looked more distressed, twisting and turning. *It really doesn't like it out here,* Spidey thought. *Maybe the noise. Maybe the background radiation. And it* really *wants the isotopes, too. But it seems to be learning from experience. It can't just take them by frontal attack—*

The creature turned and headed uptown, away from the noise and the flames and smoke. Spidey went after it cautiously, not wanting to lose it, not wanting to let it do any more damage, but wanting to see where it was headed without himself influencing its decision, if possible. It looked over his shoulder at him, then stooped to the ground, produced more tentacles, and used them to heave open the manhole cover it had been approaching when he first saw it.

That's the ticket, Spidey thought and headed after it in a hurry. He didn't want to lose it in the sewers, either. At least down there it was less likely to endanger innocent bystanders.

The creature vanished down the manhole head-first, its tentacles helping it go. Spider-Man followed it down, though not too closely—he was acutely aware of the danger of the thing turning suddenly, in a tunnel too tight for him to maneuver in, but in which it would have its tentacles to help it. He could still clearly hear the rustling sound of it as it made its way downwards and onwards.

As he entered the manhole and headed down the ladder along its side, he heard more scuffling as the creature headed off southward along the connecting tunnel which the manhole met. Spider-Man followed, listening hard, letting his eyes get used to the darkness, and waiting to see if his spider-sense warned him of anything.

No warnings, nothing but the faint sound of the creature making its way downtown. Down here, where the city sounds didn't wash it out, he could hear another sound, a sort of soft moan, repeating itself at intervals of several seconds, and decreasing with increasing distance. *Is that it breathing?* he wondered. *Or doing something else? I don't have any proof that the thing's metabolism cares one way or the other about oxygen—or any other kind of atmosphere, for that matter. And with its fondness for radiation—*

At the bottom of the manhole, Spider-Man stopped and looked around. This wasn't access to a sewer line, as far as he could tell. Among other things, it didn't smell like it. This was a general access tunnel, one of the "utility" tunnels that honeycombed the island just ten or twenty feet under the sidewalks and streets. They carried all kinds of utilities, sometimes several kinds together in separate conduits in one tunnel—steam, electric, cable TV, phone lines, water mains—never giving away their presence or location except by occasional plumes of steam. This tunnel, as far as he could tell, carried phone and cable. Bundles of waterproof-sheathed cable conduit ran down the sides of it, with occasional "spurs" vanishing upward through the ceiling of the tunnel, to buildings that they served. Here and there, very occasionally, were faint lights meant to guide the utility workers who toiled down here, in case their own lights failed. Down toward the southward end of the tunnel, he could hear the faint scrabbling sounds of his quarry hurrying away.

He followed a long way. The creature seemed unwilling to let him get too close. When he sped up a little, it did too, increasing its pace until he was hard pressed to keep up with it. The creature took its turns at great speed—right, left, left and down, down again, right, right—and Spider-Man quickly lost any sense of direction. All he could do was follow. *I'm never going to be able to follow my path to get back out,* he thought. *I should have brought a ball of string, like the guy in the fairy tale.* But he doubted he could have gotten a ball of string big enough—he'd have to head upward, instead, and pop out of a manhole cover somewhere else.

I hope, he thought, for the creature was heading deeper and deeper, going down a level every few minutes. *I think it knows where it's going,* he thought. *And that may mean something bad for me. It's a bad move to fight on ground of your enemy's choosing.*

Ahead of him, dimly seen down the dark length of the tunnel, the creature paused, looking both ways. *Confusion?* he thought. *Or is it tired? Or*—It was making that "sniffing" motion again, hunting something. Down under his feet, Spidey started to feel something: the faint rumble of a train. They were near one of the subways. *We've come a long way east,* he thought. *Maybe south too.*

He headed for the creature, trying to be stealthy about it—running along, half-crouched, on the ceiling of the tunnel rather than on its bottom.

Then his spider-sense hit him like a club in the back of his head just as the tentacle came slithering out of the shadows at the bottom of the tunnel, reached up, snagged him by the leg, and pulled him down.

The next few minutes were like a nightmare of being attacked by an octopus—except that once you've webbed up eight of an octopus's tentacles, theoretically the nightmare is over and you can leave. *This* creature produced more tentacles each time Spider-Man webbed up the ones attacking him. It had apparently decided that cutting the webbing was a waste of time and was now simply working around it instead. The tentacles swarmed over him. As fast as he could throw them off or web them down, more emerged to hold and pull at him—and at the canister webbed to his waist.

And he realized all of a sudden that he couldn't move at all: the thing had him thoroughly tied. It shredded the webbing on its imprisoned tentacles, and then one tentacle flashed in, developed an edge, and slashed down—

The webbing holding the canister parted, though not completely: for a moment the canister dangled. Another pair of tentacles snatched at it, and the canister, not designed to take such stresses, fell apart, clattering to the tunnel floor. One of the little packets of americium isotope fell out.

Somewhere nearby a train's rumble began, got louder. The creature roared too, that high piercing roar again, released Spider-Man, and leapt on the fallen canister.

Not with Dawn's science project, you don't! thought Spidey. He jumped straight at the creature's face. The fangs parted—though not to bite, to roar— and then more tentacles whipped around and hit Spider-Man broadside.

It was like being hit by a train: Spidey was lifted off his feet and flew straight across the tunnel. His head, side, and right leg crunched into the far wall and bounced off. In a blaze of pain, Spider-Man slid down to the floor, unable to stop himself or do anything but lie there, wheezing, and in agony from trying to breathe, *having* to breathe.

The creature clutched at the isotope packet, bent over it and stuffed it into its maw. *Get up, get up, get up,* Spider-Man could hear one part of his brain ineffectively exhorting his body.

He managed to lever himself up onto one elbow, then wavered to his feet. The creature froze in what might have been a moment of after-dinner digestion and paid him no mind. Spider-Man shot a quick line of web at the first half of the canister, then at the second half, and pulled them to him. Then he shot one last line of web at the remaining packet of isotope just as the creature turned its head slowly, beginning to come out of its moment of assimilation.

He quickly sealed the isotope back into its canister, rose unsteadily, and fled down the tunnel, not sure where he was going, not caring, as long as it was away from *that.*

The soprano roar went up behind him again, but Spider-Man kept running. The sound of trains grew louder, drowning out the roar behind him. He plunged through the dimness, every breath a stab in his side, stumbling, clutching his ribs. *Broken. Has to be at least one broken.*

That roar sounded behind him again, closer. Desperate, Spider-Man ran for the trains. *Can't let it get the rest of this stuff. If it gets it—if it finishes it—it might just go on with* me—*as an hors d'oeuvre—since I was so close to the radioactives.*

The roar seemed to be fading in the increasing roar of the trains. He could hear no sound of pursuit. He fell down once, got up and staggered on, but not far. Then he fell again and couldn't get up, no matter how the back of his mind yelled at him. His whole side, from head to foot, was one long line of pain, which washed the thought out of him, left him sitting, then lying, helpless, on bare cold concrete, in the dimness, which grew darker…

…went black.

EIGHT

MJ stared in horror at the TV screen. It cut to a game show, in which a well-dressed woman turned over letters in a row, while contestants tried to guess the words of the phrase they spelled. Normally MJ was of the opinion that this game was intellectually challenging only to those with IQs lower than that of a banana slug. Now, though, she stared at the impending words and couldn't make head or tail of them. *Peter!* she thought.

She hoped for some kind of continuation of the bulletin, but nothing came. An explosion at ESU—she knew what the science building there looked like. Maybe not as solid as the main building, but solid enough. Not something you could blow up easily. *He was right,* she thought. *He knew Hobby was coming. Sometimes I wish he didn't have to be so—*

She looked around nervously. There were fewer women in the reception area now than there had been before, but not that many fewer. Obviously a lot had been asked to stay, possibly to do a second reading, maybe even to read for some other part. That happened sometimes. It might happen to her. She couldn't leave now. She hadn't even read for the first time yet.

At the same time, even if she was free to leave now, what could she do? There was no telling exactly what had happened over there at ESU, and nothing was to be gained by her shooting off in that direction without a good reason or a plan. She would be much smarter to sit still and bide her time. Peter would be annoyed with her if she just ran out of an impending audition because—

"Ms. Watson-Parker?"

"Here," MJ said, standing up, the mask of the professional falling into place—though not with the usual assured slam. She followed the AP toward the audition room, feeling a lot less excited about it all than she had been just a few minutes before. *I wish I'd never seen that bulletin,* she thought—then smiled at herself, a little ruefully. *If he can be a hero,* she thought, *you can too, even if only by staying at your post.*

Head high, she went in.

IT was a good reading. She had always been able to memorize quickly, even at school, and her work on *Secret Hospital* honed that talent to a fine skill, especially since lines changed even as they filmed episodes. Several times they had even broadcast live, with several of the staff writers scribbling hectically away on the sidelines to cover up mistakes made by actors, or by another writer who had somehow slipped out of continuity. At such times, you had better be able to plaster the words onto your brain while four thirty-second commercials were airing. To actually have lines that *weren't* going to be changed was something of a luxury.

So MJ stood up in front of them confidently enough. The older woman producer, Rinalda, was there; the younger woman, the AP; the young male AP; and a suit, a handsome enough man with gray hair and a weary look. *Executive producer,* MJ thought. At least, that seemed most likely. Her resume, duplicated, was on the table in front of them. They had her still, and they were looking at MJ speculatively.

"Please, sit down," the woman AP said, and there followed the usual two or three minutes of pleasant chatter about what she'd been doing recently ("job-hunting"), had she had any other work since *Secret Hospital* ("no"), her schedule for the next year—it was hard to throw caution to the winds and say, "Empty," but she did it.

"There's a little more modeling work coming free this year," the young female AP said thoughtfully.

MJ simply sat back and said, "I like this better."

Then they asked her to read. MJ went into the ten-page excerpt they had given her without pausing for more than a breath or two—delivered the first few lines of it sitting, as the social worker in the script might have. Then she got up and began to work with the lines moving-pacing a little, playing to Rinalda as if she were the other character in the scene.

She let herself fall into feeling like Maureen as best she could: that passion and compassion, clear-eyed, a little humorous, a little edged when it needed to be, letting the anger come out at the hopelessness, the hunger. Hopelessness—that was accessible right now. MJ couldn't get her mind off what she had seen on the TV in there, even while she was in the middle of the part. Maybe that was all right. It gave the reading a bit more edge than it had had at home, when she was comfortable and unworried.

She didn't usually look at the rest of her audience while she was reading, but once she stole a glance and saw the rest of them looking at her with much more lively and intent expressions than they'd had when she'd first come in. The young female AP was smiling slightly as she scribbled something on her legal pad. The smile was not a nasty or bored one; it was genuinely pleased. That was more than MJ often saw during a reading— too many producers prided themselves on being poker-faced—and it encouraged her, oddly.

As usual, when she finished, no one told her whether they thought she'd done well or badly. Rinalda simply paged through a script in front of her, curled the pages back at one spot, and said to MJ, "Would you read this?"

MJ took the script, swallowing. Her character's parts had been highlighted in pink. That was a courtesy on the producer's part—some liked to make it harder by just letting you cold-read the part as best you could and seeing whether nerves would trick you into reading someone else's lines under pressure. "Both parts," MJ said, "or just the one?"

"Both, please."

The dialogue, as she instantly saw from scanning just the first page, was between her social worker and a young, inexperienced doctor who obviously thought very well of himself—the tone of his dialogue was pompous, the vocabulary unnecessarily complex. MJ thought she could see where this was going. She read the social worker's dialogue as patient, at first, then a little annoyed. The doctor was using heavy medical vocabulary, and MJ rocked forward on her feet a little as the social worker explained to him that he didn't need to use long words to intimidate her, and that if shorter ones like "caring" and "commitment" were beyond him, he should practice them a little until he got familiar with them. It got to be a noisy piece as it continued for page after page—and MJ began to wonder how much they had stuck her with—as the two characters began shouting at one another. MJ felt she had some shouting in her at the moment, so that came out well too, her uneasiness inside translating itself most effectively into annoyance at the idiot doctor—at any establishment that hindered her pursuit of what really mattered.

She took the reading straight through to the act break. They didn't stop her. And when she was done, the man with the silver hair was nodding. "We have a few more to go through," he said to MJ, speaking directly to her for the first time. "Will you wait?"

"Of course," MJ said. And then added, on the spur of the moment, "I might need to step out briefly—"

"We won't be too long, I don't think," said Rinalda, looking at her. MJ tried to read the expression, trying to work out whether it was one that said, *Go ahead, step out, it's okay,* or *I'd stay where I was, if I were you.* Impossible to tell; she simply didn't know the woman well enough.

MJ smiled, nodded, stepped out into the front room again.

She sat down where she had been. One of the other auditioners, a short-haired blond woman, looked over at MJ and smiled a little. "Tough in there, huh?" she said.

MJ nodded. "Tough bunch…"

After a few minutes, the AP came out of the audition room and began to step around to some of the women in the reception area, one after another, having a few quiet words with each, smiling, shaking them by the hand. The message was clear: they weren't being considered for the part. MJ waited.

The AP did not come to her.

In a few minutes the room had cleared a little more. There were about six actresses left now, and MJ. They all looked at each other, and at her, with the polite expressions that MJ knew perfectly well concealed a desperate desire that everybody else in the room should be sent home except *them.* MJ was wearing the same expression herself, she knew. She tried to get rid of it, on general principles, and wasn't sure how well she was doing.

Now more time went by in which nothing happened. The game show edged toward its end. On the last commercial break she watched a trailer for the end-of-the-week episode of the network's big soap. MJ could hardly bear the banality of the characters' conflicts and troubles, their petty jealousies and rivalries, considering what was going on in the real world at the moment down at ESU.

But after a moment, even she had to laugh softly under her breath. Doubtless, to the average person in the street, *her* problems would seem fairly fantastic. "I'm worried," she imagined herself saying, "because my husband is out chasing a raving lunatic who flies around on a jetglider and throws pumpkin bombs at things, and being chased by another nut case who's in cahoots with a sentient suit of tailor-made clothing from another planet. And they're both chasing something which appears to eat fissionables for lunch. Did I mention that *it's* from another planet too?" Any sane person would have her carted away to Payne Whitney, or some other similarly therapeutic refuge for the extremely confused. *People just have no understanding of the problems of super heroes' wives,* she thought. *Maybe I should found a support group.*

The trailer flashed on from confrontation to confrontation. MJ looked at her watch. It was pushing five o'clock: the network was about to start its local evening news. Maybe there would be something about whatever was going on at ESU.

After some more commercials, the news came on. MJ watched eagerly, and she tried to get control of her face as the first graphic to go up behind the newsreader was a picture of Hobgoblin.

"Just minutes ago," the newswoman said, "we received copies of a videotape from the costumed criminal known as Hobgoblin. In the tape, Hobgoblin claims to have planted a nuclear bomb somewhere on the island of Manhattan. He threatens to detonate this bomb unless one billion dollars in cash is paid to him within twelve hours—by five-thirty A.M. local time."

Everyone in the place was now staring at that TV, not just MJ, as the station began to play Hobgoblin's tape.

The tape showed Hobby sitting behind a desk, like a bad parody of a corporate executive about to give a pep talk. "People of New York City," he said, "such as you are. This being, according to actuarial figures, the richest and most successful city in the United States, I have decided it's time you plowed some of that wealth back into your local infrastructure. That is to say, me. Using that traditional American trait, good old-fashioned entrepreneurship, in the spirit of free enterprise, I have caused to be built one of the little toys with which the great nations of the world have been cheerfully threatening each other these last fifty years: an atomic bomb. It is rated at one point two kilotons and is more than sufficient to scour Manhattan Island down to its original native granite and basalt. Being that materials for so-called 'clean' bombs are increasingly hard to lay hands on these days, it will doubtless make life uncomfortable in the four surrounding boroughs and New Jersey—in fact, probably as far north as Albany and as far south as Baltimore, depending on how the winds blow.

"To demonstrate that I am not wasting your time," said Hobby, "and that I can in fact carry through with what I'm proposing, I have, at the time of this tape's airing, delivered to municipal authorities in New York a sample of the material I have acquired, which has allowed me to construct the tidy little device which at present sits so happily ticking to itself in some snug and secure corner of this great metropolis. Along with the material in question are instructions for how and where the payment is to be made. Any attempt to make the payment spuriously, or to lay a trap for me or any of my associates, will unfortunately result in the device being detonated—as will the failure to make a payment at all. Manhattan, in either case, will be history."

He folded his hands and grinned a little more widely. "About time, anyway. The architecture's been getting out of hand. Now, it may be that some of you will agree with me, especially about the architecture, in which case my advice to you is to sit back, do nothing, and wait for the fireball. Those of you who desire to put your affairs in order should feel free to do so.

"However, for those of you who might have breakfast or lunch dates to keep, or who for whatever other reasons desire to continue your wretched mundane little lives in what passes for their normal fashion, I strongly suggest that you call your local city councilmen, your mayor, your borough councils, your Congressional representatives, and anyone else you think may be of any use, and tell them to pay me. Otherwise—" he shrugged "—those of you who have had to deal with city bureaucracy over the years will understand that, as one more person routinely oppressed by it, especially by the doings of what are euphemistically referred to as New York's Finest, my patience with such bureaucracy is rather limited— just as yours is. Therefore, I hope you'll understand when I say that no extension of this deadline will be made. The city has twelve and a half hours from the initial broadcast of this tape, which I have embargoed until five P.M. local time. At five thirty this morning, either I am going to go away independently wealthy, or the sun is going to come up in New York. *In* it. So please, call your representatives in Government… and just say yes.

"Thank you for your attention, and—" another nasty grin "—have a nice day."

The view on the screen went back to the newsroom staff. One of them said to the female anchor, "June, we have a report from the Fourteenth Precinct downtown, which states that a canister labeled as nuclear material was delivered by courier to the Precinct a few minutes ago, and that it is currently being checked by experts from City University and the New York City branch of the Atomic Energy Commission. We hope to have a reporter down there shortly to bring you news of this development. Meanwhile, the response from Gracie Mansion—"

The room erupted in a hubbub of confused and anxious voices. MJ shut it all out. She couldn't care less about the mayor's reaction—or anyone else's, at the moment. All she could think of was, *He went to deal with Hobgoblin. And now here's Hobby on the news—but no news of* him. The hair was standing up all over her. The feeling she was having now was one she had had many times before, and repetition never made it any easier to bear.

That tape could have been made just a few minutes ago, she thought, *or days ago. There's no way to tell. If it was a few minutes*—That wasn't a thought that she much liked. It would imply that Spider-Man had met Hobby this afternoon, and Hobby had gotten away from the encounter— while Spider-Man hadn't been heard from since. It would imply that Spider-Man couldn't stop him.

"Ms. Watson-Parker?" MJ turned to see Rinalda standing in the doorway with a somewhat urgent expression on her face, beckoning MJ back into the audition room.

MJ nervously followed her in. The others were all gathering their things into briefcases and portfolio packs. "Ms. Watson-Parker, we'd like to offer you the role." MJ's eyes widened. "But with what's going on here, we're flying out to LA tonight instead of in the morning. Can you come with us? We have to start shooting tomorrow."

I got the part, was her first thought. *But Peter's in trouble,* was her next one.

She bit her lip. *Do you know how many people would kill for a chance to get out of New York right now? But I can't just leave Peter—he could be hurt or dying or worse, for all I know.*

In the end, there really was no choice.

"I'm afraid I can't leave New York tonight. I'm going to have to turn it down."

Rinalda stared at her in disbelief, her mouth twitching. Before MJ had the chance to talk herself out of it, she turned and left. She did not look back.

Outside, everyone was still standing around staring at the TV, pointing, arguing—shaking their heads, not believing it, believing it all too well. Not even the receptionist saw MJ head out, take the elevator downstairs, and rush out into the street.

SHE stood there on the sidewalk and had no idea what to do next. The back of her brain was still shouting recriminations at her, things about making a fool of herself, losing the job, not getting out while the getting was good, being blacklisted in this town, and other nonsense which she listened to briefly and then decided to ignore. She had more important fish to fry.

Peter, she thought, *was at ESU.* That, at least, gave her a place to start. She hurried down the little side street to a public phone, picked up the receiver, and listened for the dial tone. There wasn't one. MJ slammed the receiver savagely back into its cradle and went back up to the street, crossing to where she'd seen another one.

Someone was heading for it at the same time she was. MJ practically leapt across the street, got there first, said, "Sorry, emergency!" to the poor guy she pushed in front of, fed the slot money and started dialing. Normally she had trouble remembering the ESU main switchboard number, since when she called Peter there, she usually called the lab direct. But now she remembered it with no trouble.

It was busy. She hung up, dialed again. And did this five more times, while the guy waiting behind her nearly expired with impatience.

"I know, I know," she said out of the side of her mouth. "Just hang on." The sixth time she dialed, it rang… and rang, and rang, and rang. After a while it was answered by a harried woman's voice which said, "ESU—"

"Listen," she said, "my husband was back in the science building when—Has anyone seen him?"

"Who's your husband?"

"Peter Parker. He's a doctoral candidate in Biochem."

"Just a moment. I'll inquire." The woman put her on hold. MJ stood there practically stamping her feet in frustration and fear, while a deranged computer sang "Greensleeves" at her. "I could punch you right through this phone," she hissed at the hold music, the switchboard, and the composer of "Greensleeves," some five hundred years distant. The man behind her, intimidated by her tone, took a couple of cautious steps backward.

"Not you," MJ said. "Sorry—" The music seemed to go on for weeks. Finally the voice came back, saying, "Peter Parker?"

"Yes!"

"Sorry, no. No one's seen him."

"Oh, great," MJ muttered. "Listen, what was going on there, anyway?"

"It was just on the TV," said the operator wearily. "Hobgoblin did it." MJ suspected that she had been saying this to everyone for the last half hour. "He flew in on his little whatsis and stole one of the safes with some radioactive stuff inside it. Then Spider-Man showed up, and they started to fight, and then that other one. Venom, you know, the one with the weird suit? He showed up, and there was some kind of big argument."

"I bet," MJ breathed. "But they're not there now?"

The operator laughed shortly. "Do you think I'd be here if they were? And if I'd known they were coming, I'd have called in sick, I can tell you. No, they've all left, I don't know where for, and good riddance. You should see the science building. It looks like someone crashed a train into it."

"Did they leave in any particular order?"

The operator laughed again. "You working for the *Post* society column or something? They're just gone, ma'am. Don't ask me who took precedence. Anything else I can help you with? My phone's lit up like a Christmas tree."

"No—thank you. Thank you very much."

MJ hung up and walked away, staring at the sidewalk and thinking. *Gone, simply gone. But where would they go?*

She walked, trying to put it all together.

They were all there, she thought. *They met. They must have talked.* She tried to imagine what the conversation would have been about, extrapolating from what Peter had told her last night. Venom wanted whoever was impersonating him, she thought. So Peter said. Hobgoblin wanted the radioactive stuff.

She stopped there. Venom knew about the radioactive waste in the warehouse and the way the creature took it. Suppose he came to ESU because he, too, suspected Hobgoblin would try to take some more radioactive stuff, or because he suspected Hobby of being the impostor?

Now, Peter's pretty sure the creature that escaped from the sub is responsible. But did he get a chance to tell Venom about it? She had no way of knowing.

But Venom has obviously made the connection between radiation and Hobgoblin. So that's why he was at ESU. *Fine. I still don't know where I'm going to find Spider-Man…*

She stopped in the middle of a cross street, having walked a couple of blocks while she was thinking, and stepped back to let a car pass in front of her. *I wonder if he's called home and left me a message?* she thought and walked quickly to the next phone she saw, dropped a quarter in, and called home.

The phone rang three times. She hung up quickly before the fourth ring, when it would pick up. It only did that when there were no messages. *Nothing,* she thought, retrieving her quarter. *Either he didn't think to call… or he can't.*

She'd go home and wait for him. If he needed her, she'd be there.

THE voices were screaming again.

Sometimes Fay McAvoy thought the noise would drive her crazy. She heard things—always had—but down in the tunnels below the city it should have been better. Usually she could sleep here, bothered only a little by the rats and the trains. It was the voices she tried to escape.

Those voices were starting again, a little whisper at the back of her head. She pressed her hands to her ears. *No no no,* she thought. *You're not real. You're not real.*

Fay had been homeless for the better part of a decade, sometimes scavenging, sometimes living on charity, always just getting by. The voices made it impossible for her to work, impossible for her to hold a job of any kind. Half the time she just wanted to crawl into herself and disappear. Once, long ago, before her medical insurance had run out, the doctors had tried to help. She'd been in and out of institutions for years. Nothing had been able to get rid of the voices in her head, though.

Fay suddenly froze in her tracks. *What was that?* It had sounded like a footstep behind her.

She whirled, straining to hear. Footsteps—and they were getting closer. "Who's there?" she called.

"Well, look what I found," said a voice. And then, very low, Fay heard a chuckle.

It was not the sort of voice she wanted to hear. About six feet in front of her, she could see the tall, shadowy shape. Even under the rags he wore, she could tell he was broad in the shoulders, certainly stronger than she was, possibly faster. *Don't wait,* said one of the voices in her head. *Run. Run now. Knock him down, get past him, and keep going.*

She was just taking a deep breath to start her charge at him when something brushed against her leg, quite high, from behind. She screamed at the top of her lungs. Something ran by underneath her—rats, several of them. She knew all too well the abhorrent little pitty-pat of their footsteps.

The next thing she heard shocked her even more, for the man now screamed too. Then Fay heard his footsteps running in the other direction—rat-scurry and shoes mixed together.

Not one to miss an opportunity, Fay ran. She vaulted up sideways, over the third rail, and into one of the diveins that led to an access tunnel. This went at right angles to the train tunnel, and then curved around to parallel it again. One dim utility light was all she could see in this stretch, but it was enough to see that this particular spot, at least, was deserted.

The voices in her head had grown quiet for the moment. Then Fay heard a sound behind her—boots, not crunching on trainbed gravel, but coming down hard on concrete. *He's behind me!* Again, Fay ran.

She kept it up for nearly five minutes. Several times Fay had to stop, holding her side as the stitch started. She couldn't keep up such a pace much longer. Between bouts of panting, she strained to hear. The footsteps seemed to be getting closer over time.

When she stopped, what would she do? Scream? Certainly, for all she was worth—and for all the good it would do down here. Fight? The best that she could. She had been successful at fighting off the occasional mugger in the past. But that had been above ground and, despite the fabled noninvolvement of New Yorkers, you always knew you had a better chance to get away, to survive, when there were other people in the neighborhood. Here she was alone.

She hurried on into a bigger, more open space, as poorly lit as the one she had left. She stopped for a second, gasping, trying to get her bearings—

—and saw a red-and-blue shape, walking towards her.

After a moment, she realized it was a man in a red-and-blue outfit. Then she recognized the outfit—it looked like it had been rubbed threadbare in a couple of places, and it was covered in grime, dirt, and sewage, but none of that mattered. He was a real super hero. She'd seen him before from the streets, and she knew he'd help her.

"Spider-Man!" she hissed. "You gotta help me!"

He looked at her. He seemed poised and ready for action, despite the somewhat bedraggled state of his costume. "What is it?" he said.

"Help me!" Fay whispered fiercely. "There's someone after me! Please, Spider-Man!"

Spider-Man threw back his shoulders, and turned toward the spot where Fay pointed.

The big, dark shape which had been following Fay came in that doorway. It was another homeless person, with long hair and a scraggly beard—and a knife in his hand.

Hands on his hips, Spider-Man glared menacingly.

The man looked back, stunned for a moment. Then a big grin split his face. "Awright!" he said. "Nice Spider-Man costume! Whadja raid a Halloween shop or somethin'? Well, 'hero,' you gonna rescue the lady?" He moved slowly closer. "Let's see you rescue her from this." He approached Fay with the knife. Fay's mouth widened, about to form a scream.

But it was the man who screamed as the line of web shot out, fastened to the knife, pulled it out of his grip, and flung it across the tunnel.

"All right," Spider-Man said calmly, his voice sounding comfortingly strong and vibrant, "I rescued her. But who's gonna rescue *you* when I'm done with you?"

He took one step toward the man. The guy went wide-eyed, backed away stammering something that Fay couldn't make out, and fled through the entrance to the tunnel again, back into the dark.

They stood there for a moment, just waiting, but there was no sound save the receding footsteps, still running far up the tunnel.

"Are you all right?" Spider-Man asked.

"I—I think so," Fay said. The voices were still silent. "How about you? You look like you were in a real bad fight."

"I'll live," Spider-Man said. "Can you show me the fastest way out of here? I need to get to the East Side."

Fay turned slowly, getting her bearings. She'd been in this tunnel before, she realized. "That way," she said, starting out. "Follow me."

A bit less than half an hour later, Spider-Man returned home. There he found MJ, who nearly bowled him over with a hug.

"You're all right! I was so worried!" She pulled out of the embrace. She wrinkled her nose, probably from the smell of the sewer Spidey had been lying in, but she said nothing about it.

"Good to see you, too. Just came back to restock the web-shooters."

"You're going to need them," she said gravely, and then Spider-Man noticed her look of apprehension, which he realized was about more than her husband's welfare. He removed the mask from his sweat-stained face.

"Bad news, I take it," he said, opening the drawer where he kept his spare web cartridges.

MJ quickly filled him in about what she'd seen on the news. "I was worried sick. After hearing how ESU's been torn up, and that you and Venom and Hobgoblin were all there, what was I supposed to think? And then the next thing I know, Hobgoblin is on the TV, threatening to blow Manhattan up with a bomb if the city doesn't give him a billion dollars by five thirty this morning!"

"Five thirty. Boy," Peter said softly, putting a hand to his head, "some people just can't sleep in, you know?"

"I guess he wants to get to the bank early, so he has the rest of the day free." MJ shook her head. There were times when she noticed that her husband's turn of phrase had contaminated her. "Anyway, he says he has an atomic bomb. He gave some radioactive material to the city to prove he could do what he said he was going to."

"He could certainly send them quite a bit of stuff," Peter said. "He stole two safe-fulls from ESU."

"But how did he get away?"

"Venom and I had a little, uh, disagreement about how to handle him—I guess that would be the best way to put it."

"Well, never mind that, we have more important things to think about."

"I'll say we have. When I ran into our little friend, a while back—"

"Who, Venom?"

"No, the critter from the sub."

"You caught it!"

"Um, no," Peter said, rubbing the back of his neck meditatively. "I would say offhand that it's about fifty-fifty as to who caught who."

He told her in some detail about his encounter with the creature. "No question that it looks like Venom," he said finally. "There are small differences, but you don't see them until you're pretty close up—and by then you're too busy trying to keep yourself in one piece to pay much attention to them. And it's a lot stronger than Venom. Brock's no pushover, but he doesn't usually push over trains, either."

MJ shook her head. "Where can that thing have come from? Wherever did they find it?"

"The Captain didn't tell me much," Peter said. "Couldn't."

"It's a pity he couldn't have told you how to catch it," said MJ. "I wonder how they did it?"

"No telling. And in the final analysis, even having caught it once didn't help them much, the thing melted its way right out of a nonstandard radiation confinement when it was ready. We're going to have to think of some other way to keep it. Meanwhile—" He took a long breath, and winced. "Ouch. But I still can't get over how much it looked like Venom."

MJ looked doubtful. "Has it tried to shapechange, that you've seen?"

"No, but that doesn't mean that it can't." He turned towards her, really looking at her for the first time since he came in. "You're all dressed up. Were you out today?"

"I had an audition," she said.

"What, for the social worker thing? I thought that was tomorrow."

"No," she said. "They called this morning. They had to move it up."

"So how'd it go?"

"Not too bad," MJ said. "I'll tell you about it later."

Peter nodded and rose and put his mask back on. "Back to work," he said.

MJ glowered at him. "You are out of your alleged mind," she said. "Look at you! You can barely stand up! You're in no condition to fight anybody or anything."

"I can too." He struck a heroic pose.

MJ looked at him cockeyed, not convinced. "Look at the way your knees are trembling. And don't think I can't see you wincing when you breathe." She reached out to feel his ribs on the right-hand side, and sure enough, he sucked in breath and almost moved away from her. "You cracked them again! And after they just healed from the last time. Doctor Spencer's never going to believe that you fell down the stairs again. He's going to start thinking I'm abusing you or something."

"MJ, never mind. I have to go!"

She had had this argument with him before. She knew where it was going, but she had to have it. "Look," she said. "This is hardly fair to you. Where are all the other super heroes in this town? Let one of them take over. Call the Fantastic Four or somebody."

Spider-Man sighed. "Hon," he said, "half the time when I call there, all I get is their voice mail system. What am I supposed to do? Call and leave a message that says, 'Hi, guys, it's Spidey. Listen, I'm not feeling real well at the moment, but I just want you to know that if you haven't seen the news, you should turn it on, because Hobgoblin has a bomb, and he's going to blow the city up at five thirty this morning. I'm going home to take an aspirin; can you take care of this one for me?' It doesn't work."

"It's still not fair to you," MJ said. "And what about me? One of these days, one of these guys is going to catch you when you're hurt, and I—I don't know what I'll do."

He gathered her close. "You knew the job was dangerous when you took it, MJ," he murmured. "You having second thoughts?"

"No," she said. "I just wish there were something I could do to help."

"Can't think of anything at the moment," Spidey said. "If something occurs to me, I'll give you a call. But don't wait up for me… I'll be late."

"That's what I was afraid of to begin with," MJ said dryly. "That you would be late in the funeral-parlor sense of the word."

"Well, reports of my death are greatly exaggerated. Come on, MJ, cheer up."

"It's not that easy."

"Is there anything else you can remember from the newscast that might be a help?"

She recited to him, word for word, as best she could, the text of the news report. Spidey shook his head. "I'm not sure there was anything even in the big safe that would have done Hobby any good. And he wouldn't have known that until he got it home, wherever home is, and opened it. Then he probably figured that he might as well make some use of it, and gave a batch of that stuff to the authorities as a sample."

"So he got the material for his bomb somewhere else entirely."

"That's right."

"He has to have been storing it somewhere, then."

Spider-Man nodded. "The 'where' is the problem."

"Well, I've got a suggestion. Marilyn, the homeless lady I met in the shelter the other night, told me that the place where people have been getting sick lately is over by Penn Station."

"Penn Station," Spidey said. "You know, when the critter came out into the rail yards and knocked the train over, it ran back into the tracks that would have come out of Penn."

"Interesting," MJ said.

"Well, I'll find out. I managed to put a tracer on both of the safes that Hobby took—"

"Your spider-sense is back, then!" MJ said, relieved.

"That's right."

"Well, that's good. Though, I don't know… it was kinda fun to see you tripping over things like a real human being. Oh well. I knew it couldn't last."

"You like seeing me fall on my nose! When I get back after all this, I'm going to tickle you until you can't breathe."

"You'll have to catch me first," MJ said mildly, but there was loving challenge in her voice. "I just want you to know that I love you," MJ said, "and I was worried for you. I want you to be real careful, and don't give me any more cause to worry, okay?"

"Okay." He pulled up his mask just enough, and gave her a long and enthusiastic kiss.

She refused to let him go for another moment. "Hon," she said, "if I don't see you by five thirty this morning—"

"You will," said Spider-Man. "Never fear."

SWINGING from weblines, Spider-Man headed downtown. The buzz from his spider-tracer grew stronger all the time—its signal undiminished from being underground, if indeed it was underground as he suspected.

The alien was still on his mind. *How did they manage to capture it for as long as they did?* he wondered. *What were they keeping it in? Lead, almost certainly, if the ambient radiation around the creature had to be minimized. Probably reinforced with other substances—though maybe not reinforced enough.*

All the same, he wondered at the wisdom of sending a nuclear sub to carry such a creature. It would have been like shipping a tiger in a truck full of meat. He sighed, then. Friends who had gone into the armed forces had joked with him, telling him that the words "military" and "intelligence" appearing in the same phrase were an oxymoron, with the emphasis on the moronic side of things. *It may be that the Navy scientists really thought whatever confinement vessel they were using was sufficient. Well… they'll have to think again.*

Spider-Man was still bemused enough by the thing's likeness to Venom. But it was certainly nothing more than a coincidence. Though he hadn't had the symbiote-costume for very long, he'd never noticed it to have any affinity for radiation, so their resemblance wasn't a family one. He did wonder very much what kind of evolution would produce such a creature, especially one with bipedal and bilateral symmetry which also involved the ability to use those tentacular pseudopods. He would have to leave a message on Reed Richards's voice mail about it at some point, but there was no time for that right now. Maybe in the morning—assuming there was still a city with a phone system.

And the poor alien creature—he doubted that even it could survive dawn at ground zero. If it did, it would certainly get such a blast of radiation from the bomb that even *it* would get a bellyache.

Spider-Man swung up onto the top of the hotel across from Madison Square Garden and stood looking down at the entrance to Penn Station. Was he imagining it, or was the traffic a little less busy than usual this time of day? He wouldn't be surprised if people who had heard about Hobgoblin's threat might very well have decided to hurry home to their families and stay there, if this was going to be the city's last night. He wished he could do something of that sort himself, but when he could possibly do something to stop Hobgoblin, he couldn't afford such a luxury.

He swung down to ground level, and got onto one of the escalators which headed down into Penn. People stared at him with some surprise. Some waved and called his name, others just looked at him as if they saw him every day and he was just one more commuter.

He came out on the lower concourse level. His spider-sense guided him to the right... back and down. He went along past the Long Island Rail Road ticket windows into the main concourse, paused a moment to get his direction from the tracer. Looking up, he saw the guy who made track announcements gazing at him thoughtfully from his little glass box high up on the west wall. Spider-Man gave the guy a wave, then headed toward one of the track doors on the west wall. Its indicator light was lit, to show that the train was boarding.

Spider-Man joined the commuters crowding in through the door and headed down the stairs. Again, some looked at him curiously while others barely spared him a glance. But all of them were moving with a speed which suggested they thought a bomb might go off under their feet right now instead of later.

He left them getting into the big silver LIRR train and continued down the platform, following the buzz of his spider-sense. It was getting stronger. *Somewhere off this track and farther down.* He walked to the end of the platform, found the steps that let onto the tracks, and began to stroll down them, keeping an eye out behind him to make sure Venom wasn't sneaking up behind him.

He came to a railed stairway leading downwards between two of the tracks. *Downwards,* his spider-sense said to him, so down he went. At the bottom, he discovered another long, barren access tunnel. He followed it to another set of steps. Down he went again.

Following his spider-sense, he came to a place where half a dozen tunnels met. The spider-sense indicated that the source of the tracer was quite close. Just off to the right—downward again.

He followed the rightward tunnel. This one almost immediately dead-ended into a stairwell, which he took very slowly and softly in the increasing dark, for he heard voices. At the bottom he paused, looking ahead. Light poured through air vents set into the walls of the tunnel in which he now stood. The voices were louder here. He listened but couldn't quite make out the words. Then came a very familiar laugh.

Hobgoblin.

NINE

EDDIE Brock's was not what one would normally consider a meticulous personality. He had been told by friends that this lack might get him into trouble one day. Sure enough, one time during his days as a journalist, he ran with a story as it seemed to be going, confident it would turn out as he'd expected. And, as his friends predicted, he got into trouble.

That, however, had been Spider-Man's fault. His career, his relationships, everything lay in ruins now because of Spider-Man. His life since then, it seemed, had been one long stroll through dark places—the sewers of San Francisco, and the basements of his soul.

At least today he had some slight hope for a modicum of satisfaction. He would catch the Hobgoblin. He would extract the last possible measure of terror and repentance from him. And, when that was done, he would disassemble him into his component parts. Nothing about Hobgoblin's life would suit him so much as ending it.

Eddie was not going about his plan in a slipshod manner. He had taken some care, while researching CCRC's connections, also to look into the Map Room at the New York Public Library's 42nd Street research library. There he had pulled the Con Edison maps for the access tunnels in the Midtown and West Side areas.

It was fortunate that his memory had always been sharp, for the whole place was a tangled warren of crawlways, passages, flights of stairs, and access holes of such complexity that anyone trying to navigate it without aid would be hopelessly lost. There were too many traps and pitfalls for the unwary—dead ends; pathways that seemed to go nowhere but led for miles, twisting, turning on themselves; old accesses added to new ones; old ones blocked up without being noted in the maps except as footnotes. It was all very complicated.

Eddie knew well enough, though, the kinds of places he was interested in. He had started, logically enough, at the CCRC headquarters.

He came after closing hours, having just had his little *contretemps* with Hobgoblin and Spider-Man. *Spider-Man...* All over Eddie's skin, the symbiote ruffled, a quick movement like the skin of a horse trembling when a fly bites it, a gesture of mingled disgust and desire. The symbiote's moods were clear enough to him from inside. But that gesture was diagnostic of one of the most common of its emotions. The symbiote's hatred for Spider-Man was a refreshing thing next to his: simple, straightforward, but at the same time, always tinged with longing.

His pain was always a trouble to it, and its pain to him, especially when he pitied it for what it couldn't be, for the one thing that was lacking. It had sentience—it existed, and it knew it did. But personality, it had none. A sort of a yearning toward his personality, and a sort of sad longing for something of the same kind, like the Tin Man wishing for a heart. But that was all. And when you came right down to it, sentience without personality was not enough to be *company.*

Even so, from Eddie's point of view, their relationship was better than being alone. Now, as he stood in the silence of the deserted downstairs of the CCRC building, next to the old warehouse, he got from the symbiote a sense of excitement—of interest and desire—and, very restrained at the back of that interest, the hope of something to tear, devour, consume.

That was the one danger of dealing with the symbiote, Eddie thought, as he stood gazing down into that hole. If you were careless, you could easily fall into its mindset—to slash and feed when it desired to, rather than when prudence or necessity dictated. Its frustration that it could not subsume the one being it desperately desired sometimes drove it, hungrily, to try to consume others, like people desperate for protein who stuff themselves full of empty calories because there's nothing else. Sometimes these gorges left Eddie exhausted; other times they left him simply annoyed and enervated. But they were something he had learned to put up with in good grace. There had to be some give-and-take, after all, and his partner had plenty of positive aspects.

Now he stood looking down into that hole and said, "He's down there somewhere." The symbiote stirred and rustled all around him, starting already to send out questing tendrils that waved in the air as if testing it for scent. The symbiote had been attuned to his rage all day, reacting with eagerness and pleasure, knowing it was going to feed if they caught the one its partner was after. The symbiote wasn't picky. It had grown to like the taste of blood. Eddie's problem—their joint problem as Venom—was to make sure it got only blood that needed to be shed.

He judged the hole. No more than about fifteen feet down. Tendrils swarmed out, anchoring themselves to the edges of the hole. Eddie jumped and was let down easily.

He glanced up the length of the tunnel in which he found himself. Its bare concrete had been stained by years' passage of water, rust, and other, less healthy, things. Rats' squeaking could be heard further down. There was no light here, but far down he saw an inequality in the darkness which meant there was light elsewhere. He headed for it slowly and silently, knowing that what he pursued could go silently, too, when it pleased.

Hobgoblin... he thought. *Now there will be a dainty morsel for a leisurely postmortem.* Eddie confined himself to criminals, to those who preyed on the innocent. Occasionally you might find a criminal who, given the right time, the right money, and sufficient resources, could eventually have been rehabilitated. Trouble was, there wasn't enough time, and resources generally could better be used on other things. They were wasted on criminals. So often all the good intentions failed. That was the problem with life in general, from his point of view.

If there was anything Venom knew at this point, it was that justice started and ended in one's own hands, and at the business end of whatever tools you could bring to bear to enforce your power. He was justice, now. Rough justice it might be, but it worked a lot better than the milk-and-water, etiolated kind of justice that various costumed crimefighters, bumbling police, and the corrupt judiciary were trying to impose.

He paused as the light grew from a hint to a halo before him. It came from a single bare bulb set in a concrete wall where this tunnel met another. To his left, the new tunnel dead-ended. To his right, it stretched away for at least a hundred yards before either ending or turning; he couldn't see which.

That would be north, he thought. *Uptown.* "Let's go," he said.

He made his way up the tunnel, listening carefully. It was not as quiet down here as might have been expected. Even now, the incessant noise of the city managed to force its way through the layers of concrete and brick and earth: bumps and clanks from far above, as traffic hit some occasional manhole cover, the toothaching sound of someone working with a jackhammer blocks away. The low-frequency city roar didn't carry here as it did above ground, but knockings and bumpings, the hiss of steam in conduit pipes, the occasional hum of an exposed transformer box—

—and the murmur of voices.

He stopped, listened. *Nothing.* Then a sound, indistinct, but the pattern was that of someone speaking. And then, unquestionably, a cough.

Quietly, now, he thought to the symbiote. They made their way to where the tunnel did not end, but turned right again, east. Eddie was taking care to keep his directions straight; he might need to find this place again.

He headed eastward for perhaps half a long block, and then once again the tunnel turned. Now he saw the muted glow of light coming from the northward leg. This time the voices rose much more clearly.

He padded forward as quickly as he could, but took more care about being silent. Every now and then a rat bolted out from under his feet, and the symbiote stretched out a hungry tendril for it, but always Eddie would pull those reaching tentacles back. "You'll spoil your supper," he muttered. The symbiote's desires and hungers were something he had learned to exploit, and he wanted its hunger at its sharpest when they met Hobgoblin. Spider-Man had been right about one thing—he wasn't too sure where a spleen was. But he had done a little research after looking at the utility tunnel maps, and he thought Venom now had a good chance of finding it and seeing whether that particular morsel was all it was cracked up to be.

He came to the second turning of the tunnel, paused, and looked around the corner cautiously. Voices again rang out. The light ahead had a different quality than the dim, dusty-bulbed utility lights strung sparingly through the tunnel itself. It was a cleaner white, and he caught a faint whiff of kerosene.

Around him, the symbiote stirred and shifted excitedly. Eddie said softly, "Not this time. Just wait. And considering who we're going to be dealing with… street clothes, please."

Obediently it shifted. The spider logo across his chest faded as the black flushed into a beige shirt, jeans, boots. He looked himself over and said, "A little more used-looking."

Quickly the symbiote reshaped itself to his thought: frays and holes appeared in the jeans, a convincing patina of dirt, the collar and rolled-up cuffs of the shirt went threadbare. There was no point in frightening these people. He knew their kind: suspicious of strangers, always afraid of being driven out of their hard-won hiding places, or worse, made to live there on a new boss's sufferance. Venom had seen enough of that in the city under Golden Gate Park where he now served as protector—a portion of San Francisco buried in the 1906 earthquake and subsequently forgotten. The underground city had become a haven for society's outcasts.

He looked himself over one more time, ruffled his hair a bit, felt his chin. Well, the stubble was there, no need to do anything about that.

Slowly he walked down the tunnel, letting his footsteps echo. Ahead of him, people fell silent, listening. He was listening, too, for the sound of a weapon being gotten ready. Not that it was likely that people in these circumstances could do much to him, especially with the symbiote at hand. But all the same, he liked to be careful. "Hello?" Eddie said, trying to sound nonthreatening.

"Hello? Who's that?" came a voice from down the tunnel, fairly nearby now.

"Nobody," Eddie said. "Nobody much. I won't hurt anybody here."

"Well, Mister Nobody," said the voice, and it was female, "you just come down here nice and slow, and you keep your hands where we can see them."

Eddie did that, having no reason to disobey and hearing no overt threat in the voice, just the kind of toughness one needed to survive in these tunnels. Slowly he walked forward.

There were small "bays" in the sides of the tunnel, faired-in places six or eight feet deep. In one of these, the voices he heard were concentrated. He came abreast of the place and found himself looking at a tidy, neat little campsite, such as you might expect to find in the backwoods somewhere. Except that here they all were, any number of feet underground.

Eddie came up to the group—there were three of them—and stood there, letting them see him, keeping his hands in the open. Two women—an older one, red hair going pink as the white came in; a middle-aged one, blond, still pretty in anybody's book; and an old man, weary-looking, his face flushed with red, peppered with big broken blood vessels, some of them ulcerated. *Looks like alcohol or chemical abuse*, Venom thought, *Sterno, possibly....* There was no telling. It was something he had seen enough of both in San Fran and here.

"That's an old trick," the little old red-haired lady said to him, looking up at him genially.

"Which one, ma'am?"

"'Nobody.'" She smiled, and there was some humor in the expression. "I remember another time a youngster came calling on people who weren't expecting him. They asked him his name too, and he said 'Nobody.' Then when the youngster's host started abusing his guests, and the young fella arranged to have a sharp stick poked into his host's big eye, all the poor monster could yell was, 'Oh my gosh, Nobody's hurting me!' And all his friends yelled back, 'Better pray for relief, then.'"

Eddie smiled. "A classicist," he said. "Well, the wily Odysseus we are not, no matter who else we might be."

"Who might you be, actually? Queen Victoria, maybe, with all that 'we' nonsense."

He raised an eyebrow. "To tell a name is to control the thing," he said. "A classicist would know that. But never mind. Just call us Eddie."

"Eddie. Well, tell us, Eddie, would you be planning to stay?" said the younger woman.

He looked at her. Really very pretty, she was, with a small round face that looked sweet—until you saw something behind the eyes that belied the sweetness. A hard look. "No, ma'am," he said, "we're just passing through."

"Well, that's good," she said, but she didn't say why. Eddie noticed, though, that her hand was near her pocket, and her pocket bulged in an angular way suggestive of a small pistol.

"Can we sit?"

The older lady made a gracious gesture, like a queen offering a commoner a seat in front of her throne. Eddie slumped down with his back against the wall and looked at the trio. The man was paying no attention to him. Eddie glanced briefly in his direction and said, "Is he all right?"

The younger woman acquired an annoyed expression. The older one raised her eyebrows. "He hasn't been well lately," she said. "He's been sleeping in the wrong parts of town."

An odd way to put it, Eddie thought then. "What brings you down here?" Eddie said, looking at them.

"Usually the guest says first," said the older lady. "I'm Alma, by the way. This is Linda, that's Chuck."

"Alma," Eddie said, nodding. "We're just looking for someone. Someone in particular. A fellow we need to have a talk with."

Alma nodded. "And you'll be moving on, you say."

"That's right."

"Well, Eddie," she said, stretching her legs out, "you'll understand a person has to be cautious, talking to someone they've never seen before. But let's just say my marriage wasn't working out quite the way I thought it should. And I had nowhere else to go. The women's shelters were all full the night my husband tried to beat me to death. There was no way I could wait until there was an opening. So I grabbed my things and got out the best I could. Couldn't have stayed with any of my friends, because he'd have hunted them down and beat them too. So I took myself out of the way." The smile got grimmer. "I treated this as if it was a camping trip." She glanced around her, and Venom saw that they were well equipped: a little camping stove, one of those which give heat and light both, a kerosene lamp, hissing softly to itself, backpack, sleeping bag, foam mattress.

"Money has to be a problem," Eddie said softly.

"When isn't it?" she said. "I get by."

Alma looked over at Linda, who now looked at Eddie and said, "Family trouble. Alma had trouble with her husband. I had trouble with my uncle. Uncle Sam." She sighed. "I've been homeless for a few years now."

"Vietnam?" said Eddie softly.

She nodded. "I was a nurse. What I didn't realize was that, depending on where you worked, you were just as likely to be exposed to Agent Orange as you were if you were out slogging in the jungle. When I got sick, I knew what the problem was, but I was never able to prove it to the medical tribunal's satisfaction. So…" She shrugged. "I couldn't work. I lost my apartment. I went under—literally." She looked around at the tunnels. "All I can do is keep an eye on Alma and Chuck here."

Eddie looked at her pocket and nodded, knowing that she knew he knew the gun was there. "Chuck," he said. "You said he was sleeping in the wrong places. Where would that be?"

Alma jerked her head, indicating someplace up the tunnel and to the right. "Over by the Garden. Something's going on over there, I don't know what. But lately it's been less healthy than usual."

"I've heard," Eddie said. "Someone—" He was *not* going to say, *pretending to be Venom.*

"Something," Alma said. "This town is getting so full of super heroes, and super villains, and things from other planets that it's hard to know whether you're coming or going." She chuckled. "Remember those T-shirts you used to be able to get that said 'Native New Yorker'? There's a store downtown selling shirts that say 'Native Earthling.'"

Linda smiled as well. "No, there's something down here that has a taste for people," she said, "or chunks of them. Some poor guy got his hand bit off last night."

"Over by the Garden?"

"By the Garden," said Alma. "The place is usually fairly busy because of all the traffic in and out of Penn. You can get in and out of the tunnels there without being noticed, usually. These days—" She shook her head. "A lot of the 'residents' are clearing out, heading over to Grand Central instead."

Eddie was opening his mouth to ask how things were over there, when footsteps echoed from the other direction. Everyone's head but Chuck's whipped around. Linda's hand went into her pocket without trying to look as if it did so. Eddie sat quiet. The symbiote, without doing so visibly, was moving against him, eager. *Now calm down,* he said to it silently. *You don't know—*

But it *did* know, sometimes. He suspected it knew now.

Up the tunnel, three men came stalking around the corner, stopped, and stared. Because of the way the little bays were built into the side of the tunnel, and the way Alma and her people were tucked into the one they shared, all the three could see at first was Eddie. The men, though hardly more than shadows at that distance, looked briefly at each other, and the soft sound of snickering came down from that end of the tunnel.

It does know, Eddie thought. *All right... let's be ready....*

The three sauntered down into the light, easy and confident. None was older than about twenty-five, and they all, to some extent, looked like a bad cross between goths and the Hitlerjiingen. They favored the present style in soiled urban camo, and black leather with as many studs and zippers hanging off it as possible. There was not much else to choose between them, other than that the first one coming along had a brash cut which appeared to have been done with a weed-eater. The second one had apparently gone for the bald look, which didn't do much for him, since he had pimples on his skull. The third had lank greasy hair hanging down so far in front of his eyes that he could have passed for a Yorkshire terrier.

"Well, well, well," said the putative leader, he of the weed-eaten hair, "what have we here?" His hand was in his pocket too, and Eddie studied the pocket for bulges. It was hard to tell, in those baggy pants, what was concealed. It might have been a gun. It might have been a knife, either for the practical reason that knives are more complicated to take away from people than guns are, or the nastier reason that knives are intrinsically more frightening than guns, and many people who can deal with being shot will nonetheless run away screaming at the thought of being cut.

"Were it not for the possibility that you're as deaf as you're possibly blind," Eddie said mildly, "we might tell you. But why waste time or breath?"

"Oh, a wise guy, huh?" said the leader. The other two snickered behind him. "A wise guy, huh, huh, heh heh, yeah—"

The symbiote was beginning to twitch with excitement, and Eddie knew exactly what was coming, but could only laugh. "My God," he said, "we've fallen into a Three Stooges movie. Not only are you three the most hopeless and pitiful excuses for human beings that we've seen in a month of Sundays, but you don't even know how to be threatening properly! We suggest you go out and try it again. Better still"—and he eyed the leader—"we suggest you just *go out*."

Now the leader pulled his weapon. Yes, it was a knife, one of the little brass-collared Italian-style switchblades. Venom smiled gently, for he had seen this particular model several times before, back in San Fran, and it had a tendency to jam. Several of them had also been jammed into him, with responses that varied from useless to amusing. It didn't matter: all those knives' owners were history.

"Man, you're gonna get slice-n-diced now," said the Little Hitler leading the group. Behind him, the bald one doing the Il Duce impression said, "Hey, yeah, slice-n-dice…."

Not the Three Stooges after all. Venom thought sadly. *Nothing so high-class. More like MTV.* "Pitiful," he said. But there were certainly people up on the streets, and down here in the tunnels, who would be frightened by these idiots.

He spared a glance for Alma and Linda. The two of them wore the flat, straight faces of people trying to decide how they're going to fight to save their lives. Afraid, but resigned. The third of them, old Chuck, simply sat looking blankly at the floor.

"Well, come on, Cyrano," Venom said, grinning at the leader. "Let's see what you've got."

The leader moved, with what he probably thought was a strike as fast as a snake. But he was hardly half-wound up for what was going to be a roundhouse slash to Eddie's gut before a thick tentacle had whipped out and caught his arm, wrapping around it exactly as one of those striking snakes might have. The young man's eyes bugged out somewhat satisfactorily, then bugged harder, and he screamed at the top of his lungs. The tendril twisted and broke the arm straight across the radius and ulna, leaving two perfectly matched greenstick fractures sticking up out of the flesh of the arm, blood spurting from the torn brachial artery which the splintered bone of the radius had sliced on its way out.

All right, Eddie thought to the symbiote. But it was already flushing dark all around him again, its protective mask growing and stretching up over his head, growing all its teeth. It whipped out about thirty more tentacles, pinioning the three from elbows to knees, their arms strained behind them, a few tentacles wrapping around their mouths for best effect. Their muffled moans and shrieks that couldn't escape were music to Eddie's ears.

He turned his head quickly and ordered the symbiote back off his face for a moment, shedding the teeth and tongue again just for the moment. To Alma he said, "Look… I'm not going to mess up the area with this—" He gestured at the straggling three. "What's the saying? 'Pack out your trash'?"

She looked up at him, wide-eyed, and finally managed a curt nod.

"The place where Chuck's been," he said, "it's over by the Garden?"

"That's right. Listen," she said.

Eddie stopped as the symbiote lifted the three punks in its tentacles, and he prepared to carry them away. "Listen now," Alma said. "You be careful. Whatever it is over there—"

"I think I can manage," he said gently. "Thank you, Alma. You take care too."

As he lifted the punks up high, the teeth and talons and long slavering tongue settled upon him again. Venom carried the three a good way into the darkness. He waited until he was at least half a mile further down the tunnel, and a level further down, before he allowed the screaming to start. Even then, he muffled most of it, not wanting to alarm Alma too much, or her young friend with the gun, and most of all not wanting to alarm the silent man who didn't speak or look up.

It took him a while to clear away the bodies, but he did it with some care. He had no idea how many others like Alma and her group—innocent refugees from the world above—might be down here. Those people he had no desire to frighten. The others who roved this world—the predators, the cruel ones—he didn't mind scaring them as badly as possible. But at a distance, they were sometimes hard to tell apart.

Once he was finished, Venom went on. It was slow work, finding his way. Even though his memory of the maps was good, the tunnels twisted, confusing even someone who knew where he was supposed to be going. With care he worked his way upward and over into the general neighborhood of Seventh Avenue and 34th Street.

For courtesy's sake, and in case he should meet any more innocents, Eddie returned to his "street clothes." But he met no more people. Perhaps it was early for most people to be heading underground, yet. He saw enough signs of where they had been; not everyone down here was as tidy as Alma and her group. He began to see, as well, indications that something else had been down here.

He started finding scraps of metal on the floor, and splashes of— it was hard to say what. It had no specific color, coming in dark sludgy splashes here and there on walls or floor. The metallic pieces, though, had definitely been torn from barrels or canisters.

In one long dark corridor where many of the lights were gone, he found four or five scraps of the same color—that sort of bilious yellow which marks the barrels in which toxic waste is stored. Using the symbiote's tendrils to handle them—as far as he knew, the symbiote was radiation-proof—he picked up two of these scraps and examined them as closely as he could in the dim light. On one, the edges were sliced clean, as if someone had used a knife sharp enough to cut steel. On another, though, one of the edges was jaggedly cut. *You could almost use it for a saw,* Venom thought, looking at it carefully. He knew the bite pattern of a mouthful of big fangs by now. But to see it in metal was a bit of a surprise.

He put the fragments down and continued, going very carefully and listening constantly. As he had gone along, there had been several places where two or three tunnels conjoined and ran together—different utilities, usually, phone in one, cable or steam in another. Then after a quarter-mile or so, they might part again. Normally, these multiple-joint tunnels were better lit—probably, Venom suspected, because the utility people had to be in them more often. But as he continued now, he noticed that there were progressively fewer working lights in the tunnels.

He examined several of the lights as he passed them. They were not smashed, but appeared to have been cut open cleanly as if someone had come along with a diamond-bladed glass saw, slashing both the bulb protector and the bulb itself.

The tunnel was growing very dark now. Venom came to one of those places where there were almost no lights, where several tunnels met again. Ahead of him he saw, although most dimly, walls which were further apart, a ceiling higher than the one he stood under now.

Into that space Venom came, stopped, looked around him. All the floor of the place was littered with torn and shredded metal; here and there, almost invisible, was a splash of something darker than the walls. *Not blood,* he thought, *something else.* There was a rank, chemical smell about the place.

Now then, he thought, and stood very still, and listened.

He heard a faint scraping sound—coming, not from further down the tunnel, but from somewhere nearby. He cast around him. Off to one side, he saw another access shaft, with a ladder reaching straight down into the next level.

He listened hard. With the echoes down here, it was sometimes hard to tell, but the noise seemed to be coming from down there. *All right,* he thought. *Let's not jump to conclusions. Let's just check this quickly.*

The symbiote was shivering with excitement now. It flushed dark again, surrounded him with its full complement of fangs and the flickering, slavering tongue, blazoned itself with the white spider-shape across his chest. It was eager; it wanted more of what it had just had.

Patience, he thought to it. He went over to the open access shaft and stood looking down, listening. There was only the very faintest light down there—perhaps just one of these dim bulbs left burning. And he could hear the sound of something scraping, rattling, rustling—metal against metal. Not rats—too big for rats.

This is the point, he thought to himself with a slight smile under the cowl, *in a horror movie, when the person hears those noises and goes down to see what's making them, and the audience immediately understands that the character in question is brain-damaged. But never mind. In this movie, I am the monster.*

Very slowly and softly, using tendrils and hands and feet, he went down the ladder. Halfway down, he reached for the next rung—and found that there wasn't any more. Air gaped under him. The tentacles let him down, but not too softly. He came down with a clang, some three or four feet further down than he'd thought the floor would be. The ladder might have had an extension once, but it was gone now.

Venom stood dead still in the near-total darkness, letting his eyes get used to it as quickly as they could. The rustling stopped abruptly, and then, very slowly and softly, started again.

Should have brought a flashlight, he thought. But it was too late for that now. He could have cursed his eyes for taking so long to adapt, but cursing wouldn't have helped and would only have attracted more attention—and he already had more of it fixed on him than he wanted.

He found himself staring at a shape so black it nearly vanished into the darkness. He gaped at it in shock. Slowly it opened great pale moons of eyes, and by their glow he could see, though dimly.

It is unnerving enough to come around a corner in a big city, even one as big as New York, and nearly run into someone who looks so much like you that you're tempted to stop with your mouth hanging open, and stare. It's worse yet to run into such a person deep under the ground, in near-total darkness. And, Eddie discovered, it's worst of all when you are Venom.

The creature at which he was staring—and open-mouthed, for whether out of generalized bloodthirstiness, or specific jealousy, the symbiote was slavering at the sight of the thing—was bipedal, with bilateral symmetry and a head at the top. At the moment, it was crouched slightly, looking at him, and line after line of writhing tendrils wound away from it, wreathing in the air, reaching toward him. Its head was up, and the weaving motion was too swift and purposeful to have anything hypnotic about it. *Smelling*, Eddie thought. *Smelling for what?*

Reluctantly, after that, came the second thought: *It's not Hobgoblin himself, then.* Possibly some creature of his, though. "We don't know what or who you are," he said softly, moving toward it, "but you've picked the wrong person to impersonate."

Those pale eyes stared at him. Some of the tentacles, he saw, were still clutching the remnants of a torn-up canister. "Who are you?" he said. "Some new punk super villain who doesn't have the guts to work out an identity of his own? Some kind of shapechanger? There have been some of those around every now and then. But it doesn't matter." He stalked forward. "You have been killing innocent people," Venom said, "in our likeness... our name. And for that"—the symbiote began reaching hungry pseudopodia toward its rival—"there can be only one punishment!"

He let the symbiote go. Instantly it flung a hundred tentacles at the thing, wrapping it around. Venom was not surprised when the creature wrapped as many around him. But he was very surprised when it effortlessly picked him up and threw him halfway down that tunnel, to land with a bone-bruising crash among the torn pieces of canister.

He struggled to his feet, the symbiote helping him with outflung tentacles that whirled and writhed around him now like angry snakes. The symbiote was not used to being tossed around like this. Come to think of it, neither was he. The symbiote caught his rage, and after a breath or two he could hardly see his quarry for the storm of tendrils streaming out toward the fake-Venom as he headed back toward it.

"How many other innocents have you killed?" Venom hissed angrily. "People who won't be missed because no one knows that they're here and no one cares? How many—" He reached out, directing the symbiote to make the tentacles thicker, stronger this time. He wrapped them around the creature like vines around a tree, exerting an awful pressure to crush, and the tongue lanced out too, meaning to wrap around the head and rip the top of it off, anticipating the sweet brains inside.

Only something else grabbed his tongue, and nearly pulled it right out of the symbiote. The symbiote screamed soundlessly inside him, a feeling like a nail through his brain, a sound Venom had heard in fights before, and had learned to dread. Physical pain was something it rarely felt until it was driven very close to what it could no longer bear.

It was definitely time to worry now. The creature he was fighting still had him by the symbiote's tongue, and was pulling with such brutality that he thought his own head would be pulled off, no matter how the symbiote resisted. It was pulling him toward its fangs, fangs which had had no problem dealing with metal canisters full of nuclear waste. He tried desperately to push himself away, his bones cracking with the strain.

The creature pulled him closer and closer, its tongue flickering out, wrapping itself around Venom's head in a parody of what the symbiote had planned. The pressure began crushing in on him.

Sheer revulsion did what calculation hadn't been able to do, as the symbiote caught his terror and despair. It flung out tendrils to either side, anchored itself to the walls, insinuated other tendrils between him and the creature, and simply pushed all at once, one mighty leverage-breaking movement that shot him right across the tunnel again and into the far wall. He hit hard and slid to the floor, the tentacles unable to react quickly enough to cushion the impact.

The cure's almost worse than the disease, he thought, struggling back to his feet again. There was a roaring in his head, partly the pounding of blood vessels recovering from a moment of much-increased intracranial pressure, partly the rage of the symbiote—occasionally he would hear it this way, frustrated, angry. It pushed him to his feet and launched itself toward the creature.

He tried to stop it, preferring a more considered kind of attack, but the creature's tentacles and the symbiote's were already tangling together. Venom found himself at the far end of an increasingly violent tug-of-war—wreaths and ropes of pseudopodia knotting and pulling. The symbiote had anchored itself behind some cable conduits on the far wall. They were beginning to creak dangerously as the stress of the tug-of-war began pulling them out of the wall. *All right,* Venom thought savagely, *let's finish this!*

He began to coach the symbiote, showing it where to put the tentacles around their adversary to best advantage—head, limbs, waist. They pulled. The pains in his joints began again, and the pains in his back, and still they pulled. Venom was braced as well as he could be, as well as the symbiote could manage, but it wasn't enough. He felt the pains as his knees, helping to brace, started to bend forward the wrong way; in his arms, as his shoulders threatened to dislocate; in his neck and upper back, as slowly, slowly, the creature pulled him closer. The pair struggled, as each tried to get another grip on the other's head. *Come on!* Venom urged the symbiote. *Save us! Help me save us! Only you can do this—only we can do this—come* on!

Little by little he felt its desperation, its determination to be what he wanted—and little by little they pulled back, an inch, two inches, five. Pulled back toward the wall, began to pull the creature with them. *Now!* Venom said. *Now! While we can, while it's off balance!* The symbiote sprouted tendrils edged like knives, ready to tear, to rip—

The other let go. Venom reeled back against the wall again, in a clatter of torn metal and old broken glass. He fell down most ignominiously on his butt.

The creature was standing there, moving away from the wall, now, letting go of its mooring. Its head was up, all those tendrils up too, weaving in the air again, smelling. It looked over at Venom. Dazed, he looked back. The symbiote reached for the thing—

The creature looked at him, then raced away down the almost pitch-black tunnel northward and eastward, toward Madison Square Garden.

Cursing in earnest now, Venom struggled to his feet, feeling like one big bruise. He could feel the symbiote's dejection, disappointment, rage. It had wanted *that,* whatever that was.

So do I, Venom thought. *And shortly we'll have it.* He looked after the creature. *Worth noticing, though: don't attack it and it doesn't attack you. It loses interest as soon as you stop. And it can be distracted.*

Let's go find out by what. Discovering what distracts it may be the key to what will kill it. And once it's dead, then we go after its master: Hobgoblin.

With all the speed they could muster, Venom went down the tunnel after their dark twin.

TEN

SPIDER-MAN crept slowly down the passage toward the gratings. The clear, bluish fluorescent light spilling out almost blinded him after the dimness of the other tunnels.

He edged silently over to the far wall, hunkered down, and peered through. The grating was more like heavy chicken wire than anything else, and it appeared to have been cemented into the wall. Spider-Man thought they could probably be peeled out of the concrete even by someone without spider-strength. Clearly they had been designed for ventilation rather than security.

He had a bird's-eye view of a room about eighty feet square. Three men, two wearing overalls, the third wearing a shirt and jeans and boots, were talking as they assembled a very large piece of machinery. A welter of pallets and large wooden crates surrounded them.

The spider-tracer wasn't going to be able to tell him anything more. Indeed, the buzz he was getting from the tracer was now as strong as it was going to be: he could see one of the big safes stowed over in the corner, its door pried open, the safe emptied out. Spidey's gaze went back to that big piece of machinery in the middle of the room.

Now what the heck is that? Spider-Man thought, watching them work. The men had several "passive pullers," flatbeds on low wheels, each with a handle at the front and hydraulics attached to the handle: pull on the handle and the hydraulics pushed the flatbed forward to relieve the pressure, a standard "negative feedback" device. One of these pullers held a huge, gray metal box, with wiring and power inputs showing off to one side, which one of the men was trying to maneuver into place in a bay of a much larger installation which stood in the middle of the room. The other two were working at the edges of the main installation, folding doors away from the now-open bay, tidying up cables and getting ready to make connections to the new piece of equipment.

Then Hobgoblin stalked into view. Spider-Man spotted his jetglider sitting off to one side. Hobby looked unusually nervous. "Come on," he was saying to his henchmen, "I don't have all day, here! Or all night. This thing has to be in place and running before one!" *What in the world does he want* this *for?* Spider-Man thought.

The henchmen began making placating noises, not that Hobby paid that much attention to them. He just kept stalking up and down, railing at them. Spider-Man settled on the floor of the passageway for the moment to watch the developments and evaluate that big piece of machinery.

It looked like a generator of some kind. Its side doors hung open, showing a little of its guts, and Spider-Man could see what looked like sealed housings of a shape that suggested gigantic wound coils, such as you might expect to see in a power station's generators. But he couldn't imagine for the life of him what this had to do with an atomic bomb.

It's not as if an A-bomb has to be this big, he thought, *or anything like it.* Long ago, in the days of the Manhattan Project before the birth of the transistor, an atomic bomb had to be fairly hefty. *But nothing like this. You couldn't have gotten this thing into the* Enola Gay *with a crowbar.* Nowadays, with transistors and highly compacted explosives to drive the two critical-mass components together, an A-bomb could fit in the back of a car or truck. A truck would probably be best: the uranium and other fissile components were so massive, most cars' shocks and suspension would simply give up under such a trunkload.

The man with the puller wrangled a big "add-on" box into approximately the right position, and the other two men were trying to muscle it into the sort of giant "socket" for which it seemed destined, while Hobgoblin kept stalking around the machine, haranguing them and generally getting in their way.

It's only midnight, Spider-Man thought. *I wonder what his rush is?* Silently he pulled out his camera and its little tripod out of its bag, setting them up. Later, he would move them to whichever grating he finally chose to pull away.

For the moment, a possibility occurred to him. *Could it be a hiding place for the bomb itself? This isn't something he could move easily,* Spider-Man thought. *If the bomb itself is a more reasonable size, it could be hidden somewhere in this structure. You could spend a lot of useful time taking this thing apart, trying to find where the bomb part is hidden.*

It was a possibility. Hobgoblin could be awfully clever. He might assume that he was going to be caught and made a contingency plan. He might have seen to it that whoever caught up with him would waste precious time looking for the bomb——time Hobby could use to escape, possibly with a remote-control trigger.

Spider-Man shook his head. *It might just be a hiding place, but I can't believe he would have taken this long to set it up. If not that—then maybe it's something else, something he's going to need later. But what?*

He watched Hobby's henchmen as they started connecting a new module into the main generator, while Hobby rubbed his hands together and chuckled.

Let's say you've just held the whole city hostage, Spider-Man thought. *Blackmailed them into giving you a billion bucks. Then what? Logic says you get as far away from the scene of the crime as you can. Brazil... heck, Antarctica. Or the moon. Somewhere you can't be extradited from, somewhere you can't be found. But what if Hobby decided that the best place to go to ground after committing a big crime in the middle of New York City, is the middle of New York City itself? They never catch you, because you don't leave. You make yourself a nice comfy little lair with plenty of food, water, whatever else you consider necessary for life the way you like to live it—including a private generator for power. Using what for fuel, though?* And the answer immediately suggested itself: *fissiles! Atomic piles aren't the size they used to be, either. So you set up an atomic reactor for your own private use. This is the perfect place. Use a city main as the water for your reactor to heat and push through the generator's turbines as steam, giving you all the heat and power you need.*

He looked around quickly, eyeing the walls for signs of pipes or tubes. Sure enough, he spotted some in the far wall. There were enough extra pipes to reach the installation in the middle of the room. *It could be,* Spider-Man thought. *Carry out your little blackmail, get paid off, and then just snuggle down under the streets of the city, biding your time until the heat's off.* If that was what Hobby had planned, it had its points.

And if not... then I have no idea what that generator's about. The thing I need to do is get a good look around inside. But that's not going to happen with Hobby in place.

He looked down thoughtfully at the henchmen and then at the grilles farther down his passageway. He edged along quietly to examine the other gratings. When he came to the third, Spider-Man smiled to himself. Someone had been pulling at it—there was no way to tell when—but one corner had completely separated from the concrete, and all around the edges, the metal had rusted. It would be a simple enough matter to peel it open and slip in.

No sooner said than done, he thought, and he set to work on the wire, very quietly. That chamber below was well littered with pallets and crates and other nondescript machinery, so there would be plenty of things to hide behind.

Slow and easy, he told himself—though at this point his eagerness was getting the better of him. His anger at the sheer, calculated nastiness that enabled Hobgoblin to blackmail a whole city without even twitching made him very eager indeed to come to grips with the man. Nevertheless, he slowed himself down and concentrated on making as little noise as he could. The last thing he wanted to do was give himself away prematurely.

He began peeling the wire back, bending over a few jagged bits of metal that had broken off the grille and now stuck out of the concrete. *No sense catching the costume on the way down,* he thought.

Hobgoblin had begun to harangue his men again. "Come on, come on," he was snarling, and the nervousness in his voice was really rather surprising. *Can it be,* Spider-Man thought, *that he's finally realized that he's riding a tiger, and he's suddenly not too sure that he can keep hanging onto its ears?* That was possibly something that could be used to Spidey's advantage. Despite having made this bomb, or having had it made for him, Hobby was still nervous of his ability to handle it. *He might yet make a mistake... something I can exploit.* Spider-Man just hoped it wouldn't be the kind of mistake which would leave Manhattan a smoking crater.

With a final small jerk, the grating came loose in his hands. Even as it did. Hobby, muttering something under his breath, stalked off into the next room. Spider-Man smiled under his mask, got up silently, fetched his camera, and repositioned it.

The three henchmen were still wrestling and sweating at the job of fitting the new module into the generator. One of them went around the far side of the big main machine, and while the other two were watching him, Spider-Man slipped through the now-empty opening and let himself down to the floor level on a webline.

Spidey found a convenient pallet loaded with crates and tucked himself behind it, watching the men move.

"Aah, this is crap," the sandy-haired one of the pair wearing overalls said quietly to his companions. "He doesn't need this thing tonight. He's just paranoid."

The other two grunted assent, but quietly. "No use arguing with him when he's like this," said the second one, the man wearing the shirt and jeans. "Otherwise you wind up with one of those little pumpkins stuffed up your nose."

The sandy-haired man went around the far side of the machine again. "Aah," said the third one, "you know what his problem is?"

"He's a raving loony," said the sandy-haired man.

"Nah. You know what he has? A bad management style. Give him one of those executive seminars, he'd be okay."

The second man stared at the third, disbelieving. The first one was still around the far side of the machine, hammering at something with a rubber mallet. While the two discussed management technique and whether a seminar would do Hobgoblin any good whatever, Spider-Man crept closer.

The sandy-haired man in the overalls gave the installation one last desultory whack with the rubber mallet. "The contacts are in," he said, dropping the mallet on the floor. "I don't care if he does want it perfect. It's not going to fit smooth. I think they screwed it up at the factory."

"They did what?" said one of the others.

"They screwed it up, and it's not our fault, I don't care what he says." He sat on one of the crates looking disgusted.

"He'll say we did it," said the man in the shirt and jeans.

"Well, let him. He has a negative attitude," said the second man.

This might have been true, but Spider-Man didn't see any point in waiting for further analysis. He promptly stood up from behind the pallet of crates where he was hiding and jumped the sandy-haired man from behind. There was a brief but utterly silent tussle, at the end of which the sandy-haired man was as well swathed in a web as any fly after the spider's through with it. Effectively gagged, unable to utter a sound, he lay there squirming. On the other side of the machine, Spider-Man heard the man in the shirt and jeans say, "No wonder he keeps getting into trouble at work."

Spider-Man smiled to himself, while busily webbing the first man to one of the pallets, so he couldn't squirm out into sight. Then, crouching down behind another stack of crates, he turned his attention to the other two.

Henchmen, he thought. *What the heck is a hench? Is it something you carry around, like luggage? Something to eat? Maybe some kind of animal, if it had a henchman to take care of it?*

He slipped behind another pallet and looked at the other two men. They had finished taking the load-puller out from under the new installation, and the one in the jeans and shirt was standing back from it, lighting a cigarette. The other one looked at him with mild reproof and said, "You shouldn't do that in here—You Know Who gets cranky."

"Aah," said the smoker, taking a long drag.

"Besides," said the other man in the overalls, "you said you were giving it up."

"I did give up. Last week."

"You gotta try harder. They say now that if you can go cold turkey for two weeks, you'll probably give it up clean."

"Huh," said the smoker. He looked up at the installation. "That thing still isn't fitting right around the edges," he said. "Hank, where's that hammer?"

He dropped the cigarette and stepped on it, then went around the corner of the generator to where he had last seen the first man. "Oh, here it is. Where's Hank?"

"Probably went off to take a leak."

"He didn't even say anything."

"He's been that way a lot lately," said the man in the overalls. "Kinda short tempered."

"I don't know," said the man in the jeans, taking a long look at the spot that Hank had been working on. "He's never been too big on social skills, has he?"

"Nah. I think it's 'cause'a not having much family."

Spider-Man spun a length of web between his hands, judged the length and thickness of it, and paused.

"Probably. I think he doesn't have much to take his mind off his work—"

Spider-Man leapt. The ensuing struggle was mercifully brief: in a matter of seconds, the man in the jeans was as thoroughly swathed in webbing as the first, and, also like him, fastened down to the back of another of the pallets. Silently, Spider-Man slipped around to the generator.

"I don't know," said the remaining man, looking absently at the stepped-on cigarette. "I think what he needs is something to do besides work. Maybe a bowling league, or a softball team, or something. If he just—mmmf!"

Spider-Man struck a few seconds later, and the third man joined his cohorts, trussed up like a Thanksgiving turkey and stowed behind yet another pallet full of crates. *Now then,* Spider-Man thought, and he slipped into a new hiding place behind the generator itself.

Hobgoblin's voice could be heard, loud and getting louder, as he came in from the next room. "Look at that," he said testily, "it looks terrible. What am I paying you people for, anyway? Can't you even put simple machinery together straight? Look at that join, it's a mess. And then you stand around gabbing, after what I've paid you. Don't you understand that—Men? Where are you?"

Hobgoblin came through the door. "Where are you?" he demanded. Then he looked around in shock. "I can't believe it," he muttered to himself. "Look at this! This is not a time for a lunch break!" He stalked around—and Spider-Man watched Hobgoblin's face change as he realized it was not a matter of lunch breaks or anything else. He looked up and noticed the window where the grating had been torn out. "They're gone. Where'd they go?" And then his face changed under the mask from confusion to anger.

"Spider-Man!" he hissed. "All right, you two-bit web-slinger, I know you're in here somewhere! Come out!"

Hobgoblin ran for the jetglider. It rose under him, and he began swooping around the room, desperately trying to locate his enemy.

Spider-Man, grinning to himself, cried, "Two can play at this game, Hobby!" He bounded for the ceiling when Hobby was near the floor, for the floor when he was near the ceiling, always using the big installation in the middle as a way to stay out of sight. The effect, Spidey knew, would be utter confusion for Hobgoblin—he wouldn't know which way to turn.

"You've interfered with me for the last time, bug," Hobgoblin shouted, and abruptly, not five feet away from Spider-Man, in transit between a wall and the floor, a flash bomb went off. Warned by his spider-sense, Spidey ducked out of the way easily. It was followed by another, and another a few feet to Spidey's other side. He laughed to himself, though: Hobgoblin was chucking them around randomly, having no clear sense of where Spider-Man was.

"Spiders aren't bugs," Spider-Man called cheerfully as he dodged another flashbomb, "they're arachnids. But then you were never very strong on anything but the applied sciences." A few more flash bombs went off quite close to him. *Trying to draw me out,* Spider-Man thought as he leapt again. He felt exhilarated. After the time spent tonight walking in dark tunnels, the crouching and the claustrophobia, Spider-Man was glad of an excuse to stretch and move. Flash bombs popped and boomed all around him, but Hobby still hadn't seen where he was. Which was just as well; he had no desire to catch one of those up close, even though they were a lot less harmful than the pumpkin bombs were.

That caution, in itself, was diagnostic. *He doesn't want to hurt his generator,* Spider-Man realized. *He doesn't dare. So long as I stay in here, we're okay.*

But—and he grew thoughtful as another flash bomb zipped harmlessly past—*there may be no point in staying, since I don't have any proof the bomb is here. And if it's not here, I'm wasting my time.*

Hobgoblin was wheeling and screaming around, now, with much more animus than usual. "I'll get you! I'll get you and squash you like the bug you are, arachnid or no damned arachnid—!"

"Yeah, yeah," Spider-Man called brightly, continuing with his evasive maneuvers, "the same old song. You couldn't hit your own mother with a flyswatter. Did you *have* a mother? Jeez, she must be embarrassed—!"

Hobgoblin was not amused. "I'll show you—"

There was a sudden crumbling noise from off to one side of the room. Hobby paused in mid-glide, hovering, staring at the wall. Spider-Man, momentarily hiding behind another tall pallet-full of crates, peered around to see what was happening.

The wall was bulging in a very unnerving way. With a sound like a gunshot, a big crack appeared in the concrete, in the place where the bulge was most pronounced. The bulge got bigger, and the crack spread, starfishing out from what seemed like an impact point, a place where the wall was being hit, and hit hard, by something from the outside.

The concrete floor began to vibrate faintly. The other walls thrummed in response, and the thrumming slowly rose to a rumble like distant thunder. The crack stitched wider under the repeated blows from outside, multiplied itself up and down the width of the wall. Then—*smash!*—all at once, the wall fell in.

Hobgoblin threw a couple of flash bombs at something big and black pushing through the rubble, but they had no effect. Another *smash!* and broken concrete and pieces of steel-reinforcing rod came raining down into the room, leaving a great hole into blackness.

Through the hole, striding out of the darkness, came Venom. *Not now!* Spidey thought. *Not again!*

Spider-Man glanced up at Hobgoblin. The jetglider slowly backed away.

"You!" Hobgoblin snarled at Venom. He seemed to be trying hard to sound outraged, but his nervousness showed much too clearly. "Get out of here before I put an end to your nuisance once and for all!" He hefted a pumpkin bomb, but didn't throw it.

Venom stood there, arms folded, while the symbiote's tendrils writhed about him, and the symbiote's tongue licked the air and reached toward Hobgoblin hungrily. "If you could do anything about us," Venom said calmly, "you would have by now. Which means you can't do anything about us. Or won't." He eyed the big lump of machinery in the middle of the room. "And if this is what we think it is—we believe we know why you won't, and can't, do anything."

Up until now, Spider-Man had been avoiding being seen by Hobby, mostly to see what the crook might do next, where he might lead him. Now, though, it occurred to him that if he didn't do something quickly, Hobgoblin would shortly no longer be a factor in this or any other equation. He leapt out from the wall, where he had briefly been hanging upside down behind yet another stacked-up pallet, and landed between Hobgoblin and Venom. "Listen," he said urgently, "Venom, if I were you—"

The symbiote turned on him with considerable scorn. "You are not us," he said. "Something for which we give thanks, morning and night. You had your chance to be us, and you blew it. Now stand back and let someone deal with this"—Venom glanced at Hobgoblin with the kind of look someone might give a carton of sour yogurt—"this *thing* who can do the job properly."

Hobgoblin's jetglider lifted suddenly, as if he were about to soar away. He never had a chance. The tendrils flung out at him like ropes, caught the jetglider in several different places, anchored to it, and dragged it closer while Hobgoblin fought to get away. Other tendrils sought out and swathed Hobgoblin's hands in steely bands, making the flinging of bombs or the activation of energy gauntlets impossible.

"For you," Venom said, "we have only one desire. Besides ridding the world of you, but we'll get to that shortly. We want to know about this creature which is running about the sewers and tunnels of this city, impersonating us and killing innocent people in our likeness. A simple enough business, it must have seemed to you. Distract attention from yourself by presenting what ill-informed people consider another so-called 'super villain' so you can continue your schemes uninterrupted. Meantime, blameless men and women are terrorized and killed. It's all just a game to you, of course. But now"—grinning, Venom pulled the jetglider closer, while its engine screamed in protest and useless resistance—"now the reckoning time has come. You've outdone yourself this time, Hobgoblin. You've created a creature sufficiently robust that even *we* have a difficult time subduing it. So you are going to tell us everything we need to know to destroy it. If you're quick, we will be fairly merciful, and we'll be no longer about eating your probably slightly rancid and tasteless brain than necessary. If you waste any more of our time, though, we will start by tearing your arms and legs off."

Spider-Man's first impulse was to let Venom go ahead, but there were more important matters to be dealt with. "Venom," he said, "wait a moment. I take it you've met up with your lookalike down here somewhere—"

"Met it—" A look of annoyance passed over the fanged face. The teeth gnashed as the symbiote expressed its partner's frustration. "We met, yes."

"You came away with your skin intact, but not your ego, I can see that. Listen to me! Good as Hobby here is at stuff like bombs, hasn't it occurred to you that what you ran into is, well, beyond his expertise?"

"This is difficult to say," Venom said, looking at Spider-Man with a slight glimmer of interest, "but we must confess we haven't exactly made a study of this thing's 'expertise.'"

"Then think about it," Spider-Man said. "I don't think what attacked you, what attacked me, has anything to do with him. It's not even from here."

Venom suddenly looked even more interested, a dismaying effect on that sinister face. "We take it you refer to an origin a lot further away than the Five Boroughs."

"It's not from Earth."

"Is this some project of yours that went astray?"

"I can't take credit for this one," Spider-Man said, shaking his head.

"Who then?"

"Look," Spider-Man said, "I can't discuss it now. But it's nothing to do with him. There's more important business of his to deal with at the moment."

"Yes," Venom said cheerfully enough. "Rending him limb from limb sounds like a good place to begin." The tendrils began to pull. Hobgoblin screamed.

"No!" Spider-Man launched himself at Venom, trying to web as many of those tentacles as he could, and pull them away from Hobgoblin. The tendrils, though, just kept welling out between the strands of web. "Venom, he's got a bomb down here somewhere, and we have no way to know how it's supposed to be set off! He may have some kind of dead-man switch hooked up to his lifesigns, or God only knows what else he's managed. But if you kill him now, there'll be no way we can be sure of how to deactivate the thing!"

Venom looked at Spider-Man, though the pressure on Hobgoblin did not appear to decrease, and Hobby's screams continued. "Believe me," Spider-Man said, "if we could stick him and his little tinkertoy bomb in the same garbage can, shove them off the planet together, and let them blow, do you think I wouldn't do it? But his finger is on the trigger of an A-bomb, and millions and millions of innocent lives are at stake!" Spider-Man came down hard on the word *innocent.* "This is not the time to go around eating people's brains!"

There came a sudden shriek of the jetglider's engines as they pushed the glider, not back, but forward. All the tension went out of the straining tentacles, and Venom, suddenly pulling against no resistance, fell backwards.

The screaming jetglider engines almost rammed Hobgoblin into the ceiling of the big room. He ducked barely in time, recovered, dove down low, and zoomed off past Venom again—then out through the hole Venom had made in the wall.

Venom staggered to his feet and stared, astonished and enraged. Then he whirled on Spider-Man. The tendrils reached out menacingly toward him, and Spidey got ready to web as many of them as necessary to keep them from closing around his throat, or doing any rending-limb-from-limb on *him*.

"This is the second time you have interfered in our vengeance against this wretched creature," Venom growled. "We should kill you now, but if we waste time with you, we're going to lose him. You may assume, therefore, that our next meeting will be our last."

"I'll save a spot for you on my dance card," Spider-Man said. "And whatever you do, if you want to save this city's life, don't give in to your little urges. You need Hobgoblin, alive and functioning, to disarm that bomb."

Venom threw him a furious look and swarmed out after the swiftly retreating whine of the jetglider.

Spider-Man hurried back up the wall and through the opening he had made, recovering his camera and packing it away. *Those flash bombs should have given it good light cues to go by,* he thought. *Hope they didn't fool the strobe into overexposing. We'll see.... But if there's any New York City left tomorrow morning, these are going to look brilliant in the afternoon edition.*

Meantime, Spider-Man had an idea. It might take some doing to set up. If it worked, though, the results could be excellent... and the main problem was to get the results *fast*. This was, as he had pointed out to Venom, a gamble, one for millions of lives. In this case, though, it was better to gamble than to do nothing.

Spider-Man plunged back toward the subway tunnels, the way he had come, in pursuit of the last best chance to save New York.

ELEVEN

THE next two hours moved with dreadful slowness and terrible speed.

Spider-Man knew he and his quarry were going to have to find their way back to the underground generator, so he took care to remember his route, marking it with spider-tracers. Several times, where numerous train lines crossed, his spider-sense warned him of an express coming up behind him, unheard because of the omnidirectional clatter and thunder of its brethren. Then he would leap to the ceiling, clinging to it while the metallic juggernaut shrieked and sparked as it passed, inches from his back. There was a certain grim humor in it. New York City might be about to end at five thirty in the morning, but until then, the subways would keep running.

The whole thing was a longshot, of course, but most of the creature's appearances seemed to be on the west side rather than the east. Perhaps the creature found the middle of the city too populous, too dangerous, too full of machinery and trouble. He was beginning to feel for it, in a way. Here it was, alone in a strange place, confused, frightened, alone. It was more analogous to a lost animal than anything else; it hadn't shown much evidence of high intelligence. Most likely on breaking out of the sub, it had headed straight for open water and had been borne southwards by the prevailing currents where the East River emptied into the harbor. Then eventually it had struck up the far side of the island, westward, coming to a sewage outfall or another entry into the tunnel system. From there it could easily have sought out or stumbled into one, then made its way further underground, where the ambient radiation was less.

As Spider-Man made his way through the tunnels, he again mulled over the creature's bizarre physiology, for exploiting that physiology was now his best chance. The creature was sensitive to very small amounts of radioactive material. Its reaction to the little canister of isotope he was carrying was evidence enough of that. It had sensed that clearly, even through a lead container. *And there,* he thought, *lie the possibilities.*

Spider-Man paused at the junction of two tunnels. Too many of these tunnels looked alike, the only differentiating characteristics being the graffiti on the walls, and sometimes the smell.

He pulled out another spider-tracer. Spider-Man had five or six more tracers left. He leapt up onto the ceiling and slapped this latest tracer there, where it gave off the usual tiny reassuring buzz to his spider-sense.

Spider-Man came down to the floor again, paused. *All right,* he thought. *This should be—what? About Seventh Avenue and Fiftieth. So, about four or five long blocks further west, a few more up. A good way to go yet.*

He started working his way westward again. He was into the utility tunnels again, something for which he was profoundly grateful—the noise of the trains got on his nerves. Still, there would be more interesting things to watch for in the next while. *What time is it?*

He checked his watch. *One forty-eight. Four hours… less! This is* not *great.* His mission depended on speed, and here he was crawling around in tunnels. Spider-Man desperately wanted to be up in the clear air, swinging on a webline, out where he could see where he was going. But you can't always get what you want. *But hopefully,* he thought with a small grin, *I'll get what I need.*

His mind started drifting as he trudged forward. *I had promised to get something for MJ,* he thought. *What was it?* He laughed ruefully as he ran upside down along the ceiling of a tunnel whose floor was littered with rubble. *Woolite, that was it. I promised I would bring some back.* Even down here, among all the dreadful smells, he was acutely aware that his costume needed washing again.

He stopped at a big intersection, looking around. *Aha,* he thought. Faintly he could hear train rumble again, possibly one of the Broadway lines. *We're in the neighborhood.*

He turned left, slapping another spider-tracer high on the wall, and continued. Another two hundred yards on, an archway opened before him, and he gazed through it into the tunnel where he fell unconscious before. He remembered some broken concrete rubble off to one side.

That's the ticket, he thought. *Now then!*

Spider-Man began retracing his steps with more certainty. These were the tunnels in which he had lost the creature. He followed the path of his escaping bounds and leaps, recognizing a splash of spray paint on a wall here, a dropped cigarette box there. Everything was surprisingly clear in his memory, despite his weary and battered state at that point. But he was feeling a little less battered now. Weary, yes, and he could do serious damage to a steak. Twenty hours of sleep would be nice, too.

Whether he was ever going to get any such things, of course, was another matter. But it was nice to think about, down here in the dark, amidst the stench, on the trail of something which could probably wad him up like a ball of paper and slamdunk him through the nearest wall.

That's an interesting question, he thought, as he made his way through the ever-more-familiar tunnels. *The creature's strength is all out of proportion to a normal life-form that size.* To determine the cause, of course, the creature itself would have to stand still for analysis, and if there was one thing Spider-Man had noticed, standing still was not high on its list of things to do.

Like a hummingbird, he thought. *It's got to eat all the time to keep going. Its intake of residual and background radiation must be very carefully balanced against its intake of harder, more concentrated sources of radiation. Too much of one or the other might have serious consequences.*

He reached one of the tunnels he had passed through before and stopped. Torn-up metal lay around in strips and shreds. He picked up one piece and fingered it thoughtfully. It reminded him of the metal of those canisters which had been stolen from CCRC. He lifted it to his face and sniffed, but caught nothing more than a vague chemical smell.

Something made a scratching sound not too far away. Spider-Man stopped, listening, and softly put the piece of metal down. *A rat?* he thought. But it was not a rat. It sounded like it might have been underneath. *Below me somewhere?*

Well, he thought. *Let's see. Spend a few minutes here: then if that doesn't work, I'll move a little further on, try again.* All the same, the thought of having to do this six or eight times frightened him. He had wasted enough precious minutes finding his way back here.

Spider-Man chopped the thought off. Slowly he reached to the canister webbed to his belt. There was no time to rig any protective gear for himself and there was no realistic way to calculate radiation dosage. And there was hardly time to go back to ESU to get a lead apron.

He unscrewed the canister. There inside it lay the little glass capsule, very innocuous-looking. Americium isotope wasn't something you could carry around in lumps; it was enough trouble making it in thousandths of a gram, and half the time you wound up cutting it with talc so you could work with it at all. No matter. No time to worry about it.

Slowly he held up the open canister—and stood there with it open, feeling his skin begin to itch.

Somewhere, below him, came a rustle. Then another.

It can't really make you itch, he reassured himself. Nonetheless, he swore he could feel the stuff burning through his hand. It was ridiculous. His hand was protected by the lead container. Radiation escaping from the end of the canister moved in a straight line. It did not go around corners; otherwise that concrete shield back at ESU would have been useless.

Spider-Man stood there in the darkness, waiting for the creature to hurry up and take the bait. He grew impatient, and muttered, "Oh, come on."

And to his surprise, his spider-sense began to tingle. He turned, looking for the source.

There was a stairway leading downwards, off to one side of the tunnel. Many tunnels had these. Spider-Man had been ignoring them, by and large, trying to stay on one level and not confuse himself too much. Now he saw something come wavering up that stairway. *A snake?* As far as he knew, the New York sewers and tunnels were not famous for snakes.

After that first one came wavering up another of the long, sinuous shapes: not a snake at all, but a long black tentacle. The rustling grew louder as more of those dark tentacles came whispering up out of the stairwell to the lower level. And behind them, the larger shape, dark, humanoid, bigger than a human—

For a moment Spider-Man's heart clenched, as he thought he was looking at Venom. *No, it's bigger than Venom!*

It paused near the top of the stairwell, holding the two sides of the opening with its arms, crouched down, staring at him with those pale patches of eyes. Slowly Spider-Man held up the little canister with the americium inside.

As fast as any number of cobras striking, the creature leaped at him. But Spider-Man was ready for it this time. He leapt faster and away.

On spider-agile feet and single-handedly, he went galloping along the ceiling of the tunnel, retracing his steps, heading for the nearest of his tracers. The creature rushed along after him, bumping, scattering the trash and the rubble, grasping at Spider-Man with its tentacles. Once or twice he felt the wind of one or another of them missing him from behind as it made a hurried grab at him, but fast moves, quick rushes on his part, and the warnings of his spider-sense kept him one jump ahead. Spider-Man began to feel like the snack cart at the college cafeteria, with a whole class of hungry undergrads after him.

He burst into a big chamber, ran right around the walls of it, and was about to turn into the hallway he had marked, when he noticed dark, crouched forms in it, staring at him in astonishment. *Oh, no,* he thought, *people!* Behind him he heard, once again, the bizarre soprano screech of the creature as it came up behind. It was not used to its food running away with such energy. It was taking exception.

I can't bring it there, he thought, and instead led it down a secondary tunnel that led to the train tracks. Here, at least, there wouldn't be too much trouble. It was the middle of the night, the trains were few and far between.

Fat chance, he thought with a gasp of a laugh as he dived out the door, over the third rail, and came down on the tracks running. He sprinted down to the platform, ignoring the almost-empty station, and out again. The creature galloped after him at full speed.

They ran on. Another platform came into view down a long straight run of track, and he could see the glaring lights of a train facing him head-on. No matter for the moment. This tunnel intersected with the one he had marked. He could feel the tracer not too far away.

Behind him there was a bump, followed by a splatter of brightness, a fizz of furious sparks, and a shower of light, as the creature touched the third rail. That soprano shriek went up again, angry this time.

Spider-Man glanced back. The creature was barely thirty yards behind him. *Didn't even slow it down,* he thought in wonder. He kept running. At the end of the tunnel, the glaring lights of the train began to move forward, and he heard the squeak of its wheels as it began to pick up speed.

Where is that opening? he thought. *It was down here, before the station—where is the thing?* Behind him he could hear gravel crunching as the creature closed in on him. Its scream rang out again, sounding frustrated and annoyed.

I've done a lot of interesting things in my career, thought Spider-Man, *but I've never yet played chicken with an A train. Where is that opening?* Then he saw it, about fifty yards ahead of him. He sprinted. So did the train. Behind him, the creature was gaining on the straightaway. Not close enough to get him with the tentacles as yet, but they were reaching, and the scream was getting closer. *Okay,* he thought, *just follow me on in here, don't let the nice train hit you, all right?*

Spider-Man dived sideways over the third rail, into the opening of the utility tunnel. His spider-sense told him that his tracer was no more than another thirty yards behind him, and the way to it seemed clear. He paused in the doorway, panting for breath, and turned for a moment—and then heard the scream of brakes as if the train's driver, no doubt used to placid after-midnight runs, suddenly noticed something unusual on the tracks and realized it might be better not to hit it.

The brakes' squeal went up together with the creature's screech—louder and louder as the two closed on one another. Spider-Man peered out from the doorway to see that the creature made no move to get out of the train's way. Perhaps it felt it didn't need to—anything that could knock over a Penn Central diesel had little to worry about from an IRT train. The IRT train, though, and the people on it, had plenty to worry about.

Spider-Man leapt out of the alcove with all the strength he could muster and kicked the creature out of the train's direct path. He used his webbing and the momentum of the kick to bring himself up from there to the ceiling in order to keep himself safe.

The train came to a shuddering halt. There was a long pause, but then the crunch of gravel resumed as the creature made itself thinner and oozed out from between the wall and the train. *Well, it's still alive,* Spider-Man thought. He began to retreat. As the creature pulled itself into the opening of the utility tunnel, neatly missing the third rail this time, Spider-Man turned and ran.

The path was a little more familiar. Spider-Man had the tracer to guide him. Left, then right, right again, left once more—and there was the tracer; he was back on known ground. The creature was right behind him, though. Once or twice he felt the quick swipe of wind on the back of his neck as those tentacles made a grab for him, and a different swipe of cold wind further down as it went for the belt, remembering that the isotopes had been there before. But both times it missed, and both times Spider-Man just raced on, not even pausing to look behind to see if it was catching up. *Satchel Paige would be proud of me.*

The utility tunnels grew quiet as they ran. *As quiet as it ever gets this time of night,* Spider-Man thought, *with the train traffic at its lowest.* The only really noticeable noises were the frustrated screeches of the creature behind. It was a pitiful sound, in its way, and if Spider-Man's breath had not been coming so hard he would have felt actively sorry for it. Not only alone, and the only one of its kind on this planet—if that meant anything to it—but hungry, and afraid it wouldn't get what it needed to survive. *Well, after it finds the bomb for me, it can have this,* Spider-Man thought.

He grinned under his mask as he ran. The shielding on an atomic bomb generally isn't much, so as not to interfere with its being easily transportable. *If my buddy here goes after a little americium like this, it should have no trouble finding Hobby's little Tinkertoy. And once we've found it, it can be disarmed. Even Hobby's scientists won't have bothered working up anything more sophisticated to attach to the stolen trigger device than you'd find in a good James Bond movie. Probably I could defuse it myself... though if there's time, I'd sooner call in the folks from the Atomic Energy Commission.*

His spider-sense kicked into overdrive, warning of another tentacle swiping at his ankle; he scooted out of its way. His breath was coming harder. *Can't slow down now.*

He passed another spider-tracer, encouraged. This one he remembered as the third one he had put down. He ran past it, leapt for the ceiling again, kept scurrying on. He threw a quick look over his shoulder, wished he hadn't, turned, and kept on going. *Can't run outta speed now. MJ'll be really upset if the city's blown up at five thirty.*

He was hyperventilating. *It's bigger too,* came a thought. And that was true—the creature was bigger than when he had last seen it. Not incredibly so, but enough to notice. The bit of isotope it had gotten when they met first—*Just that little dose,* Spider-Man thought. *A gram or two, no more. It grew from that. What a physiology!*

He dropped from the ceiling and scurried along the floor again, past the second tracer, the one he had left on the ceiling. *Real close,* Spider-Man thought. *Real close. Pretty soon now, it should stop homing on me, and home on—*

He turned a corner, ran down that last long hall, saw the light of the gratings ahead of him—

—and was knocked flat by the creature, who sprang at him. His spider-sense warned him, but the creature came too fast for him to capitalize on the warning in time. It felt exactly like being run over by a train: legs, arms, tentacles, the creature scrambled at Spider-Man, flung him to the side, and swarmed across him, to his absolute astonishment, completely ignoring both Spider-Man and the canister he carried.

Spider-Man levered himself up on his forearms and stared down the dim-lit tunnel at the creature. It was battering at the wall. It screamed that high unearthly scream one more time, and then arms and tentacles together fastened themselves onto the wall—and the concrete began to crumble. It didn't quite melt, though the stone did run; it didn't quite crumble, though dust sifted down. The whole big patch of concrete simply slumped in and away from the creature. Spider-Man had a sudden and irrational urge to hide his eyes, as if from an atomic blast. But if that thing were throwing hard radiation at the wall, no amount of eye-hiding would help him—he was toast, every cell of his body sleeted through with gamma rays of such intensity that he would simply come apart in a few days like wet tissue paper. But he felt not the slightest tinge of heat, and people getting lethal doses of gamma typically reported the feeling of a flash of heat.

The creature scrabbled at the wall, and the wall continued to give way in front of it. Spider-Man scrambled to his feet. The effect was occurring only where the creature actually touched the wall. *Not radiation,* he thought, *not as such. It's as if it were disorganizing the shells of the atoms of the wall on a local basis. Collapsing them?* Possibly. Maybe in an earlier time, this creature's kind had normally eaten this way. Fissiles didn't usually occur in pure form, but as very sparse ore. *Maybe this was how they got the good stuff out, and threw away what they didn't need. I guess anyone can get too much bulk in their diet.*

There was no way to tell. Bracing itself with some tentacles, the creature pulled away at the wall, and the concrete and the metal slumped and fell away until they were gone. The creature dived through into Hobgoblin's generator room.

Spider-Man went after it, impressed, but all the same careful not to touch the edges of the hole. The creature tore its way toward the middle of the big room, ignoring both the generator and the piled up crates and pallets, which was fortunate, considering that the goons Spider-Man had webbed up earlier were still stuck down there.

The creature screamed, louder than before. Up came the tentacles again, questing, wreathing around it. "Aha," Spider-Man said softly. "You know it's down here somewhere, don't you?"

The creature began scrabbling at the floor. The floor began to give. *Uh-oh,* Spider-Man thought, hurriedly shooting a webline at the ceiling, and got himself up off the floor before it did something sudden.

The floor beneath the creature crumbled. It looked like a bowl of damp brown sugar being stirred, everything settling inward and downward. A hole appeared, then a space ten feet or so wide fell away from beneath the creature. It dove through roaring, but this time the roar had an odd note in it, one which Spider-Man hadn't heard before. In a human being, it might have been triumph.

Well, let's not miss the fun, Spider-Man said to himself. He swung down on his webline to drop through that hole after the creature—but at a slight angle, so as not to come down right on top of it; he did not want to distract it at this of all moments.

He only had a second or two to take everything in, but there was quite a bit to take in. There was another chamber down here, about the same size as the one above. There had been a lot of equipment in it, big machines like the generator upstairs, a little mainframe computer, some smaller stand-alone PCs. But the phrase "had been" was germane in this case, because a great deal of the machinery lay in broken, shattered piles around the floor: busted circuit boards, smashed monitors, all kinds of plastic and metallic rubble.

Then Spider-Man saw the cause of the destruction: Venom and Hobgoblin. Off to one side, the symbiote had cornered Hobgoblin, who stood on a battered but still hovering jetglider, with one hand clenching a pumpkin bomb and the other something that looked like a cell phone but which Spider-Man suspected was the trigger for the bomb.

I've missed all the excitement, he thought ruefully. *There's been one heck of a fight here. But even Venom wasn't willing to take any more chances with blowing up the city. We're right into the Mexican standoff stage now.*

But now the equation had another element. The creature took only enough time to hit the ground and recover itself. Then all its tentacles and its head whipped around to face a metal box four feet tall and two feet wide that sat by itself in a corner.

The creature flew at it with another of those cries of both hunger and delight, a sound that Spider-Man thought he had only ever heard before from MJ when you took her into that really good Szechuan restaurant at Second and Sixty-Third. It also occurred to Spider-Man at this point—as the creature flung itself at the container of the bomb and began ripping it to shreds—that there was no way for anyone, least of all Hobgoblin, to stop the Interplanetary Gourmet from having what, under present circumstances, was probably the meal of a lifetime.

Hobgoblin stared at it. Venom stared at it too, but Hobby's look was one of much greater horror. At first, Spider-Man thought the bomb's case might have been booby-trapped, and this was about to be the last second of life for all of them. But then he realized Hobby's horror wasn't at the thought of being blown up, but that his bomb was being ignominiously noshed down like a corned beef sandwich at the Stage Deli.

"No!" Hobgoblin shrieked, "no, no, *no!*" and flew at the creature on his jetglider, pressing the button on his little box. Spider-Man stared in horror.

The creature, busy with the bomb, threw a great wad of wiring and circuitry at Hobby as he came. There was a small explosion which scattered almond-scented shrapnel all around. Warned by his spider-sense, Spider-Man threw himself to the ground—then slowly stood up again, to the sound of more ripping metal. Off to one side, Hobgoblin and his jetglider were on the ground, twisted metal and twisted man trying to disentangled themselves from each other. Spider-Man recognized the almond smell: *semtex,* he thought.

Meanwhile, the creature was still tearing at the bomb, and after a moment it came up with the only thing that mattered to it: a shape very like a giant cold capsule made of lead-coated steel, slit all open down one side.

Spider-Man blinked. One of the most annoying things about an A-bomb is the basic design, which even the most ill-educated terrorists and impecunious foreign governments have managed to duplicate. Any mass of plutonium over a certain size will blow up; it can't help it. The only way to delay this process is to divide the critical mass into two parts and only slam them together when you want the explosion to happen. The slamming is done by a shaped charge of high explosive, this being what had gone off—but, thanks to the creature's hurry to get at its meal, the explosion hadn't been properly confined, and had done nothing but blow out one end of the bomb's containment vessel. Out of this, the creature hooked out the hemisphere of plutonium that had been closest to the charge, and started eating—crooning with joy as it stuffed bite after bite of metallic plutonium-uranium alloy into its face.

Spider-Man was of two opinions whether or not to breathe, since plutonium is about the most toxic thing on the planet. But by this time the creature had put that whole first lump of fissile into its gut, and was hooking the other piece out of the lead and steel capsule. And he didn't feel any warning from his spider-sense.

"No!" Hobby screamed, staggering across the room toward the creature, "don't, you dumb—"

Spider-Man never found out how Hobby intended to describe the creature, for several tentacles promptly came out and backhanded Hobby halfway across the room again. The creature was oblivious: it took bite after bite out of the second dark, shining hemisphere. In a matter of seconds that too was gone.

"No!" Hobby moaned, struggling to his feet again, fumbling for something, anything, another pumpkin bomb perhaps. "You lousy little— you ruined my—I'll—"

"No, I don't think so," Spider-Man said calmly, and going over to Hobgoblin, he reared back and awarded him a roundhouse punch in the jaw that sent him flying as far as the creature's tentacle-whack had.

Hobby didn't move again. Spider-Man strolled over to him, took a good look to make sure he was breathing, saw that he was, then webbed him up and hung him from what remained of the ceiling. With that out of the way, he turned to see that the creature, finished eating, was now holding still. It had slumped into a tired-looking puddle of tentacles on the floor, bowed over, like someone overstuffed after a very good meal.

Spider-Man looked past it at Venom. The symbiote looked furious and a little ragged around the edges. The big eyes glared, though.

"How long did it take you to catch him?" Spider-Man said.

"We would estimate," said Venom, looking at the creature sprawled on the floor, "probably about the same time it took you to catch that. He led us a merry chase. He is rather too maneuverable when airborne."

"But he came back here at last," said Spider-Man.

"Oh yes. Home is where the heart is, they say." And Venom looked at the wrecked bomb. "His plan, we're sure, was to lead us as far from here as possible, then to return and wait for his ransom—or do something worse. Who knows what spite lurks in that black heart? We have no desire to."

The creature stirred a little at their feet, and moaned. "So," Venom said softly. "Now it only remains what to do with you."

"I think so, yeah," Spider-Man said, thinking, *I'm in no shape for this. But Venom is still a fugitive and a killer, and I've let this go too long as it is.* He began to edge sideways.

"This is the time, we think," Venom said, "for the settling of old debts. Once and for all, the scores tallied, the books closed, with one gross inequity resolved."

Venom's tendrils lanced out at Spider-Man. He webbed a couple of them as quickly as he could, struck a few aside with fists and feet, and leapt sideways as Venom leapt after.

From behind them both, the moaning sounded again. There was something more urgent about it this time, though, and even Venom stopped to look. "What?" he breathed.

Spider-Man followed Venom's gaze to the creature. Still slumped among its tentacles, which were now stirring and twitching feebly around it, the creature lay—but there was considerably more of it than there had been.

"It's bigger—" Venom said.

"It was bigger before," Spider-Man said. His spider-sense began to tingle. "It's worse now. I think we need to be a little worried about this—"

"Agreed," Venom said, and Spider-Man heard the alarm in his voice too.

The whole creature twitched, and, there was simply no other word for it, *surged.* It was as if its physical structure had suddenly become debatable. *Shell changes,* Spider-Man thought. *The atoms of its own structure suddenly in flux. Energy levels renegotiating themselves—shifting into new patterns—shorter-lived—less stable—*

It surged again. Suddenly it was twice as big as it had been. And another surge, like another breath, and it tripled in size. Venom stared.

And Spider-Man cried out, "Get down! *Get down!*"

He flung himself at Venom. The impetus of his tackle hurled them both to the floor just behind one of the big half-smashed pieces of machinery. *Hobby!* Spider-Man thought, but there was no time. The creature surged one last time—

—and *blew.*

TWELVE

HOW long the rumbling and roaring went on, he wasn't sure. Spider-Man had heard a fair number of explosions in his career, some of them at a safe distance, some from entirely too close up. This one unquestionably fell into the latter category. He wasn't entirely sure that he hadn't been unconscious for some seconds in the wake of the initial blast, and the ensuing commotion was so unbelievable that Spider-Man wasn't sure that his protesting brain hadn't simply gone on strike until the noise dropped to a level he could handle.

The problem, of course, was that above ground, an explosion had freedom to move through the air and dispel its force upward. Down here, confined on all sides, the experience was much like being inside a bomb's casing when the explosive detonated. Anything weak enough to be demolished *was* demolished. Anything with any ability to resist the explosion nonetheless had to do something with the huge energy imparted to it, and most of the surfaces in here gave it up as sound, resonating to destruction—ringing like terrible crumbling bells, the walls falling down as they shook themselves to pieces in the aftermath, their reinforcing metal rods letting off prolonged howls like giant guitar strings suffering from terminal feedback. It was a long while before the noise faded to the point where one was conscious of anything but wanting it to stop.

It was almost totally dark, then. Paradoxically, the only light came from a small source which had been attached to the bomb—probably a battery backup of some kind, Spider-Man thought. By the glow of a few red and white status lights, burning stubbornly over switches which no longer worked, Spider-Man levered himself up on his elbows and looked around. Not too far away, a dark form moved feebly again: Venom. Many of the symbiote's tendrils were caught in mid-extension by the blast, but most particularly by the noise. Sound was one of the symbiote's weak points, and now all those usually fearfully active tentacles lay pitifully flat and still on the floor, as if they had been through a wringer. Still, Venom's breathing seemed steady enough. He would recover.

Spidey looked behind him, then, and saw that Hobgoblin lay on the floor, moaning. *I'm glad I webbed his mouth up,* Spider-Man thought, sitting up with a groan and dusting himself off. *The last thing I could cope with now would be him going on about his stupid bomb.*

In the rubble, something else stirred: a quick rustle, quickly gone, and a squeaking noise. *Rats,* Spidey thought, and actually laughed. After what he had been dealing with until now, a rat or two was no big deal. *But I bet they're wondering what the heck happened to their quiet home.*

More subdued squeaking followed, and more sounds of movement, but closer. Spider-Man turned. "Venom," he said. "You okay?" *Though why I'm asking, I don't know. He'll be a lot easier to deal with in this state, anyhow.*

"Nnnnngh." The dark shape stirred, hunched itself slowly up into a sitting position. "We… are still in one piece. Figuratively speaking, that is…"

"Uh, good." The squeaking was getting louder. "Listen," Spider-Man said, "I think it might be a good idea if we took Hobgoblin and got out of here. I don't know what the structural damage is, but I'd hate to have a building fall down into this hole, now that this *is* a hole. That is, mo—Yikes!"

His spider-sense buzzed just as something was about to run across his leg. He jumped and slapped at it.

"Heel, boy!" he said, and started to scramble to his feet, but before he had a chance, something else ran across his leg, into his lap. He slapped at that too. Then another tried to attack.

He jumped away, guided by his spider-sense to a clear spot in the scattered rubble. The small dark things followed. They were not rats, he knew. No rat alive could jump like that—and even as Spider-Man leapt away, several of them leapt at him. They were small dark creatures—

—with tentacles! Twenty or thirty of them. Bipedal, but not very humanoid-looking as yet, as far as he could see them in the light from the former bomb's telltales. They were little things, maybe about the size of chihuahuas. Shining black, fanged, clawed, squeaking frenziedly—in a tinier, shriller version of their parent's soprano shriek—they went plunging and leaping after Spider-Man, hungry, wanting their first meal.

For a few seconds Spider-Man was lost in a basic and for him slightly ironic response: hatred of swarming things that came at you like bugs, biting, too numerous to stop. They were all over him now, biting, clinging with tentacles, ripping with claws, scrabbling at his midsection. There were only so many he could avoid in his fatigue, even with his spider-sense. The sound of Venom's laughter, still weak but slightly sinister, didn't help at all. Spider-Man jumped and danced and clawed them off, then started webbing them up as fast as he could. But still they kept coming. The floor seethed like an anthill with hungry alien life, newborn, wanting its first meal more than anything.

He jumped to what was left of one wall, but it was no refuge—they fastened themselves to him and clawed and bit all the harder, shrieking with hunger and frustration as he shook some off, webbed others and dropped them in a package, jumped again to another wall, was followed and bitten once more. *Well,* he thought frantically, *MJ did suggest that feeding it might be a dumb idea. After this I'll listen to her.*

Feeding it—oh my gosh!!

He stopped what he was doing and fumbled at his belt. The creatures there bit his hands and arms, protesting; others, encouraged by not being shaken off him, now concentrated there as well. Their little fangs and claws were like razors. He wanted to scream, but Spider-Man concentrated on getting the webbing loose from the canister still at his belt. Revolted at the feeling of them crawling over him, shrieking and biting anything they could reach, Spider-Man flung the canister as far out into the middle of the chamber, or what had been its middle, as he could.

There was a sort of depression in the floor there, a crater blown in the solid concrete by the creature when it detonated. The canister bounced into it. The little creatures stormed into the depression in a black wave, scrabbling, tearing at each other, completely hiding the canister now in a tumble and fury of little black bodies. Hundreds of tiny shrieks filled the air.

Spider-Man brushed off a last couple of confused baby aliens, possibly clinging to him because of residual radiation from when he had been holding the canister in the open position, and watched them fall toward their ravenous brethren. There was already less noise, and Spider-Man suspected it wasn't because they had gotten the canister open—which they had—but because some of them, desperate, had begun feeding on their brothers and sisters. *Probably some residual fissile material left over in their structure from their parent,* he thought. *It might not have managed to metabolize it all before it went blooey. Or who* knows *what?* He was reminded, slightly sadly, of the sight of some kinds of spider hatching out; an egg-case suddenly releasing hundreds of baby spiders no bigger than a pinhead, only a few of which survive—those fast enough to spin some silk and float away before their brothers and sisters have them for breakfast.

He swung down near the hole in the floor and sprayed a bowl-shape from his webbing, then shot a line of web down into the depression and pulled the halves of the canister up. The young aliens followed—those which hadn't already disappeared into their siblings' gullets. Spider-Man dropped the canister pieces into the middle of his webbed bowl, and the little creatures piled on top of it. When they were all in one place, he used more webbing to cover the bowl, turning it into a tight-woven bag that would hold them all in one place until he could get help.

That left one more problem. Spider-Man turned to face Venom.

Except that the symbiote wasn't there.

Spider-Man blinked. "Venom?"

There was no sign of him. Spider-Man looked around, but it was not in Venom's style to hide behind something, in circumstances like this, and then jump out without warning. He had a bit too much love of the open challenge, the threat that gave you time to realize what he planned to do with you. He was gone.

Well, he thought, *Brock and I will have our reckoning. Right now, I've got Hobby and a bunch of baby aliens I have to get off my back.*

He picked up the webbed-up Hobgoblin under one arm. Hobby immediately began making strangled noises of rage. "Oh, put a sock in it," Spider-Man said genially. "You're going for a nice trip to the country. People pay to do that in this weather, and you're going to get to do it for free. What're you complaining about? There's just no pleasing some people."

He then picked up the bag of aliens, threw it over his shoulder, and began making his way back up to the surface, feeling like a slightly retro and downmarket Santa Claus, one who comes up from the cellar rather than down through the chimney. Soon enough he found himself in one of the subway tunnels. There were, for once, no trains in sight. Spider-Man walked to the next platform, climbed up its steps, and went out past the token booth, waving at the astonished man who sat there. "Ho ho ho," Spider-Man said cheerfully, heading up the stairs and into the beginnings of dawn.

There was enough light on the streets for things to start being active, and sure enough, with no news to the contrary, New York had started about its business as if there were no bomb theoretically about to go off. Milk and laundry trucks were buzzing around, the traffic was beginning to build up, the morning papers already lay in bundles by the news stands, and were being stacked up on the counters. "THE BIG BANG!" shouted the *Bugle's* front page, with one of Peter's pictures of Hobgoblin, looking suitably insane and menacing, prominently displayed.

Spider-Man was pleased, and even more pleased by the present contents of his camera, which he had picked up on his way out—assuming the flash and the motion-control system had once more worked properly. *Can't assume, though,* he thought. *The circumstances were different, and with all those flash bombs going off.... Oh well.*

He dropped Hobby to the sidewalk and stopped by a pay phone. Hobby made angry but muffled complaints. "Well," Spider-Man said equably as he dialed 911, "if you wouldn't threaten to blow the city up, you wouldn't *get* dropped on your head. Now shut up. Hello? Oh."

Spider-Man found himself listening to the recording that you get when the 911 system is overloaded. *Probably half the city is calling the cops demanding to know what they're doing about the bomb. Or alternately,* he thought, and grinned, looking at a bank's digital clock down the street, *why the bomb hasn't gone off when it was supposed to.* It was quarter of six. He chuckled. Some people would complain about a hoax, and the distress it had caused them, how shameful it was, the city ought to *do* something... and on and on. It was true enough: there *was* no pleasing everybody.

"Nine one one, can I help you?" said a weary, inexpressibly bored voice.

"Yeah, this is Spider-Man—"

"Oh?" The cop on the other end sounded skeptical, but said nothing to refute him.

"Listen, I'm at the corner of"—he craned his neck to look at the street sign—"Eighth Avenue and Thirty-Third. I've got Hobgoblin here, all wrapped ready for pickup, and also a bunch of little alien critters that we're gonna have to do something with pretty quick—"

"Wait a minute, Spider-Man," said the cop, suddenly sounding a lot less skeptical. Then again, "I've got Hobgoblin" were probably the words they most wanted to hear right now. "Bernie? Hand me that sheet there, will you? Thanks. Right. Spider-Man, there's a mobile patrol from S.H.I.E.L.D. out looking for you at the moment. I'll call their beeper and give them your location. They should be there pretty fast. They've been working the west side for the past couple of hours."

"Hey, that's great."

"Meanwhile, Eighth and Thirty-Third? We'll send a wagon for Hobgoblin. What happened to his bomb?"

"It was delicious," Spider-Man said.

The cop sounded slightly dubious. "Does that mean it's defused?"

"Defused, destroyed, the fissile material inactivated. If you'll give me the number of the AEC people out on the street, I'll call them and give them the details."

"Right." More paper rustling. "Ready?" The cop rattled the number off.

"Got it," Spider-Man said. "Thanks. Hey, here comes the cavalry already." For down the street he could hear, faintly, the scream of sirens as the first of several police cars turned onto Eighth and roared toward him.

"We aim to please," said the cop on the other end. "Have a nice day." He hung up.

The police cars came howling to a stop all around Spider-Man, and cops piled out, looking delighted to see Spider-Man and to have their hands on the man who had held their city for ransom for the last twelve hours. The police officers who took custody of Hobby had numerous unkind names for him, but one big handsome dark lady simply shook her head and said, "Unrealistic."

"What do you mean?" Spidey asked, surprised.

"This boy," she said, looking at Hobgoblin as they manhandled him away and put him into the newly arrived high security van, "he has no grasp of the economic realities. With the city budget in the state it's in, where did he think we were going to get a billion dollars?"

"You mean," Spider-Man said, "the city wasn't going to pay?"

The police woman looked at him mildly. "What were they going to pay *with*? Now, I hear there were some pretty noisy phone calls from Gracie Mansion to Washington, at about three this morning. Oh, I guess they would have sorted something out in a while. But this boy"—she looked at the van's doors as they clanged shut—"he was just too greedy. A million, the city *would* have given him to get off their case, I bet. Even a hundred million if the feds or Trump or Stark or someone got involved. But a billion? No way." She sighed. "But I guess times change. Maybe a million dollars doesn't go as far as it used to."

Another van pulled up, this one more sleek and streamlined-looking than the police van, with the logo of the Strategic Hazard Intervention, Espionage, and Logistics Directorate, one of the country's premiere military intelligence organizations, painted on the side. Uniformed men stepped out, holding futuristic-looking scientific instruments and futuristic-looking guns, which they pointed at the web-bag lying on the sidewalk. The bag heaved and squirmed, and loud squeaks rose from it.

"We've been looking for you for most of the evening," said the S.H.I.E.L.D. team leader—a tall, dark, crewcut man who looked at the bag with polite interest—to Spider-Man. "Sorry we couldn't find you sooner."

"Who sent you?" Spider-Man said curiously.

"Navy Department," said the team leader. "They said they had lost an item and that you were looking for it on their behalf. This it?"

"More or less," Spider-Man said, and he took the team leader off to one side, explaining as much as he could about the creature without letting on that some of the information had come to him from the captain of the *Minneapolis*—no sense getting Captain LoBuono in any trouble. He put special emphasis on keeping the little critters away from any source of radiation. The team leader nodded when Spider-Man was done. "Fine."

"Okay," Spider-Man said. He watched the S.H.I.E.L.D. team seal the bag into a small containment vessel in their van and shut the van doors. "Give my best to Nick."

The team leader nodded, then went back to the van. It headed away more silently than the police van had. After a minute or two Spider-Man stood alone on the corner, being passed by incurious traffic, looking up at the sky. It was brightening to full blue now. Eastward, on the other side of this wall of skyscrapers, the sun was peering past Roosevelt

Island and up over Brooklyn. Morning, when there had been a strong possibility of there not being a morning, all very pleasant. Even the air smelled less smoggy than usual.

Spider-Man smiled to himself, raised an arm, and shot a line of webbing into the air. It fastened to the top corner of a handy building. He hauled himself up and swung around the corner, heading inward and uptown. He had to make one more stop—then he could go back home and hug MJ.

It was actually more than one stop, and something like three-quarters of an hour later, when he came in through the bedroom window and found MJ lounging in front of the TV, watching news coverage of the police van unloading Hobgoblin, to the delight of the assembled reporters, and Hobby's evident frustration (his webbing-gag was still in place). MJ jumped up and ran to him.

He hugged her hard, pulled off his mask, kissed her, kissed her some more, and then held her away a little. "Did you stay up all night?" he asked.

MJ looked at him as if he was out of his mind. "Could you have slept under these circumstances?"

Peter had to admit she had a point. "Any calls for me?"

"One," she said, with an odd look on her face, and went over to the VCR.

Peter looked at her with amazement, pulling off the top of his costume. "Since when do I get calls on the television?"

"Since this," MJ said, and hit the play button.

It seemed that MJ had been taping the news overnight, including the coverage of Hobgoblin's arrest. The first news that anyone had had of this appeared to have come with a phone call to 911.

"This is Venom," said a voice which Peter recognized all too well, while the news show displayed a file picture of him, with a banner over it saying "POLICE RECORDING—5:30 A.M." "We have just been involved with the capture of the criminal called Hobgoblin, who will shortly be delivered to the authorities, and the dismantling of the nuclear device with which he threatened the people of New York City. We have also participated in the destruction of the creature which has for a short time caused the people of this city to believe that we, Venom, were murdering its innocents." There was a pause, and then the voice became, to Peter's informed ear, tinged with just a bit of grim amusement. "Spider-Man, an equal participant in these matters, will be able to confirm to the authorities that it was this creature, and not ourself, Venom, who was responsible for the murders in question. In return for this service, and other favors recently rendered, we find it appropriate for the moment to leave New York to pursue other matters which require our immediate attention—of which, for the moment, Spider-Man is not one."

Peter sat there, looking slightly stunned. Then he yelled at the television, "Well, don't say 'thank you' or anything!"

MJ looked at him, and very, very softly, began to laugh. After a few seconds, Peter joined her.

"So," he said, "how *did* that audition go, anyhow?"

"Actually, they offered me the role—"

"That's great!"

"—but I turned it down."

Peter blinked. "What? Why?"

"Because, thanks to Hobgoblin, they were urgent to fly out to LA— immediately. I couldn't just leave when I wasn't even sure if you were okay or not."

Peter stared at her. She had been going on for ages about how she wanted nothing more than to work. Obviously, there was at least one thing she wanted more. He pulled her into a hug. "What did I do to deserve you?"

"You were just yourself," she whispered. She kissed him on the cheek, then broke the embrace. "Now tell me what's in the bag."

"Bag? Oh." He opened it, handed her the bottle. "Is the city having a run on Woolite, or something? I had to try three places."

She grinned. "You remembered! And you need it, tiger, you and that costume both. Get it off."

Peter unpacked the camera and the last few spider-tracers, and the change from the Woolite, all of which he left on the table. "Which of us you going to scrub first?" he said, heading down the hall after MJ.

Her nightgown hit him in the face as he came up even with the bathroom door. "Come find out," MJ said, playfully splashing hot water at him as she climbed into the tub.

Peter smiled and went after her.

THE VENOM FACTOR

Book Two

THE LIZARD SANCTION

Diane Duane

**For Joe Motes, Ruthanne Devlin,
and the many other nice people
associated with SeaTrek '89:**

with thanks for a happy trip to Miami and southward,
not forgotten yet—not by a long shot…

PROLOGUE

"NOW, just take a look at that," said a voice out of the predawn darkness. "Did you ever see a bug that big in your life?"

It was a fair question. Southern Florida was famous for a lot of things, but one that didn't get as much attention as the tourist attractions and the balmy climate was the insect life. There in the near-darkness, Airman Ron Moore stood gazing down at his feet and shook his head. He shifted the machine gun he was carrying from the crook of one arm to the other, eyeing the glossy brown-black palmetto bug that wandered past his shoes, waving its antennae in apparent nonchalance as it went about its business. It must have been at least four inches long from its head to the ends of its wing-cases.

"I don't know," Ron said as his friend Lyle came up from behind him. "I would have thought something this big would violate the square-cube law, huh, Lyle?"

"From the size of it," Lyle said, "I bet it could violate any law it liked, as far as bug laws go."

"No, I mean the law about how big critters can get without having backbones."

"Oh." Lyle breathed out, a small laughing sound in the night as the palmetto bug wandered off. "I'd say this one ought to get at least a ticket, then. A moving violation—walking while invertebrated." He peered at it as it trundled past him. "Or exceeding the federally mandated number of legs. Would that be a misdemeanor or a felony?"

"Bug misdemeanors," Ron said, sighing. "You need a reality transplant, you know that, Lyle?" He turned to look behind them at the one source of light besides the setting moon, a few days short of being full.

The moonlight glistened rough on the marshland all around them and the water close by, but the next best source of illumination was Launch Complex 39, a mile and a half east of them.

It was not lit up like a Christmas tree, as it would be in eleven days' time when STS-83 went up. With the budget as tight as it was these days, there was no point in leaving the lights on all night. Anyway, it upset the migrating birds, not to mention the local bats. With the Shuttle still just behind them in the Vehicle Assembly Building, pad 39-A itself was quiet, though not quite all in the dark: two of the forty big Xenon spots were on, trained down low on the Fixed Service Structure near ground level, and giving light to the people running final inspections on the huge north-side LOX tanks before they were filled in the next couple of days. That was not a job that Ron would have wanted, himself. Being that close to high explosives made him twitch.

Not that tonight's job was exactly the equivalent of being rocked to sleep, either. He glanced over at Lyle, who had turned away from his examination of the palmetto bug and was giving other matters his attention again.

"No sign of it yet," he said, shifting his gun again.

"Nope," Ron said. "I thought we would have seen it by now."

Lyle shook his head, scuffed his boots on the concrete a little, and whistled a few notes' brief imitation of the little peeper-frogs whose tiny voices filled the night. Ron had wondered whether Lyle knew something more about this cargo than he was letting on. That wouldn't have been out of the ordinary. Ron was Air Force; Lyle was NASA Security, and though in the strictly military pecking order he didn't count, Lyle could sometimes be counted on to know things that the military side wasn't told.

"Transport came in at two," Ron said. "Or so I was told."

Lyle nodded. Canaveral Air Force Base saw a fair amount of freight traffic, but little cargo came in so late unless it was somehow sensitive. Night flights attracted notice just by their relative scarcity. This one had come in with a jet escort: a pair of Phantoms, with all the hard points occupied and the safeties off the fighters' guns. The big C-130 transport had touched down on 12 Left, its escort sweeping by on either side as it decelerated, and then both jets had circled overhead, keeping watch until the Here got onto the taxiway and down to the apron, where the security detachment in their jeeps and trucks were waiting for it.

"Not late," Lyle said, "I don't think. They just wanted to make sure that everything was in order before they started moving things around."

"Things," Ron said softly. Lyle laughed again, and looked down the canal.

The big concrete apron on which they stood was somewhat better lit than 39-A, though, again, not overly bright, for the sake of the birds and bats, and so as not to attract attention in other ways. Right behind them, the VAB towered up, the flag and Bicentennial star on its upper reaches showing in pale and dark grays in the moonlight, its lower walls much brighter in the mercury lights shining down on the parking and haulage aprons. The apron on which Ron and Lyle stood was part of the main haulage and access area, right between the pool at the end of the barge canal and the VAB proper, and just in front of its east door. Ron and Lyle were only two of about forty USAF and NASA security people scattered around to secure the VAB perimeter, and the barge docking and loading area on the west side of the canal's terminal pool. There were other people there too, not uniformed—mission supervisors and scientists, mostly from Johnson, consulting various kinds of instruments, or else just standing, waiting, empty-handed, gazing out toward the water, down to where the other end of the canal met the Banana River.

Ron looked out too. Lyle said, "See that? On the left."

Very faint, far out on the dark water of the river that splits the Cape in two the long way, a little light moved like a red star. Shortly thereafter, a green one showed to its left. A breath or so later, a loud annoyed sound came floating up from the eastern end of the canal, like an aging comedienne going "Haaah, haaah, haaah" at someone's bad joke.

"Ducks," Lyle said. "There's a bunch of them nesting down there."

Ron raised his eyebrows. The wildlife around here had never paid much attention to the act of Congress that turned this scrubby, marshy coastline into Cape Canaveral. NASA, seeing no reason to be a bad neighbor, especially to endangered species, let them be most of the time—though at launch times most of the birds were encouraged by Air Force falconers to clear out for a day or so. They always came back without much fuss, though, and complained at passing traffic in the air and on the water as if they thought they owned it.

Now the barge coasted silently past the nesting sites in the reeds at the canal's far end, and the ducks got quiet again.

"There were a lot of guys sent out to do far-perimeter work earlier," Ron said. "Out by the public road."

Lyle nodded. "I heard about that. Guess the trouble they were expecting didn't materialize."

"Just as well," said Ron. "I guess the hour helped."

Lyle laughed softly. "More likely telling people that the thing wasn't coming in until next week helped, too."

They walked a few steps together, keeping one eye on the canal as they examined the flat bare area of concrete they had been told to police. Past them went a couple of NASA specialists, one in a lab coat with a radiometer, one in a T-shirt that said "The Dream is Alive," both wearing the proper new ID badges: Ron and Lyle nodded to them as they went.

"Interesting," Lyle said, "the way they changed the badges all of a sudden last week."

Ron nodded. Such things happened often enough, but rarely without a few weeks' warning, bureaucracy being what it was. This change, though— new badge format, new photos, holographic fingerprints embossed into the badges, new scanners with which to read both them and the wearer's hand—had been imposed on both sides, USAF and NASA, with no warning at all. "You get the feeling," Ron said, "that someone Upstairs was worried about—?" He wouldn't name any names, just pointed with his chin at the barge lights coming toward them from down the canal.

Lyle scuffed again, paused, looked up: they both turned and slowly started to pace back the way they had come. "Hard to tell," he said. "You hear a lot of scuttlebutt, you don't know what to make of half of it. Most of it's bull. All the same…" Lyle frowned. He was a big, heavy-featured man; in the dim reflected light from the VAB, his eyebrows and his cheekbones had more shadows than they usually did, making him look slightly sinister. "You've heard the news lately. I don't think it's the public protest that's bothering the higher-ups, so much—the people who've been marching out there aren't violent—"

"With this much explosive stuff around," Ron muttered, glancing back toward 39-A, "I wouldn't want to get violent, either."

"Well, no. But I think there may be more to it. We've been seeing a lot of the Coast Guard people lately—"

"So have we," Ron said. It was something he had been wondering about. "Normally they're busy further south."

Lyle nodded. "Something's up. Nothing really major, to judge by the signs, but all the same, cutters are popping up like mushrooms after a rainstorm, and people are acting pretty nervous. Were you told particularly not to listen to any excuses from people not wearing the proper ID?"

"Just run 'em in, the Boss told me," Ron said. They came down to the barge-landing dock again, and stood there, with several other USAF and NASA security people, now, watching the barge drift slowly down the canal toward them. Ron could hear the faintest *putt-putt-putt* noise emitting from it.

"And if trouble started, shoot first, ask questions later?"

Ron looked at Lyle just a little sidelong. These were not matters one normally discussed "in the clear." Their different services usually had slightly different approaches to such problems. But Ron nodded slowly. "Unusual," he said, very softly. "Normally they would want to wring someone out pretty conclusively, rather than..."

There was a small silence. "It suggests," Lyle said in as low a voice, "that the people who might be, shall we say, breaching security wouldn't be expected to know anything worth wringing out of them. Or, if they did, then whatever they're up to is likely to be so dangerous, the Folks Upstairs would rather they were shot out of hand—even at the cost of intelligence about what they were after."

Ron nodded. "Not nice," he said. "But you're right. There's an atmosphere as if people think someone is taking an unhealthy interest in things down here. Unusual." He shivered a little, an odd response on a warm night.

The *putt-putt-putt* was loud now, threatening to drown out, however briefly, the noise of the peepers. The barge was almost out of the canal and into the docking pool, its ghostly reflection preceding it in the water. Another brief ruffle of duck squawks, then quiet again as it passed the reed beds at the near end where the canal and the pool met.

The barge was one of the typical long, low ones that usually carried the Shuttle's pairs of reusable solid-fuel boosters to the VAB for mating. The boosters were flown into Canaveral Air Force Base from the contractor in Utah, then boated over and up, this being considered safer than subjecting them to the shocks of even brief overland travel. One side of the pool was flattened to take the barge side-on, and the dock there was reinforced to take the heavy unloading cranes necessary to lift the boosters off and truck them into the VAB.

The usual long cargo was missing from the barge's upper deck this time, but the barge still rode very low in the water. There were a couple of men on deck—one in a NASA windbreaker, another in USAF uniform. Dim red lights showed in the ship's cabin, and very dim white ones from the belowdecks hatchway.

There was no rush forward to warp the barge in. The guys with the instruments stepped forward and moved toward the barge as cautiously as if they expected it to blow up at any moment. Ron cocked an eye at Lyle. "I thought they said that this cargo was fairly routine."

Lyle looked at him. "Compared to what? I think these things can get awfully relative. And it strikes me that Upstairs has no problem giving us a little disinformation. They've done it before."

They watched the science team holding out their various instruments: things that might have been Geiger counters, one that looked more like a prop from a science fiction movie than anything else, and another one that looked like a fly-fishing pole. Lyle chuckled a little under his breath. "What're they gonna do," he muttered, "check it for trout?"

Ron smiled slightly. "Well, at least we've got past the bug jokes. Think we'll make it any further up the evolutionary ladder before our coffee break?"

One of the scientists looked up then. "Hey, Maddy," he said, "come take a look at this, would you?" Another of the team, one of the windbreaker-wearers, came over and put his head over the railings, looked in slight alarm at the barge.

There was a splash. All around the dock, heads snapped toward the water. Ron lifted his gun a bit higher.

On the barge, a figure came out of the wheelhouse, looked around. From behind the boat came the much louder and closer "Haaah, haaah, haaah" of another duck. The officer on the barge—its captain, Ron judged from the stripes on his windbreaker's sleeves—looked over at the ripples spreading in the water, then over at the people on the dock, and said, "One of you guys drop something?"

People on the dock muttered, peered, denied anything to do with the splash. The duck went on with its noisy protests for perhaps a minute or so; the barge's second officer came out of the wheelhouse as well, and the two of them looked around the boat, seeing nothing which might have caused the noise. The two scientists who had been conferring now looked over at the barge's officers.

"You about ready?" said the captain.

"In a moment, Cap'n," said the man with the "fishing pole." "Not quite sure why you should be spilling so much beta."

The duck started quacking again, a louder and more insistent noise. People on the dock laughed. "Sounds like you forgot to pay toll on the way up," one of them said.

The suggestion was greeted with chuckles from the barge crew. "Heaven forbid anybody on this run should be denied their proper overtime," the captain said. "Mike's got a sandwich—we'll take care of them on the way out."

More splashing ensued—and then a single much larger splash. The captain turned, looking out toward the pool.

The problem was not there. Something vaguely human-shaped, but much bigger, with an odd, slick sheen to its skin, was clambering up out of the water onto the dock. Ron, gazing at this, first thought that someone from the barge or the dock had fallen in—but that wasn't the case. Anyway, no one on the security team looked like that. No uniform—was that some kind of diving suit? It looked almost scaled. But since when did diving suits have tails?

That tail whipped fiercely from side to side as the creature clambered up onto the dock, glared around it. It braced itself then with its forelimbs, and with its hind legs and tail gave the barge a great push and sent it almost staggering back into the water, away from the dock. The barge wallowed and rocked, and big backwash ripples came rushing and splashing up onto the dock. The creature leapt off the dock then, splashed down into the water, and in two strokes and a leap, was clambering up onto the side of the barge.

Ron glanced at Lyle, who stood there understandably slack-jawed, and then at the others. All around, weapons were being leveled at the barge, but all the other security people were exchanging the same shocked, horrified looks. Their instructions had been clear enough. Use weapons as they must, but under no circumstances must the cargo be shot at: it was too delicate, or too dangerous, to risk a bullet. People had drawn their own conclusions from those instructions, some of them probably erroneous, but in any case no one wanted to be the first to fire—and certainly not without a clear target.

The barge captain had one, though, if no one else did. As the creature jumped back into the water after pushing the barge away, he was already drawing his gun. By the time the thing had climbed up the side of the barge and was putting its head up over the gunwale, the captain already had the gun leveled and took aim right between the thing's eyes. As calmly as anyone could have under such circumstances, the captain said, "Hold it right there, mister!"

The scaly creature paid no attention, but went straight for him—and the gun might as well not even have been there. A great inhuman noise, halfway between a roar and a snarl, was the only answer the captain got. He managed to get just one shot off. Where it went, there was no telling: judging by the whine of the ricochet, it missed. Barely a moment later, the creature was on him. Ron had one shocked sight of the captain's face, frozen in astonishment and horror, as he went down. The second officer came at the thing, but the great green scaled shape backhanded him to one side as if he was a rag doll.

Behind Ron, Lyle was indulging himself in a splendid flow of language which Ron really wished he'd heard while still in grade school, and lifted his gun to sight as the second officer went down.

"In this light?" Ron said softly. Lyle squinted down the length of the barrel, then let it drop, and let out one helpless breath that was more of a curse than anything he'd said out loud. Things were moving too fast: in this light, it would be too easy to hit one of their own by accident, never mind the cargo they weren't supposed to hit. Closer to the dock, two of the security men slung their guns over their shoulders, kicked their shoes off, and dove, two clean, fast splashes.

Over the quick, short, economical sounds of their strokes, came other sounds. The creature on the barge went thundering and thumping down the stairs from the deck into the barge's below-decks cargo space. A crash, as a door was burst open: a breath's space, and then semiautomatic fire— several short bursts. Lyle cursed again at the sound of an immense crash— then a moment's stillness. The people on the dock looked at each other in horrified surprise.

Then sound again: thrashing, bumping, shouts—"No, what are you—!" "Get away from that!" "No!!" Another crash. Another silence, longer. The men in the water swarmed up over the side of its barge by the access ladders at the bow and amidships.

From belowdecks came one last immense crack of sound, a splintering, breaking noise. The barge swayed, listed to its port, away from the dock. The security men began to unsling their weapons but had no time to do anything more. With dreadful speed, that big, lithe bipedal figure came swarming up out of the barge's cargo hold again. The first of the security men went at the thing, catching one outflung arm and pulling it back behind the creature, not bent, but straight—the first part of the old elbowbreaking move, usually a surefire crippler and guaranteed to give an assailant so much pain to deal with that there wouldn't be time or inclination for resistance. This creature, though, simply jerked its arm forward again. All the security man's strength couldn't stop it, and the creature flung him forward and right into the bulkhead, to lie beside the captain and second officer.

The second security man launched himself in a splendid front snap kick at the thing's knee that should have brought the creature crashing down. But the blow had no more effect than if he'd kicked a tree, and the creature merely grabbed him by the scruff in one huge clawed paw or hand, shook him, and threw him overboard.

Abruptly, from behind the creature, a third security guard, whom Ron hadn't seen, came up over the gunwales behind the creature. He leapt and took it right around the throat with one forearm and pulled back hard. Ron gulped, waiting to hear the crack. But there wasn't any. The creature bent itself convulsively forward, threw the hapless security guard over its back, and as he hit the deck and rolled, and even then tried to bring his gun to bear, it grabbed the gun from him and bludgeoned the man away with it—then threw the gun overboard after the last man.

The barge was listing further and further to port. The creature paused there, threw a look over its shoulder at the crowd on the dock. A clear shape, briefly isolated, everyone else down: it was the moment. Ron cocked his rifle and fired, then cocked and fired again. All around him, shots winged and whined through the air. There was the occasional shower of sparks, a ricochet from a bulkhead—someone's marksmanship going very awry: their bosses would have words with them later. That roar went up again. Then the creature leapt into the water. A mighty splash, and it was gone.

A hubbub and brangle of angry voices broke out in the dock area: orders were shouted, and more people jumped into the water, swam out with lines. The barge was reefed in, tied up. The scientists standing around with their "fishing poles" and Geiger counters put them down or dropped them, and hurried over to help.

Ron was one of the first aboard, Lyle close behind him. Others were already trying to help the captain and his second officer. Someone else was on the honker, calling for assistance. Away back on the dock, in the direction of the VAB, the stuttering red lights of the emergency vehicles could be seen approaching.

Ron and Lyle and others moved among the hurt men, helping them up where possible, making them comfortable when it wasn't. Others got down in the water and helped fish out the man who had been chucked overboard. He had come up for air, spluttering, not much the worse for wear, except for some nips from outraged ducks. The question everyone was asking him, and the captain and the first officer, was simply, "What was that?"

The captain sat against the bulkhead, still rather stunned, but clear enough that he knew what he'd seen. "I thought the dinosaurs were all extinct," he said. "That thing—it had big jaws, like a Gila monster's. Mean little eyes. It looked at me before it hit me. Something in it enjoyed what it was doing." He shook his head, moaned a little as one of the security men tried to straighten out his arm. "No, don't—it's busted. Wait for the EMTs."

Ron noticed again the way the boat was leaning in the water. Downstairs, other people were checking the cargo. One of them, a NASA security man named George, came up the stairs, and Ron said to him, "How is it down there?"

George shook his head. "Got a big hole in the side—she's taking water pretty quick. We need to get her unloaded and then up onto the ramp, before she swamps and sinks."

"I thought these couldn't sink," Ron said.

"They're not supposed to get holes punched in 'em like that, either," George said. He gestured with his head down the stairway. "Looks like our boy lost his temper pretty good down there."

One of the scientists down in the hold stuck his head up into the stairwell. "Milissa, you want to come down here and check me on something?"

A small handsome brunette woman came down the deck and went

downstairs to join him. A few minutes of bumping, grunting, and shifting noises ensued. Then Milissa could be heard saying, not loudly, but with great feeling, "Mist!"

Ron looked over at Lyle. "'Mist'?"

"Computer game of some kind, isn't it?" Lyle said.

"Not the way she said it."

Ron went over to where a couple of the other security people were still working with the captain. Milissa and George both came upstairs, then, and they both looked as grim as a month of rainy Sundays. "Harry," Milissa said to another of the scientists, "you'd better get on the horn to Ops *right* now. We have a big problem."

"Why? What? Didn't—" His eyes widened. "Oh, no—"

"The cargo manifest," Milissa said. "We went through it twice... and we're short one object down there. Just one."

"Not—"

"Item fourteen eighteen."

Harry went ashen, even in this light. "I'll call the front office," he said, and jumped off the barge, hit the dock, and kept on running.

The ambulance had pulled up now. Kurt, one of the night-shift EMTs, slipped past and knelt down beside the captain, and seemingly from nowhere, without asking questions, produced an inflatable splint for his arm. The captain, who had been following Milissa and George's conversation, looked paler than a broken arm alone would suggest—so much so that Kurt stopped to check his pulse a second time, halfway through the splinting. Ron looked at the captain and said, "Fourteen eighteen?"

"If we don't find it," the captain said, again too calmly for the circumstances, "we are all in for a very difficult... uh, rest of our lives, I would say." He sighed. "And here I was two months off retirement..."

"The minor payloads are all in place," a voice was saying to another figure coming rapidly up the dock. "However—"

"What's missing?"

"Fourteen eighteen."

Backlit by the yellow flashing light of the car that had brought him in, a lean tall dark-haired man stepped from the dock onto the deck, and took in everything in one long sweeping glance: the injured men, the pale, sweating scientists, the list of the barge.

"Evening, Dan," said the barge captain.

Dan looked down at him. The expression was cool, and not one Ron ever wanted turned on him. This man was the Cape's night Ops supervisor, widely believed to be capable of roasting even four-star USAF generals with a look and a choice word when they got in the way of the smooth running of what he considered his operation. "You look awful, Rick," he said. "Get your butt over to the hospital right now. Then I want a debrief. You, you, you—" he pointed at Milissa and George and the head of the USAF security team "—I want a debrief in five minutes. Mike—" this to another of the NASA security people "—get onto the CG and have them get a cutter and the Harbor Patrol out. I want divers down, and I want the Banana River exit sealed and netted. Where did whoever that was go?"

"Down... but it didn't come up, sir."

"Diving gear?"

"No evidence of any."

"Doesn't prove a thing. If they move fast, they may still have time to catch it. Go."

The security man to whom Dan had been speaking went off in a hurry. Another one whispered, not meaning to be heard, "And what if we can't find it?"

Dan turned slowly and looked at him—a look that could have been sliced, curled, and dropped into the bottom of a martini. "I hear Outer Mongolia is very nice this time of year," he said.

As if on cue, several people jumped into the water behind him. Ron hefted his gun. "Boss," he said to Lieutenant Rice, the senior USAF security officer who had just climbed onto the barge, "I got a clean shot at that thing. I *know* I hit it. It wasn't just some guy in a Kevlar bodysuit."

"No," the lieutenant said. "That much at least is plain. Not that it's going to make any difference to our careers." He sighed. "Come on— let's help them shift that cargo out of there before this boat goes down. Then—" He flicked a glance back at Pad 39-A.

"Will it go anyway?"

"Oh, it'll go," Lieutenant Rice said. "Question is... will we."

Ron gulped and went below to help move cargo.

ONE

SPIDER-MAN swung across the rooftops of Manhattan. The summer sun shone down on New York City, reflecting off the buildings like rows of skyscraping jewelry. Today, he barely noticed. Web-swinging, which was often a release and a joy for him, one of the things that made being Spider-Man so much fun, held no allure even on this bright, sunny day. Ever since Mary Jane went away, he frankly hadn't had much taste for anything.

He stopped that train of thought and chucked it out, pretending to drop it to the pavement dozens of yards below. It wasn't like she was going to be gone forever.

She had turned to him one morning a couple of weeks ago, after the business with Venom and the Hobgoblin had had ten days or so to settle, and she'd said cheerfully, and in the kindest possible way, "Sweetie, I need a rest from your life."

"Excuse me?" Peter had said.

She'd touched his cheek, then. "I didn't mean to make it sound that permanent. Look, Tiger... I just need a break. I got a card from Aunt Anna last week. She said, 'Why don't you come down and see me next week?' And, well, why don't I? I've been telling her for the past three years that I would come down to Miami as soon as work permitted. And things have gotten busy..."

"Yeah," Peter said, "I know, I've been meaning to find a way for us to get down there."

"So, look," MJ said, "the time for this trip isn't going to just happen. That doesn't even happen in normal people's lives, let alone ours. I think I need to make the time. I think I need to go see her... if only to get her off my case.

The tone of that last card was edging just a little bit toward sharp. So I'm going to head on down. I'm not going to hurry. I'll take the train. I haven't taken the train for a long time—it's a lot better now, they say, than it used to be."

"I don't know, MJ," Peter said. "Trains get derailed. They get delayed. And besides, the plane's cheaper…"

"It's cheaper because they get rid of you in two hours," MJ said. "Whereas this takes you overnight."

"But people get killed on trains—"

"Only in novels," MJ said firmly. "And only on classy trains. I am sure no one ever got assassinated on an Amtrak train. The atmosphere'd be completely wrong. You," she said, winding her arms around his neck, "just don't want me to go anywhere without you."

"That's absolutely right," Peter admitted, shamefaced, and hugged her. "Am I that transparent?"

She smiled at him gently. "You'd make a great window," she said. "You missed your calling. Except that somebody has to be Spider-Man."

He chuckled.

"You just don't want me to leave."

Several minutes later, when he came up for air, Peter said, "No, I don't. Ever."

She looked at him sidewise. "It's going to get crowded in the bathroom."

"You know what I mean."

"Yes," she said, "but do you know what I mean? Peter—" She hugged him again. "To let the other person breathe, sometimes you have to let go just a little. I know it's an act of faith. But do you seriously think that if you let go just a little, I wouldn't come back?"

"Well, no—but—"

"Then relax." She smiled at him. "I'll miss you too. A lot. I just need—" She shrugged. "Call it a vacation in the normal world. Where super heroes and super villains are something you hear about on the news but don't see much of."

"You're sure it's just two weeks?" Peter said, pulling MJ close again.

She smiled, and hugged him. "For a hero," she said, "you can be such a weenie sometimes. Anyway, there's something else that needs doing. I've got to see about scaring up some work. There simply doesn't seem to be any film or TV work for me in this town lately."

"I noticed," Peter said. She was being a lot kinder about this statement than she had to be. MJ had had to walk out on her last near-commitment on discovering that New York was apparently about to be blown up, and Spider-Man was apparently going to be stuck in the middle of it. It still astounded Peter, in those dark moments he sometimes experienced in the middle of the night, that MJ had not taken the offer which the producers of that show had made her, and immediately flown out to Los Angeles with them. He wouldn't have blamed her. In retrospect, on that particular night—with Hobgoblin preparing to nuke Manhattan if he wasn't paid a staggering ransom—Peter actually would have preferred knowing MJ was on her way to somewhere relatively safe. But she had her own priorities. Since then, though, either because word of her bolting from a successful audition had gotten around, or just from good old-fashioned bad luck, there had been no more TV work for her anywhere.

"Seriously though, hon," MJ said. "We've got enough money to last us a little while, but not that long. Right now I don't see anything happening at the *Bugle* that'll allow you to raise your prices significantly. Do you?"

"Well," Peter said, "no. There are only about thirty other people jockeying for the same work I'm trying to get. Some of them are better photographers than I am..."

"You have something marketable," MJ said. "You have a gift for getting good shots of super heroes... and super villains. No one else seems to have quite the knack for it that you have." Her eyes glinted at him. "But there's only so far you can make that stretch. Listen—I've been taking a look to see where the modeling market has been moving lately. And all of a sudden there's a lot of action in the Miami area. A lot of modeling agencies, PR agencies, and so forth are beginning to concentrate down there. They like the tropical ambiance: the weather's dependable, and it's a good place to shoot. And they like the fact that all those other agencies are gathering down there: everybody's scratching everybody else's back, and they can all do a lot of business. I think it might be very smart if I saw about scaring up some modeling work. It won't be expensive: Aunt Anna will put me up as long as I want to stay."

Peter nodded. "Just two weeks?"

"Well, it takes time to get known in an area, check out all the possibilities. And what if I find work?"

"Stay there," Peter said, immediately and with energy. "Work. Make millions of dollars. Be that way. I'll come down there and be your kept man."

MJ smiled at him. "And they say chivalry is dead. Now, you know I'd rather stay here with you! But if someone has to go out and bring home the bacon…" She shrugged. "No point in me sitting around here with my feet up waiting for something to happen."

"It's disgusting," Peter said. "When I win the lottery, I will keep you for the rest of your life in sinful luxury. You will lie in bed on silk sheets all day and eat chocolates."

"None of this Godiva junk, either," MJ said. "Teuscher or nothing."

"And you'll never have to lift another finger—"

"Boooring!" she said. "But anyway, I know the agency can find someone to place me with down there—just enough to keep me going while I case the joint. And if I hit something larger—say, a steady contract—it'll pay back more than the costs of the trip."

Peter sat down and sighed. "I guess we have to, don't we?"

MJ sat down by him. "Yes. That's life at the moment, Tiger. But it'll sort itself out eventually. You wait and see. Meanwhile… Florida."

And so it had come to pass. He had put her on the train, Am-trak indeed, though from Penn Station rather than Grand Central. MJ had been disgusted at that. "Romance is dead," she said. "There is no romance in going anywhere from Penn!" But she had climbed on readily enough, ensconcing herself in the unassigned seat on which she had insisted when Peter started making noises about the price of the train ticket. She had waved good-bye as the train pulled out, and dabbed at one eye expressively as she went, making a sad-happy mouth as the train pulled off down the track.

For the first couple of days, there was no mistaking it: he moped around. He went out and had a pizza, and it tasted like paste. Life just wasn't the same without her there—or, rather, without her available to be there; knowing that even if she wasn't across the table at the moment, she would be later that evening. The next day was about the same. He couldn't bring himself to go out: he puttered around the apartment developing some contact sheets, reveling (however briefly) in the knowledge that he could use the bathroom as a darkroom without having to clear curlers off the counter, and knowing that MJ wouldn't come barging in despite the fact that he had put the Red Light sign up outside. But none of the contacts looked any good when he processed them.

This is silly, he had thought. *I was a bachelor for years. Did just fine on my own. Why is this so difficult?*

The next day, though, at seven-thirty in the morning, the phone rang. He wasn't able to get to it before the machine went off. By the time he came staggering out of the bedroom, rubbing his eyes and lurching into the living room, all he heard was a few words in Kate Cushing's voice: "… here pronto. Bye."

His editor at the *Daily Bugle* rarely called him herself: usually her assistant did it. Peter hurriedly wound the message back and replayed it.

The machine beeped, then said: "Parker, Kate Cushing. I've got a work opportunity for you up here today. I'd appreciate it if you'd present yourself about nine, or if you can't make it here by then, just get up here pronto. Bye."

After wrestling with the shower and clambering into his Spidey suit, he leaped across the rooftops and swung along weblines at about eight-thirty, wondering what was quite so urgent. Kate had told him that it would be all right for him to have a couple of weeks off, after that stupendous set of pictures he had brought her of Venom and the Hobgoblin.

He sighed. It seemed about five minutes ago, some ways. He had had an interesting couple of days last month when first Venom and then Hobby had shown up in New York, with (literally) explosive results. It hadn't actually been Venom, at first, but someone who looked like him… and killed, not what Venom would have considered the deserving guilty, but the uninvolved innocent. Venom himself had turned up on the scene fairly quickly, certain that someone was impersonating him, and determined to stop it. It still amused Peter, in a crooked way, that Venom had been concerned about having his reputation ruined. As Spider-Man, Peter naturally had to try to deal with Venom when he showed up: the man/symbiote team was a criminal by everybody else's lights, if not by Venom's own. And then, on top of that, Hobgoblin had shown up, first getting involved in a few odd thefts, and finally presenting the city with a nasty *fait accompli* hidden under its streets: a small nuclear weapon, but plenty big enough to leave a glass-lined crater where Manhattan had been. He had attempted to hold the city hostage, and a most peculiar set of circumstances had stopped it: a not-very-holy alliance between Spider-Man and Venom, and the intervention of a bizarre extraterrestrial creature—the very same being that had been misidentified as Venom—that had gotten loose in New York and considered radioactives, even a nuclear bomb, to be tasty dinner fare.

When that dust settled, Peter had presented himself at the *Bugle*—rather sore and the worse for wear—with a spectacular set of photos of the final battle royal involving Spider-Man, Hobby, Venom, and the eater of fissionables. Kate had been very impressed and had noticed Peter's very worn-out condition and told him to get lost for a little while. *I wonder why she wants me found so soon?* he thought. *But I'll find out soon enough....*

He came to a graceful landing on the roof of the *Bugle* building, right behind the huge sign that declared the identity of both edifice and newspaper to the city at large. A quick, long-practiced change of clothes, a trip down the stairs from the roof access, and he was in the City Room.

That room was in its usual stir and roil of activity, heading for the deadline for the mid-afternoon edition. Peter made his way through the many lined-up desks of editorial. The air was full of the earnest miniature-machine-gun sound of many people all pounding frantically at their keyboards. Only a few heads looked up, and only a person or two waved, as Peter went by.

He made for the rear wall, where the glassed-in offices were, Kate's among them. Coming to her door, Peter checked his watch: just nine-oh-five. *Not too bad,* he thought.

From inside the office, a hand reached into the Venetian blinds covering the window, pulled them down: eyes peered out at him, and then the hand let the blinds spring up again. The door opened, and a voice from inside said, "On time for a change. Come in, sit down."

Peter did so, perching himself on her sofa in an alert edge-of-the-cushion position: one good way to get yelled at in Kate's office was to sprawl, especially as there was nowhere much to sprawl in—the sofa, along with every other flat surface, tended to be covered with books and papers and photos and all other kinds of whatnot. Kate went back to her desk, and started (or, Peter thought, resumed) pacing back and forth behind it as she talked. This mannerism Peter knew well: almost everybody associated with J. Jonah Jameson seemed to pick it up sooner or later, so that an editorial meeting at the *Bugle* looked very much like feeding time in the lion cage (and with JJJ there, it tended to sound like one as well).

"I can't do it, Jim," she said to the speakerphone. "You know I can't. Certain parties will have my head on a plate."

"Not my problem," said Jim, whoever he was, on the other end of the conversation. "You're just going to have to cope."

Kate muttered something incomprehensible, chewed her lip for a moment. "All right. On your head be it. But unless you get the goods, I am *not* going to reimburse. And until you get the goods, I'm going to assume this is some sleazy scam to get more time on the beach at La Croisette."

"Aww, Kate…"

"Don't aww-Kate me. Get out there and ask him when he's running for President. And get an answer, you hear me?" She punched the hang-up button on the speakerphone forcefully, then sat down behind her desk and started rummaging for something. "This is a nuisance," she said. "That's the man I was going to send to Florida with you."

"What?"

"You *are* free to go to Florida?"

"Uhh," Peter said, flabbergasted. "For how long?"

"Till the story breaks," Kate said. "Knowing you, it shouldn't take forever: I'm sending you partly as a good-luck charm this time."

"What's the story?"

She came up with her address book, started paging through it. "The Space Shuttle *Endeavour* goes up week after next," she said.

"That's good news," Peter said—he had forgotten about the semi-impending launch in his post-MJ malaise—"but why send a reporter to cover it? Or a photographer, for that matter? The local stringers have been good enough in the past. And the NASA publicity staff have some of the best photographers around—"

She waved at him in annoyance. "I don't want pretty pillar-of-fire pictures, Peter. Do you know Vreni Byrne?"

"No."

"She's a stringer who came over from the *Chicago Tribune* a few weeks back," Kate said. "She was doing overseas work, mostly… wants to do some at home now. Investigative, by preference. She's good, doesn't need her hand held. Now—" Kate chewed her lip, that nervous mannerism again. "Some of the local press down in the Miami area, down near the Space Coast, have been reporting some odd things going on around

Canaveral. Nothing huge, nothing obvious or definite, but all the same… Security down there has been a *lot* tighter than usual. The press officers at KSC haven't been as forthcoming as they usually are. There've been these funny reports of sudden changes of ID, people being ferried in and out of Canaveral AFB, all very hush-hush. And at the same time, there've been some disappearances down that way. Not the usual missing-persons stuff, but people who are characterized as being otherwise very stable, very dependable—just gone. And some odd thefts and attempted thefts, all in the same general area, about a hundred miles across." She shrugged. "I don't know that there's a connection, but when things like this start happening in a physical location so close to each other, it just makes me wonder. Anyway, the sudden boost in security down there is reason enough to be interested, especially since no one's even attempting any explanations. Usually they tell you flat out that something classified is going on: NASA does enough missions for the military, after all, putting up spy satellites and so forth. This mission is innocent enough, at least on paper: they're putting up some new power equipment for the space station, doing some experiments on bees…" She shook her head. "It's all sort of odd. I want it looked into."

Peter raised his eyebrows. "Are they letting people in as usual? Tours and so forth?"

"Yes. Naturally I'll want some fresh pictures. No, I don't expect you to try to get into any place that's restricted—I don't want the paper's credentials pulled just on a hunch. But I do want you to get out and about with Vreni—mooch around the rest of the Space Coast area that's being affected by these thefts and disappearances.

"You're good at catching the unexpected stuff, the slightly cockeyed angle…"

"So we're going to be staying in the Miami area?"

Kate nodded.

Peter's heart leaped then. "Uh, well, yeah! And until the story breaks…"

"This one may take some rooting around," Kate said. "Vreni is not a fast worker, but she's thorough, and I'm reluctant to hurry her. She will drag you all over the countryside, though: be ready for that. We'll give you a travel stipend before you go, and you'll pull company credit cards for this run. Don't go overboard, either," she said, looking sharply at Peter. "I've been catching merry hell from Himself over abuse of cards." Peter smiled at the reference to JJJ. The publisher had always considered company credit cards to be little more than an excuse for reporters to take money right out of his pocket. "And why shouldn't I," Kate continued, "with Jim suddenly announcing that he's the only one Arnie wants to talk to at Cannes? So I have to put up with his shenanigans, and the damned hyperinflated hotel bills—" She caught herself, and sighed. "Never mind. I'll put up with yours as well, to a point."

Peter grinned.

"Oh, I neglected to mention," Kate said then, with a small smile. "An old friend of yours has been spotted down that way…"

"Yeah, I know," Peter said, grinning sheepishly. "She's visiting her aunt—"

Kate looked at him cockeyed. "'She'? He's had a sex change?"

"Sorry? Who'd you mean?"

"The Lizard."

Peter's mouth dropped open. He closed it again.

"Since you've consistently gotten the best pictures of him," Kate said, "it occurred to me that you would be good for this job. To Robbie, too, for that matter—in fact, he specifically recommended you."

Peter smiled. A recommendation from Joe "Robbie" Robertson, the editor in chief, was always welcome.

"And of course for the other reasons as well," Kate said with a lopsided grin.

Peter blinked and started running over the conversation in his mind, wondering which reasons she meant, exactly.

"The sex change is just a rumor, then?"

"Oh! Yeah, it is, sorry," Peter said hurriedly.

"You and MJ haven't had some kind of falling-out, have you?"

"No! No, it's just a family visit. She planned to be down there for just a couple of weeks."

Kate looked at him for a moment. "If necessary," she said, "when your card bill comes in, I will overlook a few nights' worth of extra meals and, shall we say, double accommodation."

Peter actually blushed. "Kate—thanks."

She waved him away. "I was young once, too, but it was hard to get any work done then with the damn dinosaurs all over the place. Just make sure you bring back the goods. Meanwhile, Vreni'll be along in an hour or so. Come back here around quarter of eleven and I should have finished talking to her."

"Right. Thanks, Kate!"

Peter went out, wondering.

He headed across the street to the little Stadium Deli across the way, got himself a coffee and a cheese Danish, and sat down at one of the Formica-topped tables in the back, half listening to Julio, the deli's owner, singing something low and mournful in Spanish. The rest of his thoughts were elsewhere, well back in the past.

How many years had it been, now, since that trip to Florida with JJJ? It was only a little while after he became Spider-Man. He shook his head, sipping the coffee and grimacing. It seemed like forever since the tragic saurian shape of the Lizard had first burst across the path of his life, and Spider-Man's. It had unfolded into yet another of those stories which seemed all too common in the world these days. A scientist named Dr. Curtis Connors, hardworking, dedicated, brilliant—maybe too brilliant for his own good—wandered down an avenue of research that would soon enough prove deadly for him. Having lost an arm during a tour in the Armed Forces, he had experimented with a method of regenerating the arm in much the same way a reptile could grow a new limb.

But this particular experiment, which might have been innocuous enough, went terribly wrong. It had left Connors saddled with a new kind of glandular dysfunction that the world had never seen before, one which, at unpredictable intervals, twisted his body backward down the evolutionary scale into a dreadful and untoward mixture of reptile and man, a bipedal saurian of astonishing strength, speed, and size, locked into a mental state of uncontrollable rage. The change came and went with little warning and could not be put off or cut short, turning a brilliant man into a crazed monster. What this did to his family life… Peter shuddered.

Sometimes he liked to complain to himself or to MJ about their problems. Their life together wasn't always easy: being a super hero's wife was no picnic, Peter knew. He rubbed his ribs absently; they were just now reknit after the last time Venom had cracked them. But whatever other problems they had, MJ did not have to worry that Peter would turn into a giant lizard without warning and tear up everything in sight.

Curt Connors's wife and children did, though. His wife Martha had been married to an intelligent and sensitive man, a leader in his field of biology in a quiet sort of way. Now she found herself having to try to hold the family together when Curt quit his day job, couldn't hold or find another, and tended to vanish for prolonged periods, driven by his curse, or his attempts to find ways to cure it. Peter knew, too, Curt's own fear that in one of his rages he might hurt the family he loved. Connors had taken to vanishing for longer and longer periods, driven as much by that fear as by the monster.

Both as himself and as Spider-Man, Peter had met the family on various occasions, and had forged a kind of friendship with them. It wasn't entirely pity. He knew that Curt Connors was no evildoer, no criminal by choice: he knew that the things the Lizard did weren't Curt's fault, that the Lizard was manipulable, terribly vulnerable for all his rage and strength. True criminals and villains were all too willing to make use of so blunt but effective a tool, if it should chance to fall into their hands. Curt's shame at being so used was one of the things that kept him away from his family and drove him so relentlessly to find a cure… not that the problem itself wasn't reason enough.

Peter kept in touch with the family every now and then to see how things were, checking to see whether they had heard from Curt, and how they were doing in general. It was about all he could do for them. Curt's wife was too proud to accept any other kind of help, even from the most well-meaning of their friends.

He checked his watch and sighed. It was pushing ten-thirty. Surprising how fast time could go when you were musing over something like this, but Peter felt very sorry for Curt. His own bizarre accident with the radioactive spider, so long ago, had at least left him with abilities he could control and master. Curt had not been so fortunate, and Peter was determined to do anything he could to help him.

"Hey, Mister Peter, you look sad today! Whatsamatter, is the coffee no good?"

Peter looked up. It was Julio, who ran the place: a big, friendly, florid, dark-skinned, mustached man, making his way down the Formica tables and wiping them off as he went along.

"Nah, just thinking, Julio," Peter said.

"Aah, too much of that's bad for you," Julio said. "Sours your stomach."

Peter smiled and kept to himself the thought that Julio's coffee was more likely to take care of that job. It wasn't very good as a rule, and it was amazing that he sold so much of it in a city full of coffee freaks; but at the same time there was so much caffeine in it that it could practically raise the dead, and the hacks at the *Bugle* prized it above gold when they were fighting a deadline. "Yeah," Peter said, "I'll watch out for that. Hey, Julio, I'm going to Florida."

"That's great, Pete! You go down there, you make sure you get some of that Cuban food. Better than up here; you can't get the good plantain here. You get yourself a nice fried steak, and some Cuban sandwiches, and…"

"Julio, if I start eating all this stuff, they're going to need a forklift to move me when I get back."

"If you don't eat good food when you get a chance," Julio said severely, "God will be mad at you."

"If I don't get back to the *Bugle*," Peter said, checking his watch and getting up, "Kate will be mad at me. Almost as bad. See you later, Julio!"

On the sixth floor, there was noise coming out of Kate's office when he paused outside it. A female voice, very pleasant but raised in what sounded like extreme annoyance, said something he couldn't make out, and was answered much more quietly. He knew that tone: Kate's "no nonsense" voice. Peter lifted his hand to knock: the door was pulled open, so that the knock never fell. "There you are," Kate said. "What kept you? Come on in."

He stepped in and Kate said, "Vreni Byrne—Peter Parker. Peter—Vreni."

The woman who got up from Kate's couch to shake his hand was a petite blonde in jeans and a silk shirt, no makeup, no jewelry… and possibly one of the most stunning women he had ever seen. It was difficult not to gape at her. "Uh, hi!" Peter said, trying to get his thought processes back in order. "You were with the *Chicago Trib,* weren't you?"

She nodded, pleased. "That's right. And I've seen your stuff here and there. Not bad at all. We should do all right together."

There was something about the way she said this that suddenly made it plain to Peter that Vreni thought his work was bad—or at least fairly substandard—but she wasn't going to start out by alienating a photographer with whom she was being sent out on a story that didn't particularly interest her. Peter instantly suspected that she was going to do as little work as possible on this, and intended Peter to carry it with his pictures. He'd run across this type of attitude before; it was one of many reasons why he was grateful that he was usually able to work alone. Not to mention the awkwardness of having to leave your partner to go off and change to Spider-Man. *Come to think of it,* he thought, *that may cause problems.*

Deciding to cross that particular bridge when he came to it, Peter set his face into a smile and sat down at the other end of the couch. Vreni and Kate sat back down as well. "I've explained to Vreni," Kate said, "what I was telling you earlier about the situation down at Canaveral. Since you may be away for a while, you ought to take today to get things in order for being away for a prolonged period. If you need to draw any equipment from Stores to take with you," she said to Peter, "take care of that this afternoon—have them call my office if there are any questions."

"There are some long lenses that might come in handy," Peter said, trying very hard not to let a grin of total equipment-lust show on his face. He had never had an excuse before to get his hands on such things. JJJ didn't authorize their use that often.

"Fine. Just take good care of them... those things are expensive." She looked at Vreni. "Have you got a laptop with the *Bugle* composition software in it?"

"Got it last week."

"Good, then you're all set. Today's Wednesday... I would like to have a report from you two on initial indications of what you've found by next Tuesday. Ideally, I want to put something in the Sunday supplement, the day before the Shuttle goes up. Supplement deadline is Thursday... that's for final copy. Anything newer you find that warrants followup will go in the Sunday daily edition. Anything else?"

They both shook their heads.

"Okay, then get on with it. Go see Travel and get your flights or whatever sorted out, and draw a company card each from Accounting. If at all possible, I want you two in Miami and starting work by Friday. Is that doable?"

Peter looked at Vreni: she nodded. So did he.

"Right. Now get out of here so I can get some work done."

Out they went, and Kate's door closed behind them with the air of someone who had solved a very annoying problem. Peter resolved privately to ask around and see if there was something about Vreni and Kate that she should know about: some old disagreement or piece of unfinished business. One or another of the office gossips would have the info, he was sure.

As they walked away from Kate's office, Peter said, "Ms. Byrne——"

"Call me Vreni. If I can call you Peter?"

"Right. Vreni, I get the feeling that you're not entirely overjoyed at being sent on this story——"

She breathed in and out, then chuckled a little, almost against her will. "No, I was supposed to be going to Cannes. Miami was not exactly in my plans. But when life hands you lemons, you make lemonade…" She smiled slightly. "There are good aspects to it, I suppose. I've never seen a live Shuttle launch: this will be my chance. Have you?"

"No," Peter said, though in his career as Spider-Man, he'd traveled to space once or twice, and flown in space-faring vehicles more impressive than anything NASA had yet built.

He also did not mention, right now, that there was one reason for going to Miami that outweighed any number of Shuttles, as far as he was concerned. "I'm looking forward to it."

"Right. So we'll get ourselves down there and see what we can discover about this security problem they're having. Those long lenses you were mentioning," she added, "those can be good for getting quiet photos of things a couple of miles away, can't they?"

"They sure can," Peter said. "Considering the size of Kennedy, and the fact that at least some of the things we'll want pictures of will be off-limits…" He shrugged, and then caught her smiling at him.

"I never yet saw a photographer," she said, "who didn't want to get his or her hands on one of those lenses just to play with. Nice that we're actually going to need one."

Peter laughed. "Vreni," he said, "you haven't seen one now, either. But you're right, I'll need it." He paused. "Did Kate mention the Lizard to you?"

Vreni waved a hand. "She did, but… I don't know—I find it kind of hard to take seriously. Crazed human super villains, yes: heaven knows there are enough of those running around. But I don't understand what kind of damage a big crazed lizard can do. Why doesn't someone just shoot it?"

Peter raised his eyebrows. "It's been tried," he said.

"Then somebody's not trying hard enough."

"Maybe not," Peter said, restraining himself from further comment. This was no time to get into a discussion of how the creature she was calmly suggesting should be shot was a friend of his. "But if we're lucky, we won't run into him. It sounds like there's going to be enough other things about this story to keep us busy."

"Yeah," Vreni said. "Let's go down to Travel and get those tickets organized."

That business took about an hour, while they fought with the folks down in Travel—some of the wiliest-brained cheapskates Peter had ever met; no doubt hand-trained by Jameson—to keep from being put on a flight at three in the morning for the sake of a cheap fare. They finally settled on a noon flight out of Newark on Thursday, and Peter and Vreni were left free to go off to Accounting to get their credit cards.

Vreni then went off to take care of personal business, and Peter went down to Stores and had Mike the equipment manager bring out every long lens that was presently available. One of them, a beautiful 2000-millimeter f8 lens, Peter was strongly tempted to simply grab and run away with, never to be seen again, but then he saw the scratch on the lens's achromatic coating, and shook his head and pushed the lens back at Mike with the greatest possible regret. "How the heck did that happen?" he said.

Mike, a tall handsome young black man, grinned slightly. "Jets game," he said. "A tackle went right through the sidelines, apparently. Hit Joel Rhodes—he was covering that game—knocked him on his butt and broke his leg. Knocked the lens into a bench."

"What a shame," Peter said, more for the lens than for Joel, another photographer he had met and didn't much care for; a rude and abrasive type. "Oh well. How about the fifteen, there?"

Mike handed Peter the 1500-mm lens. It was two and a half feet long and nearly a foot wide at the lens end. "Hmm..." Peter sat there briefly doing math in his head to determine the thing's range.

"Pete," Mike said, "got a little something here you should see." He turned away, went rummaging back among the steel shelves.

"What? I thought you said this was all the big lenses."

Mike came back with a box about the size of a standard personal computer case, opened it up. Peter looked inside.

"That's a telescope," he said, bemused.

Mike lifted the small cylindrical object out of its nested packing in the case. It was black, eight inches in diameter, and only about eighteen inches long.

"Questar," Mike said. "Yup, it's a telescope, but look there. See the camera fitting?" He pointed at the barrel of the telescope, where there was a standard bayonet mount. "You put your 35 right there, at the Cassegrain focus. This thing can produce virtual close-ups at five miles."

"Wow," Peter breathed. Even the 2000 wouldn't have been able to do that.

"This has been out doing nature work," Mike said. "Something to do with those owls up in timber country. You can't get close enough to them for photos, usually. You can with this, though."

"Where do I sign?" Peter said, looking over his shoulder in terror lest someone else should come in here and want it too.

"Right here." Mike shoved the usual equipment-requisition voucher at him. Peter scribbled hastily, while Mike put the Questar back in its case and snapped all the catches shut.

"Manual's inside," Mike said. "Take good care of it. Jonah finds out I gave this to a freelancer, he'll freak."

Peter seized the box and grinned at Mike. "No problem there. The question is, will you ever see me again?"

Mike chuckled as Peter hurried off.

The rest of the day was a whirl of preparation. Peter had to let the building super and the alarm company know that he was going to be away for a while, put a bigger tape in the answering machine, get rid of all the perishable food in the refrigerator, give MJ's modeling agency the phone number for the Hilton in Miami, in case they couldn't reach her themselves, and about fifty other things. When the dust finally settled, it was nearly ten o'clock at night, and he hadn't even begun packing yet. He hadn't had any dinner, and he was dead tired. However, there were a couple of phone calls he had to make: one which would be delightful, one not so.

He dialed the good one first. The phone rang about eighteen times. MJ had warned him to expect this. "It's down in the front hall," she said. "Aunt Anna doesn't like extension phones. And we're usually outside in the sun, so give us some time if you call." *It's a little late in the day for sun,* Peter thought, but all the same, he let it ring. Finally someone picked up. "Hello?"

It was Anna Watson. "Hi, Aunt Anna, it's Peter!" he said.

"Oh, hello, Peter! How are things? MJ's just out of the tub; I'll get her for you." The phone was put down, and footsteps went off out of earshot. Faintly, voices could be heard chatting in the background, and a giggle. Peter smiled; he knew that giggle. Then more footsteps, hurried, and the phone being picked up.

"Hi, Tiger! Oh, I miss you!"

"I miss you, too," Peter said. "But not for long."

"What?"

"I'm being sent to Florida."

"Really? Where?"

"Miami."

"Oh, Peter!"

He filled her in quickly on the Space Coast story, what he knew of it. Then, more quietly, he said, "They think they've seen the Lizard as well."

"Oh, no," MJ said softly.

Peter tried to sound lighthearted. "I don't know that we'll necessarily run into him. The odds—"

"Don't quote me odds," his wife said, sounding resigned, but also just slightly amused. "They're sending you down here because you're good at getting pictures of super villains. You'll run into him." She sighed. "But at least you're going to be here!"

"We should be able to see each other most nights," Peter said softly.

"Ohhh…!" Her voice clearly implied what she intended for at least some of those nights. Peter shivered, just once, with anticipation: it was amazing what a little separation could do for a relationship.

"Absolutely. But never mind that for the moment," Peter said. "How are you getting along down there?"

She chuckled. "Hon, this was actually a pretty good move. Remember I told you about North Beach?"

"Uh-huh."

"Well, it's even worse than I thought. You couldn't spit on Beach Boulevard and not hit someone toting a portfolio. A lot of them are wannabes, but a lot are genuine talent. There's plenty of work here, if you can make the right connections. And if you can cut through the talent that's already been hired…."

"How's the competition?"

Her voice sounded rueful. "Very polished. Some of these people have big careers elsewhere and are just sort of slumming for the season. Anyway, I've left my bio and CV and representative stills at about eighteen different agencies."

"There are that many of them down there?"

"I haven't hit all of them yet, by any means, just the biggest ones. 'Start at the top and work down' seems to be the best approach if I'm going to make any kind of impression with all the other talent around here."

"All those people ought to get out," said Peter righteously, "and leave the field to people like you who need the money."

She laughed. "You tell 'em, Tiger."

After that there wasn't a great deal of content to the phone call: it devolved rapidly into smoochy noises, which Peter reluctantly brought to an early conclusion. "I'll tell you everything else tomorrow," he said, "when we get in. I'm booked in at the Miami Hilton. But meanwhile I've got one more phone call to make."

"I think I know who," she said, that resigned sound again. "Well, tell them I sent my best."

"I will. I'm just hoping he's not in trouble of some kind."

MJ sounded rueful again. "I would more or less define being the Lizard as being in trouble," she said.

"Yeah. Listen, honey—gotta go."

After another five minutes of kissyface noises, Peter hung up and checked his address book for the second phone number and slowly dialed it.

Several rings, and the phone was picked up. "Hello?"

A boy's voice. "William," Peter said mock severely, "isn't it past your bedtime?"

"Peter! How are you?"

"I'm fine. Is your mom around?"

"No, she ran down to the 7-Eleven for some milk—we ran out. She'll be back in a little while."

Peter thought for a moment. "Okay. I just wanted to let her know that I'm going to be coming down your way."

"Super!" There was a pause, and William's voice dropped a little. "Dad's not here," he said sadly.

"No, huh?"

"He hasn't been here for—" A pause. "Four months. Just a little more."

"Do you have any idea where he is?"

"Not really. We knew he was getting ready to go away for a while—he packed a lot of stuff, and sent it away in boxes. He wouldn't tell us what it was, or why he was sending it, or where. I got worried, Peter… I thought maybe he wasn't going to come back at all."

"But he didn't take everything, did he?"

"No, he left a lot. But we're not sure what that means, either. He doesn't talk to us like he used to, Pete. Anyway, he went away. Then the last we heard from him was about two months ago. He sent a postcard from somewhere down by the Everglades." William stopped. "It wouldn't be so bad," he said then, "if he would write more. Sometimes I wonder if he really just wishes we weren't here."

He may, Peter thought sadly, *but not for the reasons you think.* He felt so sorry for William: he knew what it was like to desperately want a father. His own parents had died when he was very small, leaving him to be raised by his Aunt May and Uncle Ben. Ben died shortly after Peter gained his spider-powers—a death Peter could have prevented. The guilt associated with that act haunted him to this day.

But Peter had no idea how he would have reacted if he'd had a father who had Curt Connors's problem. Aloud he said, "I doubt it. Anyway, as I said. I'm coming down. It's partly about him, and partly about the Space Shuttle."

"What? The next launch? The one with the bees?"

"Yup."

"Cool!" And for several minutes William babbled happily, for apparently he and his science class, along with science classes in several hundred other schools around the country, were involved in this bee experiment—something about finding out whether bees' swarming and directional abilities were affected by microgravity, and how much. There was also something about honey-supported hydroponics which William carried on about so excitedly that Peter could barely follow him. If there was anything William had inherited from his father, it was his love of the sciences, and biology in particular; Curt had been as good a teacher as he had been a researcher.

After a while, though, William trailed off, paused. "You know, though," he said, "if it's partly about the Lizard—you be careful, Pete. You know…"

"I know. He's dangerous sometimes. But I'll have backup on this one. Spider-Man told me recently that he's going to be heading down this way himself."

"Oh, great!" William said, sounding relieved. "That's okay, then. You think we might see him?"

"I haven't seen his appointments calendar," Peter said. "No telling. But if I run across him, I'll tell him you were asking after him."

"Thanks, Pete! It'd be cool to see him—and he might know something about how Dad is."

"I hope so. Listen, William, I'm running up the phone bill. Let your mom know about what I've been telling you, okay?"

"I will. Where are you going to be?"

"The Miami Hilton, for the first few days at least. But I'll give her a call when we get in."

"Okay. Thanks, Peter!"

"Right. You take care."

Peter hung up and sighed and went off to pack.

TWO

THE trip down was uneventful. After locking up, setting the alarm, and dropping the spare key with the super, Peter caught a cab for Newark and met Vreni at check-in, where they got onto one of the most crowded commuter flights he had ever been on in his life. It took Peter a good five minutes to wrestle the Questar into the overhead baggage compartment, which was already so full that he thought he might have to spend the trip with it in his lap.

Not the best way to begin a working relationship, Peter thought, as he and Vreni wedged themselves into seats so tightly pitched and close together that they might just as well have just given up and tried to sit in each other's laps.

"They've mistaken us for sardines, these people," Vreni muttered under her breath as the plane taxied away from the gate.

"Yeah. The *Bugle* paid peanuts for the fare," Peter said, eyeing the tray that one of the flight attendants carried past, "and it looks like that's all we're going to get to eat, too."

She laughed then. "Wait till we're up," she said. For once, it didn't take long; once the plane was in the air, she reached for the tote bag she had shoved under the seat ahead of them.

Peter watched as she produced from it a package of crackers, several good cheeses from Zahar's, a couple of small bottles of San Pellegrino mineral water, and plastic cups and knives. "Self-preservation," she said to Peter, pulling down her tray. "I stopped trusting airline food, or even expecting it, a long time ago. Pellegrino?"

"Thanks," he said, delighted. She handed him one of the bottles. A short time later they were working their way through an early lunch, and getting annoyed, envious, or just plain hungry looks from all the other passengers in sight.

As they chatted over the next couple of hours, Peter started revising his original opinion of Vreni, although a little reluctantly. Vreni Byrne was quick on the uptake, and very opinionated. Occasionally she could be abrasive. But these traits made a good investigative reporter, and that was how she had gotten her start in journalism. Her talent had taken her a long way. She had been in Rwanda, and in South Africa during the worst of its troubles; she had been in Moscow for the coup that brought down the Soviet Union, in Berlin when the Wall fell, and in Latveria when Victor von Doom was deposed. She had been in the Kurile Islands when Japan and Russia almost went to war over them—a carefully covered-up business, that, and Peter shuddered as she told him more about it, and how close the world had been, once more, to its first real nuclear war. She had investigated Chinese piracy off the Philippines, pollution in Antarctica, and Atlantean attacks of offshore oil rigs. Vreni had been a busy woman.

"After a while, though," she said, "you get tired of running around foreign places. You want to rake some muck on your own doorstep." Vreni smiled a little. "The problem is, even a reporter can get typecast. My editors at the *Trib* liked the work I was doing overseas—liked it too much to let me work at home. So, I gave 'em the slip."

"What do you make of *this* story so far?" Peter said.

She shrugged. "Not sure there is one, frankly. It all seems pretty disconnected. Oh, I respect Kate's judgment, don't get me wrong. Unquestionably she has an instinct for these things. Nonetheless—" Vreni stretched as well as she could in the cramped space "—we'll see how fast the story runs away from us when we get down there."

"From us? Or with us?" Peter said, slightly bewildered.

Vreni shook her head. "From us. I've learned this over time: the faster the story runs away from you, the more it avoids you and tries not to be told, the better it is. If we start getting avoidance reactions right away—" there was a slightly feral edge to her smile "—we'll know we're onto something hot."

She laid out her plans briefly for him: "I'll go down some of the usual channels first. I should be able to make some connections in the Miami police department via my old contacts in Chicago—maybe even over the weekend, if things work out right. Then there's the initial prelaunch press conference at Kennedy on Monday. We should hear then whether there have been any changes in the Shuttle's mission to account for these sudden changes in security. You should be there for that; see if you can get some other pictures, too, background Cape stuff. Test out that widget of yours."

"Definitely," Peter said. "I'm going to see if I can get some practice with it over the weekend—it's a little idiosyncratic to work with, but it should produce some terrific results once I can figure out how to use it best."

"Right. After KSC, we should go out on Tuesday, assuming nothing else comes up, and interview some of the people who're associated with these weird disappearances and so forth. They're scattered around the northern part of the Everglades, mostly. We'll take two days over it, I would imagine, while I start assembling the first draft of the article for Kate. Second draft in on Thursday… and the launch is the Monday after."

"And then pictures of the launch."

"Of course. Make sure you pick up the launch passes on Monday— no point in leaving it till the last minute."

"No question," Peter said. Whatever else happened, he was excited about the prospect of being at the Shuttle launch; being at it with the Questar as well was the chance of a lifetime. *I should be able to show the NASA photographers a thing or three,* he thought, *if I can get enough use of the 'scope over the week to get used to it. And what practice I don't get, Spider-Man will.*

"And then there's the Lizard," Vreni said. "I'll grant Kate this: his appearances are in the same general area as these weird thefts and disappearances. But there's no proof that he's directly involved…" She trailed off, thinking, then shook her head. "We'll see what happens. If he, like the story, runs away from us…" That smile curved her lips again.

Peter privately considered that it wasn't the Lizard running away from him that he had in mind, especially when he had his Spider-Man suit on. *But as she says, we'll see what happens.*

Two hours later they touched down at Miami International Airport. As Peter and Vreni came out the ramp into the gate area, Peter turned to say something to Vreni, just behind him, and was tackled sideways by something that hit him like a ground-to-air missile—if ground-to-air missiles had flowing red hair. The kiss went on… well, Peter wasn't actually sure *how* long it went on. He was faintly aware of the sound of Vreni's amused chuckle behind him. When he broke the clinch and smiled into MJ's eyes, she raised her eyebrows at him, a teasing look, and said, "No better than eight point eight, I make that. You're out of practice already."

"Hmf."

"Do you have a lady in every port, Peter," Vreni said, politely enough, "or is this someone to whom I should be introduced more formally?"

Peter chuckled. "Mary Jane Watson-Parker," he said, taking a moment to admire MJ's miniskirt, "Vreni Byrne."

"Delighted," Vreni said, as she and MJ shook hands, and certainly she seemed to mean it. "The people at the *Bugle* all say how lucky Peter is to have caught you."

"Luck had nothing to do with it," said MJ. "'A guy chases a girl until she catches him,' as the song says. It was pretty much that way with us. But—Byrne as in the *Chicago Tribune*?"

"Why, yes."

"I thought so. I saw you on their magazine show on cable—"

They all headed down toward the baggage-claim area, chatting all the way. Peter was bemused to discover that Vreni was a fan of *Secret Hospital*, knew MJ's acting from her all-too-brief stint on that soap opera, and liked her style. After recovering their bags, the three of them caught a cab to the Hilton, and by the time they got there, MJ and Vreni were gossiping like mad over the antics of some of the other actors in the series. *What a relief,* Peter thought as they got out. He had been slightly concerned that MJ would be annoyed with him for being in the company of such a good-looking woman. *But she's above that kind of thing....*

"Are you staying here too?" Vreni said to MJ, as she and Peter went in with their bags.

"Not while he's on a job," MJ said. "I'm with relatives. We'll be visiting, though."

"Well, I hope to see more of you! I'm going to go up and get settled," Vreni said to Peter, "and then I'm going to start setting up some of our first interviews. I'll see you tomorrow morning. Breakfast?"

"You're on," Peter said.

Vreni headed off, and MJ watched her go. Then, when she was safely in the elevator and its doors shut, she turned to Peter, fisted him lightly in the ribs, and said, "Where did you find *her*?"

"Oh, MJ, come on—"

She burst out laughing at him. "I'm teasing. I'm in too good a mood to be jealous about anything, even if I didn't know Kate wished her on you. Come on."

They walked off through the lobby together, heading for the coffee shop. Peter hugged her to him as they went. "Why the good mood, then? Any luck?" he said.

They went in, waited to be seated. "A nibble," MJ said, as the waitress led them to a quiet table in the corner.

"A modeling job?"

"No. Television."

"Here? That's weird."

MJ nodded, stretched a little, and smiled. "One of the local afternoon talk shows apparently has a little modeling spot three times a week. Local couture, that kind of thing. They've just lost the model who was working for them, and now they need a replacement."

"You think you can get this job?"

"I have no idea. I think half the people in town must be trying to get it. A lot of competition…" She shrugged. "Can't do anything but try. And what about you? Where are you going to have to be?" Peter shook his head. "Up and down the coast—depends on what arrangements Vreni makes. There's going to be a lot of driving, though, between here and the north Everglades. But I'd say we'll be here for at least a week, until just after the Shuttle launch, and then maybe a little afterwards. Meantime…"

The waitress came. After they both ordered drinks, MJ said, leaning over the table and taking Peter's hand, "A lot of driving there may be, but none for you just now—or later, either."

"What exactly do you have in mind?"

"Tiger," she said softly. The smile spread to a grin. "How long has it been since we last saw each other?"

"Eleven days," he said. And added, "Fourteen hours… and twenty-three minutes. Mark." Then he eyed the key card for his room, which he'd dropped to the table. "Never mind the drinks," he said. "Never mind lunch. Come on."

"No way!" MJ said. "We have to keep up your strength. But, afterwards…"

Peter grinned back, resigning himself to the delightfully inevitable.

HE did go out, though, around six that evening. Peter stopped down at the hotel's car rental desk and took possession of a neat little compact, then drove MJ to Aunt Anna's. He spent an hour or so there with them, sharing gossip and catching up on family business. Then he left, for there was one visit he needed to make before he and Vreni got started on business the next day.

He drove most of the way. One thing he had learned was that, while Spider-Man had little trouble web-slinging his way around in his home turf in Manhattan, it was sometimes more difficult to make good speed out in open country. For long distances, a car really did work better sometimes, and he was glad enough to have one at his disposal now. Besides, with his spider-sense warning him of any kind of danger, he was probably the safest driver on the road.

He headed up and out of Miami on I-95, not desiring to get caught in the tangle of interchanges around Hialeah and Fort Lauderdale, and soon realized that being the safest driver on the road wasn't all that much of an accomplishment on the Florida highways. Once he got out of the city limits, though, the driving was a bit more sane; he went straight north along the eastern coast until he hit Route 98 near Palm Beach. There he turned west, heading inland for about thirty miles, toward the southern shores of Lake Okeechobee.

South Bay was a small city at the very southernmost point of the lake, where the North New River Canal flowed into it. The place was very much in the Floridian style of "middle America": white-shingled houses, neat front yards, palm trees, swimming pools here and there, a busy little complex of main streets in town, and a quiet, flourishing suburb surrounding it all and running up against the lake. Rough spaces of wetland were dotted here and there—a token of the presence of the northernmost part of the Everglades very nearby. Long, quiet, rural roads ran into the city from several sides, and it seemed like every other house Peter passed along these roads had a boat in the driveway—even if it was only a rowboat or an inflatable dinghy.

Around dusk, he left the car in a parking lot near a Kmart several miles outside town, and strolled off into an empty lot nearby, a tangle of undergrowth-height live oak and slash pine. It was surprisingly quiet, except for a mockingbird which sat high on a crooked palm and sang skilled and insistent imitations of every bird he knew and many he didn't.

It squawked, though, a few minutes later, and flew away hurriedly as a jet of webbing shot up into the palm tree's crown. A moment later Spider-Man swung up into the tree, crouched there among the fronds, and glanced around him, while the mockingbird settled two trees over and sang scandal and outrage at him, flirting its tail and rousing its feathers at him.

"Hey," Spidey said, "take it easy, Caruso. I'll be out of your way in a moment." He looked around and got his bearings. While still driving, earlier that evening, he had picked up a street map of the area, along with several other maps that he needed for research purposes. Now with its help, he picked out a couple of landmarks—a water tower, a radio mast—made sure of the direction in which he was headed—north, toward the lake—and set out.

It was a little less easy not to be seen in this mostly flat landscape than it would have been in Manhattan, but he made the best of his environment, enjoying it as he went. There were still some surprisingly big, surprisingly old cypresses hereabouts, a few of them big enough to be several hundred years old, and there were high-tension towers to use for anchorage (if you were careful about where you put the webbing) and plenty of other masts and poles. Spider-Man webbed his way northward, not rushing it too much, enjoying the balmy evening air, until he found the little suburban development he was after.

It was only a couple of blocks from the lakeshore: a little semicircle of shingled tract houses, one of several nearly identical cul-de-sacs radiating out from a central access road. Spidey perched on a power line tower behind the cul-de-sac and checked out the one house he was interested in. It had a neat woven-wood plank fence surrounding its backyard, which contained a small patio, numerous rosebushes, and a very beat-up lawn surrounding a pole with a basketball hoop. Off to one side was a brick barbecue, with embers still glowing in it. The house had a much-used but serviceable-looking Buick sitting in front of it, and the lawn was slightly overgrown. Off to one side, on a small trailer, sat an aluminum canoe.

Spidey smiled inside his mask—more a sad smile than anything else—looked around him to make sure he could see no one watching, and swung down into the house's backyard. There were sliding glass and screen doors opening out onto the small patio. The curtains inside them were open. Through them, Spider-Man could see a living room, and a pair of jeans-wearing legs sticking out in front of a chair. The owner of the legs was slumped or slid so far down in the chair that there was no seeing the rest of him.

Spidey slipped quietly up to the screen door. "William," he said softly, "you're going to ruin your back sitting that way, you know that?"

A frozen moment of silence, and then a blond boy leaped out of the chair and came tearing back to the screen door, staring to see out into the fast-falling darkness. "Spider-M—!"

"Sssh," Spidey said. "Can I come in?"

William slid the screen door aside, beckoned him. "Come on in," he said, and as Spidey stepped through the door, William pulled the curtain behind him, then went hurriedly to the front of the living room and shut those drapes too.

"Nosy neighbors?" Spidey said, approving.

"Yeah. Wait a minute, I'll get Mom—" William hurried off, leaving Spidey there for a moment to look around him. The inside of the house matched the outside: small, tidy, understated. Everything looked a little worn, though, a little old. The arms on some of the chairs and the sofa were rubbed almost bare, the upholstery looked slightly faded. But everything was clean. Pictures hung on the walls, some of them Martha's watercolors—she had a way with the brush. There was a particularly beautiful one of Manhattan at dusk that Spidey had always admired.

"Spider-Man—"

He turned, saw her come in through the kitchen door, drying her hands on a towel. Martha Connors had been always been an extremely attractive woman: red-gold hair, a determined face. Now she was becoming merely striking, but more formidable. Her face showed ample evidence of the pain she had lived through, but there was no surrender in it, and those cool eyes looked at Spider-Man fully expecting that there might be more pain in the offing, and not shying away from it.

"How are you, Martha?" he said.

"Not too bad," she said, and it was a lie, but a social one. "Sit yourself down. I would assume that this isn't strictly a social call."

"Not entirely. But you know I worry about you two."

"We're fine," William said. This too, was clearly a lie, but his accomplishment didn't yet match his mother's. Still, Spidey had to give him marks for effort.

"It's not too bad," Martha said, "really. It's true the work for Farrar Chemical that I was doing dried up, after Curt—left. But we're doing all right. I'm doing temp work now: teleworking, for IBM over in Boca."

"Mom's a professional Web surfer," William said with some excitement. "She gets paid to hang out on the Internet and send people questionnaires, and look at websites."

Spidey laughed softly. "Sounds pretty good."

"It's a steady paycheck," Martha said, "if nothing else. Some people still need clothes and food and books for school, after all."

"How is school?" Spider-Man said.

"It's a total bore," William said, sitting back in the chair in the backbreaking posture again.

Martha looked wry. "I'm afraid he's not exaggerating," she said. "One of our main problems is that the local school district has run out of room in its fast-track program. Curt always did insist on making sure that William read a year or two, or three, ahead of his classmates; and he picked up so much science and math from his dad that he's pretty, well, overqualified at the moment."

"I want to take my JSATs this year," William said, "and they won't let me. They're drainheads. I did a JSAT dry run last year and I got seven ninety. If they would—"

"William," his mother said dryly, "don't push it. We've been over this ground before. You're just going to have to put up with the situation for another year. And anyway, you need more work on your social studies."

"No, I don't. It's boring. I'm going to be a scientist like Dad; you don't need social studies for that."

"William," his mother said, in a sigh. Spider-Man smiled again, but they couldn't see it. He cleared his throat instead.

"Martha," he said, "I see you have your work cut out for you. One thing, though. Have you heard anything from Curt?"

She shook her head. "Did Peter tell you about the postcard?" Spidey nodded. "There's been nothing since then, unfortunately. He's actually been here very little the last year or so. Whether that means he thinks he's getting near some kind of solution to his problem, or he just thinks it's too dangerous for him to be around us right now—I don't know."

Spidey sighed. "All right," he said. "Will you do me a favor? Let me know if you do hear anything?"

"How?"

Spider-Man produced a small spider-tracer. "I know," he said, to William this time, "that the last time I offered you one of these, you told me you didn't need it, since you were going to be taking care of your mother. And you've plainly done a good job of it. Now, though, it's a question of taking care of other people, who might get hurt if I don't have all the information I need to work with. There are some things going on down here that I'd like to rule the Lizard out of, if I could, and I can't do that without your help."

William looked at the tracer for a moment, then stretched out his hand to take it. "This works the same as my other tracers. But there's something added. See the little indentation on the top?" Spider-Man said. "Just enough to take a fingernail. Press a nail in there, then talk to it. I've got it hooked to—well, consider it a very small and stupid voicemail system. It's good for about fifteen seconds of sound. When you activate it, I'll be alerted, and I'll get the message shortly." He did not say that the tiny mobile-cell connector in it would dump the message to Peter Parker's answering machine.

William glanced at the little thing, then pocketed it. "Okay."

"He's not in trouble," Martha said, "is he?"

Spider-Man shook his head. "Truly, I don't know. If I hear any report that I think can be depended upon, I'll see that it gets back to you—if you want to hear it."

She looked at him steadfastly enough for a moment, then turned her eyes away. "I very much want my husband back," she said. "William's father... we need him. A great deal. Lizard or no Lizard. But I understand what he's doing. Please tell him—" she lifted her eyes to Spider-Man's mask again "—if you see him, tell him that we love him anyway. And we miss him... and want him home again, as soon as he can come. Meanwhile... we're all right."

Spider-Man nodded, and swallowed, to try to dislodge the lump from his throat. "I'll tell him. And if there's anything I can do for you—"

"You've already done more than enough," Martha Connors said. "But take care of yourself, as well, Spider-Man. We worry about our friends, too."

He got up. "William—"

"If anything happens," William said somberly, "I'll let you know."

Spider-Man turned toward the screen door. "And get to work on that social studies," he said.

William gave him a dry look. "Puh-leeze," he said, "not you too...."

Spidey chuckled and slipped out into the night.

PETER met Vreni on Friday morning for breakfast, as planned. She had had little luck getting her police connections in order, as yet. "I'm going to make some calls today to some of the people down in the Everglades who claim to have seen the Lizard," Vreni said. "I don't think I'll need you until Monday at the press conference, and after that we can drive down to the 'Glades and take care of whatever appointments I've managed to set up."

"That's fine," Peter said. "I want to get out today and work with the Questar." *And here*, he thought, *I was worried about having to ditch her.*

"Have fun with the new toy," Vreni said, signaling the waiter for the bill.

He was loading up the rental car in the hotel's underground parking garage, and putting the Questar into the trunk with visions of a delightful afternoon of shooting lots and lots of film on expense account, when he heard a voice yell from way across the garage, "Peter!"

He turned, surprised. Vreni was practically running toward him. "What? What's the matter?"

"I'm so glad I caught you," she said as she came up to him, panting. "The hotel thought you'd left already. They've changed the day for the press conference."

"When is it?"

"Today! At noon. I didn't get the message from the hotel until just now."

"Good thing we're both early eaters," he said. "If we drive like crazy people, we can get there just before it starts."

"Let's do it," she said, and jumped into his car.

They drove up I-95 as fast as Peter dared. Vreni wanted to drive, but Peter was fortunately able to refuse. "You're not on this car's insurance," he said, and Vreni could grumble as she liked; it was true. He had other reasons, though, besides the inherent safety his spider-sense gave him. One of his newsroom cronies had told him a story about Vreni trashing a UN armored personnel carrier in Bosnia. *If she can do that to an APC,* he thought, *no way I'm going to let her do it to this poor little Chevette. Especially since the car's in my name, and I'd wind up paying for it.*

They hit the Cocoa Beach extension to the Bee Line Expressway at about twenty of twelve. A few minutes later they were at the main gate to the Kennedy Space Center, twentieth in a line of cars which seemed to be taking a long while to get in. Armed Air Force personnel, Peter saw, were looking closely at each car as it passed the gates: NASA security people were chatting with each driver.

They slowly crept up to the checkpoint, and the young NASA security man there peered in at Peter's car, while his Air Force buddy walked around it, examining it. "Can I see your driver's license, sir?" the security man said.

Peter handed it over, along with his *Daily Bugle* ID card. "We're down from New York for the press conference," he said.

"Thank you. Ma'am, may I see yours, please?"

Vreni handed her license and *Bugle* ID to the man, throwing Peter a wordless look that said, *Do you believe this security? Something's up.* Peter raised his eyebrows at her, said nothing.

The ID was handed back after a moment. "Thank you, sir, ma'am," the security guard said. "Straight ahead, turn right at the sign for Spaceport USA, and park in the Public Affairs Office lot toward the back."

They drove in and parked. Peter got the Questar out of the back of the car—he was not going to leave that piece of equipment out of his sight if he could help it—and they walked hurriedly to the main building. Spaceport USA was the Center's main public facility, a long low building housing a museum, the Astronauts' Memorial, and various free exhibits about satellites and space travel. Out behind it, dwarfing everything else, the "Rocket Garden" stood, with various old Mercury and other boosters, and the slightly sad shell of a Saturn lying on its side. "I want some pictures of those later," Peter said as they headed in through the front door.

"Tourist," Vreni said under her breath. Peter grinned. Indeed, the place was full of tourists, people in T-shirts and shorts, and sticky children eating ice cream and shouting with excitement at the sight of the Space

Man, some probably underpaid employee walking around in a space suit in this heat, and providing photo opportunities for the visitors.

To one side was a corrugated sign with plastic letters stuck to it, saying "STS-73 Press Conference." An arrow pointed off to the left, toward a meeting room down past one of the two I-MAX theaters. A crowd of people, some with tape recorders and cameras, were heading that way. Peter and Vreni followed them.

Inside the room was the usual briefing-room kind of seating, plain folding chairs and a long blue-draped table, with the NASA curved-chevron logo behind it. To one side, in back, was a table with press packs piled up on it. Vreni edged over there to pick up a couple of them, while Peter placed himself fairly well forward on the right side, in position to take pictures of the presenters.

The room was half full, no more, when the people running the press conference came in from a side door. One of them, Peter guessed immediately, was an astronaut: his hair was shorter than anyone else's there, and Peter had noticed early on that there didn't seem to be many long-haired male astronauts, at least not so close to a launch date. The other three, two men and a woman, were civil servants, NASA people. *No military*, Peter thought, *at least not openly.*

Vreni plopped herself into the chair next to Peter's and tossed his copy of the press pack down onto the floor where he could get at it, then started leafing hastily through her own as the oldest of the men sitting up at the table, a gray-haired sort with a lined and kindly face, started testing his microphone.

"Good morning," he said. "Or good afternoon. This is the press conference for STS-73, and we want to apologize to you for the sudden change in schedule. Unfortunately we discovered at the last moment that we had a schedule conflict with other launch-related activities on Monday which would have made this conference impossible then, and it seemed more logical to relocate the event earlier rather than later, since toward launch date, staff schedules become very harried..."

Peter thought the man, a Mr. Buckingham, who was involved with "Launch Processing" according to the kit, looked harried enough at the moment. He had the expression of a man with problems on his mind which he had put aside for the moment. Buckingham began discussing the upcoming Shuttle launch, detailing launch time and crew information. The Shuttle in question would be *Endeavour*; her commander this time out would be the man sitting next to Buckingham, whom Peter had spotted earlier, Commander Ronald Luks.

Peter got a few pictures of Luks, a big, tanned, good-looking man, while he spoke. Beside him, Vreni was paying little attention to this, perhaps understandably, for almost everything being discussed here was also in the press pack. She was flipping through the pack as if looking for something in particular, and not finding it. Her scowl grew deeper by the moment. Then, quite suddenly, Vreni's eyebrows went up, and she pulled out a pen and began to scribble on the press pack in messy shorthand.

Commander Luks was now talking in an easygoing way about the mission, which would be his first as mission commander, and his third flight on the Shuttle. Peter got a couple more shots of him, and then caught a look on Buckingham's face, a sudden flicker of concern as Luks mentioned the partially built space station, *Freedom*. He managed to get at least one shot of it before the expression vanished as if it hadn't been there. Peter had little time to consider what might have caused it, for Vreni nudged him and pointed at a paragraph under the one she had been making notes on.

MPAPPS, said one of the equipment descriptions: "the Mission-Peculiar Ambient Power Production System." Peter looked at Vreni, shook his head: *what's it mean?* But she flashed him a sudden smile, that feral look she had worn when speaking of the story "running away from you."

Another mission specialist, one of the ground scientists involved with project design, Dr. Brewer, was speaking now: a startlingly redheaded man in his early forties with more freckles than Peter had ever seen on a human being. Brewer chatted briefly about the birds and the bees—literally. Besides the school-science experiment with bees, some other livestock was being brought along: a pair of hummingbirds, to see how weightlessness affected their sense of balance (if at all) and their flight habits. These would be relocated to *Freedom* for long-term evaluation by the team in residence there, and would later be moved to the new space station annex, *Heinlein*, when it was ready to be assembled in orbit late next year or early the year after. When the description of these and other experiments ended, Buckingham finally asked for questions.

Vreni sat looking at her notes for a few minutes, while other reporters made inquiries about the change of schedule in the press conference, the health of one payload specialist who had had to drop out of the flight because of a broken leg, and other such queries. Finally there was a moment's pause, and Vreni put her hand up.

Buckingham nodded to her. She smiled at him and said, "Vreni Byrne, *Daily Bugle*. Mr. Buckingham, there has been a lot of discussion by various environmental groups lately of a Shuttle payload which was originally scheduled for this flight, the CHERM or Compact High-Energy Reactor Module. A lot of people were complaining about it, saying that they didn't want something which turned out to be a small, fast 'breeder' reactor containing half a kilogram of plutonium, shot off over their heads where something untoward might, God forbid, happen to it... say, a mission abort which would leave the stuff at the bottom of the Atlantic, or an explosion which would powder it all over the Southern Tier and cause deaths by cancer and mutations in the thousands. Leaving aside the thorny question of nuclear nonproliferation in space—are we to understand that the disappearance of this module from the schedule for STS-73 is a reaction to public opinion? Or has the thing malfunctioned somehow?"

A slight stir of interest went around the room. Buckingham looked completely unconcerned, an expression which Peter noted, and took a shot of. "The protests about the CHERM," Buckingham said, casually enough, "have been a matter of public record for some months now. NASA understands the public's concern in this matter, and everybody will understand that our concern for the safety of our neighbors on the Space Coast and elsewhere on the planet is a daily matter and something we take very seriously. It was decided that the CHERM equipment package, especially its security capsule, needed more study and a reevaluation before sending it aloft, in light of various issues mentioned not only in the press but in Congress and elsewhere in government. However, we are also investigating other venues for the CHERM equipment's launch, since it, or something like it, is going to be needed aboard *Freedom* eventually."

"I know people like to say that we should make do with solar power," Commander Luks said genially, "but in space, with the extremes of heat and cold we experience, and the amount of power needed to manage the backups which keep our crews safe, solar just isn't enough. The only space-sufficient power source which can safely be lifted from Earth into LEO with our present technology is atomic. We can't burn coal up there, unfortunately."

A little ripple of laughter went around the room. "Yes," Vreni said, smiling too, "Senator Lysander's line has been quoted a lot lately. The CHERM package, then, is not going up on STS-73?"

"The CHERM package is not going up," Buckingham said.

"Thank you, sir. One more thing, then. I note in the press pack the presence of the MPAPPS or 'Mission-Peculiar Ambient Power Production System.' Would you elaborate a little on the function of this, since it's listed in the cargo bay payload manifest up front of the pack, but not in the developmental test objectives supplement?"

Buckingham looked slightly bemused at that. "Isn't it? It ought to be. Briefly, the MPAPPS is an ancillary power generation system containing old-style fuel-cell technology. It's being attached to *Freedom* as a redundant backup for other energy management systems, specifically to the computer systems which handle life support for the station. With the second wing being brought on-line after STS-72/74, and new personnel coming aboard from Russia and ESA, extra planned redundancy has to be added."

"I see," Vreni said, and that smile was still very much in place, the look of a woman watching a story run away from her at full speed. "The MPAPPS isn't atomic in nature, then?"

Buckingham chuckled. "Miss Byrne, if I said that I wouldn't be very accurate, since we are all atomic in nature—"

"Please, sir, I don't think you mean to sound so disingenuous. I'm asking whether this new piece of equipment is indeed an atomic reactor—in fact, the same reactor originally scheduled to go up, but under another name."

"It is not," Buckingham said.

"Thank you, sir," Vreni said, and sat down. Another reporter jumped up and started asking questions about the Agency's possible cruelty to animals, but Vreni scribbled on her press pack again, looking profoundly satisfied.

A few minutes later, still another reporter, from the *Los Angeles Times*, stood up and began inquiring about security breaches on the KSC grounds over the past couple of weeks. "Nothing has happened," Buckingham said, "which in any way affects or threatens the launch of STS-73, if that's what you're concerned about. We are indeed breaking in a new facility-wide security system, which always means a certain number of false alarms and hiccups—as any of you know who've installed or tuned an alarm system lately. But no one's stolen the silver."

More chuckling went around the room, and the press conference turned to other topics, while Vreni turned and winked at the *LA Times* reporter, a little man with shaggy hair and wicked eyes. Finally, about an hour after it started, the conference ended, and the people up at the head table posed briefly for a photo opportunity, then left.

Peter took the opportunity, even though he didn't have to, then went off after Vreni, who was chatting with the guy from the *Times*. "Bobby," she said as Peter joined them, "Peter Parker. He strings for the *Bugle*. Peter, this is Bobby London, *LA Times,* as you heard. I owe you one, Bob."

"My pleasure," Bobby said softly. "I got wind of some craziness down this way last week. No one seems to want to talk about it: either outright denials, like this, or a lot of muttering, but no details."

"If I hear something," Vreni said, "I'll pay you back that much."

"No more?" Bobby said.

"One favor at a time," said Vreni, "and every reporter for herself. Peter? We should probably get back to Miami—there are some things I want to look into."

"Right."

They said good-byes to London and headed off to their car. "So?" Peter said.

Vreni laughed out loud as they got in and stowed their various gear. "They're running scared about something, that's for sure, and probably the reactor is at the heart of it. Usually they can't throw enough information at you at these press conferences. But I've never heard of one this short before."

"So is this the reactor that Greenpeace and everybody was protesting about?" Peter said as he started the car.

"Good question. I didn't believe Buckingham, just then… that's all I'm sure of. And here's the question—"

Peter drove out the entrance, where security people were still checking the people coming in. Vreni said nothing until they were back on the freeway again. "Look," she said, "if they wanted to send something up secretly, why didn't they just do that? They've done it before."

"Maybe," Peter said, "they thought that no one would be interested in the reactor—a mistake, granted—and now they're trying to cover up the fact that they're putting it up anyway."

"Yes, but why mention this MPAPPS thing, then? Which sounds so much like some kind of clandestine power source—a reactor by any other name? Why not just put the thing up there, hush hush, and be done with it?"

Peter shook his head. "It's beyond me."

Vreni sighed. "Well, at least I have something to run with now. I'm going to get started on those interview schedulings today, and see if I can get hold of my police buddies. Meanwhile, if I can get some interviews scheduled for tomorrow…"

"You're on," Peter said. "After I drop you, I'll be out with the camera and the Questar. I've got to get the hang of this thing. Breakfast tomorrow?"

Vreni nodded. "The Breakfast Club, that's us. Let's make it early, though. The Hilton holds these big brunch buffets on weekends, and if I see all that food, I'm going to try to eat it. Not a good thing."

Peter chuckled. "For either of us. Early it is."

SEVERAL hours later, Peter was standing in a swamp, being bitten all over by hungry mosquitoes, and was happier than he'd been in months.

After dropping Vreni off, he had called Aunt Anna's to check in with MJ. She wasn't home: Aunt Anna told him that MJ wasn't expected back until late—something about a gallery-opening party being run by one of the people with whom she had left her CV, a gathering at which it was smart for MJ to put in an appearance.

Oh, well, Peter thought, and set himself up for a day out, and an evening as well, doing work of different kinds. He packed the Questar, and one other piece of useful equipment: his police-radio scanner. He also brought an extra camera—one which he had been using, as Spider-Man, quite effectively of late. It had a motion-actuated mount, with a little circuit board, a whole PC's worth of intelligence, to drive it. A couple of weeks ago, after finishing the business with Venom, he had added one more useful piece of hardware to it—a simple vise-style C-clamp. The camera had shown a tendency to fall over, occasionally, when he left it to its own devices on a tripod. (His usual method of webbing the camera in place had the drawback of not allowing the motion sensor to move freely.)

The C-clamp, though, would leave it freer to move and less likely to do a dive from a wall or other unstable situation. Peter could even clamp it onto a pole or a tree limb, now, and be fairly certain of finding it where he left it when he got back, rather than lying on its lens in a puddle, or smashed to bits.

An hour's drive out of Miami on Route 41 brought him into the Big Cypress National Preserve. It was in the Everglades, though not part of the Everglades National Park as such. Twenty-four hundred square miles of hardwood tree islands, scattered slash pine, dry prairies, marsh, and mangrove forest. Here and there he would pass a little knot of houses, maybe with a tiny store nearby, and nothing else for miles except the huge boles of cypress and beds of waving reeds. Birdsong was everywhere: once, when Peter stopped to give himself a break from driving and listen to the wind, he heard a low coughing cry repeated several times, and it took him some minutes to realize that the sound was that of a Florida panther, somewhere out there among the tangled islands of marl and knotted tree-roots, going about its business.

He stopped several times to work with the Questar and do some wildlife photography that was as good a practice for the next couple of weeks' work as he was likely to get. The Questar's range was indeed ridiculous, and it took him a while to get used to it. He could sight a rock half a mile away and get a close-up of a cottonmouth sunning on it which suggested he was more like ten feet from the stone—though he much preferred the real distance. A flock of flamingos a mile off, an alligator a quarter-mile away, rolling lazily in a drainage canal—they seemed close enough to walk up to and touch. Peter began to wish desperately that some money would drop from the heavens so he could afford a Questar of his own. *I might as well wish for that Hasselblad they left on the moon,* he thought, and then wondered whether one of his fellow super heroes might be passing that way anytime soon. If they were….

Peter chuckled to himself and straightened up. It was getting near dusk again. He had pulled off to the side of the road to catch the moon coming up, for the Questar was after all primarily a telescope, and it would be stupid, he thought, not to experiment with that aspect of its function as well. Big and round, the moon slid up. Peter fussed over the camera's *f*-stops, looking for the best setting to catch that apparently huge disk without the diminution of its apparent size that was every photographer's bane. He blew nearly a roll of film on that alone. Behind him, in the car, the police scanner muttered softly to itself, mostly about speeders and domestic disturbances.

The moon was an hour or so up the sky when Peter stopped at last. *Vreni's not going to want to hear excuses in the morning*, he thought, *and we'll have a lot of driving to do tomorrow, I would imagine. Better pack up and go.* And he was doing just that, and had just slid into the driver's seat of the Chevette, when the scanner started talking to itself again. It had been quiet for a while; the new urgency in the dispatcher's voice caught Peter by surprise.

"Okee four one eight—"

"Four one eight, go."

"Got a report of a large reptile walking around near Deep Lake." That was one of the small towns in the area, in the heart of Big Cypress, near Route 29.

"That's the fourth 'gator today," said four one eight wearily.

"Not a 'gator," said the dispatcher, somewhat anxiously. Peter blinked.

"What?"

"No 'gator, four one eight. The report was of a reptile. Also from Deep Lake, report of a large man in distress, seen heading out of town in a hurry. And a silent alarm. The general store in Deep Lake."

Peter grabbed his road map, shook it open, and checked his position. Deep Lake was no more than two miles away.

"Okay, dispatch. ETA ten minutes. We're over by Ochopee at the moment—that break-in."

"Ten-four, four one eight."

Peter leaped out of the car, seized the Questar and his camera bag, locked the car up, and hotfooted it into a clump of cypress near the roadside. A half a minute later, Spider-Man swung down out of the trees—having first webbed the Questar, the camera bag, and his car keys tightly to the cypress's innermost trunk, about fifty feet up, just in case anyone should stop to have a look at his car with less than friendly intent. His own camera, the small C-clamped one, was tucked away in his costume should he need it.

He took off cross-country at his best speed. Here the going was better than in the suburbs: the biggest trees, the most ancient of the great bald cypresses, stood up like towers dotted across the landscape, their huge thick branches outstretched and ready to catch a slung web. Where the bald cypresses didn't grow, the lesser ones grew in plenty. Spider-Man might not get a lot of height, but he made good speed. With little chance of anyone seeing him, out here in the middle of almost nowhere, the two-minute mile was no problem.

Deep Lake was a very small town indeed: a gas station, a diner, a post office, a little general store, and a scatter of small houses on a side road behind it. The blue strobe light of the general store's alarm was flashing, and lights were on inside. Spidey swung past and glanced in the window, saw no one hurt, only some shelves knocked over and an old man looking at them, shaking his head. He would have stopped and looked in, but his spider-sense twinged hard, and he looked down past the faint aura of radiance thrown by the town's three streetlights. He thought he heard, in the vast country silence, someone or something crashing through the undergrowth.

Swiftly he went after the noise, out of town and on down Route 29, then eastward into the swamp. Swamp was probably the wrong name for it; it was wet prairie, really, mixed with dry-footed reed beds alive with the singing and peeping of frogs. Louder than the frogs, he could hear heavy footsteps thudding on soft ground, splashing through the wet, and a low, almost singsong growl. The footsteps went in a two-footed rhythm. *Definitely* not a 'gator, Spidey thought.

Here there were fewer trees to work with. Spider-Man leapt again and again, and finally, ahead of him, caught sight of what he pursued— or, rather, whom. The moon was higher, and glinted off wet, scaly hide. Color was washed out of everything in this light, but Spider-Man knew that that hide would be green by daylight. He saw the lash of the tail. The growl got louder.

One big leap brought him down right in front of it. Shocked, the creature started, then planted its huge hind claws, grounded the powerful tail behind it for balance.

"Curt," Spider-Man said. "Curt, we've only got a couple of minutes to talk. The police are coming—"

The Lizard flung his arms wide, and roared, flexing his claws. A glint in the air—*did something fly off to one side?* Or was it a bat, or some night-flying bird, flickering briefly bright in the moonlight? Spidey didn't dare take his eyes off the Lizard to see—a moment's error with this creature could leave you very dead.

"Curt, listen," he said. "Martha—"

Another roar. The Lizard shook his head wildly from side to side as if even the mention of her name caused him pain. *Maybe it does,* Spidey thought, wrenched with pity. He wanted not to have to try this tack again, but anything that might get through to Curt Connors, to the man trapped inside, was worth trying. "Martha and William—"

Half roaring, half screaming, the Lizard rushed him. Spider-Man leapt sideways and felt the wind of the Lizard's plunge brush by him, felt the claws go whiffing past his face, just missing. *Sometimes I really miss the good old days when the Lizard was semi-intelligent, and not a mindless, rampaging beast,* he thought.

He heard cars, two of them, pull up by the roadside. That was followed by car doors being thrown open and slammed shut. Flashlights came on, and people headed out into the darkness toward them.

"This is the police," said an amplified voice. "We're armed, and we'll shoot if we have to. Come out and give yourself up."

Spidey leapt up and out of the way to get a look at where the police were. He was astonished when his spider-sense warned him that one of those huge clawed hands was reaching toward him. Unable to twist out of the way in midair, the Lizard plucked him out of the air and dashed him to the ground. Stunned, he lay there just long enough to gasp and roll sideways as the Lizard's razor-sharp claws came down and slashed the ground where he had been. Spider-Man shot a web at the Lizard, but as fast as he shot it, the creature clawed it aside.

"Hold it right there!" yelled a man's voice. Enraged, the Lizard spun, took a fraction of a second to sight on the intruder—then leapt. Spidey barely had time to shoot out one last strand of web, aiming for the Lizard's legs. He caught him. The Lizard slammed down hard on the ground. "It's the Lizard!" Spider-Man shouted. "Get out of here! Get back in your cars!"

A second's silence—then gunfire. There was no way to tell in what direction the bullets were traveling. All Spidey could see were muzzle flashes, and all he could hear were ricochets. The Lizard tore the web off his legs, reared up again and made for the officers. Spidey staggered to his feet, picked the one decent-sized cypress in the area, and shot a line of web at its top. It held. *This works for Tarzan and Luke Skywalker,* he thought, *let's see if it works for me.*

The Lizard charged, claws outstretched. Right in front of his face, Spidey came swinging by, caught the first cop out of the Lizard's path, grabbed the second between his legs, and swung them both up and out of the Lizard's reach, into the cypress. The three of them thudded into the trunk, and the cops had the sense to cling on tight, while the Lizard rushed the bottom of the tree and hit it almost head-on. The crash shook the whole tree, but it held fast: three hundred years' worth of hurricanes had taught it a trick or two.

The Lizard roared rage and defiance, shook the tree, but the tree still held. Then came what Spidey had feared: the Lizard sank his talons into the trunk and started to climb it. Hurriedly Spider-Man looked around him, sighted another treetop that he thought he could hit with a web.

Out on the road, a third cop car arrived, sirens blaring and lights flashing, then a fourth. The Lizard let the tree go, roared in fury, and loped off into the swamp. Spidey tried to tell where he was going, but in the uncertain moonlight, it was hopeless—in less than a few seconds, the Lizard might as well have been invisible. And, encumbered as he was with a pair of cops, there was no opportunity to hit him with a spider tracer.

"You guys all right?" he said to his two fellow travelers.

One of them answered unprintably. The second said, "And who the hell are you, buster?"

He slid down the webline with both of them and saw them safely onto the ground before answering, "Just your friendly neighborhood Spider-Man, officer."

"Not mine," said the first policeman, and spat expressively.

The second dusted himself off, eyed Spider-Man with an expression that looked thoughtful, if not entirely friendly. "You on vacation?"

Spidey had to laugh. "No," he said. "This is a business trip."

"And was that your business?" the second cop said, gesturing after the Lizard with his chin.

"Partly," Spidey said. "I heard he'd been seen down here."

"More than seen," said another of the policemen, one of the group who had just arrived. They were carrying shotguns, and one of them had leveled his at Spidey. "They took Saunders's store apart, back there. Money missing. And, Harry? Your gun's gone from your car. So's Ed's."

"Your friend there," said the second policeman to Spider-Man, "seems to have had a friend with him."

"Not my friend," Spider-Man said. "An accomplice?" That was a new one on him. The Lizard was a loner by nature. *This puts an entirely new spin on things....*

"Never mind that," said the first policeman. "What're we gonna do with you, now, Mister Friendly Neighborhood?"

"He's a crook like the others," said one of the newly arrived cops. "Arrest 'im."

Spider-Man sighed inside the mask, and looked toward the second policeman, who looked back with that thoughtful expression again. "I think we might have trouble with that," he said. "Anyway, you did us a good turn just now, son. That thing would've fileted us. But this is *our* neighborhood, so I think it would be best if you let us handle matters around here, and took yourself on back wherever you came from."

"I understand you perfectly, Officer," Spidey said. "My pleasure to have been of service."

He shot a webline up into the tree and swung away, heading northward toward Route 41. When he got back to the spot where he had parked his car, he got in, started it up, and moved it several hundred yards farther along the road and out of sight, on a small service road running parallel with a canal by the road. *If they noticed it,* he thought, *I don't want them coming back and tracing it... it could cause uncomfortable questions.*

Once the car was seen to, and he double-checked that the Questar was still lodged in the tree, he webslung his way back to within a few hundred yards of where he and the Lizard had clashed. The police were still going over the area, so Spidey perched in one of the bald cypresses, waiting for them to leave. They took an hour or two about it, going very thoroughly over the ground where the fight with the Lizard had taken place. Finally, though, they realized there wasn't much more they could do until morning, on such varied and uneven ground, and they left.

Spider-Man came down from his tree then, slightly stiff, but no less intrigued than he had been earlier. That memory of something, faint but definitely there—flying off the Lizard? or being thrown?—was nagging him.

He went over the ground with spider-senses alert. Even so, the terrain was so variable, such a crazy unpredictable mixture of wet and dry, of bog, dirt, mud, reeds, and prickly undergrowth, and the light was so poor, that it wasn't until the false dawn began that he found it. "It" was a little can, about a foot long and matte-silvery, like a very upmarket thermos bottle.

Now then, he thought, and worked on getting the top unscrewed. It took a certain exertion of his super-strength to loosen the thing—a normal person probably wouldn't have been able to get it open without mechanical help. Finally, though, he got it off, and peered into the "thermos."

Nothing.

He shook the bottle. The faintest sound of impact inside: something, not rattling, just thumping gently against the sides of the bottle. There was something in there.

Then why couldn't he see it?

He upended the bottle over one hand. Something slid out, into his palm. Impact—but without weight.

Spider-Man peered at the object in his hand, if "object" was the word he was looking for. *It's a piece of smoke,* he thought, completely mystified, for that was what it looked like. If you had a smoke-filled room, and took a knife and cut a rectangular slice of the air, sort of the shape of a slender brick—and then took it outside into clean air to examine it, it would look just like this. The edges of the substance seemed to fade away into the air itself. The body of it was semitransparent, and grayish, just like smoke. It was lighter than an object of equivalent size made of paper or hollow plastic.

What on Earth is this? Spider-Man wondered. *Is it even from Earth? And what the heck was the Lizard doing with it?*

Spider-Man put the "smoke" back in its bottle and closed it tight, webbed it to him, and started back to the car as dawn's early light started to come up over the wetlands, and the first birds of morning started to test their voices. He was going to have to find out what this was, and what the Lizard was doing with it. But it was going to have to wait a little. In a couple of hours, Vreni would be waiting for Peter Parker, downstairs at the Hilton.

As he swung off toward the road, he yawned. *If I'd known the super hero business kept calling for these all-nighters*, he thought, *I doubt I'd ever have gotten into it.*

But this was at least partly a fib. Spider-Man swung off into the new morning, the proud possessor of a piece of smoke, and a whole new batch of unanswered questions.

THREE

WHEN Peter got back to the hotel, it was nearly seven. He'd agreed to meet Vreni for breakfast at about eight. There would be just time to get himself up to the room and run a lot of cold water over himself very quickly in an attempt to wake up.

Not that the evening's events weren't interesting enough, but Peter was having a reaction that happened sometimes after a night's excitement: the adrenaline would run out, and he would find himself totally wrecked. There was no time for that now, though. He had a long day of driving and shooting ahead of him.

Peter took the elevator up to the twelfth floor in the hotel and walked down the long hall to his room. As he slid the key card into the door, he saw to his surprise that the little light on the doorplate, which usually flashed green when the door was ready to open, was now coming up red. He tried the knob, and found the door bolted from the inside. "Hello?" he said.

"Ung," said a weary voice from inside. He heard the closet door slide aside, someone feeling among the clothes there: then the sound of the door unbolting, the chain coming off. MJ opened the door, blinked blearily at him. "If you're going to have such late nights while you're down here," she said, "I wish you'd let me know."

"What're you doing here?" he said, coming in and shutting the door behind him.

"Well, since you did slip me that spare key," MJ said, "I thought I might as well make use of it. I couldn't get back to Aunt Anna's from that party last night. It was too late, I didn't want to disturb her; and the cab would've cost a fortune." She shrugged. "So I thought I'd just crash here."

"Well," Peter said, hugging her, "I'm glad somebody got to use the room last night, because I sure didn't."

"I noticed," she said, sitting down on the bed. "Business, I take it."

He nodded. "Take a look at this," Peter said.

He rummaged among his bags and things and came up with the thermos bottle, unscrewed it, and went over to sit at the table by the window. MJ got up and looked over his shoulder as he tapped the contents of the bottle onto the table's surface. There lay, in the morning sunlight, the piece of smoke. Where the sun struck it, it seemed even less there—just a pale misty oblong, a little brick of fog. MJ looked at it, her eyes wide. "What is it?"

"You tell me."

She reached out a hand toward it, then pulled the hand back. "It's not radioactive or anything, is it?"

Peter shook his head. "Couldn't tell for sure," he said, "but if it were hot enough to be dangerous, I'd get a twinge from my spider-sense. I don't get anything like that at all, so…"

"And you found this where?"

Quickly Peter told her about the Lizard, and his encounter with him. MJ shook her head. "Strange," she said. "I thought that these days he was sort of mindless when he was the Lizard. I mean, as Curt Connors he might make plans, or do intelligent things, but—as the Lizard?"

"I don't know, MJ." And then Peter checked his watch. "Oh, jeez, look at the time. I've got to get into the shower, honey."

He headed for the bathroom, shedding clothes in all directions. MJ wandered after him. "You're gonna like that shower," MJ said. "It's so strong, it nearly rips your hair off."

"Good," Peter said. He turned it on, producing a violent stream of water and a satisfying cloud of steam. He climbed in and started to scrub.

"You'd better shave too," MJ said. "Your seven-o'clock shadow is showing."

"I just bet. How did you do last night?"

"Ohh," she said, sitting down on the sink, "not great."

"Why? Wasn't it a good party?"

"Oh, it was good. There were all these network TV people there. Lots of nice food." She sounded morose.

"Doesn't sound like you enjoyed yourself much."

"I didn't. They were all better-looking than I was."

"Oh, come on! I think that's statistically impossible."

"No, I'm serious. And in the middle of the party, they introduced the model who's going to get that part on the talk show."

"Oh, really." Now he understood where the moroseness was coming from. Peter sighed. He thought he knew what MJ was thinking: that they needed the money, but also that being passed over for a job was a personal blow to her, no matter how casually she acted about such things.

"And she," MJ said, "was gorgeous. *Gorgeous.*" She pouted slightly. "It's just not fair."

"No," Peter said, "I guess it's not. What're you going to do now?"

"I don't know. I was talking to some of the people at the party last night. Some of them were from agencies I'd applied to." She shook her head. "It's funny, but they see acting as a step down from modeling. They think that if you've gone into acting in TV, you've essentially written yourself off as a model. I don't understand it. I would have thought it'd give you more credence, not less. But that doesn't seem to be the way it works, not down here." She laughed, a somewhat bitter sound. "All of them were interested in talking to me about my TV work, but if I talked to them about modeling, they looked at me as if they thought I just wanted to come back and… slum. And it's not like that! You know that."

"You wouldn't know how to slum," Peter said, groping around for the shampoo bottle. "It's insulting for them to even think that way."

"Oh, I know, but they don't see that. A lot of these people are really kind of wrapped up in themselves."

Peter smiled slightly. This was a complaint he had heard from her before, and it was, he supposed, understandable. When your work and your livelihood depended on how good you could make yourself look to other people, the temptation to become very self-centered, it seemed to Peter, would be tough to resist. He had kept to himself, some time back, the suspicion that one reason MJ's modeling career was a little up-and-down was because she did not have that self-centeredness. But that was one of the things he loved about her, and he wasn't sure he'd trade it for any amount of success.

"Anyway," MJ said, "I had a couple of offers."

"Anything serious?"

MJ laughed again, pulled a Kleenex out of the box, and began shredding it methodically. "They weren't much better than wage slavery, really, and the travel allowances—" She shook her head. "I'd be crazy to take them. I *do* have my pride." She glanced up at him. He could just see her out the shower curtain, and the look in her eyes was an almost stern expression that he had seen before. "You start working cheap, here or anywhere, and word gets around. Pretty soon no one will have you anymore. So…" She trailed off. "Are you angry with me?"

"What? For not taking bad job offers? You have to be the judge of these things, babe. This isn't my area of expertise." He put his head out the shower curtain and smiled at her. "You want advice on how to climb up the sides of apartment buildings, or where to sock Venom to make him yell—"

"Please," MJ said. "I'd just spent a few days without even thinking of him. But I see your point."

"Well," Peter said, "I'll be guided by your opinion. If you think a job's bad, you shouldn't be taking it."

She sighed. Peter got out of the shower and hastily rubbed himself down: it was almost seven-thirty. "You know," she said, looking up at him, "you're really good to me."

"Well, I should be! You're my wife!"

"Yeah, well, you put up with a lot, you know that? Me and my insecurities."

"And you don't put up with a lot?" He hung up the towel, drew her close. "With a husband who swings around on webs and gets himself in trouble? I think you have a fairly high tolerance level, actually. I'm a pretty lucky guy."

She pulled his face down to hers. For a long minute or so, there were no words. Then MJ said, "You want me to rinse out your uniform for you?"

Peter chuckled. "It doesn't need it yet. Besides, if one of the hotel staff came in and found it hanging over the tub—"

MJ dimpled. "I see your point. Well, never mind." She stepped out and started rummaging in the closet for her clothes. "I should go back to Aunt Anna's. I left a message for her, but you know how she is. Until she sees me with her own eyes and hears everything that happened, she won't be satisfied. And she won't have anything to tell the neighbors." She chuckled. "'My Niece The TV Star.'"

"Well, give her my best."

Peter started dressing hurriedly. When he turned away from checking himself out in the mirrored sliding doors, he saw MJ staring thoughtfully at the little piece of smoke on the table. "It's so strange," she said. "It looks—" she shrugged "—illegal somehow."

"Illegal as in drugs?"

"No… just as in, it shouldn't be there. It looks wrong."

She reached out a hand, prodded it hesitantly. Then MJ put up her eyebrows. "It's a little springy. Did you feel that?"

"No." He came over to MJ and reached out a finger, poked the stuff. There was indeed a response as if he were pushing on very resistant foam rubber. But when he pushed it and let it spring back, he couldn't see any change in the object, no evidence of what he could physically feel it doing. It was very strange.

"I've got to find somebody who can tell me what the heck this is," Peter said. "But it's going to have to wait. Vreni's going to have a lot of interview appointments today, I think."

"What're you going to do with this?" MJ asked.

"Oh, I'll take it with me… there's room in the camera bag."

"Why would the Lizard have it?" she continued, as Peter shrugged into a light jacket and started packing his work bags up. "Where would he have been taking it? Where did it come from?"

"I hope I can find out," Peter said.

IN San Francisco that morning, the mist hung low, as it often did: sometimes until noon, nearly, before burning off. Many people in San Francisco paid no particular attention to this, being used to it. Others paid no attention to the weather because they couldn't see it.

Down in the darkness, below the city streets, the doings of the open sky were no concern of theirs, except on rainy days when the water made its way down through the drains and trickled into the city's underheart. Down there in the darkness, under the great buildings, under the old city, a newer one had been born. A place of tunnels and warrens, lit here and there by lamps illumined with stolen power, maintained with materials brought down quietly from the surface by night. It was a city of the disenfranchised, the homeless, the victimized, of people who had turned their backs on the mist and the sunshine both, and sought a different kind of life, private, silent, remote.

In one such quiet warren, a man sat on someone's castaway chair, and thought. It was not strictly accurate to call him a man—not anymore. The core of him was human, but things had been added. He was not a single being any longer… and had almost forgotten what it was like to be one.

He was part of a symbiosis, one that some people found deadly, others found reassuring. In a long-forgotten tunnel between two buildings, in a little makeshift "living room" containing a table and chairs, and the remains of a takeout meal, Eddie Brock, known to his friends and his enemies as Venom, sat going over some paperwork and considering his options.

The decay and destruction of something he loved was on his mind. The past month or so had been a busy one for him. San Francisco was his home, but he left it willingly enough when business called. Business, for him, meant defending the innocent, the helpless, from those who would prey upon them; defending them violently, if need be. He had gone to New York to do that, for he had gotten word that someone there was masquerading as Venom and attacking innocent people. If there was any kind of behavior he could not allow to happen in his name, it was that. Making his way to New York, he had dealt with the problem—had helped to deal with the creature which, as it turned out, had unwittingly been impersonating him by night in the streets of New York.

There had also been other satisfactions. Going to New York had also meant dealing with Spider-Man. Venom had dealt with the wall-crawler, at least to his temporary satisfaction, giving him one or two extremely conclusive drubbings and reminding him once again of the error which Spider-Man had made in rejecting the symbiote "costume" which was now part of Venom. Venom had been slightly surprised, as well, during their brief and peculiar alliance, to find that Spider-Man was perhaps slightly less a hopeless case than Venom had thought. Not that this would make any difference in the long run: Venom would destroy him eventually. The symbiote's emotions regarding Spider-Man, and Peter Parker, were too clear for Venom to ignore. Sooner or later the moment would be right, and this particular aspect of his history with the symbiote would become a closed chapter.

For the meantime, though, Venom had parted from Spider-Man, content to let him live a while longer in return for his aid against the bizarre extraterrestrial creature which had been killing people in Venom's apparent likeness, and also for his action against Hobgoblin—unquestionably a factor in keeping all of Manhattan from being blown halfway to the moon.

Other aspects of the month's work, though, were still niggling at Venom. The extraterrestrial monster had mostly killed in search of radioactive materials, its food. And there turned out to be far too much material of that kind in the city for Venom's taste... courtesy of a strange import-export firm called Consolidated Chemical Research Corporation. This firm had stored radioactive materials in odd places around Manhattan, places too accessible to normal human beings who could (and did) come to harm by them. Barrels of waste, caches of fissionable material, things that had no business being in a city full of the innocent—Venom and Spider-Man had recovered a number of caches. The New York City government, alerted to this problem, had been cleaning up the sites as best it could: as far as Venom could tell from the news, and his more clandestine sources of information, they were doing a fairly good job.

But his own concerns didn't stop there. A firm like CCRC, which had been so careless once in the middle of one of the most heavily populated areas on the planet, would likely be just as careless elsewhere. Any big company which became so cavalier with the lives of human beings was a concern to Venom, and he intended to keep working at this problem until it was solved.

He looked at one of the pieces of paper which lay on the chipped Formica table on which he sat. He didn't have to reach for it: the symbiote, which was presently masquerading as his shirt and jeans, put out a slim graceful pseudopod and flipped the page over so that Eddie could see the next one, a long list of names and addresses. Venom had continued to look into the corporate structure of CCRC.

Through his investigation of state and county documents, Eddie had found that CCRC's New York branch had been having dealings with numerous companies of varying types in various states. Some of these had been shut down abruptly over the last month: corporations were sold or otherwise divested, registrations were shifted around. Now there were only a few active links to CCRC left. Venom had found it very interesting that all of them were in Florida.

One of these was a large foreign merchant bank called Regners Wilhelm, a German-based firm, outwardly very respectable. One was a chemical supply firm called Haller Chemical. And yet another—and this one Venom found a matter for some concern—was the United States Government. CCRC seemed to be supplying something—the details were presently fuzzy—to Kennedy Space Center.

All of this gave Eddie Brock a lot to think about. He was disturbed by the government connection. He was even more disturbed by the presence of any CCRC operation in Florida. The great aquifer which underlay the state was one of its greatest assets, and was tremendously vulnerable. Already the water system there had been much damaged by the thoughtless misuse of the past century. And the flatness of the state made that aquifer very susceptible to contamination: such contamination would take months, maybe years, to purge itself completely from the ecosystem, doing who knew what damage both to animal life and the humans living there—the innocents who had no other source of water, and would shortly find themselves being poisoned if radioactive by-products were to be stored as carelessly in Florida as they had been in Manhattan.

Until a day or so ago, Eddie Brock had been content to turn all these things over in his mind, and plan, trying to figure out what was the best way in which to proceed. But then a piece of news had been brought to him that gave him much more concern.

The Lizard had been seen in Florida. All around him, Eddie could feel the symbiote twitching against his skin in the beginnings of rage. The Lizard was a thoughtless, mindless monster, one that needed to be killed: it had done enough harm to the innocent in its own time. Occasionally Spider-Man had served to contain the thing. But now, to this already dangerous cocktail of CCRC carelessness and involvement in Florida, the Lizard had been added.

Venom knew that the Lizard had been used in the past by another super villain, a woman named Calypso. At least Hobgoblin, who would love such a tool, was safely out of the picture, and put away in the Vault for the moment. But there were others who were free, and wouldn't scruple. And Curt Connors, the Lizard's human alter ego, was a scientist, one with expertise in biochemistry—but chemistry first and foremost.

It all made Venom slightly suspicious. Eddie Brock was a journalist before Spider-Man conspired to ruin his good name. And now those old instincts kicked in: he smelled something, something suspicious. Something that needed his attention in Florida.

In addition, if the Lizard was in Florida, it wouldn't be surprising if Spider-Man showed up. Venom couldn't bring himself to object to that.

Eddie smiled a little, to himself and his other, put the paperwork back in its neat pile, and stood up.

Florida is supposed to be very nice this time of year, he thought. *It's time for us to go.*

PETER met Vreni for breakfast. She looked at him with some concern. "Had a bad night?" she said. "You've got big circles under your eyes."

Peter nodded. "A late one."

"Will you be all right for today?"

"Sure, as soon as I get some coffee in me."

"All right. I've made a couple of appointments for us down in Ochopee—and a couple in the spot where the Lizard was actually seen last night. We're in good shape; we'll have fresh reports. I'll drive today, if you like—"

"No, it's okay," Peter said hastily, "I still have some work to do with the Questar—can we do it in two cars?"

"No problem."

After breakfast, they retraced the route that Peter had taken the night before. About an hour or so later, they were parking in front of Saunders's store, which Peter had passed while going after the Lizard. Vreni interviewed Mr. Saunders—"You just call me Dave now, honey"—a dear old, unreconstructed "old boy" with a halo of thin white hair, who either had never heard about women's liberation or didn't care about it. He repeatedly called Vreni "honey chile," and although Peter saw her eyebrows go up the first time, plainly she wasn't going to make an issue of it as long as the information kept coming.

"That big green thing came right in here," he said, waving his arms around at the front door, now hanging pitifully off its hinges. "Went smashing around, broke half the glass in the place—" Mr. Saunders gestured helplessly at the windows. "Gonna take me days to get all this fixed. Have to go all the way down to Ochopee for it." He glowered.

"Did he take anything specific that you could see?" Vreni said.

"Nope. Just banged around like a bull in a china shop." Mr. Saunders looked unhappily around his shelves, some of which had indeed had china on them. Now it was all swept together in a jagged pile in the corner. "There's most of my stock gone. Don't know if my insurance is gonna cover it."

"Well, certainly," Vreni murmured, "you would think…"

"Honey chile," said Mr. Saunders, turning a sharp-eyed blue gaze on her, "if you know an insurance company that routinely has clauses in its policies about damage by super villains, you let me know, okay? 'Cause I think I'm gonna have to change my coverage."

Vreni swallowed and nodded.

"He came in here, plunged around, bashed things—it was kinda funny," Saunders said, "in a horrible way. He'd bash something, and then stand still, and turn all stiff-like, and look around. Then bash something else. Then stop still again. He did that three or four times."

Peter, taking pictures of the wreckage, was bemused by that. *Doesn't match his normal behavior at all—if anything the Lizard does could be considered normal….*

"I didn't see if it took anything. I got down under the counter. So would you," Mr. Saunders said. "He was roaring. Those teeth of his—" He shook his head. "Then out he went again, out the window, crash!" He pointed with his chin. "Ran out in the wet prairie. Don't know what happened to him after that. Heard him roaring and yelling, but I wasn't gonna go out and see about it. I gave him both barrels when he came in— didn't bother him no more than spitballs would've."

Peter took a few shots of Mr. Saunders while he talked to Vreni. "Have there been any strangers in the area the last few days?" Vreni said. "Anybody you wouldn't recognize?"

Mr. Saunders shook his head. "Nope. That's half the problem with this place. No one stops. Even the gas station—" He gestured at the pumps outside. "I can't get a good price for gas out here. We're too far from the distributor. Everybody who drives up here tanks up down in Ochopee or over in Naples, places like that. They don't want to pay five cents more a gallon.… and why should they? Naah, we had three people stop for gas in the past two days, and they went straight on away again."

"And no one's stopped for longer than that—say, to sight-see?"

Saunders laughed. "Missy, anybody came hanging around here, the whole town, all four houses of it, would turn out to see. No one comes here to hang around. There's nothing here. And tell you the truth, we don't really want folks from outside hanging around here, either. This isn't no city. It's a town, our town—we like it private. We like it quiet. No crime, no one bothers us… until now." He frowned at Vreni in a way that suggested to Peter that Mr. Saunders considered them both a sign of the decadence and imminent downfall of civilization.

"Well, we won't be troubling you much longer, Mr. Saunders," Vreni said. "But thank you for your help." She turned to Peter. "You about ready?" she said.

"Yup. Let's go."

They made two other stops that day: another in Deep Lake, and then a third in Ochopee. The Deep Lake one was to Mrs. Bridger, a little old lady who lived in one of the houses built off the service road near Saunders's. The Ochopee stop was with the Melendez family, a young couple and their two baby girls who farmed about five miles from Ochopee proper.

Mrs. Bridger sat on the porch of her tumbledown little house—which would have been new in the 1950s, but hadn't been maintained or repaired since in the wake of who knew how many hurricanes—and told how she had seen the Lizard swimming down the canal, three nights before. "You're sure it wasn't a 'gator?" Vreni said, as Peter roamed around taking pictures.

The old lady, half blind as she was, knew what Vreni was actually asking. "Oh no, dear," she said. "The alligators were swimming away from him just as fast as they could. They no fools." She chuckled. "He would stop every now and then, and then go on again. But he didn't make no noise, or do anything bad."

The canal ran close to Saunders's. *Casing the joint?* Peter thought to himself. *I wonder….*

A little later, Mike and Carol Melendez took Vreni and Peter out in the back of their little farmhouse and gestured away across the fields to indicate where the Lizard had cut across their bottom thirty, frightening their cattle, until, as Carol said indignantly, "A couple of them won't even give milk now, they were so upset." Peter took pictures of everything—

those dead flat, beautifully green sorghum fields that the Melendezes were farming looked bizarre compared to the wild variation of the rest of the landscape around the Ochopee area. Mostly, though, as at Mrs. Bridger's, he concentrated on their faces—the proud, private look of them, all profoundly distrustful, Peter thought, especially of strangers. There's no way, he thought as he snapped away, that the one-armed Curt Connors could ever hide here. He'd stick out like a sore thumb. All these people had such a reserve, a resistance to strangers, that if someone new were around, Peter felt sure they would talk about it immediately.

There was something else that Peter started to notice as they talked to the Melendezes: they were afraid. He thought about it more, as he drove back toward Miami (more or less behind Vreni, who was zooming along ahead of him and apparently practicing for Le Mans). He got a sense that normally they wouldn't happily have told him and Vreni even the little they did, but they were frightened at this intrusion into their life of something so completely beyond its boundaries. Maybe they were slightly flattered that a big-city reporter and a photographer came out all this way to see them. *But there was more to it,* Peter thought. His gut feeling said that they possibly had seen more than just the Lizard, or more often than just this once. The stress had simply become too much for them, severe enough to make them want to risk their privacy. But he couldn't get rid of the feeling that there was more these people could have said, and they just weren't saying it.

Once, while the Melendez husband had been talking to Vreni, Peter saw his wife look over northwards, past their fields, into the depths of Big Cypress. The look on her face was, for that moment, one of naked fear. But when she turned back to Vreni and her husband again, the expression was gone.

Peter thought of the expression on Buckingham's face at NASA the other day, and filed the two expressions away together, for reconsideration later.

He and Vreni stopped at a diner by the Everglades Parkway for a late lunch, and didn't discuss much of the interview material there, for they were both aware of the locals watching them closely, of ears stretched in their direction. As they were walking out to the cars, though, Vreni said to Peter, "I don't know, but I get a feeling these people are withholding something."

Peter nodded. "I don't know what else we could say to get them to be more forthcoming, though. They all seem so private—"

Vreni sighed as she went to stand by her car. "Well, I'm going to keep nosing around. I'm still trying to get that police connection sorted out. Not much I can do on a Sunday, though. Tomorrow may be better. You want to do some more camera work today?"

"I think so," Peter said.

"Well, see if you can be back this evening around sevenish. I want to touch base with you then, and we can talk about this material a little more after I've had time to transcribe the tapes and think everything over. Then tomorrow we'll start some serious digging. Particularly, I want to pull some companies' registers from Okechobee and Seminole counties, and see what kind of industry is working down here besides tourism."

"No problem," Peter said. "Sevenish it is."

She sighed, climbed into her car, and roared off.

Peter, meanwhile, stopped at a roadside pay phone and dialed the Connorses, got Martha. "I'm so glad to see you made it down here all right," she said, her voice warm. "We had a visitor last night—"

"Oh? Who?"

"I don't think we should talk about it on the phone. But come on over."

About two hours later, Peter was sitting in the Connorses' little kitchen, going over much the same ground with her that Spider-Man had the other night. William was out playing ball with some friends elsewhere in the neighborhood.

Martha apparently welcomed that. "It's hard enough," she said softly, "to be, effectively, a single parent. But to be one under these circumstances—an unofficial one—" She shook her head. "You can't share all the difficulties, all the trouble, with children: it's not fair to them. It makes them think they're more of a burden than they are."

"But he's not a burden," Peter said.

"No, not at all. All the time, it's 'I'll take care of you, Mom, I'll help us.' That willingness—if work alone were enough to make the difference, I'd be a rich woman off his efforts. As far as he's concerned, nothing's good enough for me." She paused. "Your cup's empty."

Peter pushed it toward her; she refilled it. "He has friends down here," he said. "Do you?"

She raised her eyebrows. "Maybe you're going to think this sounds snobbish of me, but I don't seem to have interests anything like most of the people here. Not much in common. A lot of my neighbors seem so… fixated on their family lives, their children. They don't seem to have much of a life outside it, and to them, to have a son and not have a husband, not have the wage-earner on site…. Some of them are very old-fashioned about it. They think, some of them, that I must have done something wrong, or that he must have." Martha looked at Peter helplessly. "And of course that's not the case."

"Of course not," Peter said.

"So I let them go their way, and I go mine. They're civil enough. We meet in the store, or down at the PTA…"

Peter nodded. She spoke very lightly, but the kind of life she was describing must have been appallingly lonely.

The front screen door jerked open with a shriek, and banged shut again. "Hey, Mom," William's voice yelled, "whose car is that? Oh! Pete!"

William ran over to Peter, a skateboard in hand. There was a moment's confusion as they tried to work out whether to shake hands or hug each other, and wound up doing both. "I could say something incredibly banal," Peter said, "like how you've grown."

William rolled his eyes. "Pete—"

"Well, I'm sorry, but you have! Where did you get a whole extra foot of height?"

"Sent out for it," William said, and grinned. "Never mind. I'm glad you're here. Mom, I had an idea."

Martha looked at him curiously. "What, honey?"

"Wait." He ran off into the next room. When he came back, he was carrying several yellow manila envelopes. "It's just a thought," he said, opening one of them and peering into it, going through the contents. "I thought of it while we were playing basketball, and ran right over, and now they're all mad at me." And he laughed with the pleasure of someone who has more important things to do. "But look—"

William took some sheets of paper out of the envelope and showed them to his mother. On the backs of them, Peter could just make out a check-balancing form. Bank statements?

"I know these are private," William said, "but look. See the code numbers?"

Martha looked at the statement, then looked sideways at William. "Can I show him?" William said.

"It's not as if our bank statements have thousands of zeroes on them at the moment," Martha said, wry. "Go ahead."

William brought the pile of bank statements around to Peter. "Look. Here are checks—" He pointed. "Some more checks—then some cash machine withdrawals. But we do all our withdrawals here in town." ATM TRANSACTION FF0138, said the line William pointed at now.

"That's the machine up on Main Street. Look at this, though—" He pointed at another. ATM TRANSACTION FF0152. And another. ATM TRANSACTION FF0132. And another, ATM TRANSACTION FF0148.

"Those aren't our machine," William said to Peter. "Dad still has his card… so he must have done those. I'm not sure where they are, though."

His mother was going through the envelope now. "Now, I wonder," she was saying absently. "You open one of these accounts and you get so much junk, but I don't believe Curt would have thrown anything out. He was always—is always—so methodical about his bookkeeping." Then her expression changed. "Here!" she said triumphantly, and came up with a little credit-card-size booklet, which she opened and paged through. "Yup… I thought so." Martha handed William the booklet. "This is First Florida's list of all the machines in the state. It has the code numbers there, honey."

"Awright!" He started to page through it, went over to a table for a pen, brought it back and started to work more or less over Peter's shoulder. "This one—this is Marco. This one—it's Sunniland, and this one is Ochopee—"

"William," Peter said, "there's a career waiting for you in detection."

Martha looked thoughtful. "That's about a hundred miles southeast of here," she said. "That general area."

"I think if you drew a circle containing all those towns," Peter said, "it's a fair bet he would be there. Unless he was purposely using those machines to create a false impression that he was there—"

Martha shook her head. "I don't think so. Curt isn't the wily type… he's *too* direct, if anything. That may be what caused all this trouble, in the first place." She smiled, a rueful look that Peter was getting to know better than he liked, the expression of someone coping with her pain. "If he's using those machines regularly, it's because they're pretty nearby. He hates to drive more than he has to."

Peter looked at the most recent statement. "This is dated the week before last," he said. "Can you get anything more current?"

She thought. "You know," she said after a moment, "I think the machine will give you a mini-statement of the account activity for the last week, if you ask it. I'm not sure if that'll have the ATM code numbers on it, but we can try."

"Do you mind if I make a note of these numbers?" Peter said. "Then, when you get that statement—"

"Wait a minute." Martha went over to the kitchen counter, got her purse, and rummaged in it. A moment later she came up with a wallet and pulled a card out of it. "Here," she said, handing it to William. "He knows my PIN number. Go on up there and get a statement, honey, and get twenty dollars while you're there."

"You need anything else. Mom?"

"You," Martha said, viewing her son with a practiced eye, "just want an excuse to go to the 7-Eleven and buy motorcycle magazines. You can have *one*."

It was about a quarter-mile's walk into town. Peter and William strolled down together, chatting.

"So how did Spider-Man look?"

"Cool. He always looks cool," said William. "He was worried, though."

"About your dad?"

"Yeah. It's good to know."

"What? That he was worried?"

William nodded. "It's good to know that people care. You hear stuff about the Lizard on TV, and a lot of them think he should just be shot. I want to shout, sometimes—just yell—'Let him alone! It's not his fault!'" The words came out in a whisper, but Peter was shaken by how much force underlay them. "So," William said, a little more normally, a few seconds later, "knowing that someone knows... and would say the same thing—It's good."

Peter nodded. "Someone cares," he said.

They made their way to the bank. William slipped the card into the machine, input his mother's PIN number, and punched the button asking for the mini-statement. The machine extruded it after a moment, and William took it, glanced at it, and deftly tore it in half, handing Peter the side that didn't have the amounts on it, but did have the code numbers of the ATM machines.

"A few more uses," William said. "He's not taking a lot, though. We're okay. Is that one Ochopee again?"

"I think so," Peter said. "Interesting." That one was dated the day before, when the Lizard had passed through Deep Lake.

The two of them walked back to the house. Peter sat down and had one more cup of tea, chatting with Martha about inconsequentialities— how MJ had been redecorating the apartment, what she was up to—and then made his good-byes, promising that he would let them know as soon as he found out anything worthwhile.

He got back onto the freeway and started to think hard. Peter tended to agree with Martha that Curt wouldn't bother with driving very far from where he was actually based. It would waste too much time from whatever he was working on—and Peter was sure he was working.

Most of these ATMs take pictures, Peter thought. *I wonder if we could get the bank to release the pictures of his usages to us?* But without help from law enforcement, Peter doubted it.

He headed back to the hotel, ready to meet with Vreni. But when he checked in at the desk to pick up his room key, he was given a note from her which said: "Delayed to check something out. Tonight is off. Breakfast club tomorrow? V." And another message as well, hastily scribbled: "Call Aunt Anna's immediately. MJ."

Oh my gosh, he thought, *what's happened? What's wrong?* Peter hurried up to the room, hunted around for Aunt Anna's phone number, and dialed it.

The phone rang. And rang, and rang, and rang. Peter sat there thinking, in increasing tension, *Are they gone? Did something bad happen? What, what—*

Someone picked up the phone. "Hello?"

"MJ! I got your message—"

She squealed. The sheer joy of the sound took Peter completely aback. "I got it! I got it!" she yelled.

"You got what?"

"The job! A job!"

"On a Sunday?"

She laughed. "This town operates on strange rules. Mostly that there aren't any. I was down in one of the bars on the Strip, having a sandwich with Ellanya David, you remember her?"

She was another model, formerly based in New York. Peter was becoming more amused by the moment. "You hated her! Why were you having a sandwich with her?"

"Oh, well, that was then." MJ giggled. "But now she's down here, and she's stuck in this real awful relationship, and I really feel sorry for her. Anyway, we're having this sandwich, and a guy came over and joined her. His name is Fletch, and he's from one of the big agencies, one that turned me down. We started talking,, and Fletch found out that I knew Ellanya in New York, and he had just fired her—"

"This is getting very complex," Peter said.

"It gets worse. Or better. So Ellanya had to leave, and another guy, a friend from a different agency came along, and Fletch introduced us to this other guy, his name is Joel. *He* works for an agency called Up N Over. And Fletch talked Joel into hiring me because I knew Ellanya."

Peter blinked. This was hardly the first time he had felt he needed a program or scorecard when trying to keep track of MJ's professional connections. "Uh, I'm seriously confused now."

"You're not alone. But Joel hired me; he said I had great planes." MJ giggled again. Peter shook his head in mute amazement. "And he gave me a retainer, right then out of the cash machine. He handed me five hundred bucks, *cash*!"

"If you produce results like this in a weekend," Peter said, "I'm going to be interested to see what you can do on a weekday."

"Well, we'll find out."

"So what do you have to do for him?"

"It's standard couture. They've got a campaign coming up for one of the magazines, all high-tech scenarios, and they're going to be shooting up by IBM in Boca, and along the Space Coast. And get this: at Kennedy, too!"

"The Rocket Garden?"

"Is that what it's called, where all the rockets stand around? Probably. But Boca's first, and we leave tomorrow!"

"So you won't be commuting, then." He hadn't had time to see much of her the last couple of days; now it looked like there wouldn't be time this week, either.

"No, Tiger, you know how it is. Until they get the rhythm of the shoot established, it's going to be eighteen-hour days. The commute would be crippling. We'll be in Boca the first couple of nights... then Kennedy after that."

"You're going to be up there for the launch, then?"

"I think so, if I understand the timing right. But Joel wasn't sure. He said he still had to settle the timing with the director, and get all the people together for this—he was looking for three other models as well."

"MJ, this is dynamite! How long is this going to last?"

"I'm not sure. But money's money."

"And the deal's good enough to please you?"

"Not quite what I would be making in New York at the best of times, but—" She giggled once more. "This isn't the best of times... and this is better than nothing. So I'm coming right over. Where's the albatross?"

"The albatross?"

"Vreni."

Peter laughed. "She's got plans of her own this evening."

"Well, that's just fine. I'll be right over. And we'll have some dinner out."

"That much anyway," Peter said. "I had kind of a late night..."

"You've got your second wind—I know you. Until you have dinner: then you'll fall over." She chuckled. "I'll be there to catch you... and then—"

"Then?"

"Then we'll see where our negotiations lead us." He could hear her smiling.

So it all came to pass. They had a splendid dinner down in the hotel's fancier restaurant, which specialized in Caribbean-style food. Then they negotiated. And four or five hours later, in the hotel room, MJ turned and snuggled up against Peter and said, "So tell me about your day."

He told her. When he finished, she looked at him with some concern. "Sounds like you're starting to get close to what's going on."

"I hope so," Peter said. "I'd like to get to the heart of whatever's about to happen *before* it gets serious."

There was a little silence. Then MJ said, "I could almost wish this job hadn't come up right now."

"Why on Earth not?"

"Well, what if you need me or something?"

He chuckled. "Good point. I may need you to hold the Lizard down while I web him up."

"Peeeeter!" MJ grimaced. "It's just… I don't like it, that's all. When I got married, I promised to stay with you when you were in trouble—that's the 'worse' part of the for-better-for-worse. What if I'm not there for when you need me? When you need my help? Suppose the Lizard beats you up a little? Who's going to strap your ribs up and tell you you did okay anyway?"

There was more coming, but Peter put a finger on her lips and said, "I know. I know you're worried. I'll be okay. And you having a job, and making money to keep us both afloat—that's important. It's also important for me to know that you're doing things you like to do. That you're happy and busy. Those things are important to me."

"I don't know," MJ said. "I just… Never mind."

"It's going to be all right," Peter said. "It's been all right until now."

"Mmm," MJ said, not sounding entirely convinced. But then she smiled, and snuggled closer to him. "Never mind."

Peter reached over to pick up the phone and arrange for an alarm call, and saw that the red message light was flashing. He dialed for the front desk.

"Hi, this is Peter Parker, room twelve thirty—any messages for me?"

The operator tapped at a keyboard for a moment. "Uh—yes. 'Breakfast club is off.' Does that make sense?"

"Yes, it does."

"Right. 'Breakfast club is off, lunch instead—'" The operator paused. "This may not have been spelled right. 'V-r-e-n-i.'"

"That's right."

"What an interesting name," said the operator.

Peter chuckled and agreed, and took another moment to set up his wake-up call, then hung up and turned to MJ… and found her already asleep. *Typical,* he thought. *The one morning when we could sleep in, and we can't—she has to leave early.*

Oh well.

He turned out the light.

FOUR

HE woke up suddenly to light streaming into the room, and looked over in panic at the alarm clock. It read 8:30. *I thought I took care of the alarm call!* Peter thought. *What the—*

Then he saw that there was a note on the pillow. "Ran out to do an errand," it said in MJ's small, neat handwriting. "Back about 9, see you at breakfast."

Peter chuckled. Sometimes she was an early riser, and there was just no stopping her. This was plainly one of the times. He got up, showered, dressed, and went down.

She was there waiting for him, already halfway through a plate of scrambled eggs, with an angelic look on her face—that settled and cheerful look that she wore when she had a job, any kind of job, these days. Peter's heart clenched a little at the sight of it, and not for the first time, he wished he had a job that paid enough that MJ could work when and as she wanted to, rather than because she had to. This look of sheer pleasure was priceless for its own sake.

"You should try the pancakes," she said. "They're great." And no sooner had Peter sat down than MJ said, "And I have a present for you!"

"What?"

"Here." She handed him a box wrapped up in gift paper.

Peter tore the paper off as tidily as he could and stared at the outside of the box. It was a cellular phone. He opened the box and got the little creature out of its Styrofoam nest. "MJ! How much—"

"Not that much," she said. "They're on sale. With the connection fee and everything. It's one of those new netwide ones—it'll still work in New York."

"MJ," Peter said, still in shock.

"Now, I want you to take this with you everywhere," she said, "because they've given me one of my own. I have it right here." She got another one, twin to Peter's, out of her purse, and dangled it in front of Peter, and giggled. "Isn't this trendy? Here, write down the number." She showed it to him, on the little sticker on the back of the phone.

Dutifully, Peter got out his little address book and wrote the number down. "I want you to call me every five minutes," MJ said, "until I get back. You understand?"

She was enjoying this, Peter saw, but there was also a slight twitch to the corner of her eyes, a narrowing that said she wasn't kidding. "If anything happens," she said, and lowered her voice, "anything at all, I want to know."

"You'll be the first."

"Somebody else is usually the first," MJ said, raising her eyebrows. "Someone whose name starts with S. But never mind. Right after him—I want to know. Promise?"

Peter desperately hailed a passing waitress.

"Promise?"

Peter looked at MJ and smiled and gave in to the inevitable. "Promise."

MJ smiled and started playing little tunes on her phone's keypad, while she finished her scrambled eggs. Peter rolled his eyes, then smiled at the waitress and ordered breakfast, wondering at how complicated life could become without warning....

SOUTH of Miami proper, the Florida coastline trends gently southward and westward and becomes slightly less developed. Parkland appears, dotted here and there: places like Biscayne National Park, and Homestead Bayfront Park near the air base. Farther north, though, about fifteen miles south of Miami proper, Matheson Hammock Park rests against the water, a beautiful, flat landscape of wetland and cypress leading down to a wilderness of salt grass, and finally to the dunes and the white sand beach of the coast. The coastline itself is a long, wide welter of tidal washes, little bays, and tide-pools, alive with sea life and the land-based animal life that comes down to catch it. The busy surburban and city life of south Florida seems very far away.

Such places at night can be very quiet and very lonely. Some people count on that.

The little boat came nosing in to shore without a sound, nor a light. Northward and inland, Miami lit up the sky with a faint golden glow; southward, the lights of Homestead and Coral Gables glittered, distant sparkles flat on the edge of the flat world, unsteady through the warm night air. There was no sound but the rush of the waves.

One of the two men in the little boat peered through binoculars at the coast, saying nothing. He was a big husky man, dressed in shorts and a windbreaker. When his companion got close enough to see him, in that uncertain light, the other's face was as closed as a shut door.

Dealing with that face's owner made Satch nervous. But he was stuck with him for the time being, and so just sat, used the oars to keep the boat steady, and said nothing.

Half a mile away, on the beach, there was the merest flicker of light. "Right," said the other. "Start rowing."

Satch rowed, not arguing the point; when this man told you to do something, you just did it. Or else you got as far away as you could, as fast as you could, before he found out you hadn't done what you were told.

The other kept his gaze fixed on the coast through the binoculars, and Satch rowed steadily on. The two of them had done this run before, several times now, though in different spots, so that there was now a kind of routine. They would motorboat down from Dinner Key, say, or up from Coral Castle, and loiter when they got to the right spot—just a couple of fishermen out for the afternoon. But they wouldn't come back in. Darkness would fall, and they would wave at anyone who stopped, and say, "Night fishing…" This was common enough. Lots of people around here night-fished for pompano and blues. Occasionally, by night or day, a police boat would hurry by on business. Satch's gut would always clench when this happened, but the other man would just wave and shade his face with the bill of his cap. There wasn't a lot of Coast Guard activity around at the moment. Satch had been very relieved at that. He hadn't known quite what to make of it when the other told him that the Coast Guard were "being taken care of." If money had changed hands, well, that was common enough. But how much money did it take to buy off a whole Coast Guard cutter? Satch often thought about that, and shook his head.

"Come on," the other said, "get a move on!"

"I am, I am," Satch said, muttering. "If you're in such a rush—" He was about to say, "Why don't you row?" At the look the other gave him, though, Satch shut up and concentrated on rowing faster.

Another ten minutes' rowing and they were into the combers. The bottom didn't shelve evenly here: there were dips, and there was an undertow, and Satch had to work twice as hard as he had earlier. The other man cursed at him. "Can't you go any faster, goddammit?"

Satch didn't bother answering, just grunted and rowed.

Sand hissed softly under the keel as the boat came to shore. He could see them waiting, just above the high water. They were pretending to be fishermen, too; a couple of lawn chairs were set up on the sand, and fishing poles were stuck in the sand next to them.

Nearby, as Satch and his companion stepped out of the boat into the backward-rushing water, Satch could see evidence of recent digging, being hurriedly covered by another man. There also were the things they had come to fetch—the three small drums.

Satch's companion gave him no help with the boat. He simply strode up through the water to the beach, and up to the others. As he went, he pulled something out of his belt. Satch looked at it with some concern. He hadn't known Lugers came that big. He didn't want to *see* any that came that big. He didn't want to see this one now, or in this man's hands, where it might wind up pointed at him.

"How long have you been here?" he heard his companion say to one of the other men.

"About an hour. What kept you?"

Satch's companion gestured back at him with his head. "He's not exactly an Evinrude," he said. There was some snickering about that. Satch chose to ignore it. There were a lot of things you had to ignore about this business if you wanted to keep doing it, keep making the money. And Satch had a family to support. Hard enough to find honest work these days, and any other kind, even that was hard to hold on to....

"Okay," Satch's companion said. "Here." He reached into one pocket, came up with an envelope which he handed to one of the two waiting men.

"You want to open one up and have a look?" said that man.

More chuckling at the suggestion. Satch's companion laughed. "You want to count that?"

Less chuckling. But the man now holding the fat envelope did it nonetheless. "Price is going up, seemingly," he said, conversationally enough.

Satch's companion shrugged. "Supply and demand. When's the next pickup?"

The counting man shook his head, tucked the parcel away. "You'll be notified in the usual way."

Satch's companion showed no change of expression. He turned to Satch. "Come on," he said, "get these in the boat."

Satch sighed and did as he was told. He went to the first of the barrels, beginning to roll it slowly, edge-on, across the soft sand. Satch grunted with the strain; he never got used to how heavy these things were for their size. And when you got them down into the wet sand, it was even worse. Satch huffed and puffed and set himself low, as best he could, and grunted as he got the first barrel heaved up into the boat.

The others were speaking in low voices now as Satch made his way back for the second barrel. He could never shake the feeling, on these outings, that they were talking about him. That some dreadful joke was being made at his expense. He wondered if it had been smart for him to take this job at all… wondered whether he was actually playing the part of one of the poor schmoes in a pirate movie, who digs the hole and does the work to bury the treasure, and then gets shot or buried alive to keep the secret. Certainly, if he saw any indication of that coming, he would run like hell. But in the meantime, the money was good enough. *Besides,* he thought, *it's not like anybody's getting killed.…*

He got hold of the second barrel and started rolling it back to the boat. *At least the hours are okay,* Satch thought. It wouldn't take much longer tonight. They would row a little farther down the coast until they met the boat that would make pickup on this stuff. Then they would collect their own payment and be gone. His companion would set him ashore down at the docks, and he would catch a late bus back and see Marie and the kids.

Satch heaved the barrel into the boat, turned, and started slogging his way back to the shore. His back was killing him. His companion had turned a little away from the others and was looking toward him. "Hurry up!" he hissed. "You want to be here all night?"

"Yeah, yeah," Satch muttered. He grabbed the third barrel, said "Oof—"

Someone else went "Oof" too. Surprised, Satch looked up. One of the three men they had met, the one who had been covering up the dug hole, was standing strangely, with a shocked look on his face, and he looked taller than usual, somehow. Or there was something dark behind him, a shadow. Satch thought it was a trick of the light, at first, but there seemed to be something sticking out of the man's chest—

But there was. The breath went out of Satch with a whoosh as the scene suddenly made sense. The something was black, and it glistened in the moonlight, and then vanished as swiftly as a snake's withdrawn tongue. The man fell. The other two, and Satch's companion, took several quick steps back from him as a fifth form rose over the crumpling body.

It was a guy in a black suit, a big guy, with some kind of design or logo painted on the front of him. Satch swallowed as the thing grinned, white in a black face, and grinned, and grinned—a mouthful of great knifelike fangs that seemed to go right around to the back of his head, until the top of it looked likely to fall off because of that dreadful grinning.

Satch's companion pointed that huge shiny gun at the man. He never got a chance to fire. Satch didn't even see what happened. One minute the gun was in his companion's hand. The next minute there was a dreadful choked-off scream, as hand and gun were flensed off by some kind of knife that leapt away from the guy in black. Satch's companion bent down. Another breath, a half a scream, and that knife—it wasn't a knife at all, it was an arm or tentacle of some kind, and another one followed it, how could anyone have so many arms?—whipped out from the man's body, seemingly from a place where there hadn't been anything a moment before. It whipped itself around Satch's companion's head.

The other three men turned to run. Satch was frozen where he stood. Running did the others no good. More of those weird flexible arms shot out like glistening black rope, knotted around the men, pulled them back leisurely. The man who screamed the loudest stopped screaming first. Satch had to watch it, had to watch it all. He didn't move. He couldn't move. He just watched.

The thing in black dropped the second man and went for the third. It spent more time over him, like someone savoring a lunch break. Eventually he let the rest of the pieces fall, and turned to Satch.

Satch stood and watched. He couldn't move. The thing in black came to him, grabbed him by the lapels of his poor polo shirt. It shredded in the grip of the claws that held him. Odd, though, how delicately they did it, as if intent on doing him no more harm than was absolutely necessary.

"Now, then," said a horrible fangy voice. "We want you to take a message for us. Take it to your boss, to the person who pays you. Tell him we said, 'Cut it out.' Tell him Venom says so. You do recognize us?"

"Fuh, fuh, muh, muh," was all that Satch could say.

Those claws came up, and patted Satch's cheek, almost an amused gesture. "The dangers of celebrity," Venom said. "And you—you cut it out, too. So you have something to tell your grandchildren about. We won't tell you twice."

Venom let him fall. Satch collapsed to his hands and knees in the wet sand, panting, and didn't dare move, because if he did, he would see what had happened to the others... and then he would throw up. He hated throwing up. But mostly he felt as if he should just be very still and small, do nothing, make no sound. He held still.

That dark shape stood above him, and the voice said, very deep, very amused: "Now. About *these...*"

It was dawn before Satch got up off his hands and knees, mostly because he had to; the tide was coming in. An early jogger was approaching him along the beach, and Satch thought it would be good to get away. As he stood up, as the jogger got closer, and saw what was on the beach, and ran toward him with a horrified look on his face, Satch looked around and saw that the drums were gone. The boat was gone. Everything was gone.

DOWNTOWN Miami can be a very chic, very stylish-looking place on a Monday morning. Well-dressed people come and go, hot cars and expensive ones pass by, and everything is beautiful.

Richard C. Harkness was one of those who found it all beautiful, as a matter of course—as something he deserved. He had worked hard on his way up the corporate ladder, had sucked up to the right bosses, signed the right reports and found ways not to sign the others, and had kept his nose clean in the best corporate tradition. He was good at what he did, which was making money without getting his hands dirty.

He drove his Porsche into the parking garage at 104 West Seventh, one of those sleek glass-and-steel constructions that had risen above the smaller, less grandiose buildings of Miami these last few years. He stowed the car in the space with his name painted on it, pulled the thin briefcase out of the back, shut the car, set the alarm, and walked away. Only six steps or so took him to the executive elevator. He stepped into the shiny little lobby, put his key in and signaled. The elevator arrived quickly. This, too, was something he deserved and which he now accepted as a matter of course: the right not to have to waste time waiting, not to have to be crammed in an elevator with people in the company's lower echelons on his way to his office.

The elevator whisked him up to the thirtieth floor. Harkness stepped out, crossed the hall to the glass and gilt entrance to the front lobby. The door opened for him. The receptionist, sitting behind her big glass-brick and Italian plate-glass desk, nodded deferentially to him as he passed. "Good morning, Mr. Harkness."

"Morning, Cecile." He didn't ask her about any messages; she wouldn't be trusted with such. Down the cool gray hall, along the thick maroon carpet toward the executive offices, he made his way. There was the thick mahogany double door that had his name on it. It opened in front of him, Cecile having alerted Mary Ellen that he was coming.

"Good morning, Mr. Harkness."

"Good morning, Mary Ellen. Twenty minutes, and then you can come in and give me a report."

"Yes, sir."

He walked past her desk, past the door of the little anteroom in which her own secretary worked. The door to his private office was shut. No one touched it without his permission. He opened the door, tossed the briefcase onto the leather sofa next to it, shut the door behind him, and turned to examine, with the usual great pleasure, the view out onto the morning city, the sea, the world of business into which he had fought his way and which he handled so well.

Between him and the window stood a tall black shape. Harkness's mouth fell open in outrage and astonishment. On his five-thousand-dollar Persian carpet stood three big dirty wet barrels, shedding sand and muck onto the Kilim weave.

That dark shape looked at him, took a step closer, and said, "We believe these are yours."

PETER met Vreni that afternoon for lunch, but it was less of a lunch than he had been expecting. He stood around at the entrance of the restaurant, waiting for her, and finally at about twenty after twelve, went in and sat down, got himself a Coke, and waited. At nearly twenty of one, she appeared, hurrying across to his table. She didn't sit down.

"I have some things to take care of this afternoon," she said. "It's not stuff that I'll need pictures of... not yet anyway. Do you mind taking the day off?"

"Mind?" Peter laughed. "No problem. When should we meet again?"

Vreni thought, then made a helpless gesture. "I couldn't say. I'll leave you a message, okay?"

"Fine."

And she was off again, half running. As Peter watched, it occurred to him that he didn't remember seeing her ever go anywhere at anything less than a fast walk. She drove herself the way she drove her car. Possibly the secret of her success. *Or possibly,* he thought, as the waitress stopped at his table, *it has more to do with being shot at....* That was something Peter could sympathize with.

All the same, it left Peter with an extra day to call his own. Among other things, he could spend a little more time poring over the Connorses' bank statements. And there was also the matter of his piece of smoke. *Which to attack first?*

The smoke, he decided—if only because it was more mysterious. Peter had a sandwich and a salad, then headed up to his room to make some calls, and have another shower—this was one of those sticky mornings; even in the hotel's air-conditioning, the humidity got at you. While undressing, he flicked the TV on to one of the news channels to see what the world was up to.

"—reports of Spider-Man being seen in the east Everglades have been confirmed by Ochopee police this morning. The enigmatic super hero, or villain, depending on your sources of information, made a brief appearance near Deep Lake—"

Peter chuckled and headed into the bathroom. But he had no sooner gotten into the shower than a voice said from the next room, "Dade County police are this morning investigating an incident scene near Matheson Hammock Park. Early reports are that a jogger stumbled on the aftermath of a massive assault. Police are questioning one man, Arnold Warren Campden of Miramar, who, initial reports say, was found near the scene of the incident. Police sources say that at present they have no confirmed suspects, and no indication of a motive, though there is speculation that the crime may have been drug-related—"

This by itself would have sounded fairly dry, had Peter not climbed far enough out of the shower to look around the door into the room and see, on the TV, the news channel film crew's shots of the beach area. A patch of beach some forty feet by forty was yellow-taped off. The sand there was much churned up, as if by a struggle, and great brown splashes of blood were everywhere. Off to one side was a hole which seemed not to have been completely filled in, and there were marks in the sand leading to or from the beach, as if something heavy, several somethings, had been dragged a short distance.

Peter got back in the shower, frowning. The thought of all that blood was on his mind. He knew people who left such scenes behind them. *If* people *is the word I'm looking for,* he thought.

Never mind that now. He got out, toweled off and dressed, sat down at the room's table again, and tipped out the contents of the "thermos" once more. As MJ had, he poked it, found that slight springiness, but it gave only so much. There was an odd strength to it, for all its ephemeral appearance.

Peter reached for the room phone with one hand and his address book with the other. *What I need,* he thought, *is a specialist in materials science. And I don't know any materials scientists.*

He paged through the book for a moment. *At least it's Monday, there'll be someone up there.* He picked up the receiver, dialed nine, and then a longer number.

After some ringing, there was an answer. "Empire State University."

"Hi. Physics department, please?"

"Thank you." A pause, then another ring. "Physics."

"Rita? It's Peter Parker, from Biochem."

"Peter! How you doing? You were in last month, but you didn't stop by."

"It was a little crazy, Reets," he said.

"Tell me! With Hobgoblin and Spider-Man and Venom ripping the place up? That's one word for it. Who're you looking for?"

"I was wondering if Roger Hochberg was on campus right now."

"I think so. I certainly saw him yesterday. Any idea what department, though?"

"Not sure… he was talking about changing majors."

Rita laughed her deep dark laugh. "He does that about once a week. Wait a minute! Renee? Renee, by any chance do you know where Roger Hochberg might be?"

"Uh—" said another voice.

"Tall skinny guy, glasses. The one with the weird haircut."

"Oh, him! He's up in the main research library. I saw him go in about an hour ago, anyway."

"Pete? Did you hear that?"

"Yup," Peter said. "Can you put me through?"

"Sure thing. You come see us, now! It's not like you're that far away."

Peter laughed. "I'm in Florida at the moment."

"Oooh, how'd you swing that? Never mind, don't want to know. Putting you through. Bye!"

"Bye, Reets."

Peter waited, while yet another number rang and a seagull planed past outside his window, burning white in the sun. "Library."

"Roger Hochberg, please? I think he's up there in the stacks."

"Just a moment, I'll page." He heard the library's soft paging system say Roger's name, and then the librarian said, "Oh, there you are. Call for you." The phone changed hands.

"Hochberg."

"Rog, it's Peter Parker."

"Hey, how ya doing?" said Peter's former lab partner, his everpresent smile almost audible through the phone. "Haven't seen you for weeks."

"It's been busy. Listen, I have a question for you. What looks like smoke, but it's solid?"

"Huh? What do I win if I get this right?"

"A cookie at least. I saw this stuff the other day—on TV," he added, to avoid complicated explanations, "and I've never seen anything like it before. It's been driving me crazy. I've got to find out what it is."

"Okay. Sounds mineral, rather than animal or vegetable."

"I'd say. But past that I wouldn't venture a guess."

Peter described the stuff to Roger in more detail, and finally—on hearing about the stuff's odd unsolid look, and its minuscule weight—Roger said, "Wait a minute. You saw this on TV? I see! They must have gone public."

"Who? With what?"

"I'll tell you. There've been papers about something that's supposed to look this way. It's called 'hydrogel.'"

"What's it for?"

"I don't think anyone's sure yet. They cooked this stuff up out at Livermore Labs, out west—I think as part of their superconductor research program. The stuff is apparently no good as a conductor, but they think it may have other uses. I don't know much more about it, it's not in my line. I only read the article abstract."

"Okay. Rog, who would I talk to about this stuff—to get some detail? I'm working on a story right now, and it may actually be of some use."

"Well, let me think." A pause. "Trouble is, he's not exactly local."

"Well, define local. I'm not at home, either. I'm in Florida."

"In this weather? Jeez. You poor guy. Never mind; Florida's not bad. There's a guy I know, an alumnus, who could probably talk you through what you need to find out—he was always such a journal hound, he'll *have* to know about it."

"Where is he?" Peter said, hoping the man wasn't up in the panhandle somewhere.

"South of Miami, I think. Wait a sec—" There was a moment of scrambling. "I've got the laptop here with me. I think I have his address."

"What's this guy doing now?"

"Food science."

"Good Lord," Peter said. He got an image of someone who designed the sugar for doughnuts.

"No, he's good, don't worry." Faint keyboard clickings ensued, and then Roger said, "Here we go. Doctor Liam Kavanagh." He read off an address in Coral Gables, followed by two phone numbers. "Liam was always such a research junkie," Roger said, "that I can't believe he doesn't know about your hydrogel—lots more than I do. Will that help?"

"I think so. Rog, you've saved my life."

"Just our usual service. When are you going to get back here and go out with some of us for dinner? There are people here who want to heckle you about not finishing your doctoral project."

Peter moaned softly. "Let's not get into it. I might be back in a couple of weeks…"

"Call me, then, and we'll get together. Say hi to Mary Jane for me."

"Right. Thanks again, Rog."

Before Peter could hang up, the phone rang. After a moment, he realized it was the cell phone MJ had given him. He picked it up, fumbled with it a moment, not quite sure how to turn it on. At last, he found a button that said Receive, and hit it. "Hello?"

"Peter!" MJ said. She sounded a little breathless. "How's your new toy?"

"I haven't had a chance to play with it yet—been too busy this morning."

"With what?"

"The 'smoke.' I've got at least a hint about what it is, thanks to Rog Hochberg. He says hi, by the way. Anyhow, I have to go see somebody down in Coral Gables, if he can make time for me. Listen, MJ, I've got to try and talk to this guy right now if I can."

"Okay."

"Where are you?"

"On the way to Boca." Peter heard, quite clearly, the sound of MJ rolling her eyes. "I'm going up with one of the staff vans—we slopped for a rest break. The director for the shoot," she said more softly, "is, uh… a character."

"Oh? Good or bad?"

"I would say he had the brains of a duck, but that would be an insult to ducks everywhere. Can't seem to make up his mind about what he wants, generally. This whole thing may turn into a disaster."

"Hope not."

"We'll see. Where are you?"

"The hotel."

"Where's your friend?"

"Vreni? She had something to do this afternoon. So I'm going to Coral Gables alone."

"Right. Oh, gosh, here they come. We're leaving. Bye bye, Tiger! I'll call you later."

"Bye," Peter said, and turned the phone off, pocketing it. He got the feeling that whatever he did, MJ was going to call him every five minutes for the next while. *New toys, indeed,* Peter thought, and grinned. He picked up the thermos and the other bags and headed down for the car.

CORAL Gables was south and west of the city. Kavanagh's building was near a road called Killian Parkway, which Peter found without too much trouble. The drive down was studded with odd road signs suggesting that Peter go to places with names like Parrot Jungle, Monkey Jungle, Orchid Jungle, and the peculiar name he remembered hearing that morning, Matheson Hammock Park. The image of a forest festooned with tropical hammocks stayed with him for a while.

Kavanagh himself, when Peter had managed to reach him on the phone, had been succinct almost to the point of eccentricity. Peter explained to the scratchy voice on the other end that he had been recommended by a friend at Empire State, and the response was, "Oh, God, not that dump!"

"Dr. Kavanagh," Peter had said, "I have a research problem—"

"Don't we all, my son, don't we all. Well, bring it along." Kavanagh had issued him directions which sounded more like a football play than anything else—I-1 to 41, 41 to 826, 826 to 874, then east to 174th...

"So far so good," Peter murmured as he got onto Route 874. Then something in his pocket shrilled, and he jumped almost out of his skin. It was the phone.

Peter pulled over and answered it, knowing perfectly well who it was. "Joe's Deli," he said, "Joe ain't here."

"Peter!" MJ said. "Can I kill somebody?"

"Hmm. Don't think Florida state law permits that at the moment. Why?"

"The director. Maurice."

"Maurice."

"The ducks would be right to be insulted, honey." She was whispering now. "The man does not know what he wants. My hair is right, but the light is wrong. The light is right, but the wind is wrong. Nothing is ever all right at once. He's infuriating."

Peter sighed. *This new toy is going to be a mixed blessing,* he thought. "And also," said MJ. "Is my hair 'carroty'?"

That one brought him up short. MJ's hair was one of his favorite things about her. When they first met at his aunt's house all those years ago, it was the first thing he noticed. The blaze of it in the sunlight was a conflagration in the evening, like embers. "Well, I call you 'carrot-top' every now and then, and you don't seem to mind."

"You don't make it sound like the vegetable associations of the word should also be applied to the hair's owner," MJ hissed. "Which Maurice does."

"Ignore him," Peter said. "He's a loony."

"Murder would be quicker. He suggested I go blonde."

"Definitely a head case," Peter said. "Plainly having difficulty with reality."

MJ sighed. "It's good to hear you say that. Oh gosh… here he comes. I'd better get on with it. Thanks, honey."

"*De nada.* Have fun."

She snorted at him, and hung up.

Peter put the phone away again, resisting the urge to turn it off. *This is the first day she's got hers,* he thought. *If I turn it off, she'll kill me. I can cope with one day of this.*

As long as that's all it is.…

He finally reached Kavanagh's address, turning into the parking lot of a small professional building, the kind where doctors and dentists have their dwelling. Its lobby even had a corrugated noticeboard. Even as he had thought, there were indeed three doctors, two dentists, a chiropractor, an orthopedist, and a company called Dextro Sugar International. Underneath, in smaller letters, the sign said "DR. LIAM KAVANAGH." Peter raised his eyebrows, wondering how all the dentists felt about the company name, and went upstairs.

Peter walked up the single flight of stairs to the next level of the building, and walked around past the dentists and so forth to the door of Dextro Sugar. He knocked.

The door was pulled open by one of the single tallest people Peter had ever seen. Liam Kavanagh was seven feet tall and a bit. He stooped—Peter suspected this was likely to be a habit—and looked down at Peter the way Gulliver would have looked down at Lilliputians. "You Parker?" he said.

"That's me."

He took Peter's arm and pulled him in, then slammed the door behind him as if there were enemy agents outside. Peter managed not to react to this as if he was in a fight situation—mostly because Kavanagh was just too unusual to take seriously. He looked like a beanstalk wearing a polo shirt and jeans and a white lab coat, and big horn-rimmed glasses—the biggest and thickest ones Peter thought he had ever seen. *No one,* Peter thought, *could possibly be that nearsighted without needing to wear a radar box around their neck.*

"You want some coffee?" said Dr. Kavanagh. His accent was purest New York Bronx.

"Uh, thanks, I just had lunch."

"It's good coffee."

"Do you make the sugar for it?"

Kavanagh smiled. It was a wry smile, one that spoke of a very wicked sense of humor. "Caught the 'Dextro,' did you? No, I drink mine black."

"Milk," Peter said, "and two sugars. Thanks."

Kavanagh produced a couple of mugs and poured coffee from a filter-coffee set on one side. "It's a general tag," he said, "that's all. Our kind of life runs on dextro-rotatory molecules, ones that bend light to the right when crystallized out. Levo-rotatory ones don't do us much good. The 'sugar'—" He shrugged. "It's a private joke. What is it exactly that I can do for you, Parker?"

"May I show you a specimen of some material I found?"

Kavanagh sat down in a chair by a desk with a computer and many books on it, and leaned over to clear off a spot on a small side table. "Right there, if it can sit on a table unprotected."

Peter produced the thermos. Kavanagh looked at it and said, "Nice! European."

"Is it really?" Peter said.

Kavanagh nodded. "Better than our local brands, by and large. Whatcha got in there?"

Peter opened the container, and on the clean, white composite tabletop, dumped out the piece of smoke. Kavanagh leaned over it like a vulture examining a potential piece of prey, his eyebrows going higher and higher as he gazed. Then he glanced up at Peter. The expression was not entirely interest or surprise; there was some envy mixed in it. "West Coast connections?" he said.

"I have a few," Peter said, though he doubted they were the kind that Kavanagh meant.

"You are a genteel and nonviolent-looking young man," Kavanagh said, leaning back in his chair again. "Normally not one who I would assume was involved in industrial espionage, or any other kind. Otherwise I would have to ask you serious questions about how you got this out of Livermore. They were the last ones to be working seriously on hydrogel that I know about for sure."

"Can you tell me something about this?"

"Sorry?" Kavanagh said, looking at Peter for a moment as if he had just arrived from Mars. "You've stolen this, but you don't know what it is?"

"I didn't steal it," Peter said.

"Let's put it this way, then," Kavanagh said, leaning farther back and folding his arms. "You have—come by? come into?—a piece of a substance which is presently sufficiently rare that stable examples of it exist in only three places on the planet. Not that the technique of its making is a secret. It's simply involved, and requires a lot of specialized equipment and expertise. But you don't know what it is... and you've come to me to ask me to tell you about it."

"That's about right," Peter said, getting slightly annoyed. "Can you help me? Or should I try the orthodontist next door?"

Kavanagh gave him a long look, and then began to laugh. He took a drink of his own coffee, and then toasted Peter with it. "All right," he said. "This is a peculiar situation, but not illegal—that's my gut feeling. But when we're finished, I wish you'd tell me where you got this. For real."

The doctor sat down by the table again, and prodded the hydrogel. "It's an accident, you know," he said.

"It is?"

"Was, originally. They were looking for a spin-off from clathrate technology. You know what a clathrate is?"

Peter nodded. That was fairly elementary biochemistry, and he was much more than an elementary biochemist. "It's a sort of latticework or cage of atoms of one element, sometimes more than one. The cage holds another atom, a guest atom, trapped inside. The substance produced by that structure often has properties that don't have any relation to what a normal compound of those elements would behave like."

Kavanagh nodded. "Right. They were looking at ways to extend clathrate structure, make it more complex—possibly increase the number of atoms which could be held in one of these cages, thereby producing materials with new and unpredictable behaviors. So they tried something unusual. They mixed oil and water."

"Can't have gotten them very far," Peter said.

"Well, at normal heats and pressures, it wouldn't. Specifically, they were using silica oils, which are not structurally similar to normal oils or lipids. Then they added water, and fractional amounts of other compounds, and they mixed them together under high temperature and considerable pressure." Kavanagh grinned. "And when they did that, something happened." He nudged the little piece of smoke. "This."

Peter looked from it to Kavanagh. "What's it do?"

"Do? It doesn't *do* anything. It just sits there." Kavanagh took another swig of coffee.

"No, I mean… what's it for?"

"Ah!" Kavanagh said. "They're still working on that. But what I can tell you is that this is one of the most stable compounds ever to be produced. I don't mean nonreactive, as such, nor do I mean inert. I mean *stable*. It resists being changed. The whole molecular structure of the thing simply resists being shifted out of its present state into any other, and that makes it very valuable."

"Why?"

"Here. Have you held it?"

"Not for long…"

Kavanagh picked it up, felt it for a moment, and then slapped the piece of hydrogel into Peter's hand. Once again he felt its great lightness. It hardly felt there at all. There was also a strange, friendly warmth to it.

"Interesting, isn't it?" Kavanagh said. "The *Scientific American* articles mentioned that odd feel in the hand. They called it 're-ambient heat.' Like something else is there, isn't it?"

Peter nodded, almost reluctantly. "I'd think it was alive, if I didn't know better."

"No chance of that. However, you don't need to be alive to be useful."

He turned away from Peter and went over to several very crowded cabinets, deeper in the office. "Ah," he said, reaching up to one, and came down with a big square-headed hammer. Peter looked at it, and Kavanagh said, "May I? Thank you."

He took the hydrogel, put it up onto a workbench. "Here," Kavanagh said. He took the sledgehammer two-handed, and swung it at the hydrogel with all his might.

The hammer bounced. The hydrogel compressed no more when struck than it had when Peter poked it with his finger. "Care to try?" Kavanagh said.

"Uh, thank you, yes—" Peter took the sledgehammer, took aim, and hit the hydrogel, hard—no doubt much harder than Kavanagh suspected he hit it. The hammer bounced. There was a spatter of sparks from where the hammer hit the bench top, but nothing else. The feeling of hitting the hydrogel was like hitting a mattress, but one with more bounce.

"Not strictly an inelastic collision," Kavanagh said. "Not elastic, either. Like something yielding under the pressure, and then throwing the hammer back. Interesting, isn't it?"

Peter nodded.

"Watch this," Kavanagh said. He took the bit of hydrogel off the countertop now, came over, and handed it to Peter. Then he turned away, and when he turned back again, he was holding an orange canister with a crooked nozzle. He thumbed a ring valve by the nozzle, struck a match on his countertop, and lit the nozzle. Hissing, a blue flame leapt out.

"Now wait a—!" Peter started to say, but it was already too late. Kavanagh had already brought the flame down on the piece of hydrogel in his hand. He flinched—then realized that flinching didn't matter. The flame splattered and spread an inch and a half above his hand, and he felt almost no heat at all. No heat whatsoever was transmitted to Peter through the hydrogel itself.

"Go on," Kavanagh said. "Put it down there." Peter put the hydrogel down on some papers on Kavanagh's desk. Kavanagh lowered the torch to the hydrogel again, held it there.

Nothing whatsoever happened, to the hydrogel or the papers; nothing scorched or even curled. "Pick it up," Kavanagh said to Peter.

Peter did, waving a hand over it first to sense any residual heat. Nothing. He touched it with a finger. It was cool. The hydrogel sat there in its smoky uncertainty, completely unchanged.

He picked it up and looked at Kavanagh. "It doesn't hold heat."

"It's a peerless insulator, certainly," Kavanagh said. "So the *SciAm* article said. It's mechanically stable, chemically and physically stable, and as you see, stable in terms of molecular vibration—heat and, I would also suspect, radiation."

Peter put it down between them and sat down again, looking at it. "What you could do with this stuff…"

"Yes, but it's not easy to make. A lot of heat and pressure is required, and the process as described in the journals is very labor intensive. But once made, the substance resists everything you can do to it. It can't be broken, bent, marred, eaten, or even touched by most forces known to us. To cut it like that—" He shook his head. "How they did that I don't know: it might be a little more manipulable when it's new. Later, I suspect the molecular structure would have so robustly asserted its new integrity that it wouldn't allow any further manipulation."

He paused for a moment. "Applications—I know, because they mentioned it in the article, that they were thinking of using it for the tiles in the Space Shuttle."

"Really!" Peter said, straightening.

"Sure. You felt how light it is. An average Shuttle tile is much heavier. Shape that into a tile of the same size and thickness—" Kavanagh shrugged. "You could decrease the Shuttle's weight by, oh, eighty percent. Think of how much more payload the beasts could carry then. They *might* actually become cost-effective." He smiled. "But think of all the other industrial uses, for example. This—" He gestured at the little piece of smoke. "This stuff could change our world. It's simply one of the most extraordinary compounds ever invented."

Peter nodded.

"So, the only question I have for you at this point," Kavanagh said, leaning confidentially toward Peter, "is—where exactly did you find it?"

Peter opened his mouth, and shut it, and then opened it again and said, "In a swamp."

Kavanagh snorted, and then smiled. "You would do me a great favor," he said, "if, in return for this information, the next time you're passing through that swamp, you would pick me up a bit. This isn't exactly Livermore—" He looked around the rather shambolic combination of office and lab space in which they sat. "But I wouldn't mind taking a run at this stuff myself. Trying to work out how to make it on the cheap. An indestructible substance, light as a feather, tougher than steel, impervious to anything you can throw at it—" He shook his head, and looked slightly wistful. "The world ought to have this stuff."

Peter looked at him. "We could try leaving you a sample," he said.

They did try, for about half an hour. But no scalpel, tome, or other implement in Kavanagh's lab, not even his Swiss Army knife, could get so much as a chip or a sliver off the hydrogel. "It's too bad," Kavanagh said sadly, at last. "Take it away before I'm tempted too far. And whatever you do—" he looked at Peter seriously "—don't let the world at large know you have this stuff. I would imagine there are people who would do quite a bit to get their hands on it... and wouldn't deal kindly with you if they knew it's with you."

Peter nodded, knowing this was almost certainly true. *Curt,* he thought, *why did you have this stuff? What's going on out there...?*

Peter thanked Kavanagh for his help, got back into his car, and drove back north.

There's got to be a pile of money behind this, he thought, as he pulled back onto the freeway. *There's no way that this kind of materials engineering happens on the cheap. Either a lot of money was spent to steal this from Livermore, or a lot was spent to produce it somewhere else.*

Kavanagh had given Peter a copy of the *Scientific American* article, which gave full enough instructions for a careful chemist to synthesize it on his own, given the proper equipment. *And Curt had had it. Stolen from someone else... or synthesized by Curt, for his own purposes?*

But the Lizard was carrying it. It was hard enough to communicate with the Lizard at all, let alone make it act like some kind of courier—

The phone rang. Peter picked it up. "Hi, MJ—"

"Peter! Oh, gosh!"

"What's the matter? Where are you?"

"Up on the shoot. Oh, honey!"

"MJ, what's wrong?"

"Venom!" she said.

"What?!"

"He was on the news just now. He was up in some skyscraper—intimidated some executive, it looks like, and just walked out afterwards. By the time the police got there, he was long gone."

"Oh, that's just *wonderful*," Peter said.

"I thought—"

"MJ," Peter said hastily, "not on the cellular. People can eavesdrop on these things. Are you busy tonight?"

"No… they're putting us up at a hotel here. Do you want to come up?"

"I might do that. Which hotel?"

"The Splendide, on North Collins." She chuckled. "It's about as splendid as a landfill, but never mind. Around eightish?"

"I'll be there."

He hung up, and thought bad words, many of them.

Venom!

They had tangled last month, several times; in the middle of it, Hobgoblin had been added to the equation. Finally the alien creature had been put out of harm's way, and with Hobgoblin carted off as well, Venom had announced that, since he had other business to handle in San Francisco, he would leave Spider-Man to his own devices for the moment. *He must have handled it by now,* Peter thought. *And now that the media are announcing I've turned up here, he must feel he has leisure to come back this way and settle my hash. Not on his own turf, of course—but this isn't exactly mine, either.*

Damn! Why can't he leave me alone?

It didn't seem likely, though. The symbiote to which Venom was bound was one that Peter had rejected when he realized just how alive his new "costume" was. It had gone hunting a new host, and had found one—and the symbiote did not forget the pain of its rejection. It held a grudge, and Eddie Brock was only too glad to help the symbiote deal with its own anger. Venom had nearly killed Spider-Man several times now, and so far luck or skill in fighting had saved him. But he couldn't count on it forever.

And now they're here.

And what about the Lizard? Peter thought. *If Venom runs across him, who knows what he'll do? He thinks he's just a crazy monster, likely to harm the innocent.*

It occurred to Peter, ever so briefly, that it would be an interesting fight to watch. While he wasn't exactly invulnerable, neither was anybody going to tear the Lizard up like wet paper, not even Venom. But he very much doubted he'd have the leisure to watch any such fight, since if Spider-Man were anywhere in the neighborhood, Venom would happily put the Lizard on hold until old business had been dealt with.

Peter sighed. *I really needed this,* he thought. *Well, if he crosses my path, I'm gonna do my best to trash him. I've almost managed it, a couple of times before. Then the police can have him.*

It probably wasn't very compassionate to want so badly to pound someone into a pulp. But Venom had been making Spider-Man's life difficult for some time now—and Peter Parker's, too. Venom had not scrupled to try to get at Spidey by frightening MJ. That, if nothing else, earned him a good thrashing in Peter's opinion.

Just this once, he thought. Seeing Venom locked up in the Vault would do him no end of good.

But then there would still be the Lizard.

Curt, Peter thought, as he swung south onto the freeway toward Miami, *what's going on?*

FIVE

NOT surprisingly, the few structures standing in the Everglades have a temporary look. Heavy building materials are not easy to get in and out, and the weather makes any building situation unpredictable. The swamp and marsh are endlessly malleable by the elements. Canals that were passable last week may be drowned and lost today; ground that was dry yesterday may today be under two feet of water. And, even if you *do* manage to get your materials in and get something built, there's no predicting when or if a hurricane will come screaming through and rip up everything you've done.

As a rule, it isn't easy to see buildings in the Everglades. The lush growth makes even a cleared site look like primeval forest within a matter of years. And if you go out of your way to hide a structure, then only the spy satellites will know where you are—and even they have to be told where to look. There are places in the wetlands called hammocks where trees seed themselves prolifically, and they and their rootling trees grow so closely together that there's no seeing what lies inside the little self-contained island they create. The temperatures in such places, sealed off above by a thick canopy of leaves and surrounded by a wall of many trunks, soar far higher than elsewhere in the landscape. Rare flora—air plants, bromeliads and orchids—grow wild inside such hammocks, a kinder environment than any greenhouse.

Entering a hammock is like walking into a close, dark, humid room. The occasional song of a bird, the shriek of a shrike, are the only sounds to be heard in the acoustically close little place, and the only illumination are the few turning spots of light shifting and flowing along the interior as the sun moves. Hammocks can be as small as twenty or thirty feet in diameter, or quite large.

There was a large one, covering maybe half an acre, some miles north of Big Cypress and about ten miles from a town called Felda. No one in Felda knew much about it. In that wilderness of canals, that "river of grass," as the poet called it, filled with wetland, dry land, poisonous plants, and snakes, it was difficult enough to really know the landscape around your home, let alone that ten miles away.

But someone had found this biggest of the local hammocks, and someone had used it.

Inside the palisade of cypress, bald cypress and dwarf cypress, mangrove, and tangled banyan, a little, long, low building had been erected. It was a temporary structure of the kind built by people who supply pre-fab trailers and so forth to construction sites. It had two levels, the second accessed by a stairway up the outside. It looked as if someone made a halfhearted attempt to keep it clean, but the fiberglass of the outside was rapidly becoming festooned with Spanish moss and bromeliads, which considered the exterior of the building to be just another kind of tree trunk. The building had no windows, it was not built for pleasure or convenience, but for a specific purpose.

Upstairs in the small building, in a blank-walled office that looked just like so many others he had worked from in his time, a man in a lab coat worked busily at a personal computer. The screen was displaying an automated computer-assisted design program. He placed his left hand on the specially designed mouse—a necessity, since he had no right arm, and the typical mouse was designed for right-handed use. He clicked, and on the screen a diagram of sticks and balls, a complex molecular structure, rotated itself. The man picked up another stick and ball from a pile of them on one side of the screen, mouse-dragged them into the diagram, and hooked them onto one side of it. The new stick and ball bounced away, there was a soft chime, and the computer—using a sound-file lifted from a well-known television series—announced, in a chaste, cool female voice, "This procedure is not recommended."

The man sighed deeply. Using the mouse, he picked up a different color of ball, another stick, plugged the stick in, then thought for a moment, squashed another ball into the first one, and applied them both to the stick. There was another soft chime, but this time no protest from the autoCAD program.

The man sat back in his chair and let out a long sigh. He was good-looking, with dark hair and fine features, eyes with the slight, smile-created downturn at the corners that suggested a kind-hearted, thoughtful person. Under the lab coat, his clothes had an inexpensive look to them. They had not been tailored to accommodate his uneven proportions; the right sleeve simply hung limply. Considering what frequently happened to his clothes, Curt Conners didn't see any reason to spend a great deal of money on them when they might be torn to shreds at any moment by an annoyed Lizard—the thing at the bottom of his soul.

The lab door opened, and he glanced up to see Fischer walk in, if Fischer could ever be said to merely "walk" anywhere. To say that he hulked in might have been a more accurate description. Curt thought he had never seen shoulders so broad. On some super heroes possibly, but not on an ordinary human being. Fischer always looked as if he belonged in an action-adventure movie.

He tended to prefer wearing camouflage clothing. His hair was cropped in a Marine-style crew cut, his eyes were an astonishing, photogenic frozen blue in a broad face with high cheekbones, a big, square jaw, and a thin-lipped mouth that could wear a deceptively wide smile. He was a most improbable-looking man, and most improbably handsome, but he was real enough. He had certainly become one of the realities of Curt Connors's life in the past six or seven months. And he had to be dealt with, whether Curt liked it or not.

"How's it coming?" Fischer said.

Curt nodded. "The substrate's in place," he said, "but the beta-N ring structure is giving me some trouble—"

"I don't need the jargon," said Fischer. "How close are you to being *done*?"

Curt sighed. The man's obtuseness about science was deliberate, rather than an inability to handle it. Fischer just didn't see science as anything a reasoning being would get interested in, any more than he would get interested in, say, a screwdriver or a telephone. It was a tool, not a source of pleasure in itself.

"Very close," Curt said. "It might be a week, it might be less. Depends on how quickly I can finish putting this together. Some of it—" he shrugged, a regretful gesture "—is just a matter of trying all the pieces in different configurations until they work. And some of it, I'm afraid, genuinely does require a certain level of inspiration."

Fischer stared at him with those cold blue eyes. "Well," he said, "you'd better get inspired. Once we manage to arrange another delivery of the administration medium—"

Curt met the stare without flinching. "I don't know what went wrong with the last one," he said, "and there's really no use dwelling on it, is there? Even before the installation, the Lizard was unpredictable enough. But now that," he raised his eyebrows, "your favorite gadget's been installed, it's hardly his fault if something goes wrong. You want to have a word with the programmer. Or whoever else wrote the code. Or your pet surgeon, who put the thing in. If one of the neural implants—"

"Shut up, Connors," said Fischer. He said it jovially enough, but the tone of voice would have been more reassuring if Curt didn't know, from previous experience, that if he didn't shut up violence would follow. To Fischer, the use of force was just one more form of conversation, and Curt had seen what happened to other people who didn't shut up when Fischer told them to.

His guts began to roil a little inside him. He despised this necessary pretense of cowardice; he would have liked to wait until the inevitable happened—and then calmly take this man apart with the Lizard's bare claws. That much he would enjoy. But it would destroy the whole point of this exercise, and so he restrained himself from even thinking about what was hopeless and couldn't happen.

"Programming isn't at issue," Fischer said, leaning back against one wall with his arms folded. "What is, is that the Lizard picked up our consignment. And then he lost it again. Not very good. It's going to take us another few days to get any more. It's going to be tougher than last time, and even then we attracted enough notice."

"But you will manage it?"

"Oh yeah, we'll manage it."

"And then?"

"Then the surgery will go ahead as scheduled," said Fischer, again jovially, "assuming you have the kinks worked out of that by the time we get it."

"It's not so much working them out as working them in," Curt said ruefully, looking again at the molecular diagram on the screen. He had been hanging D-benzene rings all over the long-molecule structure like blown-glass ornaments on a Christmas tree—but no Christmas tree had ever been such a delicate construction, or so easily misbalanced. Too many balls on one side and the structure of the molecule came apart, or twisted itself into some odd configuration he hadn't planned.

Already this week he had constructed some enzymes that might prove extremely useful in the genetic engineering of vegetables, and at least one proteolytic structure that might possibly someday be part of a cure for cancer. But that wasn't the cure he was looking for, and so he put it aside— having first carefully noted the structure, and resolved to write a paper about it someday, when he was back doing normal work again. He had to hold that hope in front of himself. If he ever lost it, ever let go of it....

If that ever happens, I'll cease to be human, he thought. *Since I'm only sporadically human these days anyway, I'd better hang on to the little that I have.*

"Anyway," Fischer said, "Certain People will be very glad that you're making such good progress. Certain People wouldn't like to be kept waiting very much longer. They have their own agenda, and your price is rather small."

"I understand that."

"Good."

There were other things on Curt's mind, though. He was beginning to feel rumblings of something he knew all too well now, an array of sensations superficially like an epileptic's aura, a certain change in the way things looked, a shift in the perception of colors, a metallic taste that heralded changes in the sensorium.

"It's going to happen again shortly," he said.

Fischer's eyes widened just slightly. That was as much of a surprise reaction as you could get out of him. "How long?"

"Soon. It's never very consistent."

"All right, then. You'll want to get yourself out of here. You wouldn't want to wreck the joint after seven months of work, would you now?"

"No," said Curt. "I just want to back this up, before—"

"Fine," said Fischer. "I'll leave you to it. Just be careful not to lose anything."

"Believe me," Curt said. "That's the last thing on my mind."

Fischer turned and bulked out of the room again. Curt waited until he heard the footsteps receding down the metal stairs outside the building—probably going off to warn the rest of his people, he thought. Only when the man was safely away, for just a moment he lowered his face into his hands and breathed out a long, soft sound. A moan.

Martha... he thought.

It would be easier for him, so much easier, if he was the kind of person who could just forget about people, let them go or even shut them forcibly out of mind and memory. Keep them at arm's length. But that wasn't the way he had been raised. His parents had been loving, his relationship with his family had been good. They cared about each other.

His parents were both dead now, and his family separated; but all of them kept in touch by phone, and he knew, on the rare occasions when he called them, that they were always glad to hear him. But there was always a note in their voices that said, "Why have you become so distant? Why have you drawn away? Is it something we did? Tell us, and let us make it up."

It was, of course, nothing he could ever explain. There had seemed no point in spreading the pain Martha already suffered around the rest of the family. So he became the somewhat-lost brother, the distant uncle, the cousin who was a bit of a black sheep, who didn't keep in touch, who no one really knew much about anymore. He knew that when his relatives spoke of Martha and William, they shook their heads, and sighed, and felt sorry for them.

Not half as sorry as he did.

For maybe the ten thousandth time, Curt thought back on the day the experiment went wrong, and he wished as hard as ever that time was reversible, that you could point at a given moment, a causal linkage, and just explode it. To delete it, to hear the cosmic voice saying, "That procedure is not recommended," and watch the elements of the dumb move, the Big Mistake, separate and float back to the side of the screen, waiting for you to do it again, and this time, do it right—that would be worth almost anything.

But reality had not been so kind.

Curt opened his eyes and gulped. The taste at the back of his mouth was wrong, and the colors in the room were shifting. Hurriedly he began to take his clothes off—there was no point in ruining any more of them than he absolutely had to—and silently, looking as erect and proud as he could look when he knew that inside of ten minutes he would no longer be a man, Curt Connors went outside to await the inevitable.

Fischer watched, from his position leaning against a thick-trunked mangrove, as Connors edged sideways out of the hammock into the relatively open air, paused, then stepped down into the smooth brown water and swam slowly away. He moved with a fair amount of splashing. That gave the water moccasins and the cottonmouths a chance to get out of the way before he changed into a form less hospitable to the native wildlife.

WITHOUT looking away, Fischer beckoned over his shoulder. One of his men, a slighter version of himself, materialized at his elbow. "Get Dugan and Geraldo. Tell them to get a boat and keep an eye on him. I want to make sure that what went wrong last time doesn't happen again."

"Who's on the remote?"

"You take it."

"You want us to do anything while he's—out?"

Fischer considered, then shook his head. "No. He's been a little visible this week already. Let things quiet down. Then next week, if he's still here—" he smiled slightly "—we'll knock off one of the convenience stores in Ochopee. Go on."

The man went, and Fischer leaned there on his tree, pulled out a cigarette, tapped it against the trunk, then put it in his face and lit up, waiting for the roar.

SIX

THE next afternoon, Peter returned to Miami from Boca Raton, where he had spent the evening with MJ, and spent a long time reassuring her about what he had been up to. Or trying to, anyway; where Venom came in, she was difficult to reassure.

"I don't really like the idea of you and Venom even being in the same state," she had said as they prepared for bed.

"If I find him," Peter said as he got in beside her, "he won't be in the same state for long. I intend to pound him flat and dump him on the police and get him out of my way. I've got other things to think about just now."

MJ laughed, even though it had an uneasy sound. "Nice trick if you can do it," she said. "It's just… You know me. I worry."

"You do. And usually over nothing."

"Not over nothing," MJ said. "Venom is a legitimate problem."

"I guess so. But tell me how the shoot is going," Peter said.

MJ laughed at him. "Don't be changing the subject or anything. Tiger." Her smile went wry. "But I have to admit, this isn't going the way I'd hoped. The director… He's not exactly psychotic, but I'm going to be very glad when this job is over."

Oh dear, Peter thought. *That bad.*

"He really just doesn't know what to do. I think that's part of the problem. He seems to have a lot of trouble making up his mind. The minute he hears any suggestion from somebody else, he takes it. Even if his first idea was better. It's making a complete shambles of the shoot."

"Well," Peter said, "stick it out as best you can. But if you really can't work with this guy, you should leave."

"No," MJ said. "I went out to bring home this bacon, I went out for it on purpose, and I'm not coming back without the whole pig."

"You have the soul of a poet," Peter said.

"I'm modest, too. And gorgeous."

"Gorgeous I could have told you about. But you should try to keep from killing the director."

"Someone else may beat me to it. He's got more than one way to drive everybody crazy."

"More annoying than chronic indecision?"

"Uh-huh. He's a health nut." Peter looked at her, confused. "Look, Tiger, I don't mind people eating healthy. I mean, it's smart. And smoking is obviously a protracted act of suicide. But this guy—you can't so much as put a hamburger in your face without him screaming about saturated fat! You can't eat anything much more complex than whole brown rice without incurring a lecture."

"Sounds like a bore," Peter said. He knew that MJ had something of a taste for junk food on shoots. It was hardly her fault, either. Sometimes there wasn't much of anything else to eat, especially if the shoots had a poor caterer, and he knew how fond she was of the occasional burger.

She chuckled at him. "At one point this morning, I had this image of calling Venom—"

"Excuse me?"

"Well, if I knew his phone number. I wanted to say—" and she made a "phone" with pinky and thumb "—'Forget about my husband. Do you want some nice health food? No artificial additives, no preservatives. No brains.'"

"Oh, MJ, really! This is not a nice thing to wish on a fellow human being!"

"I have my doubts about the human part," MJ muttered. "But I just keep telling myself, 'The money's good. Stick with it.' But it's not easy. Maurice is so—I don't know—unpredictable. The sudden changes of mind and tack and God knows what else are getting on my nerves—and everybody else's."

Peter thought for a moment. "It wouldn't—" He stopped, then said, "He's not *on* anything, is he?"

MJ laughed hollowly. "Not likely. The boy doesn't even like aspirin. He saw one of the models using an inhaler this morning, and climbed all over her frame for putting unhealthy artificial substances into her body.

Never mind that they were substances her doctor had prescribed—she's asthmatic, and the air quality wasn't great up there today. I thought he was going to carry on for about an hour. Also—" She shook her head. "Odd, but I get a feeling he doesn't want to go shoot up by Kennedy, particularly."

Peter looked at her oddly. "Why?"

"He said something about the Shuttle making him nervous. You told me, didn't you, that there was something atomic going up on it?"

"It seems so. NASA's denying it, but they're protesting a bit *too* much."

"Well, he was complaining about that to Rhoda, that's the AD, this morning. If he thinks antihistamines are unnatural substances, you can imagine what he thinks about nuclear fission. To hear Maurice talk about it, you'd think all of Kennedy was one big bomb about to go off."

Peter wondered about that for a moment—then put the thought aside. *Just my own paranoia*, he thought. *Lots of people are worried about any kind of nuclear at all.*

"Well. You don't really want Venom to come and eat Maurice, do you?" Peter said.

"No," MJ said, though she sounded somewhat halfhearted. "No, I can put up with him for a *little* while longer."

"All right," Peter said. "Enough about him. What about us?"

"Yes," MJ said, and smiled slowly at him.

PETER woke up early the next morning, not entirely because he wanted to. His body still felt dog-tired, but the back of his brain was worried enough to wake him up with its own musings after only about six hours of sleep.

He lay staring at the ceiling for a few moments with a feeling of dislocation. It took a few seconds to remember where he was, why he was there, and what he had been doing.

He would have to get back to Miami. Vreni might need him today. He rolled over, saw that MJ was still sound asleep. This was unusual—usually as soon as he woke up, she did too, unless she was completely worn out.

He looked at her for a moment. There were shadows under her eyes. She looked as tired as he felt. *She really hates this work, and that wears her out. I wish she didn't have to do it.*

Peter dragged himself out of bed, showered, then switched the television on softly as he passed. The weather report was blathering about a continued spell of calm weather. That was good enough news for him. Once he had done whatever work Vreni required of him, the good weather would make his continued search for Curt a little easier.

The question, of course, was where to look? That had been niggling at him since before he went to sleep. He was pretty sure that the Lizard would not turn up again too close to where he had been a couple of nights ago. There was still too much police attention there. Judging by the news briefs, the area was apparently being searched again this morning. But if not there, where?

His dreams had been troubled by the recurring thought of the bank statements. He was sure they held the key. His first run at them hadn't been too conclusive. Curt seemed more than anything else to hit the machines down in Ochopee, but he could hardly just go and lie in wait near a bank machine.

Once Vreni had made her police connection, Peter was tempted to share a little of his information with her to see if the police could get more details on Curt's access to the machines. Most of the First Florida Bank's cash machines were now fitted with cameras, and he was hoping that somewhere within the range of the camera's lens they might be able to turn up a recurring car license plate, or maybe an actual warm body who was accompanying Curt to the machine.

Because Peter couldn't get rid of the idea that Curt Connors was, once again, being used. That strange description of Mrs. Bridger's, of him stopping and starting, kept coming back. Like someone was using him, or as if someone was attempting to control him in some strange way. It was all a mystery, but Peter hoped to get to the bottom of it.

When he was scrubbed, and shaved, and generally feeling much better, he sat down on the bed and shook MJ gently. "Honey? MJ?"

"Nnnngh," she said, opened her eyes and looked at him blearily. "What time is it?"

"About eight. Sweetie, I have to get back down to Miami."

"Okay, Tiger," she said, and reached up for a hug.

After a few seconds, Peter said, "Now, about this phone."

"Yes, dear," she said, in the voice that said she knew a lecture was coming, and that the amount of attention she would pay to it was negotiable.

"I think it would be smarter if when I'm wearing my other hat, so to speak, I shut the phone off. So if you don't get an answer sometimes, don't be surprised. Tonight in particular. I'm going out looking again."

"Okay," MJ said, though she stuck her lower lip out and pouted slightly, for effect. "But as soon as you're out of costume again, you call me. Understand?"

"I will. You can leave messages on the mobile system, anyway, even if I've got the phone shut off. I'll turn it on and pick them up when I can. But I don't want the thing going off in the middle of a swamp again."

"All right, all right." She blinked. "Eight o'clock, huh? I'd better get up and start putting myself together."

She got out of bed and stretched. "Oh, my back!"

"Is the bed too firm?"

"Not this bed," she said, "and firmer than you think. I spent the better part of yesterday tastefully draped over a large scenic rock. If Maurice asks me to do that again. I'm going to tell him to take his rock and—"

"MJ!"

"Yes," she said, "I know." She went to Peter and hugged him again.

He kissed her hard. "You're going up to Cocoa today?"

"That's right. I'll call you and let you know about the changes in plans," she said with a grim smile, "because I know there'll be some."

An hour and a half later, Peter was back in the hotel room in Miami. Vreni, when he got there, was already gone, and had left him a message saying she wouldn't be back until late. *Still chasing her police connections, I wonder?* Peter thought. *She seems awfully hung up on that.*

But he was pleased enough to have the spare time. Peter sat down at the table with the map he had picked up, and with the list of bank statements. He located Ochopee and Sunniland and several other branches of First Florida where Curt had stopped. All the bank branches sat in towns that were, in essence, along two sides of a triangle. The third side was empty of banks, empty even of towns—it ran through the heart of the Everglades.

He looked at that third side. *Martha is probably right,* he thought. *There are more usages of these two machines than any others. Curt must be closest to them, and doesn't see any point in trying to go out of his way.*

Peter was sure now that Curt wasn't staying in a town, but had found some quiet hideaway. He couldn't prove the hunch conclusively, but short of going to every tiny town in this area and asking questions, he had to let the assumption stand.

Peter gazed thoughtfully at the third side of the triangle and picked a spot about halfway along it. Whoever was working with the Lizard—if indeed there was someone at all—seemed to be keeping him fairly active. Normally, if the Lizard had a choice, he preferred to hide during his transformations, rather than be seen by people. But this time he was being seen, all right.

I have to start somewhere, Peter thought. *It's a chance: there's a lot of territory to cover there. Still…* He chuckled to himself. *A day out on the webs, working out these aches and pains, will do me good. And anyway, I don't know what else to do.*

A couple of hours later, Peter was in the Everglades, webslinging to his heart's content—and looking. You could cover a lot of ground in this part of the world if you just kept moving fast and kept your eyes open. Once you got a sense of what fit in, he figured, you would quickly start seeing what didn't.

And so he spent the best part of the day swinging around and trying to get the same feel for the 'Glades as he had for the city streets of New York. There were kinds of movement you soon came to know as normal and natural. Simple traffic patterns: the way pedestrians walked when they were untroubled, the way cars moved when the streets were clear of accidents or gridlocks, even the general sound of the place.

Here there were no pedestrians, but there was plenty of life. Peter quickly learned to recognize the different flight patterns of quite a few birds, the panicky movement of those flushed from cover by his approach, and the more leisurely evasions of others already in flight. He soon knew that a quick swirl of ripples in still water meant the same thing as a ponderous, low-slung shifting of the undergrowth, and kept well clear of the alligators both movements concealed. He even saw a couple of Florida panthers—the first was no more than a lithe, half-seen movement in the trees, but the next one was swimming. That surprised him a little, thinking the big cat had somehow fallen in or even been grabbed by a 'gator, until he saw the same thing again later in the day, and this time the panther seemed to be actively enjoying its dip.

He started near Ochopee, not too far from the Melendezes' farm, worked swiftly northward until he got as far as the Everglades Parkway about ten miles east of Deep Lake, crossed it at a quiet moment—having had to wait a while for that—and made his way over into the other side of Big Cypress, toward Sunniland. After that he moved on until he hit what he estimated were the boundaries of Corkscrew Swamp Sanctuary. There being no signs, he turned back and started working downward again a little farther east.

It was hot, and very sticky. The sun slid leisurely across the sky, and birds flapped heavily or hastily out of his path, occasionally squawking their disapproval at the intrusion. It was surprising, though, given the way this place teemed with life of all kinds, how very quiet it was.

And so it went for most of the day, as the sun dropped toward the western horizon and things finally began to cool a little. Spidey was glad enough of that. His uniform was definitely going to need a rinsing, and working in such humidity for long periods drained even his enhanced strength, as well as sweat. The sky was clearing now: earlier he had been forced to stop his swinging and head for some sort of cover, when the lowering heavens opened and the rain came pouring down in a near-solid wall of water, and lightning slashed out of the leaden sky to strike the water or, occasionally, a tree.

But the storm had passed quickly enough, and he went on again while the afternoon slipped into early evening and the sun was swallowed up by a great cloudbank to the west. Anywhere else, things would have gotten quieter with the approaching nightfall, but not here. The song of the frogs and the bugs began, peeping and shrilling and calling. The day shift of hunters and food-seekers in the animal world checked out, and the night shift took over: creatures that moved more quietly, less obviously. In the hour or two of lingering dusk before day gave way to darkness, Spidey began to get used to them, too.

He crossed the highway once again, swinging south toward the middle of the Everglades. *I could get to like this,* Spider-Man thought. *No cars, no trucks—or at least, not all over the place, like New York. Just frogs and bugs.*

He paused in the topmost branches of the cypress and looked around. It was too early for the moon, and there was only the faintest shimmer left of the sunset. A little south of him something big and silent floated by. An owl, he thought. Hawks didn't fly this late. He watched it go, perfect in its silence. *Low-tech stealth technology,* he thought, and grinned inside his mask.

From the south came a long, low roar, and with it a mild buzz of his spider-sense. The unseen grin vanished. Spidey stared into the gloom. He couldn't see anything, but he heard the roar repeated, just once. He knew that roar; it was neither 'gator nor panther.

He started swinging as fast as he could in the direction of the roar for about fifteen or twenty minutes. Then he heard another roar, much closer, and made a course correction. At a guess the source was no more than half a mile away, and he poured on some speed. He was coming into an area of fewer cypresses—more open water, with islands both solid and semisolid floating in it like dumplings in soup.

Where I can't swing, I can spring, Spidey thought, and went bouncing along, more excited now that the day's frustrating search seemed to be paying off. Only a couple of hundred yards away from him, hidden by stands of reeds, he could hear thrashing, splashing—and not just one roar anymore, but two. The first was the sound he had been tracking, the second a deep, hissing grunt. *Now what the...*

He leapt from one island to another, burst through the screening reeds, and found himself face-to-face with an alligator-wrestling match. It was not precisely wrestling: one 'gator lay on a nearby reed island, upside down with its stubby, taloned legs waving impotently and its jaws snapping at the air. But only its front legs. There was no movement from its back legs or its tail, and Spidey suspected its back had been broken.

In the water, waist-deep, the Lizard was advancing slowly, snarling, toward a second shape that was circling him. This second 'gator was bigger than the first. Its snout, eyes, and ridged, scaly back were all visible above the surface like the hull of a submarine, but its tail was lost in the swirling froth of churned-up water.

Then Spidey saw it suddenly change course, surging toward the Lizard. With two beats of that massive tail it was on top of him, jaws gaping wide, but the Lizard sidestepped the clumsy rush and grabbed the 'gator as it plunged by—then roared, strained briefly, and lifted the whole beast clear of the water and up over his head. The shocked 'gator produced that bizarre hissing grunt again, and its tail lashed from side to side, but its target was inside the arc of its swing and safely out of reach.

Spider-Man crouched down and stayed very still for a moment, sure that this was no time to distract the Lizard—no matter how much he wanted to have a chat. Then the Lizard dropped the 'gator. At first Spidey thought this was an accident, but in a flash the Lizard had grabbed the bigger saurian between his left arm and his side, holding its jaws tight shut. *He knows!* Spider-Man thought with a touch of grim pleasure. The muscles that closed a 'gator's jaws were ferociously strong, but those that opened them were much weaker.

The Lizard brought his right arm around, grabbed his left arm with it in a sort of awkward hammerlock, and began to increase the pressure. The 'gator thrashed, unable to even hiss now. Then there was a sudden, grisly snap, and the 'gator's thrashing became reflex flopping, then shuddering, until finally the huge reptile hung limp. The Lizard flung its carcass aside and roared in triumph.

Warily Spider-Man stood up, tensed and ready to dodge. "Nice going, scale-puss," he said. The Lizard whirled at the sound of his voice and threw himself at Spidey. Spider-Man leapt out of the way, tsking in disapproval. "This is no way to greet an old friend!"

The Lizard wasn't concerned. As Spidey leapt, he leapt after him. For a few seconds that part of the swamp would have looked, to an outside observer, like a particularly lively pogo-stick competition, Spidey leaping from islet to islet and the Lizard bounding after him with snake-strike speed. "Curt, listen to me!" Spidey called from a safe distance. "Listen! Stop! I just want to talk. I don't want to—"

—*fight with you!* he finished internally, springing sideways again as the Lizard pounced straight at him, claws out. His roar had scaled up and up until now it was almost a scream, a sound like sheet steel being torn in two. *It's as if it does hurt him,* Spidey thought, reluctant to be reminded, *but I won't—I can't—treat him as if he's going to be the Lizard forever. I don't want to acknowledge that identity. I've got to get through to the man inside.*

Once more the Lizard jumped him, so fast and from so close that there was no time to web him. Spidey had to club him aside, as hard as he could. The Lizard came down with a splash, half in and half out of the water, his upper body sprawled across one of the little reed islets. As he lay there dazed, Spider-Man bent down beside him. "Aw, damn," he muttered. "Curt?"

The Lizard rolled over, hissing in pain, and stared blankly at the darkening sky, slit-pupiled eyes dilating and lipless reptile mouth stretching into a snarl. Spider-Man glanced up—then threw himself sideways just as fast as he could. Even then, he was missed only barely by the pseudopod, sharp as a knife, that thudded into the reedy dirt where he had been crouching a second's fraction before. He came down on his back in the water and struggled to his feet. Even if he hadn't recognized the tendril for the alien creature that it was, he'd have identified his attacker based on the total lack of warning from his spider-sense.

"Don't you know it's dangerous to be out in a swamp after dark?" said Venom softly, and tendrils from the symbiote came boiling at Spider-Man. He jumped again, slightly hindered by the water and the clinging mud beneath, and made it to one of the islets, looking around him desperately for something to shoot a web at. There was a cypress about fifty feet away; he targeted that, and pulled himself out of the way just in time as Venom came after.

"We might have known we'd find you here," Venom said. "Well, you just keep your distance for the moment, while we deal with this." He turned back toward the Lizard. "It's ruined enough lives in its time. Now that happy chance throws it in our way, we shall put an end to it."

"*No!*" Spider-Man shouted. He charged back at Venom, leaped off one small island that was barely more than a dry patch in the midst of the water, and shot web from both hands as he passed, tangling the pseudopodia that reached out toward the Lizard to slash and kill.

The Lizard moaned, rolled over, and struggled to push himself up on his arms as Spider-Man locked off the web and used it to jerk Venom toward him. "It's not his fault!" he snapped, shooting more web—faster, he hoped, than Venom could claw it away. "None of this is his fault!"

Venom tore himself free of the webbing. "Who are we supposed to blame, then? Society?" He started toward the Lizard again.

Spidey launched himself at Venom, feet-first this time, and hit him chest-high. They went down in a heap, grappled one another, and rolled splashing in a tangle of webs and pseudopodia. "You're supposed to be such a tough guy. How come you have to try hitting people when they're down? Not very chivalrous. Not very kind to the innocent."

"Innocent?" Venom hissed, as claws and pseudopodia grabbed Spider-Man by the head and began to pull him closer to that dreadful fanged, slavering face. Spidey pushed himself back as hard as he could, but the grip was crushing. "He's no more innocent than you were when you ruined our life. If he had an accident, well, isn't that just too bad…"

Spider-Man pushed and pushed, desperate to break that lock. There was a noise on the edge of his hearing, a sound like the buzzing of bees. He couldn't make out what that would be at this time of night. "Believe it or not," he said, "I no more meant you harm than he means it to anyone. He can't help himself when he's like this. But you… You're like this on purpose. He'll turn back to Curt Connors, sooner or later. You're the way you are because you like it!"

Venom roared and went for him, clutching him tighter. Spider-Man was having a hard time keeping his distance from that awful grin. The tongue streaked out, looped around his neck, and began to tighten. Spidey braced himself against the pull of the tendrils and the strangling grip of the tongue, intent now on not blacking out; but his ears began to sing, and that buzzing got louder and louder, and his vision began to go dark around the edges.

Then there was a splashing noise nearby, and suddenly the inexorable pressures on head and throat were released as Spidey was pushed backwards into the water. He scrambled up and out of it, tangled in reeds, and looked around him. A hundred yards or so distant, he could see a low, hunched figure, indistinct in the twilight's last gleaming but with a faint sheen of water and scales about it.

It was the Lizard, heading for the horizon just as fast as he could. Venom was after him, leaping as Spidey had from tussock to tussock, but as Spider-Man watched, the Lizard dove into and under the water, cutting it as cleanly as a thrown stone. The surface closed over him, and he was gone. *Go, Curt, go!* thought Spidey as Venom continued into the darkness on the same line as the Lizard's final dive, thrusting pseudopodia into the water as he went, feeling for his quarry.

Spider-Man was distracted by that buzzing noise, now definitely not a sound from inside his battered head, but rising to a throaty mechanical drone. He turned; behind him a boat was approaching, a low, flat-bottomed boat with one of those big, wire-caged fans mounted at the stern, skimming along the open, reed-thickened water of a nearby canal. A searchlight was flickering from it, and as the beam swept from side to side it caught him square.

Fight or flight, he thought, then shook his head and stood his ground. *No. These guys are on my side, whether they know I'm on their side or not. I'm not gonna run.*

The heavy drone of the big propeller-fan died to a sound more like a domestic lawn mower as its engine was throttled back, and the boat settled down onto the surface of the canal and coasted to a stop near him. They were only vague outlines beyond the glare of the searchlight, but Spidey guessed there were about six police officers on board; he could hear the sound of rounds being racked into shotgun chambers. Then one of the figures leaned forward and said, "You again?"

He recognized the man's voice. It was the officer he had spoken to the other night, when he'd run into the Lizard earlier. "I was just passing through," Spider-Man said somewhat lamely.

"Spare me," said the officer. "We could have heard you a mile away tonight, even without all this listening-gear. Who's your buddy?"

"What? You mean the Lizard?"

"No. I mean the other one, the big one in the black suit."

"Hardly a buddy," said Spider-Man, "in my system or anybody else's. I'm afraid that was Venom."

There was a moment's silence, and a suggestion of half-seen movement as the men on the boat looked at each other. "You're keeping bad company, Spider-Man," said the cop. "And I thought we asked you to stay out of this area."

"I was looking for a friend."

"This time you *do* mean the Lizard. Company's getting worse and worse."

"Believe me," Spider-Man said, "if you had a choice between the Lizard and Venom, I'd advise you to take the Lizard any day. At least he'll run, if he has the chance. But Venom…" He shook his head. "He'll run too—but he'll go through you for a shortcut first."

If Spidey had hoped his flip remark might lighten the tense atmosphere, the attempt failed miserably. There was an awkward, distinctly unamused silence, and then the cop cleared his throat. "I'll choose not to regard that as a threatening statement," he said grimly. "Normally we don't give warnings. This is your second. I'll make it simple for you. Get out of this area. Stay out of this area. You're not wanted here. You're complicating a crime scene, and it's not making our jobs any easier. Do I make myself understood?"

"I understand you just fine, Officer."

There was another silence, and during this one Spider-Man could practically hear the cop thinking that though Spidey understood, he hadn't yet agreed. "Then you'd better be on your way."

For a moment the thought crossed Spidey's mind that, if he moved fast enough with his webbing, he might be able to tie them all up, leave them here safe enough, and continue his pursuit. *But no,* he thought. "Good night, Officers," he said, and took off.

Their engine powered up again, and a few seconds later the flatboat zoomed off in the direction taken by the Lizard and Venom. Spider-Man went after them, and despite the racket from the boat's engine and propeller-fan, he remembered what the cop had said about listening-gear, and moved as quietly as he could, trusting as always in his spider-sense to guide him. It was hard to avoid splashing near the water or crashing in the trees, but he took a Great Circle route, arcing out away from the cops and then back around to where it should intersect with Venom's and the Lizard's.

But it was too late. The Lizard had vanished into the swamp, without leaving any trace that Spidey—and hopefully Venom—could see. And as for Venom, there would be no tracking him down either, since his spider-sense never gave any hint of where Venom might be. He had often puzzled about that; probably it had something to do with the symbiote having been tailored originally for him and his special abilities. Right now the question was academic at best. They were both gone. A night's work wasted, the police even more seriously alienated than they had been before, and he was no closer to finding out what Curt was up to.

He stayed in the swamp for at least another hour, playing cat-and-mouse with the police-boat as he worked his way back toward Curt and Venom's trail—and then without warning, something shrill-voiced shrieked right beside him. For a moment, after the day's quiet, he thought it was an exotic night-bird, or a tree-frog of some kind. Then it shrilled again, in exactly the same key, and he realized it was the cell phone.

"I do not believe this," he said under his breath, and hastily pulled it out before it could ring a third time. *I cannot believe that, after all that, I forgot to turn it off!*

In the middle distance—too middle, not enough distance—he could hear the changing engine-note of the police flatboat, and then its searchlight came flickering toward him. "Hello?" he whispered.

"Peter!"

"I can't talk right now. You know," he said quietly, not saying her name, "I really wish you wouldn't call me at work!"

"Why? I thought you were going to turn the phone off when—"

"I forgot," he said, "and you can laugh at me later."

"Where are you?"

"Near some people who are getting very interested in me. What's up? Make it quick!"

"Well, we're done with… work where I am," she said. He heard the sound of MJ being cautious. "We're staying here tonight, and then we're going… farther north, tomorrow."

"Good," he said.

"That, er, garden you mentioned."

"Gotcha. Look, call me back in a couple of hours, all right?" That searchlight was getting closer, and he had a nasty feeling that its flickerings weren't as random as they had been.

"Right. Bye…" And she was gone.

By the time the police flatboat got close enough to get a positive fix on him, Spidey was gone, too. He made away at his best speed, and soon enough the light swung away and the boat's drone faded, as the cops turned back onto their original trail. This time Spidey didn't follow them. He was fairly sure that, listening-gear or not, they weren't going to find anything, either.

He sighed, and slowly made his way back to where he had cached the car, at a Seminole-run rest stop on the road—a small and amiable tourist trap kind of place that sold fry bread and souvenirs to the passersby. Anyone passing that lonely spot would have been surprised to see the figure in the red and blue costume standing l here by the beat-up little phone booth. But no one passed, and no one was left at the rest stop to see or hear as he dialed.

"Hello?" It was Martha.

"Martha," he said, "it's Spider-Man."

"How're you doing?"

"Well, good and bad. I, uh, I saw Curt this evening."

"You saw *Curt?*"

"Well, the Lizard. We had a brief set-to."

"You didn't hurt him, did you?"

"No."

"And he didn't hurt you…?"

"Not so it counts. Unfortunately, Venom ran into us before we could get into any serious conversations, if you know what I mean."

"Oh, no!"

"No, Martha, it's all right. He got away. I very much wanted to be able to follow him, because sooner or later, he would have led me back to wherever Curt is keeping himself. I just wanted to let you know what happened, though, because some of this may turn up on the news later. I had a run-in with the police."

"Are you all right?"

"I'm okay. It's just that—well, we're no further forward."

She sighed. "Thanks for letting us know, anyway. It's better to have real news than these hints and rumors."

"Whatever he's up to, Martha, it's definitely something down in this area—if only because there's a limit to the distance he can travel in a few hours as Curt, and he can't stay the Lizard all that long. At least I don't think so." He did not say that there were some things about Curt's behavior that seemed to have changed considerably since Spider-Man had seen him last. There was no point in getting her worried about something he didn't himself fully understand yet.

"You'll keep looking for him?"

"I will." He couldn't say anything more promising than that, though he wished he could.

"You know we really appreciate your help. Both of us do. William likes to make a great virtue of self-sufficiency."

"No question that it's a virtue," Spider-Man said softly. "But tell him to leave *me* something to do."

Martha chuckled softly. There was the strength of the woman: despite all the terrible things that had happened to her family, she never quite lost the humor. "I will. You take care."

"Bye, Martha."

She hung up. Spider-Man sighed, then took himself out of sight again, into the brush behind the rest stop, and changed gratefully out of a costume that was now not just itchy but muddy and smelling of an unsavory mixture of sweat and swamp-water. *Glad I brought a spare,* he thought, as he got wearily into the car and started the long drive home. *At the rate things are going, I don't think there's going to be time to stop and do the laundry.*

SEVEN

HE woke up the next morning with a massive ache in his neck and shoulders, left over from Venom's friendly embrace. Peter took a couple of aspirins, then went and stood under the shower and took mental inventory.

On the surface, it seemed to have been a wasted day. He had no new information about Curt, or about what was the matter with the Lizard. But, on the other hand, he was now a lot more comfortable with at least part of the 'Glades. Peter had a feeling that this was going to be useful, and sooner rather than later. But at the moment, he was a little weary of life in the swamp.

And then a plan materialized with a snap. *I'm going webswinging this morning,* he thought. *Among nice neat shiny skyscrapers, for a change. Since I'm here, they might as well see me. If the cops want to do anything about it, let them chase me up the side of a building.* At the very worst, he would have a nice therapeutic swing around town, and see some of the sights. It would be very relaxing. Skyscrapers were much simpler and more reliable to swing from than cypress trees. Nor were there alligators waiting beneath them, waiting eagerly to catch you as you fell.

Peter felt instantly happier. The next problem, of course, was where to go to change, in a strange city. This hotel was one of those with windows that didn't open: otherwise he would simply have gone straight out.

He left the hotel and drove north a little bit, on Biscayne Boulevard, to the big Omni shopping center. Peter had seen pictures of it in the tourist magazine in his own hotel, and had thought MJ might like to go there.

The place was very busy—they were having sales. *Yet another reason to bring MJ here, I guess—before she finds out about it, and accuses me of having known about it and not telling her.* He drove into the deepest level of the underground parking lot, and tucked the car into a shadowy corner. There he changed.

He exited then, calmly enough, in broad daylight—spidering his way along the ceiling, upside down, totally unnoticed by people as they walked out or drove in. The Questar and his other valuables he had left hidden in the trunk of the car.

Spider-Man scuttled along the ceiling to the parking lot's entrance, and then went straight up and straight out, right up the side of the main building—twenty or thirty stories of hotel and offices. He concentrated on going up only in front of closed windows; no use in ruining some jet-lagged tourist's morning by the sight of a super hero going about his business. There was a brisk wind coming in off the water; a seagull squawked, startled, as it passed Spidey while skimming past the plate-glass skin of the building.

He shot a line of web up to the top of the Omni after a while, hauled himself up, crouched briefly at the very top, and launched another webline at the nearest skyscraper, across Biscayne. It anchored and he began to swing.

It was amazing how relaxing it could be to fall back into the old routine. Building-corner to building-corner, swinging along, noting with amusement that Miami people looked up no more than New Yorkers did. There were fewer skyscrapers here, and they tended to cluster close. Most buildings here were low, as if people were reluctant to shut away the sun even though they already had so much of it. But he could still exploit the center of the city well enough to get a good look at the place—wide boulevards, traffic a little more easygoing, to his eye, than the standard New York brawl and rush of cabs and trucks. On a bright sunny morning, with the humidity not yet out of hand and the temperature still only in the 80s, it was very pleasant. Spidey smiled under the mask.

On a day like this, he thought, *it's nice to be Spider-Man—*

That was when he heard the sound.

It was familiar, and his grin got even broader under the mask. It was amazing how little real gunfire sounded like any of the sound effects in the movies, so much so that he wondered, sometimes, where they got those sounds in the first place. Bullets didn't whine: they went "pff" past you, unless they hit something and ricocheted—and even then the sound was no Lone Ranger "wheeeeenng!" but a sharp brief scratchy sound. Rifles made a sound more like someone smacking a ruler on a wooden desk, and automatic weapons generally sounded more like someone backspacing repeatedly on an old Olivetti than like the "buddabuddabudda" beloved of comics letterers.

Now Spidey heard rulers being smacked on desks, several of them, repeatedly, and fairly nearby, to judge by the way the echoes were racketing off the surrounding skyscrapers. He briefly consulted the memory of the city map in his hotel room. The sound was coming from over by North West Seventh and Flagler.

Spider-Man swung over in that direction in a hurry, fastening his web for the second-to-last swing to the top of a building with an unusual sheared-off, diagonal face. He swung low past the front of it, catching the occasional astonished look from people gazing out through the glass, and dropped down thirty or forty stories to see what was going on.

The situation was fairly serious. North West Seventh was blocked off by police cars to the east and west, about a building over in each direction. The sidewalk in front of the building to which he clung, and in front of the building directly across from it, was conspicuously empty. Across the street was a car, and from his high vantage point he could see a group of men huddled down behind it. Parked to the car's right, slewed sideways and up onto the sidewalk, was an armored car, its back doors open and smoke wafting out of them.

This was a scenario Spider-Man had seen often enough. Smoke bomb into the car's air intake, force the crew out. The details would differ, but there would always be armed men waiting nearby, wearing gas masks and ready to jump into the car and drive it off. *Not while I'm here,* Spidey thought.

He looked down and considered briefly how best to proceed. A hail of bullets was flying in several directions down there, the four men behind their car ruler-whacking and backspacing at great speed. Behind the police cars across the street and to either side, police officers crouched and returned fire, but with little effect.

Spider-Man shot a line of web over to the top of the other building, swung over, and took care to keep himself high and out of anybody's notice. Then he came up against the far building—a bank, as it happened—clung a moment, looked straight down. Only four men: he had wanted to be sure. He scurried down the face of the building until he was about ten stories above the men behind the car.

There he paused. Two of the men were firing mostly forward; the other two were firing each to his own side. None of them was paying any attention to the space behind them, which they apparently thought they had secured.

This was a mistake. Spider-Man considered his choreography for a moment—then dropped right down behind them, silently. The problem with being a stressed-out gunman, blazing away at everything you see, is that it's very hard for you to hear someone coming up softly behind you and shooting a big gob of sticky web over your head—which was what Spider-Man did to the first man, the one on the left-hand side as he faced them. He pulled the man sharply over backwards. As he fell, another jet of web hit the gun. Spidey yanked it out of his hand, released the web, and let the gun and the webline fly off to one side, well out of reach.

The man immediately to that robber's right reacted to the sudden cessation of gunfire, turned openmouthed to see that his companion was gone, spun around staring behind him, saw Spider-Man, and sighted on him. The next jet of web caught this man full-face. He staggered forward, firing, and plate glass shattered, but it was no use—Spider-Man was already somewhere else, about twenty feet to the left. He pulled on the rope of webbing. The man went down hard, face forward, and Spidey shot another webline at the gun and fastened it down immovably to the concrete.

The other two had noticed him now. One of them, a man in a T-shirt saying "Nuke the Whales," whirled, firing an Uzi at him. Spider-Man bounced and rolled, changing course twice on the way toward him. He then shot web in two directions, one at the Uzi-carrier, to snatch the machine gun out of his hands and toss it over Spidey's shoulder, the other at the fourth man, to web him and his gun solidly to the car. The one man still standing, the one who'd had the Uzi, jumped at Spidey.

"Waste of time," Spider-Man said softly, and simply decked the man in midair. Vectors add, after all; by his rush, the man added his own energy to the punch that would have hit him to begin with. He crashed to the ground, and Spidey looked down to see if he would move again. He didn't.

"It's a dumb T-shirt, too," Spider-Man said with some satisfaction. He stood still then, for uniformed cops were hammering toward him from all directions, now that the guns were silent. Casually enough, Spidey lifted his hands in a nothing-to-do-with-me gesture as they closed in on him.

"Gentlemen," he said, noticing that there were still a fair number of their weapons trained on him, "tell me if I'm wrong, but this looked more like a withdrawal than a deposit."

Some of the cops chuckled, but no one moved much until another man, one in a suit this time, came striding up to Spider-Man. He looked over the site, and then broke into a large grin. He was a big man, dark-haired, broad across the shoulders, with a big mustache over the grin, and a broad, intelligent face. When he spoke, another New Yorkish accent came out, or at least a northeastern one, so that Spidey began to wonder whether this state was entirely populated by refugees from colder climes.

"Spider-Man," he said. "Heard you were in the neighborhood. Didn't think we'd have the pleasure."

"The pleasure was all mine," Spidey said. "Detective—"

"Anderson," the detective said. "Murray Anderson."

They shook hands. "Well, on behalf of the city of Miami and the department, let me thank you," Anderson said. "Because I would have seriously disliked seeing any of my people get shot by one of these guys." He looked around at the four men, whom his officers were detaching from various globs of web, handcuffing, and taking away.

Another uniformed cop came up to them and said, "The guards in the van are coming around, sir."

"Good. Do me a favor. Run them downtown and take their statements—and have somebody from Medical come down and look them over. They might have some smoke inhalation."

"Right." The cop went off.

Anderson turned back to him. "Should I be thanking the City Tourist Bureau as well?" he said. "Are you here on vacation? Come to think of it, do super heroes get vacations?"

"Not as such," Spidey said, and laughed. "This morning I was on busman's holiday, if anything. The trip is mostly business."

"Oh really? Anything we could help you with?"

Spider-Man smiled inside the mask. "Well, since you asked..."

"We don't have to discuss it here," Anderson said. "Always wanted a chance to talk to one of you guys. Come on, I know somewhere quiet."

ANDERSON'S unmarked car was nearby. He drove them down Biscayne Boulevard to Brickell, and from there to Bayfront Park. Murray pulled up in the parking lot there, picking a spot where they could look across at the low flat green line of Key Biscayne, and, beyond it, to the Atlantic.

"Pretty spot, Detective," Spider-Man said.

"Call me Murray. Yeah," he said, leaning back in his seat and grinning, "I've sat on stakeout a lot down here. Now. What can I help you with? You strike me as a man who may have some kind of problem, seeing you're out in uniform—" he smiled "—so far from home."

Spider-Man thought for a moment, and then said, "Among other things, I'm investigating certain… anomalies in security up at Canaveral, at Kennedy Space Center."

To his surprise, Murray nodded. "Word does get around fast, doesn't it?"

"How do you mean?"

"Oh, they've had some problems recently. Something went missing, some days back—something they were taking delivery on, that *should* have gone on the shuttle. It vanished."

"The Cape," Spider-Man said carefully, "has been saying it hasn't had any security problems."

"They'd hardly broadcast it if they did. I know that's the official line. But we have our own sources up there. Some of the people in security, meaning only the best, make sure we find out things that we need to know about. Even if their bosses don't necessarily like the idea. We're all on the same side, for cryin' out loud."

"What happened, exactly?"

"Something jumped up on one of those big delivery barges they've got there. Decked a bunch of people, hurt some of them pretty badly— busted some arms and legs, poked a big damn hole in the barge—then took this object, jumped back in the water with it—was gone. They did everything up to and including drag the Banana River, but there was no sign of what was lost."

"Any reports of what this person looked like?"

Murray laughed, just a breath. "'Person'—that's not what the APB says. Six foot two or higher. Massive build. Green. Claws. Fangs. Tail," Murray said, with emphasis. "Not many perps down here answer to that description. And no 'persons.'"

Spider-Man nodded. "It's the Lizard," he said.

"No kidding." Murray looked delighted but also concerned. "But he's crazy, though, isn't he? I thought."

"If you mean he doesn't have any control over himself," Spidey said, "yes, that's right." *As far as I know.*

"Hey, a super villain on my turf!"

"He's not much of a villain, really," Spider-Man said. "Not in the classic sense."

Murray nodded, said nothing for a moment. "It wasn't accidental, then," Spidey said, "that I ran into some of your colleagues looking specifically for him, the other night?"

"Nope. The APB's been out for days. Now that there've been a couple of sightings, *everybody's* looking. Those who want to catch him, anyway." Murray's look was sly, and suggested that not everybody would particularly want to find the Lizard without ample backup on hand.

"What exactly was it that he took?" Spidey said.

Murray shook his head. "Our sources haven't been willing to say."

It was all very confusing. Theft—the Lizard shouldn't be capable of it. Unless Curt has managed to achieve some measure of control over him again. But that seemed very unlikely, given that he'd shown no sign of being conscious of his inner humanity, or even capable of being reasoned with, the last two times they'd met. Just that mindless rage.

"I have to say," Murray said, "that a little of the, shall we say, edge of immediacy has gone off the issue of the Lizard at the moment. We seem to have a bigger problem."

Spider-Man looked at him. "Venom."

"Venom," Murray said. "Now, that is *serious* trouble—somebody in full control of his faculties, and crazy as a jaybird. Or worse, crazy like a fox—and very unpredictable, especially to members of my fraternity. We've heard enough reports of what happens if you get between him and somebody he's chasing."

"At the moment," Spider-Man said, "I think that's probably me."

"Well," said Murray, "I was going to mention… You might want to be careful about the height of your profile for the next little while. You want to limit the collateral damage, you might say. To innocent bystanders—if Venom catches up to you."

"Oh, believe me," Spidey said, "the bystanders are high on both our lists. Possibly the only good thing I can say about Venom."

"And you're sure it's you he's after."

"I *think* so," Spider-Man said.

"But you don't sound certain."

"No," Spider-Man said, "I'm not. Venom doesn't do things without a reason. They might not be what you or I would consider sane reasons, but he has them. These two little escapades—that guy in the skyscraper, and the people on the beach—"

Murray frowned. "We haven't yet released any information about Venom having done it."

"I know what scenes look like after Venom's been there," Spider-Man said. "A crime scene that looks like that one did, paired with a definite sighting of Venom a day later—the coincidence is too big."

"You sound like you have inside info."

"No, I just know Venom," Spider-Man said, and shuddered just a little. "Too well."

"Either way," Murray said, "the modus for these crimes isn't clear. Our one witness has been hard to get anything out of. The doctors say he's in traumatic incurse, whatever that is. Mostly it seems to mean that he can't do anything but stammer. And as for the bank executive—" Murray shrugged. "There seem to be some smuggling connections; they're being followed up. But the guy's very white-collar, and whatever tracks he might have left are well covered. So…" He shrugged, and looked out across the bay.

Spider-Man gazed out too, for a moment, and watched the boats go by. "Did you hear about his last appearance in New York?"

"A little."

Spider-Man told Murray something about the CCRC connection on which he and Venom had stumbled when they last ran into one another—the smuggled radioactives and so forth. "It's a name we know," Murray said, "but not for hot stuff. Or not from that kind of hot stuff, anyway."

"Oh?"

"DEA has been investigating them," Murray said. "We've had a few liaison meetings with them, and the Coast Guard. Again, the trail is very well covered, and they haven't been able to pin anything really conclusive on them. A lot of talk, a lot of rumors, but no smoking gun, as yet, nothing concrete. Then this vice president in charge of buffed nails at this German bank gets attacked by Venom, and even the DEA has to start asking itself, why him? Why out of the blue? So the investigation will heat up again now. There's a little annoyance," Murray added, "in the Department at the moment. My department, you understand. Venom brought some barrels along to the scene, the second one. DEA came in and confiscated them."

"Barrels," Spider-Man murmured. There had been a lot of barrels of toxic waste stowed around various CCRC buildings and caches in New York. "Something radioactive?"

"I truly don't know," Murray said. "They just came in there and took the stuff before there was anyone on the scene really senior enough to stop it. Jurisdiction problem. Messy," he said, and chewed his mustache reflectively for a moment. "You think they were nuke stuff?"

"Could have been," Spider-Man said, "but it's a wild guess at the moment. I'd have to see them."

"Tough to do," Murray said, "unless you want to break into DEA HQ and try."

"No, thanks."

"And another thing," Murray said, shifting in his seat. "They've sold that bank."

"Who?"

"CCRC, if I understand the scuttlebutt correctly. The ownership is incredibly convoluted, of course, there are about eight shell companies involved. But the German bank's parent company divested itself of them two days ago. And the 'parent' is a 'child' of CCRC. Apparently the rumors about shipping illegal stuff didn't bother them—I'd bet every big bank in this town has such, sooner or later. But this was apparently too much for someone several corporate levels up. Sold." Murray made a "skrit" noise and a throat-cutting gesture. "To some Arabs, I think. Just like that."

Spider-Man digested that. "What were these rumors?"

"Mostly about illegal shipments coming into the Miami area. Other materials going out again. But no one knew what."

"Where was the cargo supposed to be going after Miami?"

"That," Murray said, "was the peculiar thing. They weren't going anywhere, at least nowhere that could be traced. We do get, from the DEA, estimates of what's coming into the U.S. from the so-called 'southern gateway.' That's the whole stretch of land and water between here and the Leewards, every month. They're rough estimates, of course, but these shipments, whatever they were, would come in, and there would be no sudden jump in the local market, the way there almost always is." Murray chewed his mustache again. "If someone was caching contraband for later use," Murray said, "that would fit the picture. But they almost never do that. Too much chance of the stuff being found, by the competition or by us, and then their investment's shot. In any case, DEA, and police all over the state, are watching for any large sudden movements of merchandise. It's all we can do."

Spider-Man shook his head. "I would bet that those barrels, and those other shipments you're discussing, have something to do with radioactives. Probably toxic."

"There's a nasty logic to it," Murray said. "After all, the channels for smuggling the stuff are already in place. The handoff points, the clandestine transport, everything's ready. But then—" It was Murray's turn to shudder. "The thought of toxic waste getting loose in the Aquifer…" he muttered. "The whole state would be glowing in the dark in a matter of days. And it would take centuries to get rid of it."

"We'll just have to make sure it doesn't happen," Spider-Man said, somber-voiced. The thought haunting him at the moment was not of CCRC specifically, but of Hobgoblin. He'd thought Hobby had been the major mover behind much of the business that CCRC had gotten itself involved with. But Hobby was in jail now, and those illegal operations had been shut down—he thought.

Someone else is managing this, Spidey thought. *Not Hobgoblin. Who?*

"Murray," Spider-Man said, "would you be willing to help out a guy in need of some information?"

Murray laughed. "I thought I had been."

"You have… and I'm grateful. But I may need some more. Is there somewhere I can reach you privately? There may be some info I'll need badly in the next few days. It may make a difference either to the Kennedy problem or to the Lizard situation. Or the one with Venom."

Murray fished out a business card from his jacket pocket. "That's my home machine. You leave a message on that, tell me where to call you, and I'll call you back as fast as I can. My pager number's on there, too."

Spidey pocketed the card. Murray said, "Anytime, you let me know. I'll do what I can for you." And he grinned like a little kid. "I don't often get to deal with super heroes, after all."

"Aw, shucks," said Spidey.

Murray smiled and started the car. "They used to tell me, you stay in Miami long enough, you'll see every kind of person there is. Now I believe it."

SPIDER-MAN webbed his way back to the Omni, back to his car, and had changed back to Peter Parker with no hassles. Peter drove back down to his own hotel, checked in, and found messages from Vreni and MJ waiting for him.

"Call me," MJ's said simply. Peter, bemused, took out the phone—which he had been carrying with him that morning—and turned it on again, half expecting it to ring instantly, then glanced at the other message. It said, "Interesting high-finance connection. Meet me Howitzer's, Miracle Mile…" and an address.

Peter looked at it and tried to see the map in his head again. That was over toward Coral Gables, he thought. More interestingly, that was where Regners Wilhelm, that German investment bank, had its main offices. The message had come in about twelve-thirty; it was one now. Peter got moving.

Howitzer's was a little coffee bar in the Mile, in the shadow of yet another tall, handsome, concrete-and-steel confection: though it was not as huge and obvious as some of the buildings downtown. Vreni was waiting for Peter with a cup of coffee in front of her, and was scribbling furiously on a notepad.

"How are you holding up?" she said.

"Pretty well. I'm about to go find a developer for most of my film. If you have any requests, I'll take care of them today before I drop the stuff off."

"That's exactly what I was calling for. I need you to get me some of that building over there." She pointed at it with her chin.

"Got a hot tip?"

"As hot as any so far. I *finally* made some police connections down here. Why are you smiling?"

"Nothing, just a passing thought. Sorry. What did you find?"

"Well." Vreni sat back. "That bank over there—very respectable for a lot of years—has more rumors going around about it than any other bank in this town, I think. Mostly regarding money laundering."

"Oh, really?"

She nodded. "So far, only one genuine conviction—a very very junior accounts executive, fired about a year and a half ago. But there are persistent reports of illicit funds transfers, stolen and counterfeit cashier's checks, money going missing. And then something very strange happened in their computer department, just a little while ago. An employee was fired. A virus invaded their accounting computers, trashed *everything*. The usual thing: a grudge, the employee left a Trojan, as they call it, in the system where it would go off if he didn't deactivate it periodically. Sort of a computer version of a nasty dead-man's switch."

"Bad," Peter said. "But you can always restore from the backups."

"Not if the building containing the backups is torched the same night," said Vreni. And she got that feral grin.

"Tell me," Peter said. "This was just before some kind of investigation happened?"

"Federal," Vreni said. "RICO."

Racketeering as well, he thought. It was all getting very tangled.

"The destruction of the backups was complete," Vreni said. "The destruction in the computer itself was a little more selective. What the virus ate seems mostly to have been material pertaining to a company called CCRC."

Peter's eyes widened. "What are they up to?"

Vreni shook her head. "I hope to find out. This story is a lot bigger than even Kate thinks—that I'm sure of. I have a suspicion that the whole Cape Canaveral story is going to come in second to this." She finished her coffee, closed her notebook. "Come on, let's go get your pictures."

Peter went out with her and snapped the exterior of the building, then got some long-lens expose-type shots of the building's reception area and of a guard glowering at them through the half-mirrored glass of the entrance. "This is all we're going to get from these guys," Vreni said. "Once they realized what I was interested in, they very politely threw me out. I've got stills of their executives from one of the corporate yellow pages sources, though. They'll do all right."

Peter shot the end of his last roll and got it out of the camera. "What's next, then?"

"I'm going to go interview that junior executive who got fired," Vreni said. "He's out on bail, somewhere in the area. Meanwhile, the Shuttle launch is getting closer." She looked suddenly tired. "And my sources don't seem able to tell me anything about what's going on at Kennedy."

Peter stood still and quiet for a moment, considering. Finally he said, "I had a favor that I was able to call in." He told her, without attributing the information, what Murray had told him about the Kennedy situation. Vreni produced her pocket recorder and listened to what he had to say, then looked at him sharply when he finished. "Is this source reliable?"

I only met him this morning, Peter thought. *It's a fair question.* But aloud he said, "In my opinion, yes. I *could* be wrong—"

Vreni looked at him. "I think your judgment is trustworthy. I wish I knew what to make of it all. I thought the Lizard was just—" she shrugged "—sort of a crazy thing running around, not something that you could order to do things. But if he's actually committing thefts... How is he doing it?"

Peter shook his head. Vreni smiled again. "This story is not only resisting being investigated," she said, "it's damn well taking the Fifth. I *love* it."

Peter was glad she was enjoying herself so. His problems were unfortunately not quite so abstract.

"All right," Vreni said, as they walked away from the Regners Wilhelm building together. "I've got some more interviews today, then starting this evening, I'll be in the hotel. We're getting close to our first deadline. I suspect I'll spend the afternoon hunting down this Jürgen Gottschalk, our fired exec."

"Right," Peter said.

THE Intercoastal Waterway runs up between Miami Beach and Miami proper, starting at the Port of Miami and flowing up past the opulent houses and hotels of Miami Shores and Bal Harbour. Between Biscayne Boulevard on the "mainland" side, and Collins Avenue on both sides of the Waterway, many a beautiful house leans down to a private pier or a dock. The palms around them sway and glitter when the sun hits their polished leaves, the landscaping looks pincushion-perfect, and an odor of exclusivity clings to white houses and pink bungalows and mansions done in peach stucco and glass brick. Here and there such houses rise above a strip of private beach.

One such house, shaded by palm and bougainvillea, perched by the bay shore, lights gleaming from inside as the dusk settled in. By a blue pool surrounded by pink paving, raised above the line of the waters of the bay, a man sat at a white cast-iron table, drinking an iced tea and staring out at the water.

He was quite young, blond, with a thin, fine-featured face, and very blue eyes. He had been sitting by this pool, staring at that bay, for almost three weeks now.

House arrest was a polite name for it, but that was what it was. There were police outside his front door, police outside his side doors, police staked out in boats down by the water. Some of them were not police officers per se, but federal agents of one kind or another. If he put a foot outside his property, they all went with him—and they let him know that they didn't like him to go outside, not for very long. So mostly he didn't bother going out. If the phone rang, he didn't answer it because he knew it was bugged—a friend on the force had tipped him off before the court order went through, and he had had just time enough to slip out and make a few vital calls from a pay phone before the house arrest started as well.

He sat still and did nothing, because others had told him to. It would all be straightened out in a while, they'd said. Be patient. The heat will come off. The feds will get off your case. He had not inquired how, or why—he was sure that money was changing hands somewhere. Money *always* changed hands. Not even the feds were invulnerable to that.

Evening was fading into night. He looked at the glitter of lights across the Bay Causeway and thought how very much he just wanted to get onto the Causeway, drive until he got down to the airport, catch a Lufthansa flight home to Munich... But there was no point in it. Even if he could get away from the house without his watchdogs—highly unlikely—even if he managed to successfully exit the country with one of several spare passports the others had given him, the German government would only extradite him right back here again. They were entirely too willing to show cooperation to the U.S. in these matters.

No, better to sit still. He got up, strolled over to the edge of the terrace, and leaned on it. Twenty feet straight down was the water, and not too far away was the police boat. He gave its occupants an insouciant wave and strolled back to the table, sat down again. He lifted his iced tea.

Under the nearby bougainvillea there was a rustling. *Palm rats,* he thought, exasperated, and turned to look.

The breath caught in his throat. His mouth dried. From the darkness under the big spreading tree came something darker: a man's shape, tall, broad in the shoulders, wearing some kind of dreadful-eyed mask, horribly fanged. A white design was plastered across the front of him. A spider—

The mask smiled, and a long, slime-dropping tongue flicked out. Jürgen Gottschalk gulped, and choked, dry. He watched the news. He knew who this was. More, he knew what had happened to his colleague in the Miami satellite office of Regners Wilhelm just the other day.

Slowly, Venom advanced on him. He stood up.

"No point in running, Mr. Gottschalk," said that soft, deep voice, a voice with teeth in it.

Jürgen's mouth worked, but no words came out. The blank eyes, the awful grin, transfixed him as if he were a spotlit deer, with someone sighting down a rifle along the beam. "Some people we know," Venom said softly, "suggested we go talk to your friend Mr. Harkness the other day. He told us some things we needed to know, but not as much as we had in mind. We had to check some of his files before we left his office, just to reconfirm some of the things he didn't tell us. And your name figured very prominently. We think we should have a talk."

"Aba... ba... bout what?"

Venom sat down very casually in the other white iron chair at the table, picked up the iced-tea glass, and sniffed it. "No alcohol," he said. "That's good. We like people who have their wits about them when we talk to them." Those blank eyes fastened on Jürgen's. "Those files," Venom said conversationally, "indicated times and dates for some very interesting meetings out in the water which have been taking place of late. We attended one of those meetings the other night. It was fascinating."

Jürgen swallowed. He had seen the news report. *Fascinating* was not the word he would have chosen.

"Now," Venom said, leaning in, and a pseudopod rippled out of his upper arm and patted Jürgen on the cheek, while Venom leaned his chin on his hand, "we're afraid we weren't able to get those people to deliver the message we gave them. We suppose it's better to do such things oneself, after all. We were going to tell their boss to cut it out." He smiled more widely yet. "It was rather distressing, though, that we couldn't get them to tell us anything about the source of the barrels they were handling that evening. And the people who had come to pick them up couldn't help us very much—well, we gave them a chance, but it's the usual problem: keep the lower echelons in the dark and they can't spill too much information. They may spill something else, of course…"

That grin spread wider, until it seemed to have more teeth in it than a museum of dentistry. "We weren't able to investigate those barrels too closely," Venom said, "but we want you to tell us everything about what was in them, and where it comes from, and where it goes.…"

Jürgen shook all over. "Now, we know what you're thinking," Venom said. "You're thinking that if you tell us, the people who you're involved with in this business will kill you. And so they probably will, eventually. At least they'll try. What you need to know, though, is that if you don't tell us, right now, we will kill you." The pseudopod, wavering in front of Jürgen's eyes, sharpened itself into a thin stiletto, and delicately, delicately traced a line across the front of his throat, just enough to let him feel the nick of the razor's edge.

"We can make it take quite a while," Venom said. "You won't be able to yell for help, because your larynx is one of the first things we'll cut out. After that—" Venom shook his head and shrugged. "We could be here all evening, couldn't we? The people in the boat down there won't come up here unless they see or hear some reason to. Your guards out in the street won't bother coming in—they know there's no way out except by the front or side doors, and they checked those long ago. No, we'll just have a lovely evening together. The longest one of your life."

"It's ruh… ruh… ruh—" Jürgen's mouth was just too dry to get anything out.

"First word?" Venom said helpfully. "Sounds like? Here." He pushed the iced tea toward Jürgen.

Jürgen clutched the glass and drank. When he set it down a moment later, gasping, it hadn't helped all that much, but he was able to croak. "Radioactives."

"What kind?"

"Transuranics."

Venom waved that knife-pseudopod casually in front of Jürgen's face. His eyes fixed on it as if it were a snake about to strike. "Do be a little more forthcoming, or we'll start getting the idea that you're being purposely obstructive."

"Oh, no, no!" Jürgen said, *"nein! Ich weiss nicht—"*

"English, please," Venom said gently. "We never did finish that last Berlitz course. Life got too busy."

"I don't know!"

"You'd better. What kind of radioactives?"

"It's waste of some kind. Radioactive waste."

"You're telling us," Venom said gently, and a bit of deadly edge was beginning to show in his voice, "that someone in Florida is shipping toxic radioactive waste out of the United States in those little barrels? Not a very cost-effective way to do it. Where is it going?"

"No, it comes in—"

"Where is it coming from?"

"Eastern Europe. I don't know where, exactly. Russia, maybe."

Venom's blank eyes narrowed a little. "And they're shipping it to Florida?"

"Brazil first."

"From Brazil to Florida. And then what's happening?"

"Then it gets shipped back."

"Not as toxic waste, surely."

"No. Treated—reclaimed—refined somehow."

Venom nodded. "We only know of one plant that does that kind of work," he said. "It's *in* Europe, in England, at Sellafield. The THORP facility. Nasty filthy thing," he said softly. "Think of all the fish in the Irish Sea that one can't grill without counting their heads first, because of the waste from that place. But never mind that for the moment. You're telling us that there is a nuclear waste reprocessing plant. A secret one, for no government would be so stupid as to try to site such a thing here openly—"

"I didn't tell you that."

"Oh, but you implied it. Clever, to let me draw the conclusion, so that you can truly tell your masters, when they catch up with you, that you didn't tell the main part of the secret." Venom leaned closer. That pseudopod rippled out again, forked, grabbed a pinch of Jürgen's cheek in it, and wiggled it back and forth playfully. "Very clever indeed. You may survive this. So. Toxic waste is shipped from Eastern Europe, heaven only knows how many miles overland, and then to some seaport, and then is shipped thousands of miles to Brazil in those drums—labeled as what? Industrial oil? Fertilizer? And then shipped again, from Brazil up through the Caribbean past the Leewards and the Windwards, some of the most delicately balanced ecosystems in the world, and up to Florida—and then stored here. In what have to be fairly significant quantities, to produce— what? Plutonium, surely, is what would be extracted if there was enough waste of the right kind. And no one would bother for anything less. It's much too much trouble."

Jürgen nodded.

"And then," Venom said, "that refined plutonium is shipped back the same way, all that distance, mislabeled as who-knows-what, through some of the world's most crowded sealanes, and across the Atlantic, where the currents would carry this material, if it leaked, halfway around the world before anyone knew. Killing everything in the water where the concentration exceeded a part per billion in the seawater. But then, back to Europe—and someone in Europe is getting significant amounts of plutonium, 'unmarked' as it were, leaving no records with the various atomic energy commissions of the countries which deal in such things. And there it vanishes."

Venom grinned, leaned even closer. "Into the hands of... Well, there are too many people who would pay good money for untraceable weapons-grade plutonium, here and there. Very slick indeed. And then your bank launders the payments for these services. Isn't that how it works?"

Mute, Jürgen nodded, took another drink of iced tea.

Venom stood up. Jürgen cowered down against the table, covering his head. If he was going to die now, he didn't want to see it coming. From above him, the dark, deep, smiling voice said, "You've been fairly helpful. We won't kill you just now. That might suggest to your bosses that someone's getting too close to them, and they would attempt to elude us. We don't want that. Anyone so careless with the lives of billions of innocent people deserves to be caught totally by surprise—by me. So, no warnings. You will speak of this meeting of ours to no one. Anything that makes us think that you have spoken, and we'll be back." Venom chuckled. "No one will be able to stop us. No one will be able to get to you in time to stop what will happen, or even to cut it short. All you need to do is be quiet."

A long silence ensued. It was nearly twenty minutes before Jürgen dared look up. That dark presence was gone. The city, unconcerned, glittered across the bay.

Jürgen staggered to his feet, then fled back toward the house, ran into the bathroom, and threw up.

EIGHT

"TWO more days down in Cocoa," MJ's voice said.

Peter sighed. It was the next morning, and he was just out of the shower again, getting ready to go meet Vreni before she retreated into her room to write for the day.

"So you're not going to be up to Kennedy for the launch tomorrow?"

"No," MJ said, "I don't think so. Maurice isn't a big fan of early mornings anyway, and the Shuttle goes up at—I think it must be seven-thirty."

"That's right," Peter said. "So you're not going to do the Rocket Garden after all."

"Maybe the day after. He *does* keep changing his mind. The other production staff, the AD and the wardrobe people, they're going crazy. No sooner are they ready for one shot, everything set up and the lighting right, than he changes his mind and wants to do something else."

Peter shook his head and reached over to the table for the top contact sheet of many on the pile he was looking through. "Sounds like you're beginning to think it would have been smarter not to take this job at all."

"Pleeease," MJ said, and she sighed too. "I thought we were going to see each other every night."

"Oh, I know. But look, I appreciate what you're doing."

"I know you do, Tiger. At least the clothes are nice. And the swimsuits are really lovely." Peter could hear the wicked smile in her voice even though he couldn't see it. "You'd like the swimsuits."

Peter secured the phone between shoulder and head while he riffled through the contact sheets again. *"Sports Illustrated* swimsuit issue, huh?"

"Not quite that high quality, maybe, but pretty neat anyway. The only problem is, we can't swim in them."

"Why not? Will they shrink?"

"No, that's not the problem. They've been having shark alerts all up and down the coast."

Peter came up with one sheet, the pictures of his first fight with the Lizard, and put it aside. "Don't let me hear that you've been trying to lure Maurice near the water," he said. There was a pause, and then MJ chuckled.

"Don't tempt me. Still, if I got a nice big bucket of low-calorie tofu and threw it in."

"That's the spirit," he said. "Always assuming the AD is expert enough to take over."

"Oh, she is. It's amazing she hasn't already tried to electrocute him. I'll tell you, though, I'll be glad to be done with this."

"What? You're shooting on the beach! That should be wonderful!"

"Oh, please. Between coating ourselves with sunscreen and getting sand in every orifice, we all look like a bunch of jelly doughnuts by the end of the day." Peter burst out laughing. "It's easy for you to laugh, buster! Miss one spot, and it burns! Being out in the sun all day is no joke. And we don't even have a tent or a marquee to shelter under. Maurice decided we wouldn't need it. It's the only permanent decision he's made all this week."

"Well, you make sure you cover up as well as you can. I don't like jelly doughnuts when they're overdone."

"Trust me, it's on my list. How're you doing?"

Peter laid one hand on the pile of contacts as if to hide them from himself. "Officially I've got another quiet day," he said. "Vreni's writing."

"That's 'officially.' But..." MJ trailed off.

"Oh, of course," said Peter. "I have other business to attend to." He had grown cautious about saying anything out loud or in the clear, since it had occurred to him the other night that it was possible the hotel operators could occasionally listen in on their clients' conversations. "I have to go looking for our missing friend this evening."

"He's still missing, is he?"

"Uh-huh. But I think I may have a slightly better idea of where to look for him."

"Oh, really?"

"Well, while I was swinging through town the other day—" MJ giggled a little "—I met a gent who's been able to help me cut through some red tape. I'll tell you all about him when we get around to seeing each other. But he's really been extremely useful, and he's given me some equipment that's going to be very handy for what I'm doing."

"What, better than that big goggle-eyed thing you've got?"

"Please!" Peter rolled his eyes. "I've done some nice wildlife photography with it, but nothing much else. Not so far, anyway. Tomorrow morning I think I may do better."

"Going to take it up to the launch, then? I wish I could be there."

"You'll be close enough; you'll be able to see it go up. It'll take off right over your head."

"Assuming the woodpeckers don't get it," MJ said.

Peter laughed. A lot of people at Kennedy still hadn't gotten over the embarrassment of the aborted STS-68 launch, when it was discovered, just a week before launch date, that the insulation cladding of the main fuel tank had nearly a hundred holes drilled in it by woodpeckers—one of the local varieties of flicker, actually—and *Discovery* had had to be moved back inside the VAB so that the damaged fuel tank could be swapped for a new, unpecked one. The Wildlife Management people had put up decoy owls and broadcast flicker distress calls in an attempt to drive the birds away. It seemed to have been successful so far, but the Kennedy Center falconers had been standing eighteen-hour watches for the past three days, with instructions to get rid of any flicker that showed its beak around 39-A—with extreme prejudice, if necessary, but at least to run them well downrange. Local radio stations had been getting a good deal of mileage out of the story over the past few days; for Peter's part, he doubted he would have been quite so lenient with the woodpeckers.

"Look, honey, I've gotta go—or I'm gonna be pecked to death by angry reporters. She wants a look at the contacts to pick the best one for her story, then I'm going to have to run and find a processor who'll do me some reasonable prints for less than an arm and a leg. The people who did these contacts were really terrible."

"That's funny. I would have thought with all the modeling shoots around Miami, you could have found people who'd do decent prints."

"Don't bet on it," Peter said regretfully. He had tried to travel light on this trip, and now he was wishing desperately that he had brought his entire darkroom setup with him. "They seem a little slipshod down here, at least by New York standards, but never mind, look, I'll probably be in and out for most of the day. You can safely try to reach me until, oh, mid-afternoon, but after that..."

"I won't call you," she said, more or less in the voice of an annoyed child forbidden to play with a new and favorite toy. "But if you don't call me, I'm going to get worried."

"You're just going to have to be worried, then. MJ, I'm doing all right."

"No you're not," she said. "Venom is in the neighborhood. 'All right' is at best an inadequate description. I don't like the thought that he might get anywhere near you."

"Don't worry. If he does. I'll kick sand in his face. Or something."

"Promises, promises," MJ muttered. "You call me tonight."

"I will."

PETER spent all that morning and the better part of the early afternoon going over the contacts with Vreni. She was in a bad mood, and she didn't like any of them. The angles were wrong, the lighting was poor, they were underexposed or overexposed, they included more material than she wanted or excluded things that she claimed would have made a better shot, they were badly composed, they had too many verticals or too few...

Peter sat and listened to her carping criticisms and wondered if this was the kind of thing that MJ was putting up with from Maurice. *Maybe I should offer to introduce them.* About twenty minutes into the critique session, Peter looked thoughtfully at Vreni and said, "How's the article coming?"

She fixed him with an unfriendly stare. "Better than these pictures."

"Now, Vreni." Peter smiled at her and he meant it. She sagged back in the chair on the other side of the table in her hotel room, and sighed.

"All right," she admitted, "I'm not happy with it. Not at all. There's material about this whole mess that I'm missing. I've found a lot of guns, but none of them are smoking. Lots more interlocking company registries, and shell companies, linking CCRC and the German merchant bank. Public records seem to indicate that they've been selling these shell companies back and forth as a way to launder money. But no one seems any too sure where the money's coming from."

"Don't tell me," Peter said. "The information got lost when their computer had its little fit."

Vreni nodded. "That seems to be the story. And the information on where that money is coming from is really the heart of the whole business. As for the security situation at Kennedy, I haven't been able to find out any more than we already know. Whatever happened, whatever was taken, *everyone* is stonewalling."

Peter sat quiet for the moment. He found himself wondering if his meeting with Murray was an example of the Old Boys' Network in action—with the emphasis on the "boys." It would be annoying if it were. Then again, his connection with Murray seemed to stem from Murray's excitement at working with a real-live super hero, gender notwithstanding. Still, he could see how frustrating this must be for her. "Vreni," he said, "I don't know what to tell you. You're the reporter, and I'm sure you'll find out what you need somehow in time for Kate."

Vreni looked at him blearily. "From your mouth to God's ear," she said.

"Meantime," Peter said, spreading the contact sheets across the desk again, "you're going to have to make some kind of choice from these. I've got to go to the processor and try to beat some kind of decent results out of them. Look here…"

They spent the next half hour or so with their heads bent over the contacts, until finally Vreni came up with five or six shots that she liked for the feature, and four or five second-string photos as standbys. Peter jotted down the exposure numbers, but looked up at one point to find Vreni gazing thoughtfully at one of the shots of the Lizard.

"Anything more on why he's here?" Peter said.

Vreni shook her head. "Some of my sources think that there's some connection with Venom." She was ticking off the exposures one by one, and her pen paused by one exposure number, the picture of Spider-Man and Venom which had been taken by his little camera. "That Questar," she said, impressed, "does get some brilliant results. I could swear you were right on top of them."

"It's a good piece of equipment," Peter said, which was undeniably true.

"Okay," Vreni said. "Take that last one, that should hold Kate. Could you have this stuff ready by—" she looked at her watch "—six o'clock? That's the latest the courier company can pick up."

"I'll have them for you then."

AT something like ten of six, Peter came tearing back into the hotel again with an envelope under his arm. He was suffering from a case of extreme annoyance. It had taken him most of the afternoon to find a processor who would even admit to being able to produce professional-quality color stills before the end of the business day. It had taken the rest of the afternoon to bludgeon them into doing the prints correctly, sending one picture back four times because the developer kept pushing it too hard. *It's a pity,* he had thought at the time, *that I can't just get these done at Kmart. But it's too late now. Even Kmart needs a couple of hours.*

He took the elevator up to Vreni's floor and jog-trotted down the corridor to her room. When he knocked on the door, she snatched it open at the first tap. There was a Federal Express envelope already in her hand. "Are those them?" she said ungrammatically. "Here. Hold this." She shoved the FedEx wrapper at him, grabbed the prints, sat down at her desk, and started to leaf through them. "Yes," she said "yes, yes, yes, yes—no!"

"What d'you mean, 'no'? It's just the way you wanted it."

She groaned and put her head in her hands. "It's so underexposed!"

"You should have seen it before I made them redo the print. Four times." Peter glanced around. The room looked very much as if a small localized hurricane had passed through it, littering the floor with pages torn from notebooks and crumpled bits of paper, and her laptop computer was standing open on the table, beeping a plaintive complaint about low batteries.

"All right," Vreni said finally. "It'll have to do." She squared the photos' edges and slid them back into their manila envelope, grabbed the FedEx pack from Peter and jammed the manila into it, and sealed the whole thing up. "There," she said. "Let's get it down to the front desk and meet the courier. And then I am going out."

"For a night off?" Peter suggested.

She looked at him sardonically. "Not a chance," she said. "I have a date with a cop, whom I intend to question thoroughly. What are your plans for the evening?"

"I'm going to call MJ and let her harangue me about her work conditions," Peter said, "and then I've got an old friend to look up out of town."

Vreni locked her room and they made their way down to the front desk together, where Vreni broke into a run and did a good imitation of someone trying to qualify for the hundred-yard dash. She caught up with the FedEx courier just as he was walking out the front door of the hotel. Airbills were exchanged, the package was taken away, and Vreni came back sighing with relief. "That's something, anyway," she said. "The story's already up in the *Bugle*'s computer, so Kate will have the hard copy and the comp boys will have the electronic. And here comes my date!" Peter turned, and was very hard put not to react. It was Murray Anderson.

"Peter, this is Murray Anderson. Murray, this is Peter Parker, the photographer who's riding shotgun with me on this jaunt."

"Pleased," Peter said, and shook Murray's hand. He glanced from him to Vreni. "Where'd you two meet? Have you known each other a while?"

"Since yesterday afternoon," she said. "We ran into each other downtown."

Murray smiled slightly. "Rear-end collision," he said. "Fortunately, not too serious."

"It seems to have turned into a beautiful friendship," said Vreni, "even if he did give me a ticket. The swine." She managed to both smile and glower at him; it was an amusing effect. Vreni took Murray by the elbow and steered him away from Peter, then paused and looked back at him. "If you want to join us…"

"Thanks, but no. Other plans, remember? And that friend of mine is expecting me. But have a good time."

ABOUT two hours later, darkness had fallen almost completely in Big Cypress, and a silent figure in red and blue was webswinging through the trees, intent on picking up a trail that had gone cold. But now, at least, he was better equipped for cold trails—or for hot ones. When he had spoken to Murray the second time, the policeman had sounded thoughtful. "Can't be easy," he had said, "chasing people around in the 'Glades with just your naked eyes."

"Well," Spider-Man had said to him, "what are you recommending I use?"

"Can you meet me down at Bayfront Park in, say, about an hour?"

"No problem."

Spider-Man had met Murray there, the cop having taken the precaution of slipping into a private little space created by a stand of sword-leaf palm. Spidey, webbing in, had joined him there and found Murray holding something that looked like a cross between a pair of binoculars and a VR eyeset.

"Here," Murray said, holding it up for him to see.

"Infrared night glasses?" Spider-Man said curiously. "Or a starlight 'scope?"

Murray shook his head. "Better than both. This is a thermal imager."

Inside the mask, Spider-Man raised his eyebrows. The gadget was military—or in this case, more probably SWAT—technology, something that made it possible to see people and vehicles by their own heat emissions without using an active infrared source to illuminate them. It would work in fog or smoke as well as darkness, and, unlike standard low-light optics, needed no light at all.

"If you're going to be out in the 'Glades again," said Murray, "and especially at night, this should do you some good. Most animals run hotter than people, and most of our local reptiles run cooler. At night they'll be cooler still. A little practice and you'll be able to tell one from the other easily enough. This—" he tapped a small knurled wheel at the side of the big lens-cover "—is an adjustable thermograph. Right now it's set between 95 and 100 degrees; that should catch most people."

"As low as 95? I thought everyone was 98.6?"

Murray laughed. "That reading's based on an average taken from a hundred people nearly a hundred years ago. Not what I'd call a very representative sample. So the default setting is 95 to 100. Once you've found out the temperature of the person you're trying to find, you can fine-tune the viewer to find that signal in your field of vision, tag the target with a color or an ID letter, even—" he turned the viewer over and pointed to a row of tiny buttons "—keep track of up to six different traces at any one time."

"Murray," Spider-Man said, "where did you steal this from?"

"Steal?" Murray said, drawing himself up and looking offended. "Hardly. The word you're looking for is *requisition*."

"With extreme prejudice?"

Murray laughed. "Not that extreme. The DEA guys use these for surveillance, and they've left us a couple. But I signed this out in my name, so for God's sake don't lose it, and whatever you do, don't break it!"

"Is that worse than losing it?"

"Probably. Losing it I could explain as someone else requisitioning it from me. With extreme prejudice. Breaking it, though, and I'd have to explain how it got broken."

"That settles it," Spider-Man said. "If worse comes to worst, I'll lose it."

"Please don't!"

"Only kidding. I'll bring it back to you safe and sound. With, I hope, some answers."

Now, he was swinging along through the cypresses, doing his best to retrace his way to the spot where he and Venom had clashed. Once he found that, he could also find the bearing on which the Lizard had taken off, and follow that. And then… That was always the question. And then what?

What will you do when you catch him? Spidey asked himself as he swung. *Hit him over the head, tie him up, and take him home to Martha and William? It's not likely to be that simple. You'd better hope the police are nowhere near when you find him, because they'll just hit him over the head, tie him up—and then toss him in jail.*

There are worse possibilities, he mused. *What if he's actually getting close to finding a cure? What if, wherever he's hiding out here, he's close to the solution? Whatever else has been going on with him*—and again Peter thought of the old lady's strange description of the Lizard stopping and starting, like a machine, like something being run by remote control—*he has a right to go about his own business. But what if it's not his business? What if he is being used as a tool to commit crimes? That's gotta be stopped. And not just for other people's sakes; for his too.*

It was all so tangled, and the thought of the hydrogel was on his mind, too. Was the hydrogel somehow wrapped up in the issue of Curt's cure? That wasn't an idea Peter particularly liked. It suggested that Curt had acquired at least enough control over the Lizard that he was stealing for a purpose.

"No," he said aloud. "I don't believe it." Then he slowed down and looked about him in the darkness. This was the place. He dropped down onto one of the small islets where he, the Lizard, and Venom had fought, recognizing the torn and trampled reeds and the place where one of the alligators had fallen. There was no sign of that 'gator now. Whatever else you could say about the scavengers in the Everglades, they were both efficient and thorough.

He pulled out Murray's present, which had been webbed to his back, carefully put it on and lowered the visor. At first it was a little difficult to get used to focusing both through the eyepieces of his costume and the lenses of the viewer, but he managed at last, and drew in a sharp breath.

These weren't like the stark, pallid infrared pictures of a TV wildlife show, or even the ghostly green visuals transmitted through starlight scopes during Desert Storm. Instead they were color images that showed up as clearly as on a cloudy day, or maybe even a bit brighter. Trees and undergrowth all had their colors; not exactly those of nature, but the minicomputer built into the headset recognized each separate heat wavelength in its programmed temperature band and assigned each source its own specific color. Cool was dark, warm was light, but only the water and the sky were dead black.

Slowly Spidey turned his head, getting his bearings—and also getting used to the slightly skewed perspective of a landscape illuminated by heat instead of light. It would not be comfortable to use this visor for long, especially on the move, but if he was lucky he wouldn't need to use it for very long.

He took off along the line where he had last seen the Lizard swimming, heading more or less due east. A moment later, as he swung slowly along, webbing his way from tree to tree with more care and less speed than usual, he saw that under the image a faint line of data was giving an inertial tracking readout that even included latitude and longitude. The visor had its own satellite tracker built in, and displayed the exact location of whatever object was centered in its field of view.

Very handy, Spidey thought, becoming more determined than ever not to drop or break this thing. If he had thought the Questar was expensive, the thermal viewer was an order of magnitude more so. He paused under one cypress to fiddle with the temperature setting on the right temple of the headset, and as he clicked it up and down, various parts of the landscape—a tree here, a reed-bed there—flared brighter or dimmed down.

That was all very well, but to make best use of the visor, the one piece of information that he needed was the one he didn't have. What was the Lizard's body temperature? The question probably came in two parts. Was Curt's metabolic rate as the Lizard closer to the human or to the reptilian end of the scale? And was that the modern, cold-blooded reptilian metabolism, with its reliance on ambient temperature, or was it that of a small, warm-blooded dinosaur?

Spidey shook his head and adjusted the readout to "see red" at 95 degrees. Without any hard information, splitting the difference might just work. He went off on the Lizard's trail again, holding to that due-east course and watching the water, studded with reedy islets, as he went.

Of course, there was no hope at this late stage that he would find any trace of the Lizard's passage actually left in the water. The day's heat, the night's cold, the currents stirred up by passing alligators, and the slow percolation of water through the aquifer would all have long obliterated his trail so far as temperature was concerned. But if he just kept his eyes open, there was a chance of spotting the less high-tech traces of broken branches or trampled undergrowth.

He headed steadily eastward, and after about twenty minutes of swinging, he paused and looked around him. Nothing but a soft, hazy glow near the horizon, like sunrise. It was a little late in the night for that—or a little early—but he kept going east, and as the minutes passed, that glow on the horizon grew. Through the visor it was an astonishing light, rapidly becoming blinding. Spider-Man swung on toward it, sweeping the visor from side to side. He went on that way for a long time, seeing no sign of anything in the temperature range he had set.

The visible-light end of the spectrum showed him an alligator sluggishly pulling itself up and out of the water before flopping its scaly bulk down onto a reedbed. Here and there an owl or a night-hunting kite went by in a brief, brilliant blob of light that left a trailing afterimage across his vision. And the glow in the east got brighter and brighter, until it was like looking at the dawn.

Shortly Spider-Man stopped. He was running out of trees, at least for the moment. Farther east he could see several small clumps of them gathered together. These, he had found out from one of the tourist books, were the "hammocks" that Hammock Park had been named for: knots of trees growing so closely together that they formed a living palisade, with a little isolated biosphere inside each one. He sprang toward the area where the hammocks began, passed the first one, and kept going. The first limb of the moon came up over the flat edge of the world, looking molten-white through the visor.

Spider-Man paused on one island of trees to turn the gain down, readjusting for temperature as he did so. As he jiggled the click-stopped wheel it went too high for a moment, right up over the hundred mark. The rest of the cool, nighttime world went briefly black, but far off to his right a heat source glowed, then faded as he adjusted the control again.

What the…?

Spidey held still for a moment, staring toward the visual memory of that spark of light, and delicately racked the visor's setting back up again. The spark grew again, then stabilized, radiating at 106 degrees. *At this time of night?* he thought, for it was well past midnight.

He made for the pinpoint of light, and as he closed to within five hundred yards, he could see it for what it was: a hammock, but a huge one. Spidey noted the latitude and longitude on the tracker display, and memorized it. *This,* he thought, *is distinctly fishy—or reptile-y. Whatever.*

About a hundred yards away, he paused, lifted the visor—blinking under the mask as he did so—then removed the entire headset and re-webbed it to his back. While other hammocks that he could see had a somewhat higher ambient heat than their surroundings, even at this time of night, none of them had been this hot. There was something in there worth looking at.

Let's just take a little peek, he thought, and moved in. As he got closer, the islets gave way to larger patches of firm ground, at least on this side. Little rivulets made their way through, but one strip of water was a canal, cut through a stand of reeds, fairly deep from the looks of it, and leading toward the hammock. *Very interesting,* he thought, and leapt across it.

Something hit him chest-high, and knocked him backwards into the water with a splash. Something else hit him again, adhered, grabbed him, and pulled him with brutal speed and strength out of the water and onto firmer ground. He struggled against what held him, but his arms wouldn't work. Spidey strained again, and this time felt strands part.

It was webbing. Very familiar organic webbing which, along with the lack of a spider-sense warning, clued him in as to his attacker's identity in short order.

Alien tentacles whipped around him but didn't manage this time to pinion his arms. *Two can play at that game,* he thought, grabbed a bunch of the pseudopodia, and pulled hard. What might have started as a leap ended as a crash as Venom came cannoning into him and they went down together, half in and half out of the water and the reeds.

"Same old places, same old faces," said Spider-Man as he struggled to his feet, threw off the rest of the web, and bounded twenty or thirty feet to one side. "Here I thought I was on vacation by myself, and it turns out I'm on a package tour with you! Don't you have any initiative? Is following me around the only thing you can do?"

"Don't flatter yourself, Spider-Man!" Venom hissed. His awful prehensile tongue came out and stroked along the fangs in his open, grinning jaws. "We're ready enough to stop for lunch, if you insist." Tendrils shot out at Spider-Man, but he wasn't there anymore. From something like ten feet in the air over Venom's head he shot webbing, two-handed, straight down, fast and hard. It tangled about Venom's head and shoulders, and plastered the first wave of pseudopodia to his body before they could extend far enough to be a threat to Spidey.

Down he came on the other side, rolled and bounced as Venom struggled in the webbing. It was only a matter of seconds, Spider-Man knew, before he would break free. As regarded webbing, they were fairly evenly matched.

"I don't have time for this, Venom," he said, bouncing again as the first strands of web shredded and more pseudopodia came streaming out at him. "It's not you I'm after!"

"Oh, no doubt. Just where is your confederate the Lizard?" Venom burst free of the last length of web and went for Spidey in a rush. "We'll have that information at least, before we rip your useless head off!"

"Haven't got a clue, fang-face," Spider-Man said, avoiding Venom's rush. "Right now I'm a lot more interested in what's cooking in the kitchen over there." He pointed at the hammock. Venom came down in a crouch about a dozen feet distant, and simply stared at him for a moment, breathing hard.

"Indeed?" said Venom, and his voice filled with menace. "Then why—"

Crack! The first shot went between them. Spider-Man, warned by his spider-sense, had gone down flat before the gun went off, and Venom followed suit immediately thereafter. It was a good thing they did, for a second later the unseen gunman switched his weapon to full automatic and the air above their heads was filled with the whine and crackle of high-velocity rounds.

To Spider-Man, it sounded rather like the bank robbery the other morning—except that instead of being safely above it, he was slap in the middle, in the dark, in an unfamiliar place, with Venom not ten feet away. There was more firing, a lot of it and from more than one gun, then the roar of engines starting up. Spidey could hear the droning propeller-fans of flatboats like the one he had encountered the night before, and another, deeper bellow like a big outboard motor. The engines revved up, then came blaring toward them.

"While they're moving!" Spidey said. "We may not get another chance! That reed island over there. You lead a bunch of them away from it, that way. I'll go the other. We'll meet up there—" The rest of what he might have said was drowned by the hammer of more gunfire, short, controlled bursts from several automatic weapons, so that the neighborhood began to sound like a busy night in Sarajevo.

"Even you," Venom growled, "have a good idea occasionally." He took off northward. Spider-Man headed south, jumping, rolling, and occasionally crawling through reedbeds and stands of brush, slowly working his way back around to the island he had indicated to Venom. Two of his pursuers were fan-boats, and one of them was a kind of amphibious craft.

He jumped to the other side of the canal, ran farther southward, then doubled back on his tracks while out of sight and ducked deep into a thick raft of cattails. The two fan-boats droned past, closely followed by the amphibian. Each of the fan-boats was carrying about six men; from a quick glance through the cattails, Spidey could see that they were dressed in dark camouflage coveralls with their faces blackened. Every one of them was carrying an assault rifle, and it was obvious from the way they were spraying out fire that they weren't paying for their own ammunition.

When they were safely past and the ripples were splashing up against the cattail raft where he was hiding, Spidey hurriedly made his way—very low, very cautious—back to the reedbed he had shown Venom. He slipped into it and lay flat for a moment, just getting his breath back, then put his head up. A pseudopod snaked silently out of the darkness and pushed it back down again, as another of the boats came back.

The roar of its engine died down to a throaty rumble and then fell silent as it lay rocking in the water no more than twenty feet away. "Where'd they go?" somebody said.

There was a short crackle of static from a walkie-talkie, followed by another voice grumbling, "One went north an' the other went south like cats with scalded tails."

"Question is," said the first voice, "who were they?"

"Doesn't matter. Pretty sure they're gone now."

There was another burst of static, and then a third voice spoke from another walkie-talkie. "We gotta timetable here. We can't linger."

More static, and a fourth voice. "I don't like it; they can't have gotten away that fast. We should take a look around. Anything this close needs killing."

Very close to him, Spider-Man could hear a rustling as if someone was gathering himself to rise. As softly as he could, he said, "Don't do it!"

Venom growled as softly. "If we do not kill some of these people, they will not show us proper respect."

"Not after they're dead, that's for sure," Spider-Man hissed back. "And after they're dead, we can't follow them anywhere either. You just lie still for a minute."

The boat had gone quiet. "You hear something?" someone said. There was another pause, the silence dragging out so long that Spidey was tempted to say "Ribbit!" just to relieve the tension. But he had no idea of the quality of his frog imitations, and with half a dozen military-level automatics no more than a long spit away, he didn't dare risk producing a bad one. He concentrated very hard on nothing bad happening.

Spidey heard another squirt of static. "Come on, you guys. We've got a lot of ground to cover, and things to blow. North unit, echelon left; south unit, echelon right. Warm up, let's move out!"

"That's a roger," said the man with the nearest walkie-talkie, and returned it to a cradle on his belt.

"He just loves to sound so damn military," said another voice, a scornful one, from the boat.

"Yeah, sure. And if you don't want to give him the chance to use that military on you, get this thing started." There was a cough as the engine turned over; then it caught and roared into life again. The flatboat spun neatly on its axis and headed off due east, so close to their reedbed that the reeds whipped and gusted in the propwash of the thing's eight-foot fan. Had any of the men been looking behind them, they might have seen two prone figures lying in the reeds pushed flat by the wind. Then the reeds stood up again, and the boat was gone.

Spidey elbow-walked in the direction from which the pseudopod had come, and pulled some of the reeds aside. He found himself looking directly into Venom's fanged face; not the most charming view.

"Now," Venom said. "Where were we?"

"You can't be serious!" Spider-Man said. "Didn't you hear those people? They're going to blow something up. Don't you think it might be nice to find out what, just in case there are some people on site who'd rather not be blown up with it?"

Venom looked at him coldly. "If we thought you were half as concerned for the innocent as you pretend to be…"

"We don't have time for this conversation right now. And, I might ask, what brings you here?"

"It was close to here that we lost the Lizard last night," Venom said, sounding annoyed. "About two miles south, to be precise. But we have other reasons to be here."

"Something to do with that little hot-box in there, huh?" said Spidey, nodding toward the hammock.

"Is it there indeed?" said Venom.

"Is what there?"

"The base from which your precious Lizard has been working. We thank you for the information."

Oh Lord, Spider-Man thought. *What have I told him?* But aloud he said, "Glad to be of help. But don't you think we have something a little more important to think about just now? What are those guys going to blow?" Then the thought came to him, and his mouth fell open under the mask as he made a little strangled noise that made Venom shoot him a suspicious look. "Oh my God," he whispered. "It's tomorrow morning. Only a few hours from now."

"What?"

"The Shuttle launch! They've got plenty of time to get there."

"What is this about the Shuttle?" Venom said.

Spider-Man told him, quickly, about the security breaches at Kennedy. "Something funny is going on," he said finally. "There's something very hush-hush about this particular launch, despite the fact that they're trying to make it look like there's not. Now, these guys are going off saying they've got 'something to blow'—it *can't* be a coincidence."

"That may be," Venom said, getting up. "But we've let them gain enough distance. And we have other concerns. Craft very like that amphibian are being used to smuggle certain substances in and out of this country, under circumstances that will endanger many more people than a Shuttle launch gone awry." And he leapt off eastward after the people in the boats.

Spidey went after him. "I wouldn't bet on it!" he said, as, going low and carefully, they chased the boats east.

The argument went on for a good while. Those boats were moving fast, but they couldn't do better than thirty or forty miles an hour in the clear, and this was not the clear. They had to pick their way, zigzagging from canal to stream to canal again. The amphibious vehicle did better, going up and over firm ground sometimes, but mostly for speed's sake, it stayed in the water as well. Spider-Man and Venom were able to keep up with them at a safe distance.

Nearly an hour went by, and part of another. Then a much broader stripe of water lay in the near distance before them. "It's the Miami Canal," Spider-Man said. The boats were racing down a smaller waterway ahead of them, heading for where it met the canal.

"This goes north and south, does it not?" Venom said.

"That's right. Northward it empties into Lake Okeechobee, and connects to the river and canal network northward. Southward it heads for Miami and the Intercoastal Waterway."

The boats roared into the canal—one group heading north, the other south. "Come on, Venom!" Spider-Man said. "The Shuttle!"

They were leaping along the southern bank of the smaller canal which joined the Miami. "No," Venom said, "we think not. Our business takes us south. Besides, if you and we both go north, who will follow those? And as you say—who knows what they may be about to blow?"

Spidey stopped for a moment then, and looked at Venom. "Good hunting, then," he said.

Venom chuckled. "Oh, we always have good hunting. And after we deal with them—let's see how *you* like being the hunted."

He leapt off southward and swiftly vanished into the moonlit landscape. Meanwhile, the other flatboats were buzzing off northward. Spider-Man said a word under his breath, one that super heroes should not be heard saying. Nearby, a frog said reproachfully, "Ribbit."

Spidey breathed out, just a breath of a laugh, and took off after the boats.

ANOTHER two hours passed. The boats went on through the night, and Spider-Man followed. He was getting very, very tired. Only his spider-strength was keeping him going now, and even a spider's patient, mindless endurance would be tried by keeping a pace like this. At about the two-hour point, the boats stopped, and he stopped too, watching. The pause was only a brief one—they were refueling from gas drums cached on a reedy island. Spider-Man crouched under a cypress, about a quarter-mile behind, and watched, panting.

Heaven only knew how many miles he had covered since parting with Venom. Not that that had made Spidey very happy, either; the thought of what Venom might be getting up to down south somewhere, for what purposes, made him twitch. But what made him twitch more was the image of something bad happening to the *Endeavour*, something much worse than woodpeckers.

The boats started up again, headed northward. He followed.

The canal network of mid-Florida is a tangled thing, full of unexpected connections. Once it was much used for freight; now pleasure boats plied it constantly, and local county authorities were constantly digging new connections, with their eye on the tourist industry. It was possible to go from the Everglades to Lake Kissimmee completely by the inland route. But the people whom Spider-Man was pursuing didn't opt for that. Instead, once clear of the Miami cityplex, they "hung a right" out of Lake

Okeechobee into the Saint Lucia Canal, which comes out in Saint Lucia Inlet. From there they headed up the eastern coast, on the inside of the Intercoastal Waterway, in the shadow of the long thin island which runs just down the eastern coast sheltering the Florida mainland from the sea. Spider-Man followed them.

Many times Spidey wished he were driving; other times he wished he could just stop and catch a bus. Still, he plowed onward through marshland and grassland, swinging from high-tension towers and radio masts and buildings when they were handy, and bounding through wetland and dry land when they weren't—upsetting the wildlife and the occasional late driver who saw him. *But a lot besides wildlife will be upset if I don't get to Kennedy when these people do...*

Spider-Man was sure that was where they were going. He became even more certain when, at Cocoa Beach, they veered even farther inland on the west side of Banana Island, and ran up the coast near Titusville and Mims, making for the northernmost, unrestricted part of the Cape. *That clinches it,* Spidey thought, and concentrated on narrowing the gap.

He was slowing down, though, and he knew it. What frightened him more than anything else was when he heard the engines stop. He had been tracking by sound; he would have to rely on sight again.

He caught a flicker of motion off in the flat wetland, toward Kennedy. Tonight, the lights were on down there. Pad 39-A had all the big Xenon spots trained on the Shuttle. There it stood, looking small at this distance, but blazing jewel-like in white and black and the orange of the main fuel tank. Between it and him, Spidey could see running forms, crouching, going fast.

He went after them. After a very short time, Spider-Man found himself looking at a barbed-wire fence, with a sign nearby that said U.S. Government Property. Trespassing Prohibited. In the fence, someone had cut a hole big enough to let two people go through at once. Spider-Man stopped. He could hear no alarms, no sounds of trouble of any kind— and that was the worst news of all. They were in, and somehow nobody knew about it. *Isn't there some kind of perimeter security out here?* Spidey wondered, as he leapt the fence and went after the mercenaries. *Or have the damn budget cuts affected that, too?*

Softly, ahead of him, something went BOOM.

Leaping was the only form of locomotion left to him at this point; in this vast flatness, there was nothing tall enough for him to swing from. Away Spidey went, at top speed. As he went, he hurriedly got out Murray's widget again, and slipped it over his head. He had to stop just for a moment, to readjust.

The moon was no longer a problem: it was high enough in the sky to be out of his view. *Endeavour* itself, sitting there proud and shining, was not much of a heat source at this point. But the intense hot spotlights shining on 39-A were as unbearable to look at as the sun. Spider-Man turned the gain down, and then cautiously adjusted the scope's heat levels.

There. Four or five shapes, running, white, silhouetted against the indigo and super-dark green of the grass. They were running away from a blocky shape that radiated some residual heat—not at body temperature, but lower. A building. From it a glowing fog billowed upward.

Spidey bounced toward it as fast as he could. As he approached it, he could see more shapes, brighter, hotter ones—jeeps, glowing brightest from under the hoods and at the exhausts. They came roaring toward him down a service road from the direction of 39-A. Yellow hazard lights flashed on them. He could hear sirens. Searchlamps scanned ahead of them.

Spider-Man came around the corner of the building and stopped, shocked to see the amount of heat it was radiating. A bomb of some kind had exploded against the side of it, and had made a huge crater in it. Whether the building housed someting vital, he couldn't tell. He turned.

Over his head, Spider-Man heard the whistle of a single bullet, and then a fraction of a second later, the *crack!* of its firing. Spidey stood very still and put his hands in the air as the spotlights of the approaching jeeps came to rest on him.

Three jeeps pulled up, and shortly Spider-Man found himself surrounded by more pointing guns than he ever wanted to see. Some of the people in the jeeps were in Air Force uniform, and others were wearing NASA windbreakers, and they all looked very grim indeed.

Four people got out of the jeeps and came over to him slowly: three men and a woman. "Who are you," said the man in the lead, a NASA security man, "and what are you doing here?"

"Before we get into that," Spider-Man said, "it's not me you want, it's those eight people who just scattered in all directions after doing this." He glanced at the building. "They're probably re-forming up behind you even as we speak. This wasn't anything important, was it?"

"We're not going to discuss that with you," said the man. "But all the same—" He looked at the people in one of the other jeeps and jerked his head back toward the way they had come. That jeep took off, and someone in it started talking rapidly into a walkie-talkie as they went. "Now," the man said. "About you—"

"I'm Spider-Man," he said, "and I'm here about your hydrogel."

The people with the guns looked blank. But the man who had spoken, and the woman, in Air Force uniform, exchanged a shocked glance. "Yes," Spidey said. "The stuff the Lizard stole from your boat the other night. The stuff that's supposed to go up on the Shuttle this morning."

Silence. The man and woman looked at him. "The Lizard," Spidey said impatiently. "Big green guy? About six feet? Scales? Tail?"

The woman stepped forward. "A friend of yours?"

"People keep asking me this," Spider-Man said. "Let's just say he's an acquaintance. I know where the hydrogel is, and how it can be gotten back to you. But rather more to the point, what are you going to do about those people? They do not mean well, I'm here to tell you—if you need more evidence than this." He jerked a thumb at the cratered building. "And if you don't go after them, something very bad may happen. They just made a very concerted effort to kill me and someone else I know earlier this evening, because we were in a position to overhear what they had in mind. They said they were going to blow something."

The man turned quickly to the woman. "Let's put him under guard and get out of here. We've got a situation."

She looked at Spider-Man—a cool look out of a still, pretty face. "No," she said. "He's coming with us."

"But he just broke in here!"

"I don't believe so. Put a guard on him if you like, but put him in our jeep. He's coming with us. You," she said to Spider-Man, "if you please—you have some explaining to do. Tell us who those people are, and make it quick."

NINE

THE moon was gaining height when the mercenaries split, one group going north and the other south. Venom went after the southbound ones, in a very mixed mood.

He had been ready to kill Spider-Man again, and once again he had been distracted from that. It was a perfectly straightforward intention, and he couldn't understand what kept going wrong with it. If he had been of a less materialistic turn of mind, or more superstitious, Venom would have suspected there was some bad planetary aspect in his horoscope these past couple of months. Or maybe it was sunspots. All around him he could feel the symbiote twitching with frustration. It had been so close to a satisfying, messy, violent end for its worst enemy, and the sweet satisfaction of dining on part, or more likely, all of Spider-Man, before the night was out. Now once again it would have to wait.

Be patient, Venom said within himself. *It'll be worth it. When this is all over, he will still be there.*

The wave of annoyance that came back to him from the symbiote suggested that it found the reassurance less than satisfying.

Venom settled into a steady pace along the canal bank, following the mercenaries. He found himself wondering whether the symbiote had started showing any signs of its taste for blood while still with Spider-Man. Was this something these creatures normally developed? Or was this simply a by-product of its thwarted desire to bond with Peter Parker? He supposed it made sense that the symbiote's desertion by the being for whom it had tailored itself could very well have deranged it. It was Spider-Man's blood it really wanted, and if it couldn't have it by way of partnership, it wanted it for lunch. If it couldn't have Spider-Man's, it would have other people's. This was not a substitution that made it really happy, but a stopgap measure, until the day it achieved its heart's desire. And someday it would....

Not tonight, though. Venom said silently to his partner. *For the moment, we have other business.* His group of mercenaries—two of the fan-driven flatboats—sped down the Miami Canal for the better part of an hour, southeastward. He followed them as steadily as he could, alternately bounding and webswinging along the canal's western bank, occasionally veering inward to avoid a house or a farm. He wished not to be seen by anyone, neither the group he was chasing nor the people in the towns and villages they passed. The innocent could, after all, be easily frightened by them, even though he meant them no harm. As for the guilty, they would see him soon enough. And if Venom had his way, he would leave none of them alive except one, some single messenger, to take his warning back to his masters as before—making it plain what happened to people involved in such ugly business. *And I only am returned to tell thee....* Watching the boats skim ahead of him in the moonlight, Venom smiled and continued his pursuit.

He had been very busy working with various sources in the past few days. Miami's underworld was full of people who knew more than was good for them, people who tried their best to get their fingers into the pie. It was a town where dirty money was rife, and where at any hour of the day or night you could be sure to find something illicit going on, if you knew whom to ask. Venom knew whom. Or more to the point, he knew how. And he had some help from an unlikely source: the media.

Word had gone out quite quickly that he was here. As a result, there was almost no illicit bar, numbers parlor, gambling den, or other nest of crime where he would not get instant and terrified cooperation should he put in an appearance. For anyone who had not seen the TV pictures of the spot he had visited on the beach a couple of nights ago would have heard about it by now. Rumor, decorated with tongues—in this case, one large, slime-drooling, prehensile one—had already gone streaking through the city streets, making its way into the darkest recesses, telling what had been found on that beach, and what shape it was in. Because of this, whenever Venom turned up at some shady address or some dingy alley, or (in other cases) in polished boardrooms or exclusive offices, the inhabitants had been only too glad to talk to him. Some of his informants babbled information so fast that Venom would have been tempted to think they were making it up, except he knew they wouldn't have dared.

His investigation of the CCRC connection had proved particularly fruitful. He still found it hard to believe the massive recklessness of the local environment that was embodied in CCRC's importation of toxic waste here. The people running the corporation must certainly know that when the government caught them—any of them he didn't take care of himself—they would go to jail, for years and years. But regardless, the sordid business continued. It suggested to Venom either that they thought someone in their organization could protect them from prosecution, or they were going to make so much money that a twenty- or thirty-year prison sentence seemed like an equable price to pay. And that thought made Venom boggle.

Or perhaps it meant that they seriously didn't expect to be caught— that they expected prosecution to pass them by. Venom growled, smelling bribery in the air, and the symbiote rippled in response to his anger. *How much money,* Venom thought, *do you have to spend to corrupt a federal grand jury? Or bypass an investigation? Or keep it from ever starting?* Incorruptibility was becoming a rare trait these days. If you greased enough hands, no one would be left who could hold justice's scales. In this case there were doubtless thousands of hands to grease, but if CCRC was making the kind of profits Venom suspected from this tidy little trade, there would be plenty of grease to go around.

The flatboats passed under I-75, where the arching piers of the freeway took it over the canal. Venom shot web at the supports and swung under, attaching more web to a couple of cypresses, then dropped again to the reedy ground as the flatboats roared down the canal, and went on following.

Well, he thought, *we will do some serious work tonight. No more than one of these people will be allowed away to bear the news. Of all the rest of them, we will make a memorable example.* Remembering his own days as a journalist, he added to himself with a smile, *The media will have a field day.*

Now the mercenaries were picking up speed. Venom increased his pace to match. He was unsure of the actual mileage they had covered since he and Spider-Man parted. It might have been twenty, maybe twenty-five. He hadn't run this much in some time, but his anger was giving him

388 | SPIDER-MAN: THE VENOM FACTOR OMNIBUS

energy to spare, and the symbiote, sensitive to that and eager on its own behalf, was doing most of the work for him.

Venom was fairly certain he knew where they were headed. As Spider-Man had said, the Miami Canal went mostly southward and finally to Miami Beach, with connections to various other canals along the way. He thought they would most likely head into Biscayne Bay—possibly trying to lose themselves among the normal night traffic in the water—and from there, make their way down the coast to some quiet beach well south of Miami, avoiding the police attention the nearer beaches were getting at the moment. They might go as far south as Perrine or Goulds, or even Florida City. No matter: he would follow.

But now his problem became somewhat more complicated, for instead of following the Miami Canal all the way down, they turned right, due south, on one of the minor canals near Opa-Locka. Inland again; he swore softly to himself as he followed, and the symbiote caught the anger and started to get hungry for blood. It was a sensation Venom could feel on his skin, strange as it was to be able to taste something there—but ever since he and the symbiote had taken up company, Venom had gotten used to paraesthesias of various kinds, seeing or hearing or feeling things the way the symbiote did. A small price to pay, he always thought, for the advantages it gave him, and the constant sense of wordless companionship. Now, though, its anger fretted on his nerves. No surprise, since its nerves and his were inextricably intertwined.

The route their quarry now took was a more convoluted and twisting thing, always trending southward, but using smaller canals, less direct routes. Once again they had to slow down, and gratefully, Venom slowed down as well. *No telling how long this may last*, Venom told the symbiote. *We must pace ourselves.* He felt it agree, which was good; by his reckoning, they still had at least another forty or fifty miles to go before reaching the southern coast.

He shrugged, kept following, and endured, wondering idly as he went how Spider-Man was doing. Though he might despise him, his strengths were not to be sneered at; of the heroes that Venom knew personally, he was one of the best fitted to handle a chase like this. He wondered, too, whether Spider-Man had been right—whether the target of that northbound group was indeed the Shuttle. If so—despite his preferences—Venom had to wish him well. Like many others, Venom had bitter and painful memories of a morning in the mid-1980s when, at the seventy-fourth second of a seemingly routine Shuttle launch, something had gone very wrong. The memory of *Challenger's* bizarre, Y-twisted contrail was something that would not go away. At times, when Eddie Brock had watched Shuttle launches since, he would find himself holding his breath until that seventy-fourth second was past. He did not want to see something go wrong with another one. If he can stop some such thing from happening to *Endeavour,* Venom thought, it will have been worth letting Spider-Man go.

The symbiote stirred uneasily. *Oh, you needn't fret,* Venom said silently. *We'll have him yet. But there's no harm in letting him do this job first.*

Southward the mercenaries went, and Venom followed. They plunged into the Chekiko State Recreation Area, another webwork and tangle of canals and reedbed and scrub, another river of grass. From there, they went straight into the Everglades National Park. Here the trees became much fewer, except for low stands of dwarf cypress, more bushes than trees. Great flat wind-wrinkled sheets of water quivered under the moon, rippling and troubled in the still night where the flatboats' wakes tore through them. Still Venom came after, exploiting what little dry land was to be found, and leaping from island to island, staying low and far enough behind not to be seen, the symbiote changing its coloring to blend with the background.

On the flatboats went, crossing under Route 27 and making for Florida Bay. Far off, at the very edge of the horizon to the east, the lights of Homestead and Homestead Air Force Base were a soft yellow glow. Venom started to close up the gap between him and the flatboats, smiling a bit as he went at the thought of the coastline where they were heading, just north of the Keys and sheltered by them from the open sea. It had been one of the great stomping grounds for smugglers of all kinds for nearly half a millennium. Pirates had used it first, for a staging area; they had gotten water from the freshwater streams there, hunted for victuals. Men like Henry Morgan and Bat the Portuguese and the dreadful L'Ollonois had provisioned their ships there—some apparently by trading with the Seminoles—bought and sold slaves, and unloaded hot cargoes. Later, during the Revolutionary War, blockade runners had sought refuge in the Spanish ports there. Some desperate traders eager for a fast buck had brought munitions and raw sugar up the length of Florida from there, helping the southernmost colonies break the chokehold the British had on the "triangular trade." Then later still, during Prohibition, rum had been sneaked in from the Caribbean and dropped on these shores, having run the gauntlet of government vessels in and around Key West. The running of contraband continued to this day: little clandestine seaplanes, in the dead of night, would make landings there in the "river of grass," or just offshore, drop their cargoes, and go out loaded with cash.

And now these people. Venom was very sure he knew what they would be picking up—and sure they would treat it as cavalierly as any other cargo, as something to be dumped without a second thought to save their skins. The thought of barrels of this being tossed overboard to rust—It would be a bad situation even in the open water of the bay, where the delicate coral ecosystem was already under threat from pollution and changes in water temperature, and a concentrated spill of almost any kind of pollution would strain the system to the breaking point. To destroy everything, all that would be required would be a gram or two of plutonium in this water. The sea bottom for miles around would become a sky-blue desert. And if spilled in the 'Glades....

It would not happen, he swore. Venom would not let that happen.

The first hint he had that they were coming close to the sea was by the smell of the salt in the air. Looking past the boats he pursued, Venom could see the first thin silver line of moonlit sea to the south. To tell the truth, he was relieved to see it. He was tiring, and the symbiote was fretting against his consciousness in a way that suggested it was getting weary too. He had not often had a chance to push it so close to its limits. *Take it easy,* he said silently.

Venom made a little more speed, to close up the gap between him and his quarry. Then he heard the sound he had been waiting for—the engines slowing down as the flatboats dropped speed, to feel their way through the marsh where the wetlands proper merged with the littoral marsh, the salt marsh that ran down to the dunes, and after them, to the sea.

He grinned. Venom was resolved to let as much of the exchange take place as he could before he acted. One or another of these people might drop information that he would find useful, and he intended to give them the chance. He was particularly interested in any details which might surface about the actual location of this waste-reprocessing plant. Venom was sure that such a thing, which would have to be highly secret, would be hidden away somewhere inaccessible, so there would be no chance of it being found by environmentalists, or politicians, or annoying ordinary people. Venom also suspected that—from the point of view of the people who would build such an unattractive facility—the most sensible thing would be to put it right in the middle of the Everglades. It would not be the little base from which Curt Connors was working. That was much too small, and he would deal with that himself, and with either Connors or the Lizard, in fairly short order, but right now....

He looked down at the shore. The flatboats had slipped into a little tributary stream, which led down among the dunes to the shore. Softly they cruised down it, their engines *putt-putting* quietly, and the fans muted to a lawn-mower buzz. The sea grass went sparse around him in the salt water as Venom took to the shallows and followed them, and here and there white sand from the dunes shoaled up in little bars and spits. The flatboats made for one bar that was bigger than the rest.

It was low water now. Later on, by the time any daylight showed, tracks or other traces of their presence would have been washed away by the rising tide. *Very clever,* Venom thought. *But not clever enough.*

There was no cover to be found any closer to the shore. The salt grass grew only a foot or two high. Venom slipped into the water, making his way into the little stream and sinking into it until there was only enough of his head showing to let him breathe. The stream was fairly deep: there was a strong current running in its depths, one strong enough to carve a channel deep in the sand, and right down to the shore. The flatboats came one after the other into the shallows of the bay and edged up to the broad spit of sand off to Venom's right. Very slowly, so as not to ripple the water, Venom caught up with them, instructing the symbiote to blend with the background, and got as close as he could to see what was being done.

The bay was quiet. Pseudopodia questing for some distance beneath him told Venom that the bottom here shelved only very gradually, perhaps no more than one foot in a hundred. The shallow water lapped at the boats, but made little other sound. Venom caught the sound of several bursts of static from walkie-talkies as the flatboat crews beached them on the spit and shut down their engines.

"Operation Grab Bag is go," said one voice, tinny, from a good distance away. One of the men on the spit answered on his own walkie-talkie: "That's a roger. Triple Scoop is going ahead."

"Roger," said the other voice. Was it his imagination, Venom wondered, or did he hear, before the burst of static that ended the second message, the crack of gunfire? He wasn't sure. Well, if he had, let Spider-Man handle it himself. Venom had his own priorities just now.

One of the mercenaries, a tall, thin man, said to another, "All right, Joe, give 'em the light."

"Right," a shorter, stocky man said. He came up with a long, thick, police-style MagLite. In the other hand, he held something smaller. *A compass,* Venom thought. Joe began to turn carefully in an arc from southeast to southwest, then paused, taking a bearing, and began flashing the light in that direction, probably in Morse code.

Some of the men sat down to wait then. Joe and his companion stood, looking out southwestward. What with the roil and dazzle of the water under the moonlight, it was hard to make out anything definite. But sound traveled. And faintly, Venom could hear very soft, muffled engine noise approaching from the southwest.

Now, then, he thought. Slowly, dark shapes began to show themselves against the silver of the sea and the indigo-black of the horizon. Shortly Venom could identify two separate sources of engine sound.

Under his "mask," half under the water, Venom smiled. They were boats of the same kind as one he had met off Matheson the other night. That attack had gone awry, much to his annoyance. When he boarded the boat, one of the men who had been there—at the sight of Venom, understanding quite well what was going to happen to him—had shot his companion, and then had defied Venom's questioning to the point where it could no longer be restrained. Blood it had to have, and blood he had given it—sensing clearly that there was nothing further he could do with the man, anyway. He was some kind of fanatic, to have shot the other man out of hand. Now Venom could feel the symbiote's growing excitement. It recognized the boats, too, and knew, in its limited way, who was in it, and what was likely to follow.

Not just yet, Venom thought. *Tonight, my friend, we practice patience.*

The boats approached more slowly. On the spit, one of the men pulled out a spotlight and started to make a quick sweep. Venom ducked hurriedly all the way under the water well before it hit him, so that any ripples would disperse. Under the water, he saw the bloom of the light go over, lingering for a moment, then moving on. Venom stayed under for a few seconds more, then slowly, carefully, put his head up again.

The boats drew in from the bay. One of them now was close enough to make out detail. It had a big, tall man in camouflage standing in its bow holding something blocky and dark: another searchlight. Venom submerged again, waited until the beam swept past, then surfaced once again.

The boat was a thirty-foot speedboat, with significant cargo capacity—made to be able to run fast if it had to. *Probably has a good-sized fuel tank as well. One could run a good way in a boat like that. Cuba? Haiti? Further?* He would find out soon enough.

Meanwhile the first boat drifted up to the edge of the spit. There was a muffled splash as someone softly let down an anchor. The man in the bow of the speedboat said, "Everything all right so far?"

"Dead quiet," said one of the men on the spit. Venom grinned.

"Okay," said the man in the speedboat, and turned to call below deck. "Let's get the stuff up."

The transfer began. Barrels again, as Venom had expected. The second boat came in behind the first, and it too began to unload. *Three men on the first one,* Venom thought, *four on the second, and then four each on each of the flatboats.* He started taking careful notice of who was armed with what. The symbiote was resistant to bullets, but he didn't care to put it in harm's way any more than he had to; that was no way to treat a friend.

One by one the barrels were lowered cautiously from the boats bobbing at anchor, onto the spit. They were rolled across to be stacked up in the flatboats. Venom watched this process with some concern. They were loading both boats at once, which was good, in that it gave him a little more time to consider his options. *There are quite a few of them,* he thought. *If we move too quickly, though, they'll take off in all kinds of directions, and it would not do to let this cargo escape northward. If these people get the sense they're being pursued, they'll dump it. And if it leaks into the 'Glades....* A leak into the bay would be bad, too, but the bay would purge itself far more quickly than the Aquifer. And no one drank the water from the bay.

The loading progressed. The men were talking desultorily but not saying anything that was particularly useful to him. None of them seemed to know the others any too well, and he got the sense that none of them wanted to. Probably wise: the less you know about your co-conspirators, the less you can spill about them if the police or the feds catch you.

This did Venom little good, though. He edged as close as he dared, wishing that the man piloting that first boat would say something. But his speech consisted mainly of "Hurry up!" and "We don't want to get behind schedule, keep it going." But after a few minutes he reached down out of sight, saying, "Here, might as well do this now. One of the hot ones."

"Right," said another of the men, and took charge of a surprisingly small barrel, maybe the size of a one-gallon beer keg, the kind available in grocery stores. Venom looked at it curiously. It didn't seem unusually heavy, and the man carrying it didn't seem at all nervous to be holding it.

The first flatboat was gaining a little on the second in terms of being loaded. Venom started watching it carefully. One man, its pilot, stayed seated where he was, by the boat's control panel and its tiller. The other boat's pilot was not in reach; he was down helping the others load the barrels on.

All right, Venom thought. *Time to move.*

Softly, staying low in the water, he made his way to the first boat, coming at it from behind. The pilot, sitting there, looked thoroughly bored with the whole affair. "Julio?" he said to one of the other men. "You got a light?"

"No smoking!" said the man on the speedboat, quite sharply.

"What're you, allergic or something?" muttered the pilot. But he shrugged, finally, and settled back to watching the others.

He never saw the pseudopod that slipped up behind him. Spasm froze him for the moment where he sat, then he slumped, but not so much that anyone noticed.

Silently, Venom boosted himself up onto the back of the boat to the left of the fan, peered around it. Another tendril rippled away from him, found the ignition key in the boat's control panel, slipped it out, and chucked it overboard.

"Oh, c'mon," said one of the other flatboat crew, "I'm gasping for a smoke, too. If nobody's seen all those spotlights we're using, then no one's going to see a match!"

"Oh, all right," said the man in the speedboat, the apparent commander. "Way out here, the boss won't know. Go ahead."

"Mac?" said the man who was gasping for a smoke. Possibly this was Julio. "Mac, you still wanna light?" A pause. "Mac?"

They looked at him. "No point in sulking," somebody chuckled.

That, however, was the point at which the tension of the spasm started to go out of Mac's muscles, and he began to slump noticeably.

"What the—" said one of the other men loading drums onto the boat. He made his way astern and bent over Mac.

Venom couldn't wait any longer. He boosted himself up onto the second flatboat and paused only long enough to look for its ignition key. It wasn't in the control panel, and which of the other men had it, there was no telling.

A second later he was rolling and diving into the bottom of the boat as the gunfire began from near at hand. He bounced up, sent tendrils rippling at the nearest gunman, tore the machine gun out of his hands, and flung it overboard. More tentacles shot out, one wrapping around the man's neck, the other around his waist.

"Get him!" someone screamed, and someone else yelled, "Get the stuff out of here!" That was what he had been afraid of. A third man came running at Venom, spraying bullets. Pseudopodia ripped his feet out from under him, dumped him on the deck, grabbed his gun and twisted it out of shape, then flung it overboard. The symbiote's excitement ran all through him, a sound/feeling like the purr of an angry tiger, all enjoyment and rage. If it could not have Spider-Man, it would have these miscreants.

Venom was willing enough, but right now a veritable storm of bullets was being fired at him, and a lot of them were hitting. The impact, despite the symbiote's protection, was uncomfortable. He killed the man he had just knocked down, and told the symbiote silently to deal with the remaining man on the flatboat any way it liked.

It did. Screams resounded, and many shots began to go wild.

What Venom wanted to make sure of was that none of the men remaining on this boat had the key for the other's ignition, or at least that none of them could use it. Within a few seconds, that was true.

"Get it out!" the man on the first motorboat was yelling at the men in the other one. "Get it out!" Its engines were stuttering into a roar again.

Everyone from the flatboats who remained mobile was clambering over its sides, frantic to escape. And suddenly all the fire of the men who still stood abovedecks on either boat was concentrated on Venom.

The pressure of it was so tremendous that as Venom struggled to stand against it on one of the flatboats, the gunfire actually knocked him back into the water. He stayed under, making his way hurriedly toward the first speedboat under the surface. Spotlights were raking the water, followed by the downward-striking bubble traces of gunfire, and the thick, wet, dull sound of bullets hitting a noncompressible medium at supersonic speed. In the water, the roar of the second speedboat's engine getting started was deafening. To this was added the sound of the first one's engine starting as well. *Too many of them,* he thought to himself, furious. *Just too many.* He almost wished, bizarre thought, that Spider-Man were there to help.

He burst up out of the water near the first speedboat, swarmed up its anchor before they could cut the rope, and leapt on board. Venom simply backhanded the first gunman he encountered before he could turn and fire. He felt the skull crunch, and the man toppled overboard, backwards, hitting the water with a fat splash. To the second man, who was machine-gunning him earnestly. Venom strode up, took him by the throat, and let the symbiote throttle him.

A third man, seeing Venom come for him, jumped overboard and began swimming desperately for the other boat. Only the commander was left, and he pulled a high-powered automatic and pumped six very carefully placed bullets straight at Venom's forehead.

The symbiote toughened there, but the bullets still gave Venom a headache. A pseudopod batted the gun out of the man's hand, and another grabbed him around the throat, pushed him up against the bulkhead of the motorboat, and began to tighten.

"Where have you just come from?" Venom said, shaking the man slightly. The commander shook his head, his face suffusing dark red—

—and then he jumped and jittered in Venom's grip, and slumped dead, riddled with fire from the other speedboat. The boat spun, its engine roaring, and it took off into Florida Bay. As it went, Venom could see the barrels being tossed overboard.

He swore softly again and tossed the commander's body aside. Though he knew the general route these people were taking, it would have been useful to know more about the details, the way-stations. *Oh, well. There are still three boats to examine.* When he was finished with them, he would call the proper authorities and see that the hazardous materials were picked up from the boats, or where they had been dumped, and properly disposed of.

The speedboat that remained was just about empty. Venom noted its name and registration—*Lucky Day*, out of Bermuda. *Not that lucky*, he thought. He could find no trace of other identification in it. There were discarded weapons aplenty, but they could have come from anywhere.

After a few minutes he made his way back to the flatboats. On the way, he picked up the MagLite that one of the men had been using, and with it, examined the bigger barrels. They were all of them very like the barrels from the CCRC caches in New York. Some of them were even painted the same color. Standard fifty-gallon oil drums, nothing special about them—stuff that, if dumped in seawater, would rust quite readily.

More on his mind, though, was that smallest barrel—"the hot one," the commander of the first speedboat had said. Very peculiar, that.

He got onto the first flatboat, found the barrel, picked it up. It was a plain, steel barrel, no distinguishing markings. Venom shook it. It sloshed very slightly. On close examination, the container was actually more like a paint can than a barrel, with a flat tight lid.

Venom put the container down on the floor of the flatboat, carefully pried it open with one pseudopod, and peered at it thoughtfully. It was full of a dark liquid. He lifted the can, careful not to spill it, and sniffed. A strange flat chemical smell floated up from it; nothing instantly recognizable. It reminded him, though, of the ink and toner scent of the fast copy shops he used to frequent back in his reporter days.

He told the symbiote to bare the flesh on his left hand. Cautiously, he dipped a fingertip of his right hand into the liquid and rubbed it between finger and thumb. Not an oily feeling but slick and then going tacky. Not corrosive, either. He rubbed a little on his skin, looked at it under the MagLite.

Venom's mouth fell open. It was as if he had rubbed on a bit of liquid rainbow. A whole spectrum of colors chased themselves across the wet patch on his hand, becoming brighter as the stuff dried. He turned his hand, and the colors shifted, like oil rainbows on a puddle, never quite the same even when you tried to exactly repeat the motion.

Now what in the world—? he thought, staring at his hand.

Then the memory of a newscast he had seen a couple of months before came back to him, and suddenly it became clear to Venom why this, and not the waste, had been the most important part of the shipment.

The newscast had been a digest produced by one of San Francisco's main news channels with information from the channel's European affiliates. Among stories of folk festivals and the new plays in the West End of London, of troubles in Latverian politics, and the repatriation of Russian sturgeon from polluted lakes to clean ones in Finland, there had been a little feature about the European Union's new paper money.

The European Currency Unit, or ECU, had finally begun to become the multinational currency that the Common Market's architects had intended, even over the protests of some countries who felt that the power of their own currencies would be diminished by this interloper. There were simply too many attractions to a currency that had the same value right across the Union, now one of the three largest trading blocs in the world—a currency which did not have to be exchanged at constantly fluctuating rates. Once the quirks had been worked out of the underlying exchange rate mechanism, most of the EU nations had settled down and allowed paper ECUs to be printed for them.

The main problem, unfortunately, had been counterfeiting. Any currency so popular, and usable anywhere from one side of the continent to the other, was going to attract the attention of the most talented counterfeiters on the planet. The EU security people had been determined to do their best to stop this problem before it became serious by loading the ECU with more anticounterfeiting strategies than any one country's banknotes had even applied before.

They created a counterfeiter's nightmare. Its engraving was courtesy of the Swiss, in cooperation with the most talented stamp engravers from Liechtenstein. Physically, it was a work of art, with the Union's halo of stars and the intertwined national emblems of the member states all rippling and blending into one another across the faces of all the notes in a tangle of impossibly delicate engraving, in nearly a hundred colors. Any given note had embedded in it three discrete watermarks, various zones of microprinting, a band like the embedded silver strip of a British banknote—but this one of metallized plastic, microencoded and programmed with the note's serial number and a one-hundredth-inch-wide data stripe containing other audit information. All these precautions seemed quite sensible in an age when counterfeiting advanced continually on the heels of the technology meant to stop it.

But there was one aspect to the making of these notes which was unique, and that was one for which the Union acquired a license from the French. The French had invented an ink for use in note-printing which changed color on the face of the note, depending on how it was held, what and where the light source was, and how the note was moved—the same way as, say, a hologram would change when moved, in a rainbow shift of color. It was the strongest of all the anticounterfeit measures on the ECU, for it was the one which anyone picking up one of the banknotes could instantly identify as being there or not. The words and pictures printed in that ink shimmered, giving a specious but beautiful illusion of depth.

No counterfeiter had been able to duplicate it. The secret of its manufacture was possibly the most closely held secret in France. As a result, that ink had become the single most sought-after substance in Europe by the criminal fraternity. More was being offered for it on the black market than would be offered for any illicit substance—more, even, than was being offered for plutonium. Several thefts had already been attempted, according to the TV program, but they had all failed.

A keg of this stuff—even a tiny jar, for small amounts of it went a long way—was literally a license to print money in as large a denomination as you liked—and the ECU notes went up as high as ten thousand, equivalent to about five thousand dollars.

Venom crouched there, watching the rainbows chase back and forth across his hand. A nasty scenario was taking shape in his mind. CCRC, he thought, or someone working with them, managed, somehow, to source some of this ink. Possibly someone high up in the EU in Brussels, some bureaucrat with something to hide, perhaps. And one of the major powers in the EU, right now, was certainly Germany. Venom thought of the German merchant bank and wondered if the connection might be there. *Something else to take up with Mr. Gottschalk's connections when we track them down.*

But he could imagine a situation where CCRC or the people they were working with could print their own ECUs, as many as they liked, and use these to buy much more radioactive waste material from both legal and illegal sources—both of whom would accept the currency gladly. And this was only one of the kegs. They had tossed the other one overboard. If they had more, someone at CCRC was most likely this moment trying to analyze the formula. A skilled chemist could do it. It would take time, but it could be done.

Once they had a complete analysis, once they could manufacture as much of this ink as they liked, there would literally be no limit to how many counterfeit ECUs could be printed. The European market could be flooded with them in a matter of a couple months. The whole continent's economy could be permanently damaged. Unless—

Unless someone who liked blackmail could hold its whole economy to ransom, by threatening the EU with just such an action, promising not to take it... if the price was right.

Venom carefully sealed the little can up again, and stood, willing the symbiote back down over his hand and shutting the rainbow away. All these possibilities would have to be followed up. But first—first he had business to complete, north of here. There was still the matter of Curt Connors, squatting in his little hideout in the Everglades, doing heaven only knew what—but doubtless up to his neck in this smuggling somehow. If he was...

Venom smiled. It was not a nice smile. Connors would find that he was about to be paid for his work, and not in the currency he anticipated.

And then, after that—Spider-Man.

With the little can of ink, Venom turned, and at the best speed he could manage, headed north.

TEN

THREE jeeps jostled through rough grass at Cape Canaveral, got back onto the southward-running road, and tore down it, sirens blaring and warning lights flashing. The first and the last ones carried men with guns. The one in the middle carried two NASA security people, an Air Force lieutenant, and a very bemused friendly neighborhood Spider-Man.

"You could have had me thrown in the pokey back there," Spidey said to the lieutenant sitting next to him. "You could have had me shot."

"I could have," she said, smiling a small dry smile, "but it seems a poor way to say 'hello.'"

"Well," Spidey said. "Hello, Lieutenant—"

"Garrett," she said. "I'm a liaison to Kennedy security, based over at Canaveral AFB."

"You're taking all this very calmly," Spider-Man said.

"I assure you, I'm not," she said. "I could have had you shot, yes. And believe me, if the moment comes, I won't bother contracting it out." Her voice was cool and cheerful. Spider-Man gulped.

She was not a big woman—probably about five feet three, with short close-cropped red hair and big round horn-rimmed glasses. She looked a little like an owl. But the thought occurred to Spider-Man that there were some species of owl that he wouldn't like to be locked up with, either.

"Anyway," Lieutenant Garrett said, "if you're asking me why I've given you the benefit of the doubt—I have some colleagues up in the New York offices of the Atomic Energy Commission. I chat with them every now and then. I talked to them a week or so ago, and it seems they think they owe you a favor."

"If you mean the business about New York not leaping in the air and coming down on several other continents as dust," Spider-Man said, "well, yes, I did help with that." It seemed like the wrong moment for false modesty.

"Therefore," Lieutenant Garrett said, "I am more inclined to trust you than not. What I want to know is how you came by the hydrogel. And how you know what it is."

"Am I allowed to take the Fifth?"

"Oh, you can take it," she said, "but maybe I could suggest that it would be less than helpful at the moment. The security of the United States is at stake just now, and I don't have time for jokes." There was something in her eyes, though, a mocking or daring look, even in the darkness, that suggested to Spidey it would be safe enough not to go by the book for the moment.

"Lieutenant," he said, "the least I can do is give you the benefit of the doubt, too." He took a breath, then said, "I found it after someone else had lost it. At least that's how I read the signs. Having found it, I wondered what the heck it was!"

She chuckled. "Understandable. And? What did you find out?"

He thought for a second. "It may not strictly be an indestructible substance," Spider-Man said. "I suppose adamantium has the corner on that market at the moment. But it's close to one."

"That's a fair enough description," Lieutenant Garrett said.

"Then," Spider-Man said, "I found through other sources that it was originally destined for the *Endeavour*. Now, that by itself isn't so extraordinary. Lots of things go up in the Shuttle. Birds, bees."

She smiled. "Yes," Lieutenant Garrett said. "And some of them more controversial than others."

Spidey smiled under the mask. "Like the CHERM. Or should I say the MPAPPS? Or whatever its name was. As far as I can tell, it's some kind of small reactor—and I think maybe it's a breeder."

The jeeps slowed a little; they were coming to a checkpoint. Away off on their right, Spider-Man thought he could hear the sound of gunfire.

"Well," Lieutenant Garrett said, as they stopped and were inspected, "I won't get into that. And what're you all staring at?" she said to several of the security people manning the checkpoint, who stared at her companion. "Haven't you ever had a blind date? Boy, some people…"

The jeep tore off again. "It's been days since I had Socratic Method practice," Lieutenant Garrett said. "I can hear the wheels turning in there. You know you can ask me questions, even if I can't answer."

"Well—" Spidey did his best to think through the wind and the noise and the sound of gunfire getting closer "—I confess, I do keep wondering why anyone would want to put a breeder reactor up in space. A lot of people are vague about what reactors are for, but breeders—" He shook his head. "There's no two ways about it: they exist only to make more fissionable material. Specifically, to make plutonium."

"Can't argue with that," Lieutenant Garrett said. "It's common knowledge."

"And the only use *I* know of for plutonium," Spider-Man said, "is for making bombs."

"Common knowledge would seem to bear you out there, too."

"Well," Spidey said, "who would want to make bombs in space anymore? With the new test-ban treaties in place, and the agreement that no one will try to militarize space, we're not going to do anything like that. And it's not like you could do it on the sly, either. All the crews up on *Freedom*, at the moment, are multinational; none of the participants have any secrets from each other. Not that there's any room to, anyway. They're practically living in each other's pockets as it is."

Then he looked at Garrett sidewise, as a thought occurred to him. "Other facilities are being built, though."

Lieutenant Garrett returned the look, and actually batted her eyelashes, a shockingly innocent look. "Go on."

"Yes, well, as I said, why make bombs in space? If you wanted to damage people on Earth, you might as well just drop big rocks on them. Cheaper, safer, and just as destructive, if you're the kind of nasty person who's interested in that. And there's a whole moon full of them, just down the road."

"An interesting approach," Lieutenant Garrett said. "I must make a note of that one." But by her smile Spidey guessed that she had read the idea in the same book that he had and knew that the author of the book, and the name on the space station's new annex, were the same.

"Am I getting warm?" Spidey said.

"You know I can't answer specifically," the lieutenant said. But her expression was getting more wicked. "Hurry up, though. We're getting closer to the hot zone."

"All right," Spider-Man said. "So the spacefaring powers don't want to manufacture bombs in space. Sure, there are others who might want to—various super villains and nutso dictators and so forth."

"I bow to your superior experience of the first," Lieutenant Garrett said. "But as for the second, it wouldn't make much sense for them to mess with space-based delivery systems, when conventional ones would be so much cheaper, and closer to home. Why bother with space when you can take a Mercedes across Poland and out its east side, and come back with a trunkful of enriched uranium?"

"And a terminal sunburn."

"Only if you're incautious."

"I see what you mean, though," Spidey said. He frowned and thought then, while they passed another roadblock. Between them the brilliantly lit shapes of 39-A and 39-B lay in their way. It was dark and silent, except for its two big gantries, which shone faintly with red blinking altitude lights: the Fixed Service Structure, recycled from one of the old Saturn V launch umbilical towers and installed here to hold the lifts which serviced the Shuttles; and the Rotating Service Structure beside it, with the midbody umbilical unit that swung in and out to tend the Shuttle's fuel cells and life support, which installed and removed payloads from the main cargo bay.

The jeep started working its way around the huge octagonal pad. Spider-Man stopped, frankly gaping at it as they went by. Seen on television, from the discreet distance of a couple of miles, there was nothing terribly impressive about either of the pads. Seen close, they were another story. The massive gantries, the huge 400-foot flame trench, the big sound-suppression tanks, empty at the moment of the water which protected the gantries from the sound and pressure of launches—it was an extraordinary collection of structures, like a child-giant's Erector Set put aside for the night. Spidey felt slightly embarrassed and turned to Lieutenant Garrett to pick up where he'd left off.

"We all do it," she said. "Gape, that is. Someday spacecraft will be smaller, and we won't look twice at them. But right now—it's still pretty neat." She grinned. "Go on."

"I'm not sure where to go," Spidey said. "Somebody's putting reactors up in space to make something. If not bombs, then what? What other use is there for atomic energy?"

He trailed off.

"Yes?" Lieutenant Garrett said.

Spider-Man shook his head at her for a moment. "Oh, my," he said, very softly.

She watched him.

It had to have been ten years ago that he first saw the magazine article. He saw it now, though, as he had seen it last when he had been going through the aging collection of pulps that were still in the basement of his Aunt May's house. Both MJ and his aunt had urged him to either seal them up properly in plastic bags and save for another generation, or just throw them out. Their covers were all faded, the pages were yellowed and brittle, and they would flake and come apart in your fingers if you turned them carelessly. He didn't look at them much anymore, just kept them up on their shelf where he knew he could find them: old copies of *Amazing* and *Fantastic* and other magazines. The article he was thinking of was in *Amazing*. Someone, way back then, had suggested what they described as the only good use for an A-bomb.

The problem was that to make it work, you first needed a delivery system that would let you get pretty large payloads into low Earth orbit, and build things there, like a space station, or a very big spacecraft. The idea in the magazine had involved building that huge spacecraft. At the rear end of it, a huge concave shield or vessel would be built as well.

Then the premise of the article fell apart somewhat, because for that shield you needed an indestructible, or near-indestructible, substance. Once you had built this shield, the idea was that you started exploding atom bombs inside it. The shield, being indestructible, and ideally impermeable as well, would direct the blast away behind the ship, screening it from the radiation at the same time. And Newton's Laws being what they were, in space as well as anywhere else, every action has an equal and opposite reaction: the force would translate itself into a push forward for the payload. Later, when the force from that push gave out, you exploded another bomb, and pushed again. And so you went, gently, slowly, accelerating patiently, on the way to the outer planets.

It was a plan that was both brutal and elegant. It was not pretty. But fission power of this kind was easy to produce and relatively cheap—there was a whole lot of potential propellant for this kind of thrust lying around all over the planet, in the arsenals of countries that claimed they were planning to get rid of it anyway.

Naturally, you would not start the thrust process anywhere near Earth. You would use chemical propulsion to get the ships out well past the moon. But once there, there was no question of pollution. Interplanetary space was already full of radiation as hard as a nuclear explosion. And the explosions would be, by Earth standards, very clean. Most fallout, after all, is dust sucked up by the mushroom cloud from the explosion site. In space there would be none of that. The solar wind would push the particulate matter out to the boundaries of the solar system and beyond the radiopause, where the minute particles could coast harmlessly out and diffuse themselves in the endless vacuum of near space. There was literally no harm they could ever do to anyone.

Spider-Man knew the plan would work. He also knew how it would sound to some people if they heard about it. But the main problem left— now that there was a way to build space stations, and ships, in orbit—was what to make the shield out of.

He thought of the hydrogel.

"I would have thought," Spidey said, "that people would have considered adamantium some time ago for—uh, spacebased applications."

"I'm sure they did," Lieutenant Garrett said. "Think of the weight, though."

Spider-Man nodded. Just getting the pieces of an adamantium shield into orbit would use up so much valuable energy that it didn't seem cost-effective. And besides, adamantium was metallic, and repeated atomic explosions near it would render it radioactive itself. *Hydrogel, though…* Spidey shook his head. It was just possible that among its weird properties was numbered a resistance to radiation.

He looked at Garrett and said, "It'd be sensible, wouldn't it? To send up hydrogel, and at the same time, to send up the—test material? That way you minimize the danger of sending the stuff up again with every new launch. While locking it in L5 orbit where it can't fall, not for centuries anyway."

Garrett smiled. "It has to be tested," she said. "It's our cheapest way to the outer planets, until the new microwave-driven ships are ready." And he looked at her and blinked at that, but she would say nothing more.

The jeeps roared on into the night. They had come around 39-B now and were heading for A. It was about a mile and a half distant.

"All right," Spider-Man said. "Now all I want to know is, what do these people want? The reactor?"

Garrett shook her head. "They'll have to whistle for them," she said. "The payloads were locked in two nights ago—what we had of them." She looked both grim and resigned. "There's no way to get that stuff out early. Cargo bay is locked for injection and can't be unlocked without a full abort. Even if we could get the bay open, or those people could, it wouldn't help them any, because the entire reactor is sealed in a prelaunch impact shell. We have—" and this time the grim look was completely unrelieved "—learned something about what happens when a Shuttle falls down before it makes orbit. A nasty but useful sidelight of that is that we've learned something about how to build things that don't crack open no matter what you do to them—even if you drop them from a hundred thousand feet to the bottom of the sea. They don't open."

"Even if the whole Shuttle blew—"

"At whatever altitude. That shell would come down safe. Land or water, it wouldn't matter."

Even if it blew... And he heard the voice say, earlier, *We've got something to blow.*

Spider-Man's mouth went dry. "Lieutenant," he said, and touched her arm. She glanced at the hand, at him, said nothing. "Whatever you do, don't let them near the Shuttle. Don't." And a horrible thought struck him. "They're not in there, are they?"

"At T minus—" she shook her watch free of her jacket cuff and glanced at it "—T minus two hours? Of course they are. They went up half an hour ago."

"Oh, my gosh." A horrible feeling made itself at home in the pit of Spidey's stomach. "Lieutenant, you don't understand. These people are working with some of the folks who gave some of your New York friends so much trouble. They would have blown all of Manhattan sky high. You think a Shuttle and six astronauts are going to bother them?"

Over the roar of the jeep's engines, he could hear the gunfire much more clearly now, and closer, the incongruous sound of ducks quacking, outraged at the disruption of their quiet night.

As they approached 39-A the sound of sirens got louder—and so did the sound of gunfire. "Looks like we have a problem in that department already," said Lieutenant Garrett softly.

Pad 39-A was seething with activity, like a hornet's nest that had been kicked. Every one of the big Xenon spots was on now, lighting the place up like day. *Endeavour* burned white in the blaze of them, reflecting even more light in the area immediately around the pad. That was a help, except all the light showed was depressing. Jeeps and cars were converging on it from all directions, but once they came within range of the pad they tended to come slowing to a barely controlled stop, hammered by streams of bullets.

"Oh, Lord," Spidey heard someone moan from the next jeep. "The Shuttle tiles." But there were more pressing concerns than the fragile thermal tiles just now. When the people inside the various arriving vehicles came scrambling out, it wasn't to perform their security function but simply to take cover behind their cars. Nobody stood up or moved any closer, for fear of catching a bullet.

Some of the NASA and Air Force security people already had. There were unmoving figures sprawled on the pavement here and there; others crouched behind any protection they could find. Except for their own increasingly battered vehicles, there wasn't much of that in the big empty skirting surrounding the pad proper. They were firing whatever weapons they had at the attackers, but since those weapons were mostly pistols, they were badly outgunned.

Every one of the mercenary assault team seemed to be carrying something fully automatic—submachine gun or assault rifle, the difference was academic when you were on the wrong end of it—and every now and then, to make things even more interesting, one of them would throw a grenade. They were even wearing body armor; presumably it had been stowed aboard the flatboat on the way in. The mercenaries had spread themselves more or less evenly around the circumference of the pad. They weren't bothering with the short, controlled bursts recommended by the manual, preferring simply to hose slugs at anything that moved.

As Garrett's group of jeeps turned up into the pad area, half a dozen of the gunmen turned and began firing at them. The vehicles screeched to a standstill and Spider-Man piled out along with everyone else and hit the dirt. He came down next to the lieutenant, who was unholstering her sidearm and muttering under her breath. Spidey put his head up over the edge of the jeep—then was hit with a warning from his spider-sense at the same time that his eyes caught a red light, and hurriedly ducked again just before a spatter of bullets slammed into the hood of the jeep, making it rock on its springs.

"They've got laser designators on those things," he said, then glanced at the Beretta M9 pistol in Garrett's hand. "Is that all you folks have?"

"This isn't a war zone," she said, then flinched instinctively as another long stream of slugs chewed up the concrete paving behind the jeep. "Isn't *usually* a war zone," she corrected, starting to sound angry for the first time. "Normally we don't need that level of security here." Spidey could hear a hiss and crackle of static from the walkie-talkies of the people in the next jeep. "Jones!" yelled Garrett, "Jonesey—what's their ETA?"

"Three and a half minutes!"

Garrett gave Spider-Man a small, tight smile. "That'll be the choppers from Canaveral AFB. And *they'll* be loaded for bear."

Spidey shook his head. "Three and a half minutes won't be soon enough." He cautiously put his head up again and saw an Air Force man stand up from behind one of the several jeeps spaced around the pad. The man's pistol was braced in both hands and he was crouched low—but not low enough. He got off only two shots before a sparkle of bullet-strikes marched all over the jeep and the rest of the burst punched him backwards to the ground. But Spidey also saw a trio of mercenaries break away from the main group and start sprinting for the hole in the defensive perimeter that the airman's death had opened. The gunfire intensified to cover them as they ran.

"Not soon enough at all," he said grimly. "Lieutenant, one of those guys has a bomb. I'm sure of it."

Without waiting to say anything else, he sprang out from behind the jeep and went after the running mercenaries, feeling horribly exposed out there in the midst of that vast, flat space with all those lights blazing down on him.

A submachine gun chattered and Spidey leaped, rolled, sprang, crouched, then sprang again, changing course once or twice a second as the gunman tried and failed to anticipate his next move—especially since Spider-Man's spider-sense effectively anticipated the gunman's next move.

I'm getting real *tired of this,* he thought, and bounded zigzagging toward one mercenary who seemed to have chosen him as his particular target. Spiders can move very, very fast when they have to, and for the last hundred yards of his approach, Spider-Man exploited that talent to the best of his ability, bouncing across the white concrete like a demented Ping-Pong ball. His final leap took him straight for the mercenary, and on the way in he somersaulted in midair so that he hit the man's chest feet foremost. Spidey had a fleeting glimpse of shocked eyes in a pale, snarling face; then he felt the impact jarring up through his heels and heard the explosive grunt as all the air was jolted from the mercenary's lungs. By the time Spider-Man landed in a half-crouch, the man was already flattened and out for the count, flakvest or not.

Spider-Man scooped up the gun as it went clattering and spinning over the concrete, wrenched the long, curved magazine out of the receiver, threw that and the gun as far as he could in opposite directions—then a vivid red light glowed in the corner of one eye, a blare of his spider-sense, and he leaped and twisted in three directions at once. The concrete where he had been standing exploded in dust and splinters, and his ears were filled with the scream of ricochets. At least one of the mercenaries knew how to handle a gun, and the only thing that had saved him, various super powers notwithstanding, was that whoever it was had paused for that lingering, laser-lit instant to make sure of his aim.

Spidey decided not to stand in one place for too long anymore.

The next two groups of mercenaries were a good four hundred yards away on either side. At least that increased his chances, laser sights or not. Ahead of him, those three figures were running for the pad. Fire was still being directed at him from somewhere behind, but he let his spider-sense guide him away from the hail as he chased the trio. They, at least, were running too hard to shoot at him, being more intent on making it to the big pedestals at the base of the Mobile Launch Platform; but once among those, they could take shelter and fire as they pleased, while preparing to do whatever it was they had in mind.

Spidey thought he knew. *If I was going to blow up the Space Shuttle,* he thought, his face twisting with disgust at the thought as he jumped and ran and jumped again, *I wouldn't bother with the Shuttle itself. I'd go straight for the main fuel tank.* It would have been full of lox and liquid hydrogen for a couple of hours, and he suspected that was why the attack had been timed for now. Someone knew the timetable by which the Shuttle was fueled and prepped for launch, and why wouldn't they? It was pretty much public knowledge, and had even been included in the press package.

He was beginning to catch up with the running men, and the one farthest behind was just within range of his webbing, if he was careful and shot it just so. Then the trio veered suddenly to the left, and as he caught himself just in time from shooting a web at where the man would have been, he understood why. They were quite close to the six great bells of *Endeavour's* rocket exhausts, and directly under those bells yawned the huge flame-trench, a concrete chasm some sixty feet wide and another four hundred fifty feet long.

Aha! Spider-Man thought. He took aim once more, and shot web accurately enough that he hit the last mercenary square across the arms and back with it. Spidey braced himself, and pulled. The running man stopped dead in his tracks and jerked backwards, his gun flying. The other two heard his yell and jerked squat black SMGs from clips on the front of their flakvests, blazing wildly behind them as they ran. But they didn't stop, either to help their comrade or even to make sure of their target.

Spidey dove and rolled as the slugs zipped and whined around him, then came up again and made a single huge bound to where the stunned mercenary was lying on his back. Picking him up, Spider-Man tossed him into the trench and broke his fall—with the web that still wrapped his back and arms—a good six feet from the bottom. The man bounced and swung like a mad bungee-jumper as Spidey secured the other end to the edge of the trench and glanced down at him.

"Try getting out of that," he muttered. The sound of repetitive and unimaginative swearing rose like a bad smell from the depths of the trench. *Serves him right,* Spider-Man thought and took off in pursuit of the others.

Both now turned and fired again, as carelessly as before, then kept right on running. Evidently their orders were even more important than taking out the costumed pest pursuing them. But if they were relying on the hail of poorly aimed lead to keep him at bay, they had another thing coming. Then one of the men—a broad-shouldered bald black man— stopped beside the huge wall of the Sound Suppression Water System, smacked a new magazine into his submachine gun and dropped to one knee, while the last man—a tall white man who sported a ponytail—put on an extra spurt of speed.

Spidey noted the one with the ponytail. *That's my boy,* he thought. *I'll deal with you in a minute.* But not this minute; right now he had all his work cut out to get at the bald guy who was shooting, because this one was good. Now there was no wild spraying of gunfire; instead the mercenary was ripping off quick, precise bursts of no more than three or four rounds each, and some of those were coming frighteningly close.

Spider-Man jumped sideways, up onto the wall of the water tank, then scuttled and bounced along it, forcing the man to lean out from his firing position in an attempt to hit him. It spoiled his aim a little, but nothing like enough. Spidey still had to jump around like a fly avoiding a swatter—a nine-millimeter cupro-nickel-jacketed swatter—as bullets tore chunks out of the concrete all around him.

Damn laser-sights, he thought, and shot a webline to the side of the tank with a slap of one hand, then launched himself outward, spinning more web as he went. The gunfire tracked him, but not accurately enough. That outward kick had given him more momentum than the mercenary had counted on. He swung out from the tank, then back in again in a sweeping parabola, and spinning the extra web had brought him downward as well, almost directly over the gunman's head. Confused by the movement, the man triggered a burst toward where Spidey would have been had he swung in a second arc. Then the burst cut off short as the SMG clicked empty.

That was when Spider-Man hit the wall again and kicked off once more—but this time right on top of him.

The man's reactions were very, very fast in that last instant before impact, because somewhere in the final eight feet of his drop, Spidey was staring down the barrel of the gun. Not that it did the mercenary any good. He was still fumbling to clear the empty magazine when Spider-Man kicked magazine and gun together out of his hands, then hauled off with great satisfaction and no small relief, and knocked him cold.

The gunman had barely hit the ground before Spidey was off again after the mercenary with the ponytail—but he was still just a shade too late. He could see him, too far away to reach, as the man vanished into the gantry elevator of the Mobile Launch Platform. It wasn't one of the open-cage elevators that he was familiar with from news footage of earlier launches. This one was a closed car inside the structure of the platform—and it was going up.

The question is, wondered Spidey, *how many floors will it stop at on the way?* He leapt for the nearest other thing that reached all the way up, the Fixed Service Structure with its big venting arm halfway up. That was his best bet for getting at the external fuel tank.

And that, he figured, was where Ponytail would stop. As he worked his way higher up and became visible from the ground, sporadic gunfire began probing for him as he climbed, the metal girders clanking and humming under his hands as the bullets struck them.

The only good thing about that symbiote, he thought as he worked his way around the structure and out of the line of fire, *was that its black hue made you less of a target. The ol' red and blue does stand out a bit.*

He scuttled up the tower as fast as he could, leaping from one girder to the next. About halfway up, Spidey had a sudden thought, and spared a second, no more, to snatch his camera out, clamp it to a support, make sure it had free traverse, and flick the On switch for the motion-sensitive shutter control. He headed upward, relieved to hear the camera whine and turn and click behind him, reacting to his motion. Just as well; there was no time to fiddle with it now. *Maybe four hundred feet to the top of the gantry,* Spidey thought, looking up, *and three hundred or so to where I'm headed.* But could he get up there before Ponytail did? That elevator was fast. It had been above him the whole time he had been climbing, and was pulling slightly ahead. Spider-Man poured on all the speed he could.

"These people are desperate," he muttered to himself, "and this one's probably the most desperate of the lot." The prospect was unnerving; there were few things more scary than a terrorist who didn't care whether or not he got away, just so long as he did what he was there for. They would blow the Shuttle right where it sat, and not care how many people went up with it. And after the fireball died down, if what Lieutenant Garrett said about the reactor's protective shell was true, then it would be lying somewhere in the half-mile radius of scattered debris, ready to pick up and take away. There was probably another team somewhere out in the darkness, waiting to do just that.

It was a chilling thought, and made him scramble up the gantry even faster. Then the firing from below died away. Spider-Man paused for just a moment to look down, and saw that the other mercenaries, the ones who had surrounded the pad, were pulling out.

Uh-oh, he thought, knowing what that had to mean. They were clearing the blast zone. He started climbing again, and then above him saw the elevator slide to a halt at the level where the vent-arm reached out from the fixed superstructure to *Endeavour.* It was still attached, a convenient, if not exactly safe, bridge between one and the other.

Then he saw Ponytail emerge from the elevator. The man walked straight out onto a wire-grating walkway that led to the venting arm, and Spider-Man practically flew up what remained of the tower. He shot a web at the wire grating, then hauled himself up at top speed, swung onto the walkway, and started running after the man. At the sound of his footfalls, Ponytail turned, pulled a big stainless-steel revolver from a tie-down holster belted around his waist, and opened fire.

There wasn't much room to maneuver on the walkway, and when Spidey flung himself aside he still felt a shock and a stripe of hot pain across his left side as if someone had hit him with a cattle-prod.

Too close! Waaay too close! But he was still grateful that the slug had only grazed him. From the heavy boom of the gun, it had to be firing a Magnum load. Even with an ordinary bullet, that would have left a six-inch hole in his belly—and Spidey had an ugly feeling that to be so casual about firing right beside the Shuttle's main fuel tank, this guy was using something nastier than plain lead slugs. He raised one arm, shot a web at the orange surface of the main tank, and threw himself off the walkway.

The web hit squarely and stuck fast, and he swung right past the mercenary, out and down between him and the tank. He hit the insulated surface and clung to it, then twisted around and shot another line of web at that deadly gun, splatting all over its barrel. That barrel had swung to track him, but not fast enough or far enough to be pointing at him or at the huge cylinder of volatiles on which he crouched. Spidey jerked it out of Ponytail's hand like a pin out of wet paper, then shook it free and let it drop into the flame trench nearly two hundred feet below.

That was when Spider-Man got his first good look at his assailant, and saw, hooked to the other side of his pistol-belt, a package that looked like an ordinary black nylon fanny-pack. The man was unzipping it and reaching inside, feeling for something. Remembering the grenades that the other mercenaries had been using, Spidey leapt from the surface of the fuel tank straight at him, wondering at the back of his mind if he would make it in time, or even make the distance from such an awkward springboard.

He did, and they crashed together, sprawling on the walkway and thrashing to and fro, only prevented from rolling right off by the protective grating to either side—and that was already bulged and sprung in three separate places. Ponytail's hands came up, not wasting time with punches but with both thumbs already stabbing at where Spidey's eyes were hidden by his mask. Spider-Man blocked, snapping his hands out to knock the jabbing thumbs simultaneously sideways, then brought both of them back in again to chop the man hard under both ears. Ponytail went "Urk!" and tried to get up; then he sagged, his eyes closed, and he slumped forward until his lolling head clanked against the metal of the walkway.

Panting, Spidey rolled out from under the unconscious weight and got to his hands and knees, trying to rip the fanny-pack off the mercenary's belt. It wouldn't come free so, very, very carefully, he dipped his hand inside and lifted the contents out.

It was a bomb; very small, very neat, and though its contents were in a sealed plastic casing, he didn't need to lift it to his face to smell that characteristic marzipan aroma of Semtex.

The first thing he noticed was the little LED timer built into the casing. It had no controls that he could see, no buttons to push or wires to cut at the last minute. Just those little numbers, and even as Spidey looked at it, *48* became *47*. And then *46*.

He would never have had time to get off here, Spider-Man thought. *He doesn't care if he dies.* He glanced sideways at Ponytail. *And right now, I'm not one hundred percent sure if* I *care if he dies. Unfortunately there are other people involved. Including me.*

When the bomb went off it would produce a fair-sized bang, but since it didn't have a metal casing, there would be little more than blast damage. But if it was still too close to the Shuttle and its fuel when it blew, then there would be a really big bang, with enough shrapnel to scythe Kennedy Space Center clean. Spidey glanced about him, discarded the very thought of trying to swing from the tank again with a live bomb in his hand, and looked toward *Endeavour*'s wing—and the first thing he saw there was the large, red-lettered stencil that said No Step.

"Oh, no," Spider-Man said with feeling, and bounded up another thirty feet or so to where the body of the Shuttle was mated to the tank. He scrambled up to the side window of the orbiter and banged on it until a startled face inside a space-suit helmet looked out at him.

"Out!" yelled Spidey. "Get out, now!" He gestured emphatically toward the far side of the Shuttle, and the entry/exit doors, and for emphasis held up the bomb with its LED toward the window. *34... 33... 32...*

The angry, surprised expression on the face went shocked, and the head nodded; a gauntleted hand reached out and slapped a control, and everything started to happen at once. A siren on the Fixed Service Structure began to howl, and as the big access arm began to swing out with smooth, ponderous speed, explosive bolts blew the Shuttle's port door off. There was a jostling inside as people began to pile toward the door, then he heard the booted feet ringing on metal as the astronauts plunged out of the cockpit and into their elevator.

"Good," said Spidey aloud. *26* read the bomb, *25... 24.* "At least I think it's good."

He shot web up higher toward the lightning masts, and swung down past the Shuttle, leapt for the Mobile Launch Platform tower again, barely made it, then clung to it and began to web the bomb up. "Slowly and carefully, slowly and carefully," he kept muttering to himself, a mantra of caution to offset the panicky speed with which his hands really wanted to work. *I can at least confine the blast enough to keep it from setting off the main tank. But not if this isn't done right.*

The bomb was about four pounds of Semtex—enough to make a reasonable hole in a building—and at the back of his mind he started trying to calculate the stresses involved. Then he gave up. Best to just get down off the tower and leap and bound as fast as he could in any other direction.

Not just any other, he thought. *Away from the lox storage tanks would be good too!*

He slapped one palm against the tower and fastened a web there, then began to let himself down, counting under his breath as he went. "Twelve, eleven, ten, nine..." Down below him, reflecting the intense light that flooded the whole of pad 39-A, water gleamed and rippled. And then Spidey laughed out loud and yelled, "Yes!" He knew *exactly* what to do.

Of course, this still might not work.

8... 7...

"Well," and he grinned inside his mask, "it's been nice, world. Take your best shot, Spidey." He quickly covered the bomb with as much thick webbing as he could in two seconds. Then he simply opened his hand and let the bomb drop straight down into the water tank of the Sound Suppression System. It hit with a splash and its four-plus pounds of weight cut through the surface as cleanly as a diving fish.

Up, he thought, *or down?* There was no time to calculate the stresses or the trajectories, no time even for an educated guess. Just time for the body's instinctive reaction, which was to get as far away from anything threatening as it possibly could. So he went up almost thirty feet in a single bound, hurled himself behind a girder, webbed himself there with two quick squirts, then closed his eyes and hung on for dear life.

2... 1...

The actual sound of the blast was a muffled *whoomph,* more felt than heard, a giant shock as though the concrete base of the pad had been kicked by some impossibly huge foot. Then there was a vast hissing splash, and an almost solid wall of water came erupting up from the Sound Suppression tank. Spidey had seen old newsreel footage of depth-charge attacks, and the columns of white water bursting skyward in the wake of a destroyer, but he had never dreamed he would ever be on the receiving end of one himself. Everything rattled and shuddered, and the Mobile Launch Platform vibrated like a gong. But as the water—and nothing worse than water—went flying into the sky, Spider-Man began to laugh.

The reinforced concrete tank of the Sound Suppression System contained three hundred thousand gallons of water, designed to protect the launch structures from the protracted sound and blast vibrations of a Shuttle lifting off. Anything that could absorb those millions of pounds of thrust applied for seconds at a time before the Shuttle cleared the pad would have found his tiny pack of Semtex little more than a firecracker.

There was a silence so intense that it seemed to clang in Spidey's ears, and then, out of the clear night sky, it began to rain. It had soaked him on the way up; it soaked him again on the way down. And he didn't care. Unhitching himself from the girder, he crawled back up the structure to where he had left the unconscious mercenary and his camera. Both were still there, though the double drenching with cold water awakened Ponytail enough that he was able to mumble incoherently, and Spidey's webbing and its position under a girder protected the camera from the worst of the deluge. Spider-Man trussed Ponytail up with webbing and lowered him to the ground, then slowly, still being rained on and still chuckling about it, came down after him.

It wasn't over yet, though, not by a long shot. Down by the pedestals, a lot of the Kennedy and Air Force security personnel were waiting. The roar and rotor-beat of the big Blackhawk choppers from Canaveral was deafening as they settled onto the perimeter of 39-A, though several Apache gunships continued overhead to hunt for the mercenaries who had left the area once they thought the bomb was in place.

The security people gathered around him, and there was the backslapping and applause more usually reserved for Mission Control rooms after a successful launch. Lieutenant Garrett came up to Spider-Man and smiled at him.

"I must call the AEC kids in New York," she said, "and let them know that you really are useful to have around in a crisis."

"Always glad to be of service," said Spidey. A man in a space suit approached him. Spidey recognized him, even though the helmet was off now and the expression was no longer shock, but relief and gratitude. It was Commander Luks, from the press conference. He stuck out his heavily gloved hand. Spider-Man took it, shook it, then said, "Er, permission to come aboard, sir?"

"Granted, son, anytime. Anytime at all." Then he shot a thoughtful glance at the sky and looked at one of the NASA people. "Harry," he said, "your weather reports have gone skewed again. Why's it raining?" There was a lot of laughter.

"Never mind," said an older, gray-haired man. "We'll scrub for this morning."

"We couldn't go anyway," said one of the other astronauts. "All the water in the triple-S seems to have jumped out of the tank."

"Just be glad of it," said Spider-Man, and turned to Garrett. "It was Semtex," he told her. "Now, I've a question to ask you. This group was one of two. Another one was going south down a canal when they split from this one."

Lieutenant Garrett turned to one of the other Air Force officers. "Mike, didn't you say that Coast Guard had been alerted about something going on down south?"

The man nodded. "The *James D.* just moved out," he said. "Something about a big dump of radioactive waste, and other contraband. A night-boat job, apparently. Whoever found it stopped it."

"I know who found it," said Spidey. "I'm going to have to go."

"Not before you debrief," said Garrett sharply.

"Lieutenant, believe me, if I stop for a debrief now there's going to be trouble. For me, and for a lot of other people. I'll be back later, tomorrow afternoon maybe, or tomorrow evening. Then I'll give you all the debrief you want. And," he added, "I'll have your hydrogel with me. But right now—" he looked at one of the helicopters that had settled out on the pad "—I came an awful long way to get here tonight. I'd really appreciate it if someone could give me a lift back."

On his mind was the little lab in the Everglades. Venom had clearly found whatever the other group of mercenaries was involved with. With that little matter attended to, he would surely head back up to the 'Glades, to the lab, and to the Lizard, in an attempt to finish his business there as well. And unless Spider-Man was there to stop him....

IN the small, quiet stuffy room in the little lab building, Curt Connors stood over an apparatus, waiting for its little chime to go off. "This is it," he had said to Fischer about an hour before. "It has to be. It can't be anything else."

Fischer was glad enough to hear it. He had little liking for, or patience with, scientists. They all knew too much. Stuff that might backfire on you somehow—or stuff that they might find a way to use against you, if you didn't watch them all the time. That his boss was a scientist as well made his job no easier. He always had to be careful, when dealing with him, to conceal his basic dislike and distrust of the species. And truly, it was no business of his who employed him, just so long as he got paid. For his own part, Fischer was careful to be conscientious about his work, to deliver what he promised, and to make sure that whatever happened, whether his boss's doing or his own, he didn't get caught at anything.

The subject was on his mind at the moment, since this particular project was rapidly approaching the get-away-and-don't-get-caught-at-anything stage. This place, having served its purpose, was ready to be destroyed so that the project and the organization could move on. Unnecessary personnel would be offloaded, and Fischer would likely go on to another job.

He felt eyes on him and glanced up to see Connors favoring him with an expression that was mostly loathing.

"So?" Fischer said. "Is it ready?"

"A few minutes," Connors said. "One thing, though. Before the insertion, I want this out." He held out his lone arm.

Fischer glanced at the arm, noting the nearly healed scar where the implant chip had gone in. He laughed a little and shook his head. "Oh, no. I haven't had any orders to that effect from upstairs. Besides—" he glanced at the machine "—what if it doesn't work? What if the insertion makes you crazy? What if you get out of control and start trashing the joint? I need some way to manage you. No," Fischer said, "that's my little insurance policy. Just in case you get any—" his eyes narrowed slightly "—funny ideas, when your cure starts to take—*if* it starts to take."

"You," Connors said, "are a lot too fond of control."

Fischer laughed. They had been over this ground before, and he had to admit he enjoyed it. Connors showed his wounds so openly. "It's all about control, in the end," Fischer said. "People are just animals, after all. Some of them more so than others." The pained look on Connors's face amused him; it was amazing, how some people just couldn't bear the truth. "Your little accident just made that side of you more accessible, revealed the truth, whether you like it or not. Like everybody else, you need a hand on the leash."

Connors turned away from the mercenary. "It doesn't matter," Fischer said jovially. "For the first time now, because of the implant, there's a little control over what you do when you change. So if we choose to manage the Lizard a little bit when he makes his appearances, what's it to you? You wouldn't be able to manage what he does at all. At least we've kept you from killing anybody. You should thank us. I'd think your tender humanistic sensibilities would suffer terribly from something like that. And if we can make use of your changes for our cause—a little cash here, a few weapons there, while you're running around the landscape with your scales on, destroying things—what does it matter? It's all going toward your cure, anyway. Without our protection, and our money, you wouldn't be able to afford the facilities you need for all your little experiments. And the Boss wouldn't have been able to offer you that hydrogel. He wouldn't be able to get you any more of it, either, after you lost the last batch. Careless of you."

Connors turned back and scowled at him. "It wasn't exactly my choice," he said. "I was trying to run away. Somebody wanted me to stay and fight Spider-Man, to see what would happen—a little casual entertainment for a slow night, as far as I can tell. You brought it on yourself, and made sure that your lovely Boss thought it was my fault."

"Control," Fischer said, and shrugged, and smiled. "We were still working on the retinal readout, trying to clear the pictures up, for later jobs that'll matter more. If you don't like it, you can leave—or try to. But if you leave, what happens to your cure, if this doesn't work? And we're going to need you for a while yet. The organization has a lot of needs."

"Like threatening Space Shuttles?" Curt said bitterly.

"Oh, what's a Shuttle or two? The astronauts won't be hurt—they'll have plenty of time to get out. What's *in* the Shuttle, our people will probably be able to pick up. A nice bonus, since the real business tonight is further south. If they don't get it, well, they'll still have done their job. Every police, Coast Guard, and Air Force unit in this part of the state will be over there. No one'll have time for something happening out in a swamp when Cape Kennedy is being overrun by 'bad guys.'" He laughed.

He couldn't make anything of the look Connors gave him then, but Fischer had better things to do than psychoanalyze half-sane scientists. The machine made a soft ding then, and Connors bent down beside it, opened the little ultrasound compartment, and took out a small cylindrical flask of amber liquid. He looked at it, held it up to the light. The expression on Connors's face shifted to something Fischer could understand: fear. *He's afraid it won't work. Or that it will, and that he'll still be bound to us afterwards.*

His problem....

"Where's the medium?" Connors said.

"Just a moment." Fischer went into the next room, tapped in the combination to the lab's small safe, opened its door, and took out the little metal box. He brought it back in to Connors, opened the box. A small piece of hydrogel, a cube maybe half an inch across, lay there. Connors took a pair of tweezers and lifted the hydrogel onto a glass plate, put it into the microwave, and gave it a minute on full.

Fischer looked at him curiously. He knew perfectly well that microwaves couldn't affect this stuff any more than anything else did. "Sterilizing it," Connors said, catching the look. "Be a shame to have the cure work and then get blood poisoning from a chance germ floating by."

"You sure it'll take that?" Fischer nodded at the liquid in the flask. "You haven't tested it before—"

"Oh, it'll absorb it," Connors said absently, peering at the rotating table in the microwave. "The molecular structure of the serum is built to exploit the structure of the hydrogel. It'll lock into it and then disseminate molecule by molecule when it's implanted, and the fluid pressure around it goes positive."

Fischer frowned. "Like one of those time-release nicotine patches, huh?"

"Very like. The problem in the past—" it was surprising how dry Connors's voice went suddenly, when the man himself had so many times been the main subject of the experiment "—has always been with the dosage strategy. Even metered microdosages have been too high. This one, though, will come on demand from serum blood levels."

The microwave chimed. Connors took out the hydrogel on its plate, took a pipette from a rack on his worktable, slipped it into the cylinder of serum, put his thumb over the top, and lifted an inch or so of serum from the container.

Fischer watched with some slight interest. It was odd, the way it looked. The serum didn't so much flow out of the pipette as seem to be abruptly sucked out of it, and the hydrogel went instantly from smoky gray to smoky gold.

Connors looked satisfied, showed just a ghost of a smile. "Now that," he said, "is a good chemical affinity." He looked at Fischer.

"All right," Fischer said, and got ready for his part of this business. He was an able enough battlefield medic, having cut and stitched back together a good number of people under circumstances a lot more adverse than this. Connors took off his lab coat, sat down and pushed up the sleeve of his shirt, then pulled over a bottle of Betadine surgical scrub and wet a cotton pad from it. He spent about thirty seconds rubbing his upper arm with the yellowy stuff, from the point of the shoulder to the middle of the biceps, and used the last stroke of the pad to mark a line about half an inch below the shoulder's point, an inch and a half long, down to the center of the biceps. "Right there," he said to Fischer. "That long. Half an inch deep. Any longer, or deeper, and you might hit the brachial nerve—and mess up another site for your damn implant, if it has to be changed later."

Fischer nodded. From a nearby tray, he laid out a small surgical kit while Connors anesthetized his arm.

Fischer picked up the scalpel. Connors averted his eyes while Fischer worked. Fischer smiled to himself. *Typical, that someone who in his time had caused so much bloodshed and mayhem didn't like looking at his own blood.* With very little ado, Fischer pulled the edges of the wound apart with one hand, and with the other picked up the hydrogel with the sterile tweezers from the suture pack and slipped it into the incision, seating it. A moment later he pushed the wound edges back together again, close enough to start suturing the muscle proper, and began to close. Connors shivered once, hard, as the hydrogel went in, then sat still again as Fischer stitched.

"Anything?" Fischer said.

"No," Connors said, "just reaction to being cut." But there was something in his voice that made Fischer wonder about that. He got busy with the epidermis, meantime looking around the room to see where exactly he had put the control box for the implant chip. He had seen Connors mistime his estimates of change before.

Fischer finished his needlework, knotted the last knot, and cut the last black silk suture off close. Then he got up and went to find the control box.

Connors sat shivering. Fischer was not at all sure about the way he looked. *Could he be having some kind of reaction to the hydrogel?* Fischer wondered.

Connors was ashen. Then the shivering seemed to pass off, and Fischer smiled to himself. *Maybe it's just fear,* he thought, and turned away.

Then he heard the roar....

ELEVEN

THE Blackhawk chopper rode low over the 'Glades, followed by a trail of noise from distraught birds and the occasional bellowing alligator.

Through the front window, leaning between the pilots' seats, Spider-Man watched the moonlit landscape pour by. He said, or rather shouted, to the pilot, "How far does rotor noise travel on a quiet night like this?"

The pilot shouted back, "Oh, in flat terrain like this, maybe a mile and a half, two miles."

"Okay. I'd sooner the people I'm going to meet didn't hear me coming, if it's all the same to you. You suppose you could drop me—" Spidey peered out through the windshield "—oh, about two miles north of here?"

"Mister Spider-Man, sir," the pilot shouted, "my boss told me to drop you on the moon, if you said you wanted to go there. Hoped you wouldn't. I'm due for a lunch break in another hour or so."

"Thanks. You're a pal."

"You could," said the pilot, "tell me one thing before you go."

"Sure."

He eyed Spider-Man's costume. "Don't you find that a mite inappropriate for this climate?"

Spidey laughed. "Brother, you said a mouthful. But I left my tux at home."

The pilot chuckled. Several minutes later, he was lowering the chopper gingerly above a small reed island. "I'm not real eager to set this thing down," he shouted, "on account of I'm not sure I can get her up again. You mind jumping?"

"*No* problem," he said, as another of the chopper's crew pulled the Blackhawk's door open. "Thanks a lot!"

"Our pleasure, sir. You watch yourself out there, now. There's things out there with a lot of teeth."

"You don't know the half of it," Spidey said, waved, and jumped down into the wind-flattened reeds.

The chopper leaned into a turn and headed south again. Spidey crouched where he landed until the plant life began to stand up around him again; when they did, he did, too, and looked around. He thought he had his landmarks right. He recognized a pattern of smaller hammocks which he had identified as being about two miles south of the main one.

Spider-Man paused a second to put on Murray's little present, then he got moving. It really had been a long night. He was having trouble summoning up the energy he wanted, but there was nothing he could do about the problem except just keep bounding along at his best pace.

Within a matter of a few minutes, he was distracted by the sight, in the viewer, of a bright, swift, man-shaped figure, with pseudopodia streaming off it and helping it along as it made its way from island to island about a quarter-mile ahead of him. He went after it. It would be pleasant, Spidey thought, to be able to surprise Venom for a change, instead of the other way around.

Spider-Man made his way as silently across the uneven terrain as he could. There was, unfortunately, no surprise. As he got within about a hundred yards, he saw Venom's head come up and look toward him suddenly, and his jaws open in a huge, fangy snarl.

Venom paused, crouching, and Spider-Man caught up with him and stopped at a safe distance—if there was any such thing. Spidey would have preferred half a continent or so. Venom opened his mouth to speak.

"Congratulations," Spider-Man interrupted.

This was not what Venom had apparently been expecting. He looked at Spidey and said, "Good news travels fast, we take it."

"I don't think it's all that good for everyone," Spider-Man said, "but I do know what you stopped them from doing. The Coast Guard said to say thank you—off the record, of course."

Did that smile get just a little bit less dreadful? Hard to tell. "They're welcome, we're sure. But we have other business to attend to, now."

"Venom," Spider-Man said, "will you for God's sake listen to me, just this once? Curt Connors is not to blame here. These people have been using him."

Venom started moving again. "Life uses us all," he said, "for its own purposes. If Connors has been used, what better reason to set him free—once and for all."

"And what about his wife?" Spidey said, going along with Venom, matching his pace, though still at a distance. "And his son? His innocent son?"

They made their way along in silence for a few seconds. "It is unfortunate," Venom said finally, "but—"

"It's not just unfortunate," Spider-Man said bitterly. "If you defend the innocent, you have to defend *all* the innocent. You can't pick and choose the ones you like better than the others. What about that young boy, who wants to be a scientist like his dad? What about what his life will become if Curt dies? Think about it. That will be on your conscience, your fault. Not some abstract tragedy. *You* will have caused that."

"The greater good—" Venom began.

"It's an excuse!" Spider-Man shouted angrily, panting a little—the long night was beginning to tell on him. "It's a reason not to think, not to take the responsibility, to say 'I don't care about what's right, I want to do what I feel like!' This is a boy who could do anything, be anything, if his father lives—even if Curt never comes home, that hope will be with William for years. If you kill his father, you snuff that out. You end two lives. Murder, plain and simple. One of them is the victim of an accident that's gone on and on—tragic, yes, but not a criminal. The other is an innocent. Dead at your hands, if not physically, then in essence. And you can't ignore it. Kill Curt, and you betray everything you claim to stand for. What are you going to tell your people back in San Francisco about that?"

Venom said nothing, just kept going.

"I'm not going to let you kill him," Spider-Man said. "I'm going to stop you whatever way I can. I may die doing it, but you *are not going to kill Curt Connors.*"

It took about another ten minutes for them to reach the hammock. They stopped about a hundred yards from it, looked it over. The first words that Venom said, then, were, "It seems unusually quiet."

"I don't know for sure that they committed all their people to the two operations tonight," Spidey said. "I saw about seven, maybe eight people total at the Cape tonight."

"Is that device of yours any help?"

Spider-Man was trying to discover just that. He fiddled with controls. "No," he said, "it's going to be hard to tell until we get inside the hammock, and maybe not even then. The whole place is radiating at about a hundred and five degrees—it whites out anything less." He shook his head. "We should go in."

"If we find Connors—" Venom said then, looking at Spider-Man blank-eyed.

"I'm warning you," Spider-Man said.

"If, however, we find the Lizard—"

"Venom, *don't*," Spider-Man said, meaning it.

Venom slipped past him and headed for the hammock.

Spidey went after. One after another they squeezed between the trees and worked cautiously inward. There was the lab, a little prefab building, temporary-looking. It had no windows, but through the viewer Spidey could see cracks where the heat was spilling out, indicating doors. "That way," he said to Venom, indicating the left side of the building, where there was a ground-floor door.

They started for it. And then they heard the roar. It echoed, and the right-hand side of the top of the building shook, shook once more, as something hit it. The roar scaled up to a scream.

Spider-Man and Venom looked at each other. Spidey pushed past Venom and made for the right side of the building, bypassing the stairway that went up the outside by shooting a web at the top of the building and hauling himself up. Venom came after.

Oh, please, Spider-Man said to whatever deity might be handling the Everglades on the night shift, *please let me save something from this mess!* In his present state, after the night's events, he wasn't sure he could take Venom. But if he didn't, Venom would kill the Lizard, kill Curt, for sure.

Spider-Man pulled open the door at the top of the stairs. Its lock resisted him, so he pulled harder, enraged—yanked it right off its hinges, and flung the thing backward behind him, narrowly missing Venom, who was webbing up after him.

The hallway was empty. The source of the crashing and roaring was farther off to his right, through another door. Spider-Man looked both ways, saw no one, and headed for that closed door, hit it feet first, knocked it open and down.

Beyond it was chaos. He had only a second to take in the scene: scientific equipment smashed and trashed, everywhere shattered glass, twisted metal, the walls of the prefab structure itself deeply dented, here and there punched right through. Splashed liquid, overturned machinery, a slight chemical smell… No question but that this was yet another attempted cure for the Lizard gone wrong. And at the far end of the room, there was the Lizard himself, roaring, the desperate roar of a beast which does not want to be a beast, which once again suffers the curse of existence and can find no escape.

The Lizard saw Spider-Man. It flew at him, so fast he couldn't even jump aside. It grabbed him by the throat and flung him headfirst at the wall. Spidey tried to shoot out web and catch something so that he could stop himself, or at least turn. The web caught and adhered, but on a part of wall that had been weakened by blows, and broke loose. He only managed to turn himself enough to take the impact partially on his shoulder and neck, instead of head-on. He slid down the wall, nearly blacking out, trying desperately to stagger to his feet, feeling pseudopodia whip past toward the Lizard, but he could do no more than roll blearily over to at least see what was going on.

The Lizard swatted Venom's tendrils out of the air as fast as they came for him, then grabbed a great clawful of them and yanked Venom toward him. Off balance briefly, Venom stumbled—and the Lizard hit him a huge double-fisted blow in the side of the head. Venom staggered, and the Lizard picked him up as effortlessly as he had picked up Spider-Man, and threw Venom right at Spidey.

Spider-Man rolled over to try to protect his head, still woozy. Venom crashed down on top of him, slamming his head into the floor. The two of them lay there in a heap, while behind them the roaring went on and on, ever more loud and desperate. Spidey tried to rise but couldn't. He wondered whether he had broken something, or whether Venom had broken something of Spidey's on landing, and also bemoaned the Lizard's increased strength. This latest "cure" had apparently served only to make the Lizard more dangerous.

"Curt," he tried to croak, but he couldn't even speak. His vision was going dark around the edges, not that he could see much but a litter of black limbs and limp tendrils, trying and failing to rise. Venom stirred, then sagged, slumped again.

Oh, Curt! Spider-Man thought miserably, as his vision went completely. *Martha. I'm so sorry....*

And everything went away.

The sound of moaning intruded. Spider-Man tried to open his eyes and finally managed it.

He still lay on the floor with Venom on top of him. There was no telling how long he had been out. He tried again to push himself up, and this time had more success. Venom rolled partially off him. Unconscious? Dead? No telling.

Spidey managed to make it to his hands and knees. Venom rolled the rest of the way off him, to Spider-Man's right, and Spidey looked at him in concern. He didn't much like the idea of touching the symbiote, but nevertheless he put a hand to Venom's throat, felt for the pulse. It was there.

Just knocked out, then, he thought, and snatched his fingers away.

"Unnnhhh—"

A moan from off to one side. Spidey got to his knees, looked around. Over there, sprawled against a wall, lay Curt Connors, human again. He looked terrible. He was ashen, and his arm was bleeding. "Curt," Spider-Man said.

Curt opened his eyes and looked at him, registering shock. He glanced up—

—and Spidey's spider-sense went off like someone banging a garbage can lid behind his head. He went straight up, straight for the ceiling—and it was just as well, because as he leapt, machine-gun bullets stitched the floor where he had been.

MJ woke up with terrible suddenness, and sat up in the bed in the hotel room, sweating, eyes wide, breathing hard. It had been an awful dream, involving Venom. That it had also involved the Cookie Monster was no help, though now that she was awake, she could not get rid of the memory of a voice saying, "Ooo, me impressed!" at the sight of Venom's teeth.

MJ found a smile somewhere and plastered it on, more out of reflex than anything else. She had been doing little but smile for the past few days. It was generally accepted that she was no good as the "pouty" sort of model.

All the same, smiling was hard. She had not heard from Peter since fairly early yesterday evening, and at the moment that was bad news. He had promised to call her and check in but hadn't done so. She had resisted calling him, last night, as long as she could. Finally she had succumbed to the temptation, but to no avail. Her attempts to call his mobile phone had been rewarded with the sweet recorded Southern voice of the Bell Florida operator repeatedly saying, "I'm sorry, but the mobile you have called is turned off and does not have access to voicemail services. Please try again later."

"Why didn't I get him the voicemail?" she muttered as she got out of bed. It was still dark out. The bedside clock said *5:10,* or rather, *5:1C,* since the zero was missing a piece; it was that kind of hotel. Maurice's indecision had landed them here instead of the Marriott, and this place, the Splendide, was in a state which could best be described as "faded glory." "Why am I up?" MJ said, fumbling her way into the bathroom. "What color is this wallpaper supposed to be? What's the meaning of life?"

No answers seemed forthcoming, but the shower was good and hot, and she got under it, washed her hair, and came out about ten minutes later, feeling at least human if not particularly beautiful, charitable, or intelligent. *Peter,* MJ thought, *where the heck are you?*

She had never learned to stop asking herself that question when there was likely to be no answer forthcoming. *Useless,* she thought. *And here it is oh-dark-thirty in the morning, and there's no room service in this dump, like there would be in the Marriott, and breakfast won't start for another hour and a half, like it would at the Marriott. Grr. At least there's a TV.*

MJ sat down on the bed in her towel, and flicked the TV on, getting the usual amount of early-morning snow from the local channels. There were numerous Pay-TV channels, but she flatly refused to watch any of the choices, ranging from ill-advised sequels to mindless action flicks. Cable was marginally better: at least there was the Weather Channel, the Landscape Channel, the Irish Channel, the Cuban Channel, the news channel, and the InfoMercial channel.

MJ flipped from the automotive arsonist, to a restful prairie landscape, to an Irish rural soap, to a lady talking very fast and demonstrating how to make a Cuban fried steak, to last night's sports scores. All these were relatively hopeless. Finally she settled on the Weather Channel and settled back to watch one of the nice people who worked one of the most intractable night shifts anywhere in broadcasting getting all excited about a big fat high which had positioned itself over Florida, and promised good weather for the Space Shuttle launch later this morning.

"The Shuttle," she muttered, "I can watch that, anyhow." The news network always watched the Shuttle launches pretty closely—or let you look at the thing standing on its pad, anyway, while it was getting ready to go. The sports update gave way, though not to news, but to a commercial about an exercise machine, being operated by a man who, if anything, needed to stop exercising and go out and get a life of some kind.

"Argh," MJ said, and got up and went to the window, or rather, the door. This was possibly the Splendide's only good point: it not only had windows that opened (relics of a time before air conditioning), but terraces you could go out and stand on to catch a breath of breeze, and the hotel was genuinely on the beach.

MJ went out and stood there, gazing out to sea. There was a three-quarter moon high up, and its light began to be visible out on the waves. The soft restful hiss of the water and its salt smell came up to her, and MJ breathed it in and sighed.

She looked down at the sand—and was surprised to see Maurice down there, walking along toward the waterline.

It was impossible not to recognize him. Maurice had a peculiar stumpy walk for someone who otherwise looked so tall and graceful. Apparently, according to the AD, it was because Maurice had actually had polio as a kid—one of the last cases, apparently, before it was almost completely stamped out. Or so people had thought then. Watching him, MJ breathed out unhappily at the thought that the disease was making a comeback. *Not good,* she thought. *People should do something.*

Meantime, what's Maurice doing out there at this hour of the morning? MJ thought. *He hates early. That's why we're not doing the launch, he said.*

He stopped where he stood on the beach. He just stood there for a minute, then there was a soft bloom of light at his feet. And again; and again, repeated.

He's got a flashlight. He's signaling someone.

Far away, in the pale moonlit dazzle of the water, MJ saw something move. A boat?

Suddenly MJ understood. Peter had told her about his own suspicions regarding that mess down south of the city, the other day. That boat out there could very well be tangled up in the same business.

And Maurice?

MJ swallowed hard. She didn't understand what his position was. She didn't know him at all well. Could he willingly be an accomplice of these people? Or had he perhaps been blackmailed into it somehow? He was always so nervous. He had been increasingly nervous about coming here. I.ike someone who expected something very bad to happen to him.

She heard her own voice suggesting to Peter that she would feed him to sharks, or to Venom. *Well, yes,* she told her accusing mind angrily, *he's a dreadful little overbearing power-mongering loathsome indecisive toad!*

Yeah, another part of her mind said, *so what? If that's something bad out there, do you want it to come ashore without the authorities doing anything? Do you really want Maurice to go to jail for something he might have, say, been blackmailed into?*

You don't know that's the case.

Look, said the back of her mind. *So you hate intuition. Fine. You don't have to take a position on it. Just go out there and stop what's happening. Get Maurice out of it and give him one more chance—a chance never to be stupid again, no matter what's happened to him. And cover for him, while you're at it. If those are bad people out there, make sure there are plenty of witnesses here that whatever happens now, it wasn't his fault.*

MJ slipped back into the hotel room, turned down the TV, and went over to the phone. She rummaged in the drawer of the bedside table for the yellow pages. In the front of the directory, among the numbers for Fire and Police and Ambulance, there was also a Coast Guard number, toll-free and confidential, for people who thought they had stumbled into something nasty and wanted to stop it. MJ dialed the number.

"Good morning, confidential help line."

"Uh, yes. I think there are some people about to drop something, uh, questionable, off Cocoa Beach."

"Street address, please?"

"Uh—" She rummaged around the table for the hotel's stationery, and said, so as not to pin herself down, "Fifteen thousand block of Collins."

"Could you—"

"Nope," MJ said cheerfully, and hung up. She then threw clothes on as fast as she could—a T-shirt, shorts, flipflops—took her key, and ran out, locking the door behind her. She never even glimpsed the picture of the Space Shuttle appearing on the TV, or the banner that said "KSC ATTACKED BY TERRORISTS—SHUTTLE LAUNCH CANCELED" which spread itself across the screen. MJ was too busy running downstairs to ground level, out past the half-dozing desk clerk, and out the back of the hotel onto the beach.

Just on reaching the sand, MJ paused for a moment, took a deep breath, thought for a second. Then she took another deep breath and screamed, *"Maurice!"*

It echoed. She had never heard an echo at the beach before; it was impressive. Maurice turned as suddenly as if someone had shot him, and stared at her. *She would just be visible, silhouetted against the hotel doors and the light above them.*

Upstairs, she heard windows and a couple of doors open. This was the moment. *"Maurice!"* she shrieked again. *"I have had it with you, this shoot, this beach, this state, everything! I want to talk to you right now, and you are going to do some serious listening, or else I quit, and I'm going to sue, and then I'm going to the media, and* Entertainment Tonight, *and anyone else who'll listen, and I'm going to tell them how you've mistreated me and everybody else in this operation!"*

More windows opened. In fact, they started slamming open so fast, it sounded like automatic-weapons fire.

This should definitely be classified under "guilty pleasures," MJ thought. In her TV work, she had seen some world-class tantrums thrown. She had always, herself, felt scornful about the prima donnas who threw them. *Anybody who couldn't get what they wanted by quiet reasoned discussion and negotiation,* MJ thought, *was probably stuck at the mental age of three.* However—now visiting that age for the first time in a while—she had to admit it felt absolutely lovely.

Maurice stood frozen, staring at her. MJ threw her wet hair back, squared her shoulders, and marched over to him like an invading army. He looked completely astonished and very frightened, though MJ suspected that was an effect mostly due to the people out there in the boat.

"MJ—" Maurice said.

"No sweet talk!" MJ shouted, for it was indeed the first time he had called her that since the shoot began, having constantly called "MaryJa-a-a-ane" in that nasal tone that drove her nuts. "You come inside *right now,* because we're going to have a little chat! Or else I can deck you right here where you stand, you insignificant little—" *Now, now,* said another voice inside her, which MJ suspected was the voice of Damage Control, *don't go overboard* "—little man!" She came down hard on the last word, as if it were insult enough. "Now get your butt in here!"

She turned and marched away.

Maurice stared, openmouthed—threw one glance out at the water, and then came after her.

From the floors above came a patter of applause, and the sound of subdued laughter and shutting windows.

They headed for the doors together. "And for pity's sake," she muttered to Maurice, "shove the flashlight down your pants or something. And afterwards, lose it."

They went in together, Maurice looking at MJ very strangely. So did the desk clerk, as they went by. MJ nodded to him as might a queen passing a minor courtier. She and Maurice got in the elevator together and went upstairs.

As the elevator doors closed, from outside, MJ faintly heard a sound she had heard several times over the past few days: the *whoop! whoop! whoop!* of a Coast Guard cutter out in the water, followed by the two-tone Miami police boat sirens, and the faint crackle of someone using a bullhorn.

There now, MJ thought. *All I have to figure out now is what the heck it is exactly that I'm going to say to Maurice.*

MANY miles to the west, Spider-Man dropped from the ceiling again as machine-gun fire raked up toward him. "I don't even know you," he said, leaping for the wall, and clinging there somewhat uncertainly. The wall had buckled when the Lizard hit it last. "Why are you shooting at me?"

The man with the gun laughed nastily. "Breaking and entering?" He swung the gun toward Spidey again.

Spider-Man jumped again, for the other wall this time. Out the corner of his eye he saw Curt roll groaning under a fallen table, and he hoped it was enough protection. "I didn't have anything to do with the breaking," he said. "The entering, yes—"

He kept moving, though there wasn't much room to do it in. On the floor, Venom began to stir. The man with the gun glanced at him. *Guns,* Spidey corrected himself. The camouflage-clad mercenary had a weapon braced against each upper arm—one of them an Uzi, the second with a heavy power pack and an odd bell-like nozzle that Spidey didn't like the look of. The mercenary sprayed Venom with the machine gun, then made an annoyed face and shrugged when it had no effect—conscious or unconscious, the symbiote protected its master, though Spidey found himself wondering how long that condition might last.

Bullets ricocheted in all directions. *Enough of this,* Spider-Man thought, and shot a webline at the machine gun, yanked it out of the mercenary's grip, wrapped it up as useless, and dumped it behind some furniture. "Oh," the man said, and actually grinned as Venom too began to get to hands and knees, glared at him, and the symbiote began to reach out pseudopodia in his direction. The mercenary pulled the trigger of the other gun.

Spider-Man's eyes widened and he froze as a knife of sound went straight through his head, from one ear to the other. He could feel it, a horrifying sensation, as physical as a blade. His muscles stopped working, and he fell off the wall and lay there in excruciating pain, unable even to writhe. Venom fell over sideways too, and a horrible high shrilling filled the air. The symbiote, always susceptible to sonics, stripped itself partially away from Eddie Brock's body in a tangle of blind writhing tendrils, whipping around, desperate to escape and unable to, withering in the screeching torrent of sound.

Another sound began to cut through the racket. For a moment Spider-Man, dazed and blinking, having trouble even seeing, let alone moving, thought it was the weapon again. But it was not. It spoke.

"No," it said, in a low roar. And "No!" again, and furniture rattled and crashed as it was pushed aside at the end of the room, and a figure rose up there. Six feet tall, Spidey thought dazedly. Green. Scales. Tail. But mostly teeth, at the moment. They flashed, and the tongue inside them fought to make words, and the eyes above them narrowed, looking at the mercenary.

"Stop—it—Fischer," the voice said—a terrible tangle of Curt Connors's voice, the Lizard's old voice, and the hiss of something more ancient, more dreadful, the voice of the serpent. Fischer, if that was the man's name, stood still for a moment, staring in surprise at the clawed forearm it held out for him to see. The back of it was terribly torn, perhaps by gunfire, and the edges of what seemed an old scar showed above and below the torn place. Spidey wanted to moan just at the sight of it. But why did the Lizard look—pleased?

"Come on, Connors," he said. "They're helpless. They'll be dead in a minute. Let's get out of here—the Boss has work for us."

"No," the Lizard said, and tossed the furniture aside, and made slowly for Fischer. He may have been suffering from the sonics, but not so much as Spidey and Venom were. *Then again,* Spider-Man thought, still very dazed, *lizards don't depend a lot on hearing, by and large.*

"They came here to kill you!" Fischer yelled, starting slowly to back toward the door. "Finish them and come on!"

Spider-Man tried to get up on hands and knees but couldn't even manage that. His nerves and muscles seemed to be refusing to answer him. The shrieking of the symbiote was getting more deafening all the time, heading for crescendo. Spidey wasn't sure how long it could survive this onslaught.

"They—did not," the Lizard said, struggling to get the words out; he glanced at Spider-Man as he passed, stepped over him, and headed for Fischer. "He—did not."

"But, Venom!" Fischer yelled, still backing up. "He thinks you're an animal, a nut—he's a monster, kill him!"

"I doubt he is—so—simplistic," the Lizard said. Spider-Man tried to roll over again, feeling that he wanted to either cheer or weep. That was certainly Curt's voice showing through there, and Curt's words forcing their way through the saurian throat. "Venom—might kill me for his own reasons—but he would not—think me an—animal, Fischer. As you have. As you—have taunted me—again and again—even when in manshape—with being really the animal, and humanity—just a disguise. As you wear—yours, Fischer. Just—a disguise."

Fischer backed up a couple of feet more. The Lizard reached out claws to him. Fischer ducked back from them but didn't see until too late, and couldn't avoid, the huge sharp tail which came lancing around from the side and knocked the weapon out of his hands, smashing it against the wall. Immediately the horrible shrilling of the symbiote stopped, its many twisting strands fell back toward Brock's body and started to reunite, consolidating once again into the costume. Venom stirred, moaned.

"You're crazy!" Fischer screamed. "They're here to kill you!"

"They—made—no such attempt," the Lizard said, still advancing while Fischer backed away. "You, however—have made—your intentions plain." He glanced over his shoulder, saw Spider-Man getting to his feet again, saw Venom rolling over to get onto hands and knees. "You had better—get out—while there are still only—two of us, who are—prepared to deal with you humanely. The third—will not trouble—"

Venom staggered to his feet, threw a most bemused look at the Lizard, who returned it. Spider-Man swore he saw the two of them nod to each other. Then Venom turned his attention to Fischer. He opened his mouth and grinned with every fang. The symbiote's tongue flicked out.

Fischer turned and fled. Spider-Man, still weak, went after him. As he stumbled through the doorway, he saw Fischer slap a hand down on a control box in the next room, then throw himself out the door and go pounding down the stairs.

His spider-sense stung him hard, and he saw the glimmer of an LED in the next room, saying, 6... 5... 4...

"Get out," he yelled at the other two, "it's a bomb, come on!" Behind him Spider-Man got a confused image of movement, but he didn't linger to see who went where. In a situation like this it was every man, lizard, or symbiote/human team for him- or theirself. He dove out the door, the way Fischer had gone, and got the briefest glimpse of the man making quite literally for the tall timber, slipping through the trees.

Life went white. The blast caught Spidey in the back and threw him at the trees, but it propagated fast enough to catch the trees, too, and throw them out in front of him. He was dumped headfirst into a morass of moss, mud, and water, and the air whined above him as cypress wood and ripped-up orchids and pieces of prefab architecture went flying by at speeds which would normally have required filing a flight plan. The thunder of the explosion died away after a few seconds, and for the second time that day, it rained on Spider-Man. Not clean water, though, but mud and muck and leaves and more moss and slime and bugs and freshwater leeches, and finally some very surprised frogs.

After a few moments which he spent trying to sort out the ringing in his ears from the ringing silence that followed the explosion, Spider-Man staggered to his feet again and started back toward where the building had been. There was precious little of it left, or, for that matter, of the rest of the hammock in which it had been secreted. Where it had stood was mostly a large hole, rapidly filling with water.

He cursed silently. *The odds of a normal person surviving that— Except that none of us are all that normal.*

"Spider-Man," said a voice behind him.

He turned.

"Curt?"

The Lizard dropped his lower jaw in the closest approximation of a grin. "Not—for long," he said painfully. "This—won't last. A temporary effect. The last dose of serum—it was—" The Lizard fought with his breath for a moment, or perhaps with something else.

"Never mind," he said. "The hydrogel—helped a little to slow the release, but—still dosage problems—" He gasped. "Slipping now. Spider-Man—Martha, William."

"I'll take them a message," Spidey said.

"Tell them I—love them, but I—can't come home now. So close, I'm so close—just this lucid moment between states is—such a stride." He struggled for a few breaths during which nothing came out of his throat but growls, and Spider-Man wondered whether the Lizard would go for his throat again. But the Lizard shook his head, gathered his strength again. "But it won't last. There are—probably side effects from the—neural control chip they had implanted in me, when they—sent me out to make—distractions for thefts." He lifted the torn arm. "Atypical hyperstimulation and—paleotrophic myelin regeneration, I'd guess. A—good turn—they didn't mean to do. But it's a once-off effect. Will—have to reconstruct, now, do it all over. Tell them I can't come back. Not until I'm well—"

"Curt," Spider-Man said, "believe me. They wouldn't care whether you were well or not. Just go home. Let me help you—please."

The Lizard shook his head sadly, wearing an expression like a dinosaur contemplating extinction. "Home. Oh, I want to go home, and just be me, with them—"

His face twisted suddenly out of shape. The eyes went utterly saurian—but flickered back into human expression again. "Not much— time now," the Lizard said, infinitely sad. "I love them—oh, I love them. The most important thing. Never said it enough—now it seems like all I say, all I think, when I can speak—" The sheer pain in the voice choked it, turned it into a moan, then the moan turned into a roar—

Spider-Man ducked as the claw swiped out at him. When he straightened, all there was to be seen was a scaled, shining form, loping away into the paling night, under the declining moon. As it went, it roared, like a wounded thing, and there were tears in the roar.

Spidey stood still and watched him until he was out of sight, his eyes burning.

After a while he moved around the explosion site again and spent half an hour or so looking for any sign of Venom. There was none. *The symbiote is probably recovering from that sonic whammy,* Spider-Man thought. Venom was probably thrown in the other direction and decided to get out and recoup his strength somewhere quiet. *Until he can get at me later,* Spidey thought, *or the Lizard, or both of us.*

But he couldn't quite forget that strange look that Venom and the Lizard had exchanged: the "animal" and the "monster" sharing their humanity for a moment in the face of the inhuman human threatening them both.

Not a bad way to start the day, Spider-Man thought, and sighed. He made his way out past the shattered stumps of the cypresses, into the open Everglades, and looked east, where the false dawn was slowly becoming true. Then, under the mask, he acquired a slow smile, reached into the pouch under his costume, and pulled out his phone to make a call.

TWELVE

HE knocked on the door of the hotel room.

It opened. Vreni looked at him, and her eyes widened. She said, "Where have you been?! I've been calling your mobile, but you had it turned off—"

Peter handed her a yellow manila envelope and held up a finger. "Don't say anything," he said, "until you look at them."

Vreni shut her mouth, though plainly it was an effort. She sat down at the table by the window, opened the envelope, and her mouth opened again, and stayed that way, as she started going through the prints.

"My God," she said. "My *God*." And she turned over a couple more of them, and then stopped at the one which Peter considered the prize of the collection, the bomb going off in the Sound Suppression tank, water leaping in the air all over, while in the background Spider-Man looked down from high above, on the gantry. Vreni looked up at him and said, "How did you do this? Do you channel for Eastman's ghost or something? We've got to get these on the wire. Do you know how much the Associated Press is going to pay you for these? How did you *get* these?"

"That Questar," Peter said, in sincere misdirection, "is a terrific piece of equipment."

Vreni looked at him with an expression of profound skepticism. "All right," she said. "I won't ask you how you get these, if you won't ask me about the half-track in Bosnia."

"I thought it was an armored personnel carrier," Peter said.

Vreni snorted. "Never believe the first version of a story."

"So," Peter said, "where are you with yours? Did Kate like it?"

"Oh yes," Vreni said, and to Peter's astonishment, she looked sour. "She says she wants to send me to England, to look into the collapse of another merchant bank. Damn overseas assignments! I don't want foreign muck. I want to stay here and rake good old-fashioned star-spangled muck!"

"Yell at her," Peter said mildly. "She likes that."

"I know. Bad habit. She got it from Jameson." Vreni sighed then, and sat down a moment, starting to go through her purse, hunting something. "But we made good connections on this one. The German government has apparently started an inquiry of Gottschalk's bank. I finally caught up with him," she said. "Did I mention that?"

"Not since we talked last."

"Yes. Took me hours and hours to find him, but when we finally met, he seemed most eager to talk. Something to do with someone he'd seen before me. He wouldn't say who."

Peter raised his eyebrows. He had his own ideas about who that might be.

"Meanwhile, the feds are starting a RICO investigation of CCRC's doings down here," Vreni said.

"You don't look pleased."

"They should have done this on their own, six weeks ago," Vreni said, sounding disgusted, "after the New York craziness started to surface. What were they waiting for, an engraved invitation?" She came up with a soft-tip pen from her purse and started indicating crop marks at the edges of the photographs. "They'll go into more depth this time, or they'll look really stupid.

"But, my gosh," Vreni said, sounding more satisfied, "what a haul of stuff, down on the south coast. That ink! Do you know how much that stuff is worth? The story's a bombshell. Ripples are spreading all over, in Europe. Corruption in Brussels! Government collaboration with racketeering in Germany! It's a long way yet to the bottom of this can of worms." Her eyes shone.

"Wait a minute. Don't Brussels and Germany count as 'foreign muck'?"

"Well, yeah, but—" Vreni put aside a print and eyed the next one. "Anyway, the followups on this story alone are going to keep me busy for weeks. The boondoggling in NASA alone is worth a Sunday supplement." She glanced at him, amused. "Still no telling," she added, "what was going on with that reactor."

"Oh?"

Vreni shook her head. "Can't get a straight answer out of them at the moment. They're claiming that the rumors of difficulties with the security, and the supposed change of reactors, was all part of some kind of cover operation, meant to draw these terrorists who hit the place the other night out into the open. Naturally everybody's so horrified by what almost happened on the pad that no one's asking the hard questions. Give it a couple of weeks, though, and once everyone gets over being relieved for the astronauts' sake, the gloves will come off."

Peter nodded, wondering who had manufactured this particular story. He rather suspected that the change in names from CHERM to MPAPPS had had more to do with good old-fashioned misdirection, and a piece of vital "test material" going missing. He had not pressed Garrett very far on the subject, and he had an idea she wouldn't have told him if he had. "What about the Lizard angle?"

Vreni sighed. "We wasted so much time on that," she said. "I wish we hadn't bothered. What he was doing, involved in small-time thefts, I can't imagine. He seems to have vanished again, though. A blind alley. In retrospect, I wish we could have spent that time at Canaveral."

Good, Peter thought. *I'd rather leave Curt out of all of this and spare him—and Martha and William—the grief.*

She finished with the photos. "Well," Vreni said, "these are really nice. Should make you a tidy little fee from AP after the *Bugle* gets its cut. Nobody else has anything so immediate or detailed." She glanced sidewise at him. "Come on, let's get down to the bureau. Then—" She looked closely at him. "Look at those circles under your eyes! Haven't you been sleeping?"

"Well," he said, "last night was a little long."

"I know the feeling. Come on, let's go start getting you rich and me famous."

"Promises, promises."

"If promises are all that life offers you, kid," Vreni said as they headed out, "grab 'em and shake 'em till they squeak. They're better than nothing."

FAIRLY late that afternoon, as sunset was lengthening the shadows in the Connorses' back yard, a tall shape in red and blue swung down on a web from the nearest telephone pole and landed softly in the well-trampled grass. Quietly he slipped up to the patio doors and knocked.

A head poked around into the living room from the kitchen. "Spider-Man!"

"Hey, William! Is your mom around?"

"Yeah, come on in."

A few minutes later, Spidey was ensconced in the living room again. "No tea, Martha," he said, "thanks. It's a flying visit only."

"You mean swinging," William said, grinning.

Martha was wearing a smile for her guest, but it didn't quite reach her eyes. "You've seen Curt," she said.

"I've seen the Lizard," Spidey said, "and talked with him, yes."

"Talked with him?"

He told them the story, with some discreet editing. "He was very definite," Spider-Man said, "that his condition as the Lizard right now wasn't going to last; it was an accidental conjunction of temporary effects. When the Lizard appears again, it will just be the mindless beast again. But at the same time—he felt he was getting very close to the cure, closer than he'd ever been. He said he just couldn't come home until he was well. I don't think he believes it would be fair to you."

Martha looked at Spider-Man silently. "We don't care about fair," she said. "Either of us."

"I think he knows that. I know he knows you just want him home. In fact, I told him that. He said to tell you he loves you, he wants to be home with you, just as himself, but right now, he simply can't. He says he has to go back to the work."

Martha sighed and glanced at William, who was intently examining the carpet. "Where will he go now?" she said. "Did he say?" Spidey shook his head. "I have no idea. Martha, I have nothing concrete to base it on, but I get the feeling that Curt's involved in something much larger than the business of his own cure. I wouldn't know where to start looking, at the moment, but after I have a while to consider, I may be able to think of something. I'll let you know if I find out anything at all."

"You've already done a great deal for us," Martha said. "Don't let it interfere with your proper work."

"This *is* my proper work," Spidey said.

William glanced up at him then. His face was quite calm and composed, but his eyes were too bright and he sounded stuffed up when he spoke. "When he was human," William said, "how did he sound?"

Spider-Man thought of the voice that had so briefly forced its way through the Lizard's throat—dignified, powerful even in such tragic circumstances, and able to see something worthwhile even in Venom—and bent the truth ever so slightly. "He sounded just fine," he said. "Curt Connors is alive and well, never doubt it. And he'll be back."

He looked up to find Martha's eyes on him. They said, *Really?*

All he could do was nod and believe, with Martha and William, that it would be true.

THAT evening, Peter sat with MJ over the dinner table in his hotel, and listened to her bubble over. It was the best possible salve for his aches and pains, both mental and physical.

"So he offered me a hundred percent raise," MJ said.

"After you spent an hour and a half telling him off," Peter said, hunting around in his salad for the tomatoes. He always ate them first. "He must have been frightened for his life."

MJ chuckled. "Tiger, I think he was. From me, I mean, as opposed to those other people. I haven't blown up at anybody like that since—Wow, I don't know if I've ever blown up at anybody like that."

"All those years' worth of frustration at once. I'd pay money to see it."

"Be careful," MJ said, smiling sweetly, "or someday you may get a demonstration, free. I found it very liberating."

"I bet. So what about him, then?"

"Well, the cops and the Coast Guard picked up the people who'd made him set up the drop."

"So Murray told me," Peter said, "when I brought him his widget back."

"Yeah. Maurice told me later that he'd been having dealings with the smugglers on and off for a long time, under cover of the agency, and that he was tired of it but didn't dare stop. Now, though, he can take advantage of the city's witness protection plan. They'll get him out of the area and see him set up somewhere else in the country. He'll be okay. He was pretty grateful, actually."

"That's a relief. So where do you go next?"

"Nowhere." She smiled.

"Today was the last day?"

"Uh-huh. And then I'm going home with you—when was it the *Bugle* booked your flight for?"

"Tomorrow. They're pleased, apparently—Kate says she has something else in the pipeline she wants me to work on, which suits me fine. But MJ, if there's more work here for you, you should—"

"No. Honey, this is no kind of life, you running all over the landscape, and me doing the same, and us never being together. The agency down here will refer me to some of their correspondent agencies and former clients up in New York. We'll see what that brings. But I'd rather starve with you than make tons o' bucks without you."

"We might starve yet," Peter said. "Granted, these AP royalties are nice, and the next couple of months will be okay because of them. But later in the year—"

"Let's see what the future brings," MJ said. "Finish your salad. I want my main course, and the nice lady is waiting for you to stop fiddling. Are you ever going to eat those greens?"

Peter smiled and applied himself to what remained after the tomatoes were gone. After the waitress took their plates, he found MJ looking at him speculatively. "So what did he have to say for himself?" she said.

"Who?"

"That boy with the big teeth. You remember the one."

Peter raised his eyebrows. "He was argumentative," he said, "but we parted friends."

"Oh, I believe *that*!" A steak arrived, which MJ promptly started to demolish. "Tell me another."

Peter shrugged. "He didn't bother trying to kill me after Curt took off," he said, "so either he's decided to let me be for a while longer, or he got killed in that blast."

"I don't believe the second in the slightest," MJ said. "As for the first—I don't trust his reasons."

"I don't know if I trust them either," Peter said, "but I think Curt shamed him into it, somehow. It was an odd moment—but I'm glad I saw it."

"Question is," MJ said, "how long will it last?"

Peter shook his head, then reached out across the table to take her hand. "I don't know. And I have a feeling that whatever Curt's tangled up in is going to resurface eventually, more complicated than ever. But for the moment—"

"For the moment," MJ said, squeezing his hand, "you're here. And I'm here. And tomorrow, we're going to say bye-bye to Aunt Anna, and catch a plane and go home and get on with our lives in a place with lower humidity. And I will be blessedly relieved! Now eat your pasta before it gets cold, or MJ will be *very* cross."

Peter looked at her and made an eager face. "Promise?"

Her smile promised a whole lot more.

Peter ate his pasta.

ACKNOWLEDGEMENTS

MANY thanks to Jim Dumoulin of Kennedy Space Center, maintainer of the Center's home pages on the WorldWideWeb, for much useful information.

Thanks also to Paul McGrath for technical assistance, and to Peter Morwood for advice on militaria, and for secretarial and catering services.

THE VENOM FACTOR

Book Three
THE OCTOPUS AGENDA

Diane Duane

PROLOGUE

IT was 2:30 in the morning near Dolgeville, New York—which meant it was the middle of the night in the back end of nowhere, and Jim Heffernan was deadly bored.

Jim Heffernan was forty-five years old, not a tall man, yet a fairly cheerful one given the kind of life he'd lived so far. Everyone told him he looked like a pudgy version of Sam Neill, the actor. That was all very nice to hear, except that he would have much preferred to hear that he had Sam Neill's bank balance, pudgy or otherwise. He didn't let the discrepancy in their earnings bother him too much, though; it wouldn't really have helped if he did.

Jim had once been a miner. Most of the people around here had once been miners, or the wives and children of miners. That was when Jim was in his twenties, at a time when there had actually been another small town near Dolgeville, called Welleston after some Welles or other who had actually started up the coal-mining industry.

That had been a long time ago, near the end of the last century. The town and the industry had been very successful, and for many years the town's people had come to depend on "Welleston money" for their livelihoods. But things shifted. Things always shifted.

And that was why Welleston spent thirty years as a crumbling ghost town, and another thirty as the memory of a ghost town. And why Jim was now sitting in a tacky little box of a portable guardroom at 2:30 in the morning. Once again he was blinking in the harsh, faintly flickering glare of fluorescent light, trying to do a crossword puzzle that didn't interest him, trying to stay awake. Trying to be a security guard for something which was no longer a coal mine.

The room was just slightly larger than a walk-in closet. It had walls the color of adhesive tape, and no floor except the plain, poured-concrete base that it had been plumped down on. It was damp; even on a hot summer's night it was damp, and the screens on the window, though they looked effective, weren't quite fine-meshed enough, or well enough fitted to the windows, to keep out the blackflies. The insects happily descended on Jim as a kind of movable feast, and left itching red welts on any part of him that wasn't covered (as well as some that were). So, for most of the night, Jim tended to sit with the light turned off, to avoid attracting them. Should one or another of his bosses turn up (one of the rarest of occurrences, particularly after *they* had met the blackflies) his excuse came easily: having that fluorescent tube turned off helped his night-vision, and made it easier for him to see what was going on outside. Not that anything much ever *did* go on outside here, except for the sound of the occasional crazed moose or deer crashing through the woodland surrounding the place.

The quiet was endemic in Dolgeville and its environs. The township was a remote place, buried well away from any really big town. Nestled deep in the foothills at the southern end of the Adirondacks, it sat in an undulating landscape of granite-boned hills clothed in conifer and hardwood forest. Even when the coal mining had been at its height, very few people had ever come there except on business. Since that business had mostly involved coal in one form or another, society had been limited to those who dug the coal and their families, those who maintained or replaced the machinery for those who dug the coal, and those who came to truck the coal away. There had been a constant grubbiness about everything and everybody, a fine black dust that got under your nails and into your pores and into the grooves of your fingerprints. In those days, the whole world had looked the same: gray and dingy, with the exception of a brief period in autumn when the trees flamed through the coal dust and then dropped their leaves to stand bare and clean against a clear blue sky.

Now, at least, you were free of the coal dust, and you got to see the occasional unfamiliar face, especially with the new industry coming in. Jim Heffernan sighed. It was always the way: some big company got you and everybody in the area all excited, got the local government to put up money to help them move in—and then when they *did* move in, they always managed to claw back as much of that money as they could for themselves.

But at least he had this job; better than nothing, something to feed Flora and the kids, something to make him feel even a little bit useful. He was luckier than many who had been waiting for jobs and never got them.

Even if this job was, in essence, no more than watching a large hole in the ground to make sure nobody ran off with it in the night. *Yeah,* he thought, *and maybe someday I'll move up to watching the Brooklyn Bridge in case one of these super-criminals from the papers tries to steal it. Think big, fella.* He grunted with amusement at the thought, and turned his attention back to the crossword puzzle. Yet another desperate attempt to keep himself awake. He hated the night shift, but the night shift was what they had been hiring for, and there wasn't much he could do about it, not with the mortgage to take care of, and the kids needing new clothes for school in the fall. He stared at the much-corrected puzzle and tried to think.

Seven down, dockside security, six letters, ends with e-r.

"Hawser," he muttered, not exactly sure what a hawser was, but knowing it was something nautical. Except that, like most crossword answers, though the word fit seven down, it made nonsense of nine across. And, of course, he had left the crossword-puzzle dictionary that Flora had given him on the kitchen table at home.

Then he heard a soft, quick shuffling right outside. It was way too loud for blackflies.

Jim Heffernan froze for an instant. Then he quietly laid the puzzle book aside, reached out to snap off the light, and even more quietly undid the flap of his holster. He hadn't been issued an automatic pistol, but his big Ruger Security Six revolver held half a dozen very good arguments against any casual intruder doing something stupid. He sat very still for a few seconds, letting his eyes grow accustomed to the darkness and listening to a silence that wasn't so much a lack of sound as someone—or something—carefully making no noise.

"It's okay, Jim," came a voice from outside. "It's me."

Jim let out a breath he hadn't noticed he was holding, but didn't bother turning the light back on again. "You shouldn't sneak up on a guy like that, Harry!" he said. "What if I made a mistake one night?"

"You?" There was laughter like a rusty saw in a log as Jim stepped out through the door. In the light of a bright half-moon, he could see where Harry Pulaski, the other guard on this shift, was leaning against the wall of the guard hut. He was grinning. "We both know you'd sooner pick your nose with that cannon than fire it at anybody."

"Yeah, well." Jim hated guns. According to his supervisor, that made him one of the safest kinds of people to use them. He wasn't too sure about that. Being safe around yourself and your coworkers was one thing; being safe up against some young punk with state-of-the-art firepower and no scruples about using it was something else. "Quiet round?"

"What else?" Pulaski shrugged. "Still, it's an ill wind, ya know? I'm set to lose another two, three pounds this week walking around in this heat, if it keeps up."

The site lay spread out before them, monochrome in the moonlight. Not that there was much color about it even in full daylight. All but a few of the security lights had been turned out this late at night. Only the big floods around the graveled area where the heavy machinery was parked were still on.

Forty years ago this had been the biggest of several strip mines in the area, a huge concentric ulcer burrowing into the countryside, surrounded by heaps of spoil. Over the years since the supply of coal ran out and the mining company went out of business, the local county government had made several sporadic, halfhearted attempts to re-landscape the place, but Nature had proven more effective. Weeds and scrub plants that didn't mind the local coal-dust-laden soil had moved in and made a great green terraced garden of it, where at least the various wild grasses seemed to prosper.

Much of that green covering had been scraped away now as the digging started again. The site was easily half a mile from one rim of the hole to the other, with the guard hut perched high up on one side. Jim often wondered how quick their reaction was supposed to be, if something started happening clear across the crater. All around the edges of that crater were Detex watch clocks, and a rough, graveled road that would have served a better security purpose if the guards had some sort of vehicle. As it was, once every hour one or the other of them had to leave the relative comfort of the hut and walk around the site, swiping his electronic key card at each of the clocks—and, naturally, keeping an eye open for anything suspicious.

What they were watching most carefully was the wire fence around the facility, which had been cut months ago. Three heavy trucks and two wheeled diggers had been stolen from the vehicle park by the time the next guard made his round. Jim was grateful it had happened on his weekend off, because the guards on duty that night had been fired at once.

Pulaski yawned, stretched, then leaned back against the wall of the hut. "Almost makes you wish for the good old days, when there was nothing here but wilderness," he said.

"No jobs, either," said Jim sourly. "I like it just the way it is, thanks very much."

What had happened to the town was nearly miraculous. A company that specialized in manufacturing artificial composite "marble" and "granite" had come to survey the old mine site. They had been specifically looking for quartz. From what Jim could gather, they powdered it, mixed it with resins, then turned it out as slabs of high-quality fake Carrara marble for tiles and countertops. They had found a rich seam of the stuff running underneath the depleted coal veins, and it had looked like this would provide the town with at least some jobs. After years when up to eighty percent of the population had been out of work, it was better than nothing.

The company, Consolidated Quartzite, moved in, hired a couple of hundred local people as both full-time and part-time labor, and began clearing the site and sinking boreholes to find the best—and most economical—way of extracting the quartz. The process had gone on without much fanfare for several months, and the town began to take on a slight sparkle of life. People started to eat out more than they had for a long time, the bar began to fill up again in the evenings, they even began talking cautiously about a return of the good times. Or at least, as good as times were likely to get these days.

And then it happened. There was a morning when one of the Consolidated site engineers came running from the site up to the main office so fast that his helmet fell off halfway and he didn't even stop to pick it up and put it back on. And this was the man who chewed out at least three workers a day for similar infringements of the safety regulations. He shot into the site office like a rabbit down a burrow, dumped a pocketful of something indeterminate all over the table, grabbed the phone, and began babbling to someone at the head office in Nevada.

There were some abortive attempts to hush up what had happened, but in a small town on a worksite where everyone knew everyone else—

and more or less trusted everyone else as well—the truth came out fast enough. They had struck gold.

All over the world, gold and quartz are often found together—but no one had ever expected to find it *here*. Consolidated's chief geologist flew in from Nevada to look over the site for herself, and walked away shaking her head and muttering, "Anomalous, very anomalous."

But she had been smiling. Everyone was smiling. There had been the usual talk of how much fallout from this find—nobody was calling it a strike, at least not yet—would fall out onto the workers and the local economy, and for a change the result was better than anyone expected. To their credit, Consolidated took on as many more local employees to run the extraction machinery as they could. It was mostly heavy boring and digging equipment for which people had to be trained, and since they were paid while they were being trained, no one particularly minded. It was a skill that would be useful later.

In any case, by the time the quartz dust had settled, about a month after the initial find, many more people were employed, and nearly everyone was pleased. Except for the ones who had to stay up until 3:30 in the morning, or five or six, walking around a great big hole in the ground and hoping that no more machinery would go missing. Especially on their shift.

"I suppose I shouldn't complain," Pulaski said. "There's a lot of worse things we could be doing."

Jim rubbed his eyes. The brief adrenaline rush of Pulaski's arrival had worn off, and the night shift was beginning to weigh heavily again. His eyes felt grainy. "Right now, I can't think what. I'm going crazy just trying to stay awake." He knuckled his eyes again. "'Dockside security,' six letters, ends in e-r," he muttered.

"Hawser," said Pulaski at once.

"Won't fit." Jim glanced at him. "What *is* a hawser, anyway?"

"Dunno. Some sort of small boat, I think."

"Lot of help *you* are. I'm falling asleep here."

"You want to stay awake? Just start your round early."

Jim shook his head. "It'd show on the time clocks. And you know how they hate that. I could use a snack, though. Want a Three Musketeers?"

"No. I'm trying to knock the sweet stuff. The wife says she likes how I'm losing weight."

Jim laughed, barely more than an intake of breath. He had been walking around this site just as long as Pulaski, and was beginning to doubt *he* would ever lose weight by any means short of industrial-level liposuction. He gazed thoughtfully down toward the center of the site and the deepest of the boreholes sunk so far. "I heard they got half a ton of 'reef' out of that last week," he said.

"I heard it too." Pulaski frowned slightly. "Thing is, the more of the gold-bearing ore they pull out of there, the less they're talking about how much it is, or how rich it is, or how much more might be left. Guys coming off the dig have to change their work clothes, get searched as they come out. It's getting to be like those big mines in South Africa."

"I thought those were diamond mines," said Jim.

"Gold too. I read all about them once. All the ways you can sneak gold out."

"I can guess—and no, I don't want to know. But I wonder what else they might turn up. What else they're not expecting. I mean, in all the years of digging coal, nobody knew there was gold underneath it."

"Not diamonds. It's the wrong sort of ground. You need some sort of blue clay for diamonds."

"Maybe in South Africa you need blue clay. In upstate New York," Jim shrugged again, "who knows?"

They looked out across the silent site. It was surrounded by forest, pine, and mixed hardwoods, and somewhere off among the trees some nightbird was singing. "I hear that every night," said Pulaski. "What is it?"

"Nightingale."

"Here? I didn't know we had those here." They fell silent again, listening to the distant trickle of birdsong, sweet and faintly mournful.

As if in answer came another sound, a quick, sharp crack as though someone had stepped on a twig. But much louder, and somehow more metallic as well. The two security guards looked at each other; the most common source of that particular noise was a car engine cooling after the long haul from town back up to the mine. But neither of them had been down to the all-night doughnut place tonight.

The sound had come from off to their left, behind the guard hut, and Jim's right hand slipped inside the still-open flap of his holster. He didn't draw the heavy revolver, not yet, but even for a man who didn't like guns, the cold wood and metal of the Ruger's grip was sometimes very comforting. Times like now. Pulaski looked at him, then reached for his own gun.

"Come on," Jim said, and stepped softly around the corner.

Behind the guard hut, just at the edge of the site, was a little parking lot. During the day it was used by some of the site crews; at night, it was mostly empty. Jim's car was there; so was Pulaski's.

And a bunch of aliens were standing there as well.

All of them were dressed in close-fitting black, with heads too big for their bodies and huge-lensed eyes that Jim hoped were just some sort of goggles. They looked like the meaner, bigger brothers of those skinny little aliens that turned up on TV specials about government-concealed UFO landings.

Pulaski brought up his gun at once, but before he could squeeze the trigger, a black-clad arm chopped down on his wrist and the pistol clattered onto the gravel. There was another flurry of movement and then a meaty thud as one of the aliens stepped forward and slammed a gun butt hard against his head. Pulaski grunted, slumped, and followed his revolver to the ground.

Other dark hands seized Jim Heffernan, peeled his fingers from the undrawn Ruger, and jerked it from the holster, then shoved him down onto his knees. Several weapons were already leveled at him, and he guessed that whoever—or whatever—had grabbed him was already off to one side to give a clear field of fire, if he gave them reason to shoot. Jim froze, and hoped that would be enough.

One of the creatures held something that might have been the source of the crackling sound. It looked vaguely like a rifle or a submachine gun, but there was a dully glowing strip down one side of its barrel, which made a faint humming noise. The noise was building. Then he heard the sharp metallic crack again, and a little line of fire flared and died among the weeds at the edge of the parking lot. It was plainly meant as a warning, and Jim took note.

Yet when he whispered, "Harry?" the next warning was both more direct and far less unearthly: a boot rammed hard into his ribs. More of the dark shapes gathered around him as he bent over, wheezed, and sucked for air.

Jim Heffernan had done his military service in Southeast Asia and West Germany; even though he didn't like guns, he could recognize, or at least guess at, most of them. But some of the weapons these fellows carried, like the one fired as a warning, were like nothing he had ever seen before.

A vehicle came rolling into the parking lot. There was no sound of an engine; Jim only knew of its arrival from the sound of gravel crunching beneath its tires. It showed no lights, and even the moonlight reflected only dimly from its black surface. Approximately the size and shape of a big three-axle truck, it had no windows, not even a windshield. The front was a smooth, unbroken surface, and there seemed to be no doors, either, until it stopped and an oval section swung up and away from the thing's dark hide.

Out of the darkness within the black truck stepped a shape that made Jim Heffernan's stomach twist within him, a shape from a childhood nightmare.

Years ago, when he was just a kid, he had been exploring through the woods near his home and had found a dead squirrel. He had known it was dead from the smell, if nothing else. But the squirrel had been moving. When he looked closer, he found that its body was alive with maggots, literally heaving with them. The sight had made him throw up his lunch, and ever afterward, something moving in a way that eyes and sense and reason said was *wrong* had always produced the same gut-clench reaction.

He felt that reaction now.

A man had climbed from the truck; a big man, broad across the shoulders and heavy through the waist, looking not fat but massive. But something else came out with him. At first it looked as though he was carrying two armfuls of wide-bore tubing, but then, as Jim watched with increasing horror, he realized that the tubes weren't tubes at all. They were arms.

No. They were tentacles, and they writhed and squirmed as if each one had a life all of its own, rearing into the air or coiling back down again, like snakes, huge pythons like the ones Jim had once seen in the zoo, unwilling to bite the person they were constricting. Unlike the dark metal of the truck and the black clothing of the alien figures, these shone in the moonlight with the unmistakable gleam of polished steel.

Jim stared, swallowing hard to prevent himself from throwing up again. He had a feeling that retching would be regarded as an insult, and that this weird, ominous creature was not one to take insults kindly. All he could find to say was, "Please, Mister—don't hurt him. He's got kids."

The aliens moved away, and it was extraordinary how perceptions could change in the space of a few seconds; now Jim saw that they were no more than people in funny costumes, not frightening at all. Not when compared to something *really* frightening, like the broad man-shape stalking toward him, framed by the writhing silhouettes of its tentacles.

"Ah, the human condition," it said in a deep, dark voice. "Easily remedied, fortunately." Jim gulped. He didn't know what that meant, just that he didn't like the sound of it. "Secure him," said the dark voice. "And his friend with the children."

It was done quickly and effectively, not with ropes, but with the plastic binders favored by many police departments instead of handcuffs.

"Now tell me," said the man with the arms, leaning a little closer, "that new borehole at the center of the site is recently dug, is it not?"

"Yessir," Jim said. "They sank it just two days ago."

"And what security arrangements are there for that hole?"

Jim blinked and licked dry lips. If he told what he knew, he would get fired. But if he didn't tell—he risked a glance at the slowly writhing tentacles—his employment would be terminated in a far more permanent way. Getting fired was preferable. He could always get another job.

"There's a team of two down there. They make their rounds every half hour."

"Correct," said the man with the arms, gazing down at Jim through a pair of spectacles that were halfway between sunglasses and goggles. "Very wise of you not to attempt some sort of foolish deception. Alert Team Two. Have them secure the area." One of the black-clad men turned and darted off into the truck.

"And as for you," he continued to Jim. "To ensure your continued cooperation, you and your friend the family man will accompany us. Bring them."

The black-clad men didn't use their truck to negotiate the network of access roads that coiled and switch-backed along the terraces of the old strip mine. Instead, the group standing around Jim—presumably Team One—grabbed him and went scrambling on foot straight down the walls of the crater.

If Jim had been scared of the unknown, in the shape of the stranger with the tentacles, he was even more scared of something he knew all too well. Those terraces, sixty and even seventy degrees from the horizontal, had been exposed and weathering for years. The rock was friable—crumbling like old, stale pound cake, likely to give underfoot without warning and send any careless climber down to the borehole at the bottom a good deal faster than intended.

He had no choice in the matter. He was grabbed by the arms and hustled down between two of the men like no more than a piece of awkward luggage. For themselves, they moved with a sureness that suggested the function of their bug-eyed goggles, able to see every stone and crevice even with only moonlight and sky glow to work by.

By the time they were halfway down, Jim was past caring about who could see what, and how well. He could see just enough to know he didn't want to see any more, and for the rest of the descent he kept his eyes shut tight, not opening them until an end to the jolting meant an end to the climb.

They had made it to the center borehole in a matter of minutes, but Team Two had been there before them. The other two security guards had been dealt with as efficiently as Heffernan and Pulaski. Even though Hank Sullivan was unconscious, a lump the size of an egg plainly visible above his left ear, both he and Tom Schultz were propped against the wall of the lowest terrace with binders tight around their wrists and ankles. From the lack of gunshots, alarms, or even extra lights, neither had been able to do anything about it.

One of the dark-clad men approached the bulky figure with the tentacles and ducked his head in a little gesture that was half bow and half salute. "We're secure."

"Phone lines?"

"Cut, sir. We took them out before moving in, and the Detex time clocks are receiving a dummy signal from one of the portable computers."

"Very well. Let's get on. I have no wish to be here all night."

Bound as he was, there was little Jim could do after that except sit where he had been dropped like so much garbage, and watch—without trying to *look* as if he was watching. He was the only one. Pulaski and Sullivan were still out cold, and Schultz had slumped forward, head leaning against his knees. He looked like a man trying to pretend all this wasn't happening, as if by ignoring what was going on around him, it would all somehow go away. Jim knew how he felt. But when all this was over, and assuming they survived it, then the police or even the FBI would want detailed explanations and accurate descriptions. He was going to do his best to provide whatever they required.

Several of the black-clad men busied themselves around the drilling machinery for the new borehole, with a speed and precision that spoke either of considerable prior experience or equally considerable recent training. Firing up the big gasoline engine that powered its winch, they began raising the drill up and out of the shaft until at last the carborundum-diamond drill bit itself rose from the hole. It was unlatched and swung clear, the engine shut down again; and after that, they waited.

A few minutes later another group came down the terraces, moving with the same ease as the team that had carried Heffernan and Pulaski. This new group was carrying something else: a long metal cylinder, and for all that it seemed both heavy and clumsy, the team moved in a perfect unison that was almost graceful. They too had evidently practiced before going into action, so that now what they were doing looked easy.

It couldn't have been as easy as all that. When they finally came level with the boring machinery, tilted the cylinder upright, and lowered one end to the ground not too far from where Jim was sitting, he could hear and feel the ponderous thud of something far more massive than it looked. The careful way they handled it suggested something else as well: that it was dangerous in a way far beyond mere weight.

The man with the tentacles strode over to it and raised one of his real arms to touch it in a strange gesture that was almost affectionate, the way one might stroke a pet or pat the trunk of a familiar tree. One or two of the metal arms curved around to touch the cylinder, as if recognizing some odd kinship. Then the man said, "Carry on."

The lifting gear that had withdrawn the bore and its bit was now attached to linkages recessed into the shell of the cylinder; then the engine coughed into life once more, taking up the slack, and the cylinder was raised, swung into place, and slowly lowered into the waiting borehole. Jim, still making sure that his watching wasn't obvious, couldn't help but be impressed at how exactly the cylinder fitted. Someone knew exactly what equipment was being used here, even down to the width of the bore sampler—and that could change from day to day.

But what *was* that thing…?

As the cylinder dropped out of sight, he was reminded of a huge cartridge being loaded into a massive gun. For a long time after it vanished, the cables supporting it kept unrolling from their drums. He had known in a general way how deep this bore was. Two miles, someone had said once. But until you actually watched how much cable two miles really was, and how long it took to feed that huge length down into the ground, the words had no real meaning.

The bits and the samplers were always hot when they came back up, sometimes too hot to touch. That was what one of the engineers had told him. The heat wasn't just from the friction of drilling, but from the massive heat and pressure of the earth itself two-plus miles down.

One of the pieces of machinery made an odd gulping sound, and Jim looked up. There was no reading of expressions through their hoods and goggles, but there was suddenly an air of expectation in the group.

"Well?" said the man with the tentacles.

"She's hit bottom," replied the team member who had been operating the crane.

"Then check the transmitter."

Another one of the team took an object from his belt. It was oblong, with a short antenna at one end, and looked as much like a walkie-talkie or even a cell phone as anything else. He studied it, adjusted a couple of controls, then nodded. "We've got a good signal. Five by five. Heat's no problem."

"Then our work here is done. Drop as many cores as you can into the shaft, and let's be away."

The group of black-clad men, no longer separate teams but a single unit of about fifteen, swiftly set to work. They gathered the thirty or so drilled-out core samples that had been placed near the borehole and began feeding them back down the shaft, one after another. The first half-dozen were reassembled into their original carriers and lowered with almost as much care as the cylinder itself, but after that the cores were simply rolled or carried to the top of the shaft and dropped inside.

Even when every sample around the site had been disposed of, the shaft was nowhere near filled to the top. It would take a lot more than that to completely fill a hole two miles deep. But getting at the cylinder was no longer a simple matter of reversing the winch and pulling it out, not with the better part of two tons of rock plugging the exit.

The man with the tentacles clapped his real hands together, an expression both of satisfaction and completion. "Let's be away."

Most of his various teams faded at once into the shadows, but a couple of them remained with their leader as he came over to Jim and the others. "You gentlemen will forgive me if I don't give you a ride," he said. "But we have miles to go before we sleep."

Jim was cold, he ached, and this guy, though still horribly frightening, had proved himself human enough to get on his nerves. "Any promises to keep?" he asked.

The man with the tentacles smiled at him, a smile Jim Heffernan didn't want to see again for the rest of his life, but he refused to flinch or look away. If this character was going to kill him, or have him killed, then nothing he could say or do would prevent that.

"Some say humor is the greatest gift," the man said, mockery edging that dark voice. "I have little time for it myself, and even less interest in gifts. I am more concerned with what I can take. Nonetheless, gallows humor can be appreciated. If I were you, I would not linger here."

He and his remaining followers vanished into the dark.

Jim waited a long time before he dared to move, and then every movement was an agony of cramp, or cold, or cut-off circulation from the tightness of the binder on his wrists. A voice in his brain yelled at him: *Run from here, run as far and as fast as you can!* A feeling of dread rose from him like a fog—or like the wisp of smoke curling out of a gun barrel—from that dark and silent hole in the ground. But he wasn't about to leave his friends and watchmates behind. No, not even if Hank *had* Krazy-Glued his lunch box shut last week....

But he still managed to function. He concentrated first on getting himself as loose as he could. The damn plastic binders were still very tight, but he managed—with some wriggling and a pain that made him think he'd possibly dislocated his wrist or one of the little bones in the hand—to get his crossed arms under his butt, and then, more slowly, to fold his legs tight enough to get them through the looped arms as well. This involved much squirming, pushing off one shoe so he could fit the foot through, and bracing the other foot against Hank, who was convenient and (at the moment) not terribly conscious. After that, when he could get to his feet again, it was just a matter of hopping around a little to get the other shoe back on, and then finding something sharp.

Fortunately, sharp things were not in short supply around this particular building site. The men in black had left the carborundum-tipped drill bit lying with its end accessible, shoved against a wall, but not flush against it. The disk-shaped digging end of the bit had two sets of blades: the outer set consisting of small plates of industrial diamond and carborundum set alternately in a herringbone pattern right around the face of the bit. Jim picked one blade of the herringbone and started sawing away at the plastic restrainer with it.

It took a long time. Jim hated the sight of his own blood, but he saw a fair amount of it before he was finished. Fortunately he knew well enough where the big veins and arteries were—the mandatory employees' first-aid course had been pretty specific about that—and he was careful to miss them. But the palm and heel of his right hand would probably bear the marks for a long time. At first, his hands were so numb from the constriction of the plastic restrainer that they couldn't feel what was happening to them. Unfortunately, a minute or three after he got the binders off, they began shrieking at him that they hadn't had enough blood or oxygen for a long time, and were now going to repay him for the favor by letting him acutely feel every injury that had ever happened to them, with special attention to the ones he had just incurred.

Jim swore, and ignored the pain the best he could, and clumsily used his hands to sit Harry up and shake him a little. "You okay? Say something!"

Harry said something, all right: words that would have made Flora mutter something about being a bad example to the kids. Then Harry added, "I was feeling better until you started shaking my head back and forth. Cut it out!"

"All right. Can you get up? We've gotta get out of here. I haven't got my Swiss army knife with me. Go on over to the bit and cut those off you. Tom?"

Tom was still unconscious. "We're gonna have to carry him out," Jim said, "and I don't like the look of that head. We're gonna have to be real careful with him. I wish we had a backboard or something."

"There's a piece of plywood over here," Harry said, sawing away at his binders with the herringbone blade. "I guess we could use that—"

"Okay. Get it. Hank—"

Hank sat there, shivering. When Jim came to him, he said, "They said they were gonna burn me. They said they were gonna burn me, I couldn't do anything else!"

"Of course you couldn't do anything else," Jim said, furious that "they" should so casually reduce a nice, kind man to this trembling shape. *Bastards! Let me catch you sometime without your fancy guns....* "Forget it, Hank. Except for the boss, no one's going to talk to you about this—we're gonna see to it. All right? Now get up and get over there and get loose so you can help us with Tom."

Harry got himself cut free and went over to get the "backboard" while Jim helped get Hank free. Then carefully, the way they had been trained, they lifted Tom onto the piece of plywood. "Pity we can't go up as fast as they came down," Jim muttered.

"No, thanks," Hank said. "I saw you guys come down, after the first batch jumped us. Damn near gave me a heart attack."

"Well, don't have one now, for God's sake," Jim said. "What time is it?"

Harry looked at the sky. "Near enough to dawn—" He glanced at his watch. "Damn thing's not going," he said. "Yours going?"

Jim and Hank looked at their watches. Both of them were stopped as well. "Like something out of a movie," Jim said morosely. "Guys dressed like aliens.... Never mind, let's get going. He needs a doctor."

They walked up the switchback road as fast as they dared. It was not fast enough for Jim. He couldn't get rid of the idea that, down in the crater, something very bad was going to happen. And about halfway up the road, halfway up the terraces, the feeling grew stronger than before. "C'mon," he said to the others, "we've gotta hurry, let's *hurry!*"

To his great relief, none of them asked, "Why?" Hank and Harry saw him look over his shoulder, and they looked too—and they hurried. Tom, lying on his back with their jackets wadded on either side of his head to hold it still, never moved, only moaned a little every now and then. Jim hoped he wouldn't wake up just now. He was likely to slow them down, and if there was one thing Jim was sure about right now, it was that it would be very bad if they slowed down.

He could barely believe it when they actually came out at the top of the switchback road onto the ring road that led around the site.

"They've killed the phones," said Jim, "but there's that cell phone in the office. I don't think they got that. Come on."

As quickly as they dared, and making better speed now that they weren't climbing, they made their way around the ring road to the little security hut near where the chain-link fence and the gate met the road. There was no point trying to bring Tom into the hut; he was just as well left outside. Carefully, in the slowly growing light, they put him down on the ground, and Jim ran in to get the cell phone.

As he came out again he hurriedly dialed the emergency day-or-night number for the district Consolidated office in New York. A somewhat bored voice said, "Consolidated security…"

"Jeff? It's Jim Heffernan. Listen, there's been a break-in at the site." He looked out across the diggings in dawn's early light, wondering at how peaceful it seemed now after all the madness of the night.

"Break-in? Who was it?"

"A bunch of guys dressed in black like commandos or ninjas or something—and one guy who was really strange. This is gonna need a major debrief, Jeff, and we need a doctor right now for Tom. One of these guys hit him hard with a gun, and he's been unconscious for half an hour at least. These guys were fooling around with the new bore, Jeff, the deep one."

"All right, all right, listen. Let me get Ralph Molinari on the line, he's the one you want to talk to about this kind of thing. You tell him everything that's happened, and—"

Fizz. And a dead phone.

Jim, looking out over the site, saw it happen: something he thought he had seen films of, and more recently, videotape of, in the South Pacific, when people who should have known better were playing with their toys. He felt it, too—the ground booming and jumping under his feet as if a giant had kicked it, the ground rippling like a liquid thing. He saw the top of the wave, where it touched the surface of the earth, radiate outward like the ripple from a stone chucked into a pool, watched the ripple travel, the dust puffing up behind it. And then as the shock wave passed them by, making the ground right under them jump again, he saw the whole site sag. The crater subsided into itself as if half the stone and gravel and dirt in it were suddenly pulverized finer than they had been before, settling deeper, sagging down, subsiding into a shallow, churned-up crater. Dust arose and blew gently off to one side. Jim found himself desperately grateful that the dust wasn't blowing toward them.

Jim shook the cell phone again, half hoping that it would come back to life, but it wouldn't. It was dead—and why wouldn't it be, this close to an electromagnetic pulse? He doubted it would ever work again.

"Not my hundred fifty bucks, anyway," he said softly and put it in his pocket. Then he went over to one of the logs that separated the parking lot from the site proper and sat down on it.

Hank and Harry joined him. They sat there quietly, the three of them, for what seemed like a long while, none of them saying out loud what they were thinking. Jim thought he knew what those thoughts were. *If that was what I think it was, were we far enough away? Are we going to be alive in five years, or ten? I don't feel any burns—but then early on, you wouldn't....*

It took about twenty minutes for the police and the ambulance to get there, called by the New York office. One of the cops was Rod Cummings, who Jim knew fairly well. They drank and played pool together down at Bob's Bar in town. Rod looked down at the hole and said, "Dear God on a moped."

"Yeah," said Jim.

The ambulance people got busy with Tom. As they carried him away. Rod said very softly, "CalTech called the station and the state emergency services. Asked whether there had been an earthquake."

"Nope," Jim said. "Nothing like that. A disaster, though...." He couldn't get rid of the image of that stocky shape with the metallic arms, looking down at Harry as if from a great distance, and saying, "*Ah, the human condition. Easily remedied, fortunately.*"

Jim shook all over as he watched the paramedics put Tom into the ambulance, on a real backboard this time. "He'll be okay, won't he?"

"I think so. The question is," and Rod looked down at the crater, from which vague plumes of dust still very gently rose, "will we?"

ONE

"PETEY?"

"Hmmm?"

"Where's the hand cream?"

Peter Parker was in his apartment in New York. It was one of many things for which, at the moment, he gave thanks. He was in the tub, up to his nose in suds. He lay there staring at the ceiling, and considered briefly that it was going to need repainting again soon; the dampness was making the paint over the tub bubble.

"Which hand cream specifically?" Peter said after a moment.

Mary Jane Watson-Parker, resplendent in a calico cotton bathrobe with a torn pocket, put her head around the bathroom door, looking vaguely worried. "It's the apple one, with the cuticle stuff."

"What's the bottle look like?"

"It wasn't a bottle. It was a kind of little bucket."

Peter sighed. A week ago, he had been washing Everglades muck out of his Spider-Man costume, thinking that if he could just get back to New York, he'd never complain about anything again. *How quickly things can change,* he thought, and said aloud, "A little bucket…"

"It had a design on the top," MJ said. "A little apple."

Peter closed his eyes, thought for a moment. The house had been filling with peculiar cosmetics recently, but he really couldn't complain about that, as it meant that his wife was working, rather than merely making herself more attractive than she already was—a tough job, if you asked him. "Bucket," he said, and opened his eyes. "Kind of a little tub thing? Okay. In the kitchen, on the counter by the dishwasher, there are about six pots and tubs and so forth there. All the little short squat ones were there."

"I looked," MJ said fretfully. "It's not there."

Peter closed his eyes again, trying to see where he had last seen the thing. "Not there, huh? Okay. Try on top of the refrigerator."

"The refrigerator? Why would I put anything there?"

Peter restrained himself from suggesting numerous possibilities. "Just go look."

A brief silence ensued. A moment later, MJ reappeared, smiling a little sheepishly, with a pot of hand cream in one hand. "It was behind the Rice Krispies," she said.

"Yeah, I thought I saw you use it first thing this morning," said Peter.

He sank back into the bubbles, and MJ smiled at him, less sheepishly this time. "You're being awfully good about all this."

"It's money," he said, smiling back. "Why not?"

She went off, probably to do something about her cuticles. MJ's hands had become more than usually useful in the week since they had come home from Florida. In a way, Peter regretted it. He had half hoped they would have at least a week or so to themselves to sit quietly, not doing any more work than they had to, and trying to recover a little from the rather frenetic period of heat, humidity, and super heroing without skyscrapers. But it seemed that fate had intended otherwise.

It had been a lively time. Work had taken them down there initially. First MJ's intention to hunt for more modeling work in the Miami area with one of the new PR or modeling agencies relocating down that way, and then, on Peter's end, when he was sent down by the *Daily Bugle* to help investigate some strange goings-on at Cape Canaveral, things that wound up involving not only his old acquaintance the Lizard, but Venom as well. That business was now cleared up, or as much as it was going to be anytime soon. The Lizard had vanished again; Venom had taken himself away with what Peter knew he would consider "unfinished business"— namely the killing of Spider-Man—still incomplete. *But even Venom,* Peter thought, *must want a few days off every now and then....*

While Peter, as Spider-Man, had been swinging all over the countryside—a matter not made simpler by the generally low-lying quality of Floridian flora, and the fact that only in Miami proper were there skyscrapers worthy of the name—MJ had been modeling away at her best speed. She had been working, among other things, on magazine shoots and some other light photographic work. She had also been indulging in her usual fairly frenetic networking—it would not have been MJ's style to ignore the possibility of future work, even though she was presently working her butt off. Between work sessions in a bar in South Beach, she had met, completely by chance, another model who knew someone who knew someone in New York who needed a hand model.

Peter had blinked at her when she told him about this the first time. "You mean to tell me," he'd said, "that there are actually people who just show their hands and nothing else?"

"Sure," MJ said. "You see them on TV. I bet you've just never thought about it before. Commercials for jewelry and softer-than-soft dishwashing liquid and hand creams and rubber gloves—things like that. It's all hand models."

They had been sitting in a restaurant at the time. MJ had been admiring her nails in a general sort of way. "Mikey—he's the underwear model I was telling you about—Mikey said that it's really hard to find a hand model without any wrinkles or spots at my age, the way the ozone layer's been changing the past ten years. It seems everyone suddenly has freckles and stuff. Whereas I"—and she glanced again at one hand in bemusement—"I just don't seem to have had that problem."

"That," Peter said, "is because you always keep your hands in your pockets. Most unladylike."

"Yeah." She giggled. "That's what they all said when I was growing up. If I'd known then that I could get a thousand bucks a day for it, I'd have ignored them even harder than I did."

"A *thousand*—! You're kidding, right?"

She shook her head. "If you can find the work," MJ said. "It's very specialized, and there just aren't that many people who can do it—whose hands still look perfect up close to the hot lights and the big sensitive camera lenses. Once you start doing it"—she smiled; it was a slightly feral look—"they tend to keep you on, and they tend to give you as much more of that kind of work as you can take."

"A thousand bucks a day. I think you can probably take a fair amount of it."

Peter sighed at the memory and blew out so big a breath that bubbles blew off the top layer of suds. From the next room came the sound of a cheerful woman la-laing to herself as she rubbed cream into her hands. Peter had to be amused by it. Normally MJ couldn't have cared less about her hands, at least in terms of doing anything to them in the course of a day. But the photographer on the shoot she was presently working had yelled at her that she needed to be "moister," and after some confusion on all sides, it was discovered that he meant he wanted her to use more moisturizer. So she had begun doing so, and had started meeting a couple of other hand models whom the director of the present project suggested she have a chat with. Suddenly, on their advice, the house had begun filling up with—Peter rolled his eyes a little, in amusement—tubs and pots and bottles and heaven only knew what else.

Still, the timing suited him. Peter had made a fair pile of money from the pictures he took of Spider-Man in the attack on the Space Shuttle at the Cape, and the resolution of that attack. The picture that had caught the bomb going off after it had been dropped into the flame-suppression tank at the bottom of the Shuttle launch facility had made the front page of the *Bugle,* much to his delight, and he had picked up a bonus for it. But that bonus and the money from the AP wire wouldn't last him forever. MJ had satisfied herself that the Miami modeling scene wasn't everything it was cracked up to be in terms of steady work, so, happily enough, they had come home again when both their assignments were done—only to find that instead of having a few days to call their own, MJ had to go straight out and spend ten to twelve hours a day with her hands artistically decked in what the ad described as "Ever-Lovin' Bubbles." It was just dishwashing detergent, which Peter found it beyond his ability to love even temporarily, let alone forever. But at a thousand bucks a day....

He felt around under the water for the soap. Things could have been a lot worse. They *had* been a lot worse, but after this last stint of work, each of them had managed to contribute enough money to the household kitty to get the credit cards paid down—at least to the point where they could use them—and to put a small but reassuring lump into their joint savings account. It was a little bit weird, actually, to feel somewhat secure, to feel that for the next little while, they didn't have to scramble desperately just to keep groceries in the kitchen and the landlord happy.

Peter looked forward to spending the next few weeks doing assignment work at the *Bugle* again, and having the leisure, as Spider-Man, to web-swing normally again, among proper tall buildings placed close together, in a city where he knew his way around, and in a place where you could be fairly sure that if you hit the ground suddenly, you wouldn't be on top of an alligator. He had found Florida pleasant enough for a short visit, but it was a little too flat for his taste, and there were things living in the wet part of the flatness that considered human beings, Spider-Man and others, to be perfectly acceptable hors d'oeuvres.

He heard the front door *clunk* and glanced up at the clock on the top shelf above the towels. Nine-thirty: MJ was going down to get the mail. Peter lay back in the tub again, gazed up at the ceiling, and thought, *We could try a new color in here next time. That beige is really beginning to look like masking tape.*

After a few minutes the door went *clunk* again, and he heard the jingle as MJ chucked her keys onto the telephone table. "Anything interesting?" he said.

"Mmnh," she said, going through whatever she was carrying as she came toward the bathroom. "Junk mail, junk mail, restaurant menu…"

"Which restaurant?"

"Uh." A pause; she appeared in the bathroom door in jeans and T-shirt. "The Blarney Rock."

"That's a restaurant? I thought it was a bar."

"The bar's opened a restaurant. Real Irish food."

Peter made a bemused expression. "Corned beef and cabbage?"

"Nope, it says specifically they don't do that. 'Boxty'—" She furrowed her brow. "What's that? For that matter, what's 'champ'? Or 'colcannon'?"

"You've got me. Maybe they're taking big old guns away from terrorists and cooking them?"

"Best use for them, maybe. Don't think I need that much fiber in my diet, though." She put the menu aside for later perusal. "Junk mail, junk mail, you may already have won…"

"Oh, sure," said Peter. "What's the prize in this one?"

"A trip to Miami, if you go see one of their condos."

"Too humid this time of year," Peter said. "Too many super villains."

"Yeah." MJ continued going through the pile. "Junk mail, junk mail, I can't believe trees are dying for this. Oh—phone bill. Two of them."

"Two? I thought we paid the phone bill last week."

"No, these are for the cell phones." MJ smiled as she opened the first one. She had bought a matching set of cell phones for the pair of them in Florida. Each had approximately a hundred functions, only two or three of which Peter understood. He had found that his phone was one of those instruments of the technological age that was actively dangerous if you didn't know how to work it. And he was embarrassed to find that—while he could manipulate cameras and web shooters and spider-tracers with the greatest of ease—he could not for the life of him get the hang of the cell phone. Once he had tried to use the phone's "number scratch pad," and had wound up destroying its entire "address book," which had taken him hours to install. Since then, Peter had resolutely refused to touch any buttons on the thing except for the dial pad and the "accept" or "hang up" buttons.

MJ unfolded the first bill. "I've used mine about five times this month," she said, "and you've used yours maybe three times, if I'm any judge."

"I called the weather once," Peter said, "and once I called for a pizza. Everything else was incoming."

She smiled, then took a look at the bill. Her mouth actually fell open, assuming the position at which Aunt May used to warn Peter, "You'd better shut that or a fly will get in."

"What the heck—?" She said it in a tone of voice that suggested that "heck" was not the word she really wanted to use.

"What's the matter?"

"They've given us somebody else's bill," she said and walked over to the tub, holding the bill between thumb and forefinger as if it were a recently deceased rat. "Look for yourself."

He looked. The first thought Peter had about the bill was, *That's a bit long, isn't it?* There were several pages to it. The second thought he had was on looking at the total at the top of the first page, "balance payable," it said, "$4,689.72."

Four thousand...

Peter looked at MJ in total bewilderment. "They've made a mistake," he said. "It can't be your bill. What's the other one say?"

"Hm—" She reached for the other envelope, which she had stuck up on the towel shelf with everything but the junk mail she hadn't yet thrown away. She ripped it open, unfolded it. "Twenty-three dollars and eighty cents. Twenty of that is just the rental for the number—"

They both looked at the other bill. "Four *thousand*—! It's just a mistake," MJ said, riffling through the six or seven attached pages, all covered with very small print. "CellTech's computer must have had a fit or something, that's all. They can't make me pay this. I didn't make any of these calls. There's not a single number I recognize."

Peter twitched a little, under the suds. "Some of these cell phone companies," he said carefully, "can be a little sticky about billing."

"They can stick all they like," MJ said, laughing, "but I'm not paying this. I didn't make *any* of these calls."

"Better call their helpline and tell them that the computer's barfed all over your bill," he said. "If you like, I'll—"

"No, I can handle it myself, no problem," MJ said and headed out into the kitchen. "By the way, what do you want for breakfast?"

"Oh, just some toast. I'll get some coffee later."

"Right."

HALF an hour later, Peter was out of the tub, shaved, dried, and getting dressed in their bedroom—and becoming more and more determined to put off going into the kitchen for as long as he could.

MJ was still on the phone. He had heard one loud cry of, "*What?*" and another of, "But, you can't—that's—it's, it's not fair!" and another of, "But I didn't! I've only had it—"

A long silence had followed that. Then came a quieter tone of voice that Peter knew, and didn't hear often: the sound of MJ being very controlled, and probably politer than she needed to be. It was a tone of voice which suggested that the person on whom she was using it had better never run into her at a social occasion or things would turn quickly antisocial.

Finally, he heard her hang up, very softly. To Peter's educated ear, the quiet little click sounded like a bomb detonator going off. Not too quietly, and he hoped not too casually, he made his way into the kitchen.

The toast had come up about ten minutes ago; it sat cold and forlorn in the toaster. It wasn't so dark that redoing it would ruin it, so Peter pushed it down again and walked through to the little table between the kitchen and the dining area where MJ was sitting, the cell phone off to one side, and staring at the bill.

"So what did they say?" he said.

She looked up at him bleakly. "They say we have to pay it."

"But they weren't your calls," Peter said.

"They weren't my calls," MJ said, "but it looks like I'm responsible for them."

"What do you mean?"

"According to the lady I talked to—she was really very nice, she was good to me, but she couldn't help it—my phone was probably cloned."

"Cloned—someone stole the number, you mean."

She nodded, looking morose, and sat back in the chair. "There are people who wait near the ends of bridges and tunnels with scanners because when you come out of there, when you lose the shielding effect, the phone broadcasts its ID number to the system—its PIN number, more or less. Tells the cell phone network where it is. That's an easy time for them to steal your number. People wait with their scanners for cars to come out and record as many numbers as they can. Then they put them into 'blank' phones and start making free calls. Free to them, anyway."

MJ scowled at the table. "I'm so angry, Peter. It's not like I don't know about this, like I haven't heard about it. When I'm in a cab and go into a bridge or a tunnel, I usually make sure the phone is off. I'm pretty careful about it. But just one time I must have been in a hurry, on the way to a job or something, and I must have forgotten—"

Peter shook his head. "Hon, you can't remember *everything*. We've had a fairly lively time of it these past few weeks. It's only natural, when you get home, you relax, you forget something—" He sat down by her, took her hand. "Don't look so tragic!"

She looked at him sidelong and gave him a lopsided smile. "Whatever you say," she said, "just don't say, 'It's only money.' Think about it, Tiger. What have we got in the bank?"

"I guess a little less than—"

"Five thousand dollars, yes. That was going to last us a month or two—maybe more if we stretched hard. It was going to buy us some time to get a little bit ahead. You know how it is when you start a new job—it takes a little while to get the accounting department straightened out, they take a little while to get the check cut." She shrugged. "Well—"

She looked at the bill. "The due date on this is two weeks from now."

"You don't think you could make that much money in two weeks, do you?"

She looked at him. "Not after taxes, no. Probably not. Hand work tends to happen only a couple days at a time."

Peter shook his head. "It's just wrong, though. They shouldn't be able to make you pay it. They're not your calls!"

"Apparently they can," MJ said. "The law in New York at the moment is that there's a ten-day window during which you can inform them that your number's been cloned: if you do it within ten days of the first 'spurious' call, then they won't charge you." The grin she gave him now was much more lopsided. "The problem is, it's a catch-22—how do you know your phone's been cloned until you see the bill? If you're lucky, and it happens at the bottom of a billing cycle, you'll do better, but—" She shook her head.

"But there has to be some way that they can establish that these aren't your calls."

"Not yet," MJ said sadly. "Not for us. We haven't had these phones long enough to establish a billing pattern for either of us. The lady I was talking to said that the only way not to be liable for the cost of the bill was to produce concrete proof that the phone had been cloned. I don't know how we would do that. The lady said that you would have to have the phone's number turn up in an ongoing criminal investigation. If they've actually caught some crook using it, and found your number in his phone, then naturally they'd let you off."

"Oh, jeez," Peter said. The odds of this seemed poor.

In the kitchen, the toast popped up. He ignored it. MJ sniffed. "It's burned."

"It's burned? *I'm* burned! I'm not going to give them four thousand dollars of our money when we didn't use their service!"

"Tiger," MJ said, "unless we can find some way to prove the phone was cloned, we're going to have to. Otherwise this is going to trash our credit rating. We've got enough trouble keeping that straight as it is, and without it, we're sunk. We could take them to court, but who's got the money?"

"Yeah," Peter said.

MJ reached out across the table, sighed deeply, and smiled at Peter once more. This time it was a much more normal smile, but there was a sense of it being applied, like makeup. "I've got to start thinking about going," she said, "They're going to be ready to start shooting in about half an hour, and I can't take the chance of getting caught in traffic."

"What're we going to do?" Peter said.

MJ shook her hair back and looked noble and brave. "We're going to stall," she said, "until I can find out whether we really have to pay this thing. If we have to pay it—" She shrugged. "We've been worse off before."

"I was hoping we wouldn't have to be worse off again," Peter said. "There's nothing hot coming up at the *Bugle* that I know of—I'm not going to be able to be of much help to you."

"Just knowing that you're thinking of ways to be of help to me, to us," MJ said, "makes me feel just fine. Come on, Tiger. Fresh toast for you, and then I'm going to go."

She got up and made him fresh toast, and put on fresh coffee, and the more she was kind to him, and thoughtful, the more Peter began to stew and fret as well. By the time she was ready to go out, still just in her T-shirt and jeans, and (a new development) with her hands covered with the kind of white cotton gloves that commuters used to read the *New York Times* on the train, for his own part, Peter was so angry he could hardly speak. "You going to the *Bugle* later?" MJ said.

"That's right."

"Okay, give 'em my best. When'll you be back?"

"By evening, anyway," Peter said. "Today is just a mooching-around day, to see what's going on, which editors need a photographer. After that, I might do a little night work."

She nodded, recognizing their code for web-swinging. "Okay. I won't wait to eat dinner if you're not home when I get back." She picked up her cell phone, looked at it with an expression of tremendous annoyance, and dropped it into her purse. "You know the number," she said.

"Yeah," Peter said, for a moment allowing the same annoyance to show. "So does someone else. Let me know if your schedule changes. I'll call if mine does."

"Gimme a kiss," MJ said.

Peter drew her close, and for several long warm moments, even the thought of the phone company was drowned out. When she let him go at last, Peter said, "It's a waste, them only using your hands."

She waggled her eyebrows at him. "They have other uses," she said, "as you'll doubtless find out when we're both home again tonight. Bye, Tiger." And she was off down the hall.

He watched her for a moment, then shut the door quietly and began to pace a little bit, looking across the room at where his own cell phone sat. *It's not fair—not in the slightest. There has to be something we can do. Something I can do—or that Spider-Man can do....*

Peter went over to the window that looked uptown and stood for a moment. Spider-Man certainly had various friendly police contacts here and there; it had often been his pleasure to do one cop or another a good turn, and they had done him some in the past as well. *Unfortunately, there is a basic flaw in the logic here,* he thought. Spider-Man's contacts weren't guaranteed to do Peter Parker that much good, especially since to get this particular problem solved would involve showing MJ's phone bills to the police. That would raise just too many questions leading, if he wasn't careful, to the question of his secret identity. *No,* Peter thought, *that's not going to do it—at least not directly.*

He looked out over the roofs of midtown. A brief taste of freedom, of something just a little like security, and now it was gone. *Ten million people out there—certainly there couldn't be more than a million of them who were crooks. Probably a lot less.* It just *seemed* like a lot more. Turn your back for a minute, and you found them in your soup. What still staggered him was the injustice of it all—that the phone company could recognize theft as coming from one specific direction, but hold *you* responsible for it in the next breath, even if you weren't. Though they would probably say that she was careless, she wasn't careless.

Peter stalked back and forth in front of the window, getting more furious—and then sighed. Standing here being angry did no good, but there were things that would. He'd go in to the *Bugle,* see what work was around. And then, later—well...

He couldn't do anything about the phone company, but the crooks— that was something else.

Peter went to get his keys and got ready to head out.

TWO

NIGHT fell and turned the city golden.

Spider-Man knew that light pollution was a problem. He knew that the sodium-vapor lamps that lit New York City streets made astronomers crazy, blanking out the frequencies of light that they were most interested in. But when he stood in a high place, as he did right now, and smelled the cold sweet air—well, sweeter than it was in the daytime, when the sun baked the ozone stink into everything—and when he looked down at those luminous golden pathways between the buildings, all traced with ruby and diamond light, he loved the sight and he wished the people at Hayden Planetarium could find something else to complain about.

He stood at the corner of the roof of the Met Life building and looked northeast. It was a good vantage point, and a good place to jump off from suddenly if you needed to. Plenty of skyscrapers as tall or taller were just north of him: the heart of midtown, his favorite playground. Just west was the unique design of the Flatiron Building; to the north, the traffic lights of Park Avenue, all red and green down the central mall.

Spider-Man stood on the gravel, looking down. He had spent the early part of the evening web-swinging. It was amazing how much frustration you could work off that way. The wind in your face—well, against your mask, anyway—as you snagged the corner of a building with webbing, swung down, whipped around, got a grip on some wall of empty plate glass, scurried up it, then launched yourself out into the void again. Not even riding a line of webbing, just counting on the spider's leap to take you across the gap to the next building. It was exhilarating and a great way to keep an eye on things without being seen. Only rarely did New Yorkers look up, unless a helicopter crash or an alien invasion was happening over their heads. Mostly their attention was at their own level, or below. So was Spider-Man's, but for different reasons.

He was watching pickup trucks, and had been for some days just before he went off to Florida. It was a feature on the news that had started him on this particular avenue of study, a story that made it plain how hot "ram raiding" was becoming in New York.

It was uncertain where the art had originated. Some said it was first practiced in the densely packed, small shopping malls of midlands England. Others said it had been invented in the Midwest, or among corner mini-malls of Los Angeles. Wherever it originated, it was entirely too attractive a method of crime for those who were properly equipped.

The proper equipment tended to stand out: you needed a four-wheel-drive vehicle, or a pickup, or a combination of both, some chains, and several willing accomplices. The idea was that you rammed the back or front of your truck, whichever was more convenient, into a store, and then you jumped in and robbed the place, tossed your loot into the truck, and drove away. Other forms of ram raiding were slightly more opportunistic. Those with a tow point on the back of their truck and enough chain would back their truck up to a store's security shutters, or the post that anchored the shutters, fasten the chain to the shank that secured the post, and drive away at top speed, usually taking the post out. The crooks would then quickly return, loot the store, and flee.

Spider-Man stood there a moment more, breathing the mild summer night's air, and then sprang over to the other side of the roof; there he looked down toward Twenty-third Street, shot a line of web across toward the Park Avenue South corner, and swung out into the night, heading downtown. Ram raiding, he reflected, did have its dangers. You might chain something to your fender and drive away and have your fender come off. This could be embarrassing, especially if your license plate was still attached. An NYPD detective of his acquaintance had told him about how one group of ram raiders decided to steal the cash machine from a bank. They wrapped their chains around the machine and pulled it out of the bank's wall, but the bad guys had failed to notice that the back entrance to the Fourteenth Precinct was directly across from that particular branch of Chase Manhattan. While the crooks got busy securing the cash machine to the back of their pickup, some of the bemused cops who had been watching the raid from inside their offices came strolling outside, crossed the street, and arrested the guys—only to have one of the crooks explain to them, absolutely straight-faced, that the object chained to the back of their truck was in fact a washing machine. One cop laughed so hard that he tore a newly repaired hernia and had to go back three days later for keyhole surgery. Other cops, unchaining the machine, made god-awful jokes about "money laundering" as they took the crooks and the cash machine across the street. Spidey considered this yet another example of how absolutely anything can happen in New York, no matter how absurd you think it is.

The nice thing about ram raiding, though, was that it was fairly detectable. The sound of such a large amount of glass breaking at once, or of the clatter of metal shutters in the street, was much louder than mere vandalism usually produced. For a costumed hero with sharp ears, a built-in ESP-like warning system that he called his spider-sense, and an eye for trouble, it was a happy sound.

Spidey had an eye for trouble tonight. It was difficult, if not impossible, for even a super hero to punch out an entire phone company. But as surrogates for them, he would be more than glad to punch out any crooks he ran across tonight. It would be a small consolation, but better than nothing. Additionally, he had his little motion-controlled camera with him; should any action occur, he would get pictures of it, and tomorrow Peter Parker would take them in to the *Bugle* and see who might be interested in them.

He swung on down Park Avenue South a ways, humming absently to himself as he watched the traffic flow. Ahead of him, under the sodium lights, he could see several pickups of the kind favored for ram raiding, but they seemed to be going about their business peaceably enough. Nonetheless, he followed them for a while, watching the cross streets as he passed them by. It was pleasant to be doing a simple night's work for a change. The previous weeks' run-ins with Venom and the repeated revelations of the underhanded dealings of the Russian-backed import-export company CCRC had made life more complicated than he liked. Having Manhattan almost destroyed in a nuclear explosion a few weeks prior to that hadn't done much for his composure, either. "Super villains," he muttered. "Fooey. Give me punks. I'm ready for punks."

He swung right down Park, practically to the Village, hung a right at Fourteenth, and headed west, past dozens of little stores that sold discount clothes, electrical equipment, and other odds and ends. But everything was surprisingly quiet; the city was well-behaved tonight.

Typical, he thought. *When you want a crook, you can never find them, but when you don't want them, they're everywhere.*

At Thirteenth and Sixth Avenue Spidey paused thoughtfully, looking down at the Burger King there from the skyscraper where he clung. One of the problems with web-swinging in this town was that cooking smoke and steam from restaurants and snack bars rose upward in a great cloud, and he could always smell them on his rounds. If he hadn't eaten before he left, he soon wished he had, and he almost always ate before he got home. MJ's comment was that the only creature in the city to which Spider-Man was *not* a hero was his refrigerator, because he robbed it himself every night.

MJ.... He swung along up Sixth a ways, thinking of her patient look as she sat at the kitchen table after that phone call. *How does she stay so calm?* It seemed to be a natural gift. Her bubbly personality didn't usually extend to noisy complaint, but she had confessed to him what serious fun she had had pitching a major fit one evening on this Miami trip in the direction of a misbehaving director—and the astonishment it provoked from the others in the area, especially those who had known MJ for a little while and had never heard her make a loud noise before. *There may be something to that approach,* he thought. *Save it for later, and people pay more attention—*

CRASH! Glass shattered not too far from him. Spidey paused in mid-swing, swung himself around to the plate-glass front of a building at Twenty-fourth and Sixth, and there held very still, listening above the soft roar of the city for the rest of the crash-and-tinkle. It always took a little while to settle down.

North, he thought, *and west. A block up.*

He spider-scuttled around the face of the building from the Sixth Avenue side to the side facing north, and there made a huge leap onto the roof of a convenient warehouse that stood directly across the street. He came down fairly in the middle of the roof without too much difficulty. Streets were pretty easy to jump: avenues were trouble, and he hadn't jumped one without webbing in a while.

He bounced across the building's roof to where it abutted with another, slightly taller; leapt up to that one's roof, scuttled straight across it to the Twenty-fifth Street side, paused, and peered over the square-cut, fake-castellated brick rampart that topped it out.

About halfway down the block between Sixth and Seventh on Twenty-fifth, a metallic brown Dodge four-by-four pickup had rammed the front of what looked to be a small jewelry store, whose alarm was ringing forlornly. The truck was sitting up on the sidewalk, nose well in through the dark window, while dark figures danced about the truck's hood, grabbing things out of the store, and stowing them away in their coats. Two other figures held long objects—assault rifles, Spidey guessed.

"New York, New York," Spider-Man muttered under his breath, smiling under the mask as he got out the camera and set it on the "rampart" on its little tripod, switching it on. The camera went *zzzt*, turning its "head" toward the action down in the street.

Spidey swung down.

He hit the first of the robbers with no warning whatsoever—his favorite way. He simply took him feet first in the back, knocking the gun the punk carried clear across the sidewalk and under a parked car. It skittered along the concrete, spitting sparks as it went, and Spidey had just enough time to recognize the shape. *Kalashnikov,* he thought. *Very stylish—not!*

The two crooks who had clambered in through the window and loaded themselves with stuff from the counters inside now noticed him. One of them stuffed a last glittering necklace inside his jacket, pulled out a pistol, and started emptying it at Spidey.

This, the crook shortly found, was a futile tactic. Spider-Man bounced around on the sidewalk, rather like a drop of water on a hot griddle, keeping the truck between him and the other two crooks, and waiting for the sound he wanted to hear: *bangbangbangbangbangbangbangbangclick.*

"Aha," Spidey said cheerfully. "That's a Glock, and you've had your seventeen." He jumped at the man, a big heavy guy with a five o'clock shadow several time zones ahead of itself. The crook was still fumbling for the replacement cartridge when Spidey's fist caught him just under the jaw, and sent him and the gun flying, it one way, he another. As the man flopped out of the way, his coat fell open and rained jewelry on the sidewalk.

From beyond the Dodge came more gunfire: some machine-gun, some pistol. Spidey ducked as the slugs whined and ricocheted around him on the pavement. "Impatient people," he muttered. "You'd think they'd wait and take better aim. But never mind." It was half a second's work to web his first crook up against the lightpost against which he had conveniently come to rest. After that, Spidey crouched down again and bounced toward the truck, ducking down behind it.

The guy with the Kalashnikov ran around one side, and the guy with the pistol around the other. It was as much as Spider-Man could have hoped for. "Now, who says New Yorkers aren't considerate?" Spidey said, shooting out a line of webbing and neatly tripping the guy with the pistol as he came around the corner of the Dodge. The crook slammed down onto the sidewalk; the pistol flew off to one side and embedded itself in a big lump of a substance for which there was a $50 fine for leaving it on the street.

"There's a message there somewhere," said Spidey—and then his spider-sense stung him, and he jumped right over the truck. Not a moment too soon: a spray of bullets dug a little crater on the spot of sidewalk where he had been crouching.

The crook ran for the driver's-side door of the Dodge and yanked it open. He had just gotten himself in behind the wheel when Spidey did the same with the passenger-side door, climbed up onto the cab step, and shot webbing all over the would-be driver, his gun, his legs, his arms, and anything else that showed. Then Spider-Man leaned in and pulled the keys out of the ignition, smiling at the furious, struggling man. "You should have gotten out of Dodge while you could," he said and jumped out again.

Bullets rattled and whined off the truck's body. Spidey looked toward the jewelry store and saw the one remaining crook, whom he'd briefly forgotten. "Can't have you feeling left out," he said as he rolled and bounced off the sidewalk, bounced again, and wound up clinging to one of the second-floor windows of the building that had been rammed.

The last crook stared wildly around him, spraying the area with bullets. Spidey hugged the wall, only having to move a couple of times— the big jutting brownstone windowsill protected him somewhat. Then he heard the sound he wanted to hear—not so much a click, but a sort of *mmf*, as the Kalashnikov ran out of things to fire.

He jumped from the window and came right down on the fourth man. The gun spun away. The two of them rolled together briefly. The gunman struggled. Spidey reared a fist back. "Night night," he said, and struck.

A couple of moments later he stood up, breathing hard and looking around at the mess, then walked over to the truck, while hearing, in the distance, the sound of sirens approaching.

The inside of the truck's cab was surprisingly clean. *It's either brand new,* Spidey thought, *or I've come across a bunch of neat thugs.* The back of the flatbed was empty of everything but the boxes and jewelry that the crooks had tossed into it. But inside the cab, on the little parcel shelf under the back window, he found a cardboard box. On the outside it said *a&p 12 o'clock coffee*. On the inside were four cell phones.

He reached in and looked at one. Considering his current mood, Spidey was tempted to chuck the thing across the road—but it was evidence. And who knew what numbers might be inside it?

He carefully took the box out of the truck and put it on the hood. Up and down the block, as Spidey looked up at the windows, he could see a Venetian blind bend down, or a curtain twitch aside, as people looked curiously out and decided that what they saw was nothing to do with them. Inside the mask, Spidey smiled gently.

The sirens got closer. Spider-Man watched with some caution as the cop cars came around the corner, into Twenty-fifth. He was not universally loved by the police. Now two squad cars pulled up, and a third "unmarked" car: five uniformed officers got out, and a sixth, in shirtsleeves and dark pants and a tie thrown over his shoulder, a face he knew. He last saw it months ago at an NYPD sate house in the Bronx one time when Venom was in town.

"Sergeant Drew," Spider-Man said as the cops came up.

Stephen Drew nodded to him cordially enough, and said to one of his people, "See if you can't shut that thing off—it's enough to wake the dead." And for a moment he said nothing more as he walked around the scene and looked things over.

"Okay," he finally said to the others. "Get the web off these guys' hands, anyway, so we can cuff them and take them downtown. You caught them in the act, I take it," he said to Spider-Man.

"I did. Burglary anyway. Maybe grand-theft auto as well."

"Could be. Run the truck," he said over his shoulder, to one of his officers. "Now, what have we here?"

"Four cell phones, at least. There may be more hidden in the truck—"

"Not that," Drew said. "This." He took out a handkerchief, wrapped it around one hand, then bent over to pick up what was half sticking out from one of the parked cars nearby: the Kalashnikov machine gun.

"AK-47," said Spidey.

"Nope," said Drew, with odd relish.

Spider-Man blinked. "Nope? I thought I knew these guns pretty well."

"Take another look at this one." Drew held it out for Spidey to examine. "Check the muzzle."

Spidey looked at it, shook his head. "I'm not sure what I should be seeing."

"Bigger caliber," said Drew. "This isn't just Russian, it's Russian military. And—" He turned the gun over, looked at the stock for a moment, then raised his eyebrows. "Interesting. This doesn't even have the Russian Army brands or reg numbers on it."

"Is that good or bad?"

"I'd stick to 'interesting' for the moment," Drew said. "But I doubt this was bought on the street here—or, if it was, that it's been here for long."

"Russian…" Spidey said.

Drew turned the gun over again, looking at it. "Very shiny…" he said. "Oh, Russian, yeah. And not just in origin. I expect one or two of these guys are Russian themselves."

Spidey nodded. It was no news to him, or anyone else in New York, what new influence had become something to be reckoned with in the New York crime world. When *perestroika* took hold and the old USSR fell, many people who were not oppressed in the usual sense of the word suddenly found themselves free to seek out the Land of the Free. It wasn't finding work they had in mind, though—again, not in the usual sense of the word. The USSR had always had an active network of criminal organizations. At the end of the Eighties, those organizations, as individuals and groups, had actively begun colonizing the United States, in force, either to exploit what they considered a profitable new market for crime, or else to mine the U.S. for technology and new scams, which they would then export to the growing consumer economies in Russia and the former Eastern Bloc.

Drew took another look at the machine gun, unloaded it, cleared it, and then peered down the barrel, squinting a little in the golden light. "If I'm any judge of these things," he said, "this hasn't seen a whole lot of use. It's very new. Must just have come in. Possibly via Long Island. There have been reports of some odd movements among the fishing fleet, last week."

"Drew," Spider-Man said, amused, "is there any gossip about shady stuff in this town that you don't know about?"

Drew chuckled, glanced up. "If there were, I'd hardly mention it. I have my rep to think of, after all. Let's see those phones."

Spider-Man handed him the small box. Drew had a look at them. "Top of the line, these," he said. "Expensive. They may be from a legit supplier—or they may have been traded as part of some money-laundering scheme. Either way, they'll have been cloning existing numbers into these. That way these guys can keep in touch with their bosses, while they're doing their dirty little jobs, and no one can trace them. They just ditch the phones when they're done, and steal new ones."

"It's a subject," Spidey said, "which has been interesting me lately."

"You onto something?" said Drew, catching the intensity in his voice.

"I don't know yet," Spider-Man said. "I don't really know which questions to ask."

"Well—" Drew looked briefly embarrassed. "You did me a mighty favor, once upon a time. Vance Hawkins wouldn't be alive if it weren't for you. Anybody does my partner that kind of favor, I tend to remember it. Look—"

The sound of more sirens was beginning to echo in the background. "I've got to clean this scene up and get these guys out of here," Drew said. "And the town is hopping tonight—at least the West Side is. Got a lot of stuff that's going to keep me busy. But if you'll give me a day, and then call me here—" He reached into his pocket, pulled out his business card. "If you've got some questions about 'cell crime,' I've got somebody who might be able to give you some info that'd be useful to you. Would that suit?"

"It'd suit very well. Thanks, Drew."

"Hey, listen," Sergeant Drew said, as yet another squad car pulled up, "like I said, favors are no good if you don't pass 'em back. And now I suggest you make yourself diplomatically scarce. I'll talk to you later in the week."

"Right," Spidey said.

"Get outta here, bug," Drew growled, more (Spidey guessed) for the benefit of his men than anything else.

In a much better humor than he had been, Spider-Man went straight up the wall and headed for Twenty-sixth Street, and taller buildings that would let him web quickly home

PETER got up early the next morning, and spent a happy couple of hours in the darkroom, developing the pictures from the previous night. He had been experimenting with a new low-light 1200 ASA film, which got surprisingly good results under sodium-vapor lamps—even though, if you were too close to the light source, the shots tended to get a bit washed out. Luckily, these weren't washed out at all: the contrast was crisp and the color good, though flushed with the inevitable golden tint of sodium lighting.

There was the front of the jewelry store, there were the spilled jewels on the floor and the sidewalk, and there were the bad guys, also on the floor though a lot less pretty to look at, webbed into tidy or untidy packages as speed of capture had dictated. It was all very picturesque, and Peter went to his meeting with city editor Kathryn Cushing with a high heart.

Kate went through the prints one after another, picked one—a glittering strew of gemstones and jewelry catching the light, and for contrast, the dull, oiled-metal gleam of the machine gun lying alongside—and looked at it thoughtfully. "Are these guys anybody in particular?" she asked Peter.

"The cops thought they may have been Russian."

"Really?" She picked up a slick-surface pen and began making crop marks on the paper. "I like the color on this. Almost sepia tone. You do that on purpose, or is it just what the film produces under street light?"

"A little of both."

"Do I hear the sound of a man protecting his secrets? Well, never mind. It looks good. That's what matters. Russian, huh? Mel Ahrens would like this...." She pushed the picture away and leaned back in her office chair, steepling her fingers and staring at them for a moment. "Never mind that right now. You did a super job on the Miami end of things, Peter. A difficult assignment, but very good results. I wasn't entirely sure you had it in you." She grinned. "I don't mind admitting to being wrong. So now I want to start putting you on more high-profile work—and I think I have just the thing." She started rummaging around in her file drawer.

Peter had long since learned that the safest kind of response to this kind of rather mixed compliment was to smile and say nothing. But something was niggling at the back of his mind. "Forgive me for being nosy," he said, "but why would Mel Ahrens be interested in these?"

"Huh?" Kate looked up from the drawer for a moment. "Oh. He's been working on a series of stories on the Russian infiltration of the New York crime scene. Well, that's not quite right. He's been working on a book, and the paper's been printing extracts. Very interesting stuff—maybe a little too interesting." She went back to rummaging in her drawer. "Now where did I put that Belgian stuff? Now listen, Peter. Vreni Byrne spoke very highly of you in terms of—"

"Sorry," Peter said, "wait a minute. This is the guy that the mobsters keep trying to kill?"

Kate looked up, nodded. "The names change from week to week, but yes. Mel's been lucky so far, and he's such an alert guy that I could see why anyone who wanted him dead would need to move pretty fast."

"Does he need a photographer?"

She paused a moment then, and blinked. "Now that you mention it, over the past few weeks he *has* dropped some hints that he might need a photog to work with him occasionally. You were busy then, so I tried a couple of other people on him. It didn't take. He can be a hard man to get along with." Kate gave him a cockeyed look. "Are you saying *you* want to try? Wouldn't you rather go to Belgium and the South of France for a couple of weeks? I was thinking of sending you along with the stringer who's going to the European Film Festival in Brussels."

"Uhhh…" Peter stared at her. Then he said, "Kate, I really like the sound of this."

"Of what? Being shot at by men with heavy accents?"

"Not that, specifically. It's just that the Russian thing has been— interesting me for a while." *A very little while,* he thought.

Kate looked at him thoughtfully. "You haven't actually met Mel, then."

"No. I've heard the usual newsroom stuff, though. Isn't he one of the guys who made such a stink when we went over to computers?"

Kate laughed quietly. "That was diplomatically put. You mean, the only guy who made even more of a stink than I did." She gave her own desktop terminal a sidelong look. "Yeah, that's Mel. Well, I guess you might as well meet him. Be warned, though—I said he's kind of a hard man to work with. That's not just where his partners or assistants are concerned. He's got this tendency to jump in with both feet where—"

"Where angels fear to tread?" Peter suggested.

"I was going to say, where walking softly would produce a better effect. Like not letting certain people know you're there at all. If this assignment works, then remember that he'll take you with him when he jumps. That could lead to trouble."

"I think I can cope."

"Good. Come on; I'll perform the introductions."

Kate led Peter out to the City Room, right into the interdenominational desert of desks called, appropriately enough, No Man's Land. Most of these desks were for temporary use by journalists on short-term assignments, or by staffers in transition between one section of the paper and another. Robbie Robertson, the editor in chief, often referred to them as the "Flying Dutchmen."

Kate and Peter made their way across to one desk in particular. There was a computer on it, and a great drift of papers, and—set pointedly in front of the computer monitor—the hunchbacked bulk of a splendid old 1940s-period Smith-Corona commercial typewriter. Black, with gold lettering and hair-fine gold lining along what Peter could only think of as its coach work, the typewriter gleamed with that deep patina that could only have come from much polishing throughout its working life.

"Wow," he said admiringly. "Just look at this thing. It *shines*."

"He's gonna like you," Kate said with a certain air of amused resignation. "But then, he likes anybody who doesn't call it a piece of outdated junk."

"This isn't junk. It's an antique. No, it's more than an antique, it's—"

"It's a work of art," said a sharp voice from behind them.

Peter turned. From the stories he had heard about Mel Ahrens, and from the look of the desk, he had been expecting an older man. But the guy with the shock of blond hair who was advancing on him, one hand already extended to shake, couldn't have been more than in his late twenties.

"Mel," Katherine said, "this is Peter Parker. He's the photographer I mentioned to you a couple of weeks ago."

"So you're the one who keeps pulling in those action shots of Spider-Man," said Ahrens. "Good. Very good. Not like those other losers." He shot Kate a look. "Here, pull up a chair."

As they appropriated the chairs from a nearby empty desk, Peter looked around him at the other temporary desks. "Why have they stuck you over here?" he asked. "I mean, you've been working with the paper for a while now."

"A year or so, yeah." Ahrens laughed. "But I like the buzz here, the feeling of uncertainty. God knows, it's everywhere else in my work. At least this office gives me a background I'm familiar with. Sit, sit, sit."

They did.

"That's a beautiful typewriter," said Peter.

"It's a noble instrument," said Ahrens, favoring Kate with another dirty look, "and if there were any justice in an unjust world, I'd be able to submit my stories typed on good heavy paper stock rather than using that travesty." He waved an accusing, dismissive hand toward the terminal that squatted dark and silent at the corner of his desk.

"Why don't you at least leave it running?" Kate said. "We've got perfectly good screen savers in the system."

"I have no desire to sit here and be irradiated by the thing," said Ahrens, "just for what someone else perceives to be my convenience. Which it's not, particularly, but never mind. I don't want to get into that all over again."

He turned to Peter and, as he did so, gave the gleaming black bulk of the typewriter an affectionate pat. "I typed the first story I ever sold on this machine," he said. "It was my dad's. And it will have to be pried from my cold, dead fingers before I give it up."

Peter smiled inwardly. If this was the notorious Ahrens eccentricity, at least it seemed amiable enough, and the other things he had heard about the man suggested that Mel could be granted the right to a little bit of eccentric behavior. He had heard a lot of people around the *Bugle* refer to Ahrens as an old-fashioned news-hound in a young body. Very sharp, they said; a good writer who never missed a deadline, a man with an eye for detail in both story and pictures, and a real gift for helping his photographer to find just the right picture for a given story.

"Has Kathryn told you what I'm working on?" he asked Peter.

"In general."

"I just brought him over so you could fill him in," said Kate. "You mentioned something about a photo opportunity coming up."

Ahrens laughed. "Yeah, and I just bet the people involved in it think that as well. It's the night after next."

Kate raised one eyebrow. "So soon? Then I presume you've already put all your affairs in order."

"If you mean, am I leaving you my porcelain collection, then the answer is no. You're greedy, you know that?"

"Where Meissen is concerned, I've known it for a long time," said Kate, standing up. "I'll leave you to your briefing." She nodded to Peter, then headed back to the elevator.

The two of them sat back in their chairs and looked at each other. Peter was very aware that Ahrens was studying him, sizing him up, almost filing him away in a mental card file. He smiled thinly and returned the favor with a long, hard stare.

Mel Ahrens nodded at last, after a few seconds of intense scrutiny that had seemed more like minutes. "I saw the Kennedy Space Center pictures," he said. "Those were pretty impressive. You've got something of a head for heights."

Peter grinned. "A little. They've never really bothered me."

"Well, it's the depths we're heading for this time," said Ahrens, reaching into his desk drawer and coming up with a Tootsie Roll. "Want one?"

"No, thanks."

Ahrens chuckled and unwrapped the candy slowly, then swung his feet up onto the desk, narrowly missing Peter as he did so. "The Russians," he said. "This is going to sound funny, but they really have a gift for organized crime. And they're independent. The American version of the Mafia has always had associations, however distant, with the old *Cosa Nostra* from Sicily and Southern Italy. Tradition and old habits, maybe. But the Russians, no. When the reforms began, when *glasnost* and *perestroika* set in for real and the Wall came down, they realized that the West was the place to be.

"Whole families have been relocating in the U.S. for some years now, including *crime* families. One of the favorite cover stories," he chuckled a little ruefully, "was religious persecution. A very sensitive subject, that, and a very powerful argument. It would be a very determined U.S. administration that would refuse. A lot of them claimed to be Jews, and some of them even are—but nothing like as many carrying papers that say so. That way they were able to gain direct asylum in the States, or favored immigration status through Israel. Or Germany. The Germans had very liberal asylum laws."

"And again," said Peter, "that claim of religious persecution was one that Germany would be reluctant to ignore."

"Exactly," said Ahrens. "But either way, the big gangs severed their ties with the Mother Country and started moving here. Needless to say," he coughed, delicately, "certain, ah, concerns already well entrenched here didn't take too kindly to the intrusion. You get the occasional turf war. Well, more than occasional. That sort of free and frank exchange of views has been getting very active lately. Last night, apparently."

"These pictures," said Peter, pulling another sheaf of prints from their envelope and handing them over.

"Yes, indeed," said Ahrens with great satisfaction. He studied each picture in turn, then looked intently at the close-up of the assault rifle. "Well, well. This is a Kalashnikov AK-74. You can tell by the shape of the muzzle brake. Among other things."

"The policeman I spoke to at the scene said that this was an army-issue weapon."

"A *current* army-issue weapon," Ahrens corrected. "Everybody who thinks they know about military weapons in the hands of criminals goes on at length about the AK-47." Peter stifled a smile. Ahrens might well have said just that to Spider-Man last night. "After all, the old regime handed them out to satellite states and, ah, freedom fighters, rather like a jolly uncle with a box of candies.

"However," Ahrens tapped the photo, "this is another matter. It's frontline equipment, and something the Soviets *never* did was to give away or export anything they were still using themselves. Tanks were stripped to the basics, aircraft had inferior weapons and radar, that sort of thing. They called them 'monkey models.'

"The AK-74 rifle isn't quite state of the art, of course—at least, not so far as the West is concerned. *Guns & Ammo* wouldn't be terribly excited about it. No caseless ammunition, no flechette projectiles, not even an impressive rate of fire. It does its job quite adequately, however, and that's all the Soviet military ever worried about. Funny thing, though—"

"No issue numbers."

"Exactly. This was never in service. It came straight from the factory into the hands of whoever was using it last night—and I notice they weren't wearing Russian uniforms. Like every other manufacturer in the former Soviet Union, the armaments industry is desperate for hard currency now that its major customer has almost stopped buying. My guess is that this gun, and the rest of whatever consignment it came from, was acquired by barter. That method avoids leaving a trail, either paper or electronic."

"What about the end-user certificate scam?" asked Peter. "A legal arms sale to a second party, who's already arranged to pass the goods on down the line to a third. After all, counterfeit end-user certificates are supposed to be the third most popular forgery on the planet, after money and passports." Ahrens raised his eyebrows, and Peter shrugged innocently. "Hey, I'm a photojournalist," he said, then grinned broadly. "And I've been reading Frederick Forsyth for years."

Ahrens's own smile was a good deal thinner. He nodded, just once, and continued to leaf through the photographs.

"Anyway," Peter continued more soberly, "I've been hearing about a lot of Russian activity over the past few months. That CCRC thing."

"Yes. A nasty business. The whole affair was a bucket of dirty water so deep that I don't think the authorities have reached the bottom yet. There were more scams and scandals being run out of that place than—well, never mind. And I have a feeling that what wasn't discovered in time has already been hived off to other holding companies."

"They would have to be, I guess. The parent organization was supposed to be shut down. There's going to be some huge audit of it."

"The only way to audit a company like that is with a battering ram at three in the morning," said Ahrens firmly. "Anything that needed to be shredded has been confetti for a long time now. The government, the authorities, even the IRS, are never going to find all the evidence they need. It's hopeless. A waste of time and resources. You can't give people like CCRC time to cover their tracks. And they're just one aspect of what's been going on."

"So? What else?"

Mel took a moment to munch on another Tootsie Roll. "The mobs in New York," he said, "Coney Island and Brooklyn, have really stepped up their activities in the past few months. By something over a hundred percent, according to one of my better-informed sources." Peter whistled through his teeth. "They've been getting into new rackets. Oriental, some of them. Franchised from the Triads, for all I know. But it all eventually turns into money laundering, and there's been a lot of laundry done. Massive amounts. Do you know where the biggest supply of U.S. bank notes is, outside of the continental United States?"

Peter shook his head.

"Russia. It's partly because they trust our currency more than they trust their own. The government there still isn't completely stable, at least not enough to be relied on when you're dealing with sums of money the size of small national debts. They tried to cut in on money laundering at a national level a few years ago by just abruptly withdrawing all the currency and issuing a new print—but it didn't work, because nearly all the laundering was already in dollars rather than rubles anyway."

"Laundering how, specifically?"

"Mr. Forsyth hasn't gotten into this yet, eh?" said Ahrens, with a little flicker of dry amusement. "All right, here's how the laundry works. First thing is to conceal who really owns the money, and where it came from. There's no point in laundering at all if the origin is still known at the end of the process. Next, you've got to change its shape, preferably by increasing the value of each bill. If you're starting out with ten million dollars in twenties, you don't want to finish up with the same thing."

"Even if all the bills now have different serial numbers?"

"Not good enough. You want *no* leads. Also, think logistics. If you change to higher-denomination bank notes, your ten mil at once becomes a much smaller package. That's why the Treasury took the thousand-dollar bill out of circulation—"

"I never saw enough of them to notice," said Peter sourly, but Ahrens didn't even notice the interruption.

"—so that now it takes ten times as much paper, ten times as much bulk, to shift the same amount of cash from one place to another. It makes a transfer less convenient and more noticeable. Useful for surveillance.

"So." Ahrens held up one hand and started counting points off on his fingers. "You want the origin of the money hidden, and you want the size of the bundle to shrink without reducing its value. Then the actual laundry trail itself has to be hidden. Why go to all that trouble if each step can be followed backwards?"

"I see your point." Peter was beginning to understand why there had been attempts on Ahrens's life. He was hearing a lecture on theory, but that theory was based on practical knowledge. The quickest way to get rid of what someone knew had always been to get rid of the someone.

"But the last and I suppose the most important thing is that you, or people you can trust implicitly, have to retain control of the money at every step of the laundering process. If the whole purpose of what you're doing is to make sure that nobody can prove this money was yours in the first place, then if it's stolen, you're in trouble. If it's dirty money, you can't exactly go to the police, and even if it's *clean* money, the tax folks are going to take an unhealthy interest in why you were laundering it in the first place.

"Let's try the double-invoice method. One end of the laundry is, let's say, a grocery store. The other is a wholesaler who sells stuff to the grocery store. And you're both friendly. The same nationality, the same Family, whatever." He pronounced the capital letter without difficulty. "One day you order fifty barrels of borscht from your wholesaler."

"Does borscht come in barrels?"

"Who knows? I'm not a beet fan. Anyway, it might look like your wholesaler isn't a fan, either, because he only sends you forty barrels—but then the person 'doing the laundry' hands you cash to make up the shortfall. That money, dirty for whatever reason, gets into the system disguised as clean. It looks fine to the bookkeepers, fine to the tax people, and pretty soon, if that's doing well, you open another grocery store and start ordering more borscht. The more legal outlets you have, the better it gets.

"Well," Ahrens leaned back in his chair and looked at Peter, "Brooklyn and the Bronx, parts of Staten Island and Nassau County, are all awash in that sort of legal outlet, all busily invoicing for less than they've delivered, and all laundering money like it's going out of style. But that's just one of the things the Russian mobs are getting involved with. They do the usual organized crime stuff: protection, numbers, gambling, all the rest. But in the past few months, for some reason the volume of money laundering has skyrocketed. At least, so my sources tell me, and I've no reason to doubt the accuracy of their information. But nobody knows why—or if they do know, they're not telling."

Ahrens reached into the drawer again for more Tootsie Rolls. "Sure you don't want one? Fine. Anyway, something else has been happening. A lot of the big bosses made themselves very comfortable in New York. They bought themselves big apartments, they brought their families over, they settled right into the city. Like it or not, Russian organized crime was becoming just one more community—very clubby. But now all of a sudden several of them are getting ready to leave town. One of them bought himself a little private island down in the Caymans. Another bought some place in the Bahamas that Tony Stark didn't need anymore. A third now owns a chunk of rock in the British Virgin Islands, and he's having it covered with a beautiful—and heavily fortified—holiday mansion."

"Why all this sudden interest in the Caribbean?" said Peter. "More money laundering? I remember hearing that the Cayman Islands are almost as good as Switzerland for private banking."

"Could be," said Ahrens. "Certainly the BVI is a tax haven, and the status of several other islands is still under negotiation. They might be owned by the Dutch, or they might be owned by the French, or they might be completely independent—or they might be open for sale to the right buyer. One with enough money. But the coincidence struck me as odd. It can't just be conspicuous consumption for its own sake. That's not these people's style, or they'd have been doing it a long time ago."

"Are they afraid that things might be getting too legally hot for them in the States?"

"I don't think so. They've been flouting various tax laws here, almost like they're testing to see how far they can push. And so far, they've been getting away with it thanks to expert legal help. Locally sourced, of course. As for the money laundering, their trails have been professionally concealed. So far there's no evidence stronger than suspicion."

Ahrens shifted his legs, touched the gleaming typewriter slightly with the edge of one shoe, and leaned forward at once to polish away a mark Peter couldn't even see.

"Something is going on. I don't know what it is, and that's what's making me crazy. Call it just basic nosiness, but there's a connection somewhere, and I can't find out what."

That *would* drive him crazy, thought Peter. And as for this man being just "basically nosy," then water was just "basically wet." "Even if trying to find out might get you killed?" he said.

"I don't think it'll do that. I've got a fairly good rapport with some of these people, and enough college Russian to get by—though they seem to prefer practicing English on me. It's the usual thing." Ahrens chuckled dryly. "They want to become experts in the local language, since it'll make exploiting the locals so much easier. And as for the others, the real hard men, I've been able to stay out of their way."

Peter looked thoughtfully at the casual jacket Ahrens was wearing. The cut was loose enough that a fairly big handgun could be concealed beneath it. Ahrens caught the look and nodded.

"Yes," he said. "Heckler and Koch VP-70Z, if you're interested. The civilian version, not the full-auto. With a full concealed-carry permit, of course. I've done the police department a few good turns in the past—strictly on the Q.T.—and they've been more than happy to return the favor. But that's not the point at the moment. Would you be willing to work with me on this for the next couple or few weeks? As I said, things are heating up for some reason, and I—we—need to know why. I can't call it any more than a gut feeling, but that feeling tells me that something profoundly threatening to this entire city is getting ready to happen. If there's something I can find out, then maybe it won't come as a complete surprise."

"Maybe it can even be stopped dead," said Peter.

"Maybe." Then Ahrens grinned at him. "But like I said before, I'm just nosy. I want to know what these people are doing."

Peter smiled back. That kind of nosiness he was entirely familiar with. It was probably what prompted his next question. "How good a shot are you?"

"I'm okay. I shoot twice a week at the range, and I can usually hit what I'm aiming at. The rest of the time, I try not to think about it. The whole point of a Veep-70 is that it's got lots of bullets; that helps keep heads down while you vacate the premises. But don't forget that among these people, guns are a badge of rank as much as a weapon. So I wear the badge. Without it, you might not even get past the front door of some places. That's not to say they aren't something to be used. At least it doesn't happen as often as with—other import organizations."

"That sounds good enough for me," Peter said. "When do you think you'll need me?"

"Tomorrow night. I've got an interview under slightly unusual circumstances. One of the local, I guess mafiosi is the best word for them—"

"Or mafioski, maybe?"

"Very nice," said Ahrens, grinning again as he scribbled the word onto a pad. "I like it. Anyway, this character seems to have an ax to grind regarding some of the competition. If I'm reading him properly, he might be willing to shed some light on the sudden increase in local 'business'; and what's going on with these kingpins who've suddenly all decided to go ex-pat together. So far as I can make out, they're all rivals rather than allies; in a couple of cases it goes as far as hatred. So it's not a linkup or a business deal. That could be done as easily on-site. Something else is going on."

"And you think this could have links to CCRC as well?"

"It might. I'm putting out feelers in that direction, but it'll take a couple of weeks before I get any feedback."

"Okay. But in the meanwhile, you've got a photographer." He stood up. "Thanks for the background detail."

"The free lecture, you mean," said Ahrens, also rising. "I charge for the college-level one." He put out his hand again, and they shook. "Where shall we meet?"

"Here's good enough."

"Five o'clock Thursday, then."

"Five it is."

Peter flicked one hand to his brow in a casual hail-and-farewell and turned away. As he did, the phone rang, and an expression of loathing crossed Ahrens's face as various of its lights began to flash. "This thing has too many buttons," he said, jabbing one at random as he picked up the handset. "Hello?" There was no reply from the evidently wrong line, so there was a quick sequence of more buttons being punched and a steadily more irritable repetition of "Hellos" before he finally got it right.

Peter walked away, smiling at the performance. Then his smile went a little sour. If that display of technophobia was anything to go by, then Ahrens would never have a cell phone—or a four-thousand-dollar bill generated by someone else.

He shot a final glance over his shoulder as he made for the stairwell rather than the elevator. Ahrens had reluctantly moved his beloved Smith-Corona aside and switched on his monitor, but as the screen came up he could see a saver program that was plainly one of Ahrens's own devising. The words crawled slowly across the screen, black on white, as close to type on paper as the phosphors could create.

I Will Be Obsolete Some Day.

Peter went downstairs. "CCRC," he muttered to himself. That corporation had been involved in so much recently that he half expected to find them under every stone. First they had stored toxic waste in New York City. Then they had transported it covertly both crosscountry and overseas for illegal reprocessing, theft and money laundering of their own, counterfeiting…

It was a big, tangled web, and now here was another strand of it, while he remained the same small spider in the middle, trying to make sense of the weave, trying to unravel it, and at the same time doing his best not to be strangled by it in the process.

He almost wished he could get in touch with Venom, to ask him some very pointed questions about his own research into CCRC. That research had brought Venom clear across the country, from—Peter assumed— somewhere near San Francisco straight to the center of the CCRC-financed and -managed smuggling operation in the Florida Everglades. Toxic waste again, for reprocessing.

But even if he knew where Venom had gone after suddenly removing himself from the scene in Florida, Peter couldn't really bring himself to make the first move. After all, Venom and Spider-Man still had some unfinished business.

Spider-Man was still alive.

No, he told himself. *Even if you knew his phone number, calling for advice would not be a good idea. And anyway, you might be finding out a few things all by yourself in the next few days. Wait and see.*

Peter headed home.

THREE

ABOUT 9:30 the next morning, Peter was sitting at the kitchen table with the phone more or less glued to his ear. That ear was beginning to hurt, less from the pressure of the phone than from the sound of a slightly deranged computer at the other end playing "Für Elise" in a horrible electronic harpsichord-tinkle. And playing it, moreover, for the eighteenth time.

A voice said, "Are you holding for someone?"

Peter looked at the sketch pad on the table in front of him. It was covered with curly lines and little arrows, scrawled in a helpless sort of way while listening to the hold music ritually slaughtering Ludwig van Beethoven. In amongst the squiggles were several names, each one crossed out by increasingly heavy layers of scribble. "I'm waiting for, uh, Mr. Jaeger."

"He's on another line. Will you hold?"

The temptation to shriek, *Do I have a choice, since it took me the best part of an hour to get past your voicemail system?* was very strong, but he restrained himself with a massive effort. "Yes, I'll hold. Thank you." The hold music, as remorseless as a Chinese water torture, started playing "Für Elise" again.

Peter tuned out its tinkly mutilation of melody—he'd had plenty of practice so far this morning—and stared out of the window, into the bright day and the smog. A butterfly went by. It was a big monarch, and it wasn't moving with the usual aimless flutter. This particular butterfly not only had places to go and people, or at least other butterflies, to see, it was flying with the sort of purpose that suggested a flight plan logged with La Guardia Control.

Peter desperately wished he could be out there with it instead of trapped in the Seventh Circle of Hold Hell. *I brought this on myself,* he thought. Earlier that morning, when MJ had gotten up still thoroughly depressed about the phone bill, he had foolishly offered to give them a call.

She had looked at him wistfully, then after a moment said, "I guess it couldn't hurt, really. The world isn't entirely liberated yet. Maybe the sound of a guy's voice...."

"All right," he had said. "You go and get your hands ready for work, and I'll give them a try."

With a sunny dawn ahead, and a satisfying night behind him in which he had not only pounded some bad guys, but possibly also gained a lead that might help with the phone bill, there had seemed no harm in trying. After all, if it could be resolved this way, then he wouldn't have to bother Sergeant Drew's contact. And so he had innocently called CellTech, and asked to speak to someone in customer service.

Or rather, he had *tried* to ask. CellTech prided itself on the sound quality of its system, and several times Peter had started talking to what he had thought was a genuine human being, only to find that the voice was human only at one remove: a recorded voice linked to a voicemail computer possessed of all the literalness of the species.

Its courteous little voice kept telling him that "if you have a question about routine billing, please press one. If you are interested in new services, please press two. For all other inquiries, please press three."

He had pressed three and had continued to press three, early and often, as each time the system made a polite electronic hiccup and said, "Please enter your account number, followed by the number sign."

When he did so, there had been another hiccup. "Please spell your name using the alphabet keys on your phone and ending with the number sign. Please enter your last name first. For Q or Z, please use the number one."

If they already have my account number, why do they need my name as well? Peter had wondered as he started tapping at the keys. And that was when the problems began. The phone's keypad was quite small, and his fingers were quite large, and every time he hit the wrong key that dulcet voice would say, "I'm sorry, the name you have entered does not match any in our records. Please try again."

By the fourth or fifth time, he simply wanted to punch the voice in whatever passed for its face. So he hung up, took a few deep breaths, then dialed again and this time tried for a routine billing inquiry.

"If you want to verify your account balance, please press one. If you wish to add another user to your account, please press two. If you want..." It then went on at some length, detailing a number of options which he most definitely did *not* want, then finally said, "For all other account inquiries, please press six."

Peter had mashed his index finger down on six with all the pent-up fury of an exasperated world leader starting World War III. The phone hiccuped, and the voice told him what he should have been expecting all along.

"I'm sorry, all our accounts personnel are busy. Your call will be answered by the next available operator. Please hold." And that was when they began playing "Für Elise" at him.

The first real person he had spoken to had sounded seriously hungover, and a veneer of businesslike briskness hadn't done much to conceal that fact. "CellTech-Customer-Services-Brian-here-how-may-I-help-you?" was all run together like the health warning at the end of a pharmaceutical commercial and uttered in a hoarse growl.

"I have a question about a very large bill," Peter began.

There was a pause at the other end that suggested more clearly than any words that the very large bill was Peter's problem, and nobody else's. "Your account number, please?"

Peter rattled off the number, deciding that he preferred speaking it to typing it out on the keypad.

Another pause. "I'm sorry, but I'm not authorized to give you any information on that account."

"What? Oh, because it's in a girl's name and I'm a boy. That's all right. I'm her husband. Peter Parker. She's Mary Jane Watson-Parker."

"I'm sorry, but I'm not authorized to give you any information on that account." The repetition was so exact that for a second Peter thought he was back with the voicemail system again. *This guy*, he had thought, *has been spending too much time around his firm's computers*. "Ms. Watson-Parker will have to call us herself and ask for an authorization number. If she gives that to you and you give it to us, then we can give you the account information you require."

Peter raised his eyebrows a little, but the intention behind the request was honest enough: protecting the customer. "Okay, will do. Thanks."

He called MJ on her cell phone, and the first sound he heard was a yawn. At that point it was only about 8:30, and what with fretting about the bill, MJ hadn't slept well.

"Hello?"

"Hi, hon, it's me. Listen, the CellTech people won't talk to me until you talk to them and tell them that it's all right for them to talk to me."

"Uh, yeah. I got that. I think. A pity they wouldn't let anyone else use my phone number without asking me if it was all right."

"I know. Look, can you call them? Otherwise I'm not going to be able to get anywhere with them." He read her the number quickly. "Just beware of the demon voicemail. Hit one for routine billing, then go for other options; that's, uh, six."

"Okay, Tiger. I'm on it."

About ten minutes later the phone rang again, and he picked it up. "Wow," said MJ's voice, "bureaucracy is *not* dead, is it?"

"Yeah, I get that sense. But did they give you a number?"

"Eventually. Here, write it down." She rattled off a number that had no obvious connection to the account number. "Got that?"

"Yeah." He read it back, twice, to be sure.

"Great. See what you can do with them."

"And how are *you* doing?"

"Oh, fine."

"Still doing the suds?"

"Yeah." There was a snicker at the other end of the line. "Petey, I am *never* going to use this stuff."

"Why? Do they give you tons of freebies after the commercial? Does it bother you?"

"No—and if they did give me any, I'd chuck it out. They've put a sort of tea-rose scent in it, and, well…" She chuckled again, very softly, and the sound of her voice on the phone changed slightly as if she had cupped her hand around her mouth to muffle what she was about to say. "Remember the roach powder we had to get one time? It's exactly like that.…"

Peter made a face. It had taken weeks to get the smell of the stuff out of the kitchen; the stalest, most oversweet rose perfume that anyone could ever have conceived. It had smelled, well, pink. "As bad as that, huh?"

"Worse. This is their new 'flower-fresh' fragrance"—she smothered a nasty laugh—"and if this is what they think flowers smell like…. Anyway, look, they're about to start. I'll call you back. Bye."

"Bye."

Peter dialed again, fought his way through the gauntlet of the voicemail system to where the live people had been hiding, and waited until finally a familiar, still-hungover voice said, "CellTech-Customer-Services-Brian-here-how-may-I-help-you?"

"Hi, this is Peter Parker. I spoke to you a few minutes ago about getting an authorization code so that I can discuss my wife's account. I have that number now."

"Thank you, sir. What is it, please?" Peter read it out, then waited through the inevitable pause.

"I'm sorry, sir; that number isn't showing on our system."

All the phone calls my wife didn't make are sure as hell showing on your system, Peter wanted to say, but he didn't. "Maybe that's because she just got the number?" he suggested. "The authorization number, I mean."

"That wouldn't normally be the case, sir—uh-oh." This time the pause was far longer than usual.

"Uh-oh?" Peter echoed mildly. That was not a noise he liked hearing from anybody who was so plainly dominated by the technology surrounding him.

"I'm sorry, sir. The system's gone down. Can I get you to call us back in, say, ten or fifteen minutes?"

"Certainly," said Peter and hung up as gently as he could.

That exchange set the tone for the next hour. He called back three times to find the system still down. The fourth time, it was refreshing itself and wouldn't be back online for another ten minutes. That response was the first sensible thing he had heard all morning. Refreshment.

Peter got up and made himself a cup of coffee, very strong, with a lot of sugar. Then he sat at the table again, and stared at the phone, and drank his coffee very slowly, thinking that maybe Mel Ahrens's attitude to modem technology wasn't quite so eccentric after all. He also couldn't help hoping, at least a little, for some kind of emergency to crop up that required Spider-Man's presence. Web-swinging—not to mention hitting something very hard—carried a certain amount of appeal just now.

Gamely, he dialed again, battled his way through the voice mail, and this time, to his relief, failed to find Hello-this-is-Brian-nursing-his-hangover.

"CellTech-Customer-Services-this-is-Alan-how-may-I-help-you?" Well, this one sounded bright and eager to please. It made a pleasant change. He greeted this-is-Alan courteously enough, gave him the authorization code, and this time not only was it in the computer, but the computer stayed up and running.

"So, how can I help you, Mr. Parker?"

"I'm trying to work out what can be done about this particular phone bill...."

Slowly and patiently, Peter told the whole story, while Alan listened and made encouraging noises. But finally he said, "I'm sorry, there's not a great deal I can do to help you. Under the present regulations, your wife remains responsible for the calls, and when the bill comes due, she's going to have to pay it."

"That's going to be a real problem."

"I understand it's going to be a problem for you, Mr. Parker. But please bear in mind, this kind of thing is a problem for us as well. We still have to pay the government a tariff on every minute of telecommunications used by our service on the frequencies which they lease to us, and this year already CellTech has paid over two million dollars to cover what have been fraudulent calls. We have to recoup those funds somehow, and I'm afraid that until the regulatory structure changes, it has to come from our clients."

"But isn't there anything that can be done to establish where the calls came from, or who did this, or even just to prove that they weren't made by my wife or with her permission?"

They went back and forth over it, and Alan was understanding, very understanding indeed. Professionally so, Peter thought. But it always came back to the same response: there was nothing that could be done. Finally he fell silent, and in that silence thought he sensed Alan twitch just a little bit.

"Mr. Parker," he said, "I'm sorry for your trouble. I really am." There was another silence. "I can do this. I can add—we'll call it an adjustment period—two weeks onto the due date of your bill. That way you won't have to pay until the fifteenth. Would that help you a little?"

"It's certainly better than nothing," Peter said. "And it might even give us a chance to establish where those calls really came from."

"If you can get the police to help with that, it would be your best bet," said Alan. "I'm sorry I can't be more helpful, but that's about all I can do."

"Listen, I guess it's as much as we could have hoped for. Do you have an ID number or something, so that we can call you back?"

"No, sir. Just ask for Alan. Alan Soames."

"Thanks again for your help, Alan. I really appreciate it."

"Anytime, Mr. Parker. Thank you for calling Cell-Tech. Good-bye."

Peter hung up, feeling both disgusted and at the same time guilty about his disgust. The guy had really been trying to help, and had sounded genuinely sorry that he hadn't been able to do more. Now he was left with the same problem as before, except that the date of execution had been postponed a little.

If we still have to pay this, he thought, *then there goes our safety net.*

But if those extra couple of weeks gave either him or MJ or both of them the chance to make some extra money, then it might not be so bad. He stared at the coffee cup, still a quarter full of now-cold, sweet coffee, then got up, went to the sink and emptied it out, then poured himself another cupful and over-sugared that, too.

No solution for this problem, not yet. But boy, if I ever catch the guy who cloned MJ's phone. . . . He shook his head at himself, and sat down. Murder was of course out of the question, but when the guy or guys were turned in, and if Spider-Man was responsible for their capture, then he intended to make sure they got a little wasted first. For MJ's sake, as well as for his own.

The sound of keys in the lock brought his head up suddenly. At least, it sounded like keys. Was someone trying to pick the lock? The first deadbolt was thrown, then the second; and the chance of anyone doing that with a lock pick was pretty minuscule.

The door opened and MJ stalked in. She looked around, saw him sitting at the table, and threw him an expression of such fury and sadness and upset that he stood up and went straight to her. "MJ, what's the matter?"

"I cut my hand," she said and waved her bandaged left hand at him as if it were something offensive. "I cut my *hand*!" This time it was more of a wail.

Having received his share and then some of bruises and cuts during his career as a super hero, Peter assumed the worst. "Let me see. Is it bad? Do you have to go to the hospital? Will it need stitches?"

He took her hand gently between both of his, turned it over, and eased off the bandage. Then he let out a long sigh of relief. There was a gash running across the first and second knuckles, but it was thin and shallow, already dry and clotted. He hadn't known what to expect, but at least this was no worse than any kid might pick up after a fall in the schoolyard.

"Want me to kiss it and make it better?" he said.

She glared at him. "Better not. If you start it bleeding again, then I might really lose my temper." She flumped down into the chair, looking flushed and angry beyond all reason.

"You're back early," said Peter.

MJ snorted. "You're damn right I'm back early. I can't work anymore today. God knows if I'm going to work anymore, ever!" She reached for his coffee cup and eyed the contents. "Sugar?"

"A lot."

"Good." She took a long swig. "We were shooting, and things were fine, until about half an hour in. Just after we talked. Then somebody tripped over a lighting tripod behind me. You know, the tall ones with the spots on top? They fell, the tripod went over, and I tried to catch it. I should never have done that, never. Always trying to be helpful." She took another gulp of coffee. "One of those big knurled locking nuts had a rough place on it. It caught the back of my hand as it went over. So now I'm out of work."

"What? Did they fire you just because you cut your finger?"

"Well, what else could they do? Anyway, they didn't fire me. They just—let me go until this thing heals. But they're on a tight schedule. They're not going to be able to hold the shoot for me, and no one's going to use me for anything anyway until this is better. And what if it scars?"

Her frustration was palpable. Peter sat down with her, and took that hand again, and held it. "Have you ever scarred before? I mean, you must have cut your hands. Lots of people do."

"I don't, usually. At least, I don't think so." She looked at both hands. "I can't even remember the last time I got a good cut. But it doesn't matter. Scar or not, it's going to be weeks before this heals so you can't see it anymore, and at least a week before they can even think of covering it with makeup. Anyway, even if they could use makeup, it would have to be waterproof because of the suds and things, and waterproof makeup's far too thick for the sort of close-up shooting that they need…. Oh, Tiger."

She put her head down on her folded hands and let out a long breath. "So much for a thousand bucks a day."

"Aren't they even going to pay you for what you did today?"

"I don't know. When I left, they were still discussing whether they could use the footage they had, or scrap it and bring in another model. I assume that union rules mean I'll get paid for the couple of hours' work this morning; but I doubt I'll get the whole day's worth." She sighed. "This is so *infuriating*. Never mind. How did you do with the phone company?"

"Better than I expected, but nothing like as well as I had hoped." As he explained, her face fell further. "They were pretty good about it, but I've a feeling there's only so much slack they'll cut us. We'll have to cope. But I did get one scrap of information last night that might be of use."

"Yeah, last night. I was too dozy to pay much attention when you came in."

"And I was too tired to tell you much, so you didn't miss a thing." He told her briefly about his meeting with Mel Ahrens. When he got to the bit about the Russian Mafia, MJ started to shake her head.

"Those are not nice people," she said.

"Well, I would have thought that came as part of the job description."

"No, I mean… There's been so much about them in the news lately. And they're not like the Italian gangsters—they always seem to be more careful about involving innocent bystanders. But these guys—if they even think you're any sort of threat at all, they'll shoot you."

"You've been watching too many movies. They're all crooks, they're all dangerous, and they'll all involve as many bystanders as they need to get the job done. Besides, I'm not that easy to shoot. Some of them found that out last night."

He told her about the Kalashnikov-toting ram raiders. She tsked at him—then looked slyly at him from the corner of one eye. "All that jewelry, and you didn't bring me any."

"Now, now. Some of the police are uncertain enough about Spider-Man as it is. All it would take would be me seen lifting one little stone, or one pretty necklace, and that would be it. Open season on web-slingers."

"I guess so."

"Hey, you've got a girl's best friend already. You don't need any more diamonds than the one you've got on your finger right now."

"I don't know about *that*! You know what they say: you can never be too thin, too rich—or have too many sparklies."

"I don't think I've heard that last bit before."

"Maybe not. But all the same, I like this diamond a lot. And I like you a lot." Then she grinned. "But what was this other lead you were talking about?"

Peter tapped Sergeant Drew's card, lying on the table among the other paperwork left over from last night. "It seems he has somebody coaching him where cell phone fraud is concerned. I'm supposed to give him a call today or tomorrow, then go talk to his technical adviser. Whoever he is."

"Or she," MJ put in.

"Okay. Or they. Drew was walking a company line; the police are always pretty closemouthed about 'private contractors.'"

"Do you think he-she-they can help us?"

"I don't know. But it's worth investigating, anyway. Even just for the sake of general information."

MJ got up and went over to the coffeepot. "So, what's the plan?"

"I'm going out with Ahrens tonight, to cover an interview with some disgruntled Russian crook who might spill a few cans of beans on his ex-comrades."

She looked over her shoulder at him, the sunlight from the kitchen window catching in her hair and setting it ablaze. "I really don't like this, Peter," she said. "It's bad enough that Spider-Man has to deal with crooks and gangsters, but if you're going as Peter Parker—"

"Spider-Man comes too. Even if he doesn't show. You know that. If I have to move fast to get out of harm's way, then I'll move first and look for explanations afterwards. An adrenaline rush or something like that. Look, Ahrens was being cautious, but I didn't get any feeling that he was worried about his safety."

"That's fine for him," said MJ. "But it's *your* safety that *I'm* worried about."

"He wasn't concerned. Not for his life, or mine either."

MJ poured her cup of coffee, went to the fridge for milk, then stirred fiercely. "So he's always right about things like that, is he?"

He shrugged. "Well, he's still alive."

MJ came back to the table. "Did you say that he thought the Russians were connected with this CCRC organization?"

"There may be a connection. We'll know better after the interview. The guy Ahrens is talking to didn't want to say a lot up front."

"It couldn't be a trap, could it?"

"I don't think so. If they wanted to shoot him, they'd just shoot him. They wouldn't invite him to their hideout and *then* shoot him."

"Why not? If you wanted to keep it private…"

"No. At least, not if you ever wanted to use that place again. Killing people in it would count as fouling the nest. He says that they're trusting him not to have a tail—whatever 'trusting' means in the circumstances. Still, he's never let his contacts down before, so I suppose he's got a reputation to maintain."

MJ stirred her coffee again, then looked up. "Did you catch the news this morning after I left?"

"No. I was either in the shower or holding in cell phone hell."

"Then you didn't hear about the nuclear test?"

"What nuclear test?"

"In upstate New York."

"What?"

MJ nodded, looking somber. "It seems that somebody detonated a small nuke in a little town upstate."

"Dear God. Was anybody hurt?"

"No. It seems they did it underground, in some mining facility like the French did last year in the South Pacific. Mururoa Atoll, wasn't it? And the authorities are 'refusing to comment' on who they think might have been responsible."

"Meaning they haven't a clue."

"Or don't want to start a panic. Either way, the AEC won't even say how big the 'device' was." She made quotes in the air with her fingers. "But CalTech said that the shock wave they detected was equivalent to a yield of about one kiloton."

"Sheesh," muttered Peter.

"That wouldn't have anything to do with your Russians, would it?" said MJ.

Peter shook his head and got up to see if there was enough coffee for a refill. "No way to tell at the moment. Not until the authorities are more inclined to talk about what they've found. And they may not do that for a while."

He leaned against the kitchen counter, remembering what Ahrens had said about the Russian hunger for hard currency, about how an armaments industry that had once been supported by one of the largest armies in the world was feeling the pinch along with everyone else—and was very reluctant to make that final connection even in the privacy of his own head.

"Whoever exploded the bomb," said MJ, "was not very considerate."

That struck Peter as one of the great masterpieces of understatement. "In what specific way was a nuclear explosion, ah, inconsiderate?"

"Well, the local community had just started some new commercial venture up there. Mining quartz or something like that. And now all the rock is radioactive. Literally too hot to handle. And it's going to be that way for fifty, a hundred years. So everyone's out of a job again. A whole little town with a new lease on life, destroyed just like that. Whoever could do something like that is a bad person."

Of course, thought Peter grimly, *there's destroyed and then there's* destroyed. *Whoever fired off the device could as easily have done so above ground.* But he nodded in agreement. "There's no telling who it could have been," he said. "But at least the last person we caught messing with nukes is still locked up safe in the Vault."

Hobgoblin had made a determined attempt to blow up New York City, or at least most of Manhattan, and Spidey had been lucky enough—though with Venom's often-reluctant help—to stop him. But just because one super villain had been locked up, it didn't necessarily mean that there weren't others with equally grandiose schemes.

MJ stared at her coffee cup. "If I drink much more of this stuff," she said, "I'm going to get so wired that I won't sleep for a week. And it's just too early for me to be home." She held up the injured hand and wiggled her fingers, looking at the cut with much milder annoyance than when she had first come storming through the door. "I think, given the state of this, that I might as well just go down to a couple of the restaurants where the 'resting' models hang out, and pick up some gossip about other work."

Peter looked at her affectionately. "You are just so persistent," he said. "How do you do it?"

"Right now? Probably to keep from crying." She wiggled the finger again. "The last time I ever came to another human being and bawled 'I cut my finger!' like that, I can't have been much more than six. It's just too funny."

"I still think I should kiss it and make it better," said Peter. "Or at least, kiss *something* and make it better."

MJ reached out and touched his cheek, smiling. "Your kisses always make it better," she said. "Why do you think I married you?"

"I thought it was all my other sterling qualities; my wit, my savoir faire—"

MJ just laughed, then got up and stretched. "I'll go down to the Baja," she said, "and hang out there until after lunchtime, then pick up a few things to bring home. I take it you don't know what time you'll be in tonight?"

"I have no idea what sort of business hours Russian gangsters keep, but I think you can take it that I'll be late."

"The burden of the hardworking super hero's wife; or in this case, the investigative photographer's wife."

"Something you can actually talk about, for a change."

"Well, listen, if you're not here when I get back, and if you're not going to be back before you go to this interview with Ahrens and his Russian friend," she said as she took his head between her hands, "you be careful. Be nice to these people. They have weird cultural differences."

"Ours are probably pretty weird to them, but yeah, I'll be nice."

She pulled his face close and kissed him, then picked up her keys and headed out the door.

Peter listened to the sound of her footsteps going down the hall, then slid down into a chair and stretched his legs out in front of him. His mind turned back to the Consolidated Chemical Research Corporation. CCRC, he thought, had seemed quite innocent to start with. Just one more merchant bank and its associated business concerns among the horde of them in New York. But a series of accidents—including a most unusual one involving an alien creature that actually ate fissionable material—had revealed that CCRC and the companies connected to it had been storing barrels filled with toxic waste in and around their buildings in the city.

More investigation, including an early evening Spider-Man had spent going through the files in their CEO's office, had shown that the company appeared to be involved in the transfer of transuranic elements from the Eastern Bloc. In earlier years, East Germany had been the usual doorway through the Iron Curtain, but later on, as walls came down and frontiers opened, the access routes moved slowly back into what had once been

Soviet-controlled Eastern Europe. It was material that had originated in Russia; and the reason why so much of it was being channeled into the States hadn't been immediately obvious, even from files far more detailed than they should have been.

What was really disturbing was the casual way that storage areas had been established in the center of one of the world's most densely populated cities, and the equally casual means of transport from one point to another. The drums were simply relabeled as something innocuous with no apparent concern for the consequences of an accident or leak.

And there was another person—or persons, really, if you counted his symbiotic "other"—who was also very interested in this transit of lethal radioactives across the oceans of the world and up and down the roads of America and Europe as if it were no more hazardous than sugar.

He—they—knew that no precautions were taken, and why: because it would have attracted too much attention. And knew, too, that if anything had happened, it would have been the innocents who suffered most.

The innocents. They had always been Venom's great concern, or so he constantly claimed. But interference from that quarter was one factor this equation didn't need right now. Peter tore off the topmost sheet of the pad he had been scribbling on while dealing with CellTech, and started scribbling again.

CCRC had come under investigation fairly quickly after the revelation of toxic waste stored in its properties all over New York City. After a while, the DEA had become involved as well, though entering the investigation from another angle entirely. Questions were asked about large amounts of money being channeled through CCRC's Miami branch. At first the suspicion had been that this was plain old garden-variety drug money; but then a connection to some German banks was established. A lot of Deutschmark transfers had been linked to the movement of radioactive material inside and across Europe, and the investigation had widened at an exponential rate.

Shortly afterward, the German banking consortium sold all their shares in CCRC—or were told to sell them. No one was clear on the details. Spider-Man had been following up on the case during his Florida trip and had been bemused to learn that, despite this massive vote of no-confidence by their European stockholders, CCRC was still very much a going concern.

He had thought that Hobgoblin had been mostly behind its operation, but Hobby was now snug in the Vault after his failed attempt to blow New York into the Atlantic. Of course, it wouldn't be the first time that a company kept going very-nicely-thank-you while its boss cooled his heels in prison, but it hadn't been Hobby behind it after all. The true mastermind remained obscure.

More investigation had suggested that CCRC was behind the biggest shipment of nuclear waste that anyone had ever seen. The stuff was being shipped in under fake invoices from Eastern Europe to Brazil, then north across the Caribbean—past some of the most delicately balanced island ecosystems in the world—and into Florida. There it was stored in great quantities, secretly refined, again mislabeled as who-knew-what, and finally returned to Europe, where someone was recovering significant amounts of unmarked and untraceable weapons-grade plutonium without the knowledge of half a dozen national Atomic Energy Commissions. After that, who knew where it went?

CCRC had been making vast amounts of money—and the possibilities as to where they then channeled it were fairly horrific. Countries a little east, a little south, who would be only too glad to get their hands on already-refined plutonium, for example. Peter was sure that the bottom of this particular barrel hadn't been plumbed yet. Perhaps this evening's conversation with Mel Ahrens's Russian contact might throw a little more light on it.

And maybe the man could illuminate an even worse possibility, one that even now Peter was reluctant to consider: that for all the shipping of nuclear waste one way, and refined material the other, a lot of that refined plutonium was staying right here, in the continental U.S., waiting to be used for God alone knew what purpose.

Peter got up, switched on the TV, and turned to WNN, the news channel. After about ten minutes the headline news came around again, and he found himself looking at a video shot—taken from what he hoped was a safe distance—of a flat, shallow crater maybe half a mile across. It was smooth-sided, looking as if it had collapsed from the bottom instead of being dug out from the top. Peter had seen that shape of crater before, in footage of underground tests from the American West, and more recently mainland China.

Government agencies had been queuing up to take CCRC apart; he knew that much. The corporation was under too close scrutiny right now to even risk playing with cherry bombs, never mind nukes. So who was doing this? Was there somebody, somewhere, watching him tie himself in knots of wrong theory and mistaken supposition while they quietly got on with their own agenda?

Peter didn't know; and like Mel Ahrens, knowing that he didn't know was starting to drive him crazy. He got up and set about getting ready to go out to do a couple of errands.

ELSEWHERE in the city, someone else was busy with an errand of his own.

The Corporate Registry Office of the New York State Bureau of Records is a granite-fronted building. One might call it plain, especially when compared with the more classical architecture of the oldest parts of New York. Professional people, mostly lawyers and accountants, are in and out of its doors all day, so nobody paid any attention to the tall, harsh-faced man with the blond brush-cut hair and immaculate suit and tie, carrying a briefcase so thin that he appeared to deal with only the most important paperwork, summarized and refined for his convenience by a legion of subordinates.

He paused for a second to study the front of the building, then walked up the flight of ten steps into the bureau's front lobby. If he looked a bit more brutal than the normal run of professionals, well, the more rarefied levels of corporate affairs had always been something of a cutthroat business.

It was just that this man looked all too ready to take that part of it quite literally.

He stepped up to the counter and handed a letter to one of the clerks. They conversed pleasantly for a few minutes, then the clerk excused himself and went off, returning shortly with a small printed map, a set of file envelopes, and a card with a magnetic strip to allow the man to operate the Xerox machines. The man in the dark suit thanked him, then walked up the broad stairs to the right of the reception area, heading for the stacks.

These were not stacks such as might be found in a library. Instead, they contained row upon row of filing cabinets, some tall enough to need the ladders that ran on rails across the face of the stacked files. The visitor made his way to one of the polished wooden tables set in a double line between the cabinets, opened one of the file envelopes, and fanned its contents across the surface of the table like a cardsharper playing with a new deck.

He opened the briefcase, removed several freshly sharpened pencils, set them on top of the papers, and then went across to the files and began systematically going through them. Every movement was quick, economical, and without wasted effort. He carried himself like someone who knew exactly where he was going, exactly what he was looking for, and exactly where he stood in his personal scheme of things: right at the center.

He was there for several hours, reading some files on the spot, carrying others to the table for closer scrutiny, taking still others to the Xerox machine and putting the copies carefully into his briefcase. None of the other accountants or attorneys who were using the place paid him any heed, except in a general sort of way, admiring the expensive cut of his suit, wondering why they hadn't seen him before, since he was so evidently a highflier—or, more straightforwardly, trying to guess which legal firm had started insisting that its partners spend so much time in the gym.

None of them saw him go, because he was the last one—apart from the staff—to leave the building. He packed his briefcase, closed it, then strode down to the reception desk and returned the map, the file folders, and the Xerox card. When his copy charges were totaled, he paid in cash, thanked the clerk, and left.

The Wall Street area gets fairly quiet after business hours, but there are still some good restaurants an easy walk away. The dark-suited man made his way to one of these on Duane Place and ate a leisurely supper of veal saltimbocca with peppers, washed down with half a bottle of Montepulciano d'Abruzzo. He considered the tiramisu, then declined in favor of a double espresso-corto, paid again with cash, and finally stepped out into the cool of the evening and the yellow glow of the streetlights.

He looked up and down the street, then headed east and north. Again, his path was very direct and he seemed to know exactly where he was going, even if that was right into one of the less savory parts of town. The streets where he walked now didn't have boutiques and shops and restaurants in them, or even the heavier frontages of banks and accountancy firms. Instead they had shutters rolled down over warehouse garage doors, boarded-up windows, garbage in the streets, cracked curbstones, and broken streetlights.

A voice spoke to him from the shadows. "Hey, Suit," it said.

The man paused, half-turned, and stared into the darkness. "Were you speaking to me," he said softly, "or to my clothing?"

Three men materialized in the alleyway, emerging from the shadows or stepping in from either end to block the exits. One was short and dark, wearing leather and an incongruous knitted hat with a bobble on top. It might have been funny, except that his face was not one that would take kindly to jokes.

Another was tall, fair, and shaggy, in hole-riddled jeans; a younger man than the others, with a face that looked oddly young and innocent on someone carrying such a large knife.

The third was of medium height, very pallid, his hairstyle a Medusa nightmare of dreadlocks so tangled that it was hard to tell where his hair started and his head left off. He was wearing denims and a pair of the trendy sneakers that lit up with each step.

The man with the knitted hat wasn't wearing shoes that lit up, but as he stepped forward, he produced a large, shiny semi-automatic pistol with the same self-satisfied air of a cheap conjuror performing a cheaper trick.

"Desert Eagle," said the man in the dark suit. He sounded amused instead of frightened. "My, what a great big expensive gun for such a little punk. You know, if you had bought a cheaper gun, you could afford some better clothes—and even get rid of that stupid hat."

"You got a smart mouth, Suit," snarled Hat. "Maybe you like another mouth." He gestured vaguely with the gun barrel. "Jus' 'bout behind your belt buckle."

"Maybe I like the mouth I've got."

"'Nough talk," said Dreadlocks. "Briefcase is worth about five hundred. Just take the bag and waste him." The blond youngster with the knife swallowed hard, his Adam's apple bouncing in his throat, and the man with the suit watched it move up and down with the same sort of savoring expression he had earlier given to the saltimbocca as it arrived on his table in the restaurant.

"If you want some advice," he said gently, "I don't think you should do that."

"Don't remember askin' for any," said Dreadlocks. "C'mon—let's see if his fancy suit'll stop a Teflon tip. I said waste him, man!"

Even though Hat was standing no more than eight feet away, he went through an elaborate performance of taking careful aim before he squeezed the trigger. The boom of his gun's heavy Magnum load was deafening in the confined space of the alley, its muzzle blast a stab of yellow-white flame almost a yard long. In the clanging silence that followed the shot, all of them heard the tiny tinkle of the spent cartridge-case hitting the street. But none of them really noticed.

Because this suit, at least, *did* stop Teflon tips.

Hat and Dreadlocks stood with their mouths hanging open, but the blond man with the knife took a step backward, and then another to where his companions couldn't see.

"Yes," said the man in the dark suit, watching him. "You were beginning to suspect as much, weren't you? And so only you alone shall come away alive to tell the tale. Watch, now."

The suit stopped being a suit. It boiled away from its wearer's powerful body in a whirlwind of strand and threads and ribbons that flashed and hissed as they cut through the air. Then they contracted again, snuggling close, weaving and knitting until the harsh face and the cropped hair and any semblance of a well-dressed corporate lawyer had completely disappeared, and nothing showed but the jagged, angular design of a stylized white spider across his massive chest.

Two huge pallid eyes studied them, while an impossibly wide mouth crammed with jagged fangs gaped wide, and a tongue the size of a boa constrictor came drooling and coiling out at them from between the picket fence of teeth.

"Mouth…" said Hat.

"Mouth," said the dark shape, taking a step forward. "Yes, indeed. And as you can see, we don't need another. We already have one." It grinned, and the fangs dripped slime as the grin went right around, and no matter how broad the grin became, there were always more teeth behind it.

Ribbons of ferocious darkness came swirling like tentacles from the black costume that the man was wearing, and grabbed Hat around the chest and neck, lifting him up without the slightest trace of effort until his feet dangled clear of the ground. One more tentacle reached out playfully to pull off the knitted hat, then flicked it away. Under it, on Hat's shaven skull, was an impossibly elaborate tattoo, all Celtic knotwork and tangled animals.

Dreadlocks tried to run, but another half-dozen tentacles lashed out at his legs, wrenching them from under his body so that he came splatting down full-length on the filthy pavement. The tentacles wrapped around Dreadlocks's legs tightened, dragging him closer, and then lifted him clear of the ground to dangle beside Hat. "You didn't ask for any advice before," said Venom, "but we'll give you a little more. No charge. Just remember, next time, not to attack an attorney going about his legal occasions. Everybody *knows* how nasty lawyers can be. And there's always the chance they might be someone even nastier. Like us."

The blond man with the knife knew that he could run now, *should* run, but he didn't dare to move. Instead he just stood and stared, too frightened to even drop the knife in case its clatter on the ground attracted Venom's attention.

"My word," said Venom, lifting Hat even higher and then tilting him upside-down to look at the tattoo, "that must have hurt. Not, however, as much as this."

The next few minutes were noisy and unpleasant for almost all concerned, a nightmare blur of tentacles and pseudopods that was far worse for being mostly lost in shadow. Finally Venom raised the two limp, barely breathing bodies even higher, and dropped them like so much garbage into the gutter at the side of the alley.

"These streets haven't been kept too clean recently, but that will change," he said. "Don't forget what we told you." Then he turned to the blond youngster. "They roped you into this, didn't they?"

The blond nodded his head, a tiny movement that looked more like a tremor, and let the knife slide at last from between his fingers.

"So we thought. Well, we have other business this evening, so you just run along and tell your other friends that we're back in town. Tell them that we're after one of our own this time. There's a super villain busy in town and we want him. If someone helps us, then we'll help them. And in the meantime, those of you who prey on others should stop. Take our advice. No charge."

That terrible grin spread right around Venom's face again. "Because until we find the one we're looking for, we'll keep ourselves busy with you.

And after we find that one, then there are other pleasures, long deferred. There'll be time to take care of it now. So go on now—and spread the news."

The young man didn't run. Instead his eyes rolled back in his head and he slithered down the wall in a dead faint. A pseudopod reached out and delicately pulled one of the fluttering eyelids back. "Well, we suppose you've had a busy night," he said. "Rest awhile."

Darkness shimmered around Venom, and a moment later he was dressed once more in his dark suit, with the briefcase in his hand. "No rest for the wicked," he said. "At least, not while we're around."

Then he walked off into the night.

FOUR

MARY Jane Watson-Parker walked down the street in a foul mood. She had been walking for about an hour, trying to ditch the mood, so far to no success.

She glanced at her watch. It was pushing eleven-thirty, and she had walked all the way down to Seventieth Street and all the way across to First Avenue. Now she paused at the corner of First and Seventieth, looking down toward the newly constructed towers of Cornell and New York Hospital Medical Center. Over on York Avenue, a couple of blocks down, was Baja, the restaurant that was a haven for models and the occasional confused nurse who stumbled in.

She had been putting off actually going into Baja, partly because it was still fairly early, and also because she knew that the sight of other people in there with work would annoy her. *All the same,* she thought, *it'll be a poor state of affairs when you can't face down your own kind—even when they're working and you're not. The tables turn fast enough in this town.*

She walked on up to York, turned the corner, and headed back up to Seventy-third. Baja stood on the corner there, yet another pseudo-Southwestern-chic restaurant with cloth cactuses in brass pots, too much white stucco, and too much bleached oak, but fairly passable Tex-Mex food, and a bar the size of the launch deck of an aircraft carrier. There the models perched on the stools, leaned their sometimes fairly ample cleavages on the bar, and complained to each other, male and female together. MJ smiled slightly. She was in the right mood for the complaining.

The outside sidewalk terrace was empty as yet—too much sun. It would start filling when the shadows swung around to cover it. MJ stepped in through the front door into the relative dark and looked around.

Sitting back there at the long polished bar were two models she knew, one male, one female. The man was Ted Huron, one of the tall-dark-and-handsome school, with cheekbones that could have been used to chop trees down, and stunning green eyes. The other was a female model called Hendra, with trademark six-inch-long nails, and hair that was never the same color twice. It was blue today, fading to white at the punked-out tips.

"Hi, Hen, hi, Tom," she said, strolling up and sitting down by Tom. They muttered at her cordially enough. Their nonvolubility was no surprise: it was early yet, and when they weren't working, they were club people. MJ was surprised even to be seeing them up and about before noon.

Bob the bartender came up. "Hi, MJ. Whatcha having?"

"Double kiwi," she said, "heavy on the lemon."

He went off to get her the juice. She glanced at the others. "How're you two doing?"

It was a noncommittal enough question. If they were here this time of day, it *might* mean they weren't working; but then again, *she* was here this time of day.

"Resting," Tom said glumly.

Hendra rolled her eyes. "I just finished a gig," she said. "A week in Bavaria."

"Oh? How was it?"

"Rained constantly." Hendra pushed her orange-juice glass back toward Bob as he approached with MJ's kiwi juice in a tall glass with a transparent umbrella sticking out of it. "You off today?"

"I just blew a job off," MJ said.

"Oh? What?"

She held out her injured hand. Tom gazed at it for a moment, not comprehending immediately. "You need a thorn pulled out of your paw or something?"

"No, dummy. I was doing hand work."

"You won't be doing any for a couple of weeks," Hendra said regretfully. "You want to put some vitamin E on that, make sure it heals right."

"Sure, why not?"

They gabbed for a little while, talking sports (the present hopelessness of the Mets), art (Christo's intention to wrap the Statue of Liberty), the utter uselessness of TV in the summer ("They're showing reruns of *Gilligan's Island* again," Tom muttered), politics (the recent coup d'état in Atlantis and Reed Richards's dramatic, and failed, plea to the UN for assistance). All these things were generally agreed by the three of them as signs of the imminent downfall of civilization as they knew it. After that, the subject turned rapidly to the bashing of producers, directors, and shoot administrators that they had known. No more than ten or fifteen minutes into the character assassination, the door swung open, and they all looked over to see if it was someone they had been assassinating.

Lalande Joel came in. Six feet three, weighing possibly a hundred and sixty pounds, Lalande had long, raven-black hair that had caused her to be cast in a couple of commercials as a Morticia Addams clone, and beautiful cerulean-blue eyes, blue as a Siamese cat's. Lalande had a reputation as a friendly if slightly loopy sort, and they all greeted her cordially enough as she swung up to sit by MJ.

"And how are you this fine day?" Tom said.

"Very retrograde," Lalande said wearily. "Hi, Bob. Gimme a Coke?"

"Retrograde?" MJ said.

"Well, not me. Neptune."

"Oh." MJ thought for a moment. "Neptune's a long way out. Isn't it going to be retrograde for a long time?"

"Yes," Lalande said sadly. "Forty-five years, I think."

"By the time that changes, you'll be doing senior citizens' insurance ads," said Hendra. "If I were you. I'd stop worrying about it."

"Oh, I'm not worrying, it's just—I'm conscious of it, that's all." Her Coke came and she took a sip. "And I just blew off a job."

"Oh? What?"

She presented her perfect face to them, and pointed at it with an expression of profound annoyance and regret. "Look at that," she said.

They all looked. "I can't see anything," MJ said.

"That's because I've covered it up so that I can walk the streets without someone walking in front of me ringing a little bell and saying 'Unclean, unclean,'" Lalande said. "It's a *zit*."

"It's a very *flat* zit," said Tom.

"It's not flat enough to be covered up by the amount of makeup they'll let you use in a lipstick ad," said Lalande. "And see that?" She pointed at the corner of her mouth. "There's a cold sore coming up right there. It'll be the size of my head."

MJ raised her eyebrows. It was nowhere near the size of Lalande's beautiful head yet, but she understood the problem. "Yeah," she said, "welcome to the 'I am scarred' club." She held up the offending finger for examination.

Lalande looked at it, then looked at her face. "But you're fine."

"Not for hand work, I'm not."

But Lalande was still examining her face. "Have you ever done lipstick?" she said.

"Well, I did something for Max Factor a while ago. Why?"

"Look," Lalande said, "your face is in good shape. And our lips are kind of the same shape. And you still have a SAG card. Why don't you beat it over to the job I just blew off? Maybe they'll hire you."

MJ stared at her. "Lalande," she said, "that's very kind, but what makes you think they'd take me?"

"It's like I said. They're desperate, they're on a timetable, and they have to get this thing finished by, what did they say, Wednesday, Thursday? Anyway, they've got to get it moving. And they're all just standing around there right now, howling that they can't find another model. But our mouths are really kind of close—you ought to try."

"My teeth aren't as good as yours, though," MJ said.

"I don't think it's going to matter. They were doing mostly closed-mouthed stuff with me, except for one smile—but—I don't know. MJ, go try!"

"Lalande, that's really nice of you."

"I might as well be nice," Lalande said, rolling her eyes expansively, "since I'm going to have to go into a leper colony pretty soon, at this rate. I look like the poster child for Dr. Jenner's Smallpox Cure."

"La*laaaaaaande*," said MJ and Hendra and Tom, more or less in exasperated unison. And MJ added, "It's not quite that bad, yet. Where is this job, anyway?"

"Here." She pulled out a business card, handed it to MJ. She turned it over; the address was just up Third Avenue, near Seventy-eighth.

"Go, just go," Lalande said. "They were ready to start about an hour ago, when I had to walk in and show myself to them like this."

MJ finished her juice and stood up. "Well, I'll give it a try."

"One thing," Lalande said as MJ slung her purse over her shoulder. "The director."

MJ raised her eyebrows again. "What about him? Her? It?"

"It," Lalande said. "No question. Scuttlebutt has it that this guy has dumped a bunch of models over the past few weeks. Having worked with him for a whole day, I suspect it may be the other way around. He may hire you, but make sure you get his name and yours on the dotted line, and the pay amounts inked in and dry before you actually do any work. He is"—she glanced up and around as if looking desperately for a cue card—"indescribable."

"Okay," MJ said. "Lalande—do I really want this job?"

"I don't know," Lalande said. "*I* really wanted it, until I turned into Pockmarked Grandmother Ma. But the pay's not bad. They were going to give me fifteen hundred."

"What did they wind up giving you?"

"Seven. But then they shot with me yesterday, and they couldn't use me today."

"Small world," MJ said. "Okay."

"Let me know how it comes out," Lalande said, taking another drink of her Coke. "And I hope you bite the bastard for me."

MJ heard that, though she wondered whether she'd been meant to. *Yet another interesting director. Well, we'll see....*

She headed out and looked around for a cab so as not to get sweaty on the way over. She had had her share of "indescribable" directors in her time, including the unforgettable Maurice, on this last shoot in Miami: a master of the crazed waffle, a man who didn't know what he wanted whether he saw it or not. If he did see it, he usually danced around it for an hour or so before getting down to it. Now, as MJ climbed into her cab, she wondered whether she was about to be saddled with something similar. *At least,* she thought, *I probably won't find* this *guy standing on the beach, signaling to drug runners with a flashlight.*

When she got to the address on Third Avenue, she was surprised to see that it was a side building of Auve, one of the new European cosmetic houses that had established itself in New York over the past year, and was busy making inroads into Elizabeth Arden's and Helena Rubenstein's business. It was all plate glass on the outside, and trees and green marble on the inside. She walked in the front door, paused at the front desk, and mentioned—she consulted the card—Delano Rodriguez's shoot.

"Oh yes," said the young blond receptionist, with a look that suggested that MJ had asked to do a commercial shoot with Jeffrey Dahmer. "Second floor, photo studio B."

MJ nodded and headed for the elevator. She spent the next few seconds admiring the spotless white carpet on its floor, and the shining stainless-steel walls. *How do they keep this clean?* she wondered as the bell dinged and the doors opened for her to step out. *If we had any carpet like this in my house, Peter would drop a pizza on it, facedown, within the first week.*

She headed for the studio to which she'd been directed. Down yet another white-carpeted hall with brushed-aluminum walls and a softly glowing ceiling. A pair of brushed-aluminum doors finally said *studio b*. She pushed one of them open and went in.

The soundproofing was very good here. She actually had to get the door right open before she heard the voice screaming, "How the *hell* am I supposed to make this commercial without a warm body to put the lipstick on?"

The place was chaos, the usual large number of bright lights trained on a very small space, the usual small and very uncomfortable stool on which the working cosmetic model got to perch while thousand-watt lights were positioned three inches from her perfect skin. Three of the tremendous wide-aperture movie cameras used for this kind of work sat idle around the chair. People rushed around in all directions. And storming back and forth across the room, like a beast in a cage, was the director.

ADs, assistants, script people, sound people, who knew what else, ran all over, and Delano the director was banging around in the midst of them, aimless and screaming. A few quiet people stood around on the sidelines looking like they weren't going insane, but also looking like they didn't work for this director. The room, taken as a whole, looked like a commercial for Brownian motion.

MJ had seen shoots like this before, and they had long since ceased to faze her. She strolled slowly into the maelstrom, and eventually the director's eye lit on her as he careened back and forth. He more or less screamed, "Who let you in here?"

"Lalande Joel suggested that I come over," she said coolly and held out the business card she had been given. "I understand you need some lips."

There might have been a better way to put this, since the director was the thinnest-lipped, thinnest-faced, palest, narrowest little man she had ever seen; he looked like a two-dimensional life-form trying out the third dimension, and not sure whether he shouldn't just take it back to the shop. But he seemed not to notice the verbal misstep, came over to MJ, and stared at her mouth as if it were the first one he'd ever seen.

He'll ask to see my teeth next, MJ thought. "Open, please," Delano Rodriguez said, and MJ did.

"Hmm," he said. "Not bad. It's not a speaking part. Five hundred."

"Fifteen," MJ said, wondering what kind of brain this man had. Didn't he realize Lalande would have told her how much she had been getting?

"Not for half a day."

"Yes," MJ said, amazed at her own temerity, "for half a day." *He's got all these people waiting around here, and the dollars are just burning away....*

"All right, get over there."

"Not until we get a contract signed."

The director shrieked some more at that, but she stood her ground, and after a few minutes a shoot manager materialized and handed her a template contract. There were no unexpected waiver clauses; MJ made sure the amounts were filled in correctly, and signed it after the director did. It called for "one business day," which in the business meant nine to five, or a fraction thereof.

The next eight hours were—well, indescribable. Lalande had been right about that. One thing it took MJ a little time to get used to again: the makeup going on and coming off, going on and coming off, time after time, a hundred times. Then a layer of moisturizer and a break so that the lips could recover a little—and then the whole process started again.

All through this, Delano the director went plunging around, endlessly yelling. MJ hadn't thought that anyone could yell so interminably. He yelled at the lighting technicians, the camera operators, at the ADs and the script girls, and the DGA trainee, and most of all, he yelled at MJ and the makeup artists. The lipliner was too broad, too thin, the lighting wasn't right, the lipstick shade needed to be corrected, the skin tone was bad. And this accusation he lodged against MJ as if there were something she could do about it. Her pores were too big, she couldn't hold still, she didn't look moist enough, her tongue was too red....

For a very long while, MJ asked herself the question that Lalande had asked her: *Do I want this job?* Then she thought about a bill for $4,689.72 and decided that yes, she did want it. So she sat still, and opened and closed her mouth a hundred times on order, while the lipstick was put on and taken off—and the place began to smell entirely too much like skin and toning lotion and moisturizer and lipstick melting under the heat of the lights. And the powder made her sneeze.

The hours dragged by, accompanied by the sound of screaming. MJ began to wonder whether her ears might actually be damaged by this constant noise. Certainly other people didn't spend any time nearer it than they could: the parts of the crew not actively shooting seemed to spend most of their time out of the room, leaving MJ and the poor long-suffering script girl to take most of the abuse. *Honestly, now,* she said to herself around four-thirty, *this is bad—but it's not as bad as coming home to your apartment and finding Venom waiting for you. Now, that was bad.*

The screaming continued while she was filmed with an "unseen hand" applying lipstick to her somewhat down-pouted lower lip. MJ held quite still through that, momentarily transfixed by the vision of Venom meeting the director, or the other way around. *You want to scream?* she imagined herself saying. *Here. Here's something to scream about....*

"Are you listening to me?" Delano screeched, practically by her ear. "Don't you pay attention? If you don't at least get conscious, I'm going to throw you the hell out of here!"

MJ opened one thoughtful eye and looked at Delano out of the corner of it. Some of the makeup crew near her saw the motion. One of them froze where he stood, watching. *You make it sound good,* she thought. But for the moment she said nothing, and her eye slid to the big clock across the room.

It was two minutes of five.

Delano ranted in her face. She shut the sound out, catching only occasional excerpts.

A minute forty, she thought.

"Useless, redheaded bimbo—"

A minute and twenty.

"—brains of a duck—"

Forty-five seconds.

"—dragged in off the street like a—"

Thirty.

"—waste of my valuable time—"

Eleven. Ten. Nine.

"—don't know why I don't just go down to Bloomingdale's and hire a dummy—"

Three. Two. One.

As the second hand hit the twelve, MJ shot straight up out of the cramped little chair, almost into Delano's face. He staggered a step backward, banging into a light; it swayed, and for one naughty moment MJ prayed that it might fall. But it steadied itself.

"You silly little man," she said sweetly. "You distasteful, arrogant, stupid man. You don't have enough talent to grow grass on a lawn. You've got about as much brain as a retarded billiard ball. If you had another brain, you'd *still* have just one. And what's more, you're *cheap*—I bet you'd walk miles in the snow for the chance to cheat an orphan out of a nickel." She was scaling up now. "You're a legend in your own mind, Delano. I bet you speak very highly of yourself. What makes you think you have the right to abuse these nice people the way you do? You're a heel. You're a lowlife. You barely know which end of the camera to look into. If I saw you being mugged in the street, I'd offer to hold the muggers' coats and cheer. If I saw you drowning, I'd throw you a boat anchor." MJ noticed, in a clinical sort of way, how Delano's mouth was working open and shut. He looked like a flounder. "You look like a flounder," she added, at the top of her lungs, unwilling to let the chance observation go. Then she paused. "Did I call you a fish-faced moron?"

Delano, his mouth still working, said, "No."

"Well, I meant to. I quit." She stalked past him as if he were a recently anointed fire hydrant, marched over to where the shoot manager was standing with his clipboard, and said, "Give me my money!"

"Uh—"

"Cash, right this minute," she said, "or I'm going to take that rap sheet there, the one with the overinflated budget on it, roll it up very tight and small, and shove it in the first orifice that presents itself!"

The shoot manager's eyes went appreciatively wide. He came up with an envelope and handed it to MJ.

Steaming happily, she opened it and counted the cash. Delano was muttering again, something about a lawsuit. MJ ignored him, waved good-bye to the crew, and headed for the door.

One last scream, of pure wordless fury, came echoing from behind her. She smiled. "Last refuge of the illiterate," she said softly.

A couple of men stood near the door, smiling slightly at her. As MJ approached, one of them opened the door for her, almost reverently. The other, a small cheerful-looking man with dark hair, dressed in casual clothes, spoke. "Excuse me," he said, "but I couldn't help overhearing—"

MJ chuckled. "They probably overheard me in Nyack."

"Yes, well." He handed her a business card. "Would you give me a call tomorrow, if you have the time? I'd appreciate a chance to talk to you."

She glanced at the card. It had a yellow, smiling-sun logo, and said Sundog Productions and under that, a name, Jymn Magon.

"Well, certainly, Mr. Magon," she said. "Glad to. Please forgive me, though. I have to go off and spend my ill-gotten gains."

"Right. I'll look forward to hearing from you."

Outside, MJ hailed a cab, climbed in, and as it drove off, immediately began to blush and practically to vibrate with embarrassment. She hated temper tantrums. She valued the ability to talk your way through a problem almost more than anything else. Nonetheless, sometimes it felt really good to blow up—and this was the second time in a month that she'd done it. *I wonder if I'm coming down with something,* MJ thought. *But then again, there were extenuating circumstances.* She sat back in the cab. *And now I've got all this money, too. Maybe I should lose my temper more often.*

She looked at the card again. Sundog Productions—some kind of film or TV production group, maybe? It had been a long time since *Secret Hospital,* the soap opera on which she had a recurring role for a time, and the luxury of a steady paycheck. This could be very interesting.

She decided to stop in the store on the corner and pick up some things for dinner, and make herself a snack. She hoped Peter would be back from the mafiosi in good time—but she didn't know what kind of hours mafiosi kept. Probably better not to wait up. Meanwhile, she thought happily about all the money. Money always gave her a good appetite.

And with this kind of money, I could eat a horse!

THE long dark limo with the blacked-out windows met them at the *Bugle* at about seven. Peter and Mel climbed in, and Mel said amiably to the driver, "Hi there."

The driver glared and said nothing—just waited until they closed the doors, then gunned the car around the corner a lot faster than it should have gone. He started to drive, fast, toward the Midtown Tunnel.

"I don't suppose it would be wise to ask where we're going," Peter said.

Mel shrugged. "Brooklyn, somewhere," he said. "You know and I know that the greater part of the Russian-language community is down there in Bensonhurst and Coney Island and Brighton Beach. I won't be looking closely at any street signs, and I don't recommend that you do so, either." He squinted at the windows. "But I don't think we'll be able to see any."

He was right; the glass was blacked out on both the inside and the outside, an interesting effect that left them with nothing much to do but sit back and enjoy the ride. It was a very plush car, a stretch Mercedes limo with all the extras: champagne bucket, television, phone. "I'd suspect this thing of having a pool," Peter said.

"His other one does, I hear."

"His other one?"

"Yeah. Just the Russian love for hot water, I guess. But also, Dmitri is a little, well, flamboyant. That's why you're along. He likes publicity—within reason—and he'll find the presence of a photographer nice. He'll feel more like we take him seriously."

"Oh. And don't we take him seriously?"

"Absolutely. But a little coddling never hurts when you know there's an ego involved. Which there is. Try to avoid his bald spot."

Peter chuckled.

After about forty minutes, the car began making a lot of turns. "Oh," Peter said, "this is the part where we get disoriented."

Mel laughed. "I was disoriented the minute we went through the Battery Tunnel."

"It wasn't the Battery. Had to be the Midtown."

"See? What'd I tell you?"

Outside, the car engine noise seemed to change—got closer, more immediate—then a lot more echo-y. "We're inside," Peter said.

Mel nodded. The car stopped, then both the doors opened from the outside.

Peter and Mel looked at each other. Then carefully, keeping his hands in view, Mel got out. Peter did the same on his side.

They were in a parking garage, no telling on what level. There was nothing to see but unbroken concrete walls in all directions. All around the car stood a group of big, serious-looking men, some dressed more like bouncers than anything else, some dressed fashionably enough in dark pants and windbreakers or casual jackets. All had lumps here and there under their jackets, and all were holding guns, too, some of the biggest ones Peter had ever seen.

Mel turned to one of the men, who reached inside his jacket and removed his gun. There were a few grunts of admiration before the gun vanished. Then the men looked at Peter.

He held out his camera to the nearest of the large men. The man took it from him, examined it closely, and gave it back with utter unconcern. Then all of them turned toward one of the nearby doors in the concrete wall, and some of them began to head that way. Peter and Mel followed them.

They went up several flights of stairs, their many footsteps echoing together. They came to the door. One of the suited men pushed it open, and Peter and Mel went in after him.

They came out in a long hallway of what looked like an apartment building. The hallway had no windows, only doors, and all of them shut. The leading bodyguards led them down to the last door in the hallway and opened it.

Peter and Mel went in, looked around. It was an apartment, and a beautiful one: high ceilinged and very modern, with big windows, except that all the big windows had their Venetian blinds down and shut. Tasteful lamps were on here and there, sitting on handsome antique tables and among old overstuffed furniture. The room was eclectic without looking designed. The way they were kept, the things in it obviously belonged to someone who liked them and took care of them. And sitting on one of the overstuffed couches was a little man in a light shirt and dark twill trousers, reading a copy of the German newspaper *Die Welt*.

Peter looked at the man, and thought that he had never seen anyone who looked so much like a weasel. It was partly the shape of his skull, partly his odd kind of widow's peak receding hairline, partly the reddish cast of his hair. The rest of the effect was produced by little, bright, close-set eyes and a small delicate mouth. A bit of a surprise, that—Peter expected something bigger, somehow. The overall effect was of being looked at by someone who lived entirely by calculation, wits, wiles, and plotting.

As he saw them come, he tossed his newspaper aside and held out a hand for them to shake, Mel first. "Dmitri," said the little man, "Dmitri Elyonets." His voice was a light, pleasant tenor, not heavily accented at all.

Peter stuck his hand out. "Peter Parker."

"Welcome. Please sit down."

Peter looked around. "Before we get started," he said, "I'd like to know what the ground rules are. Am I allowed to take pictures in here?"

"In here, yes. One warning: of me, take the back of my head only."

That's going to make it interesting trying to avoid the bald spot, Peter thought, but this kind of challenge was what made photography interesting, especially with vain, image-conscious celebrities. "One-third profile from behind?" Peter suggested.

Dmitri considered. "Which side?"

Peter went around the back of him and had a look. "Right, I think."

"Very well. You're a smart young man, you handle it that way."

"What about your people?" All the men who had accompanied them up from the parking lot were now in the room with them.

Dmitri looked around and then waved some of them out. "Anyone here, them you may photograph."

Peter was glad of that. If all he'd had to take pictures of was the back of Dmitri's head and his furniture, it would have been a pretty bleak and limited shoot, even seen as an ego exercise. The bodyguards, by and large, had interesting faces, and looked like the population of a James Bond movie before the hero had shown up—a bunch of grim people seemingly ready to produce flying bowler hats with a sharpened rim or steel teeth at a moment's notice.

Peter began to move carefully around the room, taking pictures of the contents and the men, trying to show, without emphasizing it, the gangsterish look of them as they stood in classic bodyguard pose, hands folded in front of them. "So," Mel said. "You called for this meeting. I was glad to come. I've known about you for a while."

Dmitri laughed. "Yes, I know you have. Sooner or later we would have had to meet. I prefer it this way."

"I'd be curious," Mel said, "about exactly what the cause of our meeting is. If rumor tells the truth, you're doing well enough in business."

"More than well enough," Dmitri said. "The usual things endemic to this part of the world. Gambling." He shot a quick glance at Peter to let him know he was included. "A little asset shifting."

"You mean the laundry," said Mel.

Dmitri rolled his eyes a little. "And some newer areas. Wire work—"

"Electronic fraud, you mean," Mel said.

Dmitri laughed again. "Always the semantics, with you. Well, business has been doing well enough. But it never does exactly as well as you'd like, so one is always looking for new ways to expand, eh?"

"True enough," said Mel. "But I get a feeling that you've found some people involved in some kind of expansion that makes you nervous."

Dmitri said nothing for a moment, simply gave Mel a long cool thoughtful look. "There," he said at last, "you would be right." He hunched over a little, his hands clasped in front of him, and Peter got one of those "back of the head" shots that was still very eloquent of the man's personality: his tension, the liveliness of the man.

"There are people in my business," said Dmitri, "who are not as cautious as I am. When you're here for a while, you learn that any business, whether one like mine or not, is a renewable resource. Yes? You have to treat it with respect, not stretch it too far, not overextend it. Push it too far, it dies. But don't push it hard enough, it stagnates. Always a question of balance.

"But right now," Dmitri continued, "there are people out there who only see the push. And their dealings are somewhat—" Dmitri shook his head. "They push, but they're not afraid. They don't care about the balance. They don't look forward, not past tomorrow."

"Do you know who these people are, specifically?"

"Ah," Dmitri said, "well. You must be clear: my concern is not to go straight." He waved a hand dismissively. "If I did straight business in this town, I would have to work ten times as hard to make a third, a quarter, of the money I make now. I know what I like. But I want things stable." He leaned over to thump the coffee table in front of him. "I want things to stay the way they are. In the old days, on the collective farm when I was a boy, the world itself would show you what had to be done. Milk the cow too hard, too often, its poor old udders get sore, and the milk dries out. Milk it much too hard, and it dies, or someone takes it away from you. I don't want that—dead cows, or missing ones. I want it to give milk for a long time yet. But there are people doing things that make that impossible. So—" He threw his arms wide, an expansive gesture. "I come to you. I come to the press. Here freedom of the press is everything, and what the press says is listened to. I want people to know. So I call you, and ask you to come listen to me, while I tell you about the people who are going to kill the cow."

"What you're saying, if I understand the agricultural idiom correctly," said Mel, "is that there are people becoming affiliated with your— organization—who are pushing for such high-profile scams or amounts of money being shifted, that they would be impossible to hide. That they're likely to attract the attention of the really big law-enforcement agencies down on you: the FBI, the CIA—"

"Oh, the CIA, they're here: we know them, they know us," Dmitri said. Peter wondered briefly just what that meant. "These people, they aren't careful—they're going to make business bad for all of us. They're greedy—or else something worse than greedy, and I am not sure what that might be. But this I feel sure of: something else is going on in some of the other organizations which I do not understand."

"Well," Mel said, pulling out his notebook and a pen, "let's hold that for a moment. Let me be clear, too. Some of these people are not friends of yours—there are old feuds. I am thinking in particular of the organizational head called Galya Irnotsji."

Dmitri sat back on the couch again and rubbed his nose a little. "Well, he is an enemy of mine, yes. But that is not the reason I want to stop him. I want to stop him, and his people, because they are going to do something bad to," he waved around him, "this place. Which is my home now, which has been good to me." He shot a sidewise glance at Peter, who was taking another picture. "You'll think perhaps it's odd. I am—you know what I am." Dmitri shrugged. "But still I want to be good to the place that was good to me. I'll take what I need to live. I'll make money from the fat banks and the big companies, and hide it where it can't be found. But past that, people should live the best they can."

Peter nodded, getting the feeling that here was a modem version of something he had thought had died out in the Middle Ages: a genuine robber baron, who nonetheless had started out as some kind of skewed gentleman.

"Now let me tell you what you ask," Dmitri said to Mel. "Galya, yes. A thorn in my side for a long time now. He's started dealing with somebody, not one of us—not Russian or Ukrainian, not at all from the other community, the Italians, or any of the Chinese. This person that Galya deals with—I don't know who he is or where he comes from. Now, lately, my eyes and ears"—he waved outside, suggesting that they were everywhere—"my people tell me he's been bringing in a little hot stuff."

"Nuclear material," said Mel. "From where?"

"I cannot say. Not that I won't tell you—I don't know. I have to tell you, I have handled some of this myself, but not for here. To send away. There are always buyers for that. But the stuff that Galya's handling is not going out of the country. It's coming in, and it *stays*. Not just coming in and staying in one place, either, but being shipped many places. New York, Detroit, Chicago, Atlanta, Los Angeles, Denver—all the big cities. Everywhere, small shipments have been moving around for the past couple of months. The shipments, they're labeled 'industrial waste' or something else—it doesn't matter. We know what they are. When I started hearing about this, I didn't know what Galya was shipping. I found out eventually. It's hard to keep a secret in our business.

"Then, the other day, we hear that upstate, in the Adirondacks— here, in our state, our home—someone has blown up an atomic bomb. A little one, but a bomb. And I think about all those cans and packages of 'industrial waste,' and I wonder, What does this mean? For a while, I'm not sure that this means anything. Then, yesterday, I hear that Galya, several days ago, had a big payment—*big* payment—so that he's having to launder it all over the place. And now I hear he's gone down to the Caribbean, to Mauritius, I think it is, to see about the finishing touches, the last work on his new house. A big house, a lot of money spent on it—like a little town. You know what real estate costs down there. It must have cost a fortune, even by our standards."

Dmitri leaned forward again. "At first I thought he just wants a house on a little island so he can run drugs easily. Everyone does it down there. You rent a flying boat, it files some fake flight plans—it's easy. But I just don't like it, don't like the way it feels. All these things, together, at once—I think Galya is involved in something that's going to be bad for business, bad for my people, bad for people in this country, this good country where we came to make a life for ourselves, a living."

Peter raised an eyebrow and took another back-of-head shot.

"I want him to be stopped. I want to tell"—he almost choked on the word—"the police what they need to know to stop him."

Mel and Peter looked at each other, and Mel began making neat small shorthand notes. "Names and dates?" said Mel.

"Names and dates."

"Then let's start."

It took a long time. Dmitri was a tireless talker, who would not let Mel tape anything. Shorthand was all right, though, and for the next three hours Mel wrote as tirelessly as Dmitri talked, taking down names of nearly every crook, major and minor, who was working with his enemy Galya—phone numbers, fax numbers, details about what they were doing, numbers and illegal betting shops, legal betting shops that had been infiltrated by illegal "private entrepreneurships," candy stores that were cash laundromats, supermarkets that were too, several big banks with "pliant" managers on the take, who falsified the cash transaction reports required by the IRS, or failed to file them altogether. The recitation went on and on.

When Dmitri started talking about the businesses in Peter's part of town, Peter's eyes widened. Many protection rackets were in force: false invoicing was going on at the grocery around the corner where he liked to shop, the one with the really good cheese case, plus dry cleaners, drugstores…

Peter shook his head as he moved slowly around the room, taking pictures of an old portrait here, a bodyguard there, half-dozing as he watched his boss, or the back of Dmitri's head again, as he gestured earnestly. It was amazing how much expression the back of a head could have. And on and on, until Peter found himself unable to count how many businesses in his area were *not* on the take. And Mel just wrote it all down, nodding and asking a question every now and then.

Three hours. Peter sat down, finally, unloaded his camera and reloaded it with fresh film, but it was a token gesture. There was simply nothing left to take pictures of in the room. A little while later, Dmitri sat back and fell silent.

Mel sat back too, flipping through the pages of his notebook. Then he looked up. "How's your security these days, Dmitri?" he said.

Dmitri looked around him, waved confidently at the (admittedly, somewhat sleepy-looking) men standing around him. "I trust them with my life."

"You're going to have to. You know how news travels in this town. It's going to be a matter of hours before Galya knows I've been here. He'll know what we've been talking about. After that—"

Dmitri shrugged. "The Communists knew where I was, too," he said. "I survived them. I'll survive this too. This is important," he said, leaning forward and tapping the coffee table again. "This is business. *Galya is bad for business.*"

"He'll be bad for you now," Mel said. "Even if he doesn't sneak up behind you one dark night and do you in, he must have some of the same kind of information about your doings that you have about his."

Dmitri laughed again. "Not nearly so much. He's not a subtle man, our Galya: he doesn't look behind things. I look to my future, and to the inevitability of betrayal—and so I make it as hard as I can. But we shall see. And you—what will you do with this?"

Mel looked at the notebook. "Transcribe it first," he said. "Then start fact-checking."

"You would check *my* facts?"

Now it was Mel's turn to shrug. "Dmitri, freedom of the press doesn't mean we get to print just anything we like. It needs to be true, in all minor particulars as well as major ones. We just need to check. Money laundering is one thing: information laundering is another."

"Well, all right. But," he checked his watch, "you should go now, yes?"

"I suppose we should. I'll be in touch, Dmitri. And listen—" Mel stood up. "If all this is as you think it is, you could be doing the city, the state—maybe the country—a big favor."

"It did me a favor," Dmitri said. "It gave me a place to come and do business." The glint in his eye was cheerful, and feral, and funny. "I scratch America's back: it scratches mine. *Da?*"

"*Da,*" Mel said.

"And you, young Pyotr," Dmitri said, turning to Peter. "Those pictures better be good. I have a reputation to maintain."

"These'll be the best pictures of the back of your head that you've ever seen," said Peter.

Dmitri roared with laughter. "Too bad you can't do something about the bald spot. Hey?" He jabbed Peter in the ribs cheerfully. "Never mind. A long night, you did a good job. You get in the car, they'll take you where you want."

"I'll take the subway in," Mel said. "If your guy just drops me near a D or F train, I'll be fine."

Dmitri led them to the door, shaking his head and looking at them strangely. "You *are* a madman," he said.

THEY went back into the garage, got into the limo, drove around Brooklyn for a bit, then stopped, presumably near a subway stop, and Mel got out.

"All right," he said to Peter. "You want to come back with me? Safety in numbers."

"Sure, why not," Peter said, and went, for he wanted to keep an eye on Mel on the way home, unable to shake the notion that something untoward might happen to him.

They went down the stairs into the subway station—

—then straight back up the stairs on the far side of the station and across to where a couple of gypsy cabs were waiting by an all-night grocery for late fares. "This'll do," said Ahrens, hopped into the first cab, and told the driver, "First and Eighty-sixth, please." They sped off.

"Mel, would you mind dropping me off along the way?" said Peter.

"No problem. Where?"

"Which bridge are you going to take back?" he said to the cabbie.

The man scowled a bit at the odd question, then said, "Probably the Williamsburg."

Peter thought for a moment. "Grand Street and Union Avenue, then."

The cabbie glanced at him in the rearview mirror and raised his eyebrows. "Not a very safe area, this time of night."

"It's all right. I'm meeting somebody."

Mel looked at Peter with a half-amused, half-disapproving expression. "Does your wife know about this?"

"As a matter of fact, she does."

"Okay, then. Suit yourself."

They got to Grand and Union, looking deserted and desolate under the yellow sodium glow, and Peter got out. Mel leaned forward to peer at him out of the still-open door. "You'll be in tomorrow with those photos?"

"Yeah. About noontime."

"Great! I'll see you, then. Be careful."

"You're telling *me* to be careful!" Peter laughed, closing the cab door. It headed away down the street and left him alone on the curb.

Quickly and quietly he slipped behind a unit of stores on the corner, scanning the alleyway to make sure the alley really was as empty as it seemed. It was, and he got busy changing.

Half a minute later, a long, slender strand of webbing shot up to hit a high-tension tower not too far away, and Spider-Man went scrambling after it, swinging onto the next building and heading after Mel's cab. *Just to be sure,* he thought.

The atmosphere of danger he had been feeling all evening had sharpened abruptly when he came out. It hadn't been his spider-sense, but something else. Probably just good old-fashioned worry.

The cab, well ahead of him by now, was indeed heading onto the Williamsburg Bridge. He went after it, sending webbing in a long shot toward one of the bridge superstructures, and swung in a wide, fast arc out into the night. They were exhilarating, these big jumps. Sometimes even working from skyscraper to skyscraper down the concrete canyons of Manhattan could seem a little constricting. Swing too wide there, and there was always a vertical solid surface sixty stories high to get abruptly in your way. The feeling of openness as he looped and swung between the structures of the bridge was like a breath of fresh air.

And all the time, he watched the cab. There wasn't much other traffic on the bridge, except for a few cars heading the other way, toward Brooklyn. *Two-thirty in the morning, so I suppose—*

His thought stopped at the roar of a fast-revving engine below him. He looked down and saw a white minivan go tearing onto the bridge in what had to be hot pursuit of Mel's cab. Spidey swung lower as the van poured on speed, its engine bellowing in protest through a muffler whose packing had seen better days. There was a brief tire squeal as it changed lanes, then another burst of speed to bring it up alongside the cab. It changed lanes again—

—and this time sideswiped the cab hard into the railing.

Once, and there was a screech of grinding metal. A long tail of sparks went stuttering across the tarmac surface before the cabbie recovered and pulled away.

Twice, and something gave. It was the railing, lengths of metal popping free of their sockets like pins in wet clay and tumbling down toward the waiting river. Spidey swung down, shooting webbing from his free hand at first one support, then another. More webbing slapped against the shattered railing as the cab slewed to a teetering stop right on the edge, and as he hit the bridge and bounced, he sent a final jet across all three strands to give them a common anchor, pulled everything as tight as he could, and turned, gasping to see what would happen.

The web stretched, and the cab tipped over sideways.

Then it stopped stretching, and the cab caught. The minivan, whose driver had slowed to watch, gunned its engine and accelerated away on over the bridge. Even though the web was holding for now, Spidey clambered hastily up the bridge support and shot a couple more lines over the cab.

Okay, spider-strength—do your stuff!

Then he heaved, and heaved again. The cab shifted, bouncing in the hammock of web strands that surrounded and supported it, then slowly leaned back toward the bridge and dropped with a crash onto all four wheels again. There was a burst of noise from inside: two voices, one yelling, the other swearing. Which was which, he couldn't tell.

Anyway, Spider-Man didn't have time to attend to them right now. But anyone capable of that much foul language at such a volume couldn't be much hurt. As he webbed away down the bridge in pursuit of the white minivan, he saw Mel stagger out of the cab, stare at the webbing, touch it, and then gape around in all directions but the right one in an attempt to see what had happened.

At the other end of the bridge the minivan had gone lurching off at the first exit, swinging around onto the approach road so as to recross in the opposite direction. Spider-Man took himself up one of the supports and out of sight, watching in case the side or rear door opened to reveal the muzzle of a Kalashnikov. If they did, he could web either or both doors shut too fast for a gunman to react.

Mel watched it approach and shook both his fists in a rage as it drew level, then ducked as a hand came out of the driver's window with a pistol in it. The gun barked a few times, a quick volley of badly aimed shots from the wildly swaying vehicle that spanged and ricocheted most impressively, but came nowhere near him.

The van had no plates, and there was no point in Mel bothering with it any further. He turned back toward the cabbie and began waving his fists at *him,* instead.

Excess tension, Spidey thought. *Wonderful thing.* He watched the white van roar away beneath him and back toward Brooklyn. *Now then,* he thought, and went in pursuit.

It led him on a merry chase, all the more so because he was taking particular care not to be seen. It was a bit of a trick as they got off the Brooklyn-Queens Expressway, but he managed it, and followed the white van south. After a mile or so the driver plainly decided he was safe, because the van slowed right down, almost too much in Spidey's opinion. Any vehicle being driven that carefully was as likely to rouse a traffic cop's suspicions as one being driven too fast, particularly this late at night, and though they hadn't used an AK-74 in the drive-by, that didn't mean there wasn't one inside.

At one point, near Flatbush Avenue and Church, it actually pulled off into a side street while two men jumped out and used cordless electronic screwdrivers—he could hear the thin whine—to bolt New York plates back onto the front and rear of the van. Spidey took a careful mental note of the numbers; they probably belonged to another car, stolen or otherwise, but then again they might prove to be some kind of help. The van started up again, and so did he.

At Foster Avenue the van veered sideways, then after a few long blocks turned south onto Ocean Parkway. *Aha!* Spidey thought, for down at the bottom of Ocean lay Bensonhurst, and after that Brighton Beach and Coney Island.

Russian country.

He swung from building to building, keeping up the best speed he could and grateful that, even at this hour of the morning, there was enough traffic to keep the van from simply blasting out of sight and losing him. They headed into the depths of Bensonhurst, turned briefly toward Ocean

Avenue, then headed down a side street. There the van pulled up in front of a brownstone, turned its lights and engine off, and sat quiet.

Hmm, thought Spidey. *Are we waiting for someone?*

Farther down the street he could see an apartment building with an underground parking lot, and suddenly he began to wonder. Hurriedly dropping from his vantage point on the roof of the brownstone, he landed on the roof of the van. There were muffled exclamations from inside, but nothing that worried him particularly.

But instead of webbing the doors shut from the convenient position of the roof, he jumped to the ground before applying his own brand of external lock. It was just as well. Even before the occupants realized that they couldn't get out, some smart guy emptied half a clip of full-auto through the roof, right between where Spidey's feet had landed.

There were a couple of metallic squeaks and clatters as the doors were tried, then another three rapid shots turned the laminated windshield into a piece of sagging modern art. It was shoved from its frame, and people started climbing through the hole.

"Oh no," said Spidey in a disapproving voice, and started webbing them as fast as they got out. Their gunfire was what newscasters would usually call *sporadic;* it made an encouraging noise but otherwise didn't do much good. One after another, as though there were a stamping-press inside, the van emitted big men in dark clothing, and one after another, as they emerged, Spider-Man hit each one with a generous squirt of web fluid.

This resulted in the utterance of several words like *svoloch* and *chyort*—which Spidey assumed to be some manner of Russian swearword or other—as they cut themselves on glass, or kicked each other in the soft parts before they realized that there really *was* only space for one to get out at a time, and they swore even harder when they found themselves trussed securely by the lengths of webbing.

Four of them, finally. It had seemed like more. When people stopped climbing out of the van, Spidey carefully peered inside in case anyone else had seen what was happening outside and decided to stay under cover. No; it was empty.

But on the back shelf of the van were four cell phones.

As he looked at them, and a grim smile spread across his face beneath the mask, one of the phones began to ring. The men lying webbed on the ground all glared at him, and one of them growled something that sounded like "*prokleenyesh sookeen-sahn…*"

"Yeah, yeah, army boots to you too," Spidey said as he reached in and picked up the phone. He tapped the reply button, and a voice that seemed too big for the little handset speaker started yelling at him in Russian. "I'm sorry," he said in a fair imitation of the annoying CellTech voice mail, "but the party you are calling is all tied up right now."

That's a joke so old it appears in cave paintings, he thought ruefully, *but what the hey? Besides*—he glanced at the well-webbed Russian hoods lying at his feet—*how often is it true?*

There was a long pause at the other end of the phone, and then laughter. It was a shrill, high-pitched, and unpleasant sound that could never be a genuinely merry sound like Dmitri's guffaw. "Who is this?" said the voice at last, speaking in good though accented English.

"Spider-Man," said Spidey, just to see what the reaction would be. It was more laughter, even more shrill, even less pleasant, and on a hunch he said, "Galya?"

"Oh, very smart. Mister Super Hero. You have been talking to Dmitri Il'yevich, have you not? That was a bad mistake. And somebody else has been talking to him. That reporter—"

"Who your people just tried to kill."

"Yes, well, if they missed him this time, they'll get him some other day. Or someone else will. He doesn't make a lot of friends, your Mister Ah-rens." He pronounced the name in two distinct syllables. "Not that he will matter in the long run. Or you." There was more laughter. "After all, in a hundred years, who'll know the difference?" He laughed harder. "Or in a hundred days."

Then the line went dead, and a moment later Spider-Man was listening to a busy signal. He looked at the phone, thought about dumping it, then decided not to and secured the phones in a pouch made of webbing—but only after using one of them to call 911 and report automatic gunfire just off Ocean Avenue. The lights of the first blue-and-white were already riding their siren wail toward him along Ocean Parkway as he webbed away.

But he was unable to get rid of the sound of that laughter, the sound of a man who didn't have a care in the world—even about being caught in the act of attempted-murder-by-proxy. Who didn't care about anything because he knew that it wouldn't matter in a hundred days.

Whatever that meant.

ELSEWHERE in town, inside a huge apartment—a nearly unfurnished place where the curtains were kept closed all day—a big-shouldered, broad-bodied man sat behind a large desk, going through some paperwork. In front of him on the marble floor stood a slender red-haired man in a black jacket; not quite standing at attention, but giving that impression anyhow.

"Report," said the man behind the desk.

"Operation Stifle is going along nicely," said the redheaded man. "The last few—sanctions—are being taken care of. No one who knew about the Miami processing plant will be left alive within two days."

"Very good. It's not just a matter of 'loose lips' and possible betrayals. Loose ends are so untidy…." He turned over some of the paperwork on the desk with one hand, leaning his chin on the other, pausing for a moment to listen to the faint rumbling from outside. "I would do something about the soundproofing," he said absently, "except that, in a little while, there won't be any point, will there? How are the container shipments going?"

"They've almost all reached their secondary destinations. Our teams will be breaking them down into their final sizes over the next two days."

"Very well. Keep an eye on the timing of this phase, the pickups and so forth. It would be very annoying if the authorities discovered one of these shipments by mistake. Or detonated it, for that matter." The big man smiled slightly, turned over another page.

"Oh, and the guest suite is ready, sir."

"Excellent. I would hate to have Spider-Man miss this denouement; it will be so delightful to watch him realize that, for once, for all his meddling over all these years, there's genuinely nothing he can do to stop the process." A metal tentacle arched slowly over the man's back, bent down to tap, like someone's drumming fingers, on the table. "We'll see if it's true what they say, that heroes break hardest when they break. Are we sure the sanction teams are properly equipped?"

"Yes, sir, and there are six of them. We'll have no trouble bringing him in for the big blowoff."

The big man chuckled. "Blowoff. Yes. I do so love the vernacular. Very well. Anything else that needs my attention, Niner?"

"Not at present, sir."

Sitting back in his chair, the big man smiled. "It's always so satisfying," he said, "to be in the last stages of a project, watching all the pieces come together. You can go, Niner."

The redheaded man left quietly. The four metal tentacles attached to the big man's waist descended to curl and wreathe around him in a contemplative way as he folded his hands, closed his eyes briefly.

Day Hundred is coming.

FIVE

PETER woke up to the smell of coffee. He had come to bed very quietly, but MJ had been sprawled under the sheets, so fast asleep and looking so wrung out that she probably wouldn't have noticed if he'd played himself a lullaby on a tuba. His last thought before closing his eyes was that her day had apparently been pretty much like his.

Now, with the scent of fresh coffee filling the apartment, he rolled over and yawned. "Aha," came a voice from down the hall. "I know that sound." MJ was already fully dressed and made up, and not just the usual casual-but-pretty. This was the full nine yards.

"Where are you going?" he said, blinking the remains of sleep from his eyes.

"Work!"

"But I thought your hand—"

"Not my hand. My voice."

"Wait a minute. Wasn't lipstick involved in this somehow?"

"Yes, it was. But that unhappy episode seems to have borne a different sort of fruit. Come on and have some breakfast, and I'll tell you all about it. But first, you'd better look at the news."

Peter yawned again and got out of bed, wrapping himself in his bathrobe as he padded toward the kitchen. "The way you say that, I'm getting tempted to put an ax through the screen."

"Oh, I dunno. It's not the TV's fault."

He wandered in just as the morning newsreader was repeating her headline stories. "—muggers are now in hospital at Bellvue, suffering from serious injuries—" she was saying, but it was the placard behind her head that caught his attention. It showed Venom's tongue-lolling, grin-distorted face.

"Oh, wonderful."

"Yes," said MJ, pouring him coffee. "I don't like having to be away from you when he's around."

"It's not like we haven't tangled before, and I'm still okay—"

"'Okay,' he calls it," said MJ and snorted derisively. "With your ribs broken and your head bashed in half the time, and lumps and bumps and bruises all over your body, and cuts and scrapes and scratches and dueling wounds, this is some new definition of 'okay' that I'm not familiar with."

Then she sighed and sat down, looking at her own coffee cup. "I don't like it, Tiger. What if he's come back to settle things? He's had plenty of time to recover after the last fight."

"And so have I. But there's no way to tell with him. And I can't worry about him right now; I've got other things on my mind. And you? What was your day like?"

"Oh, please." She told him about meeting Lalande and the others at Baja, about the lipstick shoot, and finally about the small, smiling man who had come up to her and given her his card. She pushed it across the table to him, and Peter grinned.

"Film and television? Steady work, maybe?"

"I don't know yet. I called him earlier this morning to set up a meeting, and it turns out he's a voice director for this studio. They do animation, and he wants to audition me, to see"—she smiled—"that should be, to hear, if I'll be good for some series that he's working on."

"It could *be* steady work, then. How does voice pay?"

"Well, I'm still a SAG member after *Secret Hospital,* so there's no problem at the union-card end. If he wants to hire me, I can start right away." MJ picked up the business card and put it away again. "And after yesterday, it would be a real pleasure to work at something that didn't involve bright lights, and people running around screaming, and having to do the same shot over and over again because last time it wasn't just quite right. In fact, after yesterday I'd seriously consider ditch-digging."

She finished her coffee and eyed him over the rim of the cup. "You were out late. How did it go?"

"Yes, well…" Peter gave her a much-edited version of the interview with Dmitri, and its aftermath, then watched her nod dubiously.

"At least the shooting didn't break out while you were actually there," she said. "But I don't like the idea that this guy immediately tried to kill Mel. What's to say he won't try to kill you, too? After all, you both heard the same things."

Peter raised his eyebrows. "I'm not sure that his people even knew that I was there. But they sure knew that Mel was—and they knew he'd taken a cab even after that little shuffle in the subway station. He was being watched, but I must have gone unnoticed. Not important enough, maybe."

"A backhanded compliment, if you like. Let's keep it that way. There are some kinds of importance nobody needs." She checked her watch. "Gotta go, Tiger. Where'll you be today?"

"I've got pictures to develop, and then I thought I might follow up on the lead that Sergeant Drew gave me. His source of cell phone information. After yesterday we're gonna need some other source of help, because we're not gonna get it from CellTech."

"Right," she said and kissed him. "I'm off."

"Only a little, and it hardly shows."

Her eyes twinkled at him as she headed for the door. "We should try to get you on *Letterman* sometime," she said and shut it behind her.

Peter chuckled. He got up, washed, shaved, dressed, and did some morning maintenance for Spider-Man, mostly involving refilling the web-shooters. Then he took out the cell phones from the van last night and stared thoughtfully at them, especially the one on which the call from Galya had come through. Just ordinary cell phones; brand differences, design differences, model differences, and otherwise no different from every other cell phone in the city. Peter put on his Spider-Man mask to muffle his voice, picked up the ordinary phone, and dialed for Sergeant Drew.

The sergeant was up to his neck in work, as usual, and was just on his way out to a court appearance when Spidey got through. "Listen," he said, "just call this number," and he rattled off a seven-digit number. "Got it?"

"Got it. That's a 212?"

"Yeah. If there's a problem, say I cleared you. Then wait." And Drew hung up.

Peter dialed the new number, and waited. A moment later, a very soft feminine voice said, "Doris Smyth." "Uh, Ms. Smyth, my name is Peter Parker, and I'm a friend of Spider-Man, who—"

"Oh yes. Sergeant Drew called me to say that Spider-Man might be in touch. Or have someone do so on his behalf." Peter noticed the phrasing, and was briefly, cautiously intrigued by it. Did Drew suspect? Or was he likely to, after finding out just who Spider-Man had assigned to make the visit in his place? Well, there was nothing for it now but to press on—though not regardless. Rather more cautiously than that. Ms. Smyth continued, "The sergeant didn't say much more than that this involved a very interesting problem. Would you like to come up to my place and discuss it?" The voice was warm and friendly.

"Certainly. That is, if it's convenient."

"No problem at all." And she supplied him with a posh East Side address.

"Is there an apartment number?"

"Just forty-fifth floor. You'll know it when you see it." There was a small chuckle. "The building ends quite soon afterwards."

"I'll be there in, uh, twenty minutes."

And in twenty minutes, Peter was looking up at a sleek and expensive forty-five-floor apartment building and muttering, "Good grief," under his breath. A sleek and expensive doorman opened the sleek and expensive door for him, and Peter stepped inside.

As he passed, the doorman said, "Apartment?"

"Uh, I was only told the floor. Forty-fifth."

"Ah, that would be Mrs. Smyth. Right this way, sir." He directed Peter to an elevator—as sleek and expensive as everything else he had seen so far—then reached inside, punched 45, and smoothly withdrew from between the smoothly closing doors.

When it stopped, and the doors opened smoothly, he was looking out into a small private lobby with only one door leading off it. Then the door opened.

Peter wasn't quite sure what he had been expecting, but it certainly wasn't this. Standing in the doorway was a genteel little old lady, with pale, fine skin that was barely wrinkled, except for the demure pattern of smile and laughter lines around her eyes and mouth. Wearing a dressy little green tweed jacket-and-skirt set, with a dark, high-necked blouse and a discreet string of pearls, she looked as if she were going out to take tea somewhere nice and swap gossip with a couple of duchesses.

"Ms., er, Smyth?"

"Mrs.," she said, "but call me Doris. And you're Peter Parker?"

"That's right." They shook hands, and she gestured him in. Peter walked into one of the biggest and most beautiful apartments it had ever been his pleasure to see, wonderfully furnished with antiques and expensive porcelain: the Irish Belleek that MJ lusted after, the Meissen that Kate Cushing liked so much, beautiful old couches upholstered in crimson and gold Regency stripe, with wood that gleamed with the same deep, lustrous patina as Mel Ahrens's old typewriter, polished breakfronts and bureaus, and behind all of these, floor-to-ceiling windows with a truly astonishing view.

It was not at all the sort of place where he expected to find help for his and MJ's cell phone problem.

"Forgive me," Peter said, "but—Well, I'm just blown away. This view goes right 'round, doesn't it?"

"Oh yes. I have the whole floor. My late husband used to be in shipping. He was quite successful, but, well, George isn't with us anymore." She cleared her throat. "Anyway. Sit down and have a cup of tea, and tell me what your problem is."

They sat down at a handsome glass-topped table at one end of the huge main living room, and Peter explained what had happened to MJ's phone. "Yes indeed," said Doris. "There's a lot of that nonsense going around. Very nasty. And of course, the phone companies aren't wildly eager to do anything about it. All they want is to cover their assets, so to speak, and expenses too, of course. They'll happily take it out of their subscribers' pockets."

"I've noticed that," Peter said.

"Yes, quite. So much easier than trying to find a way 'round the problem. But then, *that* might cost money. You don't have the phone with you at the moment?"

"No, I don't. My wife's got it, and she's out on business."

"All right," Doris said. "Well—"

"Forgive me," Peter interrupted, "but I'm not sure that you—I mean, what do *you* do about this kind of thing?"

"Come back this way, Peter Parker, and I'll show you."

She led him out of the living room and across the kitchen, out the far side, and into another room that was as big as both the first two rolled into one. Bookshelves were here, and more beautiful old furniture, and a corridor that led along one side of the building, walled with more floor-to-ceiling windows looking out over the cityscape below.

"I just can't get over the view," Peter said again. It was true; he'd been as high, or higher, when out web-slinging, but that had never been an activity conducive to rubbernecking.

"George always said I should be comfortable in my old age, and I've always liked to see what's going on around me. This seemed to be the best way to combine both wishes. And here we are." She opened up a door on the left that might once have led into a guest bedroom.

Now the guests would have to be communications experts from the CIA. At the very least.

What had once been a bedroom was now packed with more electronic equipment than he had seen in one place since the last time he passed through the Fantastic Four's headquarters. From floor to ceiling along every wall, mounted in studio-quality instrument racks, were banks and banks of scanners, fiber-optic phone connections in bundles as thick as packs of spaghetti, ISDN linkages, phone-band radios, what seemed to be short-, medium-, and long-wave radio receivers bristling with buttons. Everything was black, very expensive, and very professional.

"George always said I should have a hobby," Doris said to Peter, "and I never could get the hang of knitting. And as for casting off, I must have created the longest single sock in history. But he left me quite a bit of money—"

That's an unnecessary observation, Peter thought, looking again at the cool, dark racks of equipment and feeling them gaze back at him with tiny LED eyes.

"—and I always did like keeping in touch with people. Listening to what was going on. And what comes through here is so much more interesting than most talk shows, don't you think?"

"But isn't it, er, sort of illegal to listen in on private communications?" he said, staring at yet another floor-to-ceiling wall of equipment, this time so complex that he couldn't even guess at what it was meant to do.

"Not if the government gives you everything they want you to listen with."

"Um," said Peter. There were some statements that went beyond words.

"You know, I had one of the first cell phones sold in New York City," Doris said. "And about ten others. I got cloned, too. It made me cross." She said it quietly enough, but there was something about the glint in her blue-gray eyes that suggested it wasn't a good idea to make Doris Smyth cross.

"I started doing some research into hacking, and phreaking, and all the other ways a phone company could be cheated. It got very interesting. So I started buying equipment to look into the problem myself, and quite soon after that I tracked down the people who had cloned my own phone. It was easier then: they left a track through the ether half a mile wide. Once I had done that, I contacted the phone company and passed the information along. They were so impressed that," she smiled up at him, "they hired me. I do fairly well. Something like a ten percent identification rate, which I gather is pretty good. The end result is that all three of the major cell companies here—including CellTech—use me as a security consultant. I charge them what the market will bear, and in some cases I do work *pro bono.* That will be you, young man. Or rather, your wife. They socked you for—how much was it?"

"Four thousand and change."

She tutted disapprovingly. "A young couple like you can't be expected to pay that kind of money. We've got to do something about these regulations. They're hurting people. It's not *your* fault that half the criminals in New York are making cell phones work for them. It's only to be expected, though. If something is worth money, then someone, somewhere, will work out a way to steal it." She led the way out of the room, and closed its door behind her.

"Surely there have to be other consultants working on this kind of thing," Peter said as they walked back up the glass-walled corridor. "So how come you're doing so well? It could just be natural talent, of course."

Doris glanced up at him again, and smiled. "Flatterer. If your wife finds that you're wasting perfectly good compliments on eighty-year-old grannies, you're going to get in trouble!"

"Eighty?"

"But I don't look a year over sixty, right?"

"Really, you don't. What's your secret?"

"Snoopiness, and having something to do. Something really interesting. Everyone should have something really interesting to do, even if they have to keep it a secret. Have you?"

"Er, I do a lot of freelance photography, for the *Bugle* and for—"

"Oh? Would I have seen any of your pictures?"

"You would have seen some in the *Bugle* over the last week, yes."

"Then you're a celebrity! Well, you have to come and sit down, finish your tea, and tell me all about it."

"I'm not a celebrity, not really," Peter said. "It's my wife—" But it was no use. He got to sit down again with Doris, and tell her all about his wife, and especially about MJ's stint in *Secret Hospital.*

"She's in *that*! Who is she? The nurse? Why, she's famous! And her phone was cloned. The very idea! Well, we're going to do something about that." Peter smiled slightly. MJ was going to love this. "And you tell her she has to come up and see me. She has a *fan.* Why, she must meet such interesting people, and do such interesting things."

Peter let her rattle on. It was plain that one of the reasons Doris was so good at her job was that she loved gossip. No scrap of information, not the most petty detail, was too insignificant for her attention.

He sat with her for what must have been the better part of the afternoon, and after the rather dodgy company of last night, she was a pleasure. But more to the point, the more he talked to her, the more he realized that under her little-old-lady exterior she was a serious professional, and a power to be reckoned with. She told him about ways that cell phones were being illegally used in the city that even he, with his daily exposure to the criminal element, had never dreamed of. Not just drugs and gambling and money-laundering, but coordinating times for burglaries, bank robberies, and even simple street muggings. One criminal gang had even been using them as detonators to blow up the gas stations they had just robbed.

"A lot of people just don't understand electromagnetics," said Doris, "much less what the various frequencies can do." She eyed Peter keenly over the rims of her glasses. "But some of us do understand. That's one of the reasons why I bought this place."

Peter glanced around him. "Well, it's a really nice apartment," he said, "and the view—"

"No, not that. Come out this way." They stepped out onto the terrace together. Doris's terrace went all the way around her penthouse, and it had emitters, microwave receivers, and relays that made the setups on the Empire State Building and the World Trade Center look seriously inadequate. Peter had never seen so many antennas together in one place in his life.

"I've got line of sight into three states," she said, "and from here I've also got line of sight down into three-fifths of the city's streets. That means a lot of the time I can do a direct ambient-radiation trace on any cell phone in use. It's really very useful."

Peter was feeling much better, reassured as well as slightly awed after seeing the quiet room that had looked so much like a starship's bridge. He was still thinking about MJ's phone bill, but also about the other phones that he had taken from the Russian thugs last night—and Galya's bizarre, threatening laughter. *I wonder, is there any way to get her to look at that one?* he thought as they went back inside to sit at the table again.

"More tea?" said Doris, already reaching for the pot.

"Uh, thanks, Doris, but I really think I should be going."

"Well, bring that phone up for me—as soon as you can get it away from your famous wife." She smiled at him. "I really would love to meet her sometime."

"And I'm sure she'd love to meet you, too. I'll get the phone just as quick as I can. By the way, there was a sort of crank call to it, just last night. Is there any way to find out where it came from?"

"That's fairly simple, as a rule. Once I've got the phone itself, I can look into it." She saw him to the door, shook his hand, and told him to have a nice day—then went back inside to resume her secret identity as a senior-citizen spook.

Peter shook his head. Little old ladies just weren't what they used to be.

SUNDOG Productions was a small, four-story brownstone in the middle Forties, near Third Avenue. She buzzed the door, and a voice said, "Yeah?" It sounded like Jymn Magon.

"It's Mary Jane Watson-Parker, for Jymn Magon," she said.

"Oh, hi there, Mary Jane! Come on up." The lock buzzed, then clicked, and MJ pushed the heavy wooden door open. She swung it shut behind her, then proceeded to climb four levels of stairs straight up from the street. There had been other doors leading off on each floor, but those were all boarded up.

The topmost door had another buzzer, and a glass window overlooking the reception area. A friendly-looking woman waved at her through the window, and buzzed the door open as she approached. MJ was fairly fit, but even so she was panting a little as she stepped inside.

"Some climb," she said.

"Yep," said the other. "But it tires the burglars out as well. Come on in. I'm Harriet."

"Pleased to meet you."

The door of one of the inner offices opened, and Jymn Magon came out. "Hi, Mary Jane," he said. "Come in, please."

"Call me MJ if you like."

"Glad to. Now, if you'll just step this way, into our corporate lair." He led her through the reception area and out to the back of the brownstone. One side of the room had a spiral staircase leading down from it into the areas beneath, and this upper floor had been partitioned into offices.

"We keep the studios downstairs," said Magon. "All the doors and windows are sealed. It's not just for security; we had to install a lot of anechoic insulation for the voice recording, because of the usual traffic noise—and because we're real close to Grand Central and all five gajillion trains that use it. Even so, we've got some of the quietest studios in the city here."

He ushered her into a comfortable office whose walls, where they weren't covered with framed animation cels, were decorated with children's drawings, and offered her a chair. "Sit down, and tell me what you've done." Behind his own desk was a big poster entitled the six stages of a project. MJ glanced at it briefly, then gave him a quick verbal résumé of her work.

He was most impressed with the *Secret Hospital* work—less for the work itself than because she had survived in one piece. "I've heard what a zoo that place was," he said, grinning. "I hear about it every time I meet someone who was ever on the show." They also talked briefly about yesterday's lipstick shoot, and about the "director of death."

"All right," said Jymn, "so the field has a tradition of eccentric, egocentric directors. But they're not all De Mille, and they certainly don't all have his talent. So they've earned the occasional dressing-down by irate lipstick models."

MJ smiled modestly.

Jymn went on, "But, while everyone appreciated the words, I also appreciated the voice that uttered them. You've got really good timbre.

When your voice drops, it gets very dry, and there's a strong sound to it. Too often, female talents think they need to shout when they're voicing a strong character, and they end up sounding like early Margaret Thatcher, all squeaky and nasal. It took years to get her to drop her voice low enough to get the men to listen to her, apparently; and once she got it right, they hated her twice as much. She was too good at making them do what she wanted."

"What exactly did you want to audition me for?" MJ said.

"Well, right now we're starting work on a new syndicated series: sixty-five episodes. It's a super hero show called *The Giga-Group.*"

MJ raised her eyebrows. "I thought the super hero trend was getting kind of old." With so many super heroes making headlines and lead news stories, people seemed to have grown tired of the fictional versions.

"No, the pendulum's swinging back again. Go figure. In any case, we've got a nice syndication deal, so *someone* thinks the trend's not dead— and insists on giving us their money as a proof of confidence—and I for one have no objection to finding out. Right now it would be 'casual' or 'fill-in' voices that we'd want you for: not running characters, but ones who appear in specific episodes as one-time characters, super villains, things like that. Do you think it's something you could do?"

"I could certainly audition for you, and we'll see how it turns out. But," and she smiled, "I've always been kinda fond of the super hero thing."

"Good. Character identification already. Come on downstairs. We'll do a brief set of readings from some scripts that have either been shot, or are about to be, and see how you sound. Oh, and one last thing: your SAG membership is current?"

"Yes."

"One less thing to worry about, then. Let's go."

She followed him down the spiral staircase and into the reception area for the third floor, a central windowed area overlooking four separate recording suites. Two of them were already occupied: people were sitting inside manipulating soundboards, and beyond, through yet another set of glass windows, other people were sitting in director's chairs with music stands in front of them, microphones hanging from the ceiling, and intent expressions on their faces.

"Some of our leads, in there," said Jymn, pointing to the suite on the left. "Mike Bright, Chris Clarens, and Orkney Hallard. They're three of our good guys. The bad guys are out to lunch. Anyway, come over here into Four, we'll get you comfortable, and then you can read some stuff for me."

MJ went along happily enough. This was the least tense audition she could remember having for a long time. Jymn brought in a stack of scripts and riffled through them, pulling pages out.

"Since we're working on such short notice," he said, "and you haven't had a chance to read any of this material ahead of time, I'm not going to give you anything too substantive. I'm looking for emotion here, the kind of crazy voice that you were doing yesterday when our friend was yelling at you. Big reactions, over the top; don't be afraid to shriek."

She gave him a wry look. "Would you believe that shrieking is the one thing I've tried to avoid most in my entire life?" she asked.

"Good. Then you'll do it here, and get it out of your system—and if this works out, you'll get paid for it." *Now there's an interesting concept.* MJ smiled. She was liking this better and better all the time.

"Most of these characters are bad guys, so don't be afraid to 'nyah-hah-ha' a little. Unfortunately, our broader viewing public is not yet *au courant* with the concept that bad guys don't necessarily *sound* bad, but it's gotten into the culture and right now we're stuck with it. Please God, twenty years from now when everyone's reading Tolstoy and Kipling again, all this will seem very silly. Okay, I'm going to shut you in here for the sound. Do you have any problems with claustrophobia?"

"Not at all. I live in a Manhattan apartment."

Jymn chuckled. "Just thought I'd check."

MJ spent the next hour reading what seemed very fragmentary lines in various funny voices: high, low, mean, menacing, scared, funny. It was surprisingly easy—or maybe it was that the director was surprisingly good. Jymn had a talent for drawing out tones and colorations of voice that you didn't know you had. It helped that he had quite a talent in the voice line himself. If you couldn't actually understand the sound he wanted, even after five minutes of explanation that could vary from earthy and graphic to highly technical, he would make it at you. Then all you had to do was imitate, and you were home free.

"Aha!" MJ would cry, pronouncing it with more or less exclamation marks as required; and "Now I've got you!" in every shade of meaning, including some that were highly inappropriate to a children's animated show; but there was something about the way she said, "Resistance is useless!" that on at least one occasion, Jymn pitched face-forward onto the mixing board and pounded it with his fists.

"I'm sorry," she said. "Should I read that one again?"

Jymn hit the talk button that let him be heard inside the soundproofed studio, and though more or less back under control, MJ could still hear tremors of laughter running up and down his voice like a piano hit with a brick. "Yes," he said. "Oh yes. The same way as last time, but louder!"

So it went, for a cheerful hour and more, until Jymn stopped, keyed his talk button, and said, "Are you thirsty? Can I get you an ice water or something?"

The thought had occurred to her in midcackle of some villainous laugh or other, about ten minutes or so ago. "Oh, yes, please," she said. "I'd love it."

"Sit tight," said Jymn. "I'll be right with you." He got up from the mixing desk and vanished out through the sound-room door.

Trapped, thought MJ. *I'm trapped.* Not so, of course. The heavy baffled door wasn't even locked, staying tight shut as much by its own ponderous weight. But the studio was so quiet, its anechoic tiling soaking up every sound. She sat for a few minutes and just listened to it. New Yorkers forget, sometimes, just what real quiet is, and if taken out into the country they lie awake at night, missing the distant or nearby sounds of subway and traffic, and the endless subliminal roar of ten million other human beings packed together into the confines of the city who were just getting on with their lives.

In here, you could almost believe that human beings weren't outside anymore. Almost, but not quite: the listening ear could detect a truck going by or the rumble of a deep train, even though it was a sensation more felt than heard. She put her hand on the tabletop nearby, but there was nothing. Complete stillness. A total lack of noise.

I wonder, thought MJ with a grin, *if we could get these people to redecorate the apartment.* The grin went mischievous. *Or at least the bedroom.*

Jymn came back in, carrying a Coke for himself and a tall cup of ice water for her, and brought them through to the studio. "Listen," he said, his voice oddly dull and lifeless as the tiles flattened all the subtleties out of it, "we don't need to do any more today if you don't want to."

"Okay. Whatever you like." She took a drink from the Styrofoam cup and glanced at him over the rim.

"Sorry about these things," he said. "Déclassé, I know, but we haven't been able to get up to the Gristede's for the good plastic ones." He sat down in another of the director's chairs. "You're very flexible," Jymn told her. "You take direction brilliantly—and you're very good-natured. It surprised me yesterday when I saw you in that madhouse. I was wondering what someone so calm could be doing there."

"Toward the end of the day," said MJ, "I was beginning to wonder myself."

"Anyway, are you available?"

"How soon?"

"Tonight."

"To*night*?" MJ blinked. "So soon? I presume you're not talking about dinner."

Jymn laughed. "No. We're taping a *Giga-Group* episode tonight, and we lost a couple of our voices. Business, sickness, the usual annoyances. I can use you as an interim voice. I'd like to do that, and I'd also like to have you work with our people a little bit, because I suspect we could use you as a regular. Semi-regular, at least. Our main character voices are all spoken for, but we've got some recurring villains, and one of them is female."

"Villains? Hey, fun!"

"Yes, I thought I heard that when you were screeching before. You don't get much chance to be *baaad*, do you?"

MJ chuckled, but couldn't really tell Jymn why. The thought running around in her head right at the moment was that, being a super hero's wife, you mostly concentrated on being *goood,* just as good as you could be. It meant maintaining your own career, while attempting to make sure that a man largely unconscious of his own needs—and especially his own stomach, even when it was growling the loudest—got enough food, enough rest, and enough love to make up for what he didn't get in the violent dark world outside that he inhabited.

"No, and I don't see that tonight will be a problem."

"Okay. As far as I can tell right now, we'll be starting at the usual time. That's around eight; it gives the city a chance to get quiet. I have to warn you, these taping sessions do run late, usually eight to midnight or a little over. We contract in four-hour blocks, we pay Guild scale per four hours, if we run past midnight, we pay Guild-and-a-half. Does that suit you?"

She did a brief bit of mental math and realized that at the moment, Guild scale for four hours was about $500 per hour. "That's fine," she said. "Do we need to sign the paperwork?"

"C'mon upstairs. We'll cut it, get the signatures—do you work through an agent?"

"Not for voice."

"You may want to look into that at a later date. If you start working with other companies"—he smiled slightly, as if remembering something—"you'll find that some of their terms aren't as advantageous as ours, and it could be in your own best interests to get an agent with great big teeth and a loud voice to do the screaming on your behalf. We can recommend a couple if you like; otherwise talk to the talent. They'll be more than happy to tell you horror stories." Jymn rolled his eyes. "Endless horror stories. Other than that, let's go write you a contract and sign it. Do you need an advance?"

She opened her mouth, closed it again, shrugged, and said, "Why not?" Then added, carefully, "You're awfully, er, easygoing about this."

"Oh, absolutely. We know where you live. If it doesn't work out— we'll sue your butt. In the meantime, I've got work to do; I'm clear that you like this work, and I know you're good at it. We'll see how you work with a group, but I'm confident enough to advance you one night's salary. We'll go down to the cash machine and fish it out, give you a chance to do your shopping before we start work." He gave her a look. "I know how awkward it is. Arranging the rest of your life gets rather interesting when you've neither days nor evenings free."

"Well, thank you," said MJ. "Thank you very much. Has anyone ever told you that you're very, well, *nice*?"

He gave her a look that was appreciative of the compliment, but somehow ironic. "Not recently. But then, after our friend yesterday, Attila the Hun would look *nice*."

Chuckling, she agreed, and followed him out.

ELSEWHERE in the city, other people were also arranging their evening. Eddie Brock had been a busy man since the previous night. He was staying in a small, quiet hotel on the Lower East Side and had spent the better part of the afternoon going over the paperwork and copies he had brought back from the Bureau of Records.

Hunting down the actual ownership of a company can sometimes be deadly dull work; at other times it can be a good deal more exciting, especially when the trail starts heating up. There are shells within shells, share percentages, and beneficial and beneficiary owners in a paper trail that can sometimes lead halfway around the world in twenty different languages. And if it should involve one of the countries that *really* take their banking secrecy seriously, like Liechtenstein, then the trail can run up against a wall that no amount of digging will ever penetrate, and the ownership of a given firm will never be truly known.

Ownership and control are only rarely the same.

Eddie Brock was nothing if not methodical. His background as a reporter had tended to make him so until, late in that reporting career, issues had so blinded him to the truth of one business he was investigating that he jumped the gun and printed material that could be proved untrue. The rebuttal…

He shook his head, hating to let the thoughts into his head again, but unable to keep them out.

Another authority had stood up in front of the world, embarrassed him, called his integrity into question—a questioning that had been applied retroactively to everything else he had ever written—and caused him to be blackballed from the one profession he had ever really cared about. But that other authority, and the person behind it, would be dealt with soon enough.

But right now, he had other fish to fry.

CCRC was being audited by the government. Everybody knew that. The IRS, the DEA—and for all he knew, the FBI, the CIA, and even the FAA—were all on its tail. And Eddie Brock was still enough of an investigative reporter to know that a company involved in the laundering of millions, and perhaps *billions*, of dollars of illegal funds is not just closed down like a bankrupt shop putting its shutters up. There is almost always warning that there's trouble in the wind and, almost always, the money goes away.

Specifically—and it was practically the standard method—other companies would be purchased or established and clean money already laundered through other sources would be channeled into them. Any companies that had previously been founded as intermediaries to service the laundering pipelines would themselves be closed down. In military terminology, it was a "withdrawal to prepared positions."

Eddie sat now in his little hotel room working on a laptop computer whose present program allowed you to construct complex graphical expressions of relationships between completely abstract factors. Those could be anything you liked, but corporate entities was what he was looking at right now.

The New York Securities and Exchange Commission and the Bureau of Records had begun to work very closely together since the days when insider trading first reared its head. There was now more information available about companies opened in New York, the United States, and, though to a lesser extent, overseas than there ever had been before.

In particular, Eddie was looking into those overseas connections, searching for large amounts of money that had been moved out of CCRC or its accounts—and especially money that had been removed from the United States—during the period immediately before the audit had been announced.

The period when Venom and Spider-Man had been tearing the place apart.

Compared with other countries, even those that didn't make an issue of it, banking secrecy in the U.S. was little more than a joke. If you had friends in the right places, say the IRS, the DEA, or even some local police departments, and you knew the right phone numbers to call, then you could access databases that would tell you far more than any private citizen had a right to know about the movement of funds in and out of the country. Put that together with the SEC's register of newly formed companies and corporations—onshore or off, it didn't matter—and you had a powerful tool for levering your way into corporate secrets. Always assuming you knew how to sort the data.

Fortunately, Venom knew how. The copies he had made yesterday in the Bureau of Records were all New York based. Some of them were hard copy because they were already too old to be worth keeping online. Say, three months old. That was how fast corporate formation turned over in

New York State. Not as fast as in some offshore havens, certainly—where if you lingered too long over lunch you could find your morning's harvest of information already well on the way to obsolescence—but fast enough.

Venom was looking for corporate formations that were immediately bolstered by large transfers of funds. Certainly bank managers, and banks in general, were required to report suspicious transfers of any value, and all transfers above a certain threshold, to the government. But if your bank manager was pliant, as it were, and kept that way by regular applications of folding grease, then such reports would never be made. He would know you, would certainly know what you were capable of doing if he let you down, and wouldn't be *suspicious* of your money because he knew full well that it was dirty.

His search was for newly established companies without a track record, whose names appeared in no previous register—but who suddenly sprouted large bank balances that they promptly wire-transfered offshore. New York being what it is, he found plenty; the difficulty was in determining which were more or less innocent, and which were the ones he was after.

Almost all had addresses of record in lower Manhattan; hardly surprising, since that was where almost all the really good corporate formation attorneys had their offices. By correlating the records of the SEC and the IRS, an interesting picture was assembling itself. Again and again he was turning up references to a company called Rothschilds Bank Securities S.A. He knew immediately that it had been purchased off the shelf and that the name was no accident. Most shell companies invoked the name of some encouragingly large and well-established concern, trying to sound legit whether they were or not, and whether their reasons were nefarious or just good business sense.

Rothschilds had a brass-plate address which was the same as that of a well-known lawyer in South Street, near the seaport. It had opened for business about three days after the break-in at CCRC's New York headquarters during which a fission-eating life-form had killed two homeless people. Even then, paranoia or merely guessing at which way the wind might blow had caused them to jump.

Rothschilds was formed on a Tuesday. By Friday of the same week, it was showing a deposit balance at Chase Manhattan of $180 million.

By the following Monday, that had already dropped to $60 million, and the rest of that week saw further deposits of $240 million come and go. Venom knew a pipeline when he saw one.

He also knew what most people did not, the actual names of the company directors. The SEC required those on the registration documents, U.S. banking policy being what it was. He noted their names and addresses, but paid most attention to one in particular, a name that had also appeared far down the list of CCRC's directors.

There may be others, he thought, *but that one will do to start.*

"Time to go," he said aloud to the symbiote he wore as a second skin, and it responded at once. The tank top and shorts he wore changed shape, and blackness wrapped itself around him. Blackness with fangs.

Twenty minutes later he was in lower Manhattan.

It was getting on toward dinnertime, and those offices not already shut were showing signs of doing so. Venom, high above it all, was calmly wall-walking up the side of another of Wall Street's latest crop of steel-and-glass monstrosities. He had never cared for the newer schools of architecture. Its soullessness appalled him, and it probably cost hundreds of thousands of dollars each year just to keep those acres of glass clean. It did, though, make it easier for a wall-climber with the proper technique to go straight up the side of a building in a big hurry, pick a window, and get inside unseen except by their potential victim.

In this case, Venom knew the window very well. He had called earlier, and the building's security people had been more helpful than they knew about which floor and which office he was most interested in. After that it was just a matter of sticking his head quickly down from above window level for a peek inside, to see who and what were in a given office. Now, in a south-facing corner suite with a nice view out over the Battery, he was correctly positioned, and he was waiting.

A man came in and closed the door.

The office was a handsome chrome-and-steel affair, late Industrial Modern. Very sleek, very Memphis. Venom had difficulty with the Industrial style of interior design. It looked, well, *industrial,* and there was no point in saying that was the intention all along. There were other, subconscious intentions being pandered to, and as for the people who willingly embraced it…

He smiled, and the symbiote smiled with him. They were hardly *people* at all.

The man sat down at his desk, and there was a long moment of stillness before Venom extruded several pseudopods and punched the window in. He was careful to strike hard enough that all the glass went inward, rather than falling on the innocent bystanders down below whose business this wasn't.

The man sitting at the desk, who had just taken off his jacket and tossed it onto the couch, jerked around, mouth and eyes wide, his curly hair practically standing on end. He was a tall man, broad shouldered and built big.

But not big enough.

Venom was on him in two pounces, and only a few seconds after that the man was well-wrapped in alien tentacles, with several others waving their razory tips in front of his face.

"We may as well call you Mr. Rothschild," said Venom conversationally, "since that name is only slightly more fake than your own, and a good deal more pronounceable."

As Venom swung in the window, a second man was coming in through the door. He stopped in his tracks, staring. The first man looked at him, then at Venom, and yelled, "*Bistrah! Ookhadeetyeh!*"

As this second man turned to run, "Rothschild" threw himself straight at Venom's huge, dark figure, struggling. This didn't discomfit Venom in the slightest, though the collision of his heavily muscled body was enough to stagger even him. And that stagger was enough for his flurry of extra pseudopods to miss the fugitive. Not by much, but by enough for him to get clean away.

There were, if that was possible, even more fangs and drool on show than usual when Venom turned his attention back to "Rothschild." "You seem unusually eager to keep us from meeting your friend," he said grimly.

"Innocent guy." The English had only a faint hint of Russian. "Nothing to do with you."

"Innocent indeed? You've been watching too much television, Mr. Rothschild. What makes you think that anything you could say would make us consider him—or you—innocent? Now then. You're evidently a well-educated man with an excellent command of language. Do you understand the meaning of the culinary term 'julienne'?"

There was a long silence, broken by gasps, whimpers, and the occasional thin scream.

After a few minutes, Venom said, "Don't imagine that anyone is going to call the police, or that even if they do, that New York's finest would be so foolish as to come in here. We really think not. Now, let us tell you why we've made this little visit. We want to know—"

"CCRC," gasped the man. He was bleeding from dozens of long, thin cuts, and what remained of his shirt wasn't white anymore, but he was still comparatively unharmed, and knew the reason for it only too well. Venom was making him last.

"No, no, nonono," said Venom, shaking his head and spattering drool all over the carpet. "The answer we want is nothing so simple. For instance, we already know that you're involved with CCRC's, er, reconstruction. *Perestroika,* isn't it? A shame to leave all that perfectly good money in a country. And we also know all about the setting up of several new foundation trusts in Liechtenstein and Switzerland. And Hungary. Interesting choice, Hungary. The country with the tightest banking laws in Europe at the moment. The country least likely to tell you where *anything* is. They know what side their bread's buttered on; they're looking to pick up where Switzerland now leaves off.

"That said, there's other business of much more interest to us. Someone has been moving large amounts of, let's call it 'cargo,' but we both know what it really is, don't we? And it glows in the dark. So this 'cargo' is transported from a processing plant in Florida, all the way up to a location in upstate New York that's not too far from the southern boundaries of the Adirondack State Park. Details are hazy, as the eight ball would have it, on where exactly that storage location is. But we're not going to ask again later. We're asking you now. And we want to know, or we will continue our investigation of cooking terminology. Julienne, until we're bored. Then frappe. Then puree, or saute, or maybe just plain old shake and bake. Your choice, *tovarish.*"

There was more stubborn silence, and then another shriek.

"Yes, we imagine that would have hurt," said Venom. "But then, you so obviously didn't hear us that it can't have been working properly anyway. However, we think we should warn you, we really *are* getting impatient. Oh—we almost forgot. Besides everything else, we also want the name and address of your friend."

"Friend?"

"The fast-moving gentleman whose escape you were so eager to cover just now. Interesting, that you would protect him with your life."

"But I—"

"Oh, but you are, you are," said Venom softly.

There was another silence, punctuated by more screams, and then a sobbing voice said, "558 First Avenue. 1-D. I don't know his name."

"Then his nickname will do. He has to answer to something, we would think. Or do you just whistle?"

"He's—he's called Niner. Niner." The voice gasped, and choked, and said nothing more.

"My," said Venom. "We didn't think it would spurt like *that*." He spent a few minutes arranging the limp body against one wall of the office, then picked up the phone, dialed 9, then 911, spoke briefly to the recording, and hung up.

Ignoring the sound of shallow breathing from the far side of the room. Venom stalked about, opening files and drawers, looking here and there. The bottom drawer of the big steel and smoked-glass desk was the one that interested him the most. As he opened it, the lock gave way with a small metallic crunch and he looked down at five cell phones.

"Well, now," he said. "Let's pack these up and take them away, shall we?" The symbiote obligingly produced several pockets in its costume, and only a few minutes later, a black shape slipped quietly out of the broken window and was gone.

LATER, in a quiet, shadowy place among the sewer tunnels under the Union Square subway stations, Venom sat calmly going through the cell phones. He would key each one to bring up its home number, the little screen would obediently display the digits, and he would dial. Every time he did so, the reply was in Russian. It wasn't a language he had ever studied in depth, but he didn't need to understand what was said to understand well enough how these phones were being misused. One by one, he set them aside. For later.

He repeated the same procedure for the fifth and last time: activate, read, dial, listen. But this time when he held the last phone to his ear, it didn't speak to him in Russian.

Instead a cheerful voice said, "Hi there! This is Mary Jane Watson-Parker. Either I'm out of cell right now, or the phone's switched off, or it's throwing another hissy fit. Don't ask me. Just leave a message after the beep, and I'll call you back as soon as I can."

As the phone beeped at him, Venom pressed the hang-up button and briefly stared into space with those huge pale eyes. "Well," he said. "Well, well, well."

His grin was ghastly.

SIX

ABOUT an hour before, Peter walked out of the door of Doris Smyth's apartment building. He had dropped off the phone with her, and promised to talk to his "famous wife," and even get an autograph for her.

Just where is my famous wife right at the moment? he wondered. There were other things to think about, though. He badly needed to be up among the tall buildings and about his business of taking care of the city. He ducked into an alleyway, changed, and went straight up the face of a building not too far from Doris's place.

He swung a little way around the neighborhood just to loosen up, then clung to a building just across from Doris's penthouse, hiding a little around the corner to peer at her. Through the floor-to-ceiling windows she was quite easy to see. The size of the apartment was still quite startling, and right around from the living and dining area he had already seen was a small office complex with a connecting door into the electronic inner sanctum.

There, Doris hammered away on a PC, pausing now and then to stare quizzically at the screen. She was one of the fastest typists he had ever seen. *God, could we use her in the newsroom,* he thought. She might be eighty but, plainly, arthritis wasn't something that she worried about too much.

Go get 'em, Doris. Find out what you can.

He swung away, heading for midtown and parts south.

It was an excellent, bright, sunny day. A breeze was blowing—down among the trees he could hear the song of an occasional bird, and as he swung around the corner of the building he met yet another monarch butterfly, going about its business with great purpose thirty stories up.

"What are you *looking* for?" he said to it in passing as he shot another jet of webbing at the next building along and paced it. "Girl butterflies?

Boy butterflies? A good pollen pizza, extra nectar, hold the anchovies?"

Apart from food and mating, he couldn't begin to guess what might be on a butterfly's mind, especially when that mind was hidden in a brain smaller than the head of a pin. Yet this butterfly seemed to have an appointment, and moreover was running late.

Crash!

He hit something—or rather it hit him, something black that left him hanging from the web, dazed and reeling. Then he realized it was swinging back at him, hard. He clutched the building to keep from falling, slapped his hands and feet against the walls, and saw what was heading for him again.

It was Venom, of course—anyone or anything else would have alerted his spider-sense. But, as a by-product of the brief time when Eddie Brock's symbiote had bonded with Peter Parker, Venom did not trigger the early warning sense that Spider-Man depended on.

Venom came at him, all claws and pseudopodia, tongue and teeth and dribble, and that enormous mocking, hungry grin.

"Okay, *that* does it. I'm losing my temper now!" Spider-Man snarled. He leapt clear, no web of his own to hold him up, only a superheated jet of his own anger at this repetitive, constant, stupid, inconclusive feuding. It wasn't just painful, it wasn't just an interruption to a crime-fighting career that was dangerous enough already, but it was also getting seriously tiresome.

Spidey slammed into Venom, wrapping himself around the barrel-chested upper body while the pseudopods wrapped themselves around him, and concentrated entirely on pummeling Venom's head.

"I didn't start this!" he yelled furiously into Venom's ear. "I didn't start this, and right now I don't need it!"

"What you need," said the dark voice, "and what *we* need, are two entirely different things." Pseudopodia wrapped around Spidey's throat, and choking, he tore at them. "And this is a need that has remained unsatisfied for far too long!"

They slammed into the side of a building and glass shattered. Even through his daze, Spider-Man found time to wonder how the people inside were going to explain that particular claim to their insurance company. Fortunately the impact wasn't as destructive as he had feared— the wrapping that the symbiote was trying to fling around him had acted as a blunt-trauma pad all down his spine.

But the high-frequency crash as the massive sheet of plate glass gave way was enough to make it shiver away from him a little. Spidey took the opportunity, thrusting out with all his limbs in an attempt to shake it loose. It let go of his legs and arms, but still clutched him by the throat, and Venom's leering face wasn't far away either.

They dropped a dozen feet as Venom's own organic webbing stretched under the double burden, and Spider-Man used the distracting jolt as they stopped to add a little more distraction, by doubling up, arching around, and doing his level best to kick Venom in the back of the head with both feet.

One heel skidded off the rounded skull, but the other hit home square and solid. This time it was Venom's turn to reel and, as they swung out and down in another descending arc, they finished against yet another window and another explosive crack of breaking glass.

"The insurance companies in this town are just going to love us," Spidey said. As the huge slabs of shattered glass shifted and screeched, the sound loosened the symbiote's grip still further. He managed to shake himself free of its grasp and jump sideways onto the vertical surface of the building. "Would you mind telling me what brought this on?" he demanded.

"You brought this on," rumbled Venom. "All of it." Strands of darkness wreathed about him as the sound-shocked symbiote recovered what passed for its equilibrium.

"You'll be claiming I bombed Pearl Harbor next," sneered Spidey, scuttling around the corner of the building. Like a huge, black steam train, Venom came around after him. It was what Spidey had been expecting, and he was ready.

A great wad of webbing from both web-shooters hit Venom full in the face, head, and upper body, and together he and the symbiote went down, spinning more webbing behind them to break their fall.

Spidey followed, bounding down the glass wall. It didn't last; these things never seemed to last. Venom shot out another stream of webbing that anchored on the corner of the building; he recovered, turned the speed of his fall into a swinging arc, and came back up and around fist foremost.

It caught Spider-Man right in the pit of the stomach. No matter how good-looking, how well-defined, or how just plain hard the human abdominal muscles might be, they remain only muscles. Flesh, not armor plate. Spidey folded over like a half-closed penknife, coughing and winded, and the next blow took him in the side of the head.

Only reflex took him out of harm's way, because he had no idea how he had wound up clinging to another building twenty feet away. Apparently his autopilot must have cut in at the right time.

Venom came at him again. Spidey leapt to meet him, wrapped his arms and legs around him, and sent them both tumbling out and down toward the street. They turned as they fell, web shooting out from Venom to anchor on a building cornice as they plummeted past it. The strand didn't just stop their fall, but snapped them back up several stories as if they had been bungeejumping. They hung at the end of the line, not even doing anything so structured as trading punches but just flailing at each other.

Then another fist caught Spidey on the forehead. "You just don't *get* it, do you?" he shouted, shaking another incursion of stars away from his vision. "I don't want to *fight* with you." He hammered each word home with a quick left-right-left sequence into Venom's lantern jaw.

"You do a good imitation," Venom snarled, punching back. They were swinging to and fro by now, a great, thrashing, furious pendulum of kicks and punches, the soggy sound of impact and the grunt of breath. One massive punch hit Spidey in the side, and there was a single new noise, a sharp, whiplash crack as one rib gave way.

That's the third time this year, said a surprisingly calm voice in the back of his head. *The doctors at the University clinic are never gonna believe this one. What are you gonna say? "I walked into a door." They're already sure that MJ beats me up!*

Then spider-sense went sizzling along his already-outraged nerve endings and made him flinch sideways—just before something that had nothing to do with Venom or the symbiote whizzed past his ear. Spidey knew exactly what it was, because he had heard the same sound too many times before: the tiny sonic boom of a high-velocity bullet, then a perceptible instant later, the slam of the shot.

Already shooting webbing for his getaway, he glanced down and saw the man with the gun. Even at this distance its long, curved magazine was unmistakable. Another AK-74 Kalashnikov. Another puff of flame bloomed from its muzzle. This time, a spout of dust and fragments exploded from a little crater higher up the building, the snap of the bullet's passage drowned out by a more Hollywood-authentic whining ricochet.

Then even that was lost in the flat, all-too-real hammer of automatic fire as the gunman lost whatever passed for patience. He flipped the Kalashnikov's selector to full rock-and-roll and tried to use quantity where quality had failed. The bucking, juddering gun proved at once that it wasn't as easy as it looked in the movies.

"Now what?" Spidey panted bitterly as he swung high and wide for a safe, solid corner. A cluster of full-metal-jacket slugs chewed masonry in his wake and left a series of appropriately spiderwebbed holes through yet another long-suffering window.

"It would seem we have company," said Venom. He was laboring a bit himself, and his chest was heaving. Spider-Man's last kick had caught him squarely over the breastbone, and the symbiote's arms were boiling around in a seethe of undirected fury.

"Anyone I know?"

"Russians," snapped Venom, trying to get his breath back. "CCRC."

"Oh really?" The gunfire stopped briefly as a magazine was replaced, then started up again. It was back to single shots again, each one probing and picking like a needle at possible hiding places. "Truce?" suggested Spidey. "For now, anyway?"

"Not much choice," Venom gasped, plainly reluctant as always to take the course of good sense. "We'll continue this discussion later." He looked down and pointed at a man in a peculiar floppy dark hat with grommets in it. "There. We need him. His name is Niner."

"I'll do what I can," said Spidey. The rib felt bad. "You take the batch on the left, I'll take the batch on the right? Okay, then *go*!"

They leapt together and bullet strikes spattered around them; but always above. It's harder to shoot at a falling object than one might think: it's a near ninety-degree deflection, and the lead required keeps changing with the acceleration of the fall. And that's only with a steady thirty-meter-per-second-squared descent. These two targets kept splaying their limbs as air brakes or balling up tight to drop faster.

Where other jumpers from tall buildings only strike the pavement and splat, these two struck the pavement and bounced. Feet and fists lashed out, and the men on the ground, who might have thought that safety lay in distance and ballistics and weight of firepower, were rapidly taught that their only true safety lay in distance alone.

The gunmen had all of their Kalashnikovs on full automatic now, spraying bullets everywhere with a complete disregard even for their own safety, never mind the locals who were scattering in all directions. The lack of blood in the street was only due to the fact that most of the firing had been directed upward.

"These people are going to get hurt!" Spidey shouted at Venom. "The innocents, remember? Save them!"

But the innocents were already doing a good job of saving themselves. They were New Yorkers, after all, and not entirely unfamiliar with the sound of gunfire, though not with gunfire that was rapidly approaching the noise level of a small war, nor of battles involving super-powered beings on the street. They knew to get under cover when they heard it.

"Him!" Venom shouted, pointing at the man in the strange dark hat, and took off after him. Niner dashed into a building and was gone, with Venom in pursuit. And that left Spider-Man all alone, facing four or five gunmen, all of them firing rather chaotically at him. Or at least in his general direction. Being given a big, shiny assault rifle was one thing, but possession didn't automatically grant mastery, and wherever these guys had been recruited, it wasn't a marksmanship school.

Spidey gave thanks for that—and also for the fact that the sight of Venom's fanged maw and his cloud of whipping black pseudopods would have been enough to unsettle even the coolest, steadiest shot. These characters were like reeds in the wind.

He bounded toward the gunmen, never moving in the same direction for more than a split second at a time, leaping up the sides of neighboring buildings for the added advantage that came when he jumped back down again. Once again it proved true that shooting at a rapidly moving, rapidly foreshortening target could quickly ruin anyone's aim—though never so much or so fast as when that same moving target finished its last leap with both feet full in your chest. Or your stomach.

Or the one man Spidey took out simply by landing on his head.

He hit the ground rolling, swung out one leg at ankle level, and neatly chopped both of another Russian's own legs right out from under him. The man's AK-74 went one way, his legs went another, and the mafioski's head hit the pavement with a satisfying, if rather hollow, *clonk*.

Two others were running toward him, firing from the hip in the best traditions of all those old newsreels from World War II. That was fine if the purpose of firing was to keep a lot of enemy heads down; it was rather less effective when trying to hit a bouncing, elusive, rubber ball of a super hero. And whether running, jumping, or standing still, using any gun on its full-auto setting guzzles ammunition and empties one of those long banana magazines in just three seconds.

That was something else films tended not to bother with, except for dramatic effect. Spider-Man had frequently been grateful for the ignorance of crooks whose knowledge of firearms came mostly from bad action movies.

As Spidey ducked behind a row of parked cars, most of them already the likely subject of yet more insurance claims, he could hear first one and then the other gun stop firing. Yet the footsteps kept on coming. Either this pair were very brave, or very stupid. And he'd seen no sign of bravery so far today.

Or maybe they were being very crafty instead. There was always the chance that they had managed to pry their fingers from the triggers before all their bullets ran out. Or maybe they had reloads, though he hadn't seen any extra magazines so far. But like traffic, it's the one you didn't see that gets you, and he wasn't about to take any chances.

Yet when the muzzle of one Kalashnikov came poking gingerly around the end of the nearest car, it was too good an opportunity to miss.

Spidey raised his arm and webbed the weapon all over its barrel, then gave the length of webbing a good, hard yank. The gun jerked from its owner's hands and went spinning high into the air. Spidey heard it come down with a skidding clatter thirty or so yards away, and he also heard the footsteps of the now ex-gunman running away even faster than he had approached.

That left one.

Spidey was glad he hadn't risked standing up too soon, because there was a hollow metallic slap that he'd heard before: the sound of a fresh magazine being smacked home. An instant later there were three quick, spaced shots, and three heavy bangs that rocked the car on its springs. Spider-Man hadn't thought the Kalashnikov could put a bullet clear from one side of the vehicle to the other, except through the windows, but the ragged, bright-edged holes that were appearing on *his* side changed his mind.

He moved along the row of cars in a spider-scuttle far faster than the gunman could have been expecting, letting the guy keep thinking he was still four cars from his present position. That suited Spidey. He squeezed between a Lexus and the 700-series BMW beside it, thinking, *Who teaches these people to park so close?* and peered out from the shadow of a convenient wheel-arch. Spidey then waited for this last one to follow his friend's lead and come too close.

He didn't. Instead he hunched down into a position that, though it looked awkward, allowed him to see right underneath each car. If he looked underneath and saw no one hiding beyond, then he slammed four bullets through the bodywork. Two went through the front door at seat and foot-well height, then two more through the back. Then he duckwalked along to the next and did it all over again.

Spider-Man didn't like the look of this one bit. All the others had been rock-and-roll players, subject to what some reporters on the *Bugle* called "Beirut Syndrome": if it puts out enough noise and enough bullets, then it must be doing *some* good.

But this guy was good, and the parking row wasn't very long. It wouldn't be more than a minute before Spidey ran out of cars that weren't in the line of fire. But then, inside his mask, Spider-Man smiled. The solution, as usual, was an obvious one.

Totally focused on someone who had to be hiding almost at ground level behind the cars, the gunman's attention couldn't shift quite fast enough to realize that a sudden flicker of movement up and over their roofline might be more than just a pigeon. Pigeons didn't jump like that, pigeons didn't bounce like that, and most of all, pigeons didn't have fists like that.

Thud!

Spidey massaged his knuckles gently, spared just one glance for the unconscious body that had skidded several feet away, then looked about for Venom and the elusive Niner. No chance; they were gone.

He winced, and pressed one careful hand to his side over the damaged rib. *Did he just crack it, maybe?* he wondered. Yes, no, or maybe, it didn't really matter. There was no time for a checkup or an X-ray, or indeed anything much except to go back to the apartment and strap himself up—a first-aid skill at which he had way too much practice—then get back out and get busy.

Spider-Man headed for home.

THAT night, about eight, MJ headed off to Sundog to do her first night's voice work. It was a little strange, now, to feel the nervousness that she hadn't felt during the audition. *I've never really done this before,* she thought as she got out of the cab. *What if I screw up in some weird way? I'd really like to do this work—oh, please don't let me screw up.*

She pushed the doorbell, and a friendly voice said, "Hi, MJ! Come on in!" The door buzzed open.

"Hidden camera?" she said to the voice from the little grille.

"Yup," said the voice. "You wouldn't believe how many people I get to watch standing there in the daytime, picking their noses."

She chuckled and went up the stairs, a little more slowly than last time so that she wouldn't arrive out of breath. At the top of the stairs, the owner of the friendly voice, Harriet the receptionist, was waiting for her with the second door held open. "You're working on *The Giga-Group* taping, huh?"

"That's the one."

"Okay. They're all down in Six: that's the biggest room. Two levels down from this one. You want some coffee or something?"

"I wouldn't mind a Coke."

"Caffeine by any other name," Harriet said, with a lopsided grin, and went off to get it.

MJ went carefully down the spiral staircase, amazed at the complete difference of tone between this job and her last one. *Maybe making cartoons sweetens your disposition or something,* she thought. Certainly Jymn was nothing like most of the directors she'd seen lately.

Two levels down, as Harriet had said, she found Recording Room Six, which took up the whole floor. The design was interesting: the inner recording room, where the cast sat and worked, was a large U shape with a very thick bottom. On the nonmicrophoned side, in the middle of a huge semicircular mixing board, were several seats for the mixer, voice director, and so forth. When MJ came in, there was already somebody working at the board, a chunky man with a graying ponytail and a beard; next to him Jymn Magon sat, going over some pages and using a scalding-pink highlighter on them. At the sound of the door opening, he turned. "Oh, hi, MJ! Any first-night flutters?"

She laughed just a little. "Now that you mention it—"

"Don't worry about it—none of us bite. This is Paul, our soundman."

"Hi," Paul said and turned his attention back to his board.

"He's always very focused during a session," Jymn said. "Don't mind him. He loosens up afterward. Come on and meet your fellow voice talent."

He pushed the studio door open for her. "Guys? Here's your new coworker."

Three men and a woman looked back at her from the director's chairs where they perched. "Halsey Robins—he's several of our good guys." A middle-aged man with a shock of startling white hair nodded to her, smiled. "Marion Archangel." She was a petite middle-aged woman, pert and blond; MJ recognized her name as that of someone who had done a lot of commercial work in the last few years, so that there were some products, specifically a brand of margarine, that MJ associated with her. She smiled at MJ, gave her a little wave. "Doug Booth." A slim handsome young blond man dressed all in black, he waggled his eyebrows at her. "And Rory Armistead." The oldest of them, a portly man possibly in his late sixties, he nodded gravely to MJ and said, "Welcome."

"Thank you," MJ said. "I hope you'll all bear with me: I'm very new at this."

Marion chuckled. "You've done live TV, though. You'll do fine—this is a lot easier."

"MJ auditioned wonderfully," Jymn said, "and she's going to be super, no pun intended. Now listen, group, let's get our act together here. MJ, you had enough time to look over the script for tonight, and the other material?"

"Sure." Jymn had given her several copies of scripts for *Giga-Group*, and the series bible; she had read it avidly after getting home from the food store. Only Jymn's high good humor during the audition had later kept her from wondering whether she was making some kind of awful mistake, for as MJ read the bible, it became plain that *Giga-Group* was probably the most politically correct super hero cartoon she had ever seen—and she thought that because of this, the concept suffered somewhat. You could not have found a more, well, *homogenized* group of super heroes anywhere: speaking racially, sexually, and culturally alone, there was at least one hero in the group of every imaginable kind. They all had "sexy" names that were supposed to be evocative of their individual super-powers: Hotshot, Tripwire, Roadblock, Wrecker, on and on. She privately wondered how (if such a group of characters ever existed) they would keep each other's nicknames straight, let alone their normal names. *There would have to be a point,* she had thought, *where, when you're forming a new super hero group, everyone has to wear name tags for a few weeks until they get each other sorted out.* All the heroes also had (to judge by the bible) periodic outbreaks of extreme *angst,* and appeared to be cursed by the show's writers to speak almost entirely in cliches. When she finished reading through the first script she had been given, MJ was laughing so hard she practically started wheezing—and not because it was *supposed* to be funny.

"Well, you get the general idea," Jymn said. "Ten super heroes, battling more or less constantly against a rotating group of super villains who are either in jail, executing devilish schemes, or sitting at home in their secret hideaways *hatching* devilish schemes."

"They're not villains," Doug said, grinning. "They're just ethically challenged."

"Oy," Jymn said. "All right, it's true enough. This show is an ungodly hybrid between the caring-and-sharing shows of the early Eighties, and the irradiate-'em-till-they-mutate-then-put-costumes-on-'em-and-let-'em-all-fight-it-out shows of the late Eighties. That said, all we have to do is try to make it sound good."

"Frankly, Jymn," said Marion, "we couldn't do that with a rewrite by God, and the Archangel Michael running a digital mastering board. As it is, we have to make do with Paul—" Paul, outside the window, gave them an enthusiastic raspberry. "Okay, okay. *Saint* Paul."

"Better," Paul said.

"Oh come on," Jymn said, "this script isn't so bad."

"You mean, it won't be when we're through with it," Halsey said in his soft drawly voice: and MJ paused for a moment, recognizing it suddenly as the voice of a famous cat in a cat food commercial.

"You people are going to teach MJ bad habits," Jymn said, despairingly.

"At least she'll learn them from professionals," Rory said. "We haven't seen a good script for this series yet. But then it's just getting started, and that's normal. Still, we'll know one when it comes along. Meantime we'll make them sound the best we can; that's what we're taking the King's Shilling for. Here, MJ, you come sit by me and look over my shoulder while you work in."

MJ took the offer gladly, perching on the next director's chair over, and putting the marked script for that evening's work on the music stand beside it.

"Okay, people," Jymn said. "You all have your parts marked. MJ, I want you to read the part of Tripwire, the one I marked for you this afternoon; she's one of the villains. And also there's a part for a cat. Can you meow?"

MJ laughed out loud, taken by surprise, and emitted her best imitation of the loud cat that lived in the garden of a brownstone a few doors down from their building.

"Not bad," Jymn said. "Paul, you get that level?"

"Yeah, it was good."

"Okay. MJ, can you make it sound like it's talking?"

"Noooouuuuw."

"Hey, that's good," Rory said. "We've got another Frank Welker on our hands here."

"Always steady work for people who make animal noises," Marion said, smiling at MJ.

MJ smiled back. "Okay, come on, people," Jymn said, "let's get settled. From the top of Act One…"

From that affable start the evening got strange, and continued to become stranger. The script they were reading was really so bad that, at first, during the read-through rehearsal, one or more of the actors was likely to break up at any moment. Rory seemed most affected by this problem, which astounded MJ, since he seemed the oldest and most experienced. But when it came to actual recording, the guffaws were nowhere to be found. MJ found herself surrounded by people generating the voices of super heroes, ringing voices full of commitment and power. She *believed* them when they spoke. It astonished her. She tried to work to make her voice resonate that way. "A little more of that, MJ," Jymn would say from outside the recording room, and she would do it again, breathing deeply, as the other actors coached her, and setting herself into the voice.

"Don't let it make you crazy, MJ," Marion said at one point. "I've seen your commercial work. If you can act like you really believe a dishwashing detergent is going to be kind to your hands, then this isn't that much of a jump." And Marion was right. It got to the point where she could cry, for her super villainness character, "Resistance is useless!"—and believe that it *was* useless—and no one laughed. The others nodded and looked serious, and got ready to read their own parts.

There were occasional bouts of hilarity, primarily when MJ did the cat voice, and another one when Doug, playing the villain called Optimum, suddenly seemed to get his voice confused with a bad imitation of Charles Laughton doing the Hunchback of Notre Dame, and half fell out of his chair to slouch and stagger around the room shouting, "The bells! The bells!" These things always seemed to happen when there was a little tension in the room, MJ noticed. Too many errors in a take, too many takes on a line, then something would happen to let the tension loose, and the next take would go all right. A couple of times, MJ caught Jymn provoking one of these releases; other times, the actors themselves would cause them. It was the sign of a team that had worked together amicably for a long time, on and off, and who trusted one another, and had fun together.

The session went by in a hurry, this way. About halfway through the evening, Jymn said, "Marion, I'd like Glaive's voice to be a little more different from Lasso's. Let's let MJ take her." So MJ became, however temporarily, the voice of a guest super heroine, Glaive, and spent the rest of the evening enjoying learning how to produce on demand what Jymn referred to as "the right hero-style delivery," and claimed she had a naural talent for. For about the millionth time that night, she bit back a reply about occupational hazards. She was almost sorry when, by midnight, they were almost through with the script, except for some patching and relooping of lines that Paul didn't like the sound of. Finally even that was done, and at twenty after twelve Jymn came into the studio and said, "That's it, crew. Next session's tomorrow night." To MJ he said, "Nice work. You'll be back tomorrow?"

Truthfully she said, "I wouldn't miss it for anything."

"That's great. A good first night, MJ! Go home, get some sleep—we start a little earlier tomorrow. Six o'clock, everybody."

So they all departed, to a line of cabs waiting outside the studio for them. "MJ," said Marion, "you're just down the block from me, aren't you? Come on, we'll split the fare."

They did, and MJ walked into the apartment, not too much later, feeling utterly on top of the world. Another couple of weeks of work like this, and the phone bill could do what it liked. "Peter?" she said, heading for the bedroom. "You up, honey?"

The bathroom light was on. He leaned out to look at her—and MJ gasped. "Oh, jeez, honey, what *happened* to you? You're one big bruise!"

"Venom," he said, sounding rather resigned.

She stared at the elastic bandage wrapped around her husband's chest. "Oh, no, he didn't break your rib again, did he?"

"No, it's just sore. But how was your evening?"

"Terrific. I am a happy, happy woman," she said, not sounding at all happy for looking at her injured husband. "But never mind that! Come sit down and tell me what happened."

"You won't like it."

And she didn't.

IN the barren luxurious apartment, not too far from there, the big-shouldered, broad-bodied man who was born with the name Otto Octavius sat behind the desk again, going through some paperwork. In front of him on the marble floor, waiting, stood the red-haired man.

"So," said Doctor Octopus, the nom de guerre he preferred. "How are our various laundries doing, Niner?"

"We washed about eleven million dollars last week alone," said the man in the black jacket. "The cell-model recruitment for laundries has worked out very well. The problem was always finding enough people to do the legwork. That's solved now."

"Good," said Octopus. "We have a lot more to do yet over the next couple of months. I want to accelerate this process so that it's finished well before Day Hundred. Have Galya look into it—his people seem to be acting like real go-getters at the moment. What's the status on the currency situation?"

"About four billion in counterfeit is now in circulation in Europe," said Niner. "The Union's economies are going to have a nasty shock in about sixty days when their governments notice the surplus."

"Just before the Dublin summit," said Doctor Octopus. "That's excellent. The yearly G7 conference is barely a week later. They'll be at each other's throats, and whatever economic coalition remains between them and the Russians will fall apart on the spot."

A long metallic tentacle came arching over, seized one of the pieces of paper in delicate grippers, and turned it over. "Our last shipment of 'emplacements'—" said Doctor Octopus.

"They're ready to roll, sir. If we ship them during the G7, every one of them will be in place within two days. That leaves nearly thirty days of the Hundred to make the final settings."

Octopus nodded, turning over the last piece of paper, and looking keenly at Niner. "And that last emplacement I entrusted to you," he said, "that's been successfully completed?"

"Yes, sir. It's right up there, where they'll never look for it, and never find it until the sky lights up."

"Excellent. Go get in touch with Galya, Niner. I want the rest of that cash dealt with while cash still works." Obedient, Niner went. Doctor Octopus got up from behind the desk and slowly crossed the bare room to where the curtains hung down. One of his metal tentacles reached out and twitched one of the curtains aside just wide enough to let him look out. Below him, Manhattan lay in the sun: shouting, stinking, pulsating with noise and life.

"Not for much longer," he said softly, to the stones of the city. "A hundred days or so, that's all. Just be patient. A hundred days."

The tentacle withdrew. The curtain fell.

SEVEN

THE next morning, Peter got up and tiptoed out of bed, leaving MJ still snoozing there, to find an early call waiting on the answering machine. "This is a call for Peter Parker," said a soft woman's voice. "It's Doris Smyth. Would you be able to come see me sometime after ten this morning? No need to return the call unless you can't. I'll be home all day."

Has she found something already? he wondered. *Wow!* As quietly as he could, he washed and dressed and had a hurried breakfast, left MJ a note to tell her where he was headed, and then left for Doris's.

When she opened her apartment door for him, Doris looked up at Peter with an expression that was slightly more muted than the sunny smiles she had been giving him when they first met. She was still smiling, but the look had a slight edge of caution to it. "Peter! Good morning, come on in. Would you like some tea?"

"Uh, yes, I'd love some, thanks."

She led him to the dining-room table, where a teapot, a cozy, and silver tea service were set out, incongruously next to a partially disassembled cell phone, various delicate tools, and a small black box with a liquid-crystal readout on the top. "Here, sit down. Milk? Sugar?"

"Sugar, please." He stirred it in and peered at the phone. "That's our phone?"

"That's the phone you brought me," Doris said mildly, sitting down herself and taking a sip of her own tea. She reached out for the bottom half of the phone's shell, the part with the most electronics in it, and turned it over thoughtfully in her hands.

Then she glanced up at him. "I've been looking for this for a while," she said.

"You've lost me."

Doris made a slightly regretful expression. "Let me be plainer. This phone is one that both its home phone company, Americell, and the police in several states have asked me to look out for. Its present calling records have been hacked several times, with great virtuosity, by someone whom the police are most eager to find. But more—look here."

She picked up one of the tools on the table, a little slender metal rod with a hook at one end and a little slanted, slotted screwdriver head at the other, and pointed into the body of the phone with it. "See that little chip there?"

"Uh, yes. It's awfully small."

"True enough. Here's another." She picked up from the table a twin to the first chip, a tiny wafer slice of green-and-gold patterned plastic no bigger than her smallest fingernail, and with great care, using her own thumbnail, split it apart. Nestled inside it was an even smaller chip, about the size of two pinheads. Peter squinted at it.

"You are seeing," said Doris softly, "one of the better-kept secrets of the telephone industry. It won't remain secret forever, but it's doing its job pretty well for us at the moment. This is a 'covert' chip, one that the phone companies are increasingly having installed in their phones without even the manufacturers being entirely sure what it does—or most of the people at any given manufacturer, anyway. The phone companies have been so concerned about the rampant cloning of phones that they came up with a microchip whose only purpose is to secretly record all the numbers that have been programmed into a telephone as its 'own' number, for the duration of its lifetime. It doesn't take a lot of memory or power, and when a professional gets their hands on a much-cloned phone, its whole audit trail is laid out for you to see. Very useful."

She put the phone down, gazed at it for a moment in a slightly unfocused way. "Very few phreaks or hackers know about the existence of the chip, and even those who stumble across it aren't going to be able to reproduce the algorithm that makes the chip dump its data, much less the one to erase the data trail. This one hasn't been tampered with, I'm certain, and its trail indicates that over three hundred different numbers have been cloned into it over the past year and a half." Now she looked up at Peter, and the expression was a little challenging.

"What I need you to tell me now," she said, "is exactly where you got this phone in the first place."

"Uh," Peter said. Those gray-blue eyes looked at him, and he said, "Uh, Spider-Man passed it on to me."

Doris looked at him. Then she nodded. "I thought so," she said and glanced over toward one of the coffee tables across the room. Peter followed the glance, and saw, somewhat to his surprise, a copy of *Webs*, the coffee-table book of Spider-Man pictures he had gotten published not too long ago.

"Yes," she said, "I did just a little checking up on you. I tend not to take things at face value, in my line of work." And she smiled slightly: that sunny look again. "Where did your web-slinging friend find it?"

"At a crime scene of some kind. A robbery, I think."

"Hmm. Yes, that would fit in." She got up and went over to an escritoire by the wall—yet another beautiful antique—and pulled its doors open. A computer and printer were hidden inside, and by the printer was some stacked-up paperwork. She brought it over to the table. "Here," she said, "is a list of all the phone numbers that this phone has 'owned' in the last year and a half. All stolen from other, legally held phones belonging to the three New York companies, and two of the Connecticut ones, and some from Pennsylvania."

She turned back to the escritoire. "And here," she said, coming back to Peter with a ream package of paper and plumping it down on the table in front of him, "is a list of all the numbers called by this phone during that period."

He stared at the wrapped package. "This is a *list*?"

"Four hundred and fifty-three pages," Doris said. "The numbers are ranked most-used to least-used. It's interesting reading. A lot of calls to betting shops, hundreds of calls to a corner grocery not far from here." She looked rueful. "I used to shop there all the time. I've stopped now. But almost all of them are calls to places that are the subject of an ongoing police investigation. So if your friend Spider-Man is interested in this kind of thing, you'd better pass this information on to him. I hope he's a fast reader." She thought a moment and added, "If he has a computer, I can give you this data on disk. It'll be easier to sort."

"Uh, he has access to one, yes."

She went to the escritoire again, did something briefly at the computer's keyboard, then left it to its own devices. "That'll be ready shortly. Now what I need you to do is let me know where the phone that your famous wife was having trouble with is. Naughty of you to slip me this one without telling me. If it hadn't been for your wife, I would have called the FBI."

Peter gulped.

"But then I found out about this other connection," Doris said, glancing at the copy of *Webs*, "and after all, Stevie Drew said you were all right to work with."

"Stevie"? Never mind.... "Uh," Peter said, "thank you, Doris. I should have told you, really, but—"

"You were being circumspect for reasons of your own," said Doris. "I'm not going to pry. Let's let it pass. But bring me your wife's phone, all right? If your problem is solvable, I want to see if I can solve it. For one thing, if her phone has the covert chip in place, we'll be able to see some other data—time and location information, other things—which the phone company's own records won't necessarily reflect. There may even be recordings of some voice material."

Peter's eyes opened wide at that. "Recordings? How?"

Doris smiled at him. "Our snoopy government. Peter, there are more intelligence-gathering bureaus running around in this country doing their gathering than most of the government would ever like you to know. They'd quote you 'national security' as a reason for it—and to some extent they might be right. But the truth is that governments are just naturally nosy, and big ones are much nosier than others, and we have one of the biggest. A lot of calls are monitored, though everyone denies it. There's no use in them denying it, really. The technology makes it easy now, especially since our cell phone systems are still almost all analog, which any kid with a scanner can listen in on. And one of the most basic human vices is the desire to look through the keyhole and see what the neighbors are *really* doing. When things go digital, the monitoring may lessen a little. The signal is harder to break, and consumers are getting more sensitive to the issue. Which is as it should be. But governments will still fight back, doing their best to fight tight voice-encryption methods. By their own lights, they're right to do so, they feel they're protecting their own interests." Doris sighed a little. "The NSA in particular monitors a lot of calls all over the country. Computers do it for them, taking random samplings of band width and searching for certain keywords in conversations—guns, bombs, drugs, that kind of thing. If something dangerous-sounding turns up, a little bell goes off somewhere, and a live monitor quietly comes into the circuit to determine whether the threat is real. Other countries do much the same. In fact, the NSA learned the technique from the British, a while after the troubles started in Northern Ireland. As far as I know, every call from Britain to Ireland and vice versa is still routinely computer-sampled for suspect content. And I think they do the same, just for general interest—and again, with an eye to Ireland, and their own drug-smuggling problems, and so forth—with everything that comes in from the U.S. and Canada via the transatlantic cable and satellite downlink stations on the south coast of the U.K. GCHQ passes on anything interesting that they 'hear' to the NSA, and the NSA returns the favor at its end."

Peter shook his head in astonishment. "Is that legal?"

Doris gave him an excessively wry smile. "It must be, dear. They're the *government,* aren't they?"

"But what about freedom of speech?"

"The Constitution guarantees you that, all right. But it doesn't guarantee that no one will be on the other side of the wall with their ear pressed to it, does it?"

Peter opened his mouth and closed it again.

"As I said, when the U.S.'s cell phones go digital, it'll be harder for the eavesdroppers, 'legal' or otherwise," Doris said. "But I don't expect to see that before well into the next century. Assuming I *am* still around to see it. All the phone companies are arguing about what standard to use, and I think they will be for years. But for the meantime, when you're on a cell phone, exactly as with a portable phone in your house, you need to *assume* that what you're saying is being overheard and recorded by someone who means to do you dirt.

"In any case, all this may work to your benefit. It's just possible that in the NSA tape archives there is some evidence pertaining to calls made on your wife's phones. I have access to those archives on a need-to-know basis, and, well," and Doris smiled that sunny smile again, "as regards this, I just need to know, that's all."

The glint of the gossip lover showed briefly in Doris's eyes, and Peter laughed. "Okay, I'll call her later and ask her to drop it off for you. You two can have a chat then, and you can cross-examine her about *Secret Hospital.*"

Doris nodded. "More to the point, though," she said, "if I can link that phone to police work presently ongoing, that will get you off the hook with CellTech." She smiled, a slightly feral look. "They listen to me. But then, they *have* to, considering what they pay me on retainer. So have your wife give me a call."

Peter thanked Doris and headed out. As he walked down the street, at one point he paused and looked back at the top of her apartment building, all discreetly crowned with antennas, and he found himself thinking, *Did I ever say anything on that phone, anything, to MJ, that might suggest to a casual listener that I was someone else besides just Peter Parker? And forget casual listeners—that might suggest it to a little old lady who could probably make toast just by sticking a slice of bread out her window?*

He sighed. There was no point in worrying about it just now. Meanwhile, he had places to be. He headed for them.

OTHER people, also, much later that day, were going about the town on their business.

The offices of Bothwell Industries, housed in a refurbished office building downtown, had closed for the day a couple of hours ago. It was a small new company, still in the process of moving into its premises: furniture was still shoved up against the bare walls in its three rooms, and boxes were stacked everywhere in the near-darkness.

Among the boxes, a lithe dark shape moved quietly, reading labels with a tiny flashlight, and making sure that the light was always shielded by his body. A handy pseudopod cupped around it, to make doubly sure.

Venom had been there for about an hour, mentally sorting out the boxes into "check it now" and "don't bother" categories. The chaos in the place at the moment actually worked to his benefit somewhat—it meant, among other things, that there had been no time to lock files away securely. That suited him very well indeed.

He paused for a moment, glancing around him. The symbiote sent out a few questing streamers in the direction of boxes it obscurely knew he was interested in. "No, no," he said softly, "patience. We'll do this systematically. We may not get another chance, and we cannot afford to lose this one."

Venom went to the first of about twenty cardboard file boxes in which he was interested, opened it, and started going through the files inside. Most of them were innocuous, as he suspected they would be, but he was in no hurry at the moment. Security in this building was on the lax side; he had been watching it for the better part of the day to make sure, and not half an hour ago he had seen the lone security guard for the place lock the back door and head down the street to a local bar. The laxity amused Venom, and rather pleased him; he had no desire to slice up some poor hired lackey while doing what he had to do tonight. And by far the *best* thing that could happen, as far as he was concerned, was that one of the company directors might use his own building key, and come in alone. Then he and Venom would have a nice little chat.

Niner, he thought, going through the files, seeing correspondence about some shipment of oranges from Spain, passing it by. Bothwell appeared to be an innocent enough import-export firm, but the research he had done at the Bureau of Records, cross-indexed with the SEC information, made it plain that vast amounts of cash had been through Bothwell's accounts in the past couple of weeks. Now, there were legitimate firms for which this might have been true, but also many illegitimate ones. He had looked over a number of them today, in a cursory fashion—either from the street, in "civvies," or from the rooftops. Heaven only knew what some of those other firms were up to—where their money came from, what they were doing with it. But this firm had distinguished itself, in midafternoon, when Venom had seen the man called Niner, the man who had gotten away the other day, walk out its front door, dressed like a businessman, with a briefcase full of what was doubtless fascinating material.

Venom wanted to talk to that man. The symbiote's tendrils writhed a little with anticipation at the thought. "Patience," Venom said again. "We'll have a chance to ask him our questions eventually. But first I want to have a better idea of what questions to ask."

The next hour or two were weary ones. Eddie Brock had been more than capable, as a reporter, of the long slog through reams of boring information; this was very much the same. Invoices, impenetrable bank statements, letters in several different alphabets (many of them Cyrillic)—none of them told him any of the specific things he wanted to know about Bothwell. The symbiote began to make little movements that Venom had long since learned to translate as the alien version of, "I'm bored, can we go now?"

He ignored it. For the time being, he had to. He opened another box, and another, and carefully and patiently went through them all. The frustration of the whole business was that vital evidence might be right under his nose but in coded form, and he might not recognize it. Many firms, even now, used various commercial or industrial code books and software to hide their immediate intentions. There was no way to tell whether "Your inquiry about the condition of the last shipment is being investigated" actually meant "Tell the chief operative we want him back in the main office, fast" or "That last deposit for twelve million has gone through as promised." All you could do was look.

He shut that box, opened another one, went through it. Nothing. Shut that box, opened another one. Went through it—

—and suddenly found himself looking at a letter regarding more oranges from Spain—with a sticky-pad note attached to it saying, in a neat precise hand, *Cross-ref with tacticals/delivery systems schedule for DO.*

Venom looked at it thoughtfully. Whatever oranges might need for their safe shipment, there would be nothing "tactical" about it—and the word "tactical" linked with "delivery system" made his hair try to stand up on end under the symbiote, and its tentacles wreathe and flutter. He put the letter aside, noted the date, and started digging through that box with ever-increasing interest.

Two files farther in, behind some more back statements with entirely too many zeroes, he found a piece of cream-colored letterhead that he lifted out of its file and held up to the light to check the watermark. Original. At the top of it appeared the letters *ccrc/internal.*

Transfer instructions, the heading of the letter said. *Sensitive materials—see file 886, 887—*

He laughed out loud. In the hurry of their move, someone had put this file in the wrong box. The box labeled 800 was across the room. He went for it.

"Aha," Venom said softly, as he opened the 800 box. There were several locked metal security-deposit-type boxes in it, of a size to take files.

The symbiote put out several willing tentacles and levered the steel box open. The lock gave with a tiny screech of metal and a loud snap. Other pseudopodia came down, lifted the files out, opened them.

Delivery system disposition—Missile launchers have been positioned near: Boca Raton, Winter Park, Miami; Atlanta, Peachtree, Mobile; Solid emplacements: Chicago: Tower, El 1, El 2, O'Hare.

Venom began to growl softly under his breath. The symbiote shuddered with his reflected, growing rage. *Fissionables transport. Miami reprocessing plant has been shut down, but Tuscaloosa remains operational and will finish present inventory. Shipments otherwise proceeding according to schedule.*

"Shut down," Venom said to the symbiote. "We should say it was. You had fun that night, didn't you? Well, it looks like more fun is coming."

"Light bombs." ERWs are now 60% emplaced for Day Hundred. Previous difficulties with the timers have been worked out. Tests on the satellite detonation system have been abandoned as too uncertain with so little time remaining in the program.

"*So little time,*" Venom thought. *What are they planning?*

And then the last note, a sticky-pad note on the cover letter of another report on "deliveries of inventory." *I am not entirely pleased with the quality control on shipment 18: rad count is below optimum. Have it recalled and replaced—we have more than enough fissiles to do so within schedule. Please remind all staff that there is no room for error: the usual sanctions will apply.—OO*

Venom stopped growling—a sound more frightening than the growl had been.

OO.

Otto Octavius.

One of the world's leading experts on radiation and its various and sundry applications.

He remembered the earlier reference to "DO," which, Venom now realized, likely referred to the name under which Octavius tended to operate since his metal tentacles were bonded to him and he embarked on a villainous career:

Doctor Octopus.

Indeed. Now it all begins to fall into place.

Eddie Brock was a methodical man. He went through all the other boxes he had deemed pertinent before he left. But his silence then, some two hours later, was more profound and terrible than all the silences before it. He stood up, stretched—even a man with a symbiote to massage his tired muscles gets stiff after a long time hunkered down among files—and headed for the stairway to the roof, working hard to contain his fury. He was going to have to be especially careful to keep the symbiote in check. There was someone he needed very much to kill but wanted more to see.

MJ went back to Sundog that evening in a very cheerful mood. She had still been worried about Peter when she got up, but when he came in carrying about a ream of paper, whistling, and told her why he was feeling so cheerful, she felt much better too.

It was pleasant not to have to get up too early, and she took her time about getting ready for the day, while Peter pored over the stacks of paper he had brought home. She then went out with both her cell phone and Peter's, and dropped hers off with Doris Smyth. She was glad she had taken Peter's phone with her; she and Doris got into one of those like-at-first-sight conversations that people sometimes have, a conversation that ranged over everything from personal philosophies to sordid gossip from the *Secret Hospital* set, and they both drank enough tea to float themselves away. She and Doris were still talking when MJ realized that it was five-thirty, and she had to go to work.

MJ promised to come back another time and continue the conversation, then she hurried downstairs and caught a cab over to Sundog. She had just enough time to call Peter and let her know what had happened to her. "It's okay," he'd said. "I thought you might have done something like that. Listen, I've got to get out and do some night work."

"Okay, Tiger. When do you think you'll be back?"

"Not too late. Probably about one."

"Okay, see you then."

She bounced out of the cab in good spirits, and headed in and up the studio stairs. When she got down to Studio Six, the same crew from last night were mostly in their places, laughing and chatting among themselves. They welcomed her like an old friend. *These are such nice people. I hope this job lasts!*

Jymn Magon came in and started trying to get everyone organized. As MJ was beginning to suspect was usual, it took a while. Finally they settled down to start the recording of the next *Giga-Group* script. "This one has a little more stuff for Glaive in it," Jymn told MJ, "and her part is somewhat bigger than the last time—she's more important to the plot. So get in there and swagger a little. Don't be afraid to go too far over the top."

"Why should she be?" said Doug Booth. "Who would notice?"

Much laughter ensued, and they started. MJ swaggered it as best she knew how, thinking of the occasional super villains she'd run across in her career, and less heroic but generally decent folk like the Black Cat. The others cheered her on, seemingly impressed, and MJ started just unashamedly enjoying the part and the way she was playing it, bold and flamboyantly heroic. It seemed to work, at least for Jymn, and even to MJ's untutored ear, the more hackneyed lines in the script seemed somewhat improved when you delivered them as if they were the truth that would save the world. The night flew by, punctuated by one bout of laughter so severe that she could scarcely breathe, when Rory (playing a character who had for some obscure reason been temporarily regressed into a Neanderthal) suddenly started refusing to come out of character when taking direction from Jymn. "I need a little more weight on the 'Me afraid—me not know what to do,'" Jymn had said, casually enough. But Rory's reply was, in character, "Oh, okay, me screw that up the last time, me do it again," and he remained stubbornly Neanderthal for the better part of an hour.

Later, in a cab on the way home, MJ wondered whether it had really been all that funny. *It seemed so then.* But it didn't matter. She felt wonderful. She had come striding out of Sundog, after a whole night of rampant heroism, feeling nine feet tall, covered in adamantium, invincible and invulnerable, and feeling pretty good about herself—especially at five hundred bucks an hour for six hours.

She looked up at their apartment window as she got out of the cab and paid the man. The light in the third window over was on, which was Peter's code meaning that he was still out web-swinging. *Well, he said he wouldn't be late. I'll fix something light for him to eat when he gets in. And boy, I could murder a sandwich, myself.*

MJ headed upstairs, strode on down to their door, unlocked it, stepped in, and locked up behind her. There, for a moment, she paused. She felt a draft. A window was open somewhere—not the bedroom one, not the one Peter usually came in by after a night of spidering around…

Someone cleared his throat. MJ's head snapped around. Her first thought was, *Oh Lord, I've disturbed a burglar.*

It was worse than that.

Over against the living-room window, black pseudopodia wreathing gently around him, stood Venom.

The blood started rushing around inside MJ, but not to her fear-clenched stomach, as she would normally have expected—instead, it went to her face with anger. Hardly knowing what she was doing, she chucked her keys over onto the telephone table and strode straight over to him.

"I'm sorry," she said, in ringing tones, "but I must have messed up my appointments calendar again. I wasn't expecting you. Or *did* you call to make an appointment first?"

That dreadful grin looked somewhat fixed at the moment—as if by brief surprise. "We did call," he said. "Your cell phone, we believe. But we fear we did not leave a message."

"People who hang up on answering services," MJ said, looking Venom up and down, more with Glaive's scorn than her own, "are a symptom of the downfall of civilization. If you're rude to machines, you'll be rude to people, too. And breaking into people's homes is also fairly rude, by the way. But now that you're here, won't you sit down? And can I get you something?" Venom opened his mouth. She didn't give him the chance. "And no wisecracks about my husband, please, since that's doubtless the cause of you giving me the pleasure of your company. Tea? Coffee?"

"Nothing right now," Venom said. MJ looked pointedly, as if expecting something. Very slowly, the pseudopodia wreathing around him, Venom added, "Thank you."

He sat down.

MJ turned her back on him, something she would never have done—but Glaive would have. She strode away from him into the kitchen, opened the refrigerator, and got out the baloney and some mustard. "If you called my cell phone," MJ said, "I would guess it has something to do with the fact that someone cloned the poor creature. Ran up a four-thousand-dollar bill, too. Did *you* have something to do with that?" She stared at him. Venom opened his mouth, and MJ turned away again, ignoring him. "No," she said, getting out a knife for the mustard, "even you wouldn't sink that low. I apologize for suggesting it. Are you sure you won't have a sandwich?"

"What I would like," Venom growled, "is to see your husband."

"He's not at home," MJ said. She composed her sandwich, put it on a plate, got herself a Coke, took them both to the little dining-room table, put them down, and sat down. She did not eat. Her mother had always told her it was rude to eat in front of people who weren't also eating, unless they were family. She looked at Venom.

He actually twitched—he, not the symbiote.

The sound of a key in the lock came from outside. All the blood in MJ attempted to relocate itself, again, in relief, but she refused to make any other sign, except to lounge back in the chair a little. The other key went into the other lock. The door opened, and Peter came in. "Hey, MJ, did you—"

He stopped. He saw his wife sitting at the table, with a slight smile on her face, and Venom sitting on the couch.

Venom stood up. "We have a guest," MJ said. "Or guests."

Peter moved slowly toward Venom, his face going dark with anger. "What are *you* doing here—"

Venom stood up, seeing at last a reaction that he understood, and headed toward Peter. "Your wife's phone number," he growled, "appears among numbers belonging to some Russian criminals who are working in town at the moment. They appear to be involved with the covert restructuring of CCRC—and with Doctor Octopus."

Peter stopped, his mouth open. "*Ock*—"

"It is difficult to say," said Venom, "but he may be one of the owners of CCRC. Or *the* owner. Unfortunately, much of the pertinent information is concealed by Liechtenstein banking laws, and many shell companies."

"Lord," Peter said.

Venom's pale eyes turned in MJ's direction. "Is it true that your wife's phone was cloned—"

"Ask *me*," MJ said, the Glaive voice again, and it was the character, not her, that made her shake her hair back when Venom turned to her, and lift her head defiantly. "What makes you think I would bother lying to you?"

Venom simply looked at her, then turned away. "So—a false trail. Well enough. We would personally much prefer the leisure to finally settle up accounts with you here and now. But there is other information much more important to be discussed, and a much more important reason why we've come here."

He quickly told Peter about his evening's foraging in the Bothwell offices possibly belonging to the man called Niner—or, on the other hand, to Doctor Octopus. MJ's eyes got wide as Venom told of what sounded like extensive shipments of covert nuclear material making their way around the country. "Useless as they often are, this must be dealt with by the authorities," Venom said. "Spider-Man has certain connections in the AEC offices in New York that we do not—and we think he had better alert them, and seek their help."

Peter eyed Venom suspiciously. "You could call them yourself. Why put me on the spot?"

"As if they would listen to me," Venom said. "While you—"

"—are as involved as you were with the near explosion of a nuclear device under Manhattan, as far as they're concerned. Why should they listen to me, either? There are still people in the office there who suspect I might have been at the bottom of the whole thing." Then Peter paused. "Well," he said, "I suppose it's worth a try. The stakes are too high not to try, anyway. And the worst that can happen is that they'll chuck me out on my ear. But Doc Ock—" He brooded a moment. "If all the events of the past few months are somehow traceable to him…"

"That will have to be looked into as well," Venom said, "but right now the main priority is that all this atomic material be found and made safe before millions of innocent people are caught in some kind of disaster— accidentally, or on purpose."

"I'll call them first thing in the morning."

"Very good. And we want you to understand that that information had best be shared with us promptly." Venom turned a long look on MJ. She returned it, with interest, as coolly as she could. She refused to look at Peter at the moment, who was already doing a slow burn. The last thing anyone needed right now was for these two to go for each other's throats. "Otherwise, we should dislike having to call on you at home again."

"The feeling's mutual," Peter said.

"We will call you in the morning, then," said Venom. He turned toward the window he had come in by, and then left.

It was a few seconds before MJ could move; then Peter's arms were around her. She hugged him back, wordless, as Glaive suddenly became just a character in a bad script again, and her stomach clenched with sudden postponed fear, and her appetite left her with a rush. "Oh, Pete—!"

"It's all right," he said, hugging her. "It's all right."

"No, it's not," she said mournfully. "My sandwich is getting all curly at the edges."

Peter shot a glance at it. "If you don't want it, I'll eat it. Tell me about your day, which obviously was a *doozy*, and then let's go to bed—'cause we're going to have a busy day tomorrow."

EIGHT

THE next morning, about ten, Spider-Man swung quietly down onto the roof of the New York City offices of the AEC. A small, stout man in a quiet business suit was standing there, a little ruffled by the wind, waiting for him.

Spidey walked over to him. "Mr. Laurentz?"

"That's right," said the little man. He looked at Spider-Man in a considering way, and Spidey considered him back: bald, an olive cast to his complexion that suggested the Mediterranean, bushy mustache. "Please call me Rob. Do you want to come down to the offices? Or would you rather talk up here?"

"Which would be wiser?" Spidey said.

Laurentz smiled suddenly, a surprisingly loopy grin. "It's a nice morning. Let's sit up here."

Spidey looked around for chairs, saw none: but Laurentz had already strolled over to the parapet that ran around the edge of the building, and sat down on it, with considerable disregard for the effect of roof dirt on such an expensive suit. Spider-Man went after him and sat down too.

"You'll understand, I guess," said Laurentz, "that there are some—doubts about your bona fides here and there in the organization. I'm not overly concerned, though. I know enough about what happened down in the tunnels not too long ago to make me glad to shake you by the hand. And if there's anything I can help you with, it's my pleasure."

"That's a relief." Spidey looked out across the city and started to explain what was on his mind.

Laurentz sat quietly for a while, letting Spider-Man expound, particularly regarding the large amount of fissionable material that seemed to be running around loose. "Well, you know," he said at one point, "there was always a lot more of it than we're generally told about—or that the public is generally told about—being shipped here and there. All under tight government control, of course. The Commission is supposed to be informed about them all, but, well, we're a *civilian* organization, and the military, which handles its own shipping, doesn't always tell us everything. One of the aspects of this job that occasionally makes it a little interesting."

"I just bet."

Laurentz sighed a little. "We've been investigating CCRC, of course—or what's left of it—ever since those first barrels of toxic waste were found downtown. To date we've found six other stockpiles scattered here and there around Manhattan: smaller ones, but significant enough. And they weren't just of waste—they were enriched uranium and processed transuranics."

"Bomb-grade transuranics?"

"Some refined plutonium, yes, but not a whole lot. Enough to cause a disaster if it got out into the environment, though. You couldn't make an H-bomb out of it all if you tried." Laurentz's brow furrowed. "But light bombs, yes. And if I were a terrorist, that's what I would go for. They're the wave of the future."

Spider-Man gulped. "Excuse me—'light' bombs?"

"Sounds like a marketing ploy, doesn't it?" Laurentz's smile was mirthless. "I'd love to kick the man or woman who came up with that asinine name. For a while, the other name for them—not much better—was 'neutron bombs.'"

"Oh," Spidey said softly. "Why are these the preferred flavor all of a sudden?"

"Cheaper," Laurentz said. "You need less trigger material. Just be sure you understand what we're talking about here. There was a lot of confusion about this end of weapons technology—the idea that these weapons wouldn't destroy buildings, only people." He laughed, a bitter breath of nonamusement. "The first models of this bomb were designed as a tactical weapon, a battlefield nuke. The idea was this: If you're in the middle of a large armored combat and you drop a conventional nuclear weapon over or on it, obviously everything at ground zero is going to be destroyed. But out at sort of ground one-and-a-half, things won't be quite so grim, at least for a while. Soldiers in tanks are afforded some protection by their tanks from the blast and heat of the direct explosion, and so afterwards they're likely—so the generals would think—to just keep on soldiering for a day or three longer until the symptoms of radiation sickness start catching up with them. Well, the generals didn't like that idea much, so they got behind the idea of designing a bomb that would release such a massive blast of neutrons that the tanks would be no more protection than tissue paper, and the soldiers would die at least within hours, if not right away."

"Nice people," Spider-Man murmured.

They sat quiet for a moment, watching a flight of ducks make its way up the East River in a vee. "Yes," said Laurentz. "Well, anyway, as it always does, word got out. There were some astonishingly mishandled press briefings about the 'neutron bomb' in '78, followed by some astoundingly sensationalistic coverage in the media. Such a stink went up from the public that the research was very quietly dropped in late '78, and for a long while nothing else was heard about it."

Spidey nodded. "I take it, though, that now, for whatever reason, people are getting interested again."

"Budget," said Laurentz, "what else? And additionally, there have been enormous leaps in technology since 1978, making the 'light bombs'—'tidies,' they also call them—a lot more practical. And the concrete technology on which to base them is already everywhere, in the storehouses of every atomic power. NATO has a lot of artillery-fired atomic projectiles—'hundred-pounders,' they call them. They use pretty small amounts of fissile material, and they're very flexible and easy to use. They're not much bigger than a mortar shell. You can shoot them or just hide them with a timer, and when they go off, their normal output of radiation is increased many times by the tamping and pumping techniques that we've invented over the years to reduce the size of much larger bombs."

"We're so inventive," Spidey said.

"We are," said Laurentz, "and it gets worse. It would be—well, not easy, but certainly feasible—to build such bombs so that they were much more effective than the NATO weapons. Radiation 'tamp' hasn't been extended to anything like its maximum efficiency as yet, and materials technology continues to produce alloys and metals that are more and more effective for tamping. You could boost one of those battlefield nukes to thousands of times its present rad output—possibly *tens* of thousands of times. Blow something like that up in a large city, and you wouldn't notice any more of a bang than you might get out of, say, a couple of tons of chemical explosive. A few buildings would be flattened, a lot of windows blown out. But a hundred-pounder with a little imaginative augmentation…" Laurentz looked off toward the river with a grim expression on his face. "Put something like that where we're sitting, and you could leave half the population of Manhattan with LD50, the lethal dose, in a flash. Three days, they're dead. Less, for most of them."

"Do you really think that many terrorists have this kind of weapon?"

"Have it? Maybe. But would they use it?" Laurentz shrugged. "I've had a little training in this—most of us at the Commission have. Their feeling, and I share it, is that, at the moment, I doubt most terrorist organizations—ones with a plan, that is, a goal to achieve, I don't mean random crazies—I don't think they would dare. I think most of them have the sense to know that the first person or country to use nuclear weapons against a target is going to have the entire rest of the world community— most especially including the nuclear powers—come down on it like a rock. That organization would then have open season declared on it. They'd be hunted down mercilessly and wiped out—possibly their host country as well. By and large, I think terrorists want to inspire *terror,* not rage. Rage makes people fight back; terror is supposed to make them tired, to make them say 'Let's give up and go home.' At least, that's how I think the logic would go. But all it takes is one person who doesn't understand the logic, and—*whoomf.*"

"It must be a constant worry."

"Oh yes. And worse than ever, after things broke loose in what was left of the USSR, and fissile material started making its way out into the hands of people you really wish didn't have it." He smiled, just a little. "Fortunately, the laws of nature are working with us a little bit on this one. Most people who try to work with transuranics don't have the training. They're working on a shoestring, in secret. Most of them are so lacking in expertise that, very quickly, while taking apart a shell or trying to build a bomb, they get contaminated by the fissile, and it kills them and everyone around them fairly quickly, and very painfully. It's something of a deterrent."

Spidey gulped again. "I just bet," he said softly.

A barge made its way down past the Delacorte Fountain's white plume of water: they watched it go, hooting at an approaching tug. "The point at which you get into trouble," Laurentz said, "is when you have *good* scientists working with the fissiles—people who *won't* have the good grace to drop a canister and LD50 themselves. People with access to money, and to the expensive specialized equipment that you need to work with fissiles safely. This is why the U.S. has been trying to hire as many former USSR scientists as it can, at the best rates, to keep them away from other countries who might be interested in building a little surprise for their neighbors."

Spidey nodded, saying nothing. His mouth was dry.

Doctor Octopus, he thought.

Ock was one of the premier scientists in the world, it had to be said, and radiation was his area of expertise. There was no ignoring the man's genius. He would not drop any canisters, nor would he hire anyone who was likely to—or keep them on, after they'd done it once. His perfectionism would be offended, and he'd have them taken out and "neutralized" on the spot. And if there was anything else that Ock did have, it was money. Lots and lots of money, some of it earned from his career as a scientist prior to the accident that bonded him with his tentacles, most of it from the countless thefts he'd masterminded in the years since. He would have more than enough to buy himself, openly or covertly, all the machinery he could possibly need for this kind of work. And all the helping hands he'd need.

"What kind of luck have you had tracing the material that you know of being illegally shipped around the country?" Spidey said.

Laurentz shook his head regretfully. "Not a great deal. Our normal sources have dried up rather dramatically over the past few months, as if someone had put the fright on them pretty conclusively. One piece of information did slip out: some fissile, which we're still trying to locate and seize, was given to a couple of small midwestern right-wing 'patriot' groups, for 'protection.'" That mirthless laugh again. "Some members of one group got curious, and peeked into Pandora's box—tried to take one of the bombs apart. Unfortunate. Only for them, anyway; the thing didn't detonate."

"And that bomb upstate?"

Laurentz looked at him and shook his head. "That, interestingly enough, was a tamped device. Very effectively tamped, too. It developed a lot of radiation and did little actual destruction—though that's little consolation to the poor people in that tiny town. They're probably going to have to move now. The thing has irradiated the area's plants pretty conclusively, and the damage is going to make its way into the food chain."

"Any indication, as yet, who was responsible?"

"No. No one's taken responsibility, anyway."

Spidey stood up and began to pace a little. A few seagulls wafted by overhead in the wind and the sunshine. "One thing we have noticed over the past few months," Laurentz said, "the last six months, anyway. Our own technology is improving too, as you might imagine, and we're getting better at analyzing ambient and background radiation than we used to be. We've been noticing an increase in the city ambient. Bear in mind, Manhattan is founded on basalt and granite, which usually have radon associated with them. But we know what *that* ambient ought to be, and the radiation we've been sensing lately is higher—as if Manhattan was running a slight fever. The only place you normally get readings that high is over by Fourteenth Street, where the earthquake fault is."

"*What??*"

"The earthquake fault. Didn't you know about it? It's only a longitudinal. It's not all that geologically significant, though every now and then it burps a little. CalTech keeps an eye on it for us, because when it burps, sometimes it leaks a little radon, we have to do street monitoring to make sure that people are safe."

"Burps, huh? How hard?"

"Almost not worth speaking of. One-point-two, one-point-three Richter—you'd notice a heavy truck going by sooner. In fact, CalTech sometimes has trouble reading it because of the traffic vibration, but fortunately the transverse wave is diagnostic."

"The things you learn about this city," Spider-Man said.

"There's an underground river there, too. Not naturally submerged, though—I think they diverted it artificially in the 1800s. At any rate, the last analysis of the radiation figures seems strongly to suggest that there's a stockpile we haven't located yet, somewhere in or on Manhattan—more likely, in it— and it's beginning to affect the ambient of the substrate around it."

"Any way to tell where?" Spider-Man said.

"Not specifically. The equipment is kind of obvious looking, and even in this town it's hard to walk around the city streets with it and not be noticed." Laurentz then added with a sad smile, "Not that we have the money to do it. Congress has cut our appropriation again this year. But there's something down there. So far we haven't been able to find anything, while investigating the CCRC records, that would cast any light on the problem."

"Well," Spidey said, "let me cast a little light of my own."

Briefly he told Laurentz about Venom's certainty that Doctor Octopus was involved, and the extent of the involvement. Laurentz looked thoughtful, then nodded.

"I think I remember seeing a couple reports from the FBI and Interpol," he said, "possibly S.H.I.E.L.D. as well, that he was connected to incidents in which material was being smuggled in from other countries. The problem's been proof, until now. Octavius seems to have been fairly good about keeping himself from being connected to whatever's going on." Laurentz looked at Spidey. "Are you going to be investigating this yourself?"

"I don't see that I have much choice. You guys can't do it—and if the situation is getting sufficiently dangerous then someone's got to do something."

"Heroism," Laurentz said, and gave Spider-Man another of those thoughtful looks. "Well. Maybe I can help. We have some fairly effective radiation sensors—sort of the great-grandchildren of the Geiger counter—though I have to admit that they're best at close range."

"That's where we're likely to be," Spidey said.

"'We.' Two of them, you'd need?"

"Yes."

"You're in luck," said Laurentz, standing up, "because two of them is all we have. Just make sure you bring them back. I can sign them out for you, but if you lose them, I'm going to have to put off getting married for about thirty years—that's how long it'd take me to pay back what they're worth."

Spider-Man nodded. "Sounds good," he said.

"Wait here," said Laurentz and went off toward the building's roof door.

About twenty minutes later he came back with a pair of harnesses, to which were attached small "black boxes" with LCD readout panels. Laurentz turned one of them on and showed Spidey a surprisingly complex readout panel, with a tie-in to a satellite navigation "finder" system. "Here. And here's the manual." He handed Spidey a small fat book about as thick as the Yellow Pages.

"I have to read all this?"

Laurentz grinned. "Just the first couple of chapters. The rest is detail."

"Couldn't you just give me the Cliff Notes?"

"This is a government document," Laurentz said dryly. "Count yourself lucky that no one's already arrested you."

"It's the story of my life," Spidey said. "Mr. Laurentz—thanks for your help. And please get the government to pay attention to what Ock's doing."

"It's always a struggle," Laurentz said, "but I'll do my best. Good luck, Spider-Man."

"I'm going to need it," he said as he webbed up the two harnesses and the instruction manual, shot out a webline, and swung away.

SPIDEY went home to change, sat down, and spent the rest of the afternoon going through paperwork. Doris's great sheaf of numbers still needed his attention, and the manual would have to wait.

He riffled through the pages for a couple of hours, until figures and signal strengths were all blurring together in his eyes. He had long since given up looking at the "most frequently called" numbers, and was now concentrating on the numbers least frequently called, and the cloned numbers that had been least frequently used.

There were, in particular, eighteen of these that were used only once. Peter looked carefully at all their associated readings—not able to make much of them—but there was one set in particular that matched up, for each of the cloned numbers.

He reached out for the phone and called Doris Smyth.

"Hello?"

"Doris, it's Peter Parker."

"Hello, dear! I'm sorry I haven't had time to call you today; business has been unusually frantic. I don't have anything new on MJ's phone, I'm afraid."

"That's okay, that's not what I'm calling about. I'm looking through those printouts you gave me."

"Oh, dear," Doris said, "I hope you're not getting eyestrain."

"I am, but it doesn't bother me. Doris, what exactly is 'Ssth' in this one column? The fifth column over?"

"Signal strength."

"Hmm," Peter said. "Am I imagining things, or do I remember you telling me that sometimes you could get *location* information from that little covert chip?"

There was a pause. "Sometimes," Doris said, "yes. If the signal strength is sufficient, the covert will try to locate itself in terms of the nearest cell emitters. If you know the emitter locations, you can work out where the phone was."

"Can you do that for a few of these?"

"I'll try for you. It may take a while. What page of the readout?"

He told her, identifying the specific numbers. "One more thing before you go," he said. "Am I wrong in thinking that it's hard to get a bad cell phone signal in New York?"

Doris laughed at him. "Dear, I'm amazed we don't pick up conversations on our *fillings*. There are emitters every block and a half, it seems. If you've got a bad signal, it usually means that you're in a building with an unusually effective Faraday cage, or one with a lot more girders than they usually use these days, or you're down in the subway."

"Faraday cage?"

"It's a network of wires or metal mesh that people use to protect computers from ambient RF radiation that might hurt their data. For example, I know one shopping center that had to build a Faraday cage around its two biggest department stores, because they were close to a big radio station, and every time the station came on in the morning, it would wipe out all the data in their cash registers' computers. You don't get many buildings here that need to be purposely caged, though. RF of that kind is rare in the States—the store I was thinking of was in Europe."

"Okay," Peter said. "Doris—thanks lots."

"You're welcome. I'll call you back as soon as I have something. Bye!"

She hung up. Peter stared at the printout.

In an old building—or in a cage—or in the subway.

Underground.

Peter thought about Hobgoblin's hideaway, where the bomb with which he intended to nuke New York had been kept.

I wonder—did he build that? Or was it just lent to him—or built for him? By Doc Ock, for example?

Peter wondered. Before he started wearing the Hobgoblin suit, Jason Macendale was a mercenary called Jack O'Lantern. Macendale had always been willing to work for anyone if the price was right.

No question but that Ock's price would likely have been right, if he actually owned CCRC.

Underground.

He reached for the phone again, called the number that Venom had left on his answering machine earlier that morning, and talked into it rapidly for a few minutes, stating that he would leave a web-wrapped package for Venom on the roof of his building, telling him what it was, and where (in a general way) he intended to be.

Then Peter hung up and started studying the manual, preparing for a night on the town—or, rather, under it.

NINE

A famous architect once said, "New York is an iceberg." He was not talking about the friendliness, or lack of it, of the inhabitants or about the climate in the winter. He meant the infrastructure, in the original form of the word: the structure below the city, under the streets and the buildings. At least as many "built things" lay below the ground as above, and possibly more.

Between thirty and two hundred feet below the streets of New York lies the biggest, most intensively built infrastructure of any city in the world. Miles of electric cable and fiber, tons of steel and iron in the sewers old and new; water mains, access tunnels, and conduits for steam and gas; and deepest of all, the skyscraper foundations, reaching in some cases four to five hundred feet into the bedrock. There are cellars and subcellars, passages between buildings, some used for years and forgotten, some newly built; train tunnels still being used by the mainline stations, and others long forgotten; the incredible tangle of subway stations, reaching from one end of the island to the other; and here and there, a secret that only two or three people knew.

Down in the dark, in a subway access tunnel, Spider-Man was making his way toward one of them, on a hunch that Doc Ock might be there—or better still, that his stockpile of radioactives might be. Spidey had strapped one of the two AEC radiation sensors to him; his camera was in its usual belt-buckle holder, and he was as ready as he was likely to be to deal with Ock. Whether he would be doing it alone or not, he had no idea. One possibility—that he might have Venom's help—was almost as bad as the idea that he might have to take on Ock all by himself. *But,* he thought as he leaped and sprang through the darkness, *this is what heroes do.*

MJ had said it to him, when she came home and understood what he was going to do. "Maybe I won't go in to work," she said.

"No point in that," he'd said, holding her close. "I don't even know if I'm going to find anything tonight. You go ahead and make money—we've still got that phone bill to think about."

She rolled her eyes. "Well, if things keep going on this way, not much longer! All the same, just one night off—"

"No. They need you. They like you. You told me so. And you like working with them, *and* it's good money, so you go on and do it. After the nightmare you had the other night, I think you deserve a little enjoyment. I'll call you if anything exciting happens."

"On what? Doris still has my phone."

"Oh."

She chuckled and kissed him. "See how preoccupied you are. Go on, my hero, and do what must be done." She threw her head back, looked at him levelly, and said it in her super heroine voice.

He laughed. "Hey, pretty good. Just don't get bitten by any radioactive bugs or anything now, okay? One of us in the house is enough."

"If you were in the house more often, I'd like it more," she muttered. "And not chasing around after—Well, it's not the chasing that bothers me. It's the being chased. Venom—"

"Honey," he said, looking into her eyes, "we can't do a thing about him. He's here. If he comes near me with intent, I'll do everything I can to clean his clock, but worrying about it just wastes energy. Right now I've got other problems. The city's sitting on some kind of powder keg again—"

"And here you come with the matches."

"Not me," Spidey said. "I've got the extinguisher. I think."

"Go on, then," she said and pushed him away gently. "You and your gadget there. Go do what you have to—and don't be back late."

"Being late," he said, "in all senses of the word, is the last thing on my mind."

It was still on his mind, though not last, as he paused in the subway access tunnel and looked out on the tracks of the Lexington Avenue local. Far down in the distance he could see the lights on the platform of the Sixty-eighth Street station. He was not headed that way, though. There was someplace odder he had to find again, and it had been a while since he had been this way.

Doctor Octopus, over his long affiliation with the city, had become as familiar with its buried side as most people become with the parts of it that stick up in the sunlight and air. He had had several hideouts here and there, some of them obvious, some of them less so. Two of the more obvious ones, large subcellar spaces found or built under old office buildings, Peter had already checked. They were, as he had suspected, empty. Ock was too smart to return to spots that were so easily accessible. Spider-Man had wanted to look at them anyway to see whether there were possibly any radioactives stored there, as much to test his sensor as anything else. So far it hadn't given so much as a peep. Nor would it, at the moment—Spidey had it set on silent running, so that it would vibrate against him like a hypertrophied beeper set on quiet if it felt anything. But this left other opportunities to be investigated.

Ock was an avid reader of history, a pastime that had led him to some interesting discoveries, and the place to which Spidey was now heading was one of them. He looked both ways before crossing the tracks, jumped them and the third rail, and made his way down to the next access and maintenance tunnel leading away from them.

About half a mile down this tunnel, he found what he was looking for: an old opening with thick sheets of heavy metal, like the kind they put down on the streets while doing repair work, riveted up over it into the masonry of the walls. The masonry here looked older than that elsewhere, and there was a good reason for this.

I'll have to let someone know about this, Spidey thought, and reached up to grab one edge of the metal sheet. He got a good grip, then slowly pulled. The metal groaned and began to bend, and masonry around it crumbled; screws and rivets popped out of the steel sheet as the whole business leaned toward him. Then suddenly it gave way. Spidey leapt aside as it crashed to the floor of the access tunnel and lay there, rocking and scraping against the wall.

Slowly and carefully he stepped in through the doorway he had revealed and switched on his spider-signal to look around in the darkness.

It was still pretty much as it had been: the matte-masked glitter of dusty crystal reflected back filmed rainbows when hit with the red light of his spider-signal. Spidey stepped into the oldest subway station in New York City, and his footsteps echoed back from marble carvings and the inlaid terrazzo of the floor.

He hadn't believed it when he saw it the first time: a little station, with mosaics and beautifully carved bas-reliefs, and one track running away under the ground to a point about three blocks away. There was another little station, identical to this one. Both stations had crystal chandeliers and vases built into the walls for flowers. The other one had had a grand piano.

During the 1800s, there had been a very wealthy businessman who had the idea that New York should have a subway system. He had taken this idea to Tammany Hall, from which Boss Tweed effectively ran the city, and set it out for the Boss himself. The Boss had laughed and said a crazy idea like this would never catch on—whoever heard of streetcars underground? And besides, the open-trench digging that would be needed for such a project would disrupt everything for years.

The businessman did not have open-trench digging in mind. He proposed to tunnel completely underground and remove the spoil gradually from one end of the hole. The wits at Tammany Hall laughed louder than ever at this idea, and refused the businessman permission to even try.

Being, however, a New Yorker of a particularly robust period, he acted typically. He went ahead and built the thing anyway, secretly, and at his own expense. Two years later, he invited the dumbfounded Tammany fat cats to come and see his subway.

They did, and they were (against their will) impressed. They were willing to start building more such subways, but the rampant corruption of the Tweed administration had used so much of the city's money that there was nothing to spend on such a project, and soon enough the Tweed machine was out of office. The new administration couldn't be bothered with subways, and the businessman's little project was boarded up, shortly after his death, and forgotten—except by one super villain who read his history books very closely. Doc Ock found it, used it as a hideout for a time; and in the middle of a particularly nasty and lively running battle, Spider-Man had followed him there, and they had fought. For a long time after, Spidey had thought with affectionate regret about how, if things had gone just a little differently, all New York subway stations might have had chandeliers and grand pianos.

Now, though, the chandelier was somewhat the worse for wear—as a result of that old fight—and the dust lay thick. No one had been here for a long time.

Something poked him gently in the ribs. He whirled to see what it was.

Zzt.

Huh?

Zzt.

"Oh," he said, and then almost laughed out loud, and stopped himself. It was the sensor, buzzing sporadically against him.

He took a couple of experimental steps down toward the platform.

Zzzt. Zzzzzzzzt. Zzzzzzzz.

Spidey headed that way. The buzzing got stronger. He headed farther on down, until he ran out of platform and had to jump down onto the ancient track. *Zzzzzzzz.*

It was getting stronger, the buzzing, and more prolonged. This was definitely not background radiation; he had the sensor set well above that. Spider-Man leaped on down the tracks, going as silently as he could—

Zzzzzzzzzzzzzzzzzzzzzzzzzzzzzzzzzzzzzzzzzzzzzzzzzz.

When he got down to the other end of the platform, the buzzing simply wouldn't stop. He stood still for a moment, looked around him cautiously with his spider signal.

Nothing. Bare walls, bare floors.

Marks in the dust on the terrazzo floor.

He went over to the marks, bent to examine them more closely. The strength of the buzz got as high as it would go, and a soft light flashed on the sensor to indicate that he needed to decrease the sensitivity setting somewhat if he wanted the buzzer to work properly again. He didn't move to do so, still looking at the marks.

Little barrels. Little drums, like we found in the CCRC buildings. And radioactive as heck, if I'm getting this much reading just from the floor and the dust they were standing on.

The thought was rather intimidating. For the moment, he tried not to breathe. Gone, though, and no way to tell how long ago that happened. *Though not a lot of dust has fallen in the scraped places where they were moved. So maybe it didn't happen too long ago. And they were taken out another way, otherwise I would have seen markings down in the dust at the other end, not to mention picking up the radioactivity.*

He looked to see where the marks led. Down toward the farthest end of the platform. *There would have been a stairway here,* Spider-Man thought, *when it was originally built.*

Maybe there had been; now there was just a wall that had been sealed up the same way as the one he had come in through. The buzzing continued here.

He reached up to the riveted-on sheet of metal, pulled at it slowly. It gave way, very gradually—finally fell, clanging and echoing, on the marble floor beside him.

Spider-Man looked through the doorway, into the dark. *Zzzzzzzzz,* said the radiation sensor.

"All right," he said softly, "let's see where this leads."

It led a long way into the dark. The ceiling of the tunnel was low, and the masonry was old at first, then newer. Then the masonry stopped and rock began: plain black basalt, the roots of the city. And then the tunnel sloped downward, often twisting and turning sharply as it went.

Spider-Man trailed a gloved hand along the wall for a short way. The wall was surprisingly smooth. *Laser drilling?* he wondered. That kind of thing was incredibly expensive.

It occurred to Spidey that there were, once again, entrepreneurs in New York willing to spend a lot of their own money—well, *somebody's* money—on private construction projects. And the way the tunnel twisted, sometimes almost back on itself, suggested that someone had been using satellite guidance, or some other similar system, to avoid the foundations of other buildings, entries to other, older tunnels, cable conduits, etc.

Spider-Man went on at the best speed he could, trusting his spider-sense to allow him to maneuver safely in this darkness. He had been making his way along for about a mile, he thought, when the tunnel's downward slope increased more acutely, and its run straightened out a good deal. At this point, Spider-Man stopped and listened very hard. Nothing. His spider-sense had nothing to say to him, either.

It was getting damp. *Surprising how the summer humidity can make it even down here. There's just no escape, is there?* And it was cooler, too. Slowly Spider-Man started on down the tunnel again, going softly, listening.

Sound began: water. Far off, very soft, a tinkle and drip and splash of water, like the sound you hear in subway stations in wet weather—except that the subway stations, as far as Spidey could tell, should be far above him at this point. *Zzzzzzzzt,* the sensor sounded against his chest. It had been maintaining a fairly even tone all this while, picking up the traces of where the barrels had passed though this tunnel, here and there spiking a louder *ZZZZ* when it passed a place where some barrel might have banged against a wall. *The contamination,* Spider-Man thought, *must have been horrendous. If all the barrels were leaking radioactivity like that....*

He shuddered as he went along. Spidey had a healthy respect for radioactivity, both in its positive and negative aspects. The negative one was most on his mind at the moment, though. It took only a speck of plutonium in your lungs to kill you dead, and not even from radioactivity: the sheer toxicity of the metal was more than sufficient.

Spider-Man went on, and the sound of the water slowly grew and grew. Then, ahead of him, away down the tunnel, he saw the slightest glow of light: a pale greenish glow, as if from fluorescent tubes. Very quietly, he made for it.

The pale glow slowly defined a doorway, quite literally a light at the end of the tunnel. He came to the end—

—and simply had to stop and stare.

Off to his right, the pathway that flowed into the tunnel he had left continued off around some outcroppings of rock, out of sight. Spider-Man stood at the edge of a wedge-shaped natural cavern nearly three hundred feet across. From high up one of its walls, off to his right, water poured down in a thin stream of waterfall, into a shallow pool. Water splashed up high from this, and flowed away off toward the side of the cavern directly across from him, down and out of sight. The floor was a pincushion tumble of stalagmites, mingled with powdery stuff that had probably fallen from the stalactites above; some of this was a powdery fungus that glowed a faint golden-green. Down the middle of the cavern ran a deep fissure with many shattered stalagmites on either side of it. *Maybe not the fault itself,* Spidey thought, *but a symptom of it.* The ceiling was not level; it arched up in a sort of earth-Gothic style, hung with innumerable stalactites, some two hundred feet sheer to a highest, narrowest point, and from that area, though he couldn't see it directly, came just a spark of real light. *Some grille on the sidewalk?* Spidey thought. *This must be the river they diverted.*

He half wished he had a cell phone, so he could test the cell. *I bet the signal would be pretty weak down here.*

Zzzzzzzzzzzzzz, said the sensor insistently. It felt stronger than it had since down in the almost-a-subway-station.

Obediently he turned to see in which direction the signal would increase. Off to the right, it got stronger, following the level path that had been cleared through the stalagmites nearest the cavern wall.

He went cautiously along the path, quietly listening. The water made it hard to hear; the echoes were confusing. Now, though, they began to fade as the cleared path led him through into another tunnel, this one much straighter than the previous one. It ran on straight for nearly a hundred yards and there were lights in it, at intervals.

Zzzzzzzzzz, said the sensor. *Zzazzzaz. ZZZZZZZZZZZZZZZZZZZ*.

It vibrated so hard that it felt slightly indecent, and Spidey stopped briefly to turn its sensitivity down a good ways. Then he went on, but the adjustment lasted only a short time. *ZZZZZZZZZZZZZZZ, ZZZZZZZZZZZZ!*

He came to a door. It was made of extremely heavy metal, like an airlock door in a submarine, but the doorknob seemed simple enough. He turned the knob and pulled. Very silently, on well-oiled hinges, the door slowly leaned open.

ZZZZZZZZZZZZZZZZZZZZZZZZZZZZZZZZZZZZZZZZZZ-ZZZZ!!!! bellowed the sensor, and with good reason.

Spidey looked into a room nearly the size of the cavern he had just left, all carved out of the living rock. It was piled high with metal drums. Every one of them had a stenciled number on it. Some had old lettering as well: waste, chemical waste, toxic: dispose of appropriately. One, not too far from Spider-Man, said cooking oil.

I don't care what it says, Spidey thought to himself grimly, *this ain't no Mazola!*

He started to shut the door. And then his spider-sense screamed.

Spidey spun around, saw a bunch of black-clad people jumping at him, and knew perfectly well that there was no point in waiting to see if they were going to be friendly. He threw himself in a double-fisted punch at the first one and decked him; rolled, bounced, shot webbing at one of the others, missed; bounced again, trying to get a count.

Six of them? Seven? There's no fighting room here. Let's make the odds a little more even. He bounced hurriedly back down the tunnel toward the cavern, made the entrance, looked up, saw the stalactites.

It's worth a shot.

Gunfire sprayed behind him. *And me without my flak jacket,* he thought. He looked up again, picked a stalactite, shot webbing at it, felt it anchor. Went up the webline, and swung, while bullets whined all around and spat glowing fungus and rock dust off the surrounding stony icicles.

Footsteps, echoing, as the guards ran into the cavern. Spidey swung hard around the first stalactite, chose another one, one of the biggest, shot webbing at it, anchored, pulled himself free of the first—

Suddenly, fire streaked past his ear and blew the other stalactite to powder. Spidey swung hurriedly around the other one, looking to see what the heck *that* had been.

A single man had come down the tunnel, the way the others had. He was dressed in jeans and a dark jacket, and he had an RPG launcher over his shoulder, or something that looked very much like it. He drew a bead on Spidey, fired again.

Spidey launched himself out into the air—he had no desire to be a guest at his own barbecue. The second blast from the RPG ruined the biggest stalactite as Spidey caromed into another one, hung on for dear life, and prepared to move on again in a hurry. *That one looks nice,* he thought and shot webbing at it, felt it anchor. *Better go—*

He swung from the web—and the stalactite detached itself neatly from the ceiling.

For one bare moment Spider-Man understood, as if from the inside, one of the principles of cartoon physics: you must *know* you are about to fall before it can actually happen. He seemed to hover there for the split second until he knew—and then, flailing, he went down. Spidey had just enough time to glimpse the really large stalagmite pointing toward where his back was about to land. He twisted spasmodically, just missed it, and crashed into two other smaller, blunt ones. One of them grazed his head. He lolled back, unable to move for a moment, literally seeing stars.

The black shapes, he could see, were picking their way toward him—

—and then there was an appalling sound: a scream. *Not me,* he thought fuzzily for a moment. *Too deep.*

He managed to lever himself up on one elbow, look around. The black shapes, at least three of them, were being waved around in the air by long black pseudopodia attached to the usually least welcome, but temporarily most welcome shape in the world. Venom stood there, arms folded as if in amusement over something odd on his chest—Spidey squinted, abruptly recognizing the twin to his own sensor. With a quick, economical gesture, the pseudopodia chucked the three men hard at the cavern wall. They hit it hard and fell, none of them in good shape at all. Venom turned, reached out a very long set of tentacles and snatched the RPG from the man who held it, then snarled, "Niner!" and poured more tentacles at him.

"Niner" just smiled, let the RPG go, stepped hurriedly back from the extra pseudopodia, and put his hand in his pocket.

Another appalling scream. *Not me. Too high. No, it* is *me.* The sonic scream got inside his head and blasted the world and the inside of his skull white with sound and pain. He just barely saw it starting to rain stalactites, saw the pseudopodia writhing in agony, heard Venom's scream of sympathy and his own scream of agony. Then for a long time there was nothing left but the screaming, and the pain, and after a while that went away as well.

"**—OFF** them now and save yourself a lot of trouble, sir."

A voice, just a voice in the darkness. *Unfamiliar.*

"Oh, no, my faithful 'ninth arm,' you misunderstand my intent. I don't *want* to save myself trouble. After the Hundredth Day, things are going to be very quiet, except for certain indulgences I permit myself. Like these two. Almost too much to hope for, the second one. I don't intend to throw away such a piece of good luck. Indeed not."

Familiar voice. Too familiar. Can't move, can't do anything.

"You've had the guest suite ready all this while. Well, we've got an extra guest, it may get a little cramped in there—but we'll have plenty of time, all the time in the world in fact, to make more room for our extra lodger. Meantime, put them in there together."

"Won't Venom—?"

"He might. Wouldn't that be interesting to watch? Still, I doubt he will for a good while yet. I don't intend to waste their entertainment value so quickly. Not for a long time, certainly—maybe never. We'll see.

Anyway, we'll dose them at intervals with enough sonics to keep his alien pet in order. Go on, Niner, put them in the suite. We've got a few other things to do this afternoon before we can enjoy ourselves."

Joy.

Make a note. No more stalactites.

No more... sta...

TEN

SPIDER-MAN opened his eyes. It hurt, everything hurt.

Very slowly and carefully, not wanting to find out too quickly about anything else that hurt, Spider-Man rolled over onto his face. His face hurt, but he had known about that already from the graze with the stalactite. His arms hurt, but not so badly that they didn't work.

A good thing, that, since he found himself staring straight at a flaccid, black, shining pseudopod between his face and the floor. It twitched.

He boosted himself up and away from it in a hurry—then groaned as many other parts of his body complained that *they* hurt, too, and what was he going to do about it? Spidey shook his head carefully, half afraid he would hear something rattle, and boosted himself into some kind of limp sitting position.

He looked around. They were in a three-walled room about twenty feet by twenty; it appeared to have been carved out of the same solid basalt as the hallway with the fissile storehouse in it. Floor, walls, and ceiling were all the same dull black. Off to one side was what looked like a black basalt toilet, no seat; in the corner of the room was a little triangular pool of water, like a tiny koi pond set into the floor.

The fourth wall fascinated Spidey. It shimmered—just a shimmering in the air, like heat haze, with no light, nor a glow—but he was sure he knew what it was anyway. *It's a force field,* he thought, *a genuine TV-science-fiction force field.* He suspected strongly that Doc Ock was out there somewhere, waiting for him to test it. Well, he could wait.

Beyond the force field was a larger room, barren, with various crates and boxes stacked up in it. Some of Doc Ock's people, some wearing the "goon uniform" that he first saw way back when Ock was going by the immodest sobriquet of "the Master Planner," others in more casual clothes. They flitted to and fro, bringing in more crates or taking them away. It looked leisurely; no one was in a rush. Some of the henchpeople threw interested glances in at Spidey, which he declined to return.

He turned his back on the outside world and examined the cell once more. It looked like it was intended for very hard wear and very extended use. *Charming,* Spider-Man thought, and looked across at his prone cell mate. Venom lay there sprawled, having been hurt a lot worse by the sonics than Spidey had: the symbiote lay strung out all around him in stricken rags and tatters.

He disliked the idea of going near the thing, but there didn't seem any point in letting Venom lie there and rest a perfectly good, if hostile, set of brains while they could be useful in getting them both out of there. Spidey hunkered himself over closer to Venom, shook his shoulder a little. "Venom. Come on, snap out of it, you big baby."

No response.

"I should think he'd be out of it for a good while," said the familiar, rasping, gloating voice from behind him. "You'll be wasting your time. But you'll have lots of it to waste, from now on."

Slowly, Spidey turned around. There stood Doctor Octopus, just outside the force field, looking at him through those bloody sunglasses of his, and smiling. He waved a hand at the field, as if through air. "Don't you want to try it?"

"Not in the slightest," Spider-Man said, "since it'd probably kill me. Or make me wish I was dead. I have this nasty feeling that killing me—us—is not on the menu."

"Oh, no, not at all. You two are a guilty pleasure," said the Doc. "Rather, *you* are: Venom was an unexpected dividend. But over the next couple of months I intend to spend a lot of time enjoying your reactions to what you see going on around you. Helplessness: the most delicious of emotions which leads to all others—rage, grief, resignation. Though I doubt you'll come to that too soon."

"I'll resign right now," Spider-Man said, "if you'll let me out of here and give me a chance to pound you properly."

"Certainly not." Doc Ock put his hands behind his back, a little primly, and smiled, while the god-awful metal tentacles wreathed and writhed around like squaredancing snakes. "And I intend to watch with enjoyment your attempts to make me angry—what's the phrase?—'so that I'll make a mistake.' I have been practicing not making mistakes for a long time now."

"You've been practicing something, all right," Spidey said, crossing his legs with a little hiss of pain, and making himself as comfortable as he could. "High finance, mostly. I never thought of you as a banker."

"You never *thought*," Ock corrected him. "That was always your problem. React first, think things through later. Annoying, how your wretched half-baked thinking would sometimes serve you well enough to interfere with my plans. A long time now I've put up with that kind of thing from you. But no more. I intend to demonstrate to you, at leisure, what real thinking can do—and you'll have leisure to appreciate it."

"Is this the part where you gloat over me?" Spidey said.

"For years," said Ock, with a smile of pure pleasure. "But, as an exercise for the student, I'm delighted to give you a chance to tell me what's been going on."

"You're destroying the world?" Spidey said.

Doctor Octopus chuckled. "What silliness. When the building is burning, you don't pour on gasoline. You put the fire out."

"Oh," Spider-Man said. "And with terrorists and loonies all over the place trying to get their hands on nuclear material, *you're* processing it and shipping it all over the place, here and in Europe, and selling it to anyone who'll pay, and this is how you put the fire out? An interesting new definition of 'saving the world': I hadn't heard this one before."

"I *am* saving the world," Doc Ock said calmly. "From the irresponsible populations that are destroying it. When I'm finished, there will be a lot fewer of those populations. But more to the point, I'm gathering every useful technology together into the hands of the people who will use them wisely—"

"In other words, you."

"Perspicacious boy."

"Gee, you know big words, Doc."

"And what to do with them, insect." Just for a moment, a glitter of pure hate showed in Doc's eyes. "In the past twenty years, this world has changed tremendously in terms of scientific advancement. Machines that were unheard of as little as a decade ago are now household appliances—

and being misused as often as used properly. The time is ripe for one person to command all the technology."

"Nice goal," Spider-Man said. "The question is, will all those other people let you?"

"There won't be that many of them to argue the point," said Doc Ock, "in a very little while."

The chill got into Spidey's bones at the sound of that.

"See what's happened in the world in those twenty years," Ock said. "The age of the superpower should have come to an end with the collapse of the Soviet Union. There should have been an astonishing leap forward in terms of science and medicine and managing the world, with that shadow lifted. But still small nations squabble and kill each other's people over wars that were fought and lost five hundred years ago. All the technology is here to make this world a paradise, but the nations of the world just go on wasting their potential. They'll waste it until there's nothing left. The time's now ripe for one person to command the world's economy, one who'll use it to best advantage, in science's service. The greatest scientist ever to live."

Spidey cocked his head just slightly sidewise, wondering whether Venom was conscious enough to get any of this. *Can't be. He'd be raving already.*

"All it takes is one man with a vision," Ock said, "and the world can be changed. *Is* being changed: the changes are already in progress. A hundred days or less, and no one will know this for the same planet."

A hundred days—Spidey thought of that phone call from Galya. "All this money-laundering," he said casually. "Whose economy are you messing with?"

"Everyone's," said Doc delightedly. "Why leave anyone out? And there are so many ways to do it. Destabilize local currencies by speculation in the local markets. Deflate a country's cash reserves."

"Counterfeiting," Spidey said, suddenly remembering a little barrel of ink that Venom had found along with other smuggled goods on a Florida beach: the "color-changing" ink used on the new European Community bank notes—called, simply, the Euro—impossible to duplicate, now the most stolen and most expensive substance in the West.

"Yes indeed. In about a month, the Euro will suffer a most devastating drop in its value when it's discovered how much of the currency is worthless, unbacked by the member banks. So will the dollar and the yen. The ruble, worth little enough as it is, will go into hyperinflation within minutes. The world's currencies will go into free fall."

"Whole economies will crash," Spider-Man said softly, horrified.

"Yes. It will start there. Many wasteful industries will die in that first shakeout—"

"First."

"Well," said Ock, the extra arms curling and wreathing gently about him, "I always did favor the belt-and-suspenders route. There are simply too many people on this planet. Resources are being wasted faster than they can be replaced. I had given some thought to smallpox and anthrax," he said, tilting his head a little, as if considering it again, "but they are unreliable agents, and difficult to control. No, the sweet compliance of the atom suits me better. Plutonium doesn't breed without help, and won't mutate into some unpredictable new form without warning. I have acquired a fair amount of it, and over time I've distributed a great deal of it, here and there, where it'll do the most good."

"All over the country, you mean!"

"Every major city. City-dwelling has not been good for our planet, by and large," Ock said judiciously. "Now nearly half this world's swollen population lives in cities. A moment's surgery, in a hundred days, and," he made an airy gesture, "the burden becomes much less. I don't have a quarrel with simple people who live on the land. I'll rule them in their best interests, and they'll provide food and the raw materials we'll need for the new sciences. At the same time, I don't want to ruin the cities totally. It's surgery—or rather, chemotherapy. Kill the cancer, save the body." He smiled again. "They'll thank me for a thousand years after."

Spidey sat very still. Then, slowly, he got up, and walked as close to that force field as he dared.

"What gives you the right to do this?" he cried.

Ock only blinked. "I'm the one best qualified to bring this result about," he said simply, "and the time is right. Wouldn't you say?"

Spider-Man stood there and just shook.

Doctor Octopus peered past him at Venom, and tsked a little. "I hope I didn't give him too much," he said. "Keep an eye on him. This has been very entertaining—I look forward to seeing how he reacts to it."

And Otto Octavius walked away, actually whistling to himself.

Spidey sat down next to Venom, still trembling with rage and fear. For a long time he was silent.

Then, so softly it was barely a breath of sound, Venom said, "And we thought we knew what madness was like."

Spidey, acutely aware that they were probably being watched, pretended to lie back down on his back, not too close to Venom but not too far away from him either, and moaned a little. The moan was genuine enough. After a few long breaths he whispered, "If you've got any thoughts on this, I wouldn't mind hearing them."

There was a very soft hiss: after a little while. Venom said, "We should consider our available assets. We ourselves are not entirely out of commission, though holding the symbiote in check is something of a strain at the moment."

"Yeah, I know," Spidey said morosely, "it wants to eat my spleen or something."

"It wants to eat *all* of you," Venom said, "but at the moment we have no intention of catering to its whims. Later, when we are free, will be another matter. We decline, however, to be entertainment for that crackpot."

Spidey paused a moment, thought about that. "Okay," he said. "Let's fight."

"Your sense of humor is as impaired as ever."

"No, I'm serious. Venom, listen to me! We didn't even have to make him angry—he's *already* made his mistake."

"In what regard?"

"How much of that did you hear?"

"To our intense regret, all of it."

"He said he built this place for me. *Not for you.* We've got so much history together, he knows my capabilities inside out—*but not yours.* There may be some weakness in this place that you can exploit that I can't."

There was a long pause. "It is well reasoned," Venom said softly. "We would suggest you wait an hour or so. The symbiote is indeed somewhat 'under the weather.'"

"You're on."

Another pause. "This is not to be taken as a waiver of my statutory right," said Venom, "to eat your spleen at a later date."

Spidey snorted and disguised the sound more or less successfully as a sneeze. "As long as the world doesn't get blown up," he said softly, "that suits me fine."

Silence.

Spider-Man lay back and took the single most unsuccessful one-hour nap of his life.

SLOWLY, over the next half hour or so, Venom's pseudopodia began working again. He pulled himself together over the course of a few minutes: the symbiote knitted itself back into a costume, and then, over another ten minutes or so, began putting new pseudopodia out and making little grabs in Spider-Man's direction. Spidey let this continue for a little while, then "noticed" it, and withdrew to his own corner.

What Spidey desperately hoped had escaped the attention of whatever surveillance was turned on them, was that while the pseudopodia were snatching at him, one of them—fined down to a hair, and practically invisible—had been investigating the force field. He had no idea what the results were, but Venom showed no sign of any ill effects, except that the look he was giving Spidey was becoming more ferocious and hungry by the minute.

Finally he spoke. "This is an opportunity we had not thought to have for a few days yet," he said. "It seems a shame to waste it—especially as it will be good practice for dealing with that slide-rule pusher when he comes back."

Spidey glared at Venom, stood up slowly. "I wouldn't bet that it's going to go the way you want," he said. "It hasn't before."

"There's always a first time," Venom said. And he leapt.

Pseudopodia whirled out and wrapped around Spidey, and he grappled with it in a very mixed state of mind: he did not want to hurt Venom because he was going to need his help later, but he also did not want to be any closer to the symbiote than he had to. They reeled back and forth, they bashed into the walls. At one point, Venom picked Spidey up bodily and dropped him headfirst on the floor, then leapt on him again.

They grappled and rolled around the floor. Those god-awful fangs dripped slime on Spider-Man and the tongue was everywhere at once.

Their faces were close together. The symbiote made a noisy wailing sound. Eddie Brock's proper human voice whispered in Spidey's ear, "The force field is permeable. We had to narrow down to less than an angstrom wide, but some got out. With time—the controls—"

"We'll see where he keeps them," Spidey gasped.

Venom punched him. Spidey, furious, punched him back, then scrambled to his feet, picked Venom up, and threw *him* at the wall.

Unfortunately, there was very little room to work in a space like this, and some disadvantages. At one point Venom held his head under water in the corner pool. He struggled for air, gasped and thrashed, and finally got free—only to have the symbiote grab him to do it again. *It's getting too enthusiastic,* Spidey thought desperately. *Does it even understand the concept that this is a put-on? And if it does, does it care?*

The pseudopodia shoved him under the water again. *Nope,* Spidey thought, and choked and gasped and came up coughing water, and grabbed Venom and attempted to throw him straight across the horizon. The room actually shook a little when he hit the wall.

And outside the other wall, Doc Ock was standing, looking pleased. "Goodness," he said, "I hadn't thought you'd have had it in you so soon."

He glanced over to one side at something. *The controls for the force field,* Spidey thought, desperately hoping that Venom had seen it, willing him to have seen it. Venom staggered to his feet. "You utter madman," he growled, stalking toward the force field, "we'll see shortly if legend is true, that you gain intelligence by eating others' brains."

"Wouldn't recommend it," Spidey remarked from the other side of the room, getting ready to leap. "Mad Octopus Disease is incurable."

Venom jumped at him. They rolled and punched again—but Spidey noticed that Venom stayed near the force field. Pseudopodia blurred the air.

They rolled. Spidey screamed as Venom struck him in the bruised rib. But through the pain he felt the slightest flash of satisfaction. He had seen the one pseudopod that was thinned down to almost literally nothing. On the far side of the force field, he saw the same pseudopod, which had fed through the field, an angstrom thick. *Buy it time,* he thought. *Let it get thick enough to do some good.*

They fought. Venom banged Spidey's head against the floor. They rolled, but not too far. Punches rained down, bruised the faces under the masks unmercifully. Spidey dragged Venom to his feet again, reared back for one last enormous haymaker, the last blow he felt he would ever have in him.

A soft sound, like a sigh. Spider-Man looked over Venom's shoulder and saw the heat haze suddenly go away, and also saw Doc Ock's face abruptly go blank with sheer surprise.

There was no need to say anything; they both dived out the door as Ock dived for the control to slap it back on.

He hit it too late—and pseudopodia whipped out and wrapped around him like ribbons around a much-longed-for present.

There was a shout from behind Ock as he struggled. People streamed into the area as if they'd been called.

He had some kind of remote on him, probably, Spidey thought: *a panic button.* He had little time left to think about it, as the people in black unholstered weapons and started shooting at him.

He was running on autopilot at the moment. Spidey webbed guns out of hands, bounced across the room, kicked and punched, and generally was a bad target. Most of his attention, though, was on Venom and Ock, struggling and swaying together, tentacles against pseudopodia, the fangs and the dread against the tremendous strength. *This is not good,* Spidey thought. *After I deal with these guys, there's still going to he Ock. How many times have we fought? And let's say I do win: then what have I got? Venom— and a very keyed-up Venom, after the last couple of hours.*

He swallowed. *When did I last update my will?*

As he was bouncing away from one more felled guy in black, Spider-Man heard an odd, inhaling sound. His spider-sense stung him like a wasp, and he jumped straight up.

The output from the flamethrower went by right underneath him. Spidey clung briefly to the ceiling, gasping and choking with the rising gasoline fumes, as someone he remembered seeing before, a guy in a floppy black hat with grommets, chased him with the flames. He scuttled along the ceiling.

"Just a little fire for the bug," said the man cheerfully. "Not like the fire that's coming, though. That'll be worth seeing—and nothing can stop it now."

With a tremendous effort, Venom lifted Doc Ock right off the floor and flung him crashing off to one side. Then he turned, murder in his gaze. "Niner," he said, and stepped toward him.

Niner turned the flamethrower toward Venom, hitching his shoulders a little to settle the fuel pack comfortably. "Should be quite a sight," he said, "all the fire, up there where the view and the food's so superior—but I don't think you'll be around to see it. You're just trouble. Better get rid of you now."

"This is Ock's sidekick?" Spidey said.

"Niner," said Venom, circling around toward him. "Amusing to see plain old garden-variety jealousy operating. We had thought the style in sidekicks now was dogged devotion."

He leapt. Spidey, off to one side, could see Doc Ock scrambling to his feet again. "Oh dear," he said softly. "My turn in the barrel."

He jumped too—catching, as he did, just a glimpse of Niner as Venom snatched the flamethrower out of his hands, ripped it off at the hose, and then wrapped the pseudopodia around him in what looked like an indissoluble embrace. Niner was no longer a threat.

He had no more time to spend on that: suddenly there were metal tentacles wrapped around him, and he was dealing with another embrace of his own.

Ock was almost purple with rage: it was nearly worth choking to death to see. *Nearly.* Spider-Man struggled to get free, but as always, it was like struggling with angry adamantium pythons. Spider-strength sufficed to get them off him. He bounced out of range for a moment, trying to get his wind, and didn't get it, as one of those pythons reached up to the ceiling and snatched him down again.

Not without cost. Ock was still flesh and blood elsewhere, and as he pulled Spidey in at full speed, he also caught, backed by his own strength, Spidey's fist right in his face. He reeled back. Spider-Man bounced away again. *Just for a breath....*

Then all four tentacles caught him, lifted him high. He shot webbing at them; they broke it, and smashed him to the floor.

The world went white. No question about the rib this time. No question about maybe three of them. The legs were refusing to work, too. Broken back? No, he wouldn't still be able to feel the legs then.

He struggled to at least get halfway up. Ock had turned his back on him, had stalked over to Venom and grabbed him the same way. They were struggling, but the contest couldn't be in that much doubt, not really. Neither of them was fresh.

The tentacles held Venom high. Pseudopodia wrapped around them, resisting. There was a moment's swaying back and forth as dark razory ribbons struck and sliced at Doc's head, but not with the usual energy, a little feebly.

"You want to hold on?" Ock said. "Fine." And then the tentacles simply bashed Venom against the wall. Once—and the wall really did shake this time. Twice. Again. Again, like you would hit a fly you really wanted to flatten. Again.

The pseudopodia lost their grip.

Doc smashed Venom down on the floor. He lay there, still. The pseudopodia didn't move.

Spidey looked at him, where Doc stood looking down at Venom, only breathing a little fast.

He barely broke a sweat, Spidey thought in thoroughgoing disgust. *Look what he did to Venom. Venom! I've never been able to do that. And now he's going to do it to me, again. And then he's going to blow up the world, and my wife, and everything!*

No! I won't let him win! I didn't let him beat me when he dropped a ton of machinery on my back, and I won't let him beat me now!

He threw himself at Doc Ock, webbing like crazy.

At least the fighting started with webbing. Where it went after that seemed oddly predetermined to Spidey, as if he were doing some dance whose rules had been established a long time ago.

You shoot webbing at him, he shreds it up.

You jump up on the ceiling and come at him from that direction with webbing and then with feet and fists. He knocks you back.

You come at him again, hitting him like a cannonball, because all you can see in your mind is the sight of mushroom clouds everywhere, and your wife getting blown up—over and over and over.

He hits you, but you always hit him back, because if you don't, everything is going to die.

Everything.

Everything.

You hit, you kick. You're so hurt, it feels like you're kicking yourself.

It doesn't matter. MJ wouldn't like it if you stopped. "This," she would say, "is what heroes do."

And when you stop, finally, it's because the other party has stopped making the next move, failed to keep up the dance. You find yourself looking at a collapsed figure on the ground, terribly bruised and battered, metal arms lying helpless for the moment. And you wonder, irrationally, what you did wrong. Now, and all the other times.

I did it.

How did I do that?

Spidey shook his head. Ock lay still. Off to one side there was a faint beeping noise. Venom lay not too far from it, groaning.

Webbing, Spidey thought, *and lots of it.* He webbed Ock's arms behind him, and his legs, and the metal arms too, with special attention to them so that they couldn't work free. Then he staggered over to Venom.

Venom was moaning softly. It was a kind of piteous sound, especially since Spidey would have liked to lie down and make it himself. "Come on," he said. "Come on. Venom."

Wait a moment. Why am I trying to wake him up? I need to get out of here.

Then he heard the little beeping noise again. He looked for the source, and his eye came to rest on a little silver thing, like a small cylinder. It had an LED display on the top, and a little button.

The LED display said *56:04.* Then, *56:03. 56:02. 56:01.*

A chill settled in the pit of Spider-Man's stomach. He picked it up.

The way everyone came. As if called. He had this with him.

He let go of it.

Dead man's switch!

He went to Venom and actually lifted him, picked him up: he needed all the help he could get. "Come on, Venom. Wake up! He's going to blow one of these things!"

"Wha—?"

"Come on! We've got to find his computers."

Venom just sagged down to the floor. Spidey could only stand and stare at him for a moment.

Then he staggered off down the hall toward Ock's lair.

Nothing was hidden there, which was fortunate as he had no time to search. Laid out neatly off to one side, in a sort of main control room, he found the radiation sensors, and all the computers up and running. The control room was deserted. Spidey suspected that a lot of Ock's people had decided that not even the wages he paid were worth staying around for at this point, with an angry super villain and an angry super hero on the premises.

He looked at all the computer screens he could find. There were a lot of them. One system, though, was running a program called inventory. There was a list on it. It was a list of hundreds of bombs.

All of them said inactive. Spidey grabbed the computer's mouse, scrolled down it. And scrolled. And scrolled—active, said one. It had a number. It had a location in latitude and longitude. Spidey double-clicked on the entry.

A map of the World Trade Center appeared.

Oh, no, not again!

But it was the perfect place for an airburst. The closest you could come to one, without dropping it from an airplane. Maximum coverage.

It's going to kill thousands of people. Maybe hundreds of thousands.

Spidey recovered his sensor, strapped it to himself again. "Got to warn them," he muttered. "Where's a phone?" He looked around desperately, couldn't see one. "Where's a phone? It's been raining phones for days, why can't I find one when I need one?"

He caught sight of one, finally, between computer consoles. He grabbed it and punched numbers into it so fast he almost sprained a finger, that being the only part of him that was *not* presently sprained.

"Not the voicemail, please not the voicemail. Thank God! Drew! Spider-Man!" he shouted. "Call the World Trade Center, tell them to evacuate, now, there's a bomb! *Yes,* another one! Don't ask, just hurry, hurry!" He glanced at the dead man's switch. "Fifty minutes! Just get them out, get everybody there as far away as you can!"

He looked for somewhere to slam the phone down, couldn't find anywhere, dropped it on the floor and ran out as best he could.

OCK'S elevator took him up into one of the access tunnels below the Union Square subway station. He made his way up onto one of the platforms and took the stairs at a run, causing some very surprised looks among the commuters.

The sirens had already begun howling. Spidey took to his weblines and swung like a mad thing across the city. As he approached the twin towers, he could see people streaming away from them. That suited him. *And here I am, the only thing in the city except for the bomb squad going toward them.*

It's all very strange.

The sensor wasn't giving him so much as a peep as he landed on the roof of the South Tower and headed for the stairs. "Come on, give me some help," he muttered. But Laurentz had warned him that the sensors were fairly short-range.

Airburst. Top ten stories, certainly. Of two towers. Wonderful....

He took the elevator down to ninety and started quartering the corridors of the floor, with the sensor turned up as high as it could go. Nothing. It took him five minutes.

He ran up the stairs, quartered the next floor. Nothing.

Ninety-two. Nothing.

He had never been so aware of time as a liquid, like blood flowing, trickling away. Everything was going to trickle away. There was no time to even call MJ and tell her he loved her. No time.

Ninety-three. Ninety-four. Ninety-five. Nothing.

And on up to the roof.

What if he put it below ten floors down? What if I miss it?

He ran back up to the roof, shot a webline over to the North Tower, and swung over, took the elevator down ten stories, while outside the sirens howled, and did it again.

Ninety. Nothing.

Ninety-one. Nothing.

Ninety-two.

Damn them all, he found himself thinking as he raced down one more set of empty corridors, and the sensor didn't say a thing to him. *Ock, and his bloody Niner. They always have to gloat. Fire in the sky—he knew about it all right.*

Spidey stopped dead, panting.

He did know.

What was it he said?

"—up there where the view and the food's so superior—"

My God!

Spider-Man burst out laughing and ran up to the hundred-and-first floor. Seven minutes left.

The place was empty. He ran down the corridor to where a beautiful wrought-iron grille stood, with a sign on it: windows on the world.

He plunged on in. No one was there; wineglasses sat abandoned on the tables, some of the most expensive vintages in the world, he'd heard.

He stood very still, and turned the sensor up.

Zzzzt.

Not a very strong signal. He took a few steps toward one bank of windows.

ZZZzzzzzt.

No? The other way.

ZzzzZZZZZT.

Right up against the window, between two tables, he stood. *ZZZZZZZZzzzzzt.*

A fairly strong signal. But nothing here to be making it.

Six minutes.

He moved away from the window.

Zzzzzt.

Weaker. But it can't be outside.

Where the heck is it?

He went back to the spot between the windows.

ZZZZZZZZzzzzzzt.

All right, where is it? Spider-Man looked around him frantically.

And suddenly saw, in the corner, not too far away, the spiral staircase, leading downward.

He leaped down it, and found himself faced with a locked iron grille, with a beautiful little sign that said, wine cellar.

Spidey laughed again. "Sorry," he said to the grille, and ripped it courteously off its hinges, setting it to one side.

The wine cellar was immense. Racks and racks and racks of wine, names like Rothschild and Grand Cru and Zinfandel and God only knew what else.

He turned the sensor up, and began working his way up and down the racks. Three minutes left.

Zzzzzzzzzzzzzzzz.

Zzzzzzzzzzzzzzzz.

ZZZZZZZZZZZZZZZZZZ.

He paused. Moved a little to one side—

ZZZZZZZZZZZZZZZZZZZZZZZZZZZZZZZZZZZZZZ!

Two minutes.

Spider-Man looked at the wine rack—and, down in the bottom, saw one of the bottles of Rothschild with an unusually thick neck.

Very carefully, he knelt down beside it and eased it out. "About the size of a mortar shell," Laurentz had said.

More like a champagne bottle, Spidey thought, *but never mind that now.*

There was a very straightforward-looking switch on one side, and a little LED that said 01:32.

He took a deep breath.

MJ, I do love you—

—and this is what heroes do.

Spidey threw the switch.

The LED went out.

Just to be sure, he sat there for much longer than a minute and thirty-two seconds. Nothing happened. Outside, the sun shone, and the wind blew.

Inside, Spider-Man breathed again. Carefully, carrying the "wine bottle" under his arm, he went off to call Sergeant Drew's office and MJ.

ELEVEN

MUCH later, Peter sat on the living-room couch with MJ and said sadly, "So only two more weeks of this?"

"Yup," she said. "Not as many stations picked it up as they'd hoped, so they're limiting the series to twenty-two episodes. They've already got eighteen. I'll be able to tape the next four, but that's it."

"It's a shame." He hugged her. "But we're in pretty good shape at the moment."

The phone rang. MJ got up to get it. "Hello? Oh, hi, Doris. Sure, he's right here." She handed Peter the phone.

"Hi, Doris," he said.

"Two things," Doris said. "One good, one maybe. CellTech will not be charging you for that phone bill. I've got eighteen of those numbers involved in an investigation into, would you believe it, cigarette smuggling."

"That's great! Thank you, Doris."

"Anytime. My special service for famous people. The other thing— you were asking about location data on those calls? The Union Square subway station, apparently."

Peter chuckled. "I'll tell Spider-Man."

"Yes," she said, "and that's another thing. When do I get to meet *him*?"

"Uh. I'll work on it."

"You do that. Let me talk to MJ now. Bye!"

"Yes, Doris," MJ said, taking the phone back. "Yes. Yes. Lunch? Sure. Where? You're on. See you tomorrow." She hung up.

"You have a groupie," Peter said, amused, as she sat down again.

"I've had a groupie for a long time," MJ said and hugged him.

They sat looking idly at WNN, which was full of news about Doctor Octopus's arrest and the unfolding of the nuclear and economic strands of his conspiracy. Spidey had had a chance to very thoroughly debrief on the subject—having been lectured on it by the perpetrator himself—and Ock was presently in the Vault, being debriefed himself, a business that would probably take some years. Various world banks were scrutinizing every piece of their currency. The AEC was running all over the American landscape, picking up and defusing small tactical nuclear weapons and weapons-grade plutonium.

And in all this excitement, Venom had fallen right out of the news.

"I wonder where he went," MJ said softly.

"He wasn't in the caves at Ock's place when I got back there," Peter said, "but according to Ock's computer, *somebody* printed a list of all the sites Ock shipped bomb material to. I suspect that he'll be busy making sure the AEC takes care of it—and stepping in if they don't. I'm still surprised he didn't stick around, though."

"Maybe he was embarrassed at Octopus beating him."

"Or maybe he just wasn't up for another fight. I kind of suspect that he's not going to forgive CCRC or its baby, Bothwell, either. He may come back to haunt them."

"Better them than you." MJ pulled Peter close. "What did Kate say about the pictures?"

"Oh, she loved them. So, a little more money for the kitty, no Venom, the phone bill is off our case, and Doctor Octopus is locked up where he belongs." Peter chuckled and leaned his head back on the sofa, repeating a line of Doc Ock's. "Paradise on earth."

"It is, isn't it?" MJ said and kissed him.

ACKNOWLEDGEMENTS

THANKS once more to Keith of the adamantium hide for taking the flak and staying with me down to the wire.

Thanks also, *in extremis,* to Peter. If *Guns & Ammo* ever needs a demon typist, I know where they can find him....

But *I* found you first.

ABOUT THE AUTHOR

DIANE DUANE is the author of nearly fifty science fiction and fantasy novels, including ten books in the Young Wizards series. Four of her Star Trek novels have been *New York Times* bestsellers, including *Spock's World*. She lives with her husband in rural Ireland.

Visit her websites at
www.DianeDuane.com and www.youngwizards.com

SPIDER-MAN
KRAVEN'S LAST HUNT

After years of crushing defeats, Kraven the Hunter—son of Russian aristocrats, game tracker supreme—launches a final, deadly assault on Peter Parker, the Amazing Spider-Man. But for the obsessed Kraven, killing his prey is not enough. Once his enemy is dead, Kraven must become the Spider.

SPIDER-MAN
FOREVER YOUNG

Hoping to snag some rent-paying photos of his arachnid-like alter ego in action, Peter Parker goes looking for trouble—and finds it in the form of a mysterious, mythical stone tablet coveted by both the Kingpin and the Maggia! Caught in the crosshairs of New York's most nefarious villains, Peter also runs afoul of his friends—and the police! His girlfriend, Gwen Stacy, isn't too happy with him, either. And the past comes back to haunt him years later when the Maggia's assumed-dead leader resurfaces, still in pursuit of the troublesome tablet! Plus: With Aunt May at death's door, has the ol' Parker luck disappeared for good?

X-MEN

MUTANT EMPIRE OMNIBUS

Magneto—the X-Men's oldest, deadliest foe—has taken over a top-secret government installation that houses the Sentinels, powerful mutant-hunting robots. The X-Men must fight to keep this deadly technology out of Magneto's hands and stop him from carrying out his grand plan: establishing a global Mutant Empire. The X-Men must join forces with old enemies to stop him—but in Magneto's brave new world, who can they trust?

X-MEN AND THE AVENGERS

GAMMA QUEST OMNIBUS

When the Scarlet Witch of the Avengers and Rogue of the X-Men both disappear under mysterious circumstances, each team's search leads them to more questions than answers. Desperate to recover their missing teammates, they must join forces to uncover the truth. But their efforts will bring them up against a foe with the deadliest power of all: to make them turn on each other!

THANOS
DEATH SENTENCE

Thanos' pursuit of the Infinity Gems has always defined him. But when the Marvel heroes defeat him once again, Thanos' beloved Mistress Death grants him one final chance. Stripped of his powers and his old skin, Thanos embarks on a cosmic walkabout to reassert his power over himself and the Multiverse. Haunted by family – or the semblances of it – the Mad Titan may become something else entirely. Will he maintain his illusions of grandeur, or is this a new path for a lost god?

BLACK PANTHER
WHO IS THE BLACK PANTHER?

A KINGDOM BESIEGED

In the secluded kingdom of Wakanda, the Black Panther reigns supreme—until a savage villain called Klaw invades with a grudge, a super-powered army, and the support of western nations. Now the Panther must defend his homeland, his family, and his very way of life against overwhelming odds. An all-new novel based on Reginald Hudlin and John Romita Jr.'s groundbreaking Black Panther tale!

For more fantastic fiction, author events, exclusive
excerpts, competitions, limited editions and more

VISIT OUR WEBSITE
titanbooks.com

LIKE US ON FACEBOOK
facebook.com/titanbooks

FOLLOW US ON TWITTER
@TitanBooks

EMAIL US
readerfeedback@titanemail.com